John Mackay

The Celtic Monthly

A Magazine for Highlanders - Vol. 5

John Mackay

The Celtic Monthly
A Magazine for Highlanders - Vol. 5

ISBN/EAN: 9783337160142

Printed in Europe, USA, Canada, Australia, Japan

Cover: Foto ©Andreas Hilbeck / pixelio.de

More available books at **www.hansebooks.com**

THE

Celtic Monthly:

A Magazine for Highlanders.

EDITED BY

JOHN MACKAY, 1 Blythswood Drive, Glasgow.

VOL. VII.

GLASGOW: ARCHIBALD SINCLAIR, 47 WATERLOO STREET.
JOHN MENZIES & CO., WILLIAM LOVE, AND ARCHD. SINCLAIR, JR.
EDINBURGH: NORMAN MACLEOD AND JOHN GRANT.
INVERNESS: WILLIAM MACKAY.   PORTREE: J. C. MACKAY
OBAN: THOMAS BOYD & CO., AND HUGH MACDONALD

1899.

CONTENTS.

CONTENTS.

CONTENTS.

DEDICATED

TO

MY MUCH RESPECTED FRIEND,

MR HENRY WHYTE,

THE "FIONN" OF CELTIC LITERATURE,

In recognition of his signal services to the Celtic cause, and in acknowledgment

of his valued aid in conducting this Magazine.

JOHN MACKAY

PROVOST J. N. ANDERSON.

MRS. J. N. ANDERSON.

THE CELTIC MONTHLY:
A MAGAZINE FOR HIGHLANDERS.
Edited by JOHN MACKAY, Glasgow.

No. 1. Vol. VII.]   OCTOBER, 1898.   [Price Threepence.

PROVOST J. N. ANDERSON, STORNOWAY.

PROVOST ANDERSON, in the discharge of his public duties, has certainly not spared himself. Indeed, we doubt if there is to be found in the whole of the Highlands a public official who devotes himself so completely to the multifarious duties of his office as Provost Anderson does to improve the condition of his fellow men—to make life brighter and better for the natives of Lewis. He has no selfish end to gain, his only reward is the warm place which he occupies in the affections of his countrymen. The subject of our remarks was born in Stornoway, 10th October, 1844. His father, James Anderson, who was a builder to trade, came from Morayshire and settled in Stornoway in 1830, and carried out a good deal of the work in connection with Lews Castle. His mother, Jane Norrie, who only died last year, aged 84, was descended of a well known family from "The Mearns." He was educated at the General Assembly School, Stornoway, from which, in 1860, he entered a Solicitor's office, continuing there till 1878, when he entered upon a commercial career. Four years later he established coal-hulks or floating depôts in the harbour, for the supply of coals to steamers bound from America to the Baltic, which has become a most important industry, and gives employment to a large number of workmen. Provost Anderson allows no work in these depôts to be done on Sundays, although the ports in the south do not observe this very commendable rule. Last year, he decided to add to his other professions that of Notary Public and Solicitor, and successfully passed the examinations. When we come to treat of the Provost's public life, we realize that nothing less than a volume would do it justice. We cannot do more in the brief space at our disposal than summarise it as follows:—He entered the Burgh Police Commission in 1881, and has been six times returned, several times without a contest. In 1885 he was appointed Bailie, and last year, Provost. The Ness division of the County Council of Ross and Cromarty was represented by him since 1890, while he acts as chairman of the Lews District Committee, the Roads Committee, Stornoway Parish Council, and in addition is a member of a number of other committees. As a member of the Stornoway Pier and Harbour Commission he took an active part in the expenditure of £30,000 which has made the Capital of the Lews the best equipped port for the herring fishing industry in Scotland. At the last School Board election he was urgently requested to stand, and was returned at the head of the pole. The cause of Secondary and Technical education has ever had a warm advocate in Provost Anderson. A Secondary School was opened this month at Stornoway by the Rev. Dr. Whyte, and the Provost hopes that before long his native town may boast the possession of a well equipped Technical School, and a Town Hall, with municipal offices and a public library.

The great interest which the versatile Provost takes in military matters is well known. He joined the Stornoway Artillery Volunteers in 1859, and rose step by step till as Lieutenant he had command of the Battery, and had charge of fifty members of the Battery who were present at the great Review before the Queen in Edinburgh in 1882. He possesses the Victoria Decoration Medal for long service, and also a beautiful sword and scarf pin which were presented to him by the men of his Battery. Perhaps one of the most tangible services which Provost Anderson has rendered to his native island was his action in forcing upon Government the necessity of making roads in densely populated parts of the island where formerly not even a serviceable footpath existed. Excellent roads now open up some of the most distant parts of Lewis, although a good deal still requires to be done. The fishing population also owe him a deep debt of gratitude for the persistent way in which he pressed upon Government the necessity of erecting harbours, piers and boat slips for the development of the fishing industry. His services were eminently successful, for piers and landing places have been erected at Breasclete in Uig and Skitgersta in Ness, while a pier to cost £2,000 is about to be constructed at Bayble. On three occasions he acted as Hon. Secretary to committees formed to relieve distress caused in the island by fishing disasters and bad harvests, and on two occasions addressed meetings in the south on their behalf.

He has strong views on the temperance question, and has taken an active part in the movement in the Highlands. Personally he has been an abstainer for eighteen years, to which fact he attributes his success in life. In connection with that burning question, the granting of the Stornoway licenses, the Provost's name is known far beyond the confines of the Highlands. He was examined before the Licensing Commission and gave valuable evidence. He is a Free Churchman, and a deacon in the Free English Church. He also acts as Vice-Consul for Denmark.

Little more need be said in regard to his public services. Suffice it to say that there is no more popular man in Lewis than Provost Anderson, a fact which shews the good sense of this warm-hearted people. He is genial and kind in disposition, impulsive in supporting all objects intended to benefit his fellow Highlanders, learned in the literature and history of his native country, and a credit to the race from which he sprung. In conclusion we may add that in 1887 he married Miss Mary Walters Peake, only surviving daughter of the late Captain Charles Peake, Plymouth, Devonshire.

THE SOCIAL CONDITION OF THE HIGHLANDS SINCE 1800.

By A. J. BEATON, F.S.A. Scot., F.G.S.E.

I.

DEFINITION—AREA.

"AN approximately straight or gently undulating line taken from Stonehaven, in a south-west direction, along the northern outskirts of Strathmore to Glen Artney, and thence through the lower reaches of Loch Lomond to the Firth of Clyde at Kilcreggan, marks out with precision the southern limits of the Highland area." Such is the definition of the Northern Highlands by Professor Geikie, and although this boundary does not define the usually accepted limits, it is, nevertheless, the true physical frontier of the Scottish Highlands. The division of Scotland recognised to-day as "The Highlands" may be strictly confined to the area occupied by the Gaelic-speaking portion of the population.

It is not, however, within the province of this essay to discuss the precise demarcation of the Highlands; and it will therefore be understood that the area herein referred to embraces the district popularly known as strictly Highland ground.

The region is wild and mountainous, intersected with many large and picturesque lochs traversing the country generally in a north-easterly and south-westerly direction; and although the country is of a wild savage nature, yet many rich, fertile straths and glens are interspersed among the mountains, and wide stretches of fruitful alluvial plains are scattered along the seaboard and along the river valleys. Except at a considerable altitude, the mountains offer rich grazing for cattle and sheep, while the higher grounds afford sustenance for deer, and a quiet retreat for the various kinds of game peculiar to the Highlands. The coast line is wild, rugged, and indented with long arms of the sea or lochs running far up into the interior, and these lochs are at seasons of the year visited by shoals of herrings, which are caught by the fishing population along the shores. The herring and other fish are a source of considerable income to the country, but as this subject is referred to in another part of this paper I will dismiss it at present. Scattered along the western seaboard are numerous islands, which are divided into two groups—called the Inner and Outer Hebrides. These islands form detached portions of the Highlands, and they have a still more rugged coast than the mainland, being shattered and battered by the incessant roll of the wild Atlantic waves.

POPULATION.

The Highlands are now very sparsely populated, even when compared with the most impoverished agricultural county of Ireland. Take for illustration the extensive and by no means barren county of Inverness, with an area of 4088 square miles and a population of 90,454, being only a density of 22·10 inhabitants to a square mile; whereas county Galway in Ireland has 103·11 inhabitants to the square mile. Again Sutherlandshire will compare still more unfavourably with county Mayo in Ireland— the latter one of the poorest counties in Great

Britain or Ireland—being situated on the bleak and barren western seaboard, which yet has 120 inhabitants to the square mile, while in Sutherlandshire there are only 11·47. Whether or not there are means of subsistence for a larger population I allow the reader to draw his own inference from the above and the following facts.

The appended table will shew at a glance the amount of depopulation that has taken place in the following counties since 1841 :—

Name of County.	Population in 1841.	1881.	Decrease.	Increase.
Argyll,	97,371	76,468	20,903	—
Caithness,	36,343	38,865	—	2,522
Inverness,	97,799	90,454	7,345	—
Nairn,	9,217	10,455	—	1,238
Perth,	137,457	129,007	8,450	—
Ross and Cromarty,	78,685	78,547	138	—
Sutherland,	24,782	23,370	1,412	—

According to this table it will be seen that in five of the above counties there is a total decrease of 38,248, and were we to take into consideration the increase of population in towns the percentage of rural depopulation would shew a corresponding decrease. Inverness, for instance, had a population of only 12,575 in 1841. The actual population within the Old Burgh boundary in 1841 was 11,575, but I have added 1,000 to include portions now embraced within the Parliamentary Boundary extension of 1847; while the burgh census of 1881 records 17,385, being an increase of 4,810, which number should be added to the rural depopulation column for the entire county, and therefore we may assume that the actual decrease in the county of Inverness, during the forty years above referred to, is something like 10,000, allowing 2,158 as a fair increase for the burgh. It will also be seen that two counties—Caithness and Nairn—shew a slight increase, but these may be accounted for by the great development, in recent years, of the herring industry at Wick, and by the popularity of the town of Nairn as a watering place and health resort. The combined counties of Ross and Cromarty shew but a small decrease between the periods quoted in table: but, were the census of 1851 taken when the population reached 32,707, we should have a decrease 4,160 in thirty years.*

---

* The total increase of population of the Highlands and Islands (including Orkney and Zetland) from 1755 to 1821 has been 118,213. Three-fourths of the population speak the Gaelic language, the number of persons understanding English better than Gaelic being 133,699, that of persons more proficient in Gaelic 303,153.—*Vide* Prize Essay by John Anderson, F.S.A. Scot., Highland Society Transactions, 1831.

II.

CHARACTER AND CONDITION OF THE INHABITANTS.

There are as distinctive characteristic features of difference between the Highland and Lowland population of Scotland as there are in the physical demarcation line of the two divisions of the country. The Highlanders, socially and physically, are an entirely distinct people from the inhabitants of the Lowlands. Their language, dress, pursuits and customs are totally unlike the Southerner. The Highlanders or Celtic Scoti at the same time have always been sub-divided into two groups—the Hebridean and the Mainland Celts. When the Irish Scoti race moved northwards from the coast of Antrim they diverged into two streams, one branching north-eastward and on the mainland, and the other streaming away north and north-west among the Hebridean Islands. The Hebridean race on their northward course encountered the Scandinavians moving southward, while the Mainland Celts came in contact with the Picts and later on with the Saxons, this contact and intermingling of the different races causing a certain amount of amalgamation and fusing as it were of the various tribes into a distinct race, essentially different from the Irish Celts their original progenitors—and also different from each other, and hence we find in the Western Highlands what we may call the Scandinavian Celt, and the Picto-Celt in the eastern and midland districts. Undoubtedly in the portions of the country originally peopled by the Celtic race lying south of the Highland boundary, and which had originally been peopled by the Celtic race, there was effected a gradual alienation from the old and rude Celtic customs, and an adoption of the more civilized institutions of the Saxons.

It took many years after the rebellion of 1745 before the hitherto turbulent spirit in the Highlands subsided; but, with the dawn of the new century, the peaceful influences of civilizing enterprise seemed to renovate the war-worn and jaded Highlander, with an amount of vigour and energy which I fear has not since then been manifesting itself in the same forcible manner; for we find that industry, education, and the general development of the natural resources of the country received at that time such an impulse that in the few years, embraced in the first quarter of this century, the country assumed a comparative position in the commercial world that perhaps no other country under the sun can lay claim to having achieved at a single stride within the same period. The powerful natural resources of the Highland people, which, previous to the pacification of the country, were wasted on petty feuds and contentious rebellions against the crown—a misconceived Celtic idea of genuine loyalty to their chiefs—we find developing and progressing to that exalted position which ranks the Scottish Highlander so high among the peoples of the world. The martial spirit of their ancestors still holds sway in the dispositions of true Highlanders; and multitudes of the sturdy sons of the "land of brown heath and shaggy wood" have displayed their warlike and chivalrous spirit on many a bloody battlefield during the present century; and should Britain's cause require his assistance to-day, the Highland warrior's arm is as vigorous to wield his broad claymore or handle the rifle, and his courage is as undaunted to face the foe, "as when heretofore he marshalled for the lawless foray, or shed his blood in the shock of conflicting clans."

A writer in "Blackwood's Magazine" in 1836, speaking of the character of the Highlander says :—"We love the people too well to praise them—we have had heartfelt experience in their virtues. In castle, hall, house, manse, hut, hovel and shieling—on mountain and moor, we have known without having to study their character. It manifests itself in their manner, in their whole frame of life. They are now as they were, affectionate, faithful, and fearless; and far more delightful surely it is to see such qualities in all their pristine strength—for civilization has not weakened nor ever will weaken them—without the alloy of fierceness and ferocity which was unseparable from them in the turbulence of feudal times. They are now a peaceful people; severe as are the hardships of their condition, they are in the main contented with it; and nothing short of necessity can drive them from their dear mountains."

Although half a century has elapsed since the above was written, it may still be applied to the average Highlander. The Saxon reckons the Celt a lazy animal; and, not only do the Irish lie under this stigma, but the Scoto-Celt is classed as equally indolent, and perhaps in a sense, John Bull, with his advanced notions of social and political economy, is partly justified in asserting this. But when we consider the circumstances and the isolated position of the inhabitants of the west of Ireland and Scotland, we should not judge too harshly. Removed far from the centres of industry, with no opportunity of obtaining regular employment, ill fed and poorly clad, need we wonder at their lapsing into a state of what some people imagine to be indolence?

(To be continued).

The Clan Menzies celebrated the birthday of their Chief at Weem on Saturday, 24th ult., in right Highland style.

THEN AND NOW.

26th JANUARY, 1885   2nd SEPTEMBER, 1898.

GORDON is dead! along the silent street
 The cry went forth upon the awestruck air,
While eager questions passed from lip to lip
 And breaking hearts re-echoed their despair.

Gordon is dead! ah! what a wail was there!
 That grand, charmed life, so great, so true,
  so true!
Which like a meteor flashed before the world,
 Passed perils through, and lived where others died.

Gordon is dead! 'To arms!' the country cried;
 Too late! what need were now of steel or strife!
When thy brave patriot had given to thee
 The noblest moment of his noble life!

Too late! what awful tragedy was this
 That the world looked upon with bated breath!
While scene on scene unrolled the palling piece
 Till the act ended with the Hero's death!

Too late! no! not too late for British blood
 To wipe the stain from off her tarnished shield,
And from the ashes of her fallen fame
 Rise, like a Phœnix, on th' avenging field.

Too late! ah! never! whilst in loyal hearts
 Burns Honor's steady, unextinguished flame,
Whilst Lion and the Unicorn unite,
 And Tommy Atkins answers to his name.

It comes at last! at last! the waited hour
 Across the dreary waste of desert years,
And who shall say it were not glorious deed
 To die for Duty and his country's tears?

Hark! 'cross the scorching sands the battle cry,
 'For Gordon!' spurring clash of lance and sword,
And thick and fast the lines of Britain's braves
 Dash on to vengeance on the Dervish horde.

See! see! at last, the flag of Victory wave!
 And brothers kneeling where he faced his doom,
While triumph and humiliation meet
 To mourn the murdered martyr of Khartoum!

Mavor Allan.

Highland Notes.—The Clan Maclean Gathering takes place in the Waterloo Rooms on 21st October. On the following Friday (28th) the Annual Gathering of the Clan Macdonald takes place in the same rooms. The Lewis and Harris Gathering is fixed for 17th November. On 2nd December the Annual Gathering of the Skye Association takes place. The Kintyre Re-union will be honoured with the presence of the Marquis of Lorne as chairman in the City Hall on 28th October.

JOHN WILLIAM MACGILLIVRAY
(Chief of the Clan).

THE CHIEF OF THE MACGILLIVRAYS.

ACCOMPANYING this sketch is the portrait of Mr. John William MacGillivray, the Chief of the Clan. For four hundred years his ancestors possessed Dunmaglass and other mountain lands in the neighbourhood of Inverness. It is supposed that the MacGillivrays are one of the many branches of the Clan Chattan. That they were closely associated with the Mackintoshes is an undoubted fact; but whether of the same stock or not must yet be left an open question. Feudally they were connected also with the Campbells of Cawdor—yea and with previous old Thanes of Cawdor who had only a territorial surname. They were also feudally connected with the Earls of Moray. But in these cases there was no blood alliance—no common origin tie at least. Perhaps it was likewise a charter and tack connection with the Mackintoshes, which many intermarriages strengthened, rather than descent from one ancestor. In very truth the Clan Chattan, from its first appearance in records, has always exhibited the characteristics of a league or confederacy, and not the usual features in a marked degree, of a clan claiming common descent from one ancestor. Mere supposition as it is, we cannot get rid of the idea that the Clan Chattan must be connected by name and cat totem far more closely with Sutherland than with a common ancestor. It is shown pretty clearly by the Sagas of the Norsemen that these invaders drove many of the native Gael inhabitants out of Sutherland and Caithness. The driven out people would be, of course, united by race, language, and the purpose of holding themselves together, for defence and offence, under a chosen leader or captain. If there was such a displacement, as this theory supposes, of driven out Caithness and Sutherland Gael before the days when Scotland—or at anyrate the kingdom of Alba—was about equally divided between Macbeth and Earl Thorfinn, the Clan Chattan puzzle would be explainable. As regards the MacGillivrays, their surname has the same flavour of Celtic dedication to saints as the surnames of Macleans, Maclelans, Maclennans, Macgilchrists, etc. They were always a clan small enough to descend from a common ancestor, and their habitat was always Dunmaglass and some places adjoining. But although a small clan they

produced many men who distinguished themselves in war, peace, church, and science. They belonged to the law-abiding section of Highlanders through all their generations, as far as superiors and bad neighbours permitted. The MacGillivray who fell at Culloden was a brave, chivalrous, single-hearted upholder of the cause of hereditary right, who deserves to be ranked with the "Gentle Lochiel" and those who were similarly upright and unselfish. After Culloden the Macgillivray estates were forfeited for a time, and young members of the Chief's family and kinsmen emigrated to Georgia and Florida, where they had countrymen and friends of the earlier emigration of Highlanders under General Oglethorpe before them. John MacGillivray, Merchant of Mobile, and a brother of William, Laird of Dunmaglass, made his first will in 1767. Lachlan MacGillivray, his cousin, designated of Vale Royal, Parish of Christ Church, Province of Georgia, likewise made his will that year. It proved to be his last. But John, the Merchant of Mobile, lived to make his last will in 1786. By that time he had retired from loyal service on King George's side, from the revolted States, with the rank of Lieutenant-Colonel, and with considerable means which he used to redeem debts on the Dunmaglass estates. The two MacGillivrays mention, in their 1767 wills, several other kinsmen and clansmen who were resident in Georgia before the War of Independence.

In 1852 the direct line of the MacGillivray Chiefs ended with John Lachlan, who died on the 6th February of that year. Chiefship and property went then to the nearest male heir. But the question which had to be decided was—who was he? Mr. Neil John MacGillivray, of County Glengarry, Canada West, and of Easter Aberchalder, County of Inverness, claimed that his ancestor, Donald of Dalcrombie and Tutor of Dunmaglass, was the second son of Farquhar, the MacGillivray Chief of 1626; and that he was his direct representative. The Rev. Lachlan MacGillivray, who denied that Donald the Tutor was Farquhar's second son, and moreover went so far as to throw doubt on the Canadian marriage of Mr. Neil John's parents; claimed descent from William, another junior son of Farquhar of 1626. The Canadian marriage of Mr. Neil John's father was fully established by witnesses who knew his father and mother; and the documentary proofs left no doubt as to Donald the Tutor's position in the pedigree. Five years after the death of John Lachlan, Mr. Neil John was legally declared his next male heir. Although born and brought up in Canada, the new MacGillivray Chief was a far better Highlander than his predecessor, the last of the old line. He married in Canada a lady of the Glengarry Macdonells, who, although Canadian born, spoke Gaelic, and was as Highland as himself. The Dalcrombie MacGillivrays were always peculiarly popular in their native district. Of Farquhar of Dalcrombie, the grandfather of Mr. Neil John, the clan bard, Iain Donn, "the son of James, son of David," says in a song in praise of the Dunmaglass Chief of the latter part of last century :—

"O Dhalcrombaidh nam beann,
Nan creagan 's nan gleanntan glas,
Thig an t-armunn 'na dheann,
An carraid nan lann nach tais ;
Bi' dh sgiath laghach nam ball.
'S lann daingean a' d' laimh ri gaisg,
'Chuireadh agreamh air a Ghall,
'Nuair ghabhadh tu 'n t-ardan bras."

The succession litigation was costly, and led, with falling rents and other causes, to money difficulties which necessitated the selling of the ancestral estates three years after the death of the late Chief.

Mr. John William MacGillivray, the present Chief of his surname, and who is in every respect worthy of his long and honourable descent, is the eldest son of the late Chief and Laird of Dunmaglass, and of his wife, Catherine Orpha Lucy Macdonell. He was born in Glengarry, Canada West, on the 4th of February, 1864, and was educated in private schools, at first in Canada, and afterwards in this country. He joined the 2nd Battalion Cameron Highlanders, Inverness-shire Militia, in October, 1882. He was attached to the Depôt of the Cameron Highlanders on the 1st March, 1885, with whom he remained, at Fort-George and the Cameron Barracks, until May, 1887, when he left the 2nd Cameron Highlanders as Captain. After two years in London he left in June, 1889, for British North Borneo, where he remained until January, 1892. On leaving British North Borneo he visited Hong Kong and Hainan, whence he returned to India, and settled down in Behar as an indigo planter. He is at present in this country, but will shortly return to his work in Behar. He came home to see his mother, who was slowly dying, but lived long enough to welcome his return and to enjoy his company for several weeks before her death. He is like the representatives of the Glengarry, Clanranald, and many other families of old renown in Highland story—including Lord Reay, Chief of the Mackays—without the ancestral lands, but who can foretell the future. Energy and youth with a fair amount of good luck can work wonders, when prudence directs and tenacity of purpose clinches efforts of retrieval which an ancient and honourable lineage elevate into a duty to clan and to fore-fathers. The MacGillivrays may well be proud of their young Chief. All who know him like him and respect him, and heartily wish him success and happiness. He saw a great deal of the world before settling down to indigo planting in Behar. He has been several times to Canada, and seen most of the places of interest between Halifax, Nova Scotia, and Duluth on the Minnesota end of Lake Superior. In the Far East, besides the places already mentioned, he visited Rangoon, Penang, Singapore, and various parts of the Straits Settlements. He served with the British North Borneo Constabulary, and acted as Magistrate during the absence of one of the officials.

MÀIRI LAGHACH.
"WINSOME MARY."

THE romance connected with the name of "Màiri Laghach"—the "Annie Laurie" of the Highlands—has always had a fascination for Highlanders, and all true lovers of our national poetry and music. Whatever the cause may have been which led to the popularity of this song, with which the name of the subject of our present sketch has been attached, there can be no doubt at all that its universal acceptance by all Gaelic-speaking people, and others, is abundant proof that it has thrown a spell over our people, and that it breathes sentiments which appeal strongly to the human heart.

The generous and loving expressions of the poet fit in with the order of nature, and they are enhanced by the fact that these two loving souls ultimately became one, and lived a long and happy life together, with the natural result, a good death, a consummation rather uncommon with the usual type of romantic lovers. We must not, however, conclude that all romantic attachments are valueless because they don't end as happily as that of the author of " Màiri Laghach." These early impressions are generally of a lasting nature, and very often have a mollifying influence upon the future lives of the individuals concerned, even when ending in disappointment, while in others the heart is really broken and beyond the aid of mundane philosophers. It is, in fact, beyond their "sphere of influence," and that of the worldly wiseacres who worship false gods. Our national poetry is full of this sentiment of love—a divine ordinance from which there is no appeal—and those who have come under its influence assert it to be a " giant cement" that nothing in this world can ever hope to sever, so in that state we must leave it for the present.

For the benefit of all our readers and future historians, it must be explained that there were two "Màiri Laghach's," each having a song devoted to her by different composers, and admirers from different points of view. Both songs are called "Màiri Laghach," and have the same chorus, but different words and objects. In order to make this point clear to our readers we shall quote a living witness who wrote a full account of the two Marys and published it in *The Highlander* some years ago. The Rev. Roderick M'Rae, F. C. Manse, Carloway, Lewis, the gentlemen in question, supplies some interesting particulars which will clear up the confusion so prevalent in regard to the two "Màiri Laghach's." Of the first song he says: "Murdo M'Kenzie—Murchadh Ruadh nam bo—composed it to his little daughter Mary, who attended the cattle at the sheiling when his dairymaid had deserted him."

Murdo's version begins:

Nuair a thig a Bhealltainn,
Bithidh a' choill fo bhl'àth,
'S coin bheaga 'seinn duinn—
A dh' òidhche 's a lò,
Gobhair agus caoirich,

JOHN MACDONALD,   MAIRI LAGHACH.   MURDO, HER SON,
POET.   RODERICK SON OF MURDO.

A's crodh-laoigh le 'n àl
'S Màiri bhàn gan saodach'
Mach ri aodainn chàrn.
Ho mo Mhàiri Laghach, &c.

"Murchadh Ruadh," who was a farmer in Lochbroom and a drover, was married to a sister of the famous Master Lachlan M'Kenzie, Lochcarron, to whom he went when farming and droving failed him. Whilst in Lochcarron Murdo composed several songs, with some of which I was familiar in my younger days. Of Murdo's 'Màiri Laghach' I suppose I could give as good an account as any one from the circumstance of her having spent some of her time in my native place Lochcarron, and that I knew her personally. Màiri Laghach is still living,* at Torran, in the island of Raasay, along with her husband, John M'Leod, a superannuated Gaelic teacher. Anyone asking for John M'Leod is likely to be asked in turn "*An e sin an duine aig Màiri Laghach?*" –Is that Màiri Laghach's husband!

The second Màiri Laghach song is the composition entirely of John Macdonald,† who died some years ago at Croleg in the parish of Lochs

---

* When the paper was written.
† See illustration.

Lewis, in his 99th year, a man of mark in his day. This song is not as some suppose, merely an improved version of Murchadh Ruadh's song: it is purely a love song to the object of his fancy, and composed to the same air which was well known to him, as both of the poets lived in the same place. John Macdonald was, when a young man, teacher in Lochcarron parish, while the famous Mr. Lachlan M'Kenzie was minister. Subsequently he was tacksman of Scorraig, Lochbroom, and owner of a vessel of which he himself was skipper. Whilst in this latter capacity he was once storm-stayed in the harbour of Stornoway. Then it was that he saw his future wife, who was only twelve years of age; and on his way to Loch Torridon, with a fair wind, he composed his famous song to the youthful maid who was to be his wife. This song will be given *in extenso* presently. Mr. Macdonald had eleven of a family, all of them born at Scorraig. As his children were growing up he removed to Stornoway where his wife had some property. Afterwards he took the farm of Crobeg and there ended his days. He was considered one of the best scholars in the Highlands in his day. It was most interesting to listen—as it was my privilege to do—to his old Highland legends, which, if they had been preserved, would fill volumes. His sons were also men of mark. His second son, Roderick, was editor of the *Pictou Observer*, another, Alexander, was captain of an East India trader. Two were merchants in Stornoway; one of them is still living.‡ The youngest, Donald, has the farm of Dun Carloway,‡ and is ground officer of the parish of Uig. This is the father of Miss Maggie S. Macdonald, authoress of "My native hills for me" and several other poems. It will thus be seen that she is not a great-grand-daughter of "Murchaidh Ruaidh nam bo" and grand-daughter of Màiri Laghach of Raasay, but a grand-daughter of John Macdonald and of Màiri Laghach the Second.§ "The facts come out that the first Mary has been better known

than the second, although the second has been more popular than the first. I did not know John Macdonald's Mary, she being a Stornoway lady and having died ere I came to the island." "Mr. John Macdonald was author of several other popular songs, one in particular on the then laird of Tulloch, who was also proprietor of a great part of Lochbroom." M'Kenzie in his "Beauties of Gaelic Poetry" says of Macdonald that he was a gentleman of great poetical talent, and that his "Màiri Laghach" is "infinitely superior to the original set," and "while M'Kenzie has the merit of having composed the air, Mr. Macdonald is entitled to the praise of having sung that most beautiful of airs, in language, which for purity, mellowness, and poetry was never surpassed." He is also mentioned as author of many excellent poems and songs,|| full of nerve, tact, talent, intelligence, and wit. It may here be mentioned as an instance of the popularity of "Màiri Laghach," that shortly after it was composed Mr. Macdonald, having occasion to be in Ireland, and putting up at an inn, heard his own song sung in an adjoining room. Mr. Macdonald was born at Corry, Lochbroom, on 22nd February 1766, was married 2nd June, 1802, and died at Stornoway 16th January, 1865. His wife, "Màiri Laghach"—of the famous song—Mary Maciver, was born at Stornoway on 1st January, 1786, and died at Stornoway on 5th July, 1869, in her 83rd year. Anyone looking at the pictures of this remarkable couple can hardly fail to notice that they were a good lot, notwithstanding their roaming in Glen Smeoil. With bible in hand they form a beautiful picture of the contentment and happiness of old age, with that calmness of countenance that indicates confidence in the future. We subjoin the famous song of "Màiri Laghach," with translation by the late Evan MacColl, who considered the air to be simple, but to his ear "uncommonly beautiful."

‡ At the time the paper was written. Since died, 1892.
§ A sketch of her life and work will be given in the *Clan Donald Journal*, under Macdonald Bards.

|| Including one in dispraise of whisky, where he
   measured weapons with William Ross, the
   great lyric poet.

K. N. MACDONALD, M.D.

MAIRI LAGHACH WINSOME MARY.

KEY F.—*Moderato.*

{| r „r : m „r : r „d | l „l : d „m : s | l „,l : r „m : f „m | r „r : m „s : l
SEISD—Hó, mo Mhàiri laghach, 's tu mo Mhàiri bhinn! Hó mo Mhàiri laghach 's tu mo Mhàiri ghrinn;
CHORUS—Hey, my winsome Mary, Mary, fondly free!   Hey, my winsome Mary, Mary, mine to be!

{| l „,l : d „d : t „,s| l „,l : d „m : s | l „t : d' „t : l „s | m „,l : s „m : r |
Hó mo Mhàiri laghach, 's tu mo Mhàiri bhinn;   Màiri bhoidheach lurach, 'rugadh anns na glinn.
Winsome, handsome Mary, who so fair as she!   My own Highland lassie, dear as life to me.

B' og bha mise 's Mhàiri
  'M fàsaichean Ghlinn-smeòil,
'N uair 'chuir macan Venuis
  Saighead gheur 'n am fheòil ;
Tharruing sinn ri chéile,
  Ann an eud cho beò,
'S nach robh air an t-saoghal
  A thug gaol cho mòr.

Ged bu leamsa Albainn,
  A h-airgiod 'us a maoin,
Cia mar bhithinn sona
  Gun do chomunn gaoil ?
B' annsa bhi 'g ad phògadh,
  Le deagh chòir dhomh féin,
Na ged gheibhinn stòras
  Na Roinn-Eorp' gu léir.

Tha d' fhalt bachlach, dualach,
  Mu do chluais a' fàs,
Thug nàdar gach buaidh dha
  Thar gach gruag a bha :
Cha 'n'eil dragh, no tuairgne,
  'N a chur suas gach là ;
Chas gach ciabh mu 'n cuairt deth,
  'S e 'n a dhuail gu bhàrr.

Tha do chaile-dheud snaighte
  Geal mar shneachd nan àrd ;
D' anail mar an caineal ;
  Beul o 'm banail fàilt :
Gruaidh air dhreach an t-siris
  Min-ruisg chinnealt, thlà ;
Mala chaol gun ghruaman,
  Gnùis gheal, 's cuach-fhalt bàn.

Cha robh inneal ciùil
  A fhuaireadh riamh fo 'n ghréin,
A dh' aithriseadh air chòir
  Gach ceòl bhiodh againn féin,
Uiseag air gach lònan,
  Smeòrach air gach géig ;
Cuthag 'us gùg gùg aic',
  'Madainn chùbhraidh Chéit.

TRANSLATION.

Long ere in my bosom
  Lodged love's arrow keen,
Often with my Mary
  In Glensmoil I've been ;
Happy hours succeeded
  By affection true,
Till there seemed 'neath heaven
  No such loving two !

What although all Albinn
  And its wealth were mine,
How, without thee, darling,
  Could I fail to pine ?
As my bride to kiss thee,
  I would prize far more
Than the all of treasure
  Europe has in store.

What a wealth of tresses
  Mary dear can show !
Crown of lustre rarer
  Ne'er graced maiden brow !
'Tis but a little dressing
  Need those tresses rare,

Falling fondly, proudly,
  O'er her shoulders fair.

Hers are teeth whose whiteness
  Snow alone can peer ;
Hers the breath all fragrance,
  Voice of loving cheer ;
Cheeks of cherry ripeness,
  Eyelids drooping down,
Neath a forehead never
  Shadowed by a frown.

No mere music art-born
  Ere our pleasures crowned ;
Music far more cheering
  Nature for us found ;
Larks in the air, and thrushes
  On each flow'ring thorn,
And the cuckoo hailing
  Summer's gay return !

We also subjoin another beautiful translation of five stanzas of this popular song by another gifted Highlander, Mr. D. Macpherson, Bookseller, London. It is more poetical, but not so near the original as Evan MacColl's.

CHORUS.

Sweet the rising mountains, red with heather bells,
Sweet the bubbling fountains and the dewy dells,
Sweet the snowy blossom of the thorny tree,
Sweeter is young Mary of Glensmole to me.

Sweet, O sweet ! with Mary o'er the wilds to stray,
When Glensmole is dressed in all the pride of May,
And, when weary roving through the greenwood glade,
Softly to recline beneath the birken shade.
  Sweet the rising, etc.

There to fix my gaze in raptures of delight,
On her eyes of truth, of love, of life, of light,
On her bosom purer than the silver tide,
Fairer than the cana on the mountain side.
  Sweet the rising, etc.

What were all the sounds contrived by tuneful men,
To the warbling wild notes of the sylvan glen ?
Here the merry lark ascends on dewy wing,
There the mellow mavis and the blackbird sing.
  Sweet the rising, etc.

What were all the splendour of the proud and great
To the simple pleasures of our green retreat,
From the crystal spring fresh vigour we inhale,
Rosy health does court us on the mountain gale.
  Sweet the rising, etc.

Were I offered all the wealth that Albin yields,
All her lofty mountains and her fruitful fields,
With the countless riches of her subject seas,
I would scorn the change for blisses such as these.
  Sweet the rising, etc.

It is with much regret that we intimate the death of Dr. Finlayson, Munlochy, a sketch of whose career, with portrait, appeared in our last issue. The Doctor was exceedingly popular in the district.

TO CORRESPONDENTS.

All Communications, on literary and business matters, should be addressed to the Editor, Mr. JOHN MACKAY, 9 Blythswood Drive, Glasgow.

TERMS OF SUBSCRIPTION.—The CELTIC MONTHLY will be sent, post free, to any part of the United Kingdom, Canada, the United States, and all countries in the Postal Union—for one year, 4s.

THE CELTIC MONTHLY.
OCTOBER, 1898.

CONTENTS.

NOTICE TO SUBSCRIBERS.

This issue commences Volume VII. As we are anxious to complete the list of subscribers for the new Volume as soon as possible, readers who desire the "Celtic" to be sent for another year, might kindly forward their annual subscriptions (4/- post free), on receipt, to the Editor, Mr. John Mackay, 9 Blythswood Drive, Glasgow. Subscribers will greatly favour us by giving this their immediate attention, as delay in remitting entails upon us a good deal of extra trouble.

OUR NEXT ISSUE.

NEXT MONTH we will give plate portraits, with biographical sketches, of Major Black, Greenock, 5th V. B. Argyll and Sutherland Highlanders; Mr. Robert Campbell, Manchester; and portrait groups of the deputation from the Clan Mackay Society which recently took part in the Mòd at Oban and visited the Reay Country.

VOLUME VI.—We will be able to supply a limited number of copies of the volume now completed, nicely bound, at 6/6 per copy. As the supply is limited an early application is advisable.

THE MINOR SEPTS OF CLAN CHATTAN has now been issued to subscribers. The press notices have been of the most favourable nature, all agreeing in describing the work as a valuable contribution to Highland history and genealogy. The volume is got up in superb style, and contains coloured plates of the tartans, *fac-simile* bonds, and numerous fine photo process illustrations. Copies can be had from the publisher, John Mackay, 9 Blythswood Drive, Glasgow, price, 21/-.

THE DEPUTATION FROM THE CLAN MACKAY SOCIETY which visited the Reay County in September, received a most enthusiastic reception in every parish. The party consisted of Messrs. John Mackay, Hereford; James H. Mackay, London; John Mackay, Editor, *Celtic Monthly*, Glasgow, Hon Secy.; Rev. Angus Mackay, M.A., Westerdale; Dr. Adam Mackay, Dunbeath; Dr. Dingwall, Renton; and Roderick Macleod, Gold Medallist at the Oban Mòd. Large gatherings were held at Melvich, Farr, Tongue, and Durness, at which various Gaelic competitions took place, followed by the concerts in the evening. The party also took part at gatherings at Lairg and Rogart. Classes are being formed all over the country for the study of Gaelic and Music, the Clan Mackay Society lending tangible encouragement. The weather throughout was excellent, and the party enjoyed a delightful holiday. Next month fuller particulars will be given, and a portrait group of the members of the deputation taken at Rhiconich.

THE CLAN MACDONALD SOCIETY have just issued an attractive syllabus for the coming session. Dr. K. N. Macdonald is to lecture on "Clan Music," and three evenings are to be devoted to music and social enjoyment.

ON THE ANNIVERSARY OF BANNOCKBURN, 1898.

THE day breaks darkly on the eastern hills,
  The flag of gold falls heavy on the breeze
  That steals the sweetness from the wood-
    land rills,
And wails a coronach among the trees.

All nature seems to mourn for honour lost,
  And sings a dirge that moans the moorlands o'er;
The flag of freedom, once the heroes' boast,
  Has fallen low, and Scotland is no more.

Oh can it be that those dark low'ring skies,
  Thick clad in clouds of sombre hue to-day,
First saw that glorious flag of freedom rise
  And the oppressors vanquished in the fray?

Ah see! the sun breaks from its cloudy pall,
  And with its new born radiance lights the scene,
And as the tassell'd pinions rise and fall
  A halo casts upon their silken sheen.

May that bright beam not tell of true hearts still
  That venture yet to honour Scotland's name,
And pay not heed to the oppressor's will,
  Nor bow the knee to share their country's shame?

Oh that this hand might wield a fiery pen,
  That I the scroll of Freedom might unfold,
To brand its message on the souls of men
  And woo them from their sordid lust of gold.

Then shall the star of Freedom brightly shine
  To see, when once again her banner flies
Free, as of yore, above the heroes' shrine,
  A nation from a nation's ashes rise.

R. ROSS NAPIER ("Rob Lom").

MINOR SEPTS OF CLAN CHATTAN.

By Charles Fraser-Mackintosh, Ll.D.

No. XVII.—The Farquharsons.
Clan Fionlay. Part First.

THE Farquharsons, like the Shaws (No. 5 hereof), are placed by Sir Eneas Mackintosh as number 3 of the Clan Chattan descended of "Mackintosh, his house."

They branched off from Alexander Ciar, the third Shaw of Rothiemurchus, who had married one of the Stuarts of Kincardine, their progenitor being Farquhar, the 4th son. Removing to Aberdeenshire, the descendants of this Farquhar were called Farquharson, and have long held a very influential position in North East Scotland. In their early history, the name of Farquhar's descendant, Finlay Mòr, Standard-bearer at Pinkie, where he fell, 1547, stands prominent, and from and after him the Farquharsons were called in Gaelic Clan Fionlay; of him also descended the surname of Mac Kerracher.

By marriage with the heiress of MacHardy of Invercauld the Farquharsons acquired, as commonly reported, a large estate, and were much favoured with the family of Mar, of whom they held their lands. Holding for a long time an independent status, it is not here intended to do more than indicate their descent, their connection with Clan Chattan, and acknowledged dependence on its head. The present family of Invercauld is descended of the latter Rosses of Balnagown, formerly Lockharts, and as it is publicly announced that selections from their valuable papers are in course of publication, there is no occasion at present to enter into full details. It is to be hoped, in the cause of truth, that there will be no repetition of the inaccuracies and falsehoods of that Farquharson historian who flourished over 200 years since, repeated in Burke (Edition 1894) asserting that the Farquharsons are direct descendants of the Earls of Fife, without referring to the Mackintoshes and Shaws as intervening.

The first time I have observed the Farquharsons formally acknowledging Mackintosh as their chief, in writing, was upon 31st March, 1595. At Invercauld, upon that day, five influential Farquharsons, together with Mackintosh of Dalmunzie, in Strathardle, and Mac-Omie of Glenshee, both in Perthshire, enter into the obligation after quoted, and it will not be overlooked, that Invercauld's name is not the first, nor placed in the leading position. In truth, Donald was the elder brother.

"At Endercauld this last day of March in the year of God 1595; It is appointed and agreed upon between honourable and discreet persons, they are to say, Lachlan Mackintosh of Dunachton on the one part; and James Mackintosh of Gask, Donald Farquharson of Tulliegormont, John Farquharson of Invercauld, George, Lachlan, and Finlay Farquharson, brothers to the said Donald, on the other part,—in manner subsequent.—That is to say the said Lachlan Mackintosh having touched the Holy Evangell by the tenor hereof upon his great oath, faithfully promises to fortify, maintain, and assist and defend the said James Mackintosh, Donald, John, George, Lachlan and Finlay Farquharsons, their sons and friends, to the uttermost of his power, as also their heirs, in all their adoes, directly and indirectly against all whatsoever persons within this Realm (the King's Majesty being excepted); and likewise that he shall never enterprize or attempt any great matter of weight or consequence, whereby he or his said friends may come or fall in deadly feud, without the advice of the foresaid persons had thereto; and gif he does on the contrary, they shall not be holden to assist or maintain him thereunto, notwithstanding of their faithful promise after specified, but they to be free thereof as if the same had never been made. For the whilk causes and upon the provision aforesaid the said James Mackintosh of Gask, Donald, John, George, Lachlan, and Finlay Farquharson,—and with them Duncan Mackintosh of Dalmunzie, and Robert Mac Homie in the Burn of Glenshee, having touched the Holy Evangells, by the tenor hereof, and upon their great oaths, faithfully promise and oblige them and their heirs, to maintain, fortify, serve and defend the said Lachlan Mackintosh, his heirs, as our natural Chief, at our utmost power in all his adoes directly or indirectly against all and whatsoever person or persons within this Realm (The King's Majesty being excepted) and the premises observed. In witness whereof baith the said parties respectively subscribing (that can write) and the rest given their oaths upon the present Bond, day and date foresaid before these Witnesses, Sir Thomas Gordon of Cluny and diverse others."

Although numerous and influential, with Invercauld in course of time as undoubted head, yet it is found that as late as 1618, Invercauld is not included amongst the Chiefs called upon by Act of Parliament to answer for their clans.

In 1634 Robert Farquharson of Invercauld, and James Farquharson, W.S., are the Judges and Arbitrators named by William Mackintosh of that ilk, while arranging the serious question with Grant, his late guardian, and the large sums claimed as owing to the minor's estate. In 1643, the said William Mackintosh procures Robert Farquharson of Invercauld and William Mackintosh of Kclachie as cautioners for a pressing debt, and grants them security over his Lochaber Estates. Robert's son, Alexander, married Isabella Mackintosh, daughter of the above mentioned William Mackintosh. Their second, and surviving son, John Farquharson,

and Lachlan Mackintosh of Mackintosh, who distinguished themselves in the '15, as after-mentioned, were thus 'cousins in the first and second degree.

In 1664 Lachlan Mackintosh, 19th Mackintosh, resolved to bring the 300 years' quarrel with the Camerons to a final issue, and summoned all his friends, vassals and kin. In the List of Deeds will be found *fac-simile* of the very important deed granted by the Clan upon this occasion. It is in the hand-writing of Lach-

From R. Ranald M'Ian's]   FARQUHARSON.   ["*Clans of the Scottish Highlands.*

Ian Mackintosh of Kinrara, the historian, whom I have so frequently quoted, and is titled "Bond be certane of the name of Clan Chattan, to their Chieff, dated 19th Nov., 1664," and is signed by 6 Macphersons, 5 Mackintoshes, 1 Farquharsons, 3 MacGillivrays, 2 Macbeans, 2 Shaws, 1 Macqueen, with two by initials, all men of position and standing. The Farquharsons who subscribed were—1. James Farquharson of Invercy. 2. Charles Farquharson of Monaltrie. 3. James

Farquharson, younger of Whitehouse, who died s. p. ; and 4. George Farquharson, without designation, probably Bronchdearg.

Thwarted by powerful ill wishers and determined foes, amongst others by the Marquis of Huntly, the Earls of Aboyne and of Moray in the North and East, with the Earls of Argyle and Breadalbane in the West and South, who created dissensions among the Clan Chattan, Mackintosh had for a time to forbear.

In the rising of 1715, John Farquharson of Invercauld, with 4 officers and 140 men, joined the Clan Chattan regiment, in which he was Lieutenant-Colonel, and accompanying it to England, was taken prisoner at Preston.

Farquharson of Inverey, Invercauld's near relative, took it upon him to raise some of the Farquharsons as a distinct body in Lord Mar's army.

Writing of the episode of 1715, Mrs. Anne Duff, the old Lady Mackintosh, in her memoirs says, "The Earl of Mar was some time at Braemar, in his vassal, Invercauld's house, who stood out some time, and a great many more thoughtful people." Referring to the affair of Preston, Lady Mackintosh says, "Mackintosh and Invercauld having the most dangerous post, behaved most manfully, with a great character from strangers as acting their part with victory and courage." Detailing her husband's capture

INVERCAULD HOUSE.

and imprisonment, she gives the highest credit to Sir David Dalrymple, King's Advocate, for his intercession, which in the end resulted in Mackintosh and Invercauld's liberation without trial. Lady Mackintosh says "they were both released the same day (9th August, 1716), having been in prison for about ten months."

In 1724 Invercauld and Inverey are parties to the Deed of Renunciation by Cluny to Mackintosh, as are their representatives, John of Invercauld and Alexander of Inverey, to the deed of 1736, before referred to. In an agreement dated Moy Hall, 20th September, 1732, twixt Mackintosh and the Dowager Lady Mackintosh, John Farquharson of Invercauld and Francis Farquharson, second lawful son to Alexander Farquharson of Monaltrie, are witnesses.

(To be continued).

THE CAMPBELLS.

CADOXTON-BARRY,
SOUTH WALES, 2nd September, 1898.

SIR.—In your issue of September I notice Mr. MacGregor Campbell points out what appears to be an error in my article on 'The Campbells.' I was quite aware when I wrote the article that the Battle of Glenfruin was fought in 1602, but I fear I worded the sentence, in which I referred to it, somewhat awkwardly. I intended the words "in 1604," which are placed between commas in the original sentence, to be read with the last clause and not with the first as Mr. Campbell has done. I hope you will excuse my writing this, but I particularly dislike to appear careless or inaccurate in what I write.

I am, etc.,
J. A. LOVAT-FRASER.

Deeds that won the Empire. ✷

By JOHN MACKAY, C.E., J.P., Hereford.

QUEBEC, 1759.

(Continued from Volume VI., page 336).

MEANTIME Montcalm repeated the experiment of fire ships on a more gigantic scale to destroy the British ships. A vast raft was constructed, composed of seventy schooners, boats, and floats chained together and loaded with all kinds of combustibles and explosives. This fire raft is described as being a hundred fathoms long, and its appearance as it came drifting on the tide, a mass of roaring fire, discharging every instant a shower of missiles, was terrifying. The British sailors were again equal to the occasion. Regardless of danger, they dashed upon it, severed it, and broke the huge rafts into pieces, and then towed them ashore. "Hang it, Jack," one sailor was heard to say to another, "did thee ever take hell in tow before."

In the midst of all these anxieties of mind, Wolfe was laid low by illness. Writing to Pitt at this juncture, he said, "I found myself so ill and I am still so weak that I begged the general officers to consult together for the public utility. To the uncommon strength of the country the enemy have added, for the defence of the river, a great number of floating batteries and boats. By the vigilance of these and the Indians round our posts, it has been impossible to execute anything by surprise."

While Wolfe was in this desponding mood, a young Scottish officer, Lieutenant MacCulloch, is said to have suggested to the General the daring but brilliant idea of attempting that which the French considered to be impracticable —the scaling of the Heights of Abraham—a feat of arms practised upon Edinburgh Castle —and thus gaining the lofty ground that overlooked the city at a part where the defences were most weak. MacCulloch had personally observed a zig zag path going up the cliffs. The boldness of the idea and plan gave Wolfe new heart and health, and roused him from a bed of sickness in which the fever of his mind had thrown him. He consulted Admiral Saunders and concerted with him to make the attempt. It was resolved that at midnight of the 12th September the grand attempt should be made. Wolfe was now in high spirits, and before moving he invited some of his favourite officers to his tent to have a farewell carouse, and sang to them a noble old military song, long known by his name, but can be traced to the days of Marlborough :—

"How stands the glass around,
For shame, ye take no care, my boys, &c."

Exactly at one a.m., amid the greatest silence and obscurity, the Fraser Highlanders, the Louisburg Grenadiers, and four battalions of the line began to cross the river in flat bottomed boats, under Monckton and Murray, officers of the same age as their leader, only thirty-three. With the tide and flow of the river the boats dropped silently down, but the current was so rapid that most of them landed lower down than the point of disembarkation proposed by Wolfe, whose daring plans were nearly baffled by several circumstances beyond anticipation, the most extraordinary of which is given by Smollett and others.

A line of sentinels had been posted by Montcalm along the banks of the St. Lawrence, with orders to challenge all passing craft and to keep each other on the alert. The first boat crowded with Fraser Highlanders, amongst whom was Wolfe, was just approaching the woody shore, when, from amid the darkness, the challenge of a French sentinel rang out, "Qui Vive." "La France," responded a Highland officer with great presence of mind, who having served in Holland, and being master alike of the French language and their camp discipline, knew in an instant the requisite reply. "A quel regiment," demanded the wary sentinel. "De la Reine," replied the Highlander, who by a lucky accident knew that this regiment was actually in Canada, and thus might form part of the convoy. "Passe, monsieur," cried the sentinel, uncocked his musket, and asked no more questions, but lower down the stream another sentinel, more wary, after the same challenges and replies, suddenly exclaimed, "Pourquoi que vous ne parlez plus haut" (why do you not speak louder). "Mon camarade tais toi, nous serons entendus" (my comrade, be quiet, we shall be overheard), said the Highlander. This proved to be sufficient. So the boats with their kilted freight drifted peacefully on to the place now called "Wolfe's Cove."

Wolfe was the first who sprang ashore, and on looking at the precipice that towered above him in the darkness, he turned to the Scottish officer and said, "I do not believe, Sir, there is any possibility of getting up here, but you must do your best." The escalade of the Heights immediately began. On this duty it was remarked that one of the most active of the Frasers was an old Highland gentleman, Malcolm Macpherson of Phoiness, who, when verging on eighty years of age, accompanied the Frasers as a volunteer. Ruined by a law suit he had been driven in old age to become a soldier of fortune. The fury and skill with which he handled his claymore in the subsequent battle so delighted General Townshend, that, through Pitt, he received a commission from King George (Stewart).

Slinging their muskets, the gallant Frasers, some with the swords in their teeth, climbed and scrambled up the steep and bushy precipice, grasping the roots of trees, tufts of grass, rocks, or whatever might aid their difficult ascent, till the summit was at length won, then rushing on, claymore in hand, they dislodged a captain's guard that manned a battery near it, and possessed themselves of a narrow path that enabled their comrades of Louisburg and the Line to reach all the sooner the plateau that stood two hundred and fifty feet above the flowing river below.

Following the daring and hardy Frasers, Wolfe was soon by their side on the plateau of the precipice, and with eagerness and ardour he formed his troops in contiguous columns as they came toiling up, and ere the rising September sun began to gild the spires and ramparts of Quebec and the far-stretching bosom of the mighty St. Lawrence he had his whole force marching in battle array along the famous Heights of Abraham, with colours flying and bayonets glittering in the rays of the morning sun. To keep the redoubt taken by the Frasers to cover the landing place, and to act as a rear-guard, he left two companies, and at once began

to descend from the slopes towards the city.

Montcalm was early advised that his daring antagonist had succeeded in scaling the Heights of Abraham. He could scarcely credit his senses when he was told that he was confronted by his indomitable enemy. There was only one course to pursue. He was now aware that a general action could no longer be avoided, and he felt too, that on its issue rested the fate, not only of Quebec but of all Canada. Drawing in his outposts he rapidly made his dispositions, and marched boldly to the front from his camp at Montmorenci, while the British forces halted about three quarters of a mile from the ramparts of Quebec, with their right flank resting on the edge of a steep precipice that overhangs the St. Lawrence.

The French forces consisted of five regiments of the line, clad in white coats, scarlet vests with gilt buttons. A twelve pounder gun was placed on each flank, and among the bushes and underwood that fringed the front of his line were posted five companies of grenadiers, 150 Canadian riflemen, 230 dragoons, and 870 Canadian militia, in all about 6000 men.

The British line was composed of the Louis-burg Grenadiers, Fraser Highlanders, the 15th, 28th, 38th, and 58th regiments. The light infantry covered the left wing. The precipice already mentioned made the right perfectly secure. The 49th, formed in divisions, was a small reserve in the rear. There was only one light gun that the jolly tars of the fleet succeeded to bring up with incredible labour and skill. All the troops, about 4000, entered the action with bayonets fixed.

(To be continued).

THE CHEYNES.

WHEN studying the history of the old counties of Sutherland and Caithness, one cannot fail to notice the number of powerful and influential families, who, though apparently not blood connections of clans in the above counties, still frequently had a great deal to do with determining the issues of the clan conflicts of long ago. Among such families may be classed the Cheynes, the Mowats (or de Monteaths), the Irvines, Dunbars, Innesses, etc.

The Cheynes can be traced back to the twelfth century. Their name is said to derive its origin from the Gaelic name for venison, the early Cheynes or Chienes having been great hunters.

Reginald, the head of the family, and his son of the same name, were among the Scottish notables, who, in 1284, accepted the Princess

Margaret, "The Maid of Norway," as Queen of Scotland. The younger Reginald, who succeeded his father, was, in 1292, Sheriff of Invernairn. He swore fealty to Edward I. of England in 1296, when that monarch overran Scotland. As a reward he was, by Edward I. in 1305, appointed one of the justiciaries for Northern Scotland. Sir Reginald died in 1313. By his wife, Mary, eldest daughter and co-heiress of Festyn de Moray, he left a son and namesake, who, besides succeeding to the estates of his father, inherited, in his mother's right, the manse and castle of Duffus, as well as lands in Moray, Caithness, and West Lothian. This son of Mary de Moray was one of the Scottish nobles, who, in 1320, subscribed the famous letter to the Pope, maintaining the independence of Scotland. Reginald died in 1350. He left no male heirs, but was succeeded by his two daughters as co-heiresses.

Tradition has it, that, when Cheyne's lady was pregnant of her first child, Reginald was most anxious that it should be a son; the child, however, was a daughter. Enraged and disappointed the father gave orders that the child should be drowned, and delivered it to one of his retainers for that purpose. A mother's love, however, defeated the enraged father's project, and the child was conveyed to a place of safety. Then the next child with which Lady Cheyne presented her spouse was also a girl, whose destruction, though likewise decreed by the father, was, in the same way as that of the elder daughter, arrested by the mother's stratagem. Lady Cheyne bore her husband no more children. She contrived to have her two daughters secretly brought up and educated in a manner befitting their birth. After they had arrived at the age of womanhood Sir Reginald had occasion to give a large entertainment, which was attended by many guests. Lady Cheyne chose this occasion for letting their father see his daughters, without telling him who they were. Among the guests Sir Reginald was much struck by the beauty of two young ladies, whose names he could not ascertain, and exclaimed : "How happy must he be who can call these girls his own!" This auspicious moment was availed of by Lady Cheyne to present the two unknown beauties to Sir Reginald as his own daughters. The overjoyed father embraced the girls and introduced them to the assembled company as his daughters and heiresses.

On Sir Reginald's death in 1350, his two daughters inherited his estates. Marriot married first Sir John Douglas, who died without issue. She took, for her second husband, John de Keith (second son of Edward de Keith, the Marischal), by whom she had a son, Andrew, who inherited his mother's estates. Mary, the other daughter of Sir Reginald Cheyne, married Nicol Sutherland, second son of Kenneth, Earl of Sutherland, who obtained with her the barony of Duffus. From this marriage sprang the family of Sutherland, Lord Duffus.

An old seat of the Cheynes was the Castle of Dirlet, on the River Thurso.

Rangoon. FRANK ADAM.

ALEXANDER POLSON, J.P.

TO those who have been interested in the social progress of the Highlands during the past fifteen years the name of Alexander Polson is a familiar one. Mr. Polson is the eldest son of the late Mr. William Polson, Captain of *The Brothers* of Brora, at which place he was born forty years ago.

He was educated at the Free Church School of his parish, and when a youth he served an apprenticeship as Pupil Teacher under Mr. William Baillie, who is well known as one of the best living authorities on the natural history of Sutherland. On the conclusion of his apprenticeship Mr. Polson secured a Queen's Scholarship and entered the Edinburgh F. C. Training College in 1876, and at the exit examinations two years later he obtained a high place in the First Division of Merit. For a year he was an assistant at Lybster and was then appointed Headmaster of Dunbeath. During the years he was there the average attendance at that school doubled and the Government grant increased threefold, so that the Education Department and the County Council recognised it as a centre for Secondary Education, and when he resigned the School Board presented him with a cheque for a large sum and an excellent testimonial, and the inhabitants of the district with costly testimonials.

That he made education a matter of study became evident when it was announced that the Royal Scottish Geographical Society had awarded him their first prize for an essay on "The Best Methods of Teaching Geography in Elementary Schools." He developed the education of the youth by evening classes in connection with South Kensington, and that he might know scientific subjects well he spent four short sessions at the Royal College of Science, London. All this time he was taking a keen interest in social questions which were pressing for solution,

ALEXANDER POLSON, J.P.

and he was one of the witnesses chosen to give evidence for his native parish of Clyne before Lord Napier's Commission. He also gave valuable evidence before the Deer Forest Commission when they sat at Wick.

He was greatly interested in the fishermen of his district, and was chiefly instrumental in collecting nearly £2000 with which to repair and extend the harbour. The people recognised his ability and energy and on two occasions have returned him to the County Council for the Berriedale division of Caithness; he was also made a Justice of the Peace of that county. His old pupils and natives of the county have twice entertained him to a public dinner in Edinburgh, and on the second occasion presented him with a beautiful illuminated address.

But Mr. Polson's leanings have long been towards literature, and he has found time to write sketches, stories, and essays for many magazines and papers, including *The Graphic*, *Scots Pictorial*, *People's Journal*, *People's Friend*, etc. He has also written the interesting chapter on "Folk-lore" in the volume on *Sutherland and the Reay Country*, as well as several papers on Highland subjects in *The Transactions of the Gaelic Society of Inverness*, one long one being on "The Social Progress of the Highlands since 1800." Now that he has in some measure retired from public life, more literary work may be expected from him, and a guide book and a volume of papers on Highland subjects from his pen will probably be published next spring.

Mr. Polson is happily married to a daughter of the late Mr. James Conacher of the firm of James Conacher & Sons, Organ Builders, Huddersfield.

Dunbeath.   ADAM MACKAY.

SIR FITZROY DONALD MACLEAN, C.B., OF DUART, AT INCH KENNETH.

THIS photo of Sir Fitzroy Donald Maclean, C.B., of Duart and Morven, Chief of the Clan, with Lady Maclean and a son and daughter, was taken by Mr. W Drummond Norie, the well-known Celtic litterateur, in July last, in the ancient Maclean burying ground of Inch Kenneth, Loch na Keal, Mull. Desirous of inspecting the ancient sculptured stones in this old graveyard, he visited it in July, and was agreeably surprised to find on arriving there that the Chief of the Clan, with members of his family, was also paying a visit that day to the place of sepulture of his ancestors, to see that the old carved stones were in a proper state of preservation. Desirous of having an appropriate memento of such an interesting meeting, he secured the annexed photo of the Chief and his family, which we have much pleasure in reproducing here with the kind permission of the Chief and Mr. W. Drummond Norie. No doubt it will greatly interest our readers, and especially the members of the Clan Maclean.

The sculptured effigy in the foreground is supposed to be that of Sir Alan Maclean, who lived at Inch Kenneth, and entertained Dr. Johnson and Boswell there on Sunday and Monday, October 17th and 18th, 1773. Judging from the costume of the figure there can be little doubt that the memorial stone is of a much earlier period, probably of the 16th century, and represents another Chief of the Clan Maclean. It was a common practice in the Highlands to place ancient carved stones over later interments, and this seems to have been done in the case of Sir Alan. We have seen in a northern churchyard part of a beautifully carved Iona cross placed over the grave of a respectable tradesman who died about the middle of this century, and upon which his name and age were carved in bold letters. The effect was very amusing and incongruous.

DUNVEGAN AND ITS ASSOCIATIONS.

ANYONE visiting Dunvegan Castle is sure to notice the improved entrance, as compared with what he reads of in ancient records describing this interesting edifice.

RORY MOR'S NURSE.

The ancient entrance rose up in flights of steps cut in the rock, and passed into a courtyard through a portal, but now an easier one, yet in keeping with the characteristics of the place, has been formed.

Near to the castle is a pretty cascade divided into two branches and called "Rory Mor's Nurse," because this renowned chief loved to be lulled to sleep by its murmuring sounds.

One of the places of sepulture of the Macleods of Dunvegan is the ancient churchyard of Kilmuir. This place of burial contains many interesting stones, as well as many unlettered graves. Here a number of the MacCrimmon pipers lie buried. One of the most famous of these was Padruig Mor. It is told that on one occasion he went to church with eight sons, the handsomest ever seen, and before the end of that year he saw seven of them buried in Kilmuir. It was this sad bereavement which formed the theme of that affecting piobaireachd "Cumha na Cloinne"— The Lament for the Children—in which the old piper poured forth the bitter sorrow which filled his soul.

It was this famous piper who composed the well-known pibroch "I kissed the King's hand." The occasion is stated by the clan historian to have been as follows:—After the Restoration of Charles II., in 1660, Roderick proceeded to London to pay his homage to the King, and was very kindly received by His Majesty. He was, however, so much cut up because Charles made no reference to the ruin of his family and the Clan Macleod at the battle of Worcester, and its mournful results in Skye, that he at once returned home. He had taken his piper, Patrick Mor MacCrimmon, who had also been at the battle of Worcester, along with him to Court, on which he was allowed "to kiss hands," as a very special honour. MacCrimmon appears to have thought a great deal more about this incident than of the slaughter of his clansmen at the battle of Worcester, and he commemorated the honour conferred upon him, and the other polite attentions paid to him by the King, by composing the famous piobaireachd "Thug mi pog do laimh an Righ"— (I kissed the King's hand)—one of the verses of which is as follows:—

Thug mi pog is pog is pog
Ciun d' thug mi pog do laimh an Righ;
'S cha d' chuir gaoth an craicionn caorach,
Fear a fhuair an fhaoilt ach mi.

I gave a kiss, I gave a kiss,
I gave a kiss to the King's hand,
He ne'er in sheepskin bag blew wind
Who got such welcome by command.

Kilmuir is also the resting place of our Highland heroine, Flora Macdonald, who died 4th March, 1790, at the age of 68. For over four score years the grave of Prince Charlie's

KILMUIR GRAVEYARD

protector remained utterly neglected. This long neglect has now been fully atoned for by the erection, in 1872, of a beautiful monument of very light coloured granite in the form of an Iona Cross, 28 feet 6 inches in height, one of the tallest of the kind in the kingdom. The inscription reads: "Flora Macdonald, born at Milton, South Uist, in 1722, died at Kingsburgh, Skye, 4th March, 1790."

Over the remains of the present chief's mother a chaste marble stone has been erected. It is surmounted by the Macleod arms and reads: "Sacred to the memory of the Honourable Louisa Barbara, wife of Macleod of Macleod, and daughter of Lord St Johns of Bletsoe. Born January 11th, 1816, Died 17th October, 1889. 'The souls of the righteous are in the hand of God.'" In the same grave lie the mortal remains of the late chief, who died in December, 1895.   FIONN.

MACLEOD MONUMENT IN KILMUIR GRAVEYARD.

THE CLAN GREGOR SOCIETY.— The Autumn Meeting of Council of the Clan Gregor Society was held on 20th September in the Royal Hotel, Edinburgh, at which the Rev. Charles Macgregor, D.D., presided. The ordinary business of the Society falling to be transacted at this time was taken up— several new members having been admitted, bursaries granted to young men and women belonging to the clan, and charitable grants made to certain old persons connected with it.

SUIDHE-CHALLAN THE STONEY SEAT.

CELESTIAL pyramid, thou makest that of
      Cheops like a mole,
  While thy confused pile of rocks by thermal
      force flung high in air,
Flouts the mean heap of laboured stone that crowns
      the hill of Gizeh by the Nile.
Primeval man has gazed upon thy peak and named
  thee as his fancy tutored him;
Whether the 'Maiden's Breast' or 'Seat of Fairy
  Queen,' or 'Mountain of the rough and rocky
  top,'
When Romans from the south swept o'er our land
  in conquering legions, thee they could not pass,
But at thy southern base, at 'Fort of Gael,' stood
  still and paused with battled arms.
When Wallace from the rage of Saxon hordes
  sought refuge in thy weird locality,
A night he passed in 'Sedmar na Stainge,' betwixt
  'Craig Vhar' and 'Craig an Fhithich;'
Whence viewed thy hardy crest towers royal in the
  sky.
And nearer at thy feet by fair 'Dun Alaister,'
'The Bruce sought refuge with his hunted queen,
Till such time as the Sassunach emerging from the
  glen in full array at 'Lassantullich' met him;
At 'Tompech' they turned and fled till on 'Dalhosnie's' plain the shout of triumph rose.
Yet stands the 'Clach na Boile,' set to tell the tale
  of victory,
Upon that ancient battle-ground, now tilled and
  fenced,
Thou still look'st down, impassive grey Schichallion!
Ride on in azure giant prism, like jewel fixt upon
  the great earth's crust,
And while that ponderous orb upon its axis spins,
  still plunging through the star-sown sphere,
Be thou a Beacon fired by solar beam blazing aloft
  at morn and dewy eve.
And as a sweet voice came from Memnon's rock, so
  may'st thou preach to men a text perpetual,
Which permeating Scotland shall extend to other
  lands,
And teach from out the infinitude, 'Be devout, be
  free!'

Rannoch, July, 1898.   K. M.

THE MACLEODS OF DUNVEGAN.

6th September, 1898.

SIR— In his very interesting article on the Macleods of Harris, "Fionn" has made a mistake in saying that Rory Mor died at Dunvegan. It so happens that he expired at the Chanonrie of Ross (Fortrose) in 1626, and his remains were interred in the Aisle of Fortrose Cathedral, where his tomb, with inscription, can be seen.

He also made a mistake with regard to the Battle of Cairinish; it was the Macleods who were defeated there and not the Macdonalds.

I am, etc.,

Waternish House,   A. R. MACDONALD.
Isle of Skye.

THE MOD AT OBAN.

THE Mòd, which has this year returned to its birth-place, Oban, was held there on 13th September, and proved the most successful yet held. The chair was occupied by Dr. Charles Fraser-Mackintosh, whose name is revered by Highlanders all the world over. He was supported by Messrs. John Mackay, Hereford (that other great leader of the Gaelic race), Kenneth Macdonald, Town Clerk, Inverness, D. A. S. Mackintosh, Rev. Dr. Stewart, Nether Lochaber, Malcolm Macfarlane, James Mackellar, John Mackay, Editor, *Celtic Monthly*, Henry Whyte (Fionn), W. Drummond Norie, William Grant, London, Archibald Sinclair, Roderick Macleod, Inverness, Niel Campbell, John M. Campbell, John Campbell, Hon. Secy., John Mackintosh, Secy., Alexander Mackay and John Mackay, Edinburgh, A. Mackenzie Macleod, A. Mackenzie Mackay, Duncan Mackenzie, the Hon. Elspeth Campbell, etc. The weather was unfavourable, and the attendance was only fairly good at the beginning, but when the music competitions commenced the hall was crowded.

On rising to address the meeting, the learned chairman was very enthusiastically received. He said that in opening the seventh Mòd in Oban, he felt very much honoured at having been asked to take the chair on a second occasion. Perhaps it would have been better had the choice fallen on some of the worthy sons of the county of Argyll. It afforded him very great pleasure to hear, from the last announcement read by Mr. Whyte, that the prizes offered by the Glasgow Skye Association to children attending Skye schools, for the best Gaelic essay on any topic of local interest, had, in every case, been awarded to children from the remote island of Rona. (Applause). It was usual at Celtic meetings to make a brief reference to some prominent Highlanders who had left them since their previous gathering. With their permission, he would refer to two very prominent men, one of whom was intimately connected with their own county of Argyll. He alluded to the late Evan M'Coll, the bard of Loch Fyne. (Applause). The other person to whom he wished to refer was the late Alexander Mackenzie, of the *Scottish High-lander*, who was as well known in Canada as he was in the Highlands of Scotland.

SCHOOL TEACHERS' COMPETITION.

Mr. Macfarlane intimated the result of the competition for school teachers showing the highest percentage of passes in Gaelic, as follows :—
1. Hylipol, Tyree, £11 ; 2. Kilchoan, £9 ; 3. Cornaigmore, £6 6s. ; and 4. Oban, £4 10s.

REPORTS BY DELEGATES.

During the proceedings in the forenoon, reports were submitted from the delegates of the Mòd to the Eisteddfod in Wales, to the Feis-Ceoil in Belfast, and to the Oireachtas in Dublin. Mr. D. A. S. Mackintosh said that he had visited both the Feis-Ceoil and the Eisteddfod, and that at both places he had received the most flattering reception. Mr. John Mackay, Hereford, who also represented the Mòd at the Eisteddfod, gave an interesting account of the proceedings, and described his election as a bard. Mr. Malcolm Macfarlane, as the delegate of the Mòd to the Oireachtas, said that he had had a most cordial reception from the Celts of Ireland. Mr. John Macneill, B.A., Mr. Macnally, and Mr. A. W. Martin represented the Gaelic League of Ireland.

THE PRIZE LIST.

The following are the names of the winners of the Literary competitions :—

Gaelic Poem or Song.—1. Donald Mackechnie, Forth Street, Edinburgh ; 2 and 3. Alexander Stewart, Glenlyon, and William Macphail, Cornaigmore, Tyree—equal.

Metrical Translation from English into Gaelic of Burns' Poem, "Epistle to a young friend."—1 and 2. Alexander Stewart, Glenlyon, and Rev. John Maclellan, Oxford Drive, Kelvinside, Glasgow—equal.

Gaelic Prose Competition.—1. Duncan MacCallum, 12 St. Clair Street, Glasgow ; 2. Rev. Charles M. Robertson, Inverness.

Gaelic Essay.—Rev. Charles M. Robertson.

Gaelic Essay by Skye School Children.—1. John Macleod, Braig, Rona, and Catherine Nicolson, Rona ; 2. Kenneth Maclennan, Rona, and Bella Nicolson, Rona.

Gaelic Recitation. — 1. Malcolm Maccallum, Ballachulish ; 2 and 3. John Macfadyen, Glasgow, and Duncan Maccallum, Glasgow—equal.

Gaelic Reading.—1. A. D. Macneill, Oban ; 2. Malcolm Maccallum, Ballachulish.

The following are the names of the winners of the Musical competitions :—

Choral Competitions for Juniors.—1. Oban Gaelic Musical Association Junior Choir ; 2. Rhinns Junior Gaelic Choir, Islay.

Solo Competition for Juniors.—Female Voices—1. Miss Jessie Duncan, Islay ; 2. Miss Jane Currie, Islay. Male Voices—1. Edmund Black, Islay ; 2. Alexander MacLellan, Islay.

Solo Competitions for Seniors.—Female Voices—1. Miss Lizzie Mackenzie, Inverness ; 2. Miss Tina Carmichael, Glasgow ; 3. Miss Macvean, Oban. Male Voices—1. D. D. Macdonald, Skye ; 2. Alexander Macleod, Inverness ; 3. W. R. Christie, Inverness.

Duet Competition.—1. Miss Kate Maccoll and Miss E. Maceachran, Oban ; and Miss Mary Ann Mackechnie and Mr. W. A. Spence, Oban—equal.

Solo Singing, with Highland Harp Accompaniment.—1. Miss Emily Macdonald, Cathcart, Glasgow ; and Miss Mary Ann Mackechnie, Oban—equal.

Quartette Competition.—Inverness Gaelic Party.

Solo Singing, (open).—Roderick Macleod, Inverness.

Choral Competition for Seniors.—1 Oban Gaelic Musical Association ; 2. Inverness Gaelic Choir ; 3. Perth Gaelic Society Choir.

Solo Singing—Skye Songs.—1. Alexander Macleod, Inverness ; 2. Miss L. Mackenzie, Inverness ; 3. D. D. Macdonald, Skye.

NEXT YEAR'S MOD IN PERTH.

At the Annual Business Meeting of the Association, held in the afternoon, it was decided that the Mòd next year should be held in Perth, probably in October. The Marquis of Tullibardine was elected President. The usual evening concert in the Drill Hall was attended by a large and fashionable audience.

PETER MACDONALD.

MR. AND MRS. MACDONALD AND FAMILY.

THE CELTIC MONTHLY:

A MAGAZINE FOR HIGHLANDERS.

Edited by JOHN MACKAY, Glasgow.

No. 2 Vol. VII.]   NOVEMBER, 1898.   [Price Threepence.

PETER MACDONALD, GLASGOW.

OF the many natives of Ross-shire who have settled and prospered in Glasgow there is no one better known or more highly respected than the Highlander who forms the subject of this sketch. Mr. Peter Macdonald, although still a comparatively young man, has already, by his indomitable perseverance and native ability, earned for himself a position of influence which reflects upon him the greatest credit, and which may be only considered as a stepping stone to higher honours.

Mr. Macdonald is a native of Portmahomack, Easter Ross, and came to Glasgow over thirty years ago as manager of the rectifying department of Messrs. James Mackenzie, Sons, & Co. On Mr. Mackenzie's death in 1876, Mr. Macdonald acquired the business, and during the intervening years he has, by close attention to business, made an extensive and valuable connection, his firm now occupying a prominent position in the wholesale trade. It is not our intention here to refer more particularly to the firm's specialties, for we have no doubt that many of our readers are quite able to speak from experience of the excellence of their blends; it is sufficient to say that they have stood the test of years, and have lost none of their popularity, than which no better test could be applied to any goods. Mr. Macdonald is the owner of the large range of buildings in which his offices are situated, but no one could have any idea of the labyrinth of vaults and cellars, filled with a vast stock of wines, spirits, and trade requisites, which underlie these buildings,

unless he had been personally through them. Just as Mr. Macdonald has been successful in business, so also has he been in other spheres. As a Highlander there are few better known in Celtic circles in Glasgow than the clansman of whom we write. At clan and county gatherings his presence is always welcome. Of course, in the Ross-shire Association there is no more prominent personality than that of Mr. Macdonald, for he has been a member for very many years, and has held nearly every office. Many a poor unfortunate Ross-shire man, "down on his luck" in this great city, has been assisted by him, and many a promising lad, now occupying a good position in Glasgow, owes his first start in life to the influence of the subject of this sketch. The Clan Macdonald Society also has a good friend in Mr. Macdonald. He is a Vice-President, while his son, Mr. John Macdonald, is the able and energetic Joint Secretary of the Society. The Annual Social Gathering of the clan, by the way, takes place in Glasgow on the 28th October, Clanranald presiding, and we hope to see a large and enthusiastic attendance.

A brief reference might be made to the masonic craft, in which he occupies a prominent place. For twenty years he was a member of Star Lodge, 219, of which he was R. W. M. for two years. This year Mr. Macdonald was the recipient of a handsome presentation from his brother masons. It consisted of a valuable silver salver, which bore the following inscription :—" Presented to Brother and Mrs. Macdonald, along with an I. P. M's jewel, fish and fruit knives, and to Miss Macdonald a diamond bracelet " His two sons, John and William, were at the same time presented with gold scarf pins.

Before concluding, reference might suitably be made to the tangible way in which he remembered the place of his birth. In 1892, Mr. Macdonald presented the busy fishing town of Portmahomack with a magnificent drinking fountain and cattle trough, which is considered the most prominent feature of the district. The event was made the occasion of great celebrations in the district, and it is hardly needful to say that Mr. Macdonald received a hearty Highland welcome.

Two years ago he was an unsuccessful candidate for municipal honours in Govan, but if he can be induced to enter the next contest it is generally admitted that the representative of the great Clan Donald is not likely to sustain a second reverse.

JOHN MACDONALD,
JOINT SECRETARY, CLAN MACDONALD SOCIETY

THE BROTHERS OF LOCH LOMOND.

HE late Sir James Colquhoun and his second brother, John, the author of the "Moor and the Loch," were singularly devoted to each other, and were never parted till the younger brother went into the army. When their sainted mother, Lady Colquhoun, bade them and their brother, William, farewell, her dying words were—"Meet me, I charge you, at the right hand of the Throne of God!"

Sir James, the eldest brother, after a life of honored usefulness, spent chiefly on his estates for the good of the people entrusted to his care, was drowned in Loch Lomond on his return passage from Inch Ionaig, the "Deer Forest"

of the Colquhouns, where he had gone with four keepers to shoot his annual present for his "retainers," December 18th, 1873. The party killed nine red deer, and it was while returning to Rossdhu in a rising gale the boat was swamped, and Sir James and the keepers met a watery grave. Had the crew been the regular oarsmen, in all likelihood the case might have been different. Sir James steered the boat himself, and his watch—an heirloom, an old gold "repeater"—told the hour (five o'clock) when the mournful accident occurred. The loch was dragged in all directions, but it was not till ten days after the catastrophe that the body of Sir James was recovered by the barge of the Duke of Montrose, under the charge of the Duke's head keeper.

On a previous occasion Sir James had a narrow escape on Loch Lomond. The boat in which he was rowing was dashed to pieces in a gale, and his companions "lost their heads" in the squall, but previously Sir James managed to get them into shallow water, and himself remained perfectly calm and collected. There was no truer friend and helper of the poor, and, indeed, of all who sought his aid or counsel. One who lived on the property said, "I loved just to see him walking about—if only to see him and know he was there!" and those words yet will find echo in many a Highland heart of the West.

When the summons came for Sir James for the "other shore," his only son was travelling in the Far East, and it can easily be imagined what his feelings were. Those of his "Uncle John" were scarcely less poignant when called to the saddened shores of Loch Lomond, on which the brothers had so often rowed victoriously in company, and were parted on that chill December by the hand of death for "a little while."

The author of the "Moor and the Loch" has been likened to Isaac Walton, and in their nobility of character, tenderness of heart, and enthusiastic love of nature, there is great similarity. Like every true sportsman, John Colquhoun was one of nature's darlings and favourites. One, a gifted author himself, wrote of him:— "As he moves along the mountain side or through the lush grass, the trees distil their gems, the herbs shed their incense, and the flowers breathe fragrance about his path."

John Colquhoun was born at 6 Charlotte Square, Edinburgh, on the 6th of March, 1805. It was at Rossdhu he and his brothers were brought up in their early days. Their mother—the "good Lady Colquhoun"—sought to guide their feet in the "narrow way" which leads to life, while the purple hills and the blue loch imparted their own impressions.

John especially was full of mischief. To leave the free, wild life at Rossdhu, and to be torn from their beloved haunts, was a bitter pain to the trio, who were sent with a tutor to the High School at Edinburgh. After several seasons there, they went to school at Winteringham, Lincolnshire, which had educated Henry Kirke White and other noted scholars.

One of the great griefs of the boys was parting with him they considered the best instructor they had ever had—the one who superintended their out-door accomplishments, Tom Yule, the footman. The said Tom was reared in the establishment of the grandfather of the present Earl of Haddington, who kept a pack of hounds, and was considered the leading Scotch hunting sportsman of the day. Tom Yule was an expert swimmer, a noted race-runner, and practical sportsman, delighting to impart his knowledge to such sympathetic pupils. The best of friends as they were, however, they were forced to say farewell to Tom, and to exchange their native hills for the flats of Lincolnshire. In the auto-biography at the beginning of the "Moor and the Loch," John Colquhoun tells amusing stories of their school life which, in truth, was a some-what melancholy experience to the boys of the mountain and the flood.

After a few years at Winteringham, John Colquhoun joined the 33rd Regiment, "The

A GLIMPSE OF LOCH LOMOND.

Duke's Own," while his much-loved eldest brother travelled abroad, and the youngest went to Cambridge. The 33rd was at that time in Ireland, and many stirring adventures John had to tell his listeners of life amongst "the Paddies" in those still-hunting days. His next exchange was to the 4th (Royal Irish Dragoon Guards), quartered at York, and it was there he was taught to become a good "soldier of the Cross." Not long after he joined the regiment he met with an accident when hunting, which laid him aside for some time, and it was then that to him "old things passed away, and all things became new." He appears at this crisis of his life to have begun to read his Bible in a way he had never done before, which is evidenced by an interesting letter to his sister at Rossdhu.

Amongst his brother officers John Colquhoun does not seem to have had any who sympathised with him in his views. On this account he was very unhappy, and before many years he "sold out" of the 4th Dragoon Guards and married Fran-cis Sara, daughter of E. Fuller Maitland, M.P., of Park Place, Oxfordshire, and Stanstead Hall, Essex. His bride was in all respects worthy of such a husband, and the union was a singularly happy one. Year after year we find entries in his journal of increased happiness as time sped on ; and in her diary, too, she speaks of her home as "one of the very brightest on earth." Four sons and five daughters were born to them, all nine being spared to grow up to manhood and womanhood, while the family tie of affection was exceptionally close and strong. It was ever impressed upon the children by their parents that their home duties were the most important of all, and while training them for "the skies," it was their especial delight to teach them the joy of making this earth the richer by ministering to the poor, the sick, and the sorrowing, both in town and in their Highland homes.

For about thirty years John Colquhoun had a district in the Grassmarket (New Greyfriars' Parish, Edinburgh), where he held meetings, and when the houses in that region were condemned and swept away, he transferred his work to Greenside Parish, near his house in Royal Terrace. Pale faces brightened when they heard the sportsman's step in their miserable garrets or at the tops of their high winding stairs, and their hearts beat with a new hope as they crowded to his meetings and listened to the words of life coming from lips not unacquainted with the hunter's "View, halloa!" His was the Celtic nature of repressed but passionate devotion to all that is best and noblest; truly, therefore, the possession of more men like John Colquhoun would make both the Church and the world richer than they are.

On the 27th of May, 1877, his beloved wife was parted from him by the hand of death, leaving a legacy in "Rhymes and Chimes," a volume published shortly before she died. When fifteen years of age she wrote the chief part of the hymn, "Much in sorrow, oft in woe," the first ten lines of which were begun by Henry Kirke White, and left by him unfinished. Till within a very few years of his death, John Colquhoun was the strongest of the strong, and up to the last he enjoyed remarkably good health, though latterly he had several sharp attacks from chills, being always too careless of himself.

It was a remarkable coincidence that the eighth anniversary of her death, from inflammation of the lungs, was the day on which they were re-united for ever. All through his illness of five weeks his mind was kept in perfect peace, having underneath him, as he said, the "everlasting arms." The day before he was taken he "saw a vision, Heaven opened!"— uttering his wife's name as if he actually saw her. On the morning of the 27th of May, 1885, he called his daughter to him, saying, "Don't you think I am wearin' awn'? I saw it in Angus's face!" The last words he spoke were to Dr Angus Macdonald, three hours before all was over, "At evening time it shall be light!"

Two of the band of his nine children, the eldest and the youngest, "crossed the stream" before their honoured father. The rest of the family group mourned him as such a father deserved to be mourned, all in happy homes of their own except one, whose delight and privilege it was to minister to him, and who still misses the touch of the "vanished hand" every hour of every day. It may be added, as the key-note of what has been told of John Colquhoun, that one day, shortly before his death, on looking earnestly at his hands for some time, he remarked to his daughter—"I sometimes think I should like to have been crucified to show my love to the Saviour."

F. MARY COLQUHOUN.

AN ELEGANT HIGHLAND EPITAPH.

ON the back of a painting in my possession, that of a child, where it was pasted about sixty years ago, is the following newspaper cutting:—" There is something singularly beautiful and affecting in the following epitaph, which an old newspaper represents as taken from one (in Gaelic, probably) in the Parish Church of Glenorchy, in Argyllshire:— 'Lo she lies here in the dust, and her memory fills me with grief; *silent is the tongue of melody, and the hand of elegance is now at rest.* No more shall the poor give thee his blessing, nor shall the naked be warmed with the fleece of thy flock; the tear shalt thou not wipe away from the eye of the wretched. Where now, O feeble, is thy wonted help! No more, my fair, shall we meet thee in the social hall; no more shall we sit at thy hospitable board. Gone forever is the sound of mirth; the kind, the candid, the meek, is now no more. Who can express our grief! Flow, ye tears of woe!'"

The deep pathos of the words which I have put in *italics*, makes one wonder whither the late Poet Laureate, Lord Tennyson, had seen the epitaph before he had written his beautiful lyric, beginning—

'Break, break, break,
    On thy cold grey stones, O sea!'

For it is in this lyric that the often-quoted, and misquoted, lines, so familiar and so expressive of the wish of many a bereaved heart, occur—

'But O for the touch of a vanished hand,
    And the sound of a voice that is still!'

The 'silent tongue' and the 'hand at rest' of the touching Gaelic epitaph are simply reproduced in the exquisite lines of the English poet.

JAS. MACKINTOSH.

THE CALEDONIAN MEDICAL JOURNAL for October has just reached us, and contains several most valuable and interesting articles by well-known Highlanders. The Annual Meeting and Dinner was held recently in Edinburgh, and seems to have been a most enjoyable function. We are pleased to notice that quite a number of our own readers take an active part in the work of the Society, Dr. M. D. Macleod being elected President, Dr. A. Campbell Clark, Vice-President, Dr. Macnaughton, Editor, and Dr. S. R. Macphail, Secretary and Treasurer.

SOME MEMBERS OF THE CLAN MACKAY AT THE OBAN MOD.

Alexander Mackay,   John Mackay, C.E., J.P.,   [Dr. Alex. Dingwall,   John MacKay,
Edinburgh.   Hereford.   Renton.   Editor, *Celtic Monthly*

THE CLAN MACKAY DEPUTATION IN THE REAY COUNTRY.
TAKEN AT RHICONICH HOTEL.

Roderick Macleod,   Rev. Angus Mackay, M.A.,   Mr. Macdonald,   Adam Mackay,   Dr. Dingwall,
Inverness.   West dale.   Chief Constable   Dunbeath.   Renton.
                                               of Sutherland.

John Mackay, Hon. Secy.,   John Mackay,   James H. Mackay, Vice-Pres.,   Alex. Mackay,
Editor, *Celtic Monthly*. Hereford.   London.   Edinburgh.

WITH THE CLAN MACKAY.

DESCRIPTIVE ACCOUNT OF THE RECENT TOUR IN THE REAY COUNTRY.

(BY ONE OF THE DEPUTATION).

CLAN sentiment is a most powerful and contagious influence. Sufficient proof is the phenomenal success which has attended the resuscitation of the numerous clan societies, of which the Clan Mackay was the earliest. By this sentiment alone, individuals, families, districts, and clansmen, not only in the Highlands but the whole world over, have been brought together and welded into one.

For the second time within nine years, a deputation of the Clan Mackay last month completed an extensive tour throughout their much beloved Reay Country. Their visit was no raid of war nor rapine, it was not political nor ecclesiastical, but one of benevolence and beneficence, to increase and stimulate interest in the language, literature, and music of the Gael, particularly in *Duthaich Mhic Aoidh.*

The deputation—which consisted of John Mackay, C.E., Hereford (convener); John Mackay, editor of *Celtic Monthly,* Glasgow (secretary); James H. Mackay, London, vice-president, originally from Kildonan; Dr. Alexander Dingwall, Renton; Adam Mackay, Dunbeath; Roderick Macleod, Inverness; Rev. Angus Mackay, M.A., Westerdale, Caithness; Alexander Mackay, St. Andrew Square, Edinburgh—travelled to Thurso from Oban, where several of the party took part in the Gaelic *Mòd.* Lord and Lady Reay, but for their unavoidable absence at the coronation of the Queen of Holland, were to have been with the deputation. They sent messages and valuable prizes. At Lairg the deputation was joined by the Rev. Dr. James Aberigh-Mackay, chief of the Abrach branch of the Clan, originally from the party took part in the Gaelic urgent business, of Provost Mackay, Thurso, the deputation were met at Georgemas Junction by his son, Mr. Donald Mackay, and were hospitably entertained for the night. The many places and things of antiquarian interest were visited and examined. Throughout the tour facts anent the *Bratach Bhan* controversy were specially kept in view, and several important discoveries were made which will, it is expected, once and for all settle this question for the Mackays, and be a conclusive reply to the ill-natured and offensive reflections as to its authenticity, recently made by a certain Inverness rector, who has made himself the "universal dictator" on all Highland antiquarian subjects. His dogmatic assertions are likely to create some amusement in the light of the evidence which the Clan are now preparing for publication.

Next morning the deputation proceeded to Melvich. At Forss House, an ancient seat of the clan, we were welcomed and entertained by Mr. Alex. Mackay and the Misses Mackay. The menu is surely worthy of publication :—

"Thoir dùbhlan agus dìon, 's bi fìrinneach gus a' chrìoch "
Saus Gearr.
Iasg-geal bruich agus Cucumber.
Coinnean.
Muilteal Ròiste.
Earagean.
Buttàt, Peasair, Pònar, Cal.
Pònar Fràncach, Smiromheas
Cearcan fraoich ròiste.
Gimeach.
Ubhlan, &c.
Toraibhean.
Uisge-beatha.

After visiting the house and grounds, we went westwards. At Reay a halt was made, and the old churchyard, church, and other places of interest were visited. Long before we reached Melvich we were assured of the cordial welcome we were to receive throughout our visit. Before we could see the crowd we could hear their hearty cheers, and flags were flying everywhere. After a brief halt, the beautiful Mackay banner, presented to the deputation by Councillor Angus Mackay, Wick, was unfurled amidst the greatest enthusiasm, and the whole crowd marched to the strains of the bagpipes by Pipers Macleod, Mackay, and Macdonald to Bass-muag, a beautiful grass-lined hollow near the sea.

Hereford, who was chief of the deputation, briefly and eloquently explained the object of the meeting. He was followed by Rev. Angus Mackay and Mr. J. H. Mackay, London, and others. The speeches were cordially received, and listened to most attentively.

The competitions were numerous, particularly in Gaelic reading. Deciding the prizes was no easy matter. Nearly every competitor could read the Gaelic Testament and Bible correctly, and it was quite impossible to differentiate until the songs of Donnachadh Bàn and Alastair Macdonald were put before the competitors. This equally applies to all the centres visited. We were extremely

MELVICH VILLAGE.

struck with the alacrity with which grey old men and women and bare-footed lassies came forward to compete, and the patience with which the crowds watched the competitions during sederunts of from three to five hours. The Gaelic singing, the pipe music, or the solo recitations for the children did not excite a tithe of the interest taken in Gaelic reading and spelling. The beautiful singing of Mr. Roderick Macleod, fresh from his premier honours at the *Mòd*, was indeed appreciated. His delightful renderings may have discouraged local candidates at the different centres to come forward this year, but his efforts cannot fail to make everyone realise the wealth of the Celtic Lyre. There are as good voices in the Reay Country (Mr. Macleod himself is a native) as in broad Scotland, going to waste for want of encouragement and proper training.

The open air meeting over, a very successful concert was held in the Public School in the evening, Hereford presided. Besides the Gaelic songs and several interesting speeches, Mr. Macleod gave an exhibition of the gramaphone, which quite tickled the audience here as it did throughout the tour.

Next morning we were early astir for Bettyhill, and everywhere our reception was cordiality itself. Flags were flying from every prominent knoll. Each township marched to the rendezvous at Farr with flags flying and pipers playing. At the school we were welcomed by Rev. Mr. Maclean and Rev. Mr. Mackenzie, Mr. Evander Mackay, and the rest of the local committee, who had everything in readiness for the competition to begin. Rev. Mr. Mackenzie, who is enthusiastic in the teaching of Gaelic, delivered a most interesting address of welcome, in which he lauded the Celtic sentiment, and warmly

THE SMITHY, TONGUE.

thanked Mr. Mackay, Hereford, for the some two score valuable prizes, besides text-books, he had already sent to the parish. Well might they say of the Clan Mackay and their real true chief, Hereford —"Gu ma fada beò thu, is ceò as do thigh." Addresses were also delivered by Hereford and the secretary (who offered to send candidates from the Reay Country at the expense of the Society to the *Mòd* at Perth next year).

Competition was then begun, and keen enough it was, particularly in reading. The remarks about Melvich apply even more so here. With no little difficulty were the prizes adjudged. The singing was on the whole much better. The deputies were welcomed with an original ode from Robert Mackay, the Bard of Ben Huitig. At each centre a silver tea-pot was presented by Mr. Mackay, London, for original Gaelic compositions. It says much for the Celtic revival that there are no lack of bards in the Reay Country. At the four centres there were several competitors, and their appearance was most creditable, both in composition and delivery. The sederunt lasted nearly till dark, when the deputies left for Tongue. The meeting was an unqualified success.

The weather so far was delightful for outdoor meetings. "Fortune, or I should rather say Providence," said Mr. Mackenzie in parting "favours the generous efforts of the Clan in gathering once more round the banner in their ancestral Reay Country." The Naver—the classic Naver, "Sutherland's pride"—was crossed before dusk. A brief halt was made, when a bonnie wee lassie presented each of us with a bouquet of bulrushes, the badge of the Clan Mackay, for which she was rewarded in kind and a kiss all round.

At Auchnabourin we were hospitably entertained by Mr. and Mrs. Mackay. The long journey to Tongue was then

TONGUE HOUSE

resumed. We were a happy party. What between songs, choruses, and discussions, antiquarian, historical, and critical, always in the best of good humour, we never allowed time to be dull or uninteresting. We were heartily cheered crossing Borgie Bridge, and betimes we gained the foot of Ben Fhreiceadan. All the way on we were greeted with cheers. Tongue Hotel was reached in good time, where we were received with the utmost cordiality and goodwill by Mr. and Mrs Maclnnes and the local committee. They always do things well in Tongue, and we were gratified in finding that the local arrangements were complete. Next day being Sunday, a short service was held by the chaplain of our party, after which the deputation divided between the three churches in the parish, Melness, Kirkiboll, and Strathan. In the afternoon a few of the party drove to Druim-na-comb and got nearly bogged near the old battlefield, the "Bannockburn" of Mackay history.

Next morning we all assembled at Tongue House, the ancient seat of the Mackays, where we were cordially received and entertained by Mr. and Mrs. Box. The house and grounds were visited, and the various features of interest were pointed out. Valuable information was obtained about the *Bratach Bhan*, the lion in the armorial bearings of the Mackays, and other matters of clan interest. Mr. and Mrs. Box were assiduous in their attentions that nothing should be left unvisited.

Returning to the hotel, we set out with the banner flying for the school at Rhitongue, which was crowded to overflowing. Rev. Mr. Macneill presided and delivered a most interesting address of welcome in encouragement of the study of Gaelic.

The address over, the large school was so crowded that the meeting adjourned to the playground, by which time the Melness contingent, with flags and pipers, had arrived. Competitions were at once begun, and lasted for hours. The Gaelic reading and singing was the best met so far. There were plenty competitors. It was most marked the intense interest taken in the proceedings, and that too by visitors from the south, who had no knowledge of the language. The singing was most satisfactory, and no less was the piping of the Macleods and Mackays, Melness. The meeting was in every respect all that could be desired. Thanks to the local committee, the work of the deputation was light and pleasant enough. Many handsome prizes, both in books and cash, were awarded.

In the evening a concert was held. The school was crowded to overflowing, and so indeed it should, for a programme more admirable, alike in selection and rendering, could hardly be submitted. For a grand concert, and we speak from experience, Tongue can hold its own with the north of Scotland. Rev. Mr. Lundie presided, and he was supported by the deputation. Space alone forbids an extended criticism. After the concert an assembly was held. A substantial sum was secured for the reading-room.

Next morning, in most forbidding weather, we set out for Durness. So pleasant was the stay in Tongue that it was difficult for us to tear ourselves away. The Kyle of Tongue crossed, we were entertained by Mr. James Mackay of the Ferry House, and after the dreary Moine, were cheerfully welcomed by Neil Mackay, Hope Ferry (the Queen's

Highlander). By the time we reached Eriboll the day cleared up, and we looked for a pleasant sail across the loch, but were bitterly disappointed. Instead of plain sailing it was tacking and tacking, and we were drenched with spray and sea drift. The senior medical member of the party, who had frequently sailed the Bay of Biscay, was the first to get sick, his *confrère*, who frequently crossed the loch before, soon followed suit, and several other members of the party despaired of landing at all. However, we got ashore on the rocks, and somehow got ourselves, goods and chattels, up to the road, where brakes had been for hours waiting us, and we got to Durness in a much bedraggled condition. Thanks, however, to Rev. Adam Gunn, and Mr. Work of the hotel, we were soon at the field and helped to finish the athletic sports which the local committee, despairing of our arrival, had been conducting all afternoon. The committee not only had most elaborate preparations made, but out of a locally subscribed fund, entertained us to luncheon, and largely supplemented our prize fund.

The competition was held in the evening in the large Church Hall, which was crowded. Rev. Mr. Gunn presided, and to save time, only the best of the readers were presented. This made judging more difficult than ever. But for this explanation the general quality of the Durness reading and singing was far and away the best. A number of interesting speeches were delivered by members of the party, interspersed with songs from the competitors, and Mr. Macleod, whose singing, with occasional exhibitions on the gramaphone, was one of the best features of the evening meetings. The meeting lasted till nearly midnight.

Spite of the experience crossing Loch Eriboll the party were early afoot next morning, when Smoo Cave and Balnakiel Churchyard, where lie the remains of Rob Donn, the Mackay Bard, and of "Iseabal Nic Aoidh" were visited. More evidence about the *Bratach Bhan* was got here. A most interesting forenoon was spent in Durness.

In the evening we drove to Rhiconich, where the market was held that day. It was too late for a meeting, so a concert was held, in which the large house party heartily joined. The weather having much improved, we left in the forenoon for Overscaig, where we were cordially received and entertained by Mr. and Mrs. Duncan Mackay. An enjoyable meeting was held in the evening.

Next day Mr. Mackay, dressed in full Highland costume, drove us into Lairg, where we were met and warmly welcomed by Rev. Dr. James Aberigh-Mackay, chief of the Abrach branch of the clan, and Mrs. Mackay. The afternoon was spent visiting the churchyard, where several more valuable finds in connection with the banner discussion were made.

In the evening a very successful concert was held. John Mackay of Hereford presided, supported by Dr. Abrach-Mackay and other members of the deputation. The large Drill Hall was crowded with an appreciative audience. The concert over, we returned to the hotel, when we met and agreed, among other things, to report to the Society the enthusiastic reception we had received throughout the country, and to recommend that a deputation for similar purposes be sent next year. This over, the health of each individual member was duly pledged, particularly our venerable leader, Hereford, whose presence and enthusiasm more than anything else made the tour the signal success it was.

With much regret we parted next day with Mr. James H. Mackay, London, and the rest of us accompanied Hereford to Rogart, where he presided at the presentation by the Duchess of Sutherland of the prizes of the Rogart Institute. Before the proceedings began, the deputation were presented to the Duchess, who had a kind word to say to each. After an interesting speech by the Duchess, and the presentation of the prizes, there were many more speeches, all more or less interesting, and to the point. A Gaelic reading competition was held, and arrangements were made for having Gaelic classes conducted during the winter. The meeting over, the deputation were hospitably entertained by Rev. Mr. Mackintosh and Mr. Murray.

In the evening, Mr. John Mackay (secretary), Dr. Dingwall, and Mr. Macleod went south. The remaining four of us stayed in Rogart till Monday morning. We parted at Golspie, when two went north, two south, and so concluded one of the most successful clan raids on record.

In conclusion, it is pleasant to record that a deputation of very dissimilar interests, mostly strangers to one another, held so many public meetings and competitions, met so many people, and that there was not even the shadow of a discordant note, either between ourselves or with the many we came in contact with during the ten days we were together. It may be stated that several hundred volumes of books, many valuable money prizes, and the four silver teapots already referred to, were given in prizes. It will be thus seen that the Clan Mackay have done something tangible in the way of furthering the objects of the *Mòd*, and in doing their duty towards their clansfolk in the old country. Classes for the study of Gaelic and music are being started all over the Reay Country, the text-books being provided free by the Clan Society. It is intended to send a larger deputation next year, to hold athletic sports on a large scale at Tongue, and to offer a greater number of prizes for the Gaelic competitions.

Handsome donations to the prize list were given by John Mackay, Hereford; Sheriff Mackay, Q.C.; Thomas Mackay, Largs; Robert Mackay, London; Major A. Y. Mackay, Grangemouth; James H. Mackay, London, &c.

We are indebted to Messrs. W. Drummond Norie and James A. Rose for the photographs of the groups which we reproduce.

AM FEAR-CIÙIL.

(The following poem by Mr. Donald Mackechnie, Edinburgh, was awarded first prize at the recent Gaelic Mòd at Oban.)

FEASGAR latha, fuar is frasach :
    Fhuair mi fasgadh an tigh-òsd
Mo dheagh charaid, Art MacAsgaill.
    Aig Port-Aiseig Chaolas-Bhòsd.
Chaisg mi m' ìota, 's dhìol mi m' acras,
    'S chuir mi phìob thombac' air seòl ;

Leig mi dhìom mo sgìos is m' airsneal,
    Togail chaisteal anns na neòil.

Obair thaitneach ach mi-tharbhach—
    'S stéidh neo-carbsach a' ghaoth-tuath—
Casad faiteach air mo chulthaobh,
    'S thuit mo lùchairt anns an luaith.

Thionndaidh mi dh' fheuch co a bh' agam—
    Duine fada, tana, crom—
Gun mhòr choltas-feòl' no saille
    Fo 'n t-sean fhalluinn 'bha mu chom.

Bha mi taingeil air son cuideachd,
    Bho 'n bha t-sìd a muigh cho trom ;
Thug mi fàilte dha le furan,
    Ged bha 'luideagan car lom.

'Dhcanadh cobhair air gun mhoille,
    Leis na goireasan a bh' ann,
Thairg mi deur de dh' uisge goileach,
    Agus—rudeigin na cheann.

Thuig mo charaid de 'bha math dha—
    Cha 'n e 'n t-amadan a bh' ann—
Deas fna chòmhradh, tuigseach, eòlach,
    Ged bha chuid de 'n stòras gann.

Thuirt e—" 'Nuair tha 'n spiorad sàraicht',
    Is air aghaidh nàduir gruaim—
'N cridhe fann an imfhios t' fhàgail,
    'S rabhadh gabhaidh anns gach funim.

" Tha na 's miosa na 'n deoch làidir,
    Dh' aiseag pàirt de 'n chàill tha uainn,
'S air an fheitheid 'tha 'nar nàdur,
    A chur càileigin de chluain.

" Ach ged tha mòr bhuaidh 's a' chopan,
    'Bhrosnachadh ar cùil 's ar smuain ;
Tha e cheart cho deas g' ar dochann,
    'S a thoirt taic an trosdain uainn.

" Math is olc, mar sin, gu minic,
    Air am tilleadh an aon dual—
Dlùth r'a chéil tha searbh is milis—
    Nithe diombuan agus buan.

" 'S an aon lus, tha bàs is ìocshlaint—
    Spiorad fìrinn anns a' bhréig—
Còir is eucoir gun gheur chriochan—
    Ard is ìosal, freumh is geug.

" Eisd a' ghaillionn, 'seinn Hosana,
    Ri séisd fharumach nan stuadh !
Druid a' chòmhladh—Bruid a' bheòlach—
    'S cluinn cho ceòlmhor 's 'tha ghaoth-tuath.

" Cluinn mar tha gach torman gleuste,
    A comh-sheirm éibhinn, fann is cruaidh—
Builg na gaillinn suas a' séideadh,
    Garbh cheol-mèarsaidh na gaoth-tuath.

" Creid nach aimhreit' tha 's na dùilean,
    Ach an t-ùrlar air an gluais,
Gach ruith sbiùbhlach, feirm is crùnluath,
    'Théid a dhùsgadh fonn an cluais.

" 'S ionnan brigh do 'n anam cheòlmhor,
    Ceileir cìoin, is toirm aig tuinn—
Còisir chiùil an lùchairt mòrachd,
    'S feadan còmhlaich 'chos an tuim.

" Cha 'n e fiodhall, 's cha 'n e clàrsach,
    Bheir do 'n cheol is àird a' bhuaidh—
Crònan màthar thar a pàisde,
    Ceòl is àille 'n taobh so 'n uaigh.

"Ma tha 'n t-inneal-ciùil so'n òrdugh,
  'S nach do chaill mo mheoirsa 'n lùgh;
Cuim' nach tairgeanaid ar feòirlinn,
  Mar ri còisir àrd nan dùl."

Shocraich mi mi-fein a' m' chathair,
  'S lìon mi phìob thombaca suas;
Dh' éisd mi greis ri ceòl mo charaid,
  A bha annasach do 'm chluais.

Co dhìu thuit orm dùsal cadail,
  No an cruitear, tana, cruaidh,
A chur seun a' chiùil mu 'm shealladh,
  Ach chaidh m' aithne car air chuairt.

Chluinninn fathast toirm na gaillinn,
  Ach air atharrachadh fuinn--
Nualan mara 'sguabadh tharuinn,
  Ach ri caiseamachd na tuinn.

Dh' éirich mi thar chnan is mòr-thir,
  Beinne 's còmhnaird, suas 's a nuas;
Gun chairt iùil, no stiùir 'g am sheòladh,
  Ach an ceòl a bh' ann am chluais.

Fad air falbh, bha ònfhadh fuaimneach--
  Tuinn a' bualadh trom air tràigh--
Machair uaine 'n cois nam fuar-bheann,
  'S bothan uaigneach fodh an sgàth.

Leum mi air mo bhonn gu h-aotrom,
  Mhothaich mi am fraoch fo 'm chàil;
Canach geal 'cur suas air raointean,
  'S a' cheare-fhraoich a' gairm a h-àil.

B' aithne dhomh gach creag is sgàirneach,
  Creachann àrd is lagan rèidh--
Mhothaich mi am glaic an Spàinntach,
  'S air mo làmhan, calg an fhéidh.

Lùghar, làidir mar a b' àbhaist--
  Smior is càil an cnaimh 's am féith--
Beatha tharbhach! Beatha shealbhach!
  'S cukaidh fharmaid, sealgair féidh!

'S bochd nach buan dhuinn seillb cho luach-
  mhor,
  C' uime 'n d' luathaich i a ceum?
O, ciod an duais, a bheirinn suas,
  Airson aon uair dhith 'n dingh a'm cheum!

Cha 'n eil fhios domh ciamar thachair,
  Fhuair mi nis mo chas air sràid,
'Measg luchd-fuadain, 's gach ni fuaraidh,
  'S cùram fuaighte rium 's gach àit'.

Foill is fòirneart, thar na còrach--
  Dìchioll brònach 'an glas-làmh;
Is fuil is feoil, mar ìobairt bhèo,
  Do dhia an òir 'dol suas gun tàmh.

Co dhìu chaill an cruitear truagh
  Air inneal buaidh, no mheòir an clì;
Cha 'n fhios domh; ach bha 'cheol a'm chluais,
  A nis gun bhunaidh--mar fhuaim gun bhrigh.

Plathadh seallaidh nis 's a rithist--
  Boillsgeadh diombuan air bheag suim--
Nithe ghluais aon uair an cridhe
  Ach a leig e tur á cuimhn'.

Ach mu dheireadh, bhuail mo chlàrsair,
  Teud 'chuir guin troimh 'm chàil gu lèir--
Bhuail e charraig anns an fhàsach,
  'S bhrùchd aisd' uisg' an àmhghair ghèir.

Dh' éirich grian air maduinn àraidh,
  'S theich roimh làithreachd sgàil na h-oidhch;

Ach an sgàil os cionn ar fardaich,
  Nach tog grian no là a choidhch.

Sgàil 's nach goir a' chuach no 'n smeòrach,
  'S anns an seac am feòirnean suas--
Sgàils 's an d' shearg mo fhlùran bòidheach,
  'S anns nach ruig mo cheòl a chuas.

Charaich sinn an leab' a bhròin i;
  A cruth bòidheach anns an ùir;
Sgaoil sinn thairte brat de neòinein,
  'S dh' uisgich sinn le 'r deòir na flùir.

'S dachaidh fhàs dhuinn gun mo fhlùran -
  Cuimhne thùrsach anns gach ni,
Cais'eart bheag air leth an cùileig;
  'S miadhbala na crùn an rìgh.

Chiar an là, 's an oidhche thàirlinn;
  Oidhch' nach d' theid a cuimhn' nis mò--
O, na druid an nochd a chòmhladh!
  'S gun m' uan bòidheach anns a' chrò.

Leum, mu dheireadh, mi á m' chathair,
  'S thuirt mi, chraitear, thana, chruaidh,
Ma's tu féin tha teumadh m' anam,
  'S miosa t' ealain na 'ghaoth-tuath!

Thug e sùil orm fo a mhalaidh,
  Mar gu 'm b' aithne dha mo smuain--
" C' àit' a nis am bheil a' ghaillionn?
  Anns an anam no air chuan?

" Creid mi, cha tig stoirm no gaillionn
  As an adhar, deas no tuath;
Mar a dh' éireas anns an anam,
  'Nuair a shéideas carraid chruaidh.

" Amadd fein tha 'n ceòl a ghluais thu;
  Air a luasgadh leis an teud;
Gleus gu tuireadh, 's gleus gu luath-ghair,
  Fuaighte riut 's gach àit' an teud.

" Ceòl o'n d'fhuair thu gach ni luachmhor,
  'S ris am bheil gach buaidh an sàs--
Ceòl a' d' chridhe--ceòl a' d' chluasan,
  Fad do chuairt, o d' bhreith gu d' bhàs.

" An ceòl 's binne 's col do 'n fhìlidh,
  Cha tog pìob no fìodhall suas;
'N ceòl thig uaircan anns a' chridhe,
  Tuillidh 's milis air son cluais.

" Chaidh an ni so thar do thuigse!
  'Bheil thu tuigsinn ni fo 'n ghrèin?
Ciod an steidh air an do chluich mi!
  Chluich air t' fhaireachdainean féin.

" Ach cha tus' a mhàin tha iubhal--
  Nàdur uile, ann an seòl;
Bho cheud bhunait gu 'chtaoch mhulaich,
  A cheum siubhail 'dol ri ceòl.

" 'S nuair a ruitheas e a chùrsa,
  Togaidh guth na dùbhaich chruaidh,
Ceòl a leaghas sìos na duilean--
  Ceòl a dhùisgeas tu 's an uaigh!"

Thug e taing is oidhche mhath dhomh,
  'S thruis é fhalluinn thais mu 'chré--
Didean faoin ri aodann gaillinn,
  Ach 'na anam--Anail Dé.

'S diomhaireachd nach beag an duine--
  Dia a' tuineachadh 'na chòm--
Teampull faoin, 's é air dhroch uidheam,
  'S gu 'n an tugha air ach ban.

MACTALLA.

TO CORRESPONDENTS.

All Communications, on literary and business matters, should be addressed to the Editor, Mr. JOHN MACKAY, 9 Blythswood Drive, Glasgow.

TERMS OF SUBSCRIPTION.— The CELTIC MONTHLY will be sent, post free, to any part of the United Kingdom, Canada, the United States, and all countries in the Postal Union—for one year, 4s.

THE CELTIC MONTHLY.
NOVEMBER, 1898

CONTENTS.

NOTICE TO SUBSCRIBERS.

Last issue commenced Volume VII. As we are anxious to complete the list of subscribers for the new Volume as soon as possible, readers who desire the "Celtic" to be sent for another year, might kindly forward their annual subscriptions (4/- post free), on receipt, to the Editor, Mr. John Mackay, 9 Blythswood Drive, Glasgow. Subscribers will greatly favour us by giving this their immediate attention, as delay in remitting entails upon us a good deal of extra trouble.

OUR NEXT ISSUE.

Next month we will give plate portraits, with biographical sketches, of Mr. and Mrs. C. A. M'Vean, of Kilninichen, Mull; Lieutenant Donald M'Vean, of the 45th Sikhs, Indian Army; and Mr. Robert Campbell, Manchester.

Volume VI.—We will be able to supply a limited number of copies of the volume now completed, nicely bound, at 6/6 per copy. As the supply is limited an early application is advisable.

The Minor Septs of Clan Chattan has now been issued to subscribers. The press notices have been of the most favourable nature, all agreeing in describing the work as a valuable contribution to Highland history and genealogy. The volume is got up in superb style, and contains coloured plates of the tartans, *fac-simile* bonds, and numerous fine photo process illustrations. Copies can be had from the publisher, John Mackay, 9 Blythswood Drive, Glasgow, price, 21/-.

Clan Mackay Society.—The Annual Social Gathering has been fixed to take place in the Waterloo Rooms, Glasgow, on Friday, 23rd December—Major A. Y. Mackay, Grangemouth, in the chair. Sheriff Æneas J. G. Mackay, Q.C., LL.D., has consented to deliver an address, and a very attractive programme is being arranged. It will take the form of a soiree, concert, and dance.— The recent clan tour in the Reay country, a full report of which we give this month, has created a great deal of interest, not only among Mackays but among all clansmen. The Society has now formally decided that a much larger deputation repeat the visit next summer, that a larger number of prizes be given, and that athletic sports on a large scale be held at Tongue, at which many valuable prizes will be offered for the usual events. In addition to this, Gaelic competitions will be held in each parish, and the Gaelic classes examined. A Gaelic music class has just been started at Rogart, and a supply of the "St. Columba Collection of Gaelic Songs" has been sent to the teacher by the Clan Society. It is interesting to mention that quite a number of distinguished clansmen have intimated their intention of taking part in next year's tour, and have offered to contribute to the prize list.

Presentation Shield to Cluny Macpherson. —Mr. Robert Scott, 8 Buchanan Street, Glasgow, to whom was entrusted the order for the Celtic Shield which the Clan Chattan intend presenting to Cluny, has just completed the work. We have had the pleasure of examining this beautiful and massive example of Celtic silver work, and were greatly delighted with the artistic taste displayed in its design. It is intended to represent an ancient Highland shield, with two broad bands of the most delicate and intricate Celtic tracery; indeed, next to some of the carvings on the ancient Iona stones, we have never seen anything to equal the beauty of this example of Celtic ornament. On the outer edge the usual Ossianic bosses are placed, also embellished with Celtic designs, while in the centre is a shield containing the following inscription :—" Presented to Cluny Macpherson, of Cluny Macpherson, chief of Clan Chattan, on the occasion of his marriage, by members of the Clan in Glasgow and Edinburgh, as a mark of loyalty and esteem. 1897." The shield weighs about 140 ounces, and is 24 inches in diameter. The Clan Chattan are certainly presenting their chief with a very handsome and valuable memento of their esteem.

Argyllshire Nursing Association.—We would like to draw our readers' attention to the Grand Bazaar which is to be held in the St. Andrew's Hall, Glasgow, on 24th, 25th, and 26th November. The object is such a deserving one that we have no doubt it will command the sympathy of our readers, and we trust that many of them will not only pay a visit to the bazaar, but contribute in a tangible way towards its success. The Kintyre Club and Clan Maclean have special stalls of their own, while the various districts of Argyll are each represented. We understand that Celtic ornamentation will enter largely into the arrangement of the stalls, each being artistically placed between two large representations of Iona crosses. We wish the bazaar every success.

MINOR SEPTS OF CLAN CHATTAN.

By CHARLES FRASER-MACKINTOSH, LL.D.

No. XVII.—THE FARQUHARSONS
CLAN FIONLAY.

(*Continued from page 13*).

IN the year 1741 Anne Farquharson, daughter of Invercauld before referred to by one of the Athole family, married Eneas, 22nd Mackintosh, and during the rising of 1745, she took such a leading part for the Stuarts as to be called "Colonel Anne." It says much for the prudence and discretion of this most honoured lady, who shares with Eva nic Gille Chattan, the deepest affection of the Clan Chattan, that in her husband's disqualification from holding a command in the old 42nd, she did not select as temporary leader from many well qualified members of her own family, but fixed on the gallant Alexander MacGillivray of Dunmaglass. Her portrait, taken from the original at Moy Hall, is given on next page.

At Culloden the Farquharsons mustered over 300 men. John Farquharson, remembering his pardon in 1716, and arrived at mature age—for I find a note regarding him in 1686—did not go out, nor permit his son, although Jacobite feeling strongly prevailed among the clan. Upon the death of James Farquharson, son and successor of John, without male issue, the old close continuous friendship and alliance with the Mackintoshes ceased. It might have been well for Clan Chattan had the views of certain sagacious looking-ahead friends, to bring about in a certain way a permanent alliance been listened to by the principals. At Culloden, the Clan Chattan were placed 5th in the right division and the Farquharsons 4th in the left, in other words both well to the centre of the front line near each other.

In the trial of Captain John Farquharson, a witness deponed that "John was Captain in Colonel Farquharson's regiment, and in the march to Nairn to surprise the English the night before Culloden." Another witness deponed that "John Farquharson was at the head of the Farquharson regiment upon the field of battle at Culloden when preparing to attack the Hanoverian forces."

Francis Farquharson of Monaltrie, nephew of Invercauld, commanded the Farquharsons. Some days before the battle of Culloden, a witness at his trial said he saw him some days before, with a big blue coat on, at the head of his own regiment, which was then drawn out with Ardshiel's regiment and some of the Macleods, upon a plain about a mile from Inverness (The Wester Haugh—C. F. M.), and that they went through their exercises, and were reviewed by the Pretender's (sic) son." Another witness describes Colonel Farquharson as "a tall man with thin face, dressed in Highland garb, with sword and pistol and white cockade." The Colonel's servant, John Reach, who had been with his master thirty years, said "his master joined at Edinburgh with 30 men, and went back to raise more." Colonel Farquharson was condemned but reprieved.

The name of Balmoral is now often heard of since its acquisition by Her Majesty, who has made Braemar her favourite residence. Let us look at the owner in 1745. James Farquharson of Balmoral's accession and acts in the '45 are described by himself, when brought to trial long after the battle of Culloden. In a Memorial to the Crown dated 21st November, 1748, he says, putting all the blame on his brother:—

"That in the month of October, 1745, your petitioner, who till then lived quiet and peaceable at his own house in the County of Aberdeen, was unhappily induced to join in the late Rebellion, at the instigation of an elder brother, whom he still regarded as a parent.

That your petitioner is informed upon this account, he is excepted from your Majesty's Gracious Act of Indemnity, and that an indictment has been lately found against him before a grand jury at Edinburgh for high treason.

That your petitioner begs leave with the greatest humility to represent to your Majesty that from the time of his appearing in arms in the latter end of October, 1745, it was his constant care to the utmost of his power to prevent distresses to your Majesty's faithful subjects, and to protect them from injury in their persons and estates, and particularly those who had the misfortune to fall into the hands of the rebels as many of them can, and the petitioner believes will, testify when called upon.

That in the beginning of February thereafter, your petitioner retired 'home again' to his own country, and has ever since lived in such a manner as not to give the smallest offence.

That your petitioner is now advanced to a considerable age, and his health impaired by the many hardships and distresses which he had suffered.

That your petitioner has presumed in these circumstances, not as an alleviation of his guilt, but in order to move your Majesty's compassion, and being heartily sorry for his offence, he most humbly submits himself to your Majesty's Royal clemency, and imploring your Royal mercy, promises for the future to live a grateful and dutiful subject.

And your petitioner shall ever pray,

(Signed) JAMES FARQUHARSON.

In support of his prayer, the Moderator and the Ministers of the Presbytery of Alford transmitted a strongly worded statement testifying to his character. It is signed by the following :—

Pat Thomas, Minister at Tough, Modr.
Pat Reid, Clatt.
Theodore Gordon, Kennethmont.
James Lumsden, Strathdon.
John Maxwell, Auchindown.
Walter Syme, Tillienish ?
Alexander Strachan, Keig.
Thomas Reid, Leochel.
Alexander Johnston, Alford.
Alexander Drew, Forbes.
William Milne, Kildrummie.

The Moderator and Ministers of Kincardine O'Neal petition in similar terms :—

George Campbell, Moderator.
W. Mackenzie, Glenmuick.
Alexander Garden, Birse.
Francis Dauncey, Lumphanan.
William Abel, Kincardine O'Neal.
Alexander Garrioch, Midmar.
Robert Michie, Cluny.
John MacInnes, Colstrew.
James Paterson, Coull.
George Shepherd, Tarland.
George Shepherd, Aboyne.

Mr. Charles Maitland, Advocate, Principal John Chalmers, Aberdeen, and James Paterson, Sheriff Depute of Stirlingshire, also bear testimony that they have been prisoners, and met with great civility, attention, and kindness from Balmoral. He was found guilty and ultimately discharged.

These extracts from the State Papers were supplied to me by Mr. D. Murray Rose, who is exceedingly well posted up in all that took place in 1745.

In 1737 James Farquharson of Invercauld executed a deed of entail of his extensive estates in Braemar and Strath Dee, and calls to the succession his only son, James, his brother, Alexander Farquharson of Monaltric, and his four daughters, Ann, afterwards Lady Mackintosh, Margaret, Frances, and Jean. By the deed it would appear that Invercauld proper extended to 1½ davoch of land, Castleton of Braemar 1 davoch, Monaltrie 1 davoch, Crathie ½ davoch, Brackley in Glengairn 1½ davoch, and there are numerous other places mentioned in the entail. James Farquharson died in 1750, and was described "as a man of great honour and merit." He was succeeded by his son, also named James, who appears to have been in 1745 a Captain of Foot in the Hanoverian army; he died in 1806, after being in possession of the estates for fifty-six years. In 1756 he signs the deed in favour of his brother-in-law, Mackintosh, recovering the Loch Laggan lands. The Farquharsons were all vassals of Mar, and on the downfall of that family did not take kindly to the new owners, descendants of Muldavit and of the meal dealing Braco. The new family not only asserted its rights but strove to enlarge its holding in Braemar. This after many years was accomplished in the year 1784, so far as regarded the important estate of Inverey, which, formerly Inverey, sometimes Inneric, has been changed by the present owners to Inveraye. Rose of Montcoffer, the active and indefatigable doer for the Muldavit family, which had broken out into the Lordship of Braco and Earldom of Fife, in that refuge for ambitious plutocratic commoners—the Peerage of Ireland—thus narrates his doings in the autumn of 1784 :—

"It was now time to strike in with Haughton for the purchase of Inverey and Auchindrane, as to which my instructions were unlimited. Met with Haughton, and after a great deal of trouble concluded a bargain for the estates at 34 years' purchase."

In the end of September, 1784, Montcoffer visited the new purchase and records :—

"Inspected the bounds of Inverey with James Stewart. Went to Glony, Cairn-a-Grinish, Dalnaglac, dividing Glony from Glen Cluny, Craignish, Altalet, and above that Hell's Glen. Travelled with James Stewart over Delrudalet and Amuchnamon, and report the extent, and formed rules and regulations for pasturages, sheilings, forests, and game."

Lord Braco had purchased the vast estate of the Earls of Mar, after that family had sunk in the troubles of 1715, but, as before mentioned, was not welcomed by the neighbours, mostly vassals of Mar, under which family they had been nourished, and greatly flourished.

Some years previous to the above purchase, a combination of the chief proprietors of the Braemar Highlands had been formed against

the Dulls, and in especial in regard to woods. This combination was headed by Invercauld, and supported by the Earl of Aboyne, the Farquharsons of Rynallan, Monaltrie, Crathinard, Inverey, and others. This powerful combination was met by Montcoffer, who records under date 1780, after the contest had been running on for years, that :—

"At Mar Lodge he attempted a compromise with Invercauld, Inverey, and Monaltrie, and proceeding to the Marlie, where Invercauld dwelt, failed with him, but going on to Balmoral settled with Inverey, and by the after withdrawal of Lord Aboyne, Abergeldie, and Crathinard, demolished the combination."

The Fife troubles did not cease, however, for next year, 1781, Montcoffer says :—

"Monaltrie at this time had done a very bare faced act, cut *breei manu* the stately firs in sight of Mar Lodge. Some evil person set fire to the woods of Badness and Beachan. Alexander Lamond, James MacGregor, James Small, and others, cut woods at their own hand, poinded cattle in Garrieduran, within the forest of Gulzie, and Invercauld's people or herds set fire to the skirts of the woods of Caich and Ballochbuie, and erected sheilings hard by."

It may be added that poor Montcoffer, who managed with extraordinary success all the Fife affairs, territorially and politically, on a miserable salary, after a service extending over thirty years, and having put many tangled matters to rights, consolidated and enlarged the estates, was dismissed, and had to pursue his late employer in the law courts for redress, ending in the House of Lords.

James Farquharson of Invercauld, at his death in 1806, left no male issue, and was succeeded under the destination of the entail by his only surviving child, Catharine. Well wishers of the Clan Chattan had, even before marriageable age, suggested a suitable matrimonial alliance for this great heiress, but it came to naught, and the person selected was one of the lucky Lockhart family, who in a previous generation had obtained possession of the great estate of Balnagown in the Counties of Ross and Sutherland. The present owner of Invercauld is Catherine Farquharson's great-grandson. As may be seen from the illustration in last issue, the house is a noble residence.

In dealing with branches of the Farquharsons, I confine myself chiefly to those more closely connected with the Clan Chattan, parties to the Bond of 1664.

(To be continued.)

- - - - - - -

"DUNVEGAN AND ITS ASSOCIATIONS." —Mr. Macdonald of Waternish, Mr. William Macdonald, and other readers have written stating that Flora Macdonald was buried in Kilmuir, Troternish, and not Kilmuir, Duirinish, as stated in our article last month.

Deeds that won the Empire. ✱

By JOHN MACKAY, C.E., J.P., Hereford.

QUEBEC, 1759.

(Continued from page 15).

PRECISELY at eleven o'clock on the 13th September, the firing began, when the dusky Indian and the hardy Canadian sharpshooters, clad in hunting shirts and moccasins, began to dart from bush to bush on the woody banks that overhung the St. Charles river, and filled the valley with reports of irregular musketry. The light scarlet uniforms of the British officers soon became fatal targets for the riflemen. In the lull of the firing, their French commanders were frequently heard to say

"Soldats! marquez bien les officiers." (Soldiers, mark well the officers).

By Wolfe's express orders, his whole line reserved its fire till within forty yards from the enemy's bayonets, when it suddenly halted and poured in a close, deadly, and running volley upon the French, whose advance was at once arrested, their movements paralysed by the sudden heaps of killed and wounded that fell over each other, causing great gaps in the ranks. This fierce volley was so sharply timed that the explosion of 1000 muskets sounded like the sharp blast of a cannon. It was again and again repeated, and the flame ran from end to end of the steadfast line. When the smoke lifted, the French columns were seen to be wrecked. By a sudden movement, Montcalm now menaced the British left, but on being roughly repulsed, a vibration seemed to pass along his whole line, and his troops began to waver. The British line instantly charged. It was at this most critical moment that Wolfe was mortally wounded

while standing on the extreme right of the 28th regiment, cheering them and the Louisburg Grenadiers to the charge. There the conflict was both close and desperate. His position rendered him fatally conspicuous. A shot had struck him first in the wrist. He wrapped his handkerchief round it to staunch the bleeding, and hastened to head the charge, when a second shot pierced his groin and a third his breast. He reeled, and faint with loss of blood, leant on one of his staff, murmuring, "Support me, do not let my brave fellows see me fall." It was easily seen that the wound was mortal. The hero was carried a little to the rear. Even then, when in the agonies of death, he could not forget his anxiety for the fate of the day. "My eyesight and strength fail me," said he to the officer supporting him.

Then it was, infuriated at seeing their beloved General fall, that the whole line simultaneously charged. The Fraser Highlanders raised a tremendous yell, the old clan spirit was aroused in them for closer combat. "Claymore! Claymore! Dirk and claymore!" was the cry, the same wild, terrific shout that had rung in a thousand clan battles, now echoed along the Heights of Abraham. Flinging down their muskets in the old Highland fashion, on rushed the Frasers with their shields and their long basket-hilted swords and daggers, making a dreadful slaughter among the French whom Montcalm was vainly striving to rally.

In the meantime, every medical assistance was bestowed on the dying Wolfe. He was laid on the sward. He refused to allow a surgeon to be called. "There is no need," he said, "it is all over with me." Then a little group about him, casting a glance at the still smoke-covered field, cried, "They run, they run! See how they run!" "Who run?" asked the dying hero. "The enemy, sir." "What! do they run already?" exclaimed Wolfe. "Then go, one of you, to Colonel Burton, and tell him to march Webb's regiment to the river St. Charles, to secure the bridge and cut off the retreat of the fugitives. Now, God be praised, I die happy." He then turned on his left side and expired in the arms of Fraser, his favourite Highland orderly, who was weeping over him.

On Wolfe's death, Brigadier Townshend assumed chief command, Brigadier Monckton having fallen mortally wounded about the same time as Wolfe. Meantime Brigadier Murray, on the left, advanced and broke the enemy's right, driving them before him towards the town and over the river St. Charles. Townshend re-formed the centre, which had become disordered in the ardour of the pursuit, and turned upon Bougainville, who was advancing with a fresh force of 2000 men in rear of the British, but the French commander, seeing that discretion was the better part of valour, precipitately quitted the field. The battle lasted only fifteen minutes.

In the pursuit towards the city, Montcalm was shot in the thigh, and was carried by his fugitive troops into Quebec, narrowly escaping the swords of the infuriated Highlanders, roused to madness by the loss of their General, who by his affability endeared himself to them. They followed the pursuit right up to the gates of the ramparts, far in advance of their comrades, and making dreadful havoc among the fugitives, losing many of their best officers, among whom were three Macdonalds, Boisdale, Keppoch, and Lochgarry; Ross, of Calrossie; and Mac-Neil, of Barra.

A letter of an officer, in the *Edinburgh Chronicle*, says:—"Our regiments that sustained the brunt of the action were Braggs', Lascelles', and the Highlanders. The two former had not a bayonet, nor the latter a broadsword, untinged with blood;" and another writes, "When these Highlanders took to their broadswords, my God! what havoc they made! They drove everything before them, and the stone walls alone could resist their fury!"

The Marquis of Montcalm expired two days after the battle. Before he died, he dictated to General Townshend a letter, bequeathing to his care the wounded and prisoners. When this was ended he exclaimed, "Thank Heaven! I shall not live to see the capitulation of Quebec. I have got my death fighting against the bravest soldiers in the world, at the head of the greatest cowards that ever carried muskets."

Four days after, Quebec was formally surrendered by the Governor, the Chevalier Ramsay (a Scottish exile of the '45), on promise that all the rights and liberties of the inhabitants should be respected, and that all prisoners taken should be sent to France.

The loss of the British, in killed, wounded, and missing, was 57 officers and 591 soldiers; while that of the French was about 200 officers and 1200 men of all other ranks, besides the prisoners sent to France. In the citadel were taken 298 brass and iron guns, howitzers, and mortars, two petards, and 1100 bombs, and all stores and ammunition.

The capture of Quebec is one of the most brilliant feats recorded in war. It is said that the heroic young General who died at the moment of achieving the victory with which his name will be for ever associated, on the previous night, when dropping down the river in a boat, observed to his orderly (Fraser), on his repeating Gray's immortal "Elegy"—"Gentlemen, I had rather have written that poem than taken yonder city." Coming from the lips of a soldier thirsting for military fame, who, as he passed under the obscurity of night the shadow of the beetling crags overhead, might well have felt a presentiment of his coming fate: this is perhaps the most eloquent of the many eulogies on that masterpiece of the English language:—

"The boast of heraldry, the pomp of power,
    And all that beauty, all that wealth e'er gave,
Await alike the inevitable hour,
    The paths of glory lead but to the grave."

On board of the "Royal William," 80 guns, the body of Wolfe was sent home to England, and Pitt wept when pronouncing a eulogy upon the fallen hero in the House of Commons. His father had only been buried a few days before the arrival of the remains of his victorious son on the 12th of November, and amid deep silence, much ceremony and sorrow, surrounded by a vast multitude, they were interred by the side of his father in the Parish Church of Greenwich. A noble monument at Westminster, a cenotaph on the Heights of Abraham, and another in his village of Westerham, have been raised to perpetuate the memory of the soldier to whom Britain owed the conquest of Quebec. Another monument, 65 feet high, in Quebec, is dedicated to Wolfe and Montcalm.

LETTER TO THE EDITOR.

THE CLAN DAVIDSON.

NEW YORK.

MY DEAR SIR—I notice in the July issue you gave some extracts from my previous letter. What may appear as interesting in a friendly rigmarole assumes a different aspect when reduced to cold printer's type. But no matter, if my remarks afford you or your readers any amusement you are certainly welcome to them. One thing is certain, Mr. James MacGregor will not object to the handsome advertisement which you so freely gave him. Mr. MacGregor is a merchant tailor, of novel methods of advertising, and although I am not personally acquainted with him it is easy to see that he is a "Child of the Mist." (I should like to know, in all seriousness, how long the MacGregors intend to retain a monopoly of this distinction "Children of the Mist?" Cannot your friend and correspondent, Surgeon Lieutenant-Colonel John MacGregor, be induced to share *some* of its delights with his fellow Gaels?)

I had intended to have deferred answering your letter until the "Minor Septs" arrived, but losing patience I began, and just as I finished the above, the work, strange to say, came in. So far as your part is concerned it has been done handsomely: the work is certainly an artistic success.

Referring to the article on Clan Dhai, in which the author in apparent absence of any *existing* chief, names Tulloch or Cantray for that title, I would say that I am glad to note that this matter is set right, and Tulloch's claims put on record, in appendix VII. The Davidsons of Tulloch have always been recognized as chiefs by their northern clansmen. I never heard of their title being disputed or of anybody else who laid claim to it. The mere fact of their chiefship being acknowledged ought to be sufficient in this case without entering further into the question.

While Duncan Davidson of Tulloch, Lord-Lieutenant of Ross-shire, grandfather of the present laird, lived, he reigned supreme I can tell you. He died, I think, in 1881. In appearance or character it would be hard to find another who more truly represented the ideal Highland chief. His hospitality was proverbial and was known far beyond the Highland line. In matters Celtic he took the deepest interest, subscribing for and encouraging almost everything that was published relating to the history, traditions and literature of the Highlands. A Highlander himself of the oldest stock, he took a pride in the Highlands and its people at a time when matters Highland were not looked at in the same light as now. The Gaels owe much to Tulloch, and such stalwarts as he, for the prouder position they occupy to-day. Dr. Fraser-Mackintosh was a contemporary of Tulloch's, and the two must have frequently met at many a Highland gathering.

There is another fact in connection with the Tulloch family which may be of interest to you: *they have got a streak of Mackay blood in them.* The Davidsons acquired the Tulloch estate some 150 years ago by purchase from the Baynes, their blood relations. The Baynes, as known to everybody born north of the Ness, were a branch of the Mackays. We all know the Mackays: their blood was as strong as their hands. Few escaped receiving an impress of one or of the other. What their hands failed to clutch, their blood—warmed and fostered for ages as it were within their own happy mountain retreats—acted as a magnate towards every hapless Macleod, Sutherland, Sinclair, Gunn, and countless other "sons of guns" that ventured within the circle of its attraction. Yes, the Mackays had blood of the truly volcanic order, with periodic eruptions which sent thousands of claymores, like living lava, to Continental war—there to receive their "baptism of fire," and there to glut their thirst for real Sassenach gore. But I fear that I am wandering: let us return to the Tulloch family.

Before the Davidsons moved to Tulloch they were styled of Davidston, Cromartyshire, on which property they lived for many generations—probably from the time of their flight from the Badenoch country. At all events, it was here that their family records got destroyed in a fire. The fire occured at Tulloch Castle in 1845, which burnt nearly all

records, pictures, etc. The willing hands which tried to save the wonderful collection of old china did so by throwing it out of the windows on to the gravel and flagstones below! Had it not been for this misfortune we might to-day have had access to papers which would have thrown considerable light on matters of interest to the sept, if not to Clan Chattan at large.

As usual this letter has stretched out longer than I had intended, but this time the good Doctor is to blame for it.

The summer number of the *Celtic* was very good; the articles on the MacEwens, Macleods, and Campbells being especially interesting. Angus Mackintosh's tuneful piping must have warmed the Fraser heart, and Torquil Macleod's short stories must stir all hearts; I regard the latter as perfect gems in their way.

Yours faithfully,
CLAN DHAI.

CAPT. WILLIAM MACLEAN, SOUTHAMPTON,

VICE-PRESIDENT, SOUTHAMPTON SCOTTISH ASSOCIATION.

THE annual re-unions of the clan and county societies are always interesting from the fact that they bring clansmen from all parts of the kingdom together to spend a social evening. The most successful gathering of the Clan Maclean which was held the other day attracted the scattered units of the clan from distant parts, and it is our intention this month to do honour to a most worthy representative of the race, who came all the way from Southampton to support his chief. Captain William Maclean is an excellent type of the Gael who, from a humble origin, has plodded his way manfully through every stage of his profession, from apprentice on board a collier to the command of a ship. He was born in the Canongate of Edinburgh, his parents, Malcolm Maclean and Jean Cumming, being of Highland birth, and not blessed with too great a share of this world's riches. Their son, William, when fourteen years of age, went to sea, and for forty years sailed in every capacity in the mercantile marine. He has sailed under the Union Jack and the Stars and Stripes in

CAPTAIN WILLIAM MACLEAN.

every part of the world. He has now settled down in the busy town of Southampton as superintendent of the Sailors' Home, and means to sail the seas no more.

Captain Maclean takes an enthusiastic interest in all matters relating to the clan, his wife and himself being life members of the society. He was never before present at a clan gathering, and goes home with the most pleasant recollections of his visit on this occasion. It may be mentioned that he is vice-president of the very flourishing Scottish Society which exists in Southampton, and which does excellent work, and is also Grand Master of the Princess Royal Lodge of Oddfellows.

THE SOCIAL CONDITION OF THE HIGHLANDS SINCE 1800.

By A. J. BEATON, F.S.A. Scot., F.G.S.E.

(*Continued from page* 4).

II.

CHARACTER AND CONDITION OF THE INHABITANTS.

THE Scottish Highlander of the littoral districts is engaged during part of the year at the fishing, or training in the Militia or Royal Naval Reserve Corps; and when these occupations are over he wanders home to his bleak moorland holding to secure his scanty crops of corn and potatoes. What can he now do during the long dreary winter but mope about in idleness; for were he even disposed to improve his land the severe Highland winter prevents him; and, were he anxious to do a day's fishing, the tempestuous sea and a dangerous coast will prohibit him. These surroundings, therefore, tend to unnerve and suck the very ambition from their souls, so that they never seek to rise from the prison house of their mean estate. Were this people taught home arts and industries, these would not only help them to pass the dreary winter, but would form a source of income, and would ultimately be the means of elevating their social position and stimulating them to uproot themselves from the "bogs of immemorial routine." *

* Since these lines were written the Home Industries Associations, in whose useful work the Duchess of Sutherland takes such a noble part, and other similar organizations, have worked a social revolution in Highland homes. In many parts of the Highlands and Islands the people are actively employed in weaving, knitting, carving, and other suitable home occupations, the remuneration for which adds considerably to their limited income.—EDITOR.

I must not, however, overlook the record made by General Stewart of Garth in his excellent work, "Sketches of the Highlanders." Speaking of the charge of indolence made against them, he mentions the fact that during the construction of the Caledonian Canal very few Highlanders availed themselves of this constant and well-paid labour offered them in the very heart of their own country. This at the time was attributed to their natural lazy disposition; while, as a matter of fact, at the very time they refused work at their doors, thousands flocked southward in search of employment. General Stewart refutes the charge of laziness by ascribing it to Highland ambition; and, undoubtedly, the recollection of their former independence under the feudal or clan system prevented them from accepting a labourer's hire in sight of the scenes which once witnessed them in better circumstances. The semi-military life they also led, together with their constant contemplation on the renown of their noble ancestors, imbued them with the notion that they were "gentlemen" in comparison with their Lowland brethren, and their supreme contempt for any commercial or servile pursuit served to make them look upon navvy work as degrading and dishonourable. Perhaps if I quote from the late Professor Walker it will illustrate more clearly what I wish to show. He says:—"Wherever the Highlanders are defective in industry, it will be found, upon fair enquiry, to be rather their misfortune than their fault, and owing to their want of knowledge and opportunity, rather than to any want of spirit for labour. Their disposition to industry is greater than is usually imagined, and if judiciously directed is capable of being highly advantageous both to themselves and to their country." This forecast has proved true; for to-day Highlanders may be found all over the world occupying positions of honour and trust.

The hospitality of the Highlanders once upon a time was unbounded; but since the Saxon has invaded their land they have become more or less contaminated, and the greed for gold has developed. Donald's erroneous idea that English tourists are actually rolling in money leads him to overreach his conscience in matters of pecuniary detail; and hence the defamatory reports of the avaricious disposition of the Highlander. A Highland Chieftain's house was always open; and the law of hospitality and politeness forbade him, until a year had passed, to enquire of his guest what business he had called upon. Perhaps nothing can more beautifully and graphically illustrate pure Highland hospitality and confidence than the circumstances attending "The Massacre of Glencoe."—

" And tho' in them Glencoe's devoted men
Beheld the foes of all who bore their name,
Yet simple faith allowed the stranger's claim
To hospitable cheer and welcome kind ;
Undreaming that a Highland hand could shame
The ancient faith the sacred ties that bind,
The guest to him, beside whose hearth he hath
    reclined."

I may be pardoned for here quoting Pennant's description of the character of the Highlanders ; and although the date of " Pennant's Tour " is somewhat earlier than the period embraced in this essay, the description would, nevertheless, be as applicable at any stage of the present century as it was in 1769. " The manner of the native Highlander," says Pennant, " may justly be described in these words : indolent to a high degree unless roused to war, or to any animated amusements ; or I may say, from experience, to lend any disinterested assistance to the distressed traveller, either in directing him on his way or affording their aid in passing the dangerous torrents of the Highlands ; hospitable to the highest degree, and full of generosity ; are much affected with the civility of strangers, and have in themselves a natural politeness and address which often flows from the meanest when least expected. Through my whole tour I never met with a single instance of national reflection, their forbearance proves them to be superior to the meanness of retaliation. I fear they pity us, but I hope not indiscriminately. Are excessively inquisitive after your business, your name, and other particulars of little consequence to them, most curious after the politics of the world, and when they procure an old newspaper will listen to it with the avidity of Shakespeare's blacksmith. Have much pride and consequently are impatient of affronts and revengeful of injuries." In the main Pennant's description still holds good when applied to the average Highlander, yet much of the original character of the genuine son of the mountain has been destroyed. The rough and ragged edges of honest simplicity have been rubbed off by the so-called polishing influences of society, and the sturdy independence and self reliance of their ancestors are now being sup planted by, I fear, less commendable qualities, and they are gradually having transfused into them the Saxon and Southern elements. This is one of the unavoidable results of the development of civilization, and although, in a sense, it may be a source of regret to the enthusiastic patriot that the good old Highland character is being gradually obliterated, still the Highlands and Highlanders have benefitted in no small degree from their intercourse with the English nation, and they still retain the inestimable virtues of integrity and charity.

Sir John Dalrymple has observed of the Highlanders :—" That to be modest as well as brave, to be contented with a few things which nature requires, to act and to suffer without complaining, to be as much ashamed of doing anything insolent or ungenerous to others as of bearing it when done to ourselves, and to die with pleasure to revenge affronts offered to their clan or their country , these are accounted their highest accomplishments."

III.

SUPERSTITIONS, ETC.

"Donald Dhu—Donald Dhu—Donald Dhu—
Lear me, and tremble

" *The gleaming path of the steel winds through the gloomy ghost. The form fell shapeless into air, like a column of smoke which the staff of the boy disturbs as it rises from the half extinguished furnace.*"—OSSIAN.

That Highlanders are a superstitious people, anyone acquainted with their finely strung imagination and the weird, wild regions they inhabit can well imagine.

" As when a shepherd of the Hebrid's Isles,
Placed far amid the melancholy main,
Whether it be lone fancy him beguiles,
Or that aerial spirits sometimes deign
To stand embodied to our senses plain,
Sees on the naked hill, or valley low,
The while in ocean Phœbus dips his wane,
A vast assembly moving to and fro,
Then all at once in air dissolves the wondrous show."
                                                —THOMPSON.

Often have I myself, while crossing some bleak moor, or traversing a lonely deserted glen, experienced a weird awe-stricken feeling, and it would require but very little imaginative power to convert a grey rock or a waving tuft of heather into a filmy ghost, a kelpie, or a brownie. Educational enlightenment has done much to dispel the darkness of superstitious beliefs which enveloped Highlanders up to near the middle of the nineteenth century; and in many parts of the Highlands, at this very hour, scores of apparently very sensible people cling to the creed of their forefathers, and are firm believers in the existence of ghosts, fairies, and witches.

Witchcraft was the most prevalent superstition; and many a poor decrepit or eccentric individual suffered—under the very eye of the church—the extreme penalty of the law, branded with the appellation of wizard or witch. Although it takes a long time to eradicate a belief, when once rooted in so tenacious and conservative a mind as that possessed by the Celt, the belief in witchcraft, to the extent of persecuting the supposed subjects of it, is well nigh extinct. Yet fairies, ghosts, and brownies are still often seen hovering about some lonely and haunted locality—if reliance may be placed on the statements of belated travellers. Another common belief, prevalent all over the Highlands fifty years ago, and in some degree believed in at the present time particularly in the western isles—is second sight, supposed to be a supernatural gift whereby the seer can see the distant future, and

* * * * * "Framing hideous spells,
In Skye's lone isle the gifted wizard seer
Lodged in the wintry cave, with fate's fell spear,
Or in the depths of Uist's dark forest dwells.

* * * *

To monarch's dear, some hundred miles away,
Oft have they seen fate give the fatal blow,
The Seer in Skye shriek'd as the blood did flow,
When headless Charles warm on the scaffold lay."

The Seer was a very reticent and mysterious person, employing enigmatical language when disclosing any of his prophecies so as to be construed to suit the circumstances of the case, and they were regarded "as men to whom strange things had happened."

(To be continued).

THE HIGHLANDER ABROAD.
BRIGADIER-GENERAL LACHLAN MACINTOSH.

F a biography of General Lachlan MacIntosh has ever been written I am not aware of the fact. As his name occurs frequently in the history of the war for Independence, it appears to be a great oversight that his life and services have escaped the attention of the biographer.

No name is more distinguished in the annals of the State of Georgia than that of MacIntosh. The head of the family, John Mór MacIntosh, was chief of the Borlum branch of Clan MacIntosh. In 1736, with a hundred of his tribesmen, he accompanied Oglethorpe to Georgia, and settled at New Inverness (now Darien), M'Intosh County. Seven of the MacIntoshes served in the Revolution. Colonel James MacIntosh, a grandson, served in the war of 1812, also on the Canada frontier, in the Crete war, and as a brigadier in the Mexican war of 1847-8, and fell mortally wounded while leading the assault at Molinodel Rey. His son, James, was a confederate general and fell at the battle of Rea Ridge, November 7th, 1862. Maria J. MacIntosh, the grand niece of General Lachlan, was a writer of popular fiction.

Brigadier-General Lachlan MacIntosh, son of John Mór, was born near Inverness, Scotland, March 17th, 1725 At the time he emigrated with his father to Georgia he was but eleven years of age. At the age of thirteen, on account of his father having been made a prisoner by the Spaniards, he was left to the care of his mother. His opportunities for an education were very limited, yet his strong mind overcame many difficulties. At the age of maturity he went to Charleston, where, on account of his fine personal appearance (he was reckoned at that time as the handsomest man in Georgia) and the services of his father, he commanded attention, and entered the county-room as clerk of, the afterwards President of Congress, Henry Laurens. Having tired of commercial pursuits he returned to his friends on the Alatamaha, married, and engaged in the vocation of land surveyor, and at the same time made himself conversant with military tactics. He occupied a prominent position in Georgia affairs, and originated the protest of the Colonists against the introduction of African slaves.

The war for Independence found Lachlan MacIntosh on the side of the oppressed. He first received the appointment of a colonelcy, and in 1776 was commissioned a brigadier. He now suffered persecution by his rival Button Gwinnett, until he could no longer forbear; and, finally, pronouncing his opponent a scoundrel, a duel ensued, in which Gwinnett was killed. On account of the troubles beyond the Ohio Washington appointed General MacIntosh to succeed General Hand in command of the Western department. In making this appointment Washington, in his report to the President of Congress, May 12th, 1778, pays the following tribute to him: "I part with this gentleman with much reluctance, as I esteem him an officer of great worth and merit, and as I know his services here are and will be materially needed. His firm disposition and equal justice, his assiduity and good understanding, added to his being a stranger to all parties in that quarter, pointed him out as a proper person."

For the defence of Fort Pitt (now Pittsburgh) and ulterior operations, General MacIntosh brought with him a small force of regulars. Having received orders to march against Detroit, the seat of all the Western troubles, he descended the Ohio, in the month of October, to a distance of thirty miles, and then erected Fort M'Intosh—the first military fort of the United States established on the Indian side of the Ohio. The expedition against Detroit was abandoned on account of its expensiveness. In lieu therof Congress ordered General MacIntosh to proceed against any of the Indian towns, the destruction of which, in his judgment, would intimidate the savages. With a thousand men he marched against the villages on the Sandusky, but arriving at the Muskingum he decided to proceed no further until spring. He at once built a fort which he named Laurens, in honour of the President of Congress, and then, with the great part of the army, returned to Fort Pitt. In 1778 he returned to Georgia and was at the siege and fall of Savannah. In 1780 he was with General Lincoln in the heroic defence of Charleston, and there, with the rest of the army, was made prisoner by the British under Sir Henry Clinton. After his release he went with his family to Virginia, where he remained until the close of the war. When he returned to Georgia he found his property, for the greater part, wasted. In retirement and comparative poverty he lived in Savannah until his death, which occurred, February 20th, 1806, at the age of eighty-one. Twice, however, he was called from this retirement, for in 1784 he was elected a Member of Congress and in 1785 he was chosen a Commissioner to treat with the Southern Indians.

Ohio, U.S.A. J. P. MACLEAN.

UNREST!

WATCHMAN, watchman, what of the night,
The night wherewith old Earth is crown'd?
Thy watch-tower glance afar, around,
Discovers it returning light?

Is there no tint on orient verge,
A whisper crystallized a ray,
A hint of the prophetic day
Which shall Unrest and darkness merge?

The wind is boisterous and strong,
A mad-birth of the womb of noise;

I scarcely hear the still small voice
Which now and then hints joy and song.

But shadows thicken on all downs,
In syrtic way and sanguine wold,
And grim Unrest is laying hold
On shepherds' crooks and monarchs' crowns!

And on yon autocratic crest,
And northern ridges of the world,
Great flaunting banners are unfurl'd
Which rob sweet sleep of many a guest!

Watchman, watchman, shall not our strength,
That has it roots in vast resource,
A lynx-eyed giant born of force,
Establish lasting peace at length?

The spirit of the dauntless Gael,
The energy of Saxon blood,
The iron swans that sail our flood—
Shall peace not reign where these avail?

Great stores of force are bridled war,
And oaks will burn that will not bend;
Such force, restrained, shall in the end
Howl out a universal jar!

Yea, synthetize historic pith,
And scan its vast and varied scope;
Read backward, does it kindle hope
More than a crumbling monolith?

But who are they that shall abide
When rocks of human strength are rent?
My friend, till night be wholly spent,
Do thou in Providence confide!

Banff, Oct. 6, 1898, JAS. MACKINTOSH.

CLAN MACLEAN ASSOCIATION.—The Seventh Annual Gathering of the members of the Clan Maclean Association and friends was held in the Waterloo Rooms. There was a crowded attendance. Colonel Sir Fitzroy Donald Maclean, Bart., C.B., Chief of the Clan, presided, and among others on the platform were Lady Maclean and Miss Maclean, Mr. Hector A. C. Maclean, London; Mr. C. A. Maclean, Wigton; Dr. Magnus Maclean; Rev. Dr. John Maclean; Captain W. Maclean, Southampton; Mr. W. Maclean, W. Hartlepool; Mr. J. A. Maclean, Forfar; Mr. Walter Maclean, President; Mr. John Maclean; Mr. Lauchlan Maclean, Vice-President; Mr. Peter Maclean, Secretary; and representatives of the various Clan Societies. The Chief, in the course of an address, said it appeared to him that in these days Glasgow was a favourite resort for Highlanders, and very justly so, because there work might be found, and honour might be gained by all those who diligently sought it. He was happy to be able to announce that the Association was progressing in a most favourable manner. They had been able to give assistance to deserving people, and they endeavoured to help clansmen to get situations when they required such assistance. As the Society was built upon such a good foundation, he hoped the day would come when it would be a lasting blessing to all Macleans. He had received reports of their Clan from various parts of the world, from Sweden, Germany, the United States, and our distant colonies, where Macleans had gone to seek their fortunes, and where, he was proud to say, many had made them. A Concert and Assembly followed.

COLIN ALEXANDER M·VEAN.

MRS. C. A. M·VEAN.

THE CELTIC MONTHLY:

A MAGAZINE FOR HIGHLANDERS.

Edited by JOHN MACKAY, Glasgow.

No. 3 Vol. VII.] DECEMBER. 1898 [Price Threepence.

COLIN ALEXANDER M'VEAN.

COLIN ALEXANDER M'VEAN, eldest son of the late Rev. Donald M'Vean, minister of Iona and Ross, and his wife, née Susan M'Lean, of the family of the M'Leans of Ross, passed his childhood at his father's manse in Iona.

Mr. M'Vean was educated in Edinburgh, and choosing the profession of a Civil Engineer, completed his studies as a pupil of Messrs. M'Callum & Dundas, one of the leading firms of engineers in that city.

In 1861 Mr. M'Vean received an appointment under the Hydrographic Office, and served some years on the Admiralty Survey of the Hebrides under the orders of the late Admiral Otter, C.B., latterly having charge of a detached portion of the Survey.

On the completion of this work he proceeded to Turkey, having received an appointment on the engineering staff of the Varna and Rustchuck Railway in Bulgaria, and served in this work from the commencement of the preliminary surveys until the completion of the railway.

Bulgaria, at that time a Turkish province, was in a very backward and disturbed condition, infested by bands of armed brigands, consequently the British engineering staff had to be armed, and to carry out their work under the protection of armed escorts furnished by the Turkish Government; skirmishes with the brigands occurred on several occasions, besides isolated attacks.

Mr. M'Vean was also engaged for a short time on Government railway surveys in Wallachia, and was present in Bucharest during the revolution in 1866, when the Hospodar, Prince Couza, was removed from the throne, and the present ruler—now King Charles I.—invited to occupy it. Serious disturbances occurred in the capital at this time.

The *Illustrated London News* of the day published an account of the disturbance, and sketch of the scene in the streets furnished by Mr. M'Vean.

On his return from Turkey Mr. M'Vean was appointed in 1868 by the Board of Trade, acting on behalf of the Government of Japan, one of three engineers (Messrs. Brunton, M'Vean, and Blundell) to go out to that interesting country

LIEUTENANT DONALD M'VEAN.

to superintend the erection of lighthouses, and generally to instruct the Japanese in engineering and surveying operations. In 1870 he was appointed Surveyor-in-Chief of Japan, and was engaged during the rest of his stay in the country in organising the Government Survey Department, and carrying out detail surveys of

Kioto and Tokio, the ancient and modern capitals.

When Mr. M'Vean arrived in Japan, the revolution which abolished the Tyconate, and restored the Mikado to full power, was in progress, and much fanatical hatred of foreigners existed, chiefly among the Samurai or hereditary official and military classes of all ranks, and many murderous attacks were made on foreigners. This rendered travelling and residence in the interior extremely unsafe, and until the revolution came to an end, and order was again restored, all work in the interior was carried on by the foreign engineers under the protection of escorts of native soldiers. During this time, even in Tokio, the capital, Mr. M'Vean's house was furnished with a permanent guard, and in walking or riding out he was always attended by two mounted men of the Bete Gumi Guard, who were responsible to the Government for his safety.

In addition to the survey Mr. M'Vean had for a time charge of the architectural and buildings office of the Public Works Department. At this time the staff under his charge numbered about three hundred in all, including ten European assistants, the remainder native surveyors, and a corps of cadets, sons of Japanese officers, being educated for the work.

He also established a complete Government Meterological Office, containing, in addition to the usual instruments, a set of seismographs for registering time and duration of earthquakes, and other phenomena relating to them. Japan being specially subject to earthquakes, some of the most violent and appalling description, excellent opportunities are obtained for studying them. On leaving Japan Mr. M'Vean received the thanks of the Government for his services.

Mr. M'Vean has thrice visited the United States and Canada, where he has many relations, and travelled extensively in these countries, visiting, among other places, the district in Upper Canada where the majority of emigrants from his father's parish had settled, and meeting there many old friends; he was greatly pleased to find nearly all of these people in a flourishing and prosperous condition. He also visited the great Sioux Indian reservation in Dakotah and spent some weeks with the Indians, afterwards furnishing sketches and an account of the tribe to the London *Graphic* at the time of the Indian rising which occurred on this reservation shortly after his visit, when some severe fighting took place between these Indians and the United States troops.

After his wanderings Mr. M'Vean returned to his native county and settled down at Kilfinichen, Isle of Mull, which he rents from the Duke of Argyll. He has represented his native parish in the County Council of Argyll since 1889, and is a J.P. for the county, and last year received the Diamond Jubilee Medal from Her Majesty for service in the Royal Body Guard for Scotland.

Mr. M'Vean married in the year 1868. Mrs. M'Vean is a daughter of the late Alexander Cowan, Edinburgh, owner of the extensive paper mills in Valleyfield, near Edinburgh, founded by his father about 1770. In 1811 the mills were temporarily acquired by the Government as barracks for the French prisoners of war, many being confined there, and numerous deaths occurred among them. Mr. Cowan afterwards erected a handsome monument to their memory, which still stands overlooking the valley.

Mr. M'Vean's oldest son, Donald, following the profession of many of his ancestors, entered the army through the Royal Military College, Sandhurst, and is now an officer in the Indian army (45th, Rattray's Sikhs), and served on the N. W. Frontier during the late war while attached to the 21st P.I., for which he receives a medal and bar.

Mr. M'Vean's oldest daughter is married to J. H. Gubbins, C.M.G., one of the Secretaries of Her Majesty's Legation in Tokio, Japan. Alexander, second son of Mr. M'Vean, is in the Hudson Bay Company's service, and presently stationed at Fort Chimo, Ungavo, the company's most northern post in Labrador. His youngest son is still a student.

MELODIOUS MINSTREL OF MY NATIVE LAND.

(In affectionate remembrance of Evan MacColl, Esq., the Bard of Lochfyne; author of "The Mountain Minstrel," "Clarsach nam Beann," &c. Died July 24, 1898. Inscribed, with warmest sympathy, to his widow and family).

Melodious minstrel of my native land,
Whose wealth of comradeship full thirty years
Was mine, with all that friendship leal endears;
Thou, crowned with ninety years, has crossed life's strand.

We grieve not, for thee 'tis rest, reward,
Thou knowest now what we yet hope to know,
Thy gold harp's strains blend with the Heavenly flow—
Not here is stilled the numbers of the bard.

Thy fame was noble on both sides the sea,
In every land thy melodies are sung,
In English pure or tunesome Gaelic tongue,
Through all a sweet pervading harmony.

While Findhorn rushes and while Beauly sprays,
Shall cherished be thy soul-inspiring lays.

DUNCAN MACGREGOR CRERAR

PRESENTATION SHIELD TO CLUNY MACPHERSON.

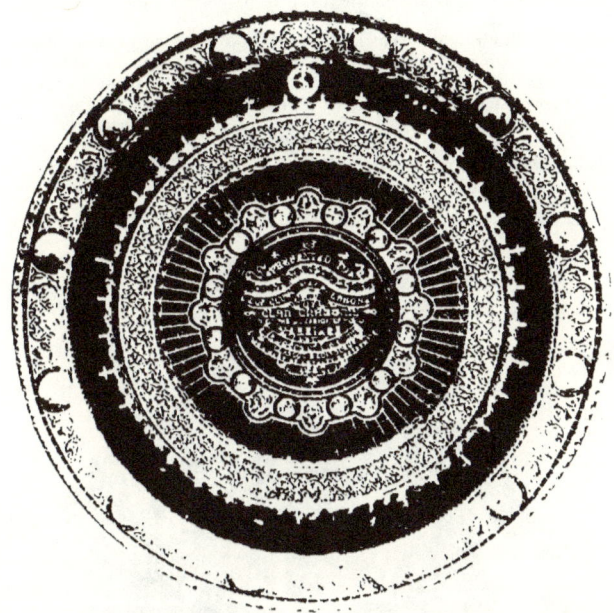

Designed and Manufactured by Mr. Robert Scott, 18 Buchanan Street, Glasgow.

THE SOBIESKI STUARTS.

TWO of the most picturesque figures in the drama of Highland history were the brothers Sobieski Stuart. The Gaelic race has never had more devoted admirers than those two. They were a strange pair, with a strange story. Their personality was enshrouded in an atmosphere of mystery and romance. The elder was known at different times as John Hay Allan, John Stuart Hay, John Sobieski Stolberg Stuart, and finally as the Count d'Albanie. The younger was known in succession as Charles Hay Allan, Charles Stuart Hay, Charles Edward Stuart, and on the death of his brother as Count d'Albanie. John was born in 1797, and died without issue in 1872. Charles was born in 1799, and died in 1880, leaving descendants. The brothers were the sons of Lieutenant Thomas Allen, of the Royal Navy. They claimed in private life to be the grandsons of Prince Charles Edward Stuart, and certainly bore a striking resemblance to the later Stuart kings. In 1837, when in Edinburgh, they were known as "The Princes." The name of Sobieski Stolberg, adopted by John, was derived from Louise de Stolberg, wife of Prince Charles Edward, and Maria Clementina Sobieski, mother of Prince Charles, and granddaughter of John Sobieski, King of Poland.

The brothers lived for many years in Scotland, and left it about 1846. During their residence there they mastered the Gaelic language, and devoted themselves to the study of the traditions, folk-lore, and ancient customs of the Highlands. They collected their information in all sorts of ways, from pipers and foresters, drovers, shepherds, and clergymen. They produced a number of works--poems, romances, historical sketches--all of which were marked by a strong love and sympathy with the Gael, and contained an immense amount of information about the Highlands. Their most notorious production was the "Vestiarium Scoticum, from the manuscripts formerly in the library of the Scots College at Douay, with an introduction and notes by John Sobieski Stuart." This work professed to be founded upon three manuscripts. The first came from the Scots College at Douay in France. The second came from the monastery of St. Augustine at Cadiz. The third was said to have been discovered in Edinburgh in 1819 in possession of an aged sword player named

John Ross, a native of Cromarty. It was said to have descended to him from his grandfather, who received it from a tutor in the family of Cromarty. John Sobieski Stuart stated that Lord Lovat (grandfather of the present Lord Lovat) had informed him that a fourth manuscript had long been in the possession of the Frasers of Inchberry, but had been taken to America. The "Vestiarium Scoticum" sets forth a system of distinguishing clans and families in Scotland by the tartans they wore. "Lest the old Scots fashion sink into oblivion," observes the author (Sir Richard Urquhart, knight), "I have taken on hande to compil accordant to my puir habilitye a trewe ensample of all or the maiste parte the pryncyppul tertains of Scotlonde sic as I may discerne them." The work was denounced as a forgery. In the *Quarterly Review* for June, 1847, Professor George Skene, of Glasgow University, attacked the "Vestiarium" in an article which appeared to his contemporaries so convincing that the reputation of the

THE BROTHERS SOBIESKI STUART.
(From a Painting in the possession of David Glen, Esq., Edinburgh.)

book was destroyed. It is but just to say that there are serious doubts as to the correctness of the forgery theory. In any case, the Sobieski Stuarts produced a number of works which were not forged, and which are well worth perusal and study. In the "Tales of the Century" they dilate on the mystery of their birth.

For a long time the brothers lived in a beautiful little river-island, Eilean Agais, given up to them by Lord Lovat. Here they surrounded themselves with ancient armour and relics of all kinds. They never wore any other costume but the Highland dress and the Stuart tartan. They were tall and extremely handsome. The father of the present writer frequently saw them, when a boy, in Edinburgh. On numerous occasions he had an opportunity of observing them as they walked along Princes Street, on their way to mass at the

JOHN CAMERON.

Roman Catholic Church, wearing the kilt and the royal tartan. He describes their bearing as singularly noble, and was much impressed by the likeness between the younger of the brothers and the portraits he had seen of Prince Charlie. It was the custom for those who passed the brothers to uncover as they did so.

Miss M'Donnell, of Glengarry, gave some interesting reminiscences of the Stuarts.* "At Glengarry," she said, "they were believed to be related in some crooked way to the royal Stuarts, and were said to have been educated in a Spanish monastery. They had pleasant conversational powers, were accomplished, drew all sorts of old Highland armour, old brooches, &c., sang one or two Gaelic and English songs, sometimes joined in the Highland games, and danced some parts of the Highland fling very well. They were obliging and good natured, and went to the Episcopal Chapel with the family, although our Presbyterian servants suspected them to be Romanists, as they had a black St. George's Cross sewed in one corner of their plaids." There can be no question about their religion. They were Roman Catholics. In the introduction to the "Costumes of the Clans" John writes as a very pronounced Romanist.

Charles the younger died in France on Christmas day, 1880. In the catalogue of his relics, which were sold after his death, he was described as "Charles Edward Stuart, Count d'Albanie, deceased, late of 52 Alderney Street, Eccleston Square," London. He left several descendants. One of the books of the brothers is dedicated to Marie Stuart, daughter of Charles.

J. A. LOVAT-FRASER.

* *Blackwood's Magazine* for April, 1895.

JOHN CAMERON, SUNDERLAND.

 THE subject of this sketch was born at Lawers, Breadalbane. He is the son of the late Rev. Duncan Cameron, who for many years laboured at Loch Tayside, a man distinguished for his piety and learning. A good Latin and Greek scholar, he devoted his spare time in educating his children, and endeavouring to instil in them a love of the beauty of the district in which they were born. His eldest brother is Mr. Robert Cameron, M.P., one of the members for the County of Durham, while his youngest is the Rev. Dr. Cameron of Ottawa.

Perhaps few men have taken a keener interest in Celtic, and all matters pertaining to the Highlands, than the subject of this sketch. Leaving the Highlands at an early age, he eventually settled in Sunderland, and for nearly forty years was head master of one of the best private schools in that district. Although Mr. Cameron was connected with most of the public bodies in the town, he yet found time to pursue his Celtic studies, and is the author of the "Gaelic Names of Plants," a book which raises him to a very high position among the scholars and scientists of his day.

The following quotation from the *Oban Times'* review of the work gives a true estimate of its value :—

"In view of this state of matters, we welcome with unmingled pleasure Mr. Cameron's book on the 'Gaelic Names of Plants.' Our perusal of it has satisfied us that it is a valuable contribution to Gaelic literature, and a valuable addition to the Gaelic student's library. As a guide to the botany of our native mountains and glens, it is simply beyond all price. Mr. Cameron has conferred an inestimable boon on his countrymen by its publication. A more delightful book to carry with one into the wilds, accompanied by an intelligent Highlander, we do not know."

The following letter from Her Majesty the Queen is worthy of notice :—

"BALMORAL, 21st Sept., 1883.

SIR—I am commanded by Her Majesty to thank you for the copy of your book, "The Gaelic Names of Plants," which you have been kind enough to forward for the Queen's acceptance, and to inform you that it will form a valuable addition to Her Majesty's Scotch Library.

I am, Sir, yours faithfully,
F. I. EDWARDS."

Mr. Cameron has also lectured on "Ancient Celtic Literature," as well as other Celtic subjects, and justly takes rank as one of our best living Celtic scholars.

THE SOCIAL CONDITION OF THE HIGHLANDS SINCE 1800.

BY A. J. BEATON, F.S.A. SCOT., F.G.S.E.

(Continued from page 39).

IV.

ANCIENT CUSTOMS AND FESTIVE AMUSEMENTS.

MANY of the ancient customs peculiar to the Highlands are being Anglo Saxonised, or gradually dying out. Halloween is still celebrated with much of its ancient rites and ceremonies, and :—

"The auld guidwife's weel hoordet nits
Are round and round divided,
And mony lads' and lasses' fates
Are there that night decided,
Some kindle, couthie, side by side,
And burn thegither trimly,

Some start awa wi' saucy pride
And jump out owre the chimlie,
Fu' high that night."

These lines from Burns's "Hallowe'en" refer to the custom of burning nuts, to decide if some secretly admired one would yet be wooed and won. But within my own recollection Hallowe'en festivities have lost much of the enthusiasm and excitement once associated with them. Many of the ancient games and pastimes of the country are neglected or abolished. The "Northern Meeting" has done more than any other institution I know of towards promoting and stimulating the continuance of the manly and athletic sports so peculiar to the Highlands. Where can you see a finer gathering of strapping, stalwart fellows, and of noble, commanding, and lovely ladies, than at the Northern Meeting in Inverness. While the institution has done much towards developing and perpetuating the national music, and in this respect I must not omit the minor kindred societies and associations, which I am glad to see springing up in almost every parish ; yet I will venture to suggest that the usefulness and, I may assert, the attractiveness of the meeting might be greatly extended were prizes offered for the best web of home spun cloth, tartan plaid, the best knitted pair of hose or other articles of home manufacture, so as to kindle the desire for industry among the peasantry.

V.—RELIGION.

Scotland is a Presbyterian nation. Roman Catholicism and Episcopacy have often endeavoured to gain the ascendency, but the former as a national religion died with James Beaton, Archbishop of Glasgow, and only in very remote regions of the Highlands did popery find space to raise its head. Recently, however, it has apparently been regaining vitality, and the re-establishment by the Pope of the Scots Hierarchy has given a stimulus to a creed which was fast falling into decay in the Highlands. Episcopacy received a very crushing blow at the time of the memorable '45, whose echo rings through Scotland to this hour, and from then till the middle of the present century it struggled to keep itself rooted in Scottish soil; but in recent years it has been asserting its position in the Highlands to such an extent, that the erection of a magnificent Cathedral in Inverness and the creation of a new See indicate that its roots have again dipped into good soil in the North, and that the solid easy-going Presbyterian creed of the Highlands is succumbing to the novelties of a new form of religion. The Established Church of Scotland is in a minority in the Highlands when compared with the Free Church and other dissenting Presbyterian bodies. In 1843 what has been called the Disruption

took place, whereby 451 ministers* of the Church of Scotland resigned their livings and formed themselves into a religious body called the Free Church of Scotland. The main causes of this secession may be ascribed partly to certain abuses in the patronage system, and partly to the looseness of the Presbyteries in licensing unsuitable persons to be preachers. Patronage had been previously twice abolished and reinstated again by Parliament. This act empowered the patron of a living to appoint as minister his own nominee without consulting either the congregation or the Presbytery. There is no essential difference between the doctrines of the Established Church and those of the Free Church, and now that the obstacle of patronage is abolished it seems a matter of regret that the two bodies do not unite, and thereby instil new life and vigour into the advancement of Christianity. It is lamentable to think that petty jealousies and ill feeling often exist between the adherents of the two churches. Notwithstanding all this the Highland peasantry are a religious people, and I venture to affirm that in no country in the world is the observance of the Sabbath day more rigorously enforced or more strictly adhered to than in the Highlands of Scotland.

"How softly, Scotia, falls the Sabbath's calm
   O'er thy hushed valleys, and thy listening hills ;
And, oh ! how purifying is the balm
   Of that day's peace which then the bosom fills !"

To some minds, perhaps, this unduly rigorous observance of the Sabbath day may seem extravagant, and when carried to extremes often appear ludicrous. Professor Blackie illustrates an instance when he ventured to pass a remark on the weather to a Skye Elder on the Sabbath day. "A fine day," said the Professor. "Ay," retorted the Elder, "a fine day indeed, but is this a day to be speaking about days ?" This morose or "gloomy religion" is chiefly confined to the Free Churchmen, the Established Church adherents, or Moderates as they are called, are somewhat more lax and advanced. Before closing these remarks on the religion of the Highlands I must touch briefly on the Sacraments or Highland Communion. The "Sacraments" is a great event in a Highland parish, and thousands of people flock from every district to attend. It extends over five days, Thursday, "the little Sabbath or Fast-day ; Friday, when the "Men" address the people and pray ; Saturday, a day of preparation ; Sabbath, the great day for the celebration of the Lord's Supper ; and Monday, a day of solemn farewell. On Sunday the Gaelic services are held in the open air, as no building sufficiently large can be found to contain so vast an assemblage.

* Of these 451, 289 were Parish and 162 *Quoad
Sacra* Ministers, or Ministers of Chapels of Ease.

VI Education.

The current belief that Scotland is such a well educated nation is erroneous in the extreme, for this supposed universal "diffusion of education," particularly in the Highlands, is anything but true; and although Scotland has long enjoyed the reputation of being the best educated nation in Europe—and as far as University education is concerned that is undoubtedly true—still we find that the Commission appointed to enquire into the educational state of the Highlands in 1818 found that portion of the kingdom sadly destitute of facilities for elementary learning. Notwithstanding the efforts made by the S. P. C. K. and the Church, little progress was made until the "Grants in Aid" system established in 1839, which gave an impetus to the educational machinery of the poorer districts of the Highlands.

Again the Free Church, shortly after the Disruption, in order to vie with the Parish or Established Church schools, erected, in almost every parish, schools in which the children of their denomination were taught, perhaps not in so efficient a degree as in the Parish school, nevertheless they created a healthy spirit of rivalry, which benefitted in no small degree the educational development of the country. The passing of the Education Act of 1872 was the means of placing all the schools in a parish under the direct management of a Board, elected triennially by the ratepayers. This School Board has full control over the teachers, regulates the course of instruction, and was empowered to levy a rate to meet any deficiency not covered by the Government Grant and school fees.* In the poorer and more thinly populated parishes the education rate was often excessive: in the parish of Lochs it reached 4 6 in the £, while in Barvas it attained to the high figure of 5 8 in the £. In these two parishes the poor rate was fixed at 1 8 and 4 6 in the £ respectively. Whether the new system is an improvement on the old Parochial one remains yet to be seen; but I fear very much that the high pressure under which it is worked does not make the same lasting impression on the young mind as did the slow, steady grinding under the old Parish Dominie. Dr. Norman Macleod in his "Reminiscences of a Highland Parish," depicts with life-like touches the quiet peaceful life of the parish schoolmaster, passed among the solitudes of some wild Highland glen. "The glory," Dr. Macleod says, "of the old Scots teacher of this stamp was to ground his pupils thoroughly in the elements of Greek and Latin. He hated all shams, and placed little value on what was acquired without labour. To master

* School Fees are now abolished in Board Schools.

details, to stamp grammar rules, thoroughly understood, upon the minds of his pupils as with a pen of iron; to move slowly but accurately through a classic, this was his delight; not his work only but his recreation, the outlet for his tastes and energies." . . . . "I like to call those old teachers to remembrance. Take them all in all they were a singular body of men, their humble homes and poor salaries and hard work presented a remarkable contrast to their manners, abilities, and literary culture. Scotland owes to them a debt of gratitude that never can be repaid, and many a successful minister, lawyer, and physician is able to recall some one of those old teachers as his earliest and best friend, who first kindled in him the love of learning and helped him in the pursuit of knowledge under difficulties." Then there is "Domsie" of Ian M'Laren's creation, whose prototype is still often met with in the Highlands.   (*To be continued*)

ARGYLLSHIRE BAZAAR—Our readers will kindly remember that the Bazaar in aid of the Argyll Nursing Association takes place from the 24th to the 28th November. It is a most deserving object and we trust that our readers will make a point of attending on at least one of the four days during which it is open.

MESSRS. CAMPBELL & CO., 116 TRONGATE, GLASGOW, the Celebrated Musical Instrument Makers, have just issued their privilege price list for 1898-9, and a most handsome and useful volume it is. Every known musical instrument seems to be stocked by this firm, pictures, particulars and prices being given of each. Pipers can here be supplied with the national instrument in every variety, with all accessories. As makers of melodions their name and products are of world-wide fame. Readers requiring any musical instrument should write to Messrs. Campbell & Co, who will send copies of their new list, post free.

We have just learned that Major-General M'Bain Farquharson of Breda died on the 12th November. He was a gallant soldier and a patriotic Highlander. His loss will be deeply regretted by his countrymen.

ROB DONN MACKAY'S POEMS.—We are in receipt of a copy of Mr. Hew Morrison's new edition of "Rob Donn." It is got up in nice style, but that is the best we can say on its behalf. It bristles with the errors of the former editions; Mr. Morrison has done practically nothing to correct them. He has devoted his energies to the revival of the old dispute regarding the bard's name, a matter that might well have been left alone, for he has given no new facts to justify his action. Indeed, his so-called impartial statement of the case is positively insulting, as it is not only a purely partisan account, but is full of what we will mildly describe as—mistakes. He charges the Mackays with giving Rob Donn the name Mackay for the first time in 1829, whereas we can prove that he was described as Robert Mackay in a Gaelic work published thirteen years prior to that date. Next month we will treat fully of Mr. Morrison's attempt to deprive the Reay bard of his rightful name.

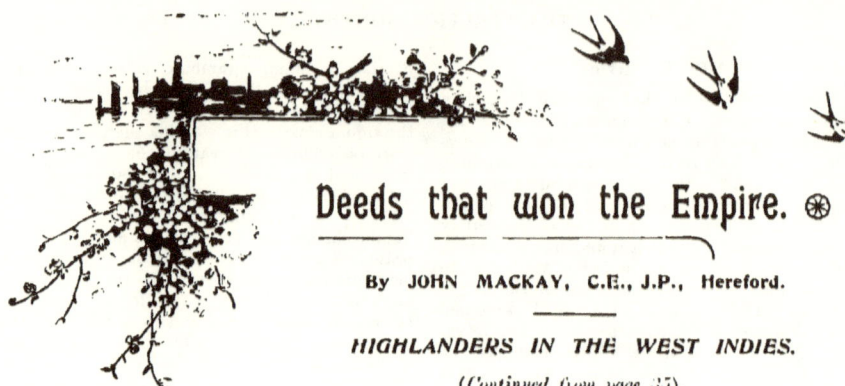

Deeds that won the Empire. ✸

By JOHN MACKAY, C.E., J.P., Hereford.

HIGHLANDERS IN THE WEST INDIES.

(*Continued from page 35*).

THE capture of Quebec by Wolfe's gallant army, of Pittsburg by General Forbes, the retreat of the French from Ticonderoga, and the capture of Niagara and Montreal by General Amherst, sounded the death knell of French superiority on the North American Continent.

The fall of Montcalm in the moment of his defeat, and the entire submission of Canada and the West, put an end to the dream of a French Empire in America.

The great Commoner's schemes met with success everywhere. The generosity and originality of his mind were displayed in his earliest measures. He quieted Scotland by employing its restless Jacobites in the service of their country, and by raising regiments among its clans to fight and conquer for it in every battle honourable to British arms. He recognised the military genius of the Great Frederick, whose prodigious efforts in the Seven Years' War would have been useless but for the aid given him by Pitt in men and money. Frederick's victory over the French at Rosbach was destined to change the fortunes of the world by bringing about the unity of Germany. To Pitt's support of Frederick, in that war, in its darkest hours, may be attributed, the events which, in our own day, led to the creation of a United German Empire.

The conquest of Canada, the expulsion of the enemy from the Ohio to the Mississippi, by the removing of this enemy, and by flinging open to the energies of the American Colonists in days to come the boundless plains and prairies of the West, laid the foundations of the United States. Britain never played so great a part in the history of mankind as then, under the commanding influence of the "Great Commoner."

During the Seven Years' War, 1756 to 1763, a period chiefly illustrated by the military genius of the Great Frederick, the British engaged their foes in every quarter of the globe. In 1758, on the West Africa coast, St. Louis, at the mouth of the Senegal, and the island of Goree, were captured, and in 1759 the island of Guadaloupe and other neighbouring islands, in the West Indies, were taken.

When Spain, in 1761, at the instigation of France, declared war against Britain, an expedition was despatched from this country early in 1772 to Cuba, Havana, and Manila. After an obstinate defence of Havana for forty days, that Spanish stronghold, reckoned by the Spaniards to be impregnable, was captured — which, this year the Americans declined to attack. So great was the booty taken that the army and navy engaged in its capture received in prize money over £736,000. Dominique, Martinique, Guadaloupe, Fort Royal, St. Lucia, Grenada, and St. Vincent swelled the list of British conquests, and the French were completely driven from the Windward islands and the Caribbean sea. In all these operations the young Highland soldiers of Pitt found a field for the display of their martial prowess, and acquitted themselves in a way worthy of their veteran companions in arms.

In a previous chapter, it was mentioned that the King had ordered a 2nd battalion to be raised in the Highlands for the "Black Watch." The recruiting for this battalion went on slowly, till a report of the heavy loss sustained by the "Black Watch" in front of Ticonderoga reached home. A cry of revenge pervaded the Highlands, men trooped off from their homes to be enrolled, in the hope that they would soon have the opportunity to avenge the fall of their gallant brothers who fell at Ticonderoga. In a very short time the ranks of the 2nd battalion were filled to nearly 1000 officers and men. Having been drilled for about five months, they were sent on the first expedition to the West Indies early in 1759. Martinique was sighted on the 13th January, and on the 15th the squadron entered the great bay of Port Royal. Next day the three ships of the line attacked Fort Negro, some three miles from the citadel, and soon the guns were silenced, and the fort taken by a body of seamen and marines landing from their boats. They scrambled up the rocks, passing through masses of mangroves, and reached the embrasures, which they entered with bayonets fixed, while the enemy precipitately fled. The Union Jack was at once hoisted with loud cheers, guns spiked, carriages broken, powder destroyed, and the detachment remained in possession. Another battery was silenced. The French troops and militia marched from the citadel to oppose any landing, but on seeing the whole British squadron with its transports full of red-coats, and Fort Negro already captured, they retired to Fort Royal, leaving the beach open, and there next morning the army landed, quietly and leisurely, as if going to exercise.

By 10 o'clock the Grenadiers, the King's regiment, and the Highlanders moved forward, and soon fell in with parties of the enemy, with whom they maintained an irregular fire, till they came within a little distance of Morne Tortueson, an eminence in rear of Fort Royal, the most important post in the island. There they maintained a sharp skirmish, during which it was said of the young Highlanders: "That though debarred the use of arms in their own country, they showed themselves good marksmen, and had not forgotten how to handle their weapons."

About 2 p.m. General Hopson informed the commander of the squadron, that he could neither hold his ground nor attack the citadel unless he was supplied with heavy guns. Oh! for an hour of a general like Wolfe! A council of war was held, the troops were recalled, and re-embarked that evening.

The inhabitants of Martinique could scarcely believe their senses when they suddenly saw themselves delivered from all fear, at a time when they were overwhelmed with apprehension, dismay, and confusion, when all their leaders had resigned the thought of all resistance, and were actually assembled in the public hall of Port Royal to send deputies to General Hopson, with proposals for capitulation and surrender. Such was the issue of the first attempt to capture Martinique. General Hopson soon after died

of fever, and the command taken by General Barrington.

It was proposed that any further attempt on Martinique should be relinquished, and the conquest of Guadaloupe suggested. Dastards: generally the result of Councils of War, and divided commands! Divided responsibilities!

THE FIR CLUB MOSS.

CLAN MACRAE'S BADGE.

WHERE sturdy boatmen gaily deck
   Loch Duich's breast with sail,
And lofty ben and mountain peak
   Keep watch o'er wild Kintail.
Where Seaforth's warlike slogan rang,
   In troubled days of old,
And from their glens responsive sprang
   His clansmen leal and bold.

Unequalled were the men who wore
   The club moss as their badge,
Behind the galley's foam-tipp'd oar,
   Or claymore, axe, and targe.
For ages long on flood and field,
   In Seaforth's plaided van,
Those giants of the sword and shield,
   With glory crowned their clan.[*]

Clan Rae's historic surname clings
   To Donan's crumbling walls,
And its romantic halo flings
   Round cold deserted halls.
In Scottish history it shines,
   Mid records of the brave,
And in the tales of other climes
   Is not unknown to fame.

While bard or minstrel tells the tale
   Of hard fought Sheriffmuir,
And Highland feet Scar Ouran scale
   With footsteps light and sure :[‡]
While, to a Gaelic song, the sail
   On western wave is set,
The ancient heroes of Kintail,
   The Gael shall not forget.

[*] The Macraes were noted amongst Seaforth's followers for stature, strength, and valour.

[†] Ellan Donan Castle, one of Seaforth's strong-holds, of which the Macraes were keepers.

[‡] Scar Ouran—a mountain in Kintail, and the slogan of the Macraes.

Hatfield.

ANGUS MACKINTOSH.

TO CORRESPONDENTS.

All Communications, on literary and business matters, should be addressed to the Editor, Mr. JOHN MACKAY, 9 Blythswood Drive, Glasgow.

—⊕—

TERMS OF SUBSCRIPTION.— The CELTIC MONTHLY will be sent, post free, to any part of the United Kingdom, Canada, the United States, and all countries in the Postal Union—for one year, 4s.

THE CELTIC MONTHLY.
DECEMBER, 1898.

CONTENTS.

NOTICE TO SUBSCRIBERS.

Readers who desire the "Celtic" to be sent for another year, might kindly forward their annual subscriptions (4/- post free), on receipt, to the Editor, Mr. John Mackay, 9 Blythswood Drive, Glasgow. Subscribers will greatly favour us by giving this their immediate attention, as delay in remitting entails upon us a good deal of extra trouble.

OUR NEXT ISSUE.

OUR issue for next month will take the form of a Grand New Year Number. It will contain portraits, and biographical sketches, of Mr. Robert Campbell, Manchester; Mr. William Matheson, President, Hebburn-on-Tyne Celtic and Caledonian Association; and Mr. and Mrs. John Maclean, Clan Maclean Association, Glasgow.

We are pleased to notice that a good Highlander, Mr. Alexander Cameron, has been elected Mayor of Stockton-on-Tees. The honour could not have been conferred upon a more deserving citizen.

GLASGOW HIGHLAND NOTES.—The many Highland societies in this city are now in the midst of their winter's work, hardly an evening passing without two or three societies meeting. It not unfrequently happens that two of the leading societies hold their Annual Social Gatherings on the same evening, which is unfortunate for both. On 28th October, while Lord Lorne was presiding over the Re-union of the NATIVES OF KINTYRE in the City Hall, Mr. J. R. M. Macdonald of Largie was addressing his clansmen at the CLAN MACDONALD GATHERING in the Waterloo Rooms. Both gatherings were well attended, although there were many

who would have liked to attend each had they been on different dates. The same mishap occurs on the 14th February, when both the INVERNESS-SHIRE and MULL AND IONA people hold their Social Gatherings. The CLAN MACDONALD DINNER, which was presided over by Colonel Macdonald of Glenaladale, was a brilliant function, and we are pleased that the Macdonalds are making such excellent progress with their society. Speeches were delivered by Glenaladale, Largie, Messrs. David Macdonald, Peter Macdonald, and other clansmen, and Mr. John Mackay, of the *Celtic Monthly*, responded for the "Kindred Societies."—THE CLAN MACKINNON are making good headway. They carry over this session a balance of £100, Mr. Duncan Mackinnon, London, as usual, giving the society the very handsome donation of £21. Mr. W. A. Mackinnon, M.A., was elected chief, and Mr. William Mackinnon, president.—THE CLAN CAMERON have done wisely in removing their headquarters to Glasgow. Messrs. Alexander and Duncan Cameron have been appointed joint secretaries, and under their guidance the society should progress. Dr. A. C. Cameron, Paisley, is president ; Mr. Allan Cameron, of Lundavra, and Mr. John Cameron, J P , Kirkintilloch, are chieftains ; Mr. Alexander Cameron of Erracht is an hon. president. The Annual Gathering will probably be held in January.—THE CLAN MACKAY have elected Major A. V. Mackay, Grangemouth, as president for the new session ; vice-presidents, Alexander Mackay, Charing Cross ; Angus Mackay ; Rev. Angus Mackay, M.A. ; Hugh Mackay, M.A. and John Mackay, West Preston Street, Edinburgh; Alex. Mackay, Thurso. Secretaries and treasurer were re-appointed. The society has a balance in hand of £1165. The Social Gathering takes place on 23rd December, a special feature being the appearance of Mr. Roderick Macleod, of Inverness, the Mòd medallist, who is to render several Mackay country songs.—THE MACMILLANS have arranged their Re-union for 7th December, in the Queen's Rooms, the Rev. Dr. Hugh Macmillan, chief of the society, in the chair. This is always one of the most enjoyable gatherings of the season.—THE NATIVES OF SKYE have their Annual Gathering in the Queen's Rooms, on 2nd December, Mr. Kenneth L. Macdonald, of Skirinish, in the chair ; and the UIST AND BARRA gather in the same hall on 13th December. Mr. James E. B. Baillie, of Dochfour, M.P., presiding.—THE INVERNESS-SHIRE hold a Grand Concert in the Assembly Rooms, on 1st December, Mr. James Grant, president, in the chair.—THE COUNTY OF SUTHERLAND ASSOCIATION at the meeting on 9th November were treated to a paper on "Rob Donn and his Times," by the Rev. Thomson Mackay, B.D., Strath, Skye. The question whether Rob Donn was a Mackay or a Calder, which Mr. Hew Morrison has again revived in his new edition of the bard, led to a most animated discussion. The meeting favoured the universally accepted opinion that he was a Mackay, and certainly Mr. Morrison has given no new evidence which is ever likely to alter that well grounded belief.—THE SUTHERLANDSHIRE ASSOCIATION had a very interesting lecture from our old friend Mr. D. W. Kemp on "Sutherland Church Tokens." We hope Mr. Kemp has not abandoned his intention to publish a work on "The God's-acres of Sutherland."

MINOR SEPTS OF CLAN CHATTAN.

By CHARLES FRASER-MACKINTOSH, LL.D.

No. XVII.—THE FARQUHARSONS.
CLAN FIONLAY.

(*Continued from page 33*).

I.—INVEREY.

THIS family descended of James, 4th son of Donald of Castleton, and were prominent in the clan. In the time of William of Inverey, second of the family, occurred a serious quarrel with the Gordons. It is thus narrated by Mackintosh of Kinrara in his Latin history, and as it took place in his own day, and came under his personal cognizance, may be taken as strictly authentic:

"In the month of September, 1666, there fell out some slaughter betwixt certain of the name of Gordon and the Farquharsons of Braemar, which bred the Laird of Mackintosh some trouble, and had engaged these two families in a far greater, if the business had not been prudently managed, and the evil for the time prevented. The matter fell out thus:

John Gordon of Breacklie having commission from the Town Council of Aberdeen for fining such

PATRICK FARQUHARSON OF WHITEHOUSE.

as killed black fish on the water of Dee, did outlaw some of the name of Farquharson and their tenants in a most rigid manner; and upon the 15th day of September foresaid, having convened a number of his tenants and followers, did beset certain Braemar men on the highway as they were coming from a fair that held at Kilmuir in Angus, and having beaten some of them, did in a very illegal manner take from them 16 to 18 pairs of horses for a poind. On the 17th day of the foresaid month John Farquharson, apparent of Inverey (so well known as the "Black Colonel"—C. F. M.), the master of the

most part of those who were robbed as aforesaid, being accompanied with the owners of the horses and others of his friends, came down to guard a fair that stands nearly at Tulloch (a mile be east the house of Breacklie), and on their way sent a message to Breacklie, desiring that in regard the foresaid poinding was unlawful, and that some of the horses poinded belonged to persons who were never outlawed for black fish, therefore he would be pleased to restore the horses to the owners, and he would engage himself that such persons as were guilty would do duty before their return from

Tulloch fair. Breacklie refused on any terms to restore the horses. Inverey was willing to dispense with the horses at that time, provided Breacklie would condescend to submit differences to well willed persons who would decide within four days after the foresaid market. As Breacklie was about to answer this overture, he perceived Alexander Gordon of Abergeldie with a number of armed men coming to his assistance, whereupon he disdained to parley any further upon the business, and in great passion and fury did pursue and assault Inverey and his tenants, with guns, pistols, and drawn swords. Inverey being most unwilling to enter in blood with his neighbours, at first gave ground, earnestly entreating Breacklie to desist from his pursuit, but Breacklie, Abergeldie, and his followers became the more insolent and eager, and in time shot two of Inverey's followers dead upon the spot. Whereupon Inverey and his tenants being forced in their own defence to resist the pursuers, faced about and killed the said John Gordon of Breacklie, William Gordon, his brother, and James Gordon of Cults, who were most forward in the pursuit. Shortly after this slaughter Breacklie's nearest relations pursued Inverey and the most part of the specials of his friends, criminally before the justices. Then Inverey makes his address to Mackintosh as his chief, who remembering the

MARJORY STEWART, WIFE OF PATRICK FARQUHARSON.

kindness he had received of Inverey not long before in the expedition of Lochaber, did set his course to act a friendly part for him ; and to manifest his forwardness and resolution to that effect, did travel from his own house to Edinburgh three several times in his defence. And by his friendship and moyen brought the business to that point that in the end there was no pursuer to appear in the cause, and in a short a deserving clansman had occasion to meet with a thankful requital from a loving chief."

The male line of William, eldest son of the above James, terminated with James Farquhar son of Balmoral, great-grandson of the above James, 1st of Inverey. This James was out in the '15 and '45, and wounded at Falkirk. Lewis Farquharson, second son of James, 1st of Inverey by his second marriage, was styled of Auchindryne. Lewis was out under Lord Dundee 1690 and again in 1715. He was contemporay with his cousin, the "Black Colonel" of Inverey, and though trained as a minister became a Roman Catholic. The line of Auchindryne terminated in 1820 upon the death of James, 4th of Auchindryne. He had sold his estates of Auchindryne, together with Inverey and Balmoral, to which his father had succeeded, to the Earl of Fife, and exchanged Tulloch and Ballater for Bruxie. James' only brother, Lewis, who assumed the name of Innes in succeeding to Ballogie, died in 1830.

ANDREW FARQUHARSON OF WHITEHOUSE,
AT THE AGE OF 19.

The representation of Inverey as the male descendants of William and Lewis Farquharson, the eldest sons of James, 1st of Inverey, must be looked for in the descendants of James Farquharson of Tullochcoy, 3rd and youngest son of the before mentioned James Farquharson, 1st of Inverey. The initials of James, 1st of Tullochcoy and of his wife, with the date 1693, still exist on a stone lintel at Tullochcoy. In 1755 James Farquharson, 2nd of Tullochcoy, obtains a charter of confirmation to the estates in his own favour in liferent, and his eldest son, Peter, in fee. This James, 2nd of Tullochcoy, and son of the first James, died at Tullochcoy in 1760. Peter, 3rd Tullochcoy, born in 1733, parted with Tullochcoy and removed to Belnabodach in Strathdon. He married a daughter of Forbes of Bellabeg (now Newe), and died in 1801. Peter Farquharson, son and successor of James, 1st of Belnabodach, was born at Tullochcoy in 1758, and died at Ballater, 1813. He left three sons, Peter, John, George, and one daughter, Mary. The eldest son, Peter, Major H.E.I.C.S., died at Ballater 1849. The second son, John of Corrachree, Lieutenant-Colonel H.E.I.C.S., married Margaret, younger sister of Andrew Farquharson of Whitehouse, and died at Corrachree, 1871, without issue, leaving his estates to his nephew, John, son of his sister Mary, above mentioned. She married the Rev. C. Macpherson, and died in 1876. John Gordon assumed the name of Farquharson in terms of the settlements of his uncle, Colonel John Macpherson of Corrachree. He entered the military service, and now Colonel, C.B., R.E., has for some years held the high position of Director General of the Ordnance Survey Department. George Farquharson, 3rd son of James Farquharson of Belnabodach, died there in 1841, leaving two sons, Francis and James. The latter is presently resident in New Zealand. The eldest son, Francis Farquharson of Belnabodach, now worthily represents the honourable house of Inverey, with its cadets of Balmoral or Balmurrel, Auchindryne, and Tullochcoy.

The burial place of the family is within the ruined chancel of the old church of Crathie.

The manner Inverey fell to the Duffs has already been mentioned, with Montcoffer's complaisant remarks on his success.

II.—MONALTRIE.—This estate, which has fallen into that of Invercauld, lies chiefly within the parish of Glenmuick and Glengairn. Charles Farquharson, last of the old family, sold the estate to Alexander, younger brother of Invercauld, in 1702, having been all his life the constant ally, friend and supporter of Mackintosh.

III.—WHITEHOUSE—This family descends from James, younger brother of Colonel Donald Farquharson (Donald Og), a distinguished soldier in the Civil Wars. The eldest son of the above James signs the Bond of 1664 as "younger of Whitehouse,"

and dying without issue, was succeeded by his brother, Henry. One of the family, Captain Henry Farquharson (whose portrait is given), fell at Culloden, a handsome gallant youth, one of the many of the flower of Highland families who fought and died for Prince Charlie. The portrait of his son and successor, Dr. William Farquharson, is given, and the line continued direct until 1896, when it terminated on the death, without issue, of Andrew Farquharson. Mr. Farquharson had been a member of the

CAPT. HENRY FARQUHARSON,
WHO FELL AT CULLODEN.

Bombay House founded by Sir Charles Forbes, and on his retirement in 1840, received a very complimentary address from upwards of three hundred of the most influential Parsee merchants of Bombay. By his settlements the estate of Whitehouse was left to his great nephew, George Leslie, younger son of Kininvie, on condition of assuming the name of Farquharson. This has been done, and the present Whitehouse (whose coat of arms is given) may be confidently expected to prove a credit to the name of Farquharson. The mansion house, erected by the late Andrew Farquharson, is reproduced, as also portraits of his parents, Patrick Farquharson and Marjory Stewart, Lessmurdie, the latter of great character; also of himself when a youth of nineteen. Andrew Farquharson lived to the great age of ninety-three. Dying in 1896, without issue, the headship of the Farquharsons, which had been in Whitehouse for about a century, fell to Farquharson of Finzean, as after mentioned.

DR. WILLIAM FARQUHARSON.

WHITEHOUSE, ABERDEENSHIRE.

TRANSLATIONS FROM THE GAELIC.

'S E 'N T-EILEAN UAIN, ILEACH.

(TRANSLATED FROM SINCLAIR'S "ORANAICHE," p. 67).

O Islay, sweet Islay, proud queen of the sea,
What land in rare beauty can e'er vie with thee?
Thy green spreading forests, thy dens and thy dells,
Thy braes and thy corries bespangled with bells.

In sleep and in waking I long in my dreams
For thy cool crystal fountains and clear winding
　streams;
Thy green bracken glens where the antler'd herds
　dwell,
And the birds of the forest their melodies swell.

Though long I may roam beneath far foreign skies,
Where the flowers of the tropic luxuriant rise,
To thy green shores for ever my memory will turn,
And love for thy braes in my memory will burn.

In all my far wanderings I long for the hour
When the prow of my bark will be turned to thy
　shore;
There once more I shall feel on thine own lovely
　strand,
The warm hearty greetings of friendship's true hand.

O Islay, sweet Islay, proud queen of the sea,
What land in rare beauty can e'er vie with thee?
Thy green spreading forests, thy dens and thy dells,
Thy braes and thy corries bespangled with bells.

THOIR MO SHOIRIDH THAR AN T-SAILE.

From Neil Macleod's *Clarsach an Doire*,
Second Edition, p. 115.

Air—"God 'tha mi gun chrodh gun aighean."

Here's far o'er the stormy ocean,
Greetings wi' my heart's devotion,

To the bonnie land o' Scotia,
　Rugged bens and glens o'green.

To her bonnie hills o' heather,
To her bonnet blue and feather,
To her tartan plaid, together,
　Wi' her lassies neat and clean.

There the heather bell is growing,
There each heart wi' love is glowing;
There the Gaelic songs are flowing
　Blythe through every Highland glen.

There the matron kind and cheerie
Greets the wanderer lone and weary,
And no heart e'er sad or dreary
　Turns in sorrow frae the door.

The land o' misty ben and mountain,
Murmuring rill and mossy fountain,
Where through greenwood bowers at Beltane
　Sweet the lilt o' sangsters pour.

Though from their homes our kin are riven,
And o'er the ocean billows driven;
While to the stranger race is given
　The glens their fathers' steel kept free.

Yet soon will fortune's wheel be turning,
The heather on the braes be burning,
And to their fathers' homes returning
　Will our Highland exiles be.

Then will our straths and fields be golden
With our harvests, as of olden,
When the Celtic step, beholden
　To no stranger, trod the lea.

　　　　　DUNCAN LIVINGSTONE.
Ohio, U.S.A.

AN ELEGANT HIGHLAND EPITAPH.

SIR,—In the *Celtic Monthly* for November,
Mr. James Mackintosh gives the translation of a
Gaelic epitaph. I am sure he and others will
be pleased to read the original. It appears on
a stone in the churchyard of Glenorchy Parish,
Argyllshire.

　　　　　　　　　　　　FIONN.

" An so na liugh ta 's an Innis
　Bean bu duilich leom bhi ann,
　Beul a chiuil, is Làmh a ghrinnis,
　Ha iad 'nioshe sho nan tàmh.

Tuill 'cha toir am Bochd dhuit beannachd ;
　An lom-nochd cha chlùthaich thu nis mò,
Cha tiormaich Deur bho shùil na h-Ainnis ;
　Có tuill' o Lagg! a bheir dhuit treòir?

Chan fhaic sin tuille thu a 's choinni :
　Cha suidh sin tuille air do Bhòrd ;
Dh 'fhalbh uain suairceas, seirc is modhan
　Ha Bron 's bi-mhulad air teachd oirn."

AN SEALLADH.

Paired for the Second Prize at Oban Mod.

DH-EIRICH mi suas gu luath aon mhaduinn,
　'Is dhir mi 'n ceann tamull ri beinn,
Chula mi ceòl an loin 'sa bharraich,
　San smeorach gu leadarra seinn,
Chunnaic mi 'n drinchd gu h-urail soilleir
　Dealradh mar mhile leug,
Na blaithean gu h-aillte lubadh fodham,
　Us cuirneach maiseach nan geug.

Bha faile nam flùr mar thùis am chuinnean,
　Sam boithe gu cùbhraidh bha fas,
Bha geug agus gair air nadur uile,
　Nuair bhris gu h-aoibhneach an la,
Bha uain air an reidhlein leum 'sa cluicheadh,
　Gach aon diubh siubhal le mhathair,
Bha coisir na coill le loinn us furan,
　Ann an laoidh, air a mhaduinn cuir fàilt'

Dhirich mi suas gu aird a biunean
　'S bu ghloirmhor 'n seolladh a fhuair
Bha ghrian anns an Ear gu morail 'g imeachd,
　'S i snamh thar mullach nan stuadh
Bha luchairtean òir 'san speur ri fhaicinn
　Fosgladh an dorsan gu fial,
Uinneagan neamh fo sgeimh 's iad laiste,
　Dearrsadh troimh dumhlas nan nial.

Bha toslachd us tamh air fonn a tighinn,
　Nuair choisinn mi circan nam beann,
Ach uiscag bheag chiar ag iadh le sigheadh,
　San osag ri torman fann,
Bha mi lean fhein an teampull farsuinn
　Na Cruitheachd, gun neach mun cuairt,
Beachdach gu geur air meud na h-aitreabh
　A dh-eirich e neo-ni aig uair.

Mun cuairt air gach taobh bha ceudan tuiread,
　A togail ri Flaitheas an cinn,
'N cois shruthanan maoth bha naomh-chill lurach,
　'S na coireachan uaigneach grinn,
Bha innealan ciuil air surd fo uidheam,
　Nuair dhuisgeadh gu h-oibhinn ceol,
Aimhnichean brais gu cas a ruitheas,
　San iar-ghaoth sheideas gu foill.

Ach dhluthaich an ceo nam choir 'us dh' fhalaich
　A ghrian a h-aghaidh 's na neoil,
Thuit air an raon na bhraonaibh ealamh,
　An t-uisge, us bhasaich an ceol,
Bha dealanach dluth na luban teine
　Boillsgeadh bho ghleann gu gleann,
Clisgeach san speur le beuchd an eagail
　Tairneanach bhris us mo cheann.

Bha mi fo fhiamh bu chianail m' aigne,
　'G eisdeachd ri bagradh nan dul,
Fasgath bho 'n stoirm le toirm cha 'n fhaighinn,
　Ach sgorr anns a chreag bha dluth ;
Nam chrubain gu truagh le sumaintean trom,
　Diblidh gun mhisnich san uair,
Creutair air geill 's e 'm feum air cobhair,
　An lathair na Cumhachd Bith-bhuan.

Na h-uairean a thrial! air sgiathan cabhaig,
　Shioladh 'n doinionn gu feath,
Shiubhail na neoil 'us shoillsich fhathast,
　A ghrian air an fhearann gu leir,

Theiriun i sios gu boidheach flathail,
Folach a h-aille 'sa chuan,
Thainig an oidhche us bhoillsg a ghealach,
Nuair dh-aom luchd cadail gu suain.

Chi sinn na speur 's na reultan uile,
Tha 'g imeachd nan cursan reidh,
Tha iad bho chian 'se 'n rian bhi siubhal,
Fo stiureadh 's fo ordugh treunn.

Tha iad 'g innseadh an sgeul gun bheul a labhairt,
Mo mhoireachd na Cruitheachd gu leir,
Tha Cumhachd a riaghl' air neamh us talamh,
Nach urrainn duinn sgrud leinn fhein.

Thig madiunn us feasgar oidhche us latha,
'Us aimsirean solais us broin,
Luighe an ceo air foun gu h-ealamh,
Thig Samhradh us geamhradh mor,
Sinne bho 'n de cha leir ach platha,
Troimh 'n dorchadas ciod th-air a chul,
Aig criochnach air reis thoir Fhein dhinn sealladh,
Do 'n t-solus mu 'n duin air suil.

"FEAR-SEALLAIDH" (Alex. Stewart, Glenlyon).

M'INTIRE OF LONDONDERRY.

RI CRUADAL.

THIS branch of the M'Intyre clan during the troubles of the 17th century moved southward, and having joined the Covenanters were driven from Scotland during the persecution of that body by James the Second, and settled at Struve, a headland on the Donegal coast of Ireland, in sight of their native land, the Mull of Cantire, Islay, and Paps of Jura being conspicuous in the north east. For the seven generations which have come and gone since their settlement in Ireland, in no instance has a member of this family intermarried with the Irish Celt, difference of religion has as a rule been a bar to the English and Scotch settlers in Ulster amalgamating with the original inhabitants. John M'Intire resided at Struve in the year 1700. His son, Robert, had by his wife, Anne Blackburne, a son also named Robert, who settled as a merchant in Londonderry, and married in 1783 Elizabeth, daughter of Ninian Boggs of that city. There was issue of this marriage two sons, Ninian Boggs and John, also a daughter, Mary, wife of Major Edward Renwick of the 72nd (Highlanders) and 83rd regiments, who, on retiring from the British army, served with the rank of Colonel in the Spanish War of Succession, and died in 1831, from which year, to their honour be it told, successive Spanish Governments, notwithstanding monetary and political difficulties, paid his widow's pension until her death in 1891 at the age of 103 years.

John, younger son of Robert M'Intire, having obtained a commission in the East India Company Bombay Army, on his outward voyage received orders to join the expedition of 1805 under Sir David Baird, which expedition eventuated in the conquest of the Dutch Settlement in the Cape of Good Hope. He subsequently served with distinction in the Pindaree and Maharatta Wars, and died, holding the rank of Major, without issue, in 1829.

Ninian Boggs, elder son of Robert M'Intire, born in 1786, was descended maternally from John Riddle, a citizen and defender of 'Derry at the period of the memorable siege of 1689. Mr. N. B. M'Intire was a merchant in Dublin, and as such a member of the Ouzel Galley, a society then existing of the leading merchants of that city, and founded in 1705, for the arbitration of disputes relating to commerce. During his latter years, on retiring from business, he resided at Clover Hill, County of Dublin, and died there in 1866. He had by his wife, Anne, daughter of Richard Litton, a family of whom three sons are now surviving, Richard Litton, Travers, and Hartley.

The Rev. Travers M'Intire, second surviving son, having graduated in Dublin University, was for many years Vicar of Langcliffe, Yorkshire, and now resides at Bedford. He married Sarah Anne, daughter of the Rev. Aaron Manby of Knaresboro, by whom he has four sons surviving, Ninian, M.A., Oxford; Arthur, of the Indian Forestry Service; Travers, B.A., Cambridge, in Holy Orders; and Walter, of London University. Hartley, youngest son of N. B. M'Intire, a lawyer, now resident at Blenheim, New Zealand, married Miss Harriet Skelton, by whom he has issue one son, Robert.

Dr. Richard Litton M'Intire, whose portrait we give, eldest surviving son of N. B. M'Intire, is now senior representative of the M'Intires of Londonderry. Dr. M'Intire was born in the city of Londonderry in 1815, three years afterwards his father moved to Dublin, where Richard was educated. Matriculating in Dublin University, he took honours in science and graduated B.A. in 1836. He joined the Medical School of the University, taking his M.B. degree in 1843, subsequently that of M.D and Fellowship of the Royal College of Surgeons, Ireland, in 1845. For some fifty years Dr. M'Intire practised his profession with ability and success; he finally left Coleraine, in the County Londonderry, the scene of his labours, in 1891, and is now resident at Kingstown, County Dublin. Dr. M'Intire married Elizabeth, daughter of Robert de Neufville Lucas of London.

A characteristic of this gentleman, which has gained him respect through life, is his high sense of honour and duty. He now enjoys, in his eighty-fourth year, a vigorous health, which is not often the lot of much younger men.

RICHARD LITTON M'INTIRE, M.D.

Upon the death of his mother Dr. M'Intire inherited the lands of Kilcoscan, in the County of Dublin, a property which has been in that lady's family for two hundred years, the original grant by patent from Queen Anne to Dr. M'Intire's ancestor, Joseph Budden, describes these lands as "the estate of the late King James."

THE ROVER'S RETURN.

TIME passed, and I retraced again
  My steps to scenes of old,
And looked and looked, but looked in vain,
  For friends now dead and cold
  Beneath the silent mould ;
While e'en the hills scarce seemed to me
The same as they were wont to be.

The bygone years had all things changed,
  Except the changeful years,
Which through their seasons duly ranged,
  Unchanged in their careers
  Of ever cycling spheres,
Through winter's gloom and summer's glow,
Which still remained as long ago.

But yet they seemed not so to me
  When I returned at last.
From roaming over land and sea,
  Through breeze and bitter blast
  Of years now dead and past,
Whose toils have tinged my locks with grey,
And changed my heart to grave from gay.

Through many lands though I have been,
  Across the ocean's foam,
Of every kind of clime and scene,
  They lacked the charms of home ;
  And so, where'er to roam
My footsteps strayed, my thoughts anew
Strayed back to Scotland's mountains blue.

Though there my forbears fought and bled,
  And suffered grievous wrong.
Their good old name dishonoured—dead,
  For ages dark and long,
  By traitors' faithless tongue ;
Yet none the less I loved the land,
That nursed Clan-Alpine's war-like brand.

Her shady glens, her airy braes,
  So bright and fair to see,
Her lakes and mountains, creeks and bays,
  Her warriors brave and free—
  Yea, these were aye to me
Meet food for fancies, wayward, wild,
Since first I wandered there, a child.

The world was then a vision bright,
  With lights of rainbow hues,
A fairy land that charmed the sight
  With clear delightful views,
  From which 'twere hard to choose
The prospect best to please the eyes,
When all assumed such luring guise.

But these delusions now are past
  Whose charms can none restore,
And so I grieve my thoughts to cast
  Behind me or before,
  The past being now no more,

Whereas the future's brief look-out
Is wrapped in clouds of care and doubt.

The morn assumes another hue
  From what it used to take.
For now its pearly drops of dew
  Seem tears that duly wake
  A sense of pensive ache,
Which makes me grieve in vain, and sigh
For other days and years gone by.

And so the evening sunset fades,
  With sadness in its light,
Until anon the twilight shades
  The landscape out of sight,
  To hail the reign of night ;
While night and day appear to toll
Sad funeral marches to my soul.

The grass-grown graves are all that mark
  The friends of years of yore,
Who hear no more the morning lark,
  Nor can the wild wind's roar
  Awake them ever more.
From out that silent sleep profound,
That recks of neither sight nor sound.

And of the few still left behind
  Of that once thriving fold,
They're all, alas ! with wrinkles lined,
  Of strength deprived and old ;
  For those once young and bold
Are of themselves but shadows now,
With feeble frame and careworn brow.

Delightful youth, how happy 'tis
  Thou know'st not what's in store !
Or else thy fleeting hour of bliss
  Would soon be bliss no more ;
  For ne'er a woman bore
A son that, when three score and ten,
Would wish to live his life agen.

Ah, God ! how vain our youthful dreams,
  How few of them turn true !
Yet what without their magic gleams
  Would men aspire to do ?
  For if they only knew
The toils that on their footsteps wait,
Their hearts would fail to face their fate.

But Hope—that cordial of the mind—
  Revives them by the way,
Against the freaks of Fortune blind
  To strive while strive they may,
  And face the future fray,
With dauntless cheer that leads them on,
To win what is but seldom won.

For somewhere up life's rude incline—
  They know not when or where,
But always short of their design—
  Grim Death abides them there,
  With fixed and fatal stare,
Their promised deeds while yet undone,
And their prospective race unrun !

JOHN MACGREGOR, M.D.,
Lieutenant-Colonel.

"MINOR SEPTS OF CLAN CHATTAN," by C. FRASER-MACKINTOSH, LL.D.—We are pleased to state that a copy of this beautiful and interesting volume, which we recently published, has been ordered for the Royal Library at Balmoral Castle.

LORD MACAULAY'S ANCESTORS.

By William C. Mackenzie.

"EVERY schoolboy" knows that Lord Macaulay was the eldest son of Zachary Macaulay, who identified himself with the anti-slavery movement in England early in the present century. But even Macaulay's famous schoolboy might have difficulty in tracing his patron's genealogy back to the sixteenth century; and still greater difficulty, perhaps, in describing off-hand any notable deeds performed by the historian's forbears. To the student of heredity, as well as the student of Macaulay, it may be of interest to learn that he came of a fighting, a writing, a preaching, and a political stock; a combination which culminated in the person of one, the pugnacity of whose political temperament was only equalled by the brilliancy and the versatility of his literary genius.

The origin of a large proportion of the Highland clans is a matter of conjecture. Historians differ in ascribing to them respectively, native and foreign beginnings. The origin of the Clan Macaulay admits of no doubt : it is pure Norse. Macaulay's forbears hailed from Lewis, the largest* of the Western Isles of Scotland, which for centuries lay under the dominion of Norse marauders. The supposed progenitor of the Macaulays is Olaus Magnus of Norway, who is the hero of an ode, entitled "Olaus the Great, or the Conquest of Mona," written by Lord Macaulay at the tender age of eight. The name Olaus has been variously rendered as Olaf and Olave, and in an ancient manuscript it appears as Olay. Macaulay is the Gaelicised form of Olaf's son, and is synonymous with the modern Scandinavian name of Olafsson. Traces of the Norse occupation of Lewis are evident in numerous place-names, as well as in certain customs and in the folklore of the inhabitants of that island. Indeed, there are Lewis Macaulays to-day, whose Scandinavian appearance is alone sufficient to attest their origin. Some of them claim relationship, necessarily distant, with the great Lord Macaulay, and are quite prepared to assert that his genius was the concentrated result of the use by his ancestors for centuries of a diet of fish and oatmeal! In this view they are supported by no less an authority than Carlyle, who, on one occasion, upon seeing Macaulay's face in unwonted repose, remarked, "I noticed the homely Norse features that you find everywhere in the Western Isles, and I thought to myself, 'Well, anyone can see that

* That is, Lewis with Harris.

you are an honest, good sort of fellow made out of oatmeal.'" The writer recollects one of the Lewis Macaulays, now dead, who was particularly proud of his illustrious connection. Although his knowledge of general literature was, to say the least, limited, he could recite the "Lays" by heart, and quotations from the "Essays" interlarded his everyday conversation. This was a tribute from a humble clansman which would probably have gratified the kindly heart of Macaulay. Hero-worship among Highlanders is by no means an uncommon sentiment, and the great figure of Macaulay was well calculated to inspire the breasts of his Hebridean namesakes with that feeling.

The first of his ancestors of whom there is any authentic record was Donald Macaulay, who lived in the reign of King James VI. It was a common practice in the Highlands in those days—a practice which is still largely followed— to distinguish the possessors of marked physical peculiarities by nicknames having reference to their infirmities. Donald Macaulay was blind of one eye, and for that reason was known by his fellow-Lewismen as Donald Cam. The one-eyed progenitor of Lord Macaulay was a man of great physical strength, which in those troublous times he had many opportunities of turning to good—or bad—account.

In a book entitled "The Highlands of Scotland in 1750," recently edited by Mr. Andrew Lang, the statement appears that, "The common inhabitants of Lewis are Morisons, McAulays, and McKivers" (Macivers); as a matter of fact they are to this day, with the Macleods, the representative Lewis families. The Macaulays were at constant feud with the Morisons, or Clan Gilliemhuire, who were located at Ness, on the north side of the island, and of whom were the Breves, or hereditary Celtic judges, of Lewis. It is more than probable that the Morisons knew Donald Cam only too well for their peace of mind. But events occurred during his lifetime which united the Lewis clans in face of a common danger; and Donald Macaulay's prowess was directed into a more patriotic channel than had hitherto been the case. The Macleods— another clan of Norse origin—who, in Donald Cam's time, were the lords of Lewis—were quarrelling among themselves, and with the Mackenzies, of Kintail, in Ross-shire, The latter were scheming to obtain possession of the island. Taking advantage of the disturbed condition of Lewis, a party of Fife adventurers applied for, and obtained from the King, a gift of the island. Their professed object was to civilize the islanders; their real intention was to supplant the inhabitants by a settlement of Lowlanders. They built houses and "skonses" about Stornoway, the capital of Lewis, and made what a certain chronicler terms "a bonny village" of it. But this settlement was of short duration, for the colony was constantly harassed by the islanders, who forgot their feuds in their common determination to drive the hated Sassenachs into the sea. The adventurers had a disastrous time of it, and were finally forced to relinquish their possessions, the right to which they sold to Lord Kintail, Chief of the Mackenzies.

Donald Cam took a prominent part in driving the Fife colonists from Lewis, and subsequently sided with the Macleods in their fruitless attempts to repel the Mackenzies when they ultimately took possession of the island. His patriotic spirit rebelled equally against the invasion of his beloved island by Sassenach or Celt, and his courageous and obstinate resistance to the encroachments of the Mackenzies has been immortalised in a Gaelic proverb, "*Cha robh cam nach robh 'crosda*," meaning, "Whoever is blind of an eye is pugnacious," the true signification of which it is that is difficult to overcome a one-eyed person. A careful student can readily see in Lord Macaulay's character more than mere traces of Donald Cam's spirit.

Donald Cam Macaulay had a son who was known as *Fear Bhreinis*, literally the man, or tacksman, of Brenish. The tacksmen of those days were the representatives of the duinewassels of former years, who formed the gentry of a clan, holding land direct from the chief in consideration of military services. This Macaulay was therefore a man of importance in Lewis; and being, like his father, a man of great bodily strength, he acquired a reputation for personal prowess, which has been commemorated in song and story.

The son of the Brenish tacksman was named Aulay Macaulay, who, forsaking the warlike traditions of his ancestors, entered the church, and after some disagreeable experiences in his earlier ministerial life, settled down in Harris, adjoining Lewis, where for nearly half a century, until his death in 1758, he discharged the duties of the manse. Of his six sons, no less than five were educated for the church, the sixth, named Zachary, being bred for the bar.

Aulay's third son Kenneth, nicknamed Kenneth Drover, transmitted to Lord Macaulay the gifts of the historian. True it is that the "History of England" has a world-wide reputation, while the "History of St. Kilda," written by the Rev. Kenneth, is now barely known even to local antiquaries. In its day, however, the book had a certain vogue. Dr. Johnson described it as "a well-written work except some foppery about liberty and slavery." The "foppery," it may be noticed, subsequently fructified in the life-work of the author's nephew, Zachary Macaulay. There is reason to believe

that Johnson's liking for the book was really due to a statement which it contained, to the effect that a curious epidemic of what would now be called influenza, spread over St. Kilda whenever the factor paid his periodical visits for the purpose of collecting the rents. The probabilities are that the islanders had just as great an aversion to the payment of rent as crofters in modern times have shown, and may possibly have shammed illness in order to move the factor's bowels of compassion.† That the coincidence of the factor's presence and the influenza were, in the author's mind, not attributable to supernatural causes, is pretty clear from the fact that in another part of the book there are slighting references to some of the superstitions of the islanders. Johnson's mind, however, imbued as it was with superstitious ideas, failed to grasp the humour of the thing, and so we find him gravely praising the author for his "magnanimity in venturing to chronicle so questionable a phenomenon, the more so," he added, "because Macaulay set out with a prejudice against prejudice, and wanted to be a smart modern thinker." Subsequently, Johnson and Boswell visited Macaulay at his manse at Calder, or Cawdor, and while staying there, according to the "Journey to the Western Islands," they visited Cawdor Castle, "from which Macbeth drew his second title." Johnson thanked Macaulay for his book, and said it was "a very pretty piece of topography," a compliment which the author apparently did not relish. Boswell tells us that Johnson afterwards remarked to him that, judging by Macaulay's conversation, he was persuaded that he was not the author of "St. Kilda." "There is a combination in it," he added, "of which Macaulay is not capable." Needless to say, Johnson's *dictum* was sufficient for Boswell, who states that he was afterwards told that the book was written by Dr. John Macpherson, of "Sky," from materials collected by Macaulay. Johnson's opinion, however, was probably biassed by a dispute which he had with his host, to whom he was simply rude. Macaulay appears to have spoken somewhat slightingly of the lower ranks of the English clergy. Johnson turned on him with a vehement rejoinder: "This," he said, "is a day of novelties. I have seen old trees in Scotland, and I have heard the

---

† Modern writers have also commented on the circumstance that the natives of St. Kilda contract severe colds whenever strangers visit the island. A plausible explanation of this phenomenon has been offered. It is suggested that a landing can only be effected when the wind is blowing in a direction which is favourable to the contraction of colds; hence the coincidence of the visits of strangers and influenza.

English clergy treated with disrespect. Sir, you are a bigot almost to laxness." That the great castigator afterwards regretted his rudeness is evident from the fact that he presented his host's son, "a smart young lad about eleven years old," with a pocket Sallust and obtained for him a servitorship at Oxford, of which, however, young Macaulay did not avail himself, as he appears to have gone abroad.

(To be continued).

AN EPISODE OF THE '45.

THE wind was moaning through the pine trees, making sweet sad melodies as it rose and fell, and ending occasionally in a long mournful sigh, as if it were weary and longed to be at rest. The moon, struggling through the drifting clouds, showed from time to time a thatched hut, half way up the hill side, within which there was no light except a red glow from the peat fire. Beside it sat an old woman, shrivelled and grey, her face brown and wrinkled with age; but the dark piercing eyes, which turned ever to the door, were full of fire and passion.

"Ochan, Alastair, *laogh mo chridhe!*" she moaned, "oh, that I could give my life for you, my son, my only son!"

She started as the door opened, and a tall slim girl entered, her young face white and haggard with terror.

"Elspeth," she cried, breathlessly, "is it true that Alastair has been taken by the *saighdeir ruadh?* He who was as strong and fleet as the deer. Elspeth! speak to me. Tell me."

"Sine," began Elspeth hoarsely, "Alastair is taken. He was with the Prince yesterday in the cave of Dun Artach, when the red-coated soldiers came; and the Prince thought it better to leave the cave and take shelter in the woods, so that when darkness came they could row over the loch to Ardrioch. The red Sassanach came too near as they lay among the bracken, and Alastair showed himself among the trees, and led them away down the Corrie of Artach, and through the woods of Dougla, letting them see him from time to time. When he knew the Prince had time to be away in safety, he bounded among the rocks, but it was too late. He had let them come too near. They fired on him, and he fell. They bound him, Sine, and are taking him to Fort-William to be hung as a rebel. Hush! What is that?" she cried, as the door shook and rattled.

"It is only the wind," answered the girl, as she opened the door to satisfy the old woman. But as she did so her face changed, and she gasped—"Alastair! Elspeth! Alastair has come back to us!" She flung her arms round him, and drew him into the house. His tartan kilt was mud-stained and torn in many places, and as he sank down exhausted beside the fire, on which Elspeth had thrown a heap of fragrant pine branches, Sine knew that Alastair would never again hunt the deer in Glen Artach, or help her to carry home the peats in the autumn evenings, while the setting sun poured its blessing on them ere it sank to rest behind the shoulder of Ben Dougla. Elspeth had pillowed her son's fair head on her lap, and was crooning soft Gaelic words of endearment over him as he lay half unconscious; but, as the fire blazed, the heat seemed to put life into his stiffened limbs, and consciousness returned.

"Mother," he whispered faintly, as he took the old wrinkled hand within his own, "they could not keep me. When I thought of you and Sine, it gave me strength, and I burst the thongs that bound me and escaped down the banks of Loch Dougla. They couldn't follow, and I knew every step of the way. I thought I couldn't get home in time to say good-bye, mother, but I am quite happy now. And the Prince, is he safe?"

"*Ha e m'eudail,*" answered Elspeth. He got safely over the loch last night, and is with the Macdonalds. He is sore at losing you, my boy. Don't try to speak more just now. We will make your bed here by the fire, and then you will rest."

They made a bed of fresh heather and covered it with a plaid, then assisted Alastair on to it. When they were doing this, his plaid fell back, and they saw that his shirt was darkly stained with the life-blood, which was slowly ebbing away.

"Sine, my loved one," he said, as he again opened his eyes, "you were to have been my wife, but it cannot be now. To-night, as I came up the hill, I saw the ghosts of my fathers riding on the storm-driven clouds, and I knew that they had come for me. They are waiting for me now. You will look after my mother, Sine, and comfort her; and some day, if a good man should love you, look kindly upon him, and know that Alastair will be pleased to see you happy."

"Alastair, *mo run,*" cried Sine, "don't leave me. I cannot live without you, Alastair! Alastair!"

His mother was moistening his lips with a little water, and he smiled to her and whispered faintly—"Kiss me, mother and Sine."

As the fire burned down, and the dawn faintly shone on Alastair's pale face, the two women knew that he had left them. They gently covered him with his plaid, while the sun rose and the wind sang his coronach among the pine trees.

ANNA NIC DHAIBHIDH.

THOMAS M·KELLAR, J.P.

THE CELTIC MONTHLY:

A MAGAZINE FOR HIGHLANDERS.

Edited by JOHN MACKAY, Glasgow.

No. 4. Vol. VII.]   JANUARY, 1899   [Price Threepence.

THOMAS M'KELLAR, J.P.,
OF LERAGS, ARGYLLSHIRE.

MR. THOMAS M'KELLAR of Lerags, who is a J.P. for Argyll and in the Colony of Victoria, and ex-member of the Legislative Council of Victoria, was born in Scotland in 1820. His father, the late Mr. John M'Kellar of Knebsworth, went to Victoria in the early days of that colony and purchased the estate of Knebsworth, where he lived till his death in 1859.

Mr. Thomas M'Kellar, the eldest son of Mr. John M'Kellar, went to Victoria in 1848, and about forty years ago purchased the adjoining Strathkellar and Croxton estates, which he still owns. He subsequently purchased the Tarrone estate in Victoria and Raglan in Queensland. Some years ago he purchased the estate of Lerags in Argyllshire from his wife's cousin, Mr. John Beverley Campbell, Mrs. M'Kellar being a grand-daughter of the late Archibald Campbell of Lerags and his wife Margaret, daughter of Captain John Campbell of Ardslignish, and sister of Archibald Campbell, 9th of Lochnell.

Mr. M'Kellar, as one of the early colonists of Victoria, has aided in making that great colony what it is, and was always to the front in support of every patriotic scheme. With Sir W. J. Clarke, Sir Samuel Wilson, and a few others, he subscribed the fund which enabled Ernest Giles, the Explorer, to undertake his second expedition through the interior of Australia. Mr. M'Kellar has been a keen sportsman and the tenant of many well known sporting estates in Scotland, till advancing age confined his shooting to his own estate of Lerags. He introduced hares on his Victorian estate, Strathkellar, from whence they spread through the western district of Victoria. Mr. M'Kellar had a family of five sons and four daughters, but his three eldest sons are dead. Two of his daughters are married. Mr. John M'Kellar,

the eldest son, resided mostly at Tarrone in Victoria, which estate he owned in conjunction with his two brothers. It was sold at his death. He married, in 1850, Edith, daughter of the late Hon. William Rutledge of Farnham Park, a member of the Legislative Council of Victoria, and by her had five sons. He died at Torquay in England, in 1885, at the age of 35.

Mr. Thomas M'Kellar, the second son, was one of the best cricket and football players of his time, a good shot and polo player. He married Mary, daughter of Roderick Urquhart, Esq., of Yangery Park, Victoria, and by her had one son. He died in 1877 at the early age of 23, only ten months after his marriage. Mr. James Allan M'Kellar, the third son, resided the latter part of his life at Raglan in Queensland, where he died, unmarried, in 1888, at the age of 33. He had travelled much, and like his brothers was a good all round sportsman. Mr. Campbell M'Kellar, the fourth, and now eldest surviving son, has published seven or eight novels and other works, some under various pseudonyms. One entitled "In Oban Town" deals with the Highlands. He published another work on Greece, copies of which were accepted in very gracious terms by the King, Crown Prince and Princess of Greece, and the Princess of Wales. Two of his books have been translated into Swedish and published as serials in Swedish newspapers. He has also written stories, sketches, and articles for London weeklies and magazines, also in Australia, and has contributed illustrations to *The Graphic*. He is a member of the Society of Authors, the Salon, etc., has been a member of the Royal Geographical Society of Victoria since its formation many years ago.

The youngest son of Mr. Thomas M'Kellar is Mr. Ernest Edward M'Kellar, who resides mostly at Raglan in Queensland. He married in 1892 Grace Violet, daughter of the late Hon. John Cumming of Terinallum and of 'Millicent,' Melbourne, a member of the Legislative Council of Victoria, and by her has three daughters.

Both Mr. Thomas M'Kellar and his wife are ardently Highland in their sympathies, though equally attached to their Australian home, and they reside alternately in the two countries, having crossed the ocean innumerable times. They are at present in Australia.

THE SOCIAL CONDITION OF THE HIGHLANDS SINCE 1800.

By A. J. BEATON, F.S.A. Scot., F.G.S.E.

(Continued from page 39).

VII.—DOMESTIC LIFE.

DOMESTIC life in the Highlands may be divided into three classes—the Lairds, large Farmers, and Crofters. The Land Lords have large and elegant castles or mansions; and the majority of them live in luxury and maintain large and expensive establishments. The extraordinary demand for land, for agricultural and sporting purposes, caused a corresponding increase in the value of this class of property, but recent depression of trade has considerably reduced the rentals of several large estates, resulting in the cutting down of expenditure, and this will be a loss very severely felt by many poor workmen who were wholly dependant on the employment they constantly obtained about the "Big Hoose." Up to the middle of this century large and middle class tenantry were ill accommodated; but now few indeed there are who have not handsome and commodious dwelling houses and offices. The crofters and cottars on the other hand, we may safely assume, are still in some places not one whit better than they were a hundred years ago. Their habitations are but miserable hovels, in many cases the walls being built of turf, with a few cabers, thatched with heather, for a roof; while an opening in the roof serves the two-fold purpose of allowing the peat reek to escape and admitting a dim light for in many cases there are no windows. The floors are formed of clay beaten down to a hard surface, which in dry weather serves the purpose very efficiently, but in wet weather forms into a slushy puddle. I am now referring more particularly to the dwellings in some parts of the Western Isles—on the mainland considerable improvements have been effected on many estates within the last ten to twenty years on the dwellings of both crofters and cottars.* Miss Gordon Cumming in her interesting work "*In the Hebrides*," published in 1883, graphically describes a South Uist crofter's "Home Sweet Home," as she calls it, in the following words:—"Right across the island the road is built upon a narrow stone causeway, which is carried in a straight line over moor and moss, bog and loch, and which grows worse and worse year by year. Such miserable human beings as have been compelled to settle in this dreary district, having been evicted from comparatively good crofts, are probably poorer and more wretched—their hovels more squalid, their filth more unavoidable, than any others in the isles—the huts clustering together in the middle of the sodden morass, from which are dug the damp turfs which form both walls and roof, and through these the rain oozes, falling with dull drip upon the earthen floor, 'where the half-naked children crawl about among the puddles, which form even around the hearth—if such a word may be used to describe a mere hollow in the floor, where the sodden peats smoulder as though they had no energy to burn. Outside of each threshold lie black quagmires crossed by stepping stones—drainage being apparently deemed impossible. Yet with all this abundance of misplaced muddy water, some of the townships have to complain of the difficulty of procuring a supply of pure water, that which has drained through the peat moss being altogether unfit for drinking or cooking.

"Small wonder that the children born and reared in such surroundings should be puny and sickly, and their elders listless

A HIGHLAND COT.

* Since the passing of the Crofter Act in many townships substantial houses have been erected by the crofters.

and dispirited, with no heart left to battle against such circumstances. Existence in such hovels must be almost unendurable to the strong and healthy, but what must it be in the times of sickness? The medical officer of this district states officially that much fever prevails here, distinctly due to under feeding. He says, two families often live in the same house, and that he has attended eight persons in one room all ill with fever, and seven or eight other persons were obliged to sleep in the same room."†

The foregoing picture, which alas! is too true, does not, however, depict the prevailing state of matters in the Hebrides generally, but taking the most advanced townships in any part of the Highlands or Islands of Scotland in this enlightened age, we find the sanitation of those dwellings in a state that should certainly claim the immediate attention of the Board of Supervision, and rather than allow a recurrence of so deplorable and so demoralising a thing as to allow sixteen persons to occupy one room—eight of whom were down with fever—the Government should step in and compel the owners to supply adequate accommodation and healthy sanitary arrangements, failing which State aid should be granted, and thus remove from our land one of the foulest stains that ever disgraced the annals of a civilized country.

Before leaving the question of dwellings I will make a short extract from the report of Sir John MacNeill, who specially surveyed the Northern districts of Scotland for the Government in 1850. Sir John says :—"The crofters' houses, erected by themselves, are of stone and earth or clay. The only materials they purchase are the doors, and in most cases the rafters of the roof, on which are laid thin turf covered with thatch. The crofters' furniture consists of some rude bedsteads, a table, some stools, chests, and a few cooking utensils. At

A HIGHLAND CASTLE.

one end of the house, often entering by the same door, is the byre for his cattle, at the other the barn for his crop. His fuel is the peat he cuts in the neighbouring moss, of which an allotted portion is often attached to each croft. His capital consists of his cattle, his sheep, and perhaps one or more horses or ponies ; of his crop that is to feed him till next harvest, provide seed and winter provender for his animals : of his furniture, his implements, the rafters of his house, and generally a boat or a share of a boat, nets or other fishing gear, with some barrels of salt herrings, or bundles of dried cod or ling for winter use."

Notwithstanding all this, sanitary improvements in the Highlands have made remarkable progress during the present century, particularly so, in towns and villages. But although in many cases rural districts have advanced considerably, still, as I have already shewn, much yet requires to be done. I presume the reader is fully acquainted with the lovely town of Inverness with its charming surroundings, its commanding views of miles of characteristic Highland landscape, with the winding silvery Ness and its wooded islands and picturesque bridges ; all presenting an air of attractiveness, which fills the beholder with ecstacy and delight. Yet what do you think of the report of the Provost of Inverness made to the Home Secretary from the Poor Law Commissioners "On an enquiry into the sanitary condition of the labouring population of Great Britain," July, 1842,‡ the worthy Provost says :— "Inverness is a nice town, situated in a most beautiful country and with every facility for cleanliness and comfort. The people are,

---

† Dr. Ogilvy Grant, Medical Officer of Health for the County of Inverness, has some very interesting statistics in his report for 1897. He finds that the average length of life is seven years shorter in the Islands than on the Mainland. Dr. Grant attributes the recent serious epidemic of typhus fever in Skye to the unsanitary state of the townships and contaminated water supply. It is, however, gratifying to learn that the District Councils are steadily forming special water supply districts, and that trained nurses are being stationed all over the district. But until the existing wretched dwellings are substituted by cottages built on modern sanitary principles, these ever-recurring epidemics can never hope to be stamped out.

‡ We need hardly add that the sanitary condition of Inverness has greatly improved since 1842.—ED.

generally speaking, a nice people, but their sufferance of nastiness is past endurance. Contagious fever is seldom, if ever, absent; but for many years it has seldom been rife in its pestiferous influence. The people owe this more to the kindness of Almighty God than to any means taken for its prevention." . . . He adds, "When cholera prevailed in Inverness, it was more fatal than in almost any other town of similar population in Britain."

The mode of living among the poorer classes is of the commonest description, indeed often bordering on starvation. Their chief fare is oatmeal porridge, or salt herrings and potatoes, while in many of the outer isles a meal has often to be made on a few cockles gathered on the sands or some limpets picked off the rocks. During the most prosperous year, the poor crofter lives but a "hand to mouth" existence; and, when a bad season turns up or the fishing proves a failure—starvation stares him in the face—hence the famine which occurred during the years 1846-47 when the potato blight visited the country, and plunged the poorer people into the severest distress. Their chronic state of almost entire poverty, together with the potato failure, landed them in a state of extreme wretchedness. Ireland was suffering in a similar manner; yet notwithstanding the heavy drain made on public generosity, in the case of Ireland, a "Destitution Fund" was raised by voluntary subscription in Scotland, England, and the Colonies, to relieve if not to check the prevailing distress in the Highlands. Sir John MacNeill, who, at the time of the potato failure, was chairman of the Poor Law Board of Scotland, in speaking of the demoralising effects of eleemosynary aid, said :— "The inhabitants of Lewis appear to have no feeling of thankfulness for the aid extended to them, but on the contrary regard the exaction of labour in return for wages as oppression. Yet many of these very men, on a coast singularly destitute of safe creeks, prosecute the winter cod-and-ling-fishing in open row boats, at a distance from the land that renders it invisible, unless in clear weather, and in a sea open to the Atlantic and Northern Oceans, with no land beyond it nearer than Iceland or America. They cheerfully encounter the perils and hardships of such a life, and tug for hours at an oar, or sit drenched in their boat without complaint; but to labour with a pick or a spade to them is most distasteful."

Highlanders are a very sociable race, and perhaps nothing is more enjoyed, by old and young, than a "Ceilidh" when sitting around the glowing turf fire, they repeat story upon story, each more wonderful than the other, about giants and witches and fairies and midnight adventures, that make the very hairs of the

head stand on end. These tales are sometimes varied by songs; and often does Donald blow his chanter and make his bagpipes skirl; and all join in a hearty country dance or in the good old-fashioned "Reel of Tulloch," and thus the long winter nights are passed by those humble people in innocent simplicity. Can we wonder at them thus trying to wile away the long dreary weary time in that desolate country and damp moorland atmosphere, where they are compelled to pass an existence in poverty, hardship, and isolated imprisonment?

(To be continued).

A MORNING SONG.

OH, bright is the glory
     That, mountains! streams o'er thee.
Behind and before me
     Your summits uprise;
The white mists are trailing,
The plover is wailing,
And Luna is paling
     Adown the soft skies.

The dark loch lies dreaming
'Neath golden light streaming;
The snow-drift is gleaming
     On yon mountain-crest;
The dew-drops are glowing
By bright waters flowing,
And zephers come blowing
     From out the cool west.

The streamlets are leaping
By dark willows weeping;
The wild stag is sleeping
     In coverts of green,
While musingly wending
With heart-songs unending,
Where spring-flow'rs are blending
     With summer's rich sheen.

The winds of the dingle
With sea-breezes mingle
O'er tangle and shingle,
     That floor the cold cave;
My happy voice singing,
Re-echoed, is ringing
On breezes high flinging
     The foam o'er the wave.

                        JOHN W. MACLEOD.
Strathy, Sutherland.

MR. AND MRS. JOHN MACLEAN.

JOHN MACLEAN, GLASGOW.

THE Clan Maclean Society is one of the most successful Clan Societies in Glasgow, and one of its most active office-bearers is Mr. John Maclean, 68 Mitchell Street, who is one of its Vice-Presidents, and Convener of Finance. Mr. Maclean is a native of Inverness, and belongs to the Dochgarroch branch of the clan (the Macleans of the North). Educated in Inverness, he served his apprenticeship to the drapery trade in that town. He afterwards came to this city and represented a Glasgow house over the North, as far as Shetland; and ultimately settled down in St. Mungo as Agent for Wholesale Clothing Manufacturers in England. He soon formed a wide connection among clothing firms in this city, and was in this way able to do much to assist young men from the North in procuring situations. He is best known as one of the most loyal and enthusiastic office-bearers of the Clan Maclean Society, and its success is largely due to his fostering care. The Society met with considerable reverses in 1894, but Mr. Maclean, having been appointed Convener of Finance Committee, framed rules for the guidance of the Society, which carried it safely over that critical period. He still holds the office to which he was then appointed, and has the satisfaction of seeing the Society flourishing under his guidance. In 1895 his clansmen acknowledged the yeoman services rendered to the Society, in a tangible form, when at the reception given by the Chief and Lady Maclean in the Bath Hotel, Glasgow, he was presented by the Chief, in the name of the clan, with a gold watch and chain, while Mrs. Maclean received a handsome diamond ring. Among those present, to whom the presentations gave great satisfaction, was their old friend Dr. Charles Fraser-Mackintosh. The name of the Convener of Finance is well known among clansmen, and he receives many enquiries regarding the clan and its history. He was among the first to suggest that Rev. A. Maclean Sinclair be requested to prepare a history of the clan.

Mr. Maclean is also a Vice-President of the Glasgow Inverness-shire Association. He acted as Secretary for that Association in 1873-74, when he was the means of resuscitating it, and placing it on a satisfactory basis. When leaving the city for the North in 1875, he was presented by this Association with a handsome writing desk, in acknowledgment of his services. When Mr. Fraser-Mackintosh was returned M.P. for the Inverness Burghs, Mr. Maclean succeeded in getting him to preside at the Annual Gathering of the Association, and now he has persuaded him once more to preside at the forthcoming Gathering in February.

Mrs. Maclean is also an Invernessian, being youngest daughter of Mr. David Roy, engineer, Inverness, a gentleman well known and respected in the North. She is in full sympathy with her husband's Celtic enthusiasm, and a loyal supporter of the Clan Maclean. They have a family of three daughters. The death of their infant son, John, last year, was a severe blow to them. We are sure all loyal clansmen will wish long life and prosperity to Mr. and Mrs. Maclean.

A h-uile latha dhaibh!

FIONN.

"SONGS AND POEMS OF ROB DONN."
BY HEW MORRISON, F.S.A. SCOT.

AS briefly indicated in our last issue, this volume is disappointing in every way. Excepting the futile attempt to foist on the Reay Country bard a Calder ancestry, on the strength of some entries in the Parish Register, it possesses no value whatever to the student of Gaelic, and is a mere reprint of the 1829 edition, with additional orthographical errors. As, however, the revival of the controversy regarding the bard's name, which, by the way, was only originated a few years ago by Mr. Morrison himself, will serve to give this edition a passing notoriety, it is only fair to our readers to estimate this fresh contribution at its true value. In doing so it need hardly be said that we shall deal as fairly as possible with the genial Librarian of the Edinburgh Free Library, while taking serious exception to his want of accuracy and methods of proof.

To begin with, the work shows unmistakable signs of haste, and want of careful revision. This was probably due to the knowledge that another edition was in course of publication, which must at all hazards be forestalled. The result is as might have been anticipated: from title-page to conclusion—in both its English and Gaelic orthography it loudly calls for the pruning knife. In this connection it is but fair to state that it is difficult to apportion the blame aright between Publisher and Editor. Everyone who has had anything to do with Gaelic publications, knows how difficult it is to get an accurate "copy" from a press in which the work is carried on by hands unskilled in Gaelic orthography. Had this work passed through the Celtic Press of Glasgow, we are confident it should have presented far fewer blemishes. As it is, such portions of it as are not a reprint of the earlier editions, are presented in a style of Gaelic orthography which is now happily a thing of the past.

Still, in fairness to the Publisher, we must take the Editor also to task in matters of greater moment. From notices appearing from time to time in a certain paper of log-rolling proclivities we were given to understand that the Editor had in his possession a manuscript of great value, in which the songs of the bard were written down to verbal dictation. It turns out, however, that any value this MS. possesses, has been already taken advantage of by Rev. Dr. Mackintosh Mackay in the first edition! It is not a "find" in any sense; not even of antiquarian interest; for now it is as the revising hands of the Rev. Mr. Findlater left it, who by the way did not come to the parish of Rob Donn, until the latter was more than *thirty* years in his grave! So much for the value of this original manuscript.

Again we were led to expect "poems and songs" which were never published before, and so prominent a feature of the new edition was this to be, that the fact is duly announced in the dedication! But where are they? Surely the tiny fragments, occupying *two* leaves of a volume extending over 500 pages, do not deserve the name of *poems*. Do they deserve even being printed at all? Certainly there is no *internal* evidence furnished by them, that they are Rob Donn's, and preceding editors did wisely in throwing them into the waste-basket, where Mr. Morrison should have left them, with one or two stanzas of indelicate allusion—pardonable it may be in the 18th century, but not now. So the "new poems and songs" have vanished into thin air like the hitherto unpublished manuscript.

We now turn to Mr. Morrison's investigation of the bard's real surname, a subject in which he took a leading part more than a dozen years ago. We hardly expected him to admit at the outset, that it was a question regarding which "those interested" must be left "to exercise their own judgment and draw their own conclusions." Surely if *conclusive* proof could be gleaned from Parish Registers that Rob was a *Calder*, such a hesitating attitude should not be adopted at the outset of the proof. But the next statement makes up for any timidity of tone in that preliminary canter. Here it is. "The name Mackay was first applied to Rob Donn on the title-page of his poems in 1829." This is business-like, and coming from a Librarian such a statement should carry weight. But it so happens that Macallum's Collection was published in 1816, and here the Reay Country bard is called Robert *Mackay*! What is more, this collection was not published by wicked and perverse Mackays at all. So much for the strength of the first link in the chain of proof; yet we were solemnly assured that in this edition of the bard's works nothing was to be taken for granted, but everything subjected to proof!

The next link is even more delusive, for it is made to bear a greater strain. "In addition to the name Mackay appearing as already stated on the title-page of the poems, one of the strongest grounds for attaching the name of Mackay to the poet is contained in a note which Colonel David Stewart of Garth quotes from Munro's narrative of the casualties at the battle of Arnee on 2nd June, 1782, as follows:—'I take this opportunity of commemorating the fall of John Donne Mackay, a corporal in Macleod's Highlanders, son to Robert Donne, the bard, whose singular talent for the beautiful and extemporaneous composition of Gaelic poetry was held in such esteem.' This John (continues Mr. Hew Morrison) who was married in Crosple, is in the Parish Register twice designated

Donn, and under date 21st January, 1773, he is further referred to as John Donn, *alias* Calder in Crosple." Then, with a flourish, Mr. Morrison asks "Which is the more likely to be correct—the recruiting list of Macleod's Highlanders, or the register of his native Parish attested by the Parish Minister?" It is almost cruel to deprive Mr. Morrison of the pleasure this "find" in the Parish Register gave him, but it must be done. We had occasion to consult a most interesting Parish Church Account Book of Durness (1765-1824) for other purposes lately. This volume, which was then in the hands of Mr. Hew Morrison, was secured for us by Rev. Adam Gunn, Durness, to whom reference is made in the preface to Mr. Morrison's edition, as supplying him with Parish Records. The Rev. Mr. Gunn, it may be mentioned, is engaged with us in editing another edition of the bard's works. Well, will the reader believe it? in this ancient Account Book, the John Donn, indentified by Mr. Morrison as Rob Donn's son, dies in the year 1778—exactly four years before Rob's son, John Donne Mackay, was killed at the battle of Arnee!! Of course they cannot be one and the same individual; and thus "the strongest grounds" on Mr. Hew Morrison's own admission, remain as strong as ever. We have this Record now in our possession, and shall be glad to shew the entry, and others bearing on the Calder theory, to any who may yet have the shadow of a doubt on the matter. The entry is as follows:—

"1778. By paid expences of John Donn's interment with 6s. to his widow £1.4." Let it be observed that this entry was in Mr. Morrison's possession, when he culled the other entries out of the Register of Baptisms.

We are, however, unwilling to believe that his eye lighted upon it, for the reason that he is quite innocent of the value, or the danger of giving dates in questions of controversy. For instance, he tells us (page 31 Introd.) that Rob's eldest son, James, married in 1774 Jean Stewart in Balnaceill; but on page 35, he tells us in another connection that his "eldest son, James, after his return from the army, marries in 1775 *Isobel* Stewart!" Again on page 35 he states that the bard's eldest daughter, Isobel, was married in 1770, whereas the Register gives the date as 1771. The William Calder whom he identifies as Rob's brother was the charity schoolmaster at West Moine, and was in no way related to Rob's family. Mr. Morrison in searching the Register picked out those who bore Calder to their name, and honoured them by making them sons or brothers of the bard. Inaccuracies of this kind might pass muster some twenty years ago, but the critical element is altogether too rampant to-day for such slip-shod work. It affords a good illustration of the danger of carrying a preconceived theory so far as to ignore dates and facts which might prove troublesome. The truth is, there were Mackay-Donns and Calder-Donns, and the minister in making entries in the Register often confused the families, for although the same person is mentioned three times, he usually describes him in as many different ways. However, the Clan Mackay Society are preparing an exhaustive reply to Mr. Morrison's statements, after which we shall hear no more of the Calder theory.

MINOR SEPTS OF CLAN CHATTAN.

By CHARLES FRASER-MACKINTOSH, LL.D.

IV.—THE FARQUHARSONS OF HAUGHTON.

THIS estate, which came by marriage to a member of the Altyre family, has after a brilliant course again descended in the female line, and now belongs to Miss Maria Ogilvie Farquharson. Her step-mother, Mrs. Farquharson of Haughton, takes much interest in Highland matters, and in her clan. Mrs. Farquharson is a great authority on Ferns, and prior to her marriage, when Miss Marian Sarah Ridley, of Hollington, Hants, published "A Pocket Guide to British Ferns, London, 1881."

The late Mr. Robert Francis Ogilvie Far-

THE LATE R. F. O. FARQUHARSON.

MRS FARQUHARSON.

HAUGHTON HOUSE, ABERDEENSHIRE.

quharson, of Haughton, who had succeeded also
to the estate of Thornton, died in 1890, much
regretted. At a public meeting of the inhabitants of the Parish of Alford, where the deceased
after returning from Australia resided as the
leading man of the Parish for thirty-six years,
a most gratifying tribute was passed to his
memory, eulogizing him a kind landlord, high
agriculturist and prize winner, as also an active
and useful man of business. A handsome
fountain erected to his memory adorns the
village of Alford.

V.—ALLARGUE AND BREDA.—General Farquharson, whose portrait is given, has had a
famous career in India, reaching his present
position after surmounting obstacles and crushing
oppression in high quarters in a manner worthy
of a Highlander and a Farquharson. Breda
died, full of years and honours, on 12th November, 1898.

VI.—FINZEAN.—I have left this family to the
last, because, so far as has been observed, there
seems no doubt that Dr. Robert Farquharson,

THE LATE MAJOR-GENERAL GEORGE M'BAIN FARQUHARSON.

who has, and is serving one of the divisions of
his County in Parliament so faithfully, is the
worthy Chief. Dr. Farquharson is directly
descended of Robert, son of Donald Farquharson,
otherwise Mackintosh, 2nd of Castleton of Braemar. Robert married Margaret, daughter of
Lachlan Mor Mackintosh of Mackintosh and
widow of Glengarry. Since the death of Andrew
Farquharson of Whitehouse in 1896, unmarried,
Dr. Farquharson has become head of all the
Farquharsons. To his very advanced political
opinions he has always adhered. Dr. Farquharson is well qualified to represent the best tradi-

tions of the celebrated house of Farquhar Mor.
Illustrations of the picturesque house of Finzean,
and of Dr. Farquharson at home, surrounded by
friends, are given.

I have to express my acknowledgments to the
four families immediately above mentioned, and
to Colonel John Farquharson of Corrachree,
Cadet of Inverey, for their courtesy in responding to enquiries and requests, and allowing so
many rare and valued illustrations to appear,
and to express my regret that the scope of the
work does not permit of my doing them the full
justice their position demands.

DR. FARQUHARSON AND FRIENDS.

FINZEAN HOUSE—SEAT OF DR. FARQUHARSON.

TO CORRESPONDENTS.

All Communications, on literary and business matters, should be addressed to the Editor, Mr. JOHN MACKAY, 9 Blythswood Drive, Glasgow.

TERMS OF SUBSCRIPTION.—*The CELTIC MONTHLY will be sent, post free, to any part of the United Kingdom, Canada, the United States, and all countries in the Postal Union—for one year, 4s.*

THE CELTIC MONTHLY.
JANUARY, 1899.

CONTENTS.

OUR NEXT ISSUE.

NEXT MONTH we will give plate portraits, with biographical sketches, of Mr. Alexander Cameron, Mayor of Stockton-on-Tees, and Mrs. Cameron; Colonel John M'Donnell of Kilmore, Ireland; and Mr. Robert Campbell, Manchester. Several articles and stories of special interest will also appear.

THE REV. DR. HUGH ROSS OF LANCASTER has been elected a Fellow of the Educational Institute of Scotland, having attained to a prominent place in the profession   Dr. Ross is of the ancient family of Morangie, Ross-shire.

GLASGOW HIGHLAND NOTES.—THE SKYE GATHERING was a brilliant success, the speech made by the chairman, Rev. R. C. Macleod of Macleod, being one of the most interesting we have ever heard.—THE MACMILLAN SOCIAL GATHERING, presided over by the learned chief, Rev. Dr. Hugh Macmillan, was one of the most enjoyable functions of the season. The chairman took as his subject "clan badges," and drew many useful lessons from them.— Mr. James E. B. Baillie, of Dochfour, M.P., presided at the UIST AND BARRA RE-UNION and gave an interesting address. There was a large gathering.—THE LEWIS AND HARRIS ASSOCIATION held their Annual Concert in the Waterloo Rooms, and had a record attendance of 1200 persons present. A splendid programme was submitted.—THE CLAN MACKAY celebrate their Annual Gathering on 23rd December, Major A. Y. Mackay, president, in the chair. Mr. James H. Mackay, London, is to present the Society with an oil portrait of Mr. John Mackay, Hereford, painted by his daughter, a talented artist. At the last clan meeting held in Edinburgh, Mr. John Mackay, Hon. Secy., read a paper on the subject of Rob Donn's name, completely disproving Mr. Hew Morrison's assertions that he was a Calder.—THE CLAN CHATTAN had a great gathering in Edinburgh, when they presented Cluny with the beautiful Celtic Shield which was reproduced in our last issue. Provost Macpherson of Kingussie, the talented clan historian, administered a severe handling to that historical humbug, Mr. D. Murray Rose, for his reflections on Cluny of the '45   The Mackays will sympathise with the Macphersons in their vindication, for really it is high time that the pretensions of this amateur historian were exposed. It was only the other day that, under a *nom-de-plume*, he maliciously attacked the Clan Mackay Society, and asserted that the Mackay banner was the property of the Grays of Skibo, although it was well known that the Skibo family never owned the armorial bearings on the flag. He was glad enough to retire ignominiously from the contest with the Clan Mackay, and now the Macphersons have taken him in hand, with an energy that will make him more careful in future, we hope, to make no assertions which he cannot prove. His reputation for historical accuracy is gone, it could hardly survive the twaddle of his recent "Historical Notes."

LETTER TO THE EDITOR.
THE CHIEFSHIP OF CLAN DAVIDSON.
INVERNESS.

SIR—My excuse for not having replied to your correspondent "Clan Dhai" before this, is that until my arrival in Inverness I was unable to obtain access to a copy of the "Minor Septs." "Clan Dhai" writes : "The Davidsons of Tulloch have always been recognised as Chiefs by their northern clansmen. I never heard of their title being disputed or of anybody who laid claim to it." Tulloch also writes that his predecessors were recognised as heads of the clan, and that he is presently acknowledged Chieftain. Can these gentlemen produce any evidence in support of these assertions?

To the best of my recollections, William Davidson married Jean Bayne about 1719, and their son, Henry, purchased the estate of Tulloch. He does not appear to have called himself Chief, this title being first assumed about 1827 by his grand-nephew, Duncan Davidson, Lord Lieutenant of Ross-shire, grandfather of the present Tulloch. I always understood from my late father that previous to his accession no such claim had been heard of.

I think your correspondent falls into an error in assuming that Tulloch is universally recognised as Chief. A large number of the Aberdeenshire and Badenoch branches of the clan do not admit his claim, and the majority of the Davidsons settled in Canada, to the best of my belief, hold to the tradition that the true Chief of Clan Dhai must be sought for among the descendants of the last Davidson of Invernahavon, who is said to have changed his name to Macpherson towards the end of the 17th century.

I regret that owing to my family papers being in Canada, I cannot enter more at length into this controversy, but I trust I have said enough to show that Tulloch's position is not *at present* beyond dispute, and it is a matter of great interest that the question of the true Chiefship should be decided.

6th December, 1898.   "QUEBEC."

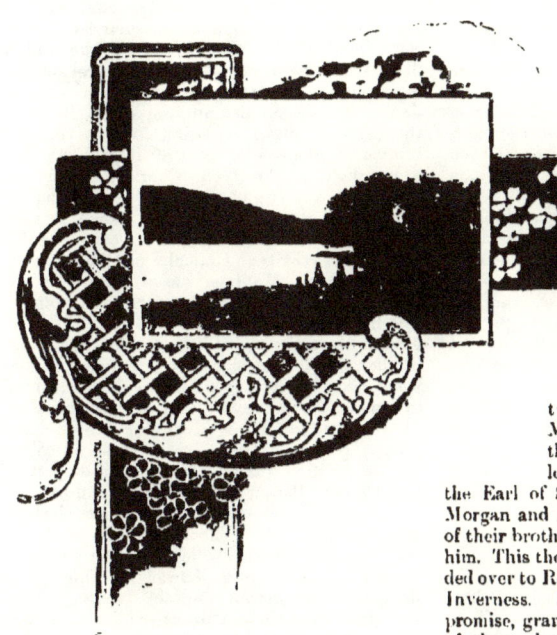

THE POLSONS.

THE circumstances by which the Creich lands, which have just passed into the hands of Miss Marget Carnegie, daughter of Mr. Andrew Carnegie of Pittsburg, first became the home of the Polsons savours somewhat of romance.

When the Lord of the Isles defeated Angus Dubh Mackay at the battle of Dingwall he took him prisoner, but thought it politic to have such a powerful chief as a friend, and therefore proposed to set him at liberty, give him his sister, Elizabeth, as wife, and endow him with lands. Angus Dubh, of course, quite agreed to these terms, and returned to Tongue with his wife and a charter confirming to him territory extending from the church lands of Skibo to the confines of Assynt, and thence to Loch Broom and the whole of Strath Halladale. The Earl of Sutherland did not like being thus hemmed in by the Mackays, and schemed as to how he should bring them low. He soon found helpers in his own relatives, the Murrays, and the Mowatts of Caithness, who forthwith began to make raids on Strath Halladale When Thomas Mackay, who succeeded, demanded redress from the Mowatts, he was haughtily refused, and not long after, while Thomas was at Creich, he heard that his enemies had passed south. He followed, Mowatt was slain, and his followers who took refuge in St. Duffus Chapel were burned there by the infuriated adherents of Mackay. For this Thomas Mackay was declared an outlaw, but the difficulty was to find anyone bold enough to apprehend him. The Murrays now came to play their part in the drama. Angus Murray of Pulrossie had two lovely daughters with whom Morgan and Neil, the brothers of the outlawed Thomas, had fallen in love, and after a consultation with the Earl of Sutherland, Angus Murray offered Morgan and Neil his daughters and a large share of their brother's land, if they would only capture him. This they did and Thomas Mackay was handed over to Royal authority, tried and executed at Inverness. King James, in accordance with his promise, granted three charters. In the second of these, dated 20th March and 24th year of King James' reign, Neil Mackay was granted "All and whole our lands of Creich, Garloch, Daane, Moy-Zebblary, Cronzcorth, Tultim-Tarwach, Langort, and Amayde, with the pertinents." This Neil was afterwards killed, together with his cruel brother, Morgan, and his scheming father-in-law, at the battle of Drum-na-coupa, near Tongue (the Bannockburn of the Reay Country), fought between the Mackays and the Murray-Sutherland host. Neil left three sons, viz. :— Angus, John Bain (the fair), the ancestor of the Bains of Ross and Caithness, and Paul, who became the ancestor of the Polsons. This Paul seems to have settled for a time at Creichmore, but was afterwards killed in battle at Cnock-wic-niel, but his descendants called themselves by the name—Paulson, Poulson, Poilsone, which is now almost universally spelt Polson.

By Cosmo Innes the Polsons are regarded as descended from Paul MacTire —'Paul the Wolf'—who got these Creich lands in 1365 and was the builder of Dun Creich, and, according to Sir Robert Gordon, he "was a man of great power and possessions. In his time he possessed the lands of Creich in Sutherland, and built a house there called Dun Creich, with such a kynd of hard mortar, that at this day it cannot be knowne whereof it was made. . . There are many things fabulourlie reported of this Paul Macktire, among the vulgare people, which I doe omitt to relate."

But whether descended from Paul MacTire or Paul Mackay, certain it is, that the Polsons must have sprung from one of the chieftains of Creich, and to this day the name of Polson is more common on the East of Sutherland than elsewhere, though it is by no means a common one even in Sutherland.

The earliest document in which the name of a Polson appears is in the will of Alexander Sutherland of Dunbeath, dated 15th November, 1456, at Roslin Castle. This will was cited in the Countess of Sutherland's case, and the passage runs as follows:—" Item I gif and assignes to my daughter Marion al the lave of landis that I have undisponyt upon, and sa money ky, old and young, as I have with Aytho Faurcharsone, or with Mackay, Benauche, and sa mony ky as scho aucht to have of William Polsonys ky."

A 'Hugh Poilson' witnessed a deed relating to Torboll, and on September 20th, 1497, King James IV. presented Sir John Polson to the Chantry of Dornoch, and on the 3rd November, 1499, to the Chantry of Caithness.

But from Creich the Polsons spread, as in 1506 it is found that the lands of Tullochglens belonged to a Duncan Polson heritably. These lands were adjacent to the Culbin sand-hills, from which the sand in successive storms drifted and covered them to a depth of several feet, so that in 1695 the then proprietor had to appeal for exemption from taxation, as the lands were merely a sandy desert. In 1542 one of these Creich Polsons—Thomas—married Elizabeth Munro, a daughter of the fourteenth baron of Foulis. In 1567 this Thomas Polson was one of the Commission that sat in the Tolbooth at Inverness, and which found "That Adam, Earl of Sutherland, grandfather of John (the then Earl), had died at the peace and faith of the King; that the said Earl John was his lawful heir, and that he was likewise the lawful heir of his grandmother, Elizabeth, Countess of Sutherland, who also died at the King's peace."

In the parish of Dornoch he is said to have been possessed of the estate of Auchenloch, and his son or grandson, Angus, was a burgess of that town in 1583. A Hew Polson was also reader for the parish of Lairg between 1574 and 1578.

About the close of the sixteenth century the ancient lands of the Polsons in Creich passed by marriage to the Grays of Skibo, and the Polsons appear to have been somewhat scattered thereafter. One branch settled in Aberdeenshire, another in Inverness-shire, and a third on the borders of Caithness. Towards the close of the

seventeenth century—probably 1697—it is found that a Catherine Polson married David Sutherland of Ousdale. Later still we find a John Polson as owner of Navidale previous to his departure for Jamaica. This John married Janet, the second daughter of John Mackay, the famous minister of Lairg, and his younger brother, William, who lived at Rogart, married a daughter of the Hon. Charles Mackay of Sandwood, and two of their children lived up to the middle of this century, viz., John Polson, J.P., Rovie, and his sister, Janet Polson. John Polson of Navidale and Jamaica had ten children, and the eldest, William, was a captain in the Virginia Rangers, of which George Washington was in command. At the disastrous battle of Monangahela River, William was killed, and his brother, John, an ensign in the same regiment, wounded. He recovered and was subsequently in command of an expedition against the Fort St. Juan in the Gulf of Mexico in 1780. Lord Nelson conveyed these forces from Jamaica, but the position was so difficult, even desperate, that Captain Polson had to send Nelson back to Jamaica for reinforcements, but after Nelson had departed Polson made a supreme effort and the fort was taken, which drew from Lord Nelson a letter which showed how highly he thought of his friend Captain Polson. It is, doubtless, from these Polsons of Navidale that those of that name who lived in Kildonan before the Clearances, and those who are now found in Helmsdale, are descended, and it is one of them who, in rather astonishing circumstances, killed the last wolf in Sutherland—a tale for another number.

The Inverness Polsons became men of importance in that town, as in a charter dated 1634 John Polson owned lands there, and was a Councillor in 1660. In 1649 there was an Angus Polson a burgess of Inverness, and in 1650 John Polson and his son, David, became proprietors of the estate of Markinch. In 1684 David Polson, junior, purchased the fine estate of Kinmylies, and became Sheriff of the County. The estate was again sold in 1730 to a Mr. Ross, who later on sold it to the family of the Baillies of Dochfour.

The burying place of the Polsons for ages was a chapel near the present churchyard of Creich.

For many of the facts in this paper the writer is indebted to an article on this branch of the Clan Mackay by the Hon. F. H. E. Palmer of Paris.

Cromore, Stornoway.   A. POLSON.

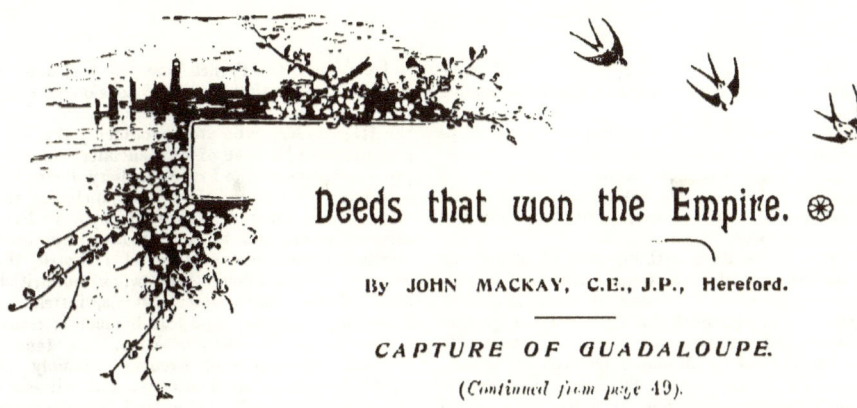

Deeds that won the Empire. ⊛

By JOHN MACKAY, C.E., J.P., Hereford.

CAPTURE OF GUADALOUPE.

(Continued from page 49).

THE attack upon Martinque having miscarried through the inaptitude and want of daring in the General in command, the squadron steered for Guadaloupe, and was soon close on shore. The ships were ranged in line with the Basse Terre, or western portion of the island. Here stands the capital of the Cambran Isle, defended by a citadel and other fortifications. This island is about 70 miles in length and 25 in breadth. It is divided by a channel, or narrow straits, called "La Rivure Saleè," or salt river about 100 yards wide. Its elevated hills consist of chiefly coral rocks, some of which are 1000 feet in height, and one, "La Soufriere," rises to an attitude of 5,400 feet. It is a mountain of sulphur. Though Martinique was at this time of more importance, yet Guadaloupe exported a larger quantity of coffee and equipped more privateers against British commerce.

A general attack upon the citadel and other fortifications was resolved upon The ships took up their various positions, and at 9 a.m. of the 23rd January, 1859, the firing began. The booming of the cannons incessantly echoed and reverberated among the wooded mountains, while the roar of small arms from the ships and the batteries filled up the intervals of sound. For several hours this was continued with unabated vivacity. Commodore Moore, 2nd brother of Sir John Moore, the hero of Corunna, shifted his broad pennant from the flagship to the "Woolwich" frigate, that he might watch the operations with more ease, and apart from the smoke of battle, gave his orders with the greatest deliberation. It was a necessity for him to do so on this occasion, that he might consult the officers of the army on the plans they had in view. The ship captains fought their ships with remarkable bravery, distinguishing themselves during the hottest of the engagement by their courage, their impetuosity, and deliberation. Two ships were blown out of range by the wind, the "Panther" was left unsustained, and two batteries turned their fire on the "Ripon," which, by two in the afternoon, silenced all the guns of the "Mont Rouge," but at the same time she ran aground. On perceiving the disaster, the exultant French assembled in great numbers on an adjacent hill, and lining a breastwork, opened from it a rolling fire of musketry, while the militia, with an eighteen pounder, raked the helpless ship fore and aft for two consecutive hours. The captain returned the fire as well as he could, though his crew were falling fast on every hand, till all his grape shot and wadding were expended, his rigging cut to pieces, and to add to his misfortune, a case of 900 cartridges blew up on the poop and set his ship on fire.

The captain threw out a signal of distress, but it was unseen amid the smoke. The flames were, however, extinguished, and Captain Leslie with the "Bristol," coming in from the sea and seeing the helpless situation of the "Ripon," ran in between her and the battery, and opened fire upon the shore, making an immediate diversion in favour of the "Ripon," which did not float till midnight, when she escaped from the very jaws of destruction.

By seven in the evening, all the other large ships having silenced the guns to which they had been opposed joined the rest of the fleet, and now in the darkness that so suddenly follows twilight in tropics, four bomb ketches anchored near to the shore, to hurl their red hissing bombs and flaming carcases into the town, which was speedily set on fire in all quarters, while ever and anon a magazine of powder blew up with a terrible explosion.

At two o'clock next afternoon the fleet came to anchor in Basse Terre roads, where the flaming hulls of many vessels were to be seen, set on fire and abandoned by the enemy. Several ships attempted to escape and get to sea, but were taken. At five o'clock the troops began to land without opposition, and taking possession of the half-ruined town and empty citadel, encamped in the vicinity.

For several days nothing took place but the establishment of some small posts on the hills nearest the town. On one of these Major R. Melville of the 38th, in after years a general officer, took up a position over against entrenchments formed by Madame Ducharmey, a lady of high spirit, who, despising the French governor, the Chevalier D'Estril, had armed her servants and Negroes for resistance to the last.

The General learned from a deserter, that the French troops before retiring had laid a train to blow up the powder magazine in the citadel after the British had entered it, one of the first measures to be done was to cut off the train and secure the magazine. A panic seemed to have seized the French here. A foot note to Smollett states, that the apprehension of cruel treatment from the British, more especially from the Highlanders, who are undoubtedly the most generous and humane of any enemies, not only prevailed amongst the French soldiery during the war, but even infected the officers, including the most distinguished of them, who ought to have known better, and to this emotion has been attributed the timid conduct of D'Estril, the governor of Guadaloupe, who, when the British attacked the citadel and batteries, instead of remaining to animate and lead his men to resist, retired to a distant plantation, and tamely watched the course of events. Possibly he might have been at Fontenoy, and witnessed the terrible havoc the "Highland furies" caused in the French ranks there by their broadswords.

The inhabitants continually harassed the scouting detachments by suddenly firing on them from thick woods and sugar cane plantations. These were set on fire in all directions, yet the bush fighting was incessant, the French Creoles and armed Negroes proved very expert at it, and much destruction took place in consequence.

GUARDING THE COLOURS.

Ever and anon, the musket shots rang sharply out among the woods and coral cliffs, while Creoles and Negroes fled from bush to bush, and tree to tree, followed by the Marines and Highlanders, who now received a reinforcement of 300 men who had arrived from Glasgow by the "Ludlow Castle" before the landing took place in Guadaloupe.

Meanwhile Madame Ducharmey was busy. At the head of her slaves and armed retainers she made many furious attacks upon the post of Major Melville. The Major felt compelled to attack and carry the entrenchments of this Amazon by storm, sword in hand. She made her escape, but her houses, entrenchments, and plantations were destroyed, and a number of her people killed and taken prisoners. The Major had 12 killed and 30 wounded, one of the latter was Lieutenant Maclean of the Highlanders, who lost an arm. He declined to leave his regiment and remained in Guadaloupe till he was convalescent. He became a great favourite with the ladies of Basse Terre. He was particularly noticed by them for his gallantry, spirit, and strange costume, especially for the manner he wore his plaid and regimental garb.

Fever soon attacked both sea and land forces. Five hundred sick were sent to Antigua, while there were many more in hospital.

General Barrington was anxious to complete with all possible dispatch the total reduction of the island, and to transfer the seat of operations to the eastern part of the isle called "Grand Terre," which was protected by a strong fort named "Fort Louis." Accordingly on the 13th February, after a six hours' cannonade from the ships, a column of Marines and Highlanders landed in boats. Their progress towards the shore being much impeded by long trailing plants and mangrove roots, the gallant Highlanders and Marines leaped into the water up to their waists, got ashore, attacked Fort Louis, and carried it at the point of the sword and bayonet. In a few minutes the flag of France was hauled down and the "Union Jack" hoisted in its place. "No troops could behave with more courage than the Highlanders and Marines did on this occasion."

Such was the vigour with which the reduction of the island had been prosecuted, that in a few days all the batteries in and about Basse Terre were blown up. The detachments were recalled from the advanced posts, and the whole force re-embarked except one battalion left under Colonel Dubrissay, an accomplished and experienced officer, in the citadel of Basse Terre.

The enemy no sooner perceived the squadron under weigh, than they descended from the hills in force, and endeavoured to take possession of the town, from which they were driven by a fire from the citadel. They now threw up a battery, from which they hurled shot and shell and began to attempt a regular attack, but were repulsed by a sally from the castle. In the midst of these operations the gallant Colonel Dubrissay, Major Trollope, and others were blown up and destroyed by a powder magazine explosion. During the commotion caused by this catastrophe, the enemy made a vigorous attack, but they were successfully repulsed, and General Barrington, on learning the fate of Dubrissay, sent Major Melville to assume the command and repair the fortifications.

(To be continued).

HONOUR TO THE MARCHIONESS D'OYLEY. On the occasion of the Ottoman New Year's Day celebration at Constantinople, November 7th, His Imperial Majesty the Sultan was pleased to confer upon the Marchioness d'Oyley the decoration of the Chefekat (Grand Cross), and as a special favour has sent to her Ladyship the insignia of the order in diamonds. This last distinction is usually granted to sovereigns (as lately to the Empress of Germany during her visit to Constantinople), or to the wives of favoured ambassadors. The Marchioness d'Oyley is a resident of Paris and is at present visiting the country of her birth, the United States. She is the first and probably the only American lady upon whom such a distinction will be conferred. The recipient was born at Baltimore, and was a Miss Annie Macdonald, of the family of Keppoch. We tender our sincere congratulations.

A CHRISTMAS WAKE.

HARK! the waits along the street
Come their carols to repeat,
With their hautboys sounding sweet
Thro' the frosty midnight air.

While the old folks at the fire
Watch the Yule-log flaming higher,
As the moments fleet expire
Like the ashes on the hearth.

And the children, in their sleep,
Dream their happy wake they keep,
Whilst their stockings O! so deep,
Santa Claus is filling full.

Sing aloud ye minstrel throng,
For without your chant and song,
O! th' wake were very long,
And our thoughts were very sad.

And the children dreaming fast
That good Noël now has passed
By their little beds at last,
Are far happier than we.

For the scythe of sharp edged fears,
Leaves a track bedewed with tears,
Thro' the harvest of our years,
As the Yule-tides come and go.

And Time wears a Crown of snow,
And the pulse of age beats slow,
And scarce feels the Yule-log's glow,
As the Christmases glide on.

But O! hark! the carols near,
Bid us cast away our fear,
Crying loud ' Be of good cheer,
For the dawn of love is nigh.'

Tho' the smould'ring Yule-log dies,
Never dark can dim our eyes
When the glorious Day shall rise
Of th' Incarnate Light of God.

MAVOR ALLAN.

DR. FARQUHAR MACRAE, ALNESS.

THERE are few, if any, medical practitioners in Ross-shire better known throughout the length and breadth of that wide country than Dr. Farquhar Macrae of Alness. Dr. Macrae, who was educated at Dingwall Academy and at Aberdeen University, from which he holds the degrees of M.B., C.M., and D.P.H., is of the Macraes of Auchtertyre in Lochalsh, a family descended from the youngest son of the Rev. Farquhar Macrae (Inverinate), who was Vicar of Kintail and Constable of Ellandonan Castle during the stirring times of Cromwell and Montrose. On his mother's side he is descended from the Mackenzies of Dochmaluak, who were lairds of Strathpeffer for nine generations. Through two of the Dochmaluak marriages he is descended also from the Chiefs of the great Clan Munro, so

ELLAN DONAN CASTLE.

that he is in every sense a genuine son of the Highland County Palatine. After completing his course at the University Dr. Macrae was for some time in England. He was afterwards, for a few years, Medical Officer of Glenelg, and about five years ago he settled at Alness, where he has succeeded in establishing an extensive and increasing practice, patients even coming from the neighbouring counties of Sutherland and Inverness to consult him. He takes a keen interest in Celtic matters, and like his brother, the Rev. Alexander Macrae, the historian of the clan, he is well versed in the traditions and history of his native county. His genial manner, together with his knowledge of the Highland people and their ways, has gained Dr. Macrae much popularity, and he has recently been elected a member of the Parish Council of Rosskeen, and is also a Fellow of the Royal Institute of Public Health.

LEABHAR NAN CNOC, LE TORMOID MACLEOID, D.D. (INVERNESS: "NORTHERN CHRONICLE" OFFICE).—For this new and handsome edition of a Gaelic classic we are indebted to the generosity of that "Grand Old Man" of the Highland race, Mr. John Mackay of Hereford. The volume is nicely got up, and should have a large sale as a Gaelic class book.

HISTORICAL GEOGRAPHY OF THE CLANS OF SCOTLAND (EDINBURGH: W. & A. K. JOHNSTON). —This is a third edition of a standard work on the clans, and will be welcomed by Highlanders. The clan lists have been largely added to, while the Highland campaigns make a valuable addition to the volume. There are twelve maps, plans and other illustrations; the book is printed in clear bold type on good paper, and is handsomely bound.

DR. FARQUHAR MACRAE.

WHERE ARE THEY?

IT is a mere historical truism that there was a time when the Highlands were much more thickly populated than they are at the present day. Districts now wild and lonely were filled with denizens engaged in industries long extinct. There was the hum of busy life in many a valley now haunted only by the sheep and the deer. It is strange, if true, that the changes were not unforeseen. Nearly three centuries ago the Brahan Seer could prophecy that the day would come when the 'awbone of the big sheep would put the plough on the rafters. "The ancient lairds of the soil," said he, "shall give place to strange merchant proprietors, and the whole Highlands will become a mighty forest for deer." The strange merchant proprietor is there sure enough and working his unthwarted will. "It is a bitter cruel thing," said Fiona Macleod, "that strangers must rule the hearts and brains, as well as the poor fortunes of the mountaineers and islanders."

Sobieski Stuart has recorded many proofs of antique industries now forgotten. Each valley had its 'margadh.' In Glenurchy a small knoll

KILCHURN CASTLE, LOCH AWE.

below Sron-miol-choin is called Tom-a-mbarg-aidh, the market-knoll. There is no 'margadh' in Glenurchy now. On the level space between the hill of Dun Bhaille Righ in Benderloch is a level area called Sraid-a-mhargaidh, the market street. No booths have been pitched there for many a long day. About a mile to the east of Fortrose stands the old mercat croce of the Ness. It marks the site of the village where the Brahan Seer was burned. He was not unavenged. There is not much trafficking done there now. In Isla the spot is still shown, where stood the forge of its once celebrated smiths. The rocks can still be seen from whence was dug the iron with which the renowned Lann Isla or Isla blades were made.

"Bows and arrows!" said Dalgetty when Ranald MacEagh presented the archers of his clan. "Have we Robin Hood and Little John back again? Ah! that Dugald Dalgetty should live to see men fight with bows and arrows!" But the making of bows and arrows was a famous industry in the Highlands once. How runs the old rhyme?

Bogha dh' iughar Easragain,
Is ite firein Locha Treig,
Ceir bhuidhe Buaile-na-gailbhinn,
'S ceann o'n cheard Mac Pheidearain.

The bow of the yew of Easragan,[*]
The feather of the eagle of Loch Treig,
The yellow wax from Galvin,[†]
And the head from the smith MacPhederan.

A single proof may be cited of the changes described. No spot was once more populous than the north end of Lochawe. On Inishail stood a convent of Cistercian nuns, "memorable for the sanctity of their lives and the purity of their manners." This did not save them at the Reformation. They disappeared, but they made Inishail "holy" unto this day. On Kilchurn stood the castle of the Campbells of Breadalbane. It is now a solemn ruin, but only a hundred years ago it was entire and inhabited by an aged domestic. One of the rooms was hung with tapestry. Wine was in the cellar for the chieftain if he should visit Lochawe on a hunting expedition. The iron door was still on the charter room. An old skull cap and mail shirt remained hanging on the wall of the armoury. On Fraoch Elan stood a fortalice of the Mac-Naughtons, granted to the first of the line by the last Celtic King of Scotland, Alexander III., on condition of entertaining the Sovereign when he visited Lochawe. The castle was inhabited as late as the '45, and if Prince Charles had passed that way the occupant was ready, in the spirit of the old Baron of Bradwardine, to fulfil the condition of his tenure by entertaining the Prince. The convent of Inishail, the castles of Kilchurn and Fraoch Elan were not planted among deserts. Hundreds of dwellers on the shores of the loch looked out across the waters at the homes of their chiefs. Where are they now? Where are the MacNabs of Barachastailan, most famous of armour makers? Where are the men who donned the armour? The life that once centred round those shores is forgotten. Holy Inishail is a name. Kilchurn is a roofless ruin. The MacNaughtons of Fraoch Elan are as utterly forgotten as the sacristans that tolled the bell for the vespers of the nuns.

[*] On Loch Etive, and long famous for its yews.
[†] In Atholl.

J. A. LOVAT-FRASER.

LORD MACAULAY'S ANCESTORS.

BY WILLIAM C. MACKENZIE.

(Continued from page 60).

CURIOUSLY enough, Johnson, a little later, had a passage-at-arms with the brother of the minister of Cawdor, the Rev. John Macaulay, eldest son of the Rev.

Aulay, and grandfather of Lord Macaulay. While passing through Argyllshire, Johnson and Boswell paid their respects to the Duke of Argyll at Inveraray Castle, whence they returned to the inn at Inveraray where they were to pass the night. John Macaulay was at that time the minister of Inveraray, and, as a matter of courtesy, paid a visit to the distinguished travellers, and passed the evening with them. In the course of conversation on the subject of profession and practice, Macaulay made the pertinent remark that he had no "notion of people being in earnest in their good professions where practice was not suitable to them." Johnson flared up at this harmless expression of opinion, and thundered, "Sir, are you so grossly ignorant of human nature as not to know that a man may be very sincere in good principles without having good practice?" Macaulay appears to have taken the rebuff in good part, for the faithful Bozzy chronicles that "being a man of good sense he had a just admiration of Dr. Johnson," and was next morning "nothing hurt or dismayed by his last night's correction." Both Kenneth and John Macaulay appear to have been good talkers, but were, of course, no match for Johnson. But one can imagine what a battle of Titans would have been fought had Johnson met the grandson instead of the grand-father!

It is possible than Johnson's trouncing of the brothers Macaulay was in a measure instigated by their political views, with which he was no doubt acquainted. They were apparently devoted to the Whig cause, and it is clear that the interest which the Argyll family exerted on their behalf was not unconnected with their politics. In 1761 Kenneth procured the parish of Ardnamurchan through the patronage of the Duke of Argyll, whence he removed to Calder, where, as we have seen, he met Johnson. We have also seen that his brother John was minister of Inveraray in the Duke's own parish. Previous to this, he had been minister successively of Barra and South Uist in the Outer Hebrides, and the island of Lismore near Mull. While minister of South Uist, he signalised his devotion to the Hanoverian cause by an act which, if successful, would have shed lustre on his name, or clothed it with infamy, according to the point of view.

A fugitive after the crowning disaster of Culloden, Prince Charles Edward Stuart was skulking in the Hebrides, and had arranged to proceed in disguise to Stornoway, where he intended to hire a vessel which would carry him to France. By giving out that he and his party were the crew of a vessel belonging to the Orkneys, which had been wrecked on the coast of Tiree, he hoped to avoid suspicion and achieve his object. This plan was suggested by Macdonald of Boisdale in South Uist, where the Prince had landed, and it appears to have come to Macaulay's knowledge. There is good reason to believe that he at once placed himself in communication with the Government through his father, the minister of Harris. Word was sent through his agency to the Stornoway people that the Prince had landed in Lewis with 500 men, and was marching on the town with the intention of burning it, carrying off their cattle, and seizing a vessel to convey him to France. On receipt of this information, the Stornoway men naturally rose in arms and prepared for a determined resistance. Luckily for the Prince he never entered the town. The guide lost his way on the moor, the result being that the party spent the night in the neighbourhood of Stornoway, on the opposite side of the bay. This circumstance afforded time for explanations, which were given by Donald Macleod, who accompanied Charles Edward. No attempt therefore was made to capture the royal fugitive, the sole condition imposed by the Stornoway people being that he should at once depart from their coasts—a request which was speedily complied with. Thus did Stornoway, in common with the rest of the Highlands, refuse to accept the blood-money of £30,000 which was offered by the Government for the capture of bonnie Prince Charlie, and thus was the great name of Lord Macaulay saved from the stigma which would have attached to it had his grandfather's plan succeeded.

As South Uist nearly led to the undoing of the Prince, so did it ultimately prove his salvation, for it was there that he met the heroic Flora Macdonald, who, by her woman's wit and daring, saved him from the clutches of his enemies.

The Rev. John Macaulay, A.M. (he had graduated at Aberdeen) ended his days as minister of Cardross, in Dumbartonshire. By his marriage with the daughter of Colin Campbell, of Inveresragan, Ardchattan, he had twelve children. It is worthy of note that the early sorrows of Aulay, his father, to which allusion has been made, were caused chiefly by the action of the Laird of Ardchattan, at whose instance the young minister was deprived of his stipend. It was while on a visit to the manse at Cardross, with Aulay, John's son, that the patron of the former, Thomas Babington, M.P., met and fell in love with Jean Macaulay, Aulay's sister, whom he subsequently married.

Another Rev. John Macaulay is mentioned in Hew Scott's "Fasti" as having been minister successively of Barra, and in 1771 of South Uist; and in the "Dictionary of National Biography" it is assumed that it was he, and not Lord Macaulay's grandfather, who gave the information which nearly led to the capture of Prince Charles Edward Stuart. This assumption, however, appears to be baseless. The John Macaulay here referred to emigrated to America, where he died in 1776. The minister of Cardross was succeeded in that parish by his son Alexander, of whom there appears to be no further record extant.

Another son, Colin, entered the Indian Army, in which he had a distinguished career, ultimately attaining the rank of General. He was present at Seringapatam, and was, with Sir David Baird, imprisoned by Hyder Ali. He afterwards entered the Civil Service, and was for a time Resident at the native State of Travancore. On his return to England, he sought and obtained Parliamentary honours, as M.P. for Saltash. Wellington appears to have held him in high esteem, and maintained a friendly correspondence with him. He died at Clifton in 1836. Macaulay's youthful fancy was fired by the exploits of his uncle, the General, and his admiration—as was usual in his callow days—was expressed in poetic form. There is no room, however, for the suggestion that the gratitude of the General had any connection with the substantial legacy which he left his precocious nephew!

Aulay, Colin's brother, to whom a passing reference has been made, possessed literary abilities of no mean order. He graduated at Glasgow University, and while there, was a frequent contributor to Ruddiman's Weekly Magazine, under the pen-name of "Academicus." After leaving college he crossed the Border to push his fortunes. He became a tutor at Bedford, and subsequently entered Holy Orders, being the first of his family to forsake the manse for the vicarage. Commencing with the curacy of Claybrook in Leicestershire, he obtained in 1789 the living of Frolesworth, and in 1796 was presented by his brother-in-law, Mr. Babington, with the living of Rothley. During the six years which elapsed between his resignation of Frolesworth and his acceptance of Rothley, he travelled on the Continent, chiefly in Holland and the Netherlands; he contributed an interesting account of those countries to the Gentleman's Magazine. In 1794 he was travelling in Brunswick in the capacity of tutor to a son of Sir Walter Farquhar. While there he gave lessons in English to the young daughter of the Duke of Brunswick, afterwards Queen Caroline, and he appears to have gained the sincere regard of her mother.

His literary efforts embraced "Essays on various subjects of Taste and Criticism"; "History and Antiquities of Claybrook"; "Two Discourses on Sovereign Power and Liberty of

Conscience" (translated from the Latin of Professor Noodt of Leyden), as well as various detached sermons. He married a daughter of Mr. John Heyrick, town clerk of Seceister, who survived him. He left a family of eight sons.

The third and most famous of John Macaulay's sons was Zachary, the father of Lord Macaulay. Zachary Macaulay was a man of remarkable force of character and strength of conviction. Possessed of high ideals and scrupulously conscientious in the discharge of what he conceived to be his duty, he never wavered in his adherence to principle. His life is a record of unshaken fidelity to the sacred cause of liberty, and his work lives after him. He commenced life as a clerk in a London office, and at an early age was appointed book-keeper, and subsequently manager, of an estate in Jamaica, where he had his first experiences of the evils of the slave trade. When the Sierra Leone Company founded a colony for liberated slaves in that island, Macaulay was appointed second member of the Sierra Leone Council, afterwards becoming Governor. With only one colleague to assist him in the discharge of his duties, his labours were almost Herculean. He was Governor, judge, paymaster, and parson all rolled into one.

His health at length broke down under the strain and he returned to England. During his visit to the old country, he met and became engaged to Miss Mills, the daughter of a Bristol bookseller, and a former pupil of Hannah More. He was soon, however, back at his duties in Sierra Leone, where he had varied exciting experiences.

Finally leaving the island which he had governed so wisely, he reached England in 1799, married, and was appointed Secretary to the Sierra Leone Company. He subsequently started business as an African merchant, in partnership with his nephew, young Babington, and for a time the firm prospered. Zachary Macaulay's heart, however, lay elsewhere than in his business; his energies being devoted to the suppression of the slave trade. He became editor of the *Christian Observer*, the organ of the so-called Clapham sect, and was the man who, while shunning publicity, pulled the strings of the anti-slavery movement. His nephew proved an incompetent business man, and the firm ultimately ceased to exist, Macaulay losing a fortune of £100,000 thereby. For the rest of his life he was largely dependent on his sons, Thomas Babington and Henry, the latter of whom had succeeded him at Sierra Leone. He died in 1838. A fitting memorial to the great Abolitionist was placed in Westminster Abbey soon after his death. To his influence was directly attributable all that was best and noblest in the life and character of his eldest son, Thomas Babington, Lord Macaulay.

[CONCLUDED.]

TEAGASG NAN SIANTAN.

Paired for Second and Third Prizes at Oban Mod.

'S a mhaduinn chéitein 's a' ghrian ag éiridh
'Nuas thar an t-slèibhe, gu 'm b' éibhinn leam,
Le cridhe céillidh 'us m' iuntinn réidh rium
Bhi 'gabhail ceum ann an tìr nam beann,
Far 'n dean mi éisdeachd, a' measg nan geugan,
Na thogas éislein o 'n chridhe fhann ;
An uiseag ghleusda a' seinn 's na speuran,
'S an smeòrach féin dhi a' togail fonn.

Mar bhàrd tha 'n còmhnuidh an sòlas glòrmhor
Nan smuaintean sòluimte tha teachd bh' uaith,
A' cur an clò dhuinn le laoidh 'us òran,
Gu 'n tugadh còir dhuinn air nithibh buan,
Gu 'n cluinn thu smeòrach le binn-ghuth ceòlmhor
'Us ceileir eòin anns gach gleann 'us cluain,
A' toirt dhuinn sòlas, 's a' dùsgadh dòchas
'S an deach tha brònach 'us deòir le 'ghruaidh.

Tha obair Nàduir an so 'n a h-àilleachd,
'Us mais' an àite cha ghabh dhuinn luaidh,
Oir 's duilich luns' ann am briathran simplidh
Mu iomadh innleachd an Tì 'tha shuas ;
Ach do 'n tì bhios aig siubhach slochail
'Feadh coille dhìreach 'us sleachd uain,
Bidh faile cùbhraidh nan iomadh flùran
'Toirt àithn' as àr dha mu 'n Ughdar bhuan.

Tha cuid de dhaoine a meas gur faoineas
Bhi còmeas caochlaidhean, 'ni an t-sìd,
Ri'r cuairt 'san t-saoghal nach mair dhuinn daonnan ;
Ach tha mi saoilsinn gu 'm bheil iad clì,
Tha 'n dràsd an samhradh, le 'blàths neo-ghann
'Tha cuir spéirid 's fonn anns na h-uile nì,
Le briathran buadhor, gidheadh neo-fhuaimneach,
Ag ràdh, "An uair so na leig a dhìth."

Ach thig an Geamhradh gu guinneach 's greann air,
'S bidh sneachd nam beann 'dol 'na dheann roimh
'n ghaoth,
Bidh gaillion 'séideadh, 's a' mhuir ag éiridh
'N a tonnan beucach gun chéill gun saod,
Bidh 'n talamh fuarail gun dad ri bhuain às—
'S an Foghar fhuaraidh gach sguab a chinn—
'S gach lus bha àillidh, gun ghaoid gun fhàillinn,
Gu 'm faigh am bàs ; 's amhuil dh' fhàsas sinn.

Oir tha ar làithean an so air 'n àireamh,
Cha 'n fhios a' màirench nach tig mu 'n cuairt
Ar geamhradh breun bhios gun éirigh gréine,
'S dubh-neòil 's an speur troimh an éirich fuaim ;
'S mar mhaoth-lus dh' fhàsas am feadh 's tha 'm
blàths ann,
Gidheadh a bhàsaicheas leis an fhuachd,
Aig òrdugh 'n Ughdair gu 'n stad ar cùrsa,
'S fo phlochd 's fo ùir théid ar dùnadh suas.

"CLAIGEAN" { WILLIAM MacPHAIL,
Cornaigmore, Tiree.

COLONEL JOHN McDONNELL.

THE CELTIC MONTHLY:
A MAGAZINE FOR HIGHLANDERS.
Edited by JOHN MACKAY, Glasgow.

No. 5 Vol. VII.]　　　FEBRUARY, 1899.　　　[Price Threepence.

COLONEL JOHN M'DONNELL, D.L., J.P.

COLONEL JOHN M'DONNELL, D.L., J.P., of Kilmore, Co. Antrim, entered the army at a very early age, and joined the Cavalry Depot at Maidstone, where he was attached to the 7th Dragoon Guards. He soon afterwards proceeded to the Cape of Good Hope, and joined H. M's. Cape Regiment of Mounted Riflemen, then about to take the field against the combined armies of the powerful Kaffir Chiefs, Sandillie, Pato, and Crelic. During the first six months of that harassing and protracted war he commanded the detachments of the 7th Dragoon Guards and C. M. Riflemen, serving with the division under Major-General Hare, and subsequently, to the end of the war, he commanded a squadron of the latter corps, with the division under Sir Henry Somerset. He was present in almost all the principal actions during the entire war, was frequently mentioned in despatches, and thanked by the Generals and other superior officers under whom he served.

From the Cape Blue Book, and other official records, we give the following extracts as shewing the harassing nature of that war:—

"A report having been received by the General in command, that Major Baker, 73rd Regiment, and four British officers had been treacherously murdered and their bodies terribly mutilated by the enemy, at the Sohota mountain, the Mounted Riflemen moved thither, marching all night a distance of 25 miles, and attacked the enemy, at daybreak, at all points; here the detachment under the command of Lieutenant M'Donnell particularly distinguished itself, killing forty of the enemy, who defended every point with great determination, but were driven across the river (Kye) with great loss, after making several attempts to turn our flank."

Referring to this affair, Sir Henry Pottinger, the Governor, in his despatch to Earl Gray, stated—

"I forward for your Lordship's information a transcript of a letter from the Lieutenant-General giving particulars of a very gallant attack, near where the murders were committed."

Sir George Berkeley states:—"I despatched the Mounted Rifles under Lieutenant M'Donnell down the side of the mountain, but on the descent they found the Kaffirs had occupied in strength a rocky neck of land by which they were obliged to pass, and being reinforced at this moment by a party of the Swellendam Levy, the two parties attacked the Kaffirs with great spirit and drove them from their position, following them into the low lands. I cannot say too much in praise of the zeal displayed by the troops, regular and provisional. They underwent great fatigue and were at least eighteen hours in constant march.

(Signed)　G. H. BERKELEY,
Lieut.-General Commanding."

Colonel, then Lieutenant, M'Donnell served in the Orange River Territory under the celebrated Sir Harry Smith against the rebel Boers, was present at the battle of Boem Plaats on 29th August, 1848, and in consequence of the senior officers having fallen severely wounded he commanded three squadrons of cavalry during the latter part of the action, and succeeded in turning the right flank of the rebels, who were posted behind rocks, with every advantage of ground, from which they opened a most galling fire upon the advancing troops.

The artillery and infantry having compelled the rebels to abandon their position on the left, the whole were driven from every point, with heavy loss in killed and wounded.

Lieutenant M'Donnell having been sent in pursuit, he drove the rebels back for many miles towards Bloemfontein, where numbers of them surrendered. The remainder escaped beyond the Vaal river under their leader Pretorius, where they settled down and ultimately formed what is now known as the "South African Republic."

On this occasion Lieutenant M'Donnell and the squadrons under his command received the personal thanks of the Commander-in-Chief. His Excellency also published a general order, from which we give the following extract:—

"The Commander-in-Chief congratulates the detachments of corps under his command in dislodging, from one of the strongest positions ever attacked, the rebel force. The gallant conduct of the troops upon this occasion is equalled only by their exertions in crossing, with very slender means, the large and unfordable Orange river, and the cheerfulness with which they have marched nearly 400 miles without intermission."

The British Resident having been reinstated at Bloemfontein, Lieutenant M'Donnell was ordered back to the Cape Colony, in command of the C. M. Rifles, a distance of 400 miles, and on his return he received the thanks of Sir Henry Somerset, then commanding the troops on the Frontier, for the efficient state in which he found the regiment, notwithstanding the hardships they had to endure on this extraordinary march of about 800 miles, to and from the scene of action, in the most inclement weather, in the depth of winter, the advance having been executed by forced marches, in frost and snow, without tents. At the time Lieutenant M'Donnell rendered these important services he was a mere youth, under four years' standing in the army.

In 1850 he was specially selected for the command of the detachment of his regiment stationed in the New Colony of Natal, where he served eight years. There, at the request of the Lieutenant-Governor, he undertook the duties of a magistrate, and was constantly employed in repelling the incursions of native marauders on the Frontier. He commanded the detachments of troops on the successful expedition against the refractory Chief Isodoie, and compelled him to submit to the authority of the Natal Government.

On the war of succession breaking out between Umbolassie and Ketchwio, sons of the Zulu King Panda, Captain M'Donnell was sent in command of detachments of C. M. Rifles and 45th Regiment to the banks of the Tugela river to guard the passes from the Zulu country into Natal, where he established Fort Scott, and remained in command for twelve months. A great battle was fought on the opposite bank, in which Umbolassie was killed and his army completely dispersed, and it was feared this might have led to the invasion of the Colony by pursuing parties of the victorious army, but from the vigilance of Captain M'Donnell and the force under his command this was successfully averted.

On Prince Alfred (Duke of Edinburgh) visiting South Africa in 1860, Captain M'Donnell was selected for the command of the escort which accompanied H. R. H. on his tour through the eastern districts of the Cape Colony.

That distinguished and gallant South African veteran, the late Lieutenant-General Sir H. Somerset, who commanded H. M's. Cape Regiment of Mounted Riflemen for so many years,

writing in support of Captain M'Donnell's claims to promotion, expressed himself as follows :—

"Bombay, 6th June, 1855.

I have much pleasure in stating that I consider Captain M'Donnell of the C. M. Rifles a most gallant, active, and efficient officer. He served under my command during the Kaffir wars of 1846-7 and in 1851-2. He was always employed on the most active and arduous services, which he conducted with great intelligence and gallantry. He is in every respect a most efficient officer.
(Signed) H. SOMERSET, Lieutenant-General."

In 1863 Major M'Donnell was appointed to the command of the depot of his regiment at the Cavalry Depot, Canterbury, where he served two years, at the expiration of which time he applied to be placed on temporary half-pay, on account of the death of his only brother and urgent private affairs. The application was recommended, but at the urgent request of the Military Secretary he proceeded to the Cape and took over the command of the regiment, reorganizing it in regard to discipline drill and the use of new arms. For these services he was highly complimented by the Commander-in-Chief at the Cape, who recommended him for the Lieutenant-Colonelcy, but his claims were passed over in favour of an officer from another corps. Having been thus deprived of any chance of promotion in his corps, he purchased an unattached Lieutenant-Colonelcy, which at that time would have given him the right to exchange back to the active list, in another regiment, but on the abolition of purchase, about this time, a new rule was introduced which deprived him of this right, thus debarring him from any further advancement in the army. In 1870 he was appointed Gentleman Usher and Master of Ceremonies in the Irish Vice-Regal Household, and afterwards as Gentleman-in-Waiting, in which position he served many years.

Clansmen will be much surprised to hear that, notwithstanding Colonel M'Donnell's distinguished and faithful services, he never received any reward or decoration beyond the ordinary war medal, on the ground that his principal war services were rendered in the subordinate ranks of Captain and Lieutenant, which seems a hard rule and should be abolished. But although Colonel M'Donnell was not fortunate in obtaining the advancement he had reason to expect, he was so in another respect, for having been twenty-two times under the fire of the Queen's enemies during his twenty-three years' active service, he never received a wound.

Colonel M'Donnell, who belongs to the section of the Clan Macdonald who have always adhered to the Roman Catholic faith, was much concerned on his first arrival in Natal, in 1850, to find there was no chaplain or pastor to minister to the religious wants of the Catholic soldiers in that Colony, which was then only in its infancy as a British Settlement. Accordingly through his influence he secured the services of the Rt. Rev. Monsr. Murphy, a zealous missionary, who soon gathered round him a numerous congregation from among the many Catholic immigrants in the Colony, and laid the foundations of the many flourishing missions now existing among the native heathens in the surrounding country. For the assistance rendered by Colonel M'Donnell in promoting the interests of religion, he was presented by Pope Pius IX. with the decoration of a Military-Knight of St Gregory.

Colonel M'Donnell is descended from the Chiefs of the Clan "Ian Mhòr," who were also Lords of the South Isles, Kintyre, and Glens of Antrim. He is fifth in descent, by father and mother, from Sir Alastair M'Donnell (MacCholla Chiotaich), Montrose's celebrated Lieut.-General, who led the Highland clans and the Marquis of Antrim's Irish contingent in the great Civil War of 1645, 46-7, and was killed, on the 13th December, 1647, at the battle of Knock-na-noss, in the South of Ireland, while second in command of the Royal Forces. (See also sketch of the Rt. Hon. Sir Alexander M'Donnell, Bart., *Celtic Monthly*, Volume IV., page 107.)

Colonel M'Donnell married, in 1870, the Hon. Madeline, eldest daughter of Thomas, Lord O'Hagan, K.P., then Lord Chancellor of Ireland. She died in 1875. He had an only brother Alexander, who died in 1862, a man so distinguished for his many virtues and works of charity, that a beautiful Celtic monumental cross, some twenty feet high (now known as the M'Donnell Cross), was erected to his memory in Glasnevin Cemetery by his numerous friends and admirers. Alexander left one daughter, Rachel Mary Josephine, who married, in 1882, Henry Thomas, eldest son of the late Mr. H. C. Silvertop, D.L., and the Hon. Mrs. Silvertop of Minster Acres, Northumberland. Mrs. Silvertop has three sons and two daughters, the eldest of whom, Francis Somerled, is heir to the family estates of Minster Acres and Lartington in Northumberland and Yorkshire.

Durban, Natal.   W. A. GREEN.

ORIGIN OF THE MACGREGOR MOTTO.—When King William the Lion was out hunting one day a wild boar rushed to attack him. Sir Malcolm MacGregor asked permission to encounter the animal. "E'en do and spair nocht," said the king. So MacGregor immediately tore up an oak sapling and killed the infuriated creature. Therefore the king gave Sir Malcolm liberty to use for a motto the words, "Een do and spair nocht."

ERIC STAIR KERR.

THE SOCIAL CONDITION OF THE HIGHLANDS SINCE 1800.

By A. J. BEATON, F.S.A. Scot., F.G.S.E.

(*Continued from page* 64).

VII.—DOMESTIC LIFE.

THE characteristic Highland weddings and funerals, with their peculiar customs, are fast becoming extinct, and of one thing I am glad, that considerable reformation has taken place in the matter of Highland funerals; and, although as yet, as a rule, no religious ceremony is conducted at a burial further than, perhaps the offering up of a prayer by the minister, still many of the scenes of revelry and apparent levity, in olden times, have been abolished. Refreshments are still dispensed; and the practice – unless abused—is commendable, as many of the mourners come from remote places and perform long and weary journeys to attend the funeral.

"Ochone, oh rie, ochone oh rie,
My love is dead and lost to me."

Lord Teignmouth, in his "Sketches of the Coasts and Islands of Scotland," thus relates the description of the funeral of a distinguished officer, as conveyed to him by an enthusiastic Highlander:—"Oh, Sir, it was a grand entertainment, there were five thousand Highlanders present; we were so jolly!" continued the guileless native, "some did not quit the spot till next morning, some not till the following day, they lay drinking on the ground; it was like a field of battle."

To those acquainted with the Highland character, the foregoing may appear uncivilized and barbarous conduct; nor will I attempt to justify it; yet for all this it cannot be attributed to their levity, as Highlanders regard death with becoming solemnity, neither is it want of attachment to the memory of the deceased; it is but the perpetuation of a remnant of a rude custom of showing respect to the dead and hospitality to the mourners. In our day, at festive seasons, the custom of "drinking the health" of friends is still indulged in, and, undoubtedly, in those "good old times," long ago, the same method was employed in paying respects to the memory of the dead.

VIII.—EMIGRATION.

The emigration question is one which requires very careful consideration before any definite conclusion is arrived at, for it is nothing less than a great national problem, a problem which, up till now, has had no satisfactory solution.

That our surplus population must be got rid of is an undisputed fact, but whether it is the wisest course to drain off the congested districts by emigration I am not prepared to say. I, however, think that voluntary emigration, whether of communities or individuals, should be encouraged, so long as it can be satisfactorily shown that those persons are qualified and adapted to undergo the life of an emigrant; but wholesale compulsory emigration cannot be too strongly condemned, as a system rotten at its very core, for while it hurls whole townships higgledy-piggledy into a howling wilderness, in a foreign land, it also forms a cloak to screen many cruel evictions that have occured throughout the Highlands. But, as I have said, we must somehow dispose of our over population; and still I question very much if it is a judicious policy to drive from their native land a race of people who, in bygone years, formed the stamina and backbone of the nation.*

"Ill fares the land, to hast'ning ills a prey,
While wealth accumulates and men decay,
Princes and Lords may flourish or may fade,
A breath can make them, as a breath has made,
But a bold peasantry, their country's pride,
When once destroyed can never be supplied."
—GOLDSMITH.

True it may be that it is next to impossible for so large a population, as now occupy the

* The Island of Skye alone has sent forth since the beginning of the last wars of the French Revolution, 21 lieutenant-generals and major-generals, 48 colonels, 600 commissioned officers, 10,000 soldiers, 4 governors of colonies, 1 governor-general, 1 chief baron of England, and 1 judge of the Supreme Court of Scotland.

—DR. NORMAN MACLEOD.

barren and swampy wastes of many of the Western Isles, to even eke out a miserable existence; yet were the Government aid which was offered to emigrants given to them, with the power to migrate and settle on some of the rich fertile lands scattered throughout the many beautiful straths and glens of bonnie Scotland, we should not only be retaining the people and their capital in our midst but also enriching the land, and, above all, feeling that we were not expatriating a people whose love for their native land is such that, when the heather clad mountains sank from their view, their hearts would

"In these grim wastes new homes we'll rear,
New scenes shall wear old names so dear;
And while our axes fell the tree,
Resound old Scotia's minstrelsy:
Stand fast, stand fast, Craig Elachie!"
—Mrs. D. Ogilvy.

sink, and their arms would shrink like ferns in the winter's frost, and when they reached that far western land, with no heart or energy to face the rough battle of life, they would say—

"The Highlands! the Highlands! O gin I were there,
Tho' the mountains an' moorlands be rugged and bare,

JOHN MACKAY, C.E., J.P.

JOHN MACKAY, C.E., J.P.

Tho' bleak be the clime, an' but scanty the fare,
My heart's in the Highlands, O gin I were there.

The Highlands! the Highlands! far up the grey
  glen
Stands a cosy wee cot, wi' a *but* and a *ben*,
And a dess at the door, wi' my auld mither there,
Crooning—' Haste ye back, Donald, an' leave us
  nae mair.' "

These simple verses illustrate the attachment
that Highlanders have for their land of brown
heath and shaggy wood, for—

" The tempest and the torrents roar,
But bind them to their native mountains more."

Why, then, should we exile our fellow
countrymen when there are thousands of
acres in our own land, equally as fertile
as the richest virgin soil in Manitoba, ay!
land far less difficult to till than the tough
prairie lands of Canada or the arid plains of
Australia, and which is now lying practically
waste—the abode of the sheep or wild red deer !
Until every available acre of tillable land is
occupied in the Highlands of Scotland, we should
have no emigration. The congested communities
we find along the sea-board of the mainland,
and in many of the islands, are the results of
continuous evictions and the gradual driving of
people down from the rich glens, until their
progress has been checked by the wild waves of
the Atlantic Ocean, where they squatted down,
multiplied and sunk into the chronic state we
now find them in. Notwithstanding that many
districts are over-populated, if we take the entire
area of the Highlands, or even of any single
county or particular parish, we see that the
country is not too densely populated, but that it
has sustained in less prosperous years a larger,
more contented and wealthier community than
we have this day in our midst.

To demonstrate this I have selected the
combined counties of Ross and Cromarty.
These counties will represent a fairer average of
the depopulation that has taken place during
this century, than will, perhaps, any of the
other counties in the Highlands; for we find no
material increase in any of the towns or villages,
thereby giving a truer idea of the actual extent
of rural depopulation.

The total population of Ross and Cromarty-
shires in 1851 was

82,707,

and in 1881, 78,547,

Decrease, 4,610 of population in 30 years.
The number of paupers on the roll
  during the year 1888, - - - 3583.
Number of poor persons obtaining
  relief in the year 1800, - 1813.

Increase of paupers, 1770.
(To be continued).

JOHN MACKAY, C.E., J.P., HEREFORD.

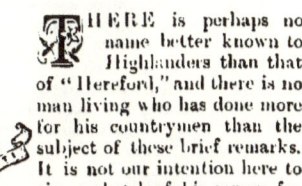

THERE is perhaps no
name better known to
Highlanders than that
of " Hereford," and there is no
man living who has done more
for his countrymen than the
subject of these brief remarks.
It is not our intention here to
give a sketch of his career, for
a very interesting account of it appeared in our
issue for December, 1892, copies of which may
still be had. The portrait which we give is
considered a life-like likeness, and was taken for
the preparation of the large oil painting which was
presented to the Clan Mackay Society at the recent
Gathering by Mr. James H. Mackay, of London,
whose daughter, Miss E. Rose Mackay, was the
distinguished artist. It is to be held by each
President during his term of office, and is now
in the possession of Major A. Y. Mackay,
Grangemouth. Clansmen in all parts of the
world will doubtless be glad to possess such an
excellent portrait of the "grand old man" of the
Mackay Clan. Before parting from this subject,
we may say that it has often been a matter of
wonder to us upon what principle Her Majesty
bestows her honours. Probably many of our
readers have shared our surprise. But what we
do think is, that if honours are given as an
acknowledgment of services performed on behalf
of our fellow men ; of a noble and lofty example
in matters calculated to inspire feelings of
patriotism ; of a generous, practical support of
every movement intended to advance the material
and intellectual interests of the Highland race ;
and for notable achievements in business pursuits
affecting the welfare of the nation at large; then,
we ask, how have the distinguished services of
such men as Mr. John Mackay of Hereford and
Dr. Charles Fraser-Mackintosh never been
properly recognised ? Of recent years several
Highlanders have been honoured, and probably
deservedly so ; but not one of them has
rendered services equal to those associated with
the names of these two outstanding representatives of the Highland race. We quite
recognise that they are gentlemen who would
shrink from, rather than court such honours; yet
it is a matter affecting the whole Highland race,
and we think that when official recognition is
given for distinguished services to the nation,
Highland sentiment ought to receive some consideration. In making these remarks, we know
that we are expressing the feelings of the
Highland people at home and abroad.

RONALD CHEYNE AND THE MACKAYS.

SIR ROBERT GORDON writes thus of Ronald Cheyne:—"In this William Erle of Sutherland his days lived Ronald Cheyne, a Catteynes man, who, during his tyme, was a great commander in that countrie, of whom many fables are reported amongst the vulgar people, and chieflie concerning his hunting, wherein he much delighted. Doubtless the Cheins had sometymes many possessions, and were once of greatest command and power in that country." Ronald Cheyne, who died in 1350, was one of those who subscribed the famous letter to the Pope in 1320, maintaining the independence of Scotland in defiance of Rome, and must have been a man of commanding importance in his day. He had lands in Caithness and Sutherland, and had also a stronghold in both counties. His seat in Caithness was Dirlot Castle, on the Thurso river, about fourteen miles from the sea, and in Sutherland a place now called "Tor an tigh mhoir" (the mound of the great house), on the right bank of the river Naver, and about half a mile from its mouth. Four miles above Dirlot Castle, and just below Loch Mor, famed for its salmon, he built a house close to the river, and cruives across the stream so arranged that, as is traditionally reported, a bell rang in the house when a salmon got entangled in them. The ruins of the house and cruives are still to be seen. A similar tradition also exists in Sutherland. It is said he had on the Naver a house with cruives and bells for salmon fishing, but I am not inclined to believe it was at "Tor an tigh mhoir," as the river is too broad and tidal there. It must have been a good many miles further from the sea, and if so it would imply that he possessed a great part of Strathnaver.

"A fable reported amongst the vulgar sort of people" concerning Cheyne is to this effect. When his lady was pregnant with her first child he made up his mind that it must be a son, and powerful man that he was, accustomed to get things his own way, he could brook no denial. The fated time came. It was night. Ronald Cheyne impatiently paced the hall of Dirlot Castle waiting for the result, and determined that it must be a son or nothing. At length the attending woman came down and told him it was a daughter. "A daughter!" roared Ronald, "Go at once and cast her into the black pool below the castle." The woman went, and anon Ronald, who stood listening at the window, heard a splash in the water. In the course of time another baby was due at Dirlot Castle, and Ronald was as determined as ever that it should be a son, but to his dismay a damsel again had the hardihood to present herself in gross defiance of his wish. Of course he could not stand this. If he did not maintain authority in his own house, how could he expect to maintain it over his unruly vassals? They would argue that if he was not able to manage women by the fireside, he was ill suited to lead bearded men in battle. No, no. Again he thundered forth his command, "Drown her in the black pool," and had the satisfaction of vindicating his authority when he heard for the second time a splashing of water. Time passed and Ronald still longed for a son, but nor son nor daughter came. As he slept he dreamt he heard the patter of little feet and the merry laughter of children

ANCIENT SCULPTURED STONE IN THE CHURCHYARD AT FARR.

SYRE, STRATHNAVER.

ringing through the hall; he awoke and found
it was a dream. He loved Lady Cheyne with
all the ardour of a strong wild nature; he could
not discard her. If fault there was it was his
own, who so ruthlessly cast away the children
God gave him. He gradually gave way to
despondency, and was often seen silently gazing
at the black pool, but such was his pride that he
would never speak of his lost children—no, not
even to his cherished wife. After all he had a
conscience and it smote him sorely, pagan
though he was. One day he got a pot, filled it
with gold, and flung it into the black pool, thinking
thus to appease the angered spirit of the waters,
who, he fancied, was torturing him. But gold
will not buy peace of conscience. At any rate
Ronald got no release in that way: his burden but
increased.

Lady Cheyne, now suspecting what was
wrong, suggested that, as Christmas was drawing
near, they should invite to the castle, for that
festive day, a company of merry
men and maidens Ronald, though
in no mood for mirth, eventually
acquiesced in his wife's proposal,
just to please her whom he had so
cruelly wronged. The day came, the
feast was spread, the guests took
their places at the table, and on
either side of it, near the top, sat
two fair girls who caught the eye of
Ronald. One of them was the very
image of Lady Cheyne, the other
bore a striking resemblance to himself. For a time he sat silent, feasting
his eyes on them, then bursting into
a torrent of tears he exclaimed,
"Wretch that I am, if I had spared
my daughters they would be like
these two to-night, and I would be
a happy man." "Calm yourself,"
said Lady Cheyne, "they are your
own two daughters, saved from the
waters by the devotion of the
woman who got orders to destroy
them, and who has since been a
good mother to them" Ronald's joy
is easier imagined than described.
The woman who reared his daughters found a home in Dirlot Castle
till her dying day; and Ronald, as
a thank-offering to God, built a
chapel on Dirlot green, where he
was buried himself when his time
came to be gathered unto his fathers.
I am told that part of the ruined
walls of this chapel could be seen
standing fifty years ago. The
stones were then, unfortunately,
used to repair the dyke round the
burial-place at Dirlot.

Sir Robert Gordon says:—"All the lands
apperteyning to this Reynold Cheyn were
divyded among his daughters . . . one of Reynold Cheyn his daughters was marcid to Nicolas
Sutherland, with whom Nicolas had the Cheines
third of the lands of Catteyness and the third of
the lands of Duffus." Mary Cheyne married
Nicolas Sutherland, and got for dowry the third
part of Cheyne's landed estate with Dirlot Castle
as seat. The other, named Marriot, married,
first, Sir John Douglas, who died without issue.
Her second husband was John Keith, by whom
she had a son Andrew, who got a third part of
Cheyne's land. Her third and last husband was
Farquhar Mackay, a brother of Morgan Mackay,
who, as traditions says, got Cheyne's Sutherland
property, and made "Tor an tigh mhoir," near the
mouth of the river Naver, his seat. About 1340,
as Sir Robert relates, the Mackays were designated "Clan vic Vorgan" (the children of

VIEW AT THE HEAD OF STRATHNAVER.

Morgan) and "Clan vic Farquhar" (the children of Farquhar), as Morgan and Farquhar were the two heads of the family. It was about this time that the Mackays historically became really powerful in the North, and one of their old seats was "*Tor an tigh mhoir*," of which so little is now known or left. The "*tigh mor*" stood on a rocky knoll jutting out towards the river, at the lower end of the land farmed by my late maternal grandfather. The old man often told me the house was built by Ronald Cheyne, and passed into the hands of "*Teaghlach Mhic Aoidh*" (the family of Mackay) when Marriot Cheyne married Farquhar. From its position the house could be made a very strong place, with the river flowing past its western face, while a deep, broad moat protected its eastern or landward side. The moat is now filled, and corn is growing where it ran, but traces of the old wall on the north side are still to be found.

At the west end of Farr Churchyard stands a massive tombstone, rising five feet above the ground, and sunk to a depth of three or four feet. On its east face there is sculptured a large embossed Celtic cross, surrounded by intertwined Celtic ropework, the west face is plain, and there is no writing on any part of the stone. I believe the stone is described in "The Sculptured Stones of Scotland," at any rate it is well known to antiquarians, and has been carefully examined. Authorities, reasoning from the character of its sculpture, differ in their views as to its probable age. Some say it is as early as the tenth century, others put it later, but the curious thing is, that they have hitherto overlooked, or rather remained in ignorance of, the name by which it is known locally. The people of the place call it "*Clach Cloinn Fhearchar*" (the stone of the children of Farquhar). I do not profess any ability to judge the age of a tombstone from its sculpture, but I am strongly of the opinion that it stands over the grave of Farquhar Mackay, Chief of the Clan vic Farquhar of Strathnaver, and Marriot Cheyne, his wife, who lived at "*Tor an tigh mhoir*." This opinion I ground solely on the local name by which the stone is known to this day among Farr people, who hold it in peculiar reverence. I may also remark that the stone is of native whin, hewn out of the Clachan rock, where the grain of the stone is exactly similar. It is nonsense to say it was imported from Denmark and marks the grave of a Danish Prince, when we can shew its original bed in the rock, not four hundred yards away, and know it by the good old Gaelic name, "*Clach Cloinn Fhearchar*," one of the ancient Gaelic designations of Mackay.

It is also interesting to notice that a kind of kinship seems to have been maintained, for a long time after Ronald Cheyne's death in 1350 between the Mackays, the Keiths, and the Sutherlands, Lairds of Duffus and holders of Dirlot Castle, owing, no doubt, to the fact that they were on the female side, of the same blood, and divided between them the landed estates of Cheyne. About 1438 the Keiths of Caithness, being sorely pressed by other Caithness clans, sent for aid to Mackay, who, as Sir Robert Gordon says, "readily came to their assistance," and combining their forces routed the common enemy, with terrible slaughter, at "Blar Tainne," near the town of Wick. About the same date a daughter of Angus Mackay, the chief, married Laird Duffus of Dirlot Castle. The eldest son of this marriage, who afterwards ruled in Dirlot, proved a worthless character. He borrowed money wherever he could, and nearly ruined his uncle, Y. Roy Mackay, the chief who succeeded Angus. Eventually he murdered Alexander Dunbar, brother of Sir James Dunbar of Cumnock, who was suing him for debt, and the matter being brought before the King, Duffus of Dirlot was "put to the horn," and Y. Roy Mackay commissioned to apprehend him. Duffus was caught, brought to Edinburgh, and there executed in 1499. Y. Roy Mackay, to recompense his losses and reward his diligence, was that year installed by the King into possession of Dirlot Castle and the lands appertaining thereto. The castle and lands continued in the uninterrupted possession of the Mackays from 1499 to 1617, when they gave them away in dowry to one of their daughters, who married Sinclair of Brims. Thus the Dirlot Castle of Ronald Cheyne passed at length into the hands of the Mackays, who stoutly held it for many a long year during those stormy times when men needed a strong arm to cover their heads and keep their own.

Westerdale,
Halkirk.   (Rev.) Angus Mackay, M.A.

MINOR SEPTS OF CLAN CHATTAN.

By Charles Fraser-Mackintosh, LL.D.

No. XVIII.—The "Kith and Kin" of Clan Chattan.

HAVING exhausted the authentic lists of the tribes as detailed by Sir Eneas Mackintosh, I finish this work with a brief account of those families known to have sprung from, or allied themselves with the Clan Chattan, more properly falling under the heading of the "Kith and Kin" of Clan Chattan.

They again may be divided into two branches

1st, those who dwelt in the county of Inverness, and 2nd, those settled in other counties; and they are placed alphabetically.

I.—Cattanach. This sept spread over Badenoch, but once important, are diminishing. The late Mr. James Cattanach, Kinlochlaggan, and the late Mr. Cattanach, Newtonmore, were both highly respected in their day.

II. Crerar. This name of late has come well to the front. Originally Mackintoshes, it is matter of tradition that the name took its rise in the person of a prominent member owing his safety to concealment from his foes in a manner somewhat similar to that connected with the Loban of Drumderfit. Mr. Duncan Macgregor Crerar of New York, and Provost Crerar of Kingussie with his promising son at present in Perth, are the zealous clansmen.

III.—Gillespie. This name is much scattered over Scotland, but many at different periods have adhered to Clan Chattan.

IV.—Gillies. Lachlan Mackintosh, 2nd son of Malcolm, 10th Mackintosh, married, according to the Kinrara History, "the daughter of the chieftain of the Clan Vic Gillies, that dwelt in Gaskmore, in Badenoch." The Gillies' of Badenoch were at one time numerous, but have almost died out. The name is at present very common in the Hebrides.

V.—Noble. This name was to be found chiefly in Strathnairn and Strathdearn, dwelling amid the Clan Chattan. Some—particularly tenants of Raigmore—are still to be found in the parish of Moy. Of the name I select three, each in different spheres showing a decided individuality, illustrating the name. (1)—Sir Andrew Noble, member of the great house of Armstrong & Co., Newcastle, of world-wide reputation; (2)—Mr. Noble, a native of Inverness, recently deceased, who, after a long service in the Cape of Good Hope, retired on a well-earned pension from the Parliament of that Colony; and (3)—my late worthy friend, Mr. John Noble, bookseller at Inverness, a most accomplished aider in building up the reputation of Inverness as a great centre for the disposal of Highland and Gaelic literature.

2. THE FAMILIES IN ABERDEEN AND PERTH SHIRES.

At the head of these families falls to be placed

1. MacHardies. This at one time influential name in Aberdeenshire and on the southern slopes of the Grampians, has of late begun to come well to the front, especially in the constabulary departments of Scotland. Histories have been written,—some with more zeal than discretion. That by Coghlan Maclean Mac-

Hardy, published in 1891, shows considerable research. There were at one time six landowners of the name in Perthshire, and the MacHardies, like the Farquharsons, were greatly favoured by the Earls of Mar.

The MacHardies of Strathdon followed the banner of Mackintosh those of Braemar that of the Farquharsons. Their lands were over-run by powerful neighbours, and it is noted that, in 1696, the fighting men of this once powerful tribe only numbered twenty-six.

Mr. Macbain, Rector of Raining's School of Inverness, suggests to me that the name may be derived from the Pictish "Cart Naigh," pronounced "Gratney," a well-known name of old in Mar. Mr. Macbain thinks that in time it changed to MacCardney or MacCarday—Mac-Cartney in Irish—and ultimately, before 1587, to MacHardy. Mr. Macbain tells me what is very pertinent to this work, and I have much pleasure in recording, viz.—that the late Donald MacHardy of Daldownie, who died in 1870, descended from Duncan, who acquired Daldownie in 1710, informed him that claiming to be head of the MacHardies, "he owned no other chief than Mackintosh."

Much material has already been gathered connected with the MacHardies, but it is not open to the public; and there is a wide field to any enterprising historian to deal with the matter in an authentic form. No time should be lost, for numerous most interesting traditions connected with Corgarff, Cairn-na-Cuinne, and other localities, presently within reach, are, from the changed mode of possession, in danger of being lost.

II.—MacOmie. They are descended from Thomas, younger son of the 6th Mackintosh, and long held an influential position in Glenshee. To the Farquharson bond of 1594, granted to Mackintosh as their chief, Robert MacOmie, in the burn of Glenshee, and Duncan Mackintosh, of Dalmunzie, are parties. In 1594, the above Robert Mackintosh is mentioned, also the name of Barbara Rattray, his wife, and Elizabeth MacOmie, his only daughter. In 1595, Elizabeth, with Duncan Mackintosh, alias MacRichie, in Dalmunzie, Lachlan Farquharson, in Bronchdearg, and others, her tutors, pay up in a formal manner on the 26th January, at Strath Ardill Kirk, a debt of 100 merks Scots, due by the late Robert MacOmie. Mr. MacCombie Smith has written a very interesting account of the MacOmies of Glenshee, of which family descended Vice-Admiral of Orkney, Sheriff Thoms. the late Mr MacCombie, M.P., Mr. MacCombie, of Easter Skene, also the well-known

(To be concluded.)

TO CORRESPONDENTS.

All Communications, on literary and business matters, should be addressed to the Editor, Mr. JOHN MACKAY, 9 Blythswood Drive, Glasgow.

TERMS OF SUBSCRIPTION.— The CELTIC MONTHLY will be sent, post free, to any part of the United Kingdom, Canada, the United States, and all countries in the Postal Union—for one year, 4s.

THE CELTIC MONTHLY

FEBRUARY, 1899

CONTENTS.

OUR NEXT ISSUE.

NEXT MONTH we will give plate portraits, with biographical sketches, of the late Duncan Macrae, M.D., Kames Castle (of the Conchra family), whose recent funeral in Ross-shire occasioned such a kindly expression of clan feeling; Mr. John M'Kerchar, treasurer of the Gaelic Society of London; and Mr. John Macgregor, Crieff.

" ROB DONN'S SONGS AND POEMS." — This most interesting volume is now nearly ready. Some little delay has been occasioned through the controversy as to the bard's surname, and a special chapter has been added to the book treating fully of the whole question, and answering the various objections put forward by Mr. Hew Morrison and others in favour of the Calder theory. Apart from this, the volume will be unique in many ways. The original music of some fifty of the bard's songs is given in both sol-fa and staff notations, edited by that gifted musician, Mr. Malcolm Macfarlane, a feature unprecedented, so far as we are aware, in the works of any other Gaelic bard. A large number of excellent English metrical translations of Rob Donn's songs are also given, which will prove of interest to the many subscribers who do not know the language. A graphic "Sketch of the Bard and his Times in Sutherland" is contributed by the Rev. Thomson Mackay, B.D., Skye, a descendant of the poet; and the Rev. Adam Gunn, M.A., Durness, supplies a treatise on the "Dialect," and an exhaustive "Glossary" of uncommon Reay country words, with their meaning. Indeed, this list alone is one of the most valuable contributions which have been made to Gaelic literature for a long time, and bears evidence of much research and ripe scholarship. Nothing to compare with this work has ever been published on a Gaelic bard, and in this respect Sutherland has set an example which Argyllshire will doubtless hasten to follow, in regard to the works of its bards. A list of subscribers is to be printed in the volume, and those desirous of possessing copies should order at once, as the edition is limited. Price 10s 6d, to be had from the publisher, John Mackay, 9 Blythswood Drive, Glasgow.

THE GLASGOW INVERNESS-SHIRE ANNUAL GATHERING takes place in the Queen's Rooms on 24th February—Dr. Charles Fraser-Mackintosh in the chair. A splendid programme has been arranged. We hope to see a crowded attendance.

PROMOTION TO A HIGHLANDER.—We are pleased to learn that that most gifted and genial of Highlanders, Mr. E. E. Henderson, of the Govan police force, has been promoted to a first-class inspectorship.

"LOYAL LOCHABER," BY W. DRUMMOND-NORIE. Glasgow: Morison Brothers.—The name of Mr. Drummond-Norie is doubtless familiar to our readers, many valuable contributions from his pen and pencil having appeared in our own pages during recent years. Hitherto he has enjoyed the reputation of being a writer of very interesting magazine articles; now we recognise in him an author of undoubted power, possessed of the rare gift of being able to write history with a fascination which we expect only to find in the realm of fiction. Mr. Norie is a keen Jacobite, and the whole key-note of the book is a eulogy of the men who "fought and died for Charlie." There is no true Highlander but would honour the memory of these gallant clansmen, but when the argument is extended to eulogise the whole race of the Stuart Kings we feel inclined to object. The Hanoverians may not have been ideal monarchs, but they made it possible for this country to establish democratic institutions such as we now enjoy, concessions which could only have been wrested from the Stuarts at the point of the sword. And what these same Stuarts ever did to recompense Highlanders for the many sacrifices which they made on their behalf is a question which perhaps our good friend, Mr. Norie, will be able to explain. But we have often agreed to differ on this point, and doubtless he will be willing to forgive our heresy when we join with him in praising the noble men who laid down their lives and sacrificed their all out of a sincere, though perhaps undeserved, spirit of loyalty. Mr. Norie need have made no apology for his book, for we are confident that most readers will be well pleased that he avoided the exact style of the historian, and described the exciting history of Lochaber with the graphic pen of the novelist. On closing the book, one cannot help feeling that in Mr. Norie we have an author who has produced such excellent work that the sooner he produces another volume the better he will please his readers, and Highland literature will be all the richer. It is pleasing to add that the publishers have done the work every justice. It is illustrated with portraits, relics, and views of Lochaber; while the binding is handsome and artistic. Author and publisher deserve to be congratulated on the publication of this really beautiful work.

LOCHABER LOVE.

THERE are some who say that in the north where the people with the fine eyes dwell, the love tales are full of sorrow and sadness and nothing more. But it is only strangers who do not know us that keep telling in books how there is always a gloom about the mountain dwellers. It is true that the mist of the hills and the moaning of the sea will for ever have a sadness in them to the men and the women who live in the glens and on the islands. But there are no blesseder souls anywhere than we who delight to call the glens and the sea and the islands our own.

In our parts the love is deep. And if it be that a man is crossed in his courting, there is always a dirk ready for the breast of the troubler. For the Lochaber lads are not the gentlest lads in the North, and as our grandfathers used to say, it is either neck or nothing with them.

THE ROARING MILL, GLEN NEVIS.

But you can enter Lochaber now without asking leave of any man. The hills and the passes and the sea-lochs are, each of them, open and free. And there are even those who will say that nowadays the men of Lochaber are as tame as the sheep that they herd on the braesides. But, indeed, the glens are all empty now, for the strangers of the South with their gold and their game bags have driven us away to their own noisesome cities, where a Macdonald is as good as a Macleod, and there is no difference betwixt a Cameron and a Chisholm.

But it was not so in the days when Ewen Cameron used to meet Little Mairi at the Roaring Mill in Glen Nevis. Strange, is it not, what way great men will court small women? Ewen was a good six feet four without the brogues, and for this wholesome reason he was called *Ewen trom*, that is, in the good Gaelic, Ewen of the Heavy Body. And who of all the women in Lochaber should Ewen Trom set himself a winning but *Màiri ghearr*, that is, Short Mary—a lightsome bit of a lass with blue eyes and sunflecked hair, that Ewen could have held at arms' length as easily as his sword or his bonnet. Yet so it is, that there is a mystery about all this love-making, such as even old Tormaid the Seer cannot make plain, and Ewen and Mairi had sworn eternal troth of love betwixt each other.

But strangely enough, fate has ruled it that the path of true love shall be a steep and crooked path. In our land of mists and rivers we do not love strangers over much, and we are wishful always that our children should marry among their own clan, or at least with those of their own countryside. So much do we look askance at the stranger that we have a name for such a one. We call him *Gall*.

And Mairi was not of Ewen's country or folk at all. She had come from the south—the land of big fields and slow rivers—and because her hair was fair and golden like the sunlight she was called *Fiona-gall*, the Fair Stranger. So it was that Ewen's folk were at feud with him for courting the little lass who spoke the Lowland tongue, and had sprung from Lowland blood.

But if the path of love be a steep one, there are always plenty of lads and lasses who are keen to spiel it. And it is not a Highland lad who will draw back when once he has pledged his word. And such was Ewen Cameron. He was big and strong, and willing to draw the dirk to any man who would come between him and Mairi Ghear. But there was need of caution in their courting, so it came about that the two lovers had trysted to meet one gloaming in the wood above the Roaring Mill, which is the *eas*, or waterfall, in the river that runs down Glen Nevis.

It was a warm summer gloaming. And on such a night there is no fairer world anywhere than the world of Lochaber. As Ewen crossed the shoulder of the hill from the sea-loch, and began to descend through the straggling wood to the glen below, he would stop again and again to look round on the landscape. He was before his time. For what man with the love deep in his heart was ever yet late for a trysting?

Far away to the north he could see up the valley of the Lochy, where the grey walls of the castle stood on the river's bank. Opposite was Loch Eil, the dwelling place of his own chief. And below him lay the still waters of Loch Linnhe, with a small barque lying becalmed in the light of evening. But leaving all that behind him, he turned and made his way in the twilight through the brackens to a little clearing, from which the roaring sound of the waterfall could be heard stealing up on the still

air. Many a time had Ewen watched the
salmon leaping at the Roaring Mill and turning
round in mid-air and falling back again into the
deep water when they could not leap the fall. But
it was of no salmon he was thinking now, but
of a dark scheme that was shaping itself in the
soul of him.

Suddenly, the stillness of the evening was
broken by the faint cry of a sea-bird. Ewen
started to his feet and listened. There it was
again—low and plaintive and clear.

"Aye, it will be Mairi, sure enough!" And
putting his fingers to his lips there soon went
echoing down the glen the quick, gurly cry of a
whaup, wild and complaining at first, and then
dying away in repeated wails. After that there
was no more bird music, but only the dull sound
of the Roaring Mill far below.

And then, through the trees in the gloaming-
dusk came a woman's figure wrapped closely in
a tartan plaid a small, slight, lissome girl, with
a whisp of a golden curl hanging over her brow,

ENTRANCE TO GLEN NEVIS.

and a white, happy light shining in the eyes of
her.

"*Luaidh mo chridhe*, come to my arms, for it
is I that am glad to see you."

"Aye, Ewen, I feel safe now. But I was
feared at climbing that steep brae in the mirk.
Aye . . . yes . . . Ewen . . . stop . . . that
is enough. We will sit down now! Where
learned ye such kissing!"

And for a time there was a great to-do
between the big man and the little lass, so fond
were they of one another. But our tale has not
to do with their private love-making—as, in
truth, it is no man's business to set down a
record of lover's caresses.

So when they had sat for some while, Ewen
began to lay aside all his bantering talk, and
drawing the little lass to his side, said -

"Mairi, my white love, it is I that am going
to tell you of a plan that is in my head. You

will be knowing all about the high words that
have passed between our folk and your father
who lives up in the big farm in the glen yonder.
I was hearing my father last night say to a man
over at Loch Eil, that he would be killing me
with his dirk before he would have you for a
daughter. It was in the dark and on the hill
that I heard him, and I have laid a plan. For
it is I that will wed you, my love, in spite of all
Lochaber. By the God above us, Mairi, I will!"
And Ewen Trom's was no pretty face to look
on at that moment.

"Oh, Ewen, dinna look so fierce like! And
how could I wed you if your folk are so ill at
me?"

"And is it my father or myself then will be
caring most for?"

"Ah, no Ewen, I will gang to the end of the
earth with you. I love you dearly."

Then there was an interruption here in the
talk that seemed vastly to the liking of the both
of them.

"Now tell me the plan, Ewen."

"Well, then, it is this. So long as you and
I will be stopping in Lochaber, there will be no
wedding for us at all. It is I that am not afraid
to fight. But what is one man against a hundred? So we must leave Lochaber, my little
one. You will meet me at the Roaring Mill
to-morrow night when the moon is just over the
Great Ben there, and we will go down to the
loch and get into old Donald Cameron's boat,
and we will sail away to the south. For it is I
that will not live another week without you."

"Ah, Ewen, but what if they come after us?"

"Let them follow who will. But we must be
for leaving this place, whatever."

So they sat and talked long over the plan,
and only when the moon had risen above the
shoulder over the Great Ben did they rise to say
good night.

The next day broke warm and still, and there
were two hearts in Lochaber that were ill at
ease. Long before the appointed time Ewen
had everything prepared. The boat was ready.
His sporran was full of gold pieces. And when
the gloaming was gathering in Glen Nevis the
great man was crossing the shoulder of the hill
above the Roaring Mill. He had a long time
to wait. Everything was as still as still could
be. Far above the hill the afterglow was filling
the sky with light, and the little clouds were
lying in the pale wan sky, like long molten
islands of gold in a glassy sea. The bog-myrtle
and the heather filled the night air with a sweet
fragrance, and far below the sound of the waterfall rose and fell on the light evening airs

Then the moon came out. And Ewen put
his hand to his lips, and immediately there rose

the cry of a whaup, long and weird and plaintive in the silence of the darkening glen. But there was no answering sea bird's note. Again the the whaup's cry rose. And again there was no reply. And the heart of Ewen Trom began to be filled with the great fear. So for half-an-hour, and yet an hour, the whaup cried—but in vain, until the moon was high in the heavens and the glen was lying steeped in white light and shadows.

"Oh, my white love! And have they taken you away! Mairi, Mairi, it is I that am full of fear for you. Where shall I find you to comfort you and speak to you. *A luaidh, mo chridhe!*"

But though Ewen Trom wandered up and down the glen all that night, and even crept round the house where Mairi and her father dwelt—there was no answer to the whaup's cry, not even a light at her window or a sound to be heard anywhere. So Ewen knew that Mairi had left home and had never reached the Roaring Mill. And turning away he walked back to Loch Eil.

The next day as he was standing at the door of his father's lodge, thinking and brooding over his grief, the old man came up with a leer in the eye of him and said—

"Ewen, my son, what will be your trouble? Is it for love of the Fair Stranger that you stand and look across at the glen? When will you be going across to the Roaring Mill, my son? And do the salmon bite in the moonlight better than in the dawn?"

"It is the man that will be asking no questions that will be told no lies," replied the tall lad with a fire in his eye. But from that moment he knew that his father had discovered the trysting place of Mairi and himself. And the thought filled him with black hatred.

Up and down, up and down, below the windows of the lodge he walked, wondering and wondering where Mairi could be hidden away. Those were the days of dirks and targes, and Ewen Trom's soul was full of bloody thoughts. A stone's throw from where he walked two blood hounds were quarrelling on the grass over a bone, and when they were like to fly at one another with rage Ewen stopped and cried out in the Gaelic with a great oath, and the dogs slunk away to the back of the house.

Then all was still again, for the day was warm and sultry. Ewen stood looking across the loch. There was not a bird chirping even in the thicket. Then suddenly he heard something fall at his side! Something like a little stone. He turned round and saw a bit of gold shining among the pebbles of the walk. But knowing that he might be watched he turned and walked up and down as usual, and only at the fourth turn did he stoop to pick up a handful of pebbles to fling at an old crow that was pecking at the bone on the grass. When he had thrown away all his stones, he turned to his walking again; but in his hand there was something bright. He stopped and looked at it. *It was the gold ring that he had given to Mairi!* And when he saw it the wild light leaped in his eyes and the black anger in his heart.

But in Lochaber the trees have both eyes and ears. So Ewen Trom, although he was in his father's house, knew that he had need of caution. So he went and sat down on the seat at the door, but he put the ring in his sporran.

After sitting five minutes, he knew that Mairi was a prisoner in his father's house, that she was in the room on the second floor immediately above the fuchsia bush, for it was there he had picked the ring up, and there was only one window directly over the bush. And the thought made his heart beat wildly.

While he sat, Morag, the servant maid, came out of the house, and as she was passing her young master, she turned and looked slowly into his eyes and said—

"Where did you learn such kissing?" And before Ewen Trom could find words to express his anger at the servant's impudence, she had vanished in the fir wood.

Then suddenly he laughed—low and quietly and gladly, like a man who has seen the humoursome point of some tale. And rising slowly he wandered into the fir wood. The words that Mairi had repeated were exactly the words that Morag had playfully used the last time they had met at the Roaring Mill! And in a moment Ewen knew that Morag, the serving maid, had been sent to him with a message from Mairi. So he took the way of the fir wood.

He found Morag gathering sticks on the shore, and owing to her young master's interruptions that day it took her half-an-hour to gather an apron full. Yet there were plenty of sticks. And after they had been on the shore together for some time, each returned by a different way to the lodge.

Ewen learned three things. First, that Mairi's door was closely watched. Second, that Morag only carried in her meals three times a day. And, therefore, that the only way of communicating with her was by means of a note sent in by Morag. So that evening Morag carried up Mairi's supper as usual, but there was a sheet of paper between two of the slices of bread.

And what was Ewen doing all day? He was gathering together a strange assortment of things— an old bow and arrow, a long piece of thread, a bit of string, and a stout rope. In the evening he went across to the Roaring Mill as usual, to avoid any suspicion and to delude the old man into believing that Ewen thought Mairi was still in her father's house in the glen.

But when the moon had risen and gone down again, Ewen Trom was standing at the edge of the fir wood and gazing up at one of the windows of the lodge. The night was still light enough to see plainly. And without moving hand or foot he stood and watched.

Then slowly, oh, so slowly, he saw the casement open. There was no sound, and there was no hand visible at the open window. No whaups or sea-birds were abroad this night.

Then Ewen Trom saw a white sheet stretched across the open casement, and he knew his time had come. So taking up his arrow, to which was affixed a long silken thread, he fitted it in the bow-string, and breathing a prayer, gently drew the string and let it free. The arrow shot silently through the night and pierced the white cloth, so that it fell quietly down from the casement inside the room without even touching the floor. Then the cloth was removed. The silken thread was gently drawn upwards, and then the stout string which was attached to it, and then the rope which was tied to the string. And when again the white cloth was waved three times at the casement, Ewen Trom knew that the rope was made fast, and that in another second Mairi Ghear would be letting herself down to the ground.

So he crept stealthily in the gloom to the wall of the house and waited patiently. An owl in the fir wood gave a great "Too-hoot!" which made Ewen's heart jump to his mouth, and he swore a big oath –but into himself. And the next moment he was watching a little woman swinging slowly down the rope. How slowly she seemed to descend! But now she was almost down. She was in his arms. At last!

"*A Inaidh, mo chridhe,*" Ewen exclaimed and at the risk of rousing the whole household the foolish man imprinted a sounding smack on the little lassie's lips, which startled her mightily, and made her whisper –

"Wheesht! wheesht! Ewen, they'll hear us, you gomeril!"

And the next thing that the owl in the tree saw with his nightly eyes was, a great Highlander running like a deer across the grass with a little lady in his arms, and disappearing in the fir wood.

When they got to the road where Morag was waiting with the horses, they made great haste to be away. At last they were seated and Morag let go the reins. They had scarcely time to give their thanks to her before they were off. But, indeed, the faithful servant was well enough contented to see their bustle. And the last thing she heard as they galloped away was the fair haired little lady asking of her sweetheart this strange question, "Ewen where learned ye such kissing?"

Then the clatter of hoofs died away in the distance.

TORQUIL MACLEOD.

A REVERIE 1899.

HARK to the midnight chimes that thund'ring roll
　　Their solemn knell : The year is dead at last,
And I in deep seclusion of the soul
　Peruse the sacred volume of the Past.

Dwell on this page !—so pure, so undefiled,
　The first impressions of unsullied youth,
When still it seemed that nature ever smiled,
　Sin was unknown, and all was love and truth.

Pass on !—and childhood now is left behind,
　As mem'ry reads the record set within.
Pages unfold, and now, alas I to find
　Their virgin purity besmirched by sin.

Pass on !! Pass on !!! -nor yet too closely scan
　The varied writings of the byegone years ;
Perfervid youth emerges in the man,
　And oft the scroll is dimmed by sorrow's tears.

A moment stay ! ! !—this page, from blemish free,
　Bespeaks some kindly word ; some deed well done.
Ah, that a page, pure and unstained, should be
　So easily, and yet so seldom won.

I may not pause. The present now I see ;
　Here is the last,—here the unwritten page.
What will the verdict of my readers be
　When headstrong youth has died in sober age.

As star that flashes o'er the ev'ning sky,
　And in dark night's infinity is lost,
Leaving no trace behind—just such am I ;
　A meteor upon life's sky at most.

Yet could I wish that, as its flick'ring ray,
　To light some wanderer's pathway may be given,
So I may cheer some fellow creature's way,
　And help to bring him nearer unto Heaven.

If I should die—would there be one to weep,
　And softly shed a tear for friendship's sake?
Would one bend o'er me in my last, long sleep,
　And with caresses, bid me to awake?

The flow'ret blooming on the mountain side,
　Its mission fills, tho' not to mortal shown,
But love in empty worldliness may hide,
　And all its wondrous sweetness be unknown.

Then, when the shadows blend with life's short day
　If hope be dead, and saddest mem'ries live,
With my last breath my faltering lips shall pray—
　"Think of me gently, and forget—forgive.

R. ROSS NAPIER

("Rob Lom.")

THE PRINCELY RACE OF THE ISLES.

"HISTORY," said the historian Freeman, " is past politics and politics is present history." From time immemorial politicians have divided themselves into hostile sections. No one can study past politics in anything like detail without unconsciously taking sides in the contests of which he reads. In studying the history of the Western Highlands, the student finds his sympathies ranging against particular houses and taking sides against particular factions. Some will side with the Scottish Kings. Some will side with the Macdonalds. Some will even side with the Campbells. The ignorant would perhaps smile at the notion of Highland politics. To them the history of the Highlands is sheer brute fighting and stupid bloodshed. This notion has been fostered by certain historians who never took the trouble to understand that of which they wrote. There were treaties and embassies, councils and judges, laws and charters among the Macdonalds of the Isles as well as among the Saxons of Scotland. It may have pleased Roland Cheyne* to talk of the "ranks sae rude" of the Highland kerne and to compare them scornfully to "moorland fern." The Highland kerne were loyal to their chiefs, and hated the sway of the domineering foreigner, and loved their old customs and reverenced Holy Church as much as Roland Cheyne and his kind. Sometimes the Highland kerne gave Roland Cheyne and his friends a good deal more than they wanted.

The history of the Western Highlands is the history of the struggle between the Gaels, led by the Macdonalds, Lords of the Isles, and the Saxons of the Lowlands. In perusing the chronicles of the contest the present writer has ever found his sympathies going out to the Macdonalds. For centuries the Lords of the Isles struggled to maintain their footing as princes of the Gael. Like the Dukes of Normandy and Brittany and the feudal potentates of mediæval France, the Scots Lords of the Isles sought to maintain their independence and refused to put their necks under the yoke of an alien sovereign. Their methods in the struggle have not commended themselves to every historian. "They were too much in English pay," says Mr. Andw. Lang† "and too correctly

*The Antiquary. †Private letter to the present writer.

described themselves as 'the auld enemies of Scotland.' " But they were the enemies not of their own ancient 'Alba,' but of that Saxon Scotland which hated and despised them. No one denies the ancient right of Scotland to spurn the English yoke, although a united kingdom of Britain would have saved endless misery and bloodshed No one denies the right of Scotland to call in the aid of France against her Southern foe. It is unjust to blame the Islander for seeking for allies against his natural enemy. He was surely entitled to combine with England against the hostile Scottish king.

They were an Imperial race, the Lords of the Isles, with something of the Roman chivalry. Their stage was small, but they filled it all and grandly. Down to the very South of the Isles they spread their sway. On the remotest part of the Isle of Arran stands the castle of Kildonan, the southernmost memorial of their ancient power. "Like a deer's skull in Wood Mamore, empty, eyeless, sounding to the whistling

THE LORD OF THE ISLES DISPENSING JUSTICE.

wind," it stands looking across to Greenan Castle on the coast of Ayr, itself for a brief season a stronghold of the Macdonalds. The Macdonalds were no mere barbarous chiefs. They were politicians and diplomatists, and patrons of the Church. Donald, the hero of Harlaw, was a student at Oxford, like Thyrsis and the Scholar Gipsy and Matthew Arnold. Like them Donald must have seen

" the warm-green-muffled Cumner hills "*
and drunk
"at some lone alehouse on the Berkshire moors" †
and known
" what sedged brooks are Thames' tributaries."‡
A race which could appreciate the fame of Oxford could scarcely fail to befriend the Church. The abbey of Saddell, in Kintyre; Trinity Church, Carnish, the priories of Oronsay and Colonsay owe their origin to the race of the Isles. Iona was enriched by their benefactions. Several of the Lords of the Isles died as monks in Paisley Abbey.

In spite of their long and noble resistance the Lords of the Isles were finally conquered. In 1517 the Isles were handed over to MacCailein Mòr, as were Lampsacus and Magnesia to Themistocles, for his bread and wine. Argyle made the most of excellent opportunities, and men can witness to-day the results of his exertions. " Vix ea nostra voco—Scarcely do I call these possessions ours,' runs the Campbell motto. " No, perhaps not, considering the manner in which they were acquired," a modern disciple of Diogenes might aptly reply.

The last blow was struck at the Macdonalds in 1616. In that year a statute was passed, which required the gentlemen of the Isles to send their children to Lowland schools to learn " godlinesse and Inglische." Godliness and English! Poor gentlemen of the Isles! "Man!" said John Splendid, " I hate the very look of those Lowland cattle sitting here making kirk laws for their emperors, and their bad bred Scots speech jars on my ear like an ill-tuned bagpipe." Such was the attitude of the true Gael towards godliness and English. The English has still to make its way. The godliness has crushed the nature of a joyous people for two centuries at least.

J. A. Lovat Fraser.

---

*†See the Scholar Gipsy by Matthew Arnold.
‡See Thyrsis by Matthew Arnold.

The Queen has intimated through her private Secretary, Sir Arthur Biggs. K.C.B., C.M.G., her acceptance of a copy of Mr. W. Drummond-Norie's "Loyal Lochaber," just published by Messrs. Morison Brothers, Glasgow.

ROBERT CAMPBELL, MANCHESTER.

AMONG the many Scots who have settled in Manchester and prospered in business, the name of Mr. Robert Campbell is well known. He was born in 1861, his father being the late Allan Campbell, of Eaglesham, whose ancestors came originally from Oban and settled at Lochwinnoch, Renfrewshire. The head of the family dying while the children were still young, Robert had to make his own way in life as best he could. In 1881 he joined his brother John in the business of Aitken, Campbell & Co., Glasgow, but six years later he removed to Manchester where he established a branch of the firm, which has proved most successful, and of which he is managing director. Indeed, the brothers may be taken as typical examples of that enterprising class, always well represented in business circles at home and abroad, the sturdy, industrious Scot who has been the " architect of his own fortune." It would be difficult to discover a place where the successful Scot is not to be found.

When not engaged at business it is always safe to assume that Mr. Campbell may be found on the golf course, for although fond of all out-door exercises, his great absorbing hobby is golf. That may be said of a great many who are not even Scotsmen, now-a-days! Indeed, he himself admits that he is fonder of golf than of business. He is a member of the Machrie Golf Club, and spends a good deal of his leisure time on the course at Buxton (The Peak Hydro., of which he is a Director, and where Scotch visitors always find in him a friend). Like a true clansman he takes a warm interest in the Highlands and its people, and always spends his holidays in Tir nam beann. In private life he is of a retiring nature, and has therefore never taken any active part in public matters, but in business circles and among his friends he is well liked for his genial, kind and hearty disposition. In 1886, Mr. Campbell married Margaret Paton, daughter of Mr. Thomas Middleton, Glasgow.

The Ross-shire Gathering takes place in the Queen's Rooms on the 9th February, Captain Macleod, of Cadboll, presiding.

Highland Association.—Perth not being prepared to receive the Mod next Autumn, it has now been decided to hold it in Edinburgh. We trust the various Highland societies in the Capital will combine to make it a success.

ROBERT CAMPBELL.

ROBERT CAMPBELL,

Deeds that won the Empire. ✳

By JOHN MACKAY, C.E., J.P., Hereford.

CAPTURE OF GUADALOUPE.

(Continued from page 75).

MEANWHILE Commodore Moore, having received certain intelligence that the French Admiral Bompart had arrived at Martinique with eight sail of the line and three frigates with troops on board, sailed to Rupert's Bay in Diminique to oppose them, leaving General Barrington on Grand Terre with only one forty gun ship to protect the fleet of transports.

Colonel Crump was now ordered with 600 bayonets to attack the towns of St. Anne and St. Frances. They were captured, in the most gallant manner, before sunrise, and, notwithstanding a heavy fire from trenches and batteries, the losses were trifling, only one officer of the Highlanders fell in the assault. On the following day, Colonel Crump pushed forward and drove the enemy from another position, and stormed a battery of three twenty four pounders. General Barrington now formed a scheme to surprise Petit Bourg, St. Maries, and Goayare. This duty he assigned to Brigadiers Clavering and Crump, but owing to the darkness of a most tempestuous night, when the wind howled amid palm and cocoanut trees, and the lightening flashed among the mountains, thus exciting the terror of their Negro guides, the attempt failed, and the general was compelled to do that by force which he intended to have done by stratagem.

He now ordered the same commanders to land near the town of Arnonville, and they did so unopposed by the enemy, who retreated to a strong position on the banks of the Licorn. Except at two narrow passes, the river, rendered inaccessible by a morass, covered by mangroves, was fortified by a redoubt and intrenchment mounted with guns.

Despite these disadvantages, the brigadiers etermined on assault, confident that their active Highlanders would surmount any natural obstacle. They were not disappointed! Under cover of a fire from their field pieces, the young Highlanders advanced to the attack, supported by the 38th regiment. As they pushed rapidly on, the enemy began to waver, then, we are informed by "Letters from Guadaloupe" that, slinging their muskets, the Highlanders drew their swords, and supported by part of the other regiment, rushed with their characteristic impetuosity, and followed the enemy into the redoubt, of which they immediately took and kept possession.

Like the rest of the troops, they had endured intolerable heat, continued fatigue, the air of a climate to which they were unaccustomed, and the toil of climbing lofty mountains and steep precipices.

In storming this work 65 officers and men were killed, or wounded. Other towns and works being carried and captured elsewhere, they pushed on to Capesterre, amid the most lovely tropical scenery, and captured from one planter alone 870 Negroes, who, being saleable, were then as valuable as prize money. There Brigadier Clavering was met by Messieurs de Clairvilliers and Duqueroy deputed to know what terms of surrender would be granted them. They were conducted to General Barrington, who, considering the smallness of his force, diminishing daily by fever and bullet, the chance of the enemy being succoured from Martinique, and the unaccountable absence of the commodore, resolved to settle the terms without delay, and they were hardly signed when a messenger came with tidings that General Branharnois had landed at St. Anne's with succour from Europe, with the squadron under Admiral Bompark. On learning that the capitulation was complete, these forces returned to Martinique.

This expedition, says General Stewart, was a tolerably smart training for a young corps, who, nine months before, had been breeding cattle and sheep on their native hills.

By private accounts from Guadaloupe, it would appear that the French had formed the most frightful and absurd notions of the "Sauvages d'Ecosse," they were led to believe that they would neither give nor accept quarter, and that they were so nimble, that, as no man could catch them, so nobody could escape them, that no man had a chance against their broadswords, and that, with a ferocity natural to savages, they made no prisoners, and spared neither man, woman, nor child. As they were always in the front of every action in which they were engaged, it is probable that these notions had no small influence on the nerves of the militia and possibly regulars. It was believed by the French that the Highlanders amounted to several thousands.

(*To be continued*).

FROM THE WEST, GREETING!

(The following humorous greeting was sent by the Bristol Caledonian Society to brother Scots celebrating St. Andrew's Day in other parts)

HERE'S a health and good cheer to our Scots
　　where they meet,
　　In the lands they have made their home;
For it's truth that the critics so often repeat—
He's a terrible fellow to roam.

But if any should say that a solemn old Scot
　Never cares to be jolly and bright,
You can shew them what Northerners are, and are not,
　If they'll come and behold you to-night.

Let them learn from your merriment—ill-judging
　folk !
As it rings to the roof of the hall,
That the joke that a Scotchman is blind to a joke
Is the mightest joke of them all.

Do you doubt of his wits, if he's up to the game ?
　Of his arm, if it's able to strike ?
You may reach down the Record of fortune and
　fame,
　And open the page, where you like !

Clifton, November, 1898.　　A. C. MACPHERSON.

THE APATHY.

BY THE HON. STUART ERSKINE

THERE was a day when Summer was turned all to grey, and the hot, steaming mists rolled slowly up and down the hills. He was in a wood when he saw that day. Listless and heedless of the chase in the wood of many colours slumbered he, and slept. The sun of the sky slept at mid-day ! It happened that the eagle and the falcon did the same.

He looked up, as he lay upon the soft, bright, green sward in the wood of many colours, and saw grey forms stealing from tree to tree. Between the dark, green pillars of the wood saw he grey shapes moving. Some of the branches dropped hot moisture ; and a young small birch cried aloud in his extremity for cold winds and rain. He thought it was only deer moving among the trees ! His bow lay unstrung beside him.

The grey shapes came down from the moist, hot hills and occupied the wood. They began to devour all the trees. There was not one left. The little grey-coated people of the wood were afraid to come out of their homes. The children of the wood were silent. Fortunate was it for the lost souls of the wood that many were not yet returned home, or, in spite of their dark, swift, silent flight, they must have been caught in the nets spread by the little grey men. As it was, some of the timid souls of the wood were caught in the shapes, and perished of terror.

He was not afraid of the grey shapes. He saw the trees disappearing one by one, and felt the hot breath of the grey men upon his cheek ; but he thought only of sleep. Even when the shapes stepped up to him, and gazed at him, he was not afraid. It was only when they began to smother him that he struggled a little, syne rose up, and went out of the wood.

He did not go far from the wood. He lay down upon the outskirts. The grey shapes came and gazed at him ; but they did not offer to smother him again. There was a little more safety out of the wood than there was in it.

The grey shapes moved down the hill of the wood of many colours, and occupied the plain. They devoured the most of what was in the plain, and stupefied the rest. After them marched a mysterious warrior, clad in partly-coloured raiment, who cried aloud for champions to fight him ; but there was none to challenge him. He was so listless, that when he heard his warrior calling, he thought it was merely the drowsy hum of bees, and slept again.

He slept till eventide. Then a sharp, clear, cool, refreshing voice called to him from the east saying that the grey shapes were fled ; and the son of the sky was rejoicing in the west. He awoke and stood upright. The pale moon was uncovered in the plain. The wood was on the hill.

He strung his bow and went into the wood. He drew upon a young roe-buck. The arrow, covered with blood, pierced a tree. He laid the buck on his shoulders and went home.

Such was the apathy of Ruadri, the son of Mastach, that day in the wood ; and of his awakening I have told you.

BRAVERY AND MODESTY.

A GALLANT CAMPBELL.

SIR—The frequent remark of how the above qualities are combined in our last great leader, the Sirdar, is not to be wondered at, for the second is born of the first. That they are a natural combination I have found borne out in the case of a humbler soldier than the Sirdar, one who gave his life for his country in India's great rebellion. His inmost thoughts on the subject of his own deed of valour have just been perused by me, his son, for the first time, his letters to his wife and to his mother having just come into my hands.

Note the contrast in this account of a brave man's action, and the way in which his inmost soul speaks of it.

Marshman, in his " Life of Havelock," page 355, thus writes of the Action of Boorhiya :—" The enemy's guns were admirably served, and their fire was the severest our men had yet encountered. All the efforts of our artillery, though superior in numbers, were unable for some time to make any impression upon them, sheltered as they were by earthworks, and it was found necessary at length to have recourse to the bayonet. The infantry of the enemy, posted behind the guns, continued to maintain a galling fire, but nothing could withstand the impetuosity of our troops. The Highlanders, now reduced in number to about 100, marched up to the guns, and when within 100 yards of them, changed their pace into a rush, and with their usual cheer, mastered and bayoneted the gunners. The infantry then broke and fled, and the Highlanders instantly turned the captured guns on them.
. . . Immediately on reaching Cawnpore the General issued the following order of the day : —
" . . . In this our eighth fight, the conduct of the artillery was admirable. The Fusiliers and the Highlanders were, as usual, distinguished. The Highlanders, without firing a shot, rushed with a cheer upon the enemy's redoubt, carried it, and captured 2 of the 3 guns with which it was armed. If Colonel Hamilton can ascertain the officer, non-commissioned officer, or soldier, who first entered this work, the Brigadier will recommend him for the Victoria Cross."

" Colonel Hamilton reported that it was difficult to decide to whom this honour belonged, as it appeared to be divided between Lieut. Campbell and Lieut. Crowe. The gallant Campbell was smitten down the next day by cholera ; the distinction fell to the lot of Lieut. Crowe."

Lieut. Campbell (just then promoted Captain) wrote thus to his wife—" First, say nothing on the subject of the cross of valour until I see how it is to be settled. It was not for valour I sprang into the battery at the head of our men, but I always maintain that for safety it is the safest place to get at the guns immediately. However, a little time will show what will turn out, Crowe deserves it as much as I do. My most joyful news is that I am at last Captain Campbell of the Grenadiers, after about sixteen years, high time. . . . I will write old . . soon, but I am perfectly shaking writing even what I have done, with only the ground for my table. Finlay, Crowe, Bouverie, Bogle, and half the men have a fever, a sort that lasts only four or five days ; it is just rest they require, nothing else."

In an enclosed letter to his mother he wrote—" Cawnpore, 14th August. (He died 16th August).
. . . Through the protection of God I am spared again to express my gratitude for his bringing me through other two actions, both of rather a severe nature. . . . We always find the artillery of the enemy most wonderfully well served, and they stand to their guns like men, their infantry are *most cowardly*, and their cavalry *deplorable*. . . . We had to advance against several discharges of grape, . . and we had a nasty breastwork to get over. Crowe and myself were first over the breastwork, and Havelock has sent to the regiment to know who was the first in, as he wished to recommend him for the cross of valour ; as it is between the two of us it may here rest, with thanks probably in general orders. After all I can't see what we did to merit it, and I think the General has quite over-valued our services individually, for with soldiers like the 78th you may go anywhere, they have made a name for themselves this war. We have but a very small part of the regiment, and out of the 320 we first took the field with we have lost about half from action, sun and disease, and I so much regret that so many of my Grenadiers[a] have been the unfortunates. Kindly say not a word about the said cross, for it is quite unlikely the reward will be given when two can equally claim it."

By a strange coincidence, my eldest son, now in the Artillery, joined the Royal Military Academy on the 16th August, 1897, as cadet, so that his first day of soldiering was the exact 40th anniversary of his grandfather's last day of service.

Yours very truly,
DONALD A. CAMPBELL, Lieutenant Colonel,
Late Royal Inniskilling Fusiliers.

P. S.—In no hiatus was there a single boastful or discontented expression, though toil and hardship are referred to as the common lot of all.

THE CAMERONS OF GLEN NEVIS.

DEAR SIR,
I have much enjoyed the short read of Mr. Drummond-Norie's book, "Loyal Lochaber"; naturally, the first thing I did was to look up the index for "Glen Nevis"—chap.xxv. p. 213,and as one of " Sliochd Shomhairle ruaidh, Glen Nevis " I was somewhat surprised to read on p. 217, it taken for granted that this branch of the Camerons is extinct.

Having left home when little more than a child, and since then having paid but visits far too short,

*Archibald Forbes, in his "Drawn from Life," writes of these Grenadiers :—" There was never a finer Grenadier Company in any regiment in the British service, and it was almost exclusively national. There were Rosses, and Mackenzies, and Mackays in it by the half dozen, and as for Donalds, Hart, the Irish Sergeant-Major, had been heard to mutter in despair over the Company roll, that ' The Grenadiers were all Donalds together, and be d—d to them !' Their captain was a naturalised Scot—Captain Bouverie—and the subalterns were Campbell, a splendid Argyleshire man, Crow, another bird from the same nest, and Walsh."

my clan knowledge may be taken to be very meagre, but when burying my father in Glen Nevis, nearly 21 years ago, there were a few members of the tribe then present.

I have heard it often related as a peculiarity of my people, that when a member died, burial in the family burying ground was insisted on by the rest of the Clan, and it is not so long ago that a member, whose wife wished to bury him elsewhere, was forcibly carried to Glen Nevis. I always thought the name of our burying-place was "Tom a charaich," but on thinking matters over I remembered having heard of an older place which had to be abandoned in consequence of the Nevis encroaching on it, and probably this is the place mentioned in the book as "Tom-cas-an-t-slinnein," as I have some recollection of hearing the name. I also heard that when the estate was sold it was omitted to reserve the burying grounds, and that my great grandfather, on learning this, charged the then chief with having sold the bones of his fathers and threatened him with penalties more forcible than legal, and I always understood that the reservation was then made.

The last owner of Glen Nevis, I believe, was John Cameron, who went to the West Indies; there were besides three daughters. I should be glad if you can tell me of any person who can inform me of the history of the family at the time the place was sold. As long, however, as there is even this remnant in Devonshire consisting of myself, six boys, and two girls left, I object to the clan being spoken of as extinct! If you are any time in Rothesay you will find a house called Glen Nevis in the Marine Parade, and another of the same near Townsville in Australia.

I am
Yours faithfully,
DONALD CAMERON.

THE NAME MACINTYRE MENTIONED IN HOLY WRIT.

Dublin.

DEAR SIR,
I was deeply interested in the account which appeared in this month's issue of the Celtic Monthly of the M'Intires of Londonderry. My mother having belonged to that old Scotch family I naturally take more than a passing interest in Scotland and Scotchmen, whom I feel proud to regard as my own kith and kin.

I would like to mention a fact in connection with the name M'Intire, and it is that it occurs in Holy Writ. I was much struck with it some years ago when reading a Celtic Bible and I came across the passage (Matt. xiii. 55,) "Nach e so mac an t-saoir?" Here we have the Celtic form of the name and applied to our Blessed Lord. Is not this an honour to those who bear that name, and is it not a strong incentive to seek that greater honour offered in the 50th verse of the preceding chapter?

Faithfully yours,
CHARLES BLACKHAM.

KILMUIR GRAVEYARD, DUNVEGAN.

SIR—In the article on "Dunvegan and its Associations," in the October number of the Celtic, the author says:—" Kilmuir is also the resting place of our Highland heroine, Flora Macdonald." This statement is incorrect, as her remains were interred in the Kingsburgh family burial place in the churchyard of Kilmuir in Troternish, a hundred and eight years ago, and were never removed from there to Kilmuir churchyard at Dunvegan. In the beginning of the present century, Flora's youngest son, Lieutenant-Colonel John Macdonald of Exeter, sent a marble slab to Skye to be placed over his mother's grave. It was unfortunately broken, and not a fragment of it was left by tourists, who carried it off in pieces as curiosities. The inscription on it was as follows :—" In the family mausoleum at Kilmuir, lie interred the remains of the following members of the Kingsburgh family, viz., Alexander Macdonald of Kingsburgh; his son Allan; his sons Charles and James, his son John, and two daughters; and of Flora Macdonald, who died in March, 1790, aged 68—a name that will be mentioned in history, and if courage and fidelity be virtues, mentioned with honour." — " She was a woman of middle stature, soft features, gentle manners, and elegant presence. So wrote Johnson." In 1834 her daughter Anne, the wife of Major Alexander Macleod, Stein, Waternish, was also buried there. None of Flora's descendants were interred in Kilmuir Churchyard, Dunvegan, excepting her grand-daughter, Miss Mary Macleod, commonly called " Miss Mary Major," who wished to be buried beside her father, Major Alexander Macleod. It is generally believed that Flora Macdonald was born at Milton in South Uist, and died at Kingsburgh in Skye, but it is alleged that it was in an uncle's house at Frobost near Milton that she first saw the light, and that she died at Peninduin near Kingsburgh on the 4th of March, 1790, while on a visit to her half-sister, Annabella, daughter of Captain Hugh Macdonald, Armadale.

I am etc.,
A. R. MACDONALD.

Waternish, Skye.

CLAN MACKAY.—The annual social gathering which took place in the Waterloo Rooms on 23rd December, under the presidency of Major A. Y. Mackay, Grangemouth, was a great success. There were about seven hundred present. Speeches were delivered by the chairman, Sheriff Mackay, and Mr. James H. Mackay, London, who presented to the society a large oil portrait of Mr. John Mackay, Hereford, painted by his daughter, Miss E. Rose Mackay, a photo reproduction of which we give this month as a plate.

THE CAITHNESSIANS met the other evening in the Queen's Rooms, and made a capital appearance. The hall was crowded, and the speeches were excellent. We have seldom heard a soiree speech which we enjoyed so much as that by the Rev. John Horne. It was homely, fragrant of Caithness manners and tongue, and went home to the hearts of the hearers like a waft of the breeze on Morven.

THE CLAN CAMERON gathered in their hundreds to celebrate their annual re-union in the Queen's Rooms. Sir Charles Cameron, M.P., was in the chair, and delivered a stirring address. We are glad to learn that the society is making excellent progress.

The late DUNCAN MACRAE, J.P, D.L.

THE CELTIC MONTHLY:
A MAGAZINE FOR HIGHLANDERS.
Edited by JOHN MACKAY, Glasgow.

No. 6 Vol. VII]   MARCH, 1899   [Price Threepence.

THE LATE DUNCAN MACRAE, J.P., D.L., KAMES CASTLE.

MacRae
or
Conchra

THE late Mr. Duncan MacRae, J.P., D.L., whose portrait is here given, died at Kames Castle, Isle of Bute, on the 14th December last, in his 83rd year. He was the youngest and last surviving son of the late Major Colin MacRae of the 75th (Abercromby's) Highlanders (now the 1st Battalion of the Gordon Highlanders of Dargai fame) who saw a good deal of service, especially during the Seringapatam campaigns at the end of last century, and was in temporary command of the regiment when last quartered in Edinburgh in 1807. His mother was Isabel, daughter of Archibald M'Ra of Ardintoul by his wife Janet MacLeod, one of the celebrated "ten" daughters of John MacLeod, 10th "Baron" of Rasay.

Mr. MacRae was the head of the "Conchra" branch of the MacRaes of Kintail, an old Ross-shire family, which has sent many representatives to the British army during the last century. The first of the family, of whom anything definite is known, was Fionnla dubh MacGillichiosd, who was contemporary with Murdoch Mackenzie, 5th "Baron" of Kintail, who died at Achilty, 1416. John, 2nd son of Fionnla dubh, was called "Vicar M'Ra." His daughter, Margaret, married Adam Gordon, 3rd son of 1st Earl of Huntly by his 3rd wife, Elizabeth, eldest daughter of William, Lord Crichton, Lord Chancellor of Scotland, from whom are descended the Gordons, Baronets of Embo, in Sutherlandshire.

Christopher, grandson of Fionnla dubh, was Constable of Ellandonan Castle, and left six sons, one of whom, Farquhar, was ancestor of the "Clann Doil vic Farquhar" or "Black MacRaes," the "Torlishich" branch of the MacRaes of Kintail.

Duncan, eldest surviving son of Christopher, Constable of Ellandonan Castle, married Isabel, relict of Sir Dongal Mackenzie, Priest of Kintail. "From him the tribe commonly called the White MacRaes are come." He killed "Donald Gorm" Macdonald of Sleat with an arrow, when acting as Constable of Ellandonan Castle, and defending it against the Macdonalds in 1539. His eldest son,

Christopher, was Constable of Ellandonan Castle, and married the 3rd daughter of Murdoch Murchison, Priest of Kintail, who was presented to the Vicarage of Loch Carron by James VI., 19th July, 1582.

Farquhar, eldest son of the above Christopher, was born at Ellandonan Castle in 1580. He also was Constable of Ellandonan Castle, and minister of Kintail, 1618. His son,

John, was born at Ardlair, 13th March, 1614. He was minister of Dingwall in 1640, and married 1st, Agnes, 3rd daughter of Colin Mackenzie, 1st of Kincraig, and died August, 1673. He was succeeded by his eldest son,

Alexander of Conchra, served heir 12th July, 1681, who married Florence Mackinnon of Corriechatachan. His eldest son,

John of Conchra, was killed at the battle of

Sheriffmuir (November), 1715. He was one of the four gentlemen of Seaforth's regiments who

DUNCAN MACRAE, SOUTH CAROLINA.

signally distinguished themselves before they were killed. They were known as "the four Johns of Scotland," viz: John MacRae of Conchra, John Mackenzie of Hilton, John Mackenzie of Applecross, John Murchison of Auchtertyre. He married Isabella, eldest daughter of Donald MacRa, minister of Kintail, 1681, by his wife, Catherine Grant of Glenmoriston. His eldest son,
John of Conchra, married Isabella, daughter of

ISABEL, WIFE OF MAJOR COLIN MACRAE.

John of Conchra, Captain 80th Regiment, killed by the French on board the "Admiral Applin" in the Bay of Bengal, 1804. His only son, James, was also on board the "Admiral Applin," and taken prisoner and carried to the Island of Mauritius. He was afterwards drowned on his way to the Peninsula with his regiment, on the 21st February, 1811, being then a Captain in the 11th Devon Regiment. His transport having been run down by H.M.S. "Franchise" off the Lizard Lights. Duncan, the second son of John of Conchra, was born at Conchra, 26th April, 1751. He went to America and became a wealthy planter in South Carolina, where he died on the 27th November, 1824. Colin, the third son, was a Major in the 75th (Abercromby's) Highlanders, he married in 1808 Isabel, 2nd daughter of Archibald MacRa of Ardintoul, and his wife, Janet MacLeod of Rasay. Major

Colin MacRae died at Banff on the 10th March, 1821, leaving six sons and one daughter, none of whom have left any male issue except his youngest son, Duncan, the subject of our sketch. Major MacRae was, by his dying request, buried in the family burying place at Clachan Duich, at the head of Loch Duich in Ross shire. The clansmen of Lochalsh and Kintail went to to meet the hearse, and carried the remains on their shoulders to Clachan Duich. His youngest son,
The late Mr. Duncan MacRae, joined the H.E.I.C. Service in January, 1839, and served through the memorable Afghan campaign of 1842 under General Pollock, when Cabul was occupied; was present at the capture of the Fort of Khytul in 1843; through the Boogtee campaign in Scinde in 1846; through the Pun-

MAJOR COLIN MACRAE.

Alexander Mackenzie of Ballone, and died in 1761, leaving three sons:

jaub campaign of 1848-49, including the siege of Mooltan and the battle of Googerat; served through the Indian Mutiny of 1857-58, was present at Umballa, Meerut, and the siege and capture of Delhi, for which services he was awarded three medals and three clasps. Mr. MacRae retired from the Indian army with the rank of Inspector-General of Hospitals. The remains, which were conveyed from Bute, were met at Dornie by a large gathering of the people of the district to the number of several hundreds, of whom the greater number were MacRaes. The melancholy cortege left Dornie to the mournful but appropriate lament:

Thèid mi dhachaidh 'Chrò Chiunntàile
(I will go home to Cro in Kintail).

The coffin was covered with a MacRae tartan plaid, and was carried all the way to Clachan Duich (a distance of 7 miles) by relays of the men accompanying the funeral. The day was fine; and as the procession wound its way slowly up the steep hill from Dornie, with no sound but the weird, sad, wail of the pipes, the scene was a most solemn and impressive one. About half-way to Clachan Duich a halt was made for refreshments, and a cairn was raised on the spot where the coffin had rested, in accordance with the old custom in the Highlands. For the last

ELLANDONAN CASTLE, ROSS-SHIRE.

lift, before reaching the churchyard, the coffin was carried by four gentlemen of the clan, namely: Mr. Duncan MacRae, Ardintoul; Mr. John MacRae, Ratagan; Mr. Christopher MacRae, Conchra; Mr. Donald MacRae, Fadoch. The pall bearers were the three sons of the deceased, namely: Mr. Stuart MacRae, Handley House, Newark-on-Trent; Major John MacRae-Gilstrap of Ballimore, Argyllshire; Lieutenant Colin MacRae of the "Black Watch"; Mr. Batten-Pooll of Road Manor, Somersetshire (son-in-law); Mr. Walter Batten-Pooll (grandson); Captain Stewart, younger of Essay, Major MacDougall of Lunga, Mr. Donald Stewart

(nephews). The coffin was covered with a MacRae tartan plaid which was buried with it, and which had been carried through the Soudan and Nile campaigns in Egypt by Major MacRae-Gilstrap, who was then a young Lieutenant in the "Black Watch," and who took part in most of the engagements in these campaigns. The family burying place has hitherto been within the walls of the ruined chapel at Clachan Duich; but no further space being available there, a new burial ground has been acquired close to the wall of the churchyard. The service at the grave was conducted by the Rev. Canon Chisholm, resident priest in Kintail. The funeral was the largest that has taken place in the district for many years. The deceased gentleman's connection with the country, as head of the Conchra branch of the MacRaes of Kintail, being very familiar to all the people of the place, as he was brought up amongst them at Ardintoul, and the memory of his father, Major Colin MacRae, who died in 1821, is still referred to in terms of esteem and respect. The fact that the people turned out in such large numbers to pay their last homage to the representative of a former prominent family in that district shows that the loyal clan feeling is yet far from extinct in the Highlands, and this manifestation of it

has been very highly appreciated by the deceased gentleman's widow and family. About 25 years ago he took up his residence at Kames Castle in the Island of Bute, and his quiet gentlemanly demeanour gained for him the esteem of all with whom he came in contact. As was said of him by the Rev. Mr. Dewar, parish minister of North Bute, on the Sunday after his demise: "He was in every way a typical Highland gentleman." During his residence in Bute he was appointed a Deputy-Lieutenant for the county, and also a Justice of the Peace.

Requiescat in Pace.

KAMES CASTLE, ISLE OF BUTE.

THE BOG-MYRTLE.

CLAN CAMPBELL'S BADGE.

I'VE sung of the heather, Clan Donald's loved
    badge,
The oak of the sons of the axe and the targe,
Mackay's bonnie bulrush by Naver that waves,
And Gregor's blue pine tree the tempest that braves,
And now I would hie to the shores of Loch Fyne,
And the daisy flecked valleys of castled Argyle,
To sing of the sons of the famed Cailein Mòr,
Whose badge is the myrtle, whose crest is the boar.

On the pages of story for ages shall shine,
The name of the martyr'd brave faithful Argyle ; *
A name to his countrymen hallowed and dear ;
A name that his clansmen for aye shall revere,
Of that house yet another the Scot does admire,
Who answered a Saxon queen's threat with true fire,
"Ere the shores of my country your hunting ground
    bounds,
I'll away to the North and let loose my stag-
    hounds." †

* Archibald, Earl of Argyll, who suffered martyr-
    dom for the religious freedom of Scotland.
† Mac Cailean Mòr's retort to Queen Charlotte's
    threat of turning Scotland into a hunting ground.

PROFESSOR DUNCAN M. M'EACHRAN.

Not only the Highland brown mountain and fell
Have echoed Clan Diarmid's proud pibroch's shrill
    swell,
" The Campbells are coming " has sounded afar,
And often decided the fortunes of war.
On the heights of far Alma - steep, frozen, and bare,
It nerved the leal clansmen to do and to dare :
And where the broad Ganges rolls through the hot
    plains,
With joy the beleaguered gave ear to its strains.

The slogan " Ben Cruachan " no longer is heard,
And hushed is the harp of the minstrel and bard,
In peaceful repose rest the brave that have been ;
Yet still the bog-myrtle waves fragrant and green,
And still undiminished in numbers and worth,
From Lorn and Breadalbane the Campbells go forth,
With unimpair'd courage, leal, brave as of old,
Their fathers' traditions afar to uphold.

Hatfield   ANGUS MACKINTOSH.

PROFESSOR DUNCAN M. M'EACHRAN,
MONTREAL.

DUNCAN M·NAB M'EACHRAN,
F.R.C.V.S., V.S. (Edinburgh), D.V.S.
(M'Gill), is a son of the late David
M'Eachran, for many years a magistrate and
senior bailie of the town of Campbeltown,
Argyllshire. He was born there November
27th, 1841, and educated in his native town
and at Edinburgh, where he graduated as a
Veterinary Surgeon in the Edinburgh Veteri
nary College.

In the autumn of 1862 he removed to Canada,
living for nearly three years at Woodstock,
Ontario, where he practiced his profession,
delivering a course of lectures during the winter
sessions in Toronto, where he aided in the
establishment of the Ontario Veterinary College.
Removing to Montreal in 1866, in connection
with the Medical Faculty of M'Gill University
and the Board of Agriculture of the Province
of Quebec, he founded the Montreal Veterinary
College, which in 1889 became the faculty of
Comparative Medicine and Veterinary Science
of M'Gill University, and he was appointed
Dean of the Faculty and Professor of Veterinary
Medicine and Surgery. He is also one of the
original Fellows of the Royal College of Veteri
nary Surgeons, England, elected in 1875, being
the only one in Canada upon whom the honour
of Fellowship by election was conferred.

Professor M'Eachran was instrumental in
establishing the cattle quarantine system of
Canada, the first station being established under
his direction at Point Levis, opposite Quebec,
which quarantine system has extended its sphere
of usefulness in the protection of the live stock
industries from ocean to ocean, he being the
Chief Inspector for the Dominion. In 1879 he
was appointed by the Canadian Government,
acting on behalf of the Imperial Government,
to make a report on the subject of contagious
diseases, more especially pleuro-pneumonia, said
to exist in certain portions of the United States,
and it was on Dr. M'Eachran's report that the
scheduling of the American cattle in 1879 took
place. As Chief Inspector he took an active
part in the discussion on the scheduling of
Canada by the Home Government for the
supposed existence of contagious pleuro-pneu
monia in Canada, stoutly maintaining that no
such disease existed. Subsequent events have
proved conclusively that he was right in his
contention.

He has also been largely instrumental in the
development of cattle breeding and exportation
of cattle from Canada. In 1881, in connection
with Senator Cochrane, he established the first
large cattle ranch at the foot hills of the Rocky
Mountains, of which he was General Manager
for two years. In 1883, severing his connection
with the Cochrane Ranch, he established the
Walrond Cattle Ranch in connection with the
late Sir John Walrond, Bart., the Board of
Directors being resident in England. Recently
Dr. M'Eachran reorganized this company, and
has associated with him as a Board of Directors
some of Canada's leading business men ; Sir
William H. Walrond, Bart., M.P., London,
being President, and Dr. M'Eachran, Vice-
President and Managing Director.

He has from time to time published valuable
contributions to magazines on subjects relating
to his profession, and is the author of a hand-
book for the use of farmers on the diseases of
horses, and other minor publications.

In December, 1896, he accompanied the
Minister of Agriculture to Washington, and
assisted in the formation of the agreement by
which the quarantines between the two countries
were mutually abolished, resulting in the
opening up of a very large market for Canadian
store cattle and pedigreed stock.

In the winter of 1897-98 he visited, on behalf
of the Canadian Government, France, Germany,
and Denmark, for the purpose of familiarising
himself with the conditions of these countries
in relation to the existence of contagious diseases
in animals and their method of dealing with
them. A valuable report of his observations
has recently been issued by the Dominion
Government.

He married in 1868 Esther, third daughter of
the late Mr. Timothy Plaskett, of St. Croix,
West Indies, by whom he has one daughter
living.

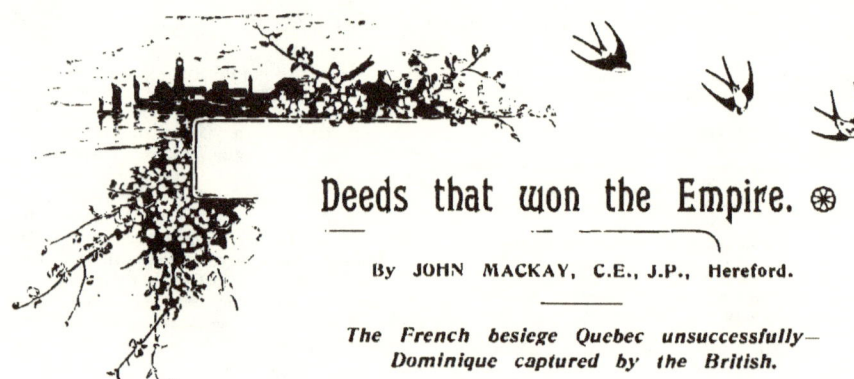

Deeds that won the Empire. ✳

By JOHN MACKAY, C.E., J.P., Hereford.

The French besiege Quebec unsuccessfully— Dominique captured by the British.

(*Continued from page* 98.)

GUADALOUPE being captured and garrisoned, the young Highland regiment, who had acted so smartly and so bravely in the conquest of the island, was ordered to join their countrymen, the Royal Highlanders, in North America, to aid General Amherst to complete the conquest and pacification of Canada. Wolfe accomplished his part on the Heights of Abraham, the result being the fall of Quebec. The French were still in great force on the Upper Lakes, and in Lower Canada along the St. Lawrence. General Townshend returned to England, leaving General James Murray in command of Quebec with a slender force, including the redoubtable Fraser Highlanders. He immediately began to repair and strengthen the fortifications to resist any impending attack by the French to recover Quebec. The winter months passed quietly away, but in April, 1760, a large force of French, Canadians, and Indians, amounting to 14,000 men, appeared in the vicinity. Murray, trusting to the gallantry of his little army, boldly, but rashly went forth to give them battle, but so overwhelming was the strength of the enemy that he was soon in danger of being completely surrounded and cut off from the city; order was then given to retire by sections fighting all the way back and checking the advance of the enemy, the Frasers in the rear fighting like lions at bay and losing many men, until at length the remains of the gallant little army got inside the ramparts of the fortifications. The Frasers were much annoyed at their defeat, and one of their officers, who had been "out" in the '45 and had shared in the defeat of Culloden, said, "From April battles, and Murray generals, Good Lord deliver me."

The French General Levi besieged Quebec, and brought his cannons to bear upon its fortifi-cations, but was gallantly resisted. At length a British fleet from Halifax under the command of Commodore Lord Colville appeared in the St. Lawrence. Colville immediately attacked the French shipping, destroying the whole of it, upon which the French raised the siege of Quebec, and retired into the interior, followed by Murray, who reached Montreal a few days before Amherst. Upon the arrival of the Commander-in-Chief, the city was summoned to surrender. The Governor General consented, and the last stronghold of the French in North America fell into the hands of Great Britain, and the conquest of Canada was complete. By the judicious arrangements of Amherst, and the spirited enterprise of Murray, the pacification of it was soon effected.

No sooner was this important service completed than orders were sent to North America to prepare a strong force for the West Indies, amongst whom the Highland regiments, then in Canada, were particularly specified, "as their sobriety and abstemious habits, great activity, and capability of bearing the vicissitudes of heat and cold, rendered them well qualified for that climate and for a broken and difficult country."

By this time George II.—"dapper little George"—died, and George III. succeeded at the age of 20. He was entirely controlled by his mother, and Lord Bute, his tutor. The Court was against the war with France, and greatly inclined to make peace, now that the object of it had been obtained—the expulsion of the French from Canada. War with Spain was imminent, and France appealed to Spain for aid. The family compact between these two nations still existed. Differences arose in the Cabinet, a change of ministers took place, Pitt, the "great commoner," lost supreme control, hence the "orders" alluded to were not followed up at home, and only a few troops from North America reached the West Indies, and the commanders, Colonel Lord Rollo and Commodore Sir James Douglas, with a small force of infantry, and four ships of war, could not undertake much. However, these brave commanders would try. After some consideration they resolved to attempt the capture of Dominique, an important French island. The capture of Guadaloupe in 1759 showed the French weak points in their harness. It warned them of their danger, and induced them to make every exertion to strengthen their fortifications, erect new ones, and maintain larger garrisons than formerly in every island, so that, what might have been easily accomplished in 1759, was now probably to be a work of time, labour and bloodshed.

The force at the command of the two gallant Scots consisted of the garrison of Guadaloupe, the grenadier and light companies of the 4th and 22nd regiments, commanded by Colonel Melville, of whom we heard at the capture of Guadaloupe, six companies of the Montgomery Highlanders and some other troops sent from New York, altogether about 2000 men. The transports conveying the New York contingent were scattered in a gale of wind. A company of the Montgomerys in a small transport was attacked by a French privateer, which the gallant Highlanders repulsed and beat off with the loss of Lieutenant Macleod and six men killed, and Captain Robertson and eleven men wounded.

Arriving at Dominique on the 6th June, 1760, they at at once effected a landing, and with little opposition marched to the town of Roseau. A very galling fire was poured upon them by the French from entrenchments above the town. Lord Rollo determined without any delay to attack them, more particularly as he ascertained that a reinforcement in a short time was expected from Martinique.

This service, being of the utmost importance under the circumstances, was performed most gallantly by himself and Colonel Melville at the head of the grenadiers, light infantry, and the Montgomery Highlanders, and with such audacity, vigour, and success that the enemy were driven successively from all the entrenchments. So sudden, so quick, and vigorous was the charge of the grenadiers and Highlanders under Rollo that very few of the British were killed or wounded, and the result was that the Governor and his staff were taken prisoners, Dominique was surrendered without further opposition, and Lord Rollo took possession of it for the British Government.

This was the only service performed in the American seas during the year 1761. In the following year greater exploits were performed

in these waters; Spain in the meantime joined France, and war was declared upon that effete nation. Our next theme will be the capture of Martinique and the Havannah, in the operations effecting which, the Montgomerys and the Black Watch, as usual, highly distinguished themselves.

(*To be continued*).

THE FIRST SUTHERLAND FENCIBLE REGIMENT, 1759.

THE recent attempt to deprive the Clan Mackay of the honour of having produced the Sutherland bard, Rob Donn, has naturally drawn attention to the first Sutherland Regiment of Highlanders of which he was a member, and a few facts regarding the regiment may be of interest at this time.

This regiment was one of two raised in Scotland in 1759 for service in Great Britain. The renowned Pitt, afterwards Earl of Chatham, who in later years so justly boasted that he had "sought for merit and found it in the mountains of the north," was the first to suggest the idea.

Britain had suffered reverses abroad, and large drafts were necessary to retrieve her honour. The militia had been raised in England, but owing to the recent disturbances in Scotland it was not thought desirable to extend the system there.

Letters of Service were therefore granted for raising a regiment of Fencibles in the county of Argyll, and a few weeks later, on the 7th of August, similar letters were granted to the Earl of Sutherland to raise a battalion of volunteers, being Highlanders in any county or part of our kingdom of Great Britain.

This order was superseded by one dated 11th August in similar terms, but restricting the recruiting area to the counties of Sutherland and Caithness and places adjacent, known to be well affected. The reason for this is obvious. About that time the Jacobite agents in this country were very active. An invasion from France was threatened, the expedition was being fitted out at Brest, and manifestoes had been prepared for the press, in which, by the use of certain words, Prince Charlie's presence in the country would be known to his supporters. Thanks to Pickle, or other traitors, the British Government was made aware of these movements, and care was taken to confine recruiting to those parts favourable to the Hanoverian cause.

The Letters of Service for raising the regiment are as follows :—

GEORGE R.

Order for raising a Battalion of Highlanders.

Whereas we have thought fit to order a Battalion of Highlanders, to be forthwith raised under your command, which is to consist of nine Companies of four Sergeants, four Corporals, two Drummers, and one hundred private men in each, besides Commission Officers, with two Pipers to the Grenadier Company; which men are not to be sent out of Great Britain, and to be entitled to their Discharge in three years or at the end of the War; these are to authorize you by beat of Drum or otherwise to raise so many Volunteers (being Highlanders) in the counties of Sutherland and Caithness, and in Places adjacent known to be well affected, as shall be wanted to compleat the said Battalion to the above mentioned numbers. And all Magistrates Justices of the Peace, Constables and other our Civil Officers whom it may concern, are hereby required to be assisting unto you in providing Quarters, Impressing Carriages and otherwise as there shall be occasion.

Given at our Court at Kensington this 11th Day of August, 1759, in the thirty-third year of our Reign.

By His Majesty's Command,
BARRINGTON.

To our Right, Trusty, and Welbeloved Cousin, William, Earl of Sutherland, Lieut.-Colonel Commandant of a Batt. of Highlanders, or to the officer appointed to raise men for our said Batt."

Particulars as to the arming of the battalion exist in the following order, but the first portion being in identical terms to the Letters of Service, above quoted, it is unnecessary to repeat.

GEORGE R.

Arms, etc., for a Battalion of Highlanders to be forthwith raised.

Whereas ....

....

Our Will and Pleasure is that out of the Stores remaining within the office of our Ordnance under your charge you cause the Arms, etc., wanting for the use of the said Battalion and mentioned hereunder to be forthwith issued and delivered to the Colonel of the said Battalion or whom he shall appoint to receive them; and you are to take the usual Indents for the same and insert the charge thereof in your next estimate to be laid before the Parliament, and for so doing this shall be as well to you as to all other our officers concerned herein a sufficient warrant.

Given at our Court at Kensington the Tenth Day of August, 1759, in the Thirty-third year of our Reign.

By His Majesty's Command,
HOLDERNESSE.

To our Right, Trusty, and Welbeloved Cousin and Councillor, John Viscount Ligonier, Master General of our Ordnance.

Iron Ramrods, 936; Firelocks with Bayonets and Scabbards, 936; Side Pistols and Straps, 972; Cartouche Boxes and Straps, 936; Halberts, 36; Drums, 18.

The halberts mentioned in the foregoing were for the Sergeants of companies. Within nine days of the Earl's arrival in Sutherland 1500 men reponded to the call to arms, and so great was the military ardour and patriotism that many of the disappointed men followed the regiment to Perth, with the result that the authorities granted permission for a tenth company to be added. General Stewart thus records the impression created by this fine body of men—

"The martial appearance of these men when they marched into Perth in May, 1760, with the Earl at their head, was never forgotten by those who saw them, and who never failed to express admiration of their fine military air. Some old friends of mine who often saw these men in Perth spoke of them with a kind of enthusiasm. Considering the abstemious habits or rather the poverty of the Highlanders, the size and muscular strength of the people are remarkable. In this Corps there was no light infantry company; upwards of 200 men being above five feet eleven inches in height, they were formed into two Grenadier Companies, one on each flank of the Battalion."

The regiment served for four years, during which time its behaviour was irreproachable, and though its duties were monotonous, being confined to garrison work, not a single man was punished. Had the opportunity occurred we may be sure that these men would have shown themselves worthy successors of the "Old Invincibles" of Gustavus.

It is a matter for regret that there does not appear to be a Muster Roll or Pay Sheet of the regiment in existence, unless it be in the possession of the Ducal family, but whether the poet was really an enlisted member of the regiment is open to doubt. Certain it is that Rob occupied a more or less privileged position in the corps, probably akin to that of bard, an interesting survival of ancient times. The story is well known how, while the regiment was stationed at Inverness, a Major Ross, who had recently joined and was a strict disciplinarian, encountered the poet roaming about when the regiment was drilling. Not knowing Rob, he demanded to know to which company he belonged, and was considerably astonished to get the reply "to every company," an answer which enquiries fully explained.

That Rob should join the regiment was not surprising, as among the officers were the following Mackays, viz.:—Lieutenant-Colonel Hugh Mackay of Bighouse, Captain John Mackay of Strathy, and Lieutenants Donald Williamson (Mackay) of Banniskirk, Alexander Mackay, younger of Strathy, and James Mackay of Skerray. It was in the family of the last named that the poet's early years of service were spent.

In 1762 the Seven Years' War was at an end, and France, crippled by the loss of Canada and most of her Indian possessions, was suing for peace, which the Treaty of Paris, signed 10th February, 1763, eventually secured.

Meanwhile orders were issued disbanding both the Argyllshire Fencibles and the Sutherland Highlanders, in the following terms :—

Order and Instructions for disbanding Colonel Campbell's Regiment of the Fencible Men of Argyllshire, and the Earl of Sutherland's Battalion of Highlanders.

GEORGE R.

Whereas we have thought fit to order our Regiment of the Fencible Men of Argyllshire, commanded by our Trusty and Welbeloved Lieutenant-Colonel Dougal Campbell, and our Battalion of Highlanders commanded by our Right, Trusty, and Welbeloved Cousin, William, Earl of Sutherland, to be forthwith disbanded. Our Will and Pleasure is that you, or such person or persons as you shall appoint for this service, do immediately repair to the respective Quarters of the said Corps and disband them accordingly, and that in the disbanding of them the following Rules be observed.

1st. Before such disbanding you are to cause an exact Muster to be taken of the several companies of the said Corps, which you may draw together in the Quarters where they now are, or any other adjacent place as you shall see most convenient ; and you are to give an account of their condition and numbers at the time of the disbanding to our Secretary at War for our Information.

2dly. You are to take care before the disbanding the said Corps that the Quarters of each Company be duly satisfied, as also that the Accounts between the non-commissioned Officers and private Soldiers hereby disbanded and their Officers be made up to the Day of their Discharge, and that they be fully satisfied and paid their arrears or other just pretensions, whereof the said Officers are to produce Acquittances and Discharges from them respectively.

3dly. That care be taken that the Arms delivered out of our Stores of Ordnance and indented for, be returned thither again, and Acquittances taken for the same.

4thly. That care be taken that each non-commissioned Officer and private man hereby to be disbanded be permitted to carry away with him his Cloaths, Belt, and Knapsack which he now wears, and that each private Soldier, Corporal, and Drummer be paid three Shillings for his Sword, which is to be delivered with the other Arms into our Stores of Ordnance ; and we being pleased to allow each Sergeant, Corporal, Drummer, and private Soldier who shall be hereby disbanded fourteen days Subsistence as of our Royal Bounty to carry them home, payment is to be made of the same to each of them respectively out of such monies as shall be advanced for that purpose, and you are to take receipts for the same from each non-commission'd Officer and private man respectively and transmit them to our Paymaster General as Vouchers for the Bounty Money so paid, and to send to our Secretary at War an authentic List attested in the best manner by yourself, or Officers commanding in chief our said Corps of the names of the non-commission'd Officers and private Soldiers so disbanded, and to give them passes in case they shall desire the same, to the places of their former residence, allowing them a convenient time to repair thither, and giving them likewise a strict charge that they do not presume to travel with any arms nor more than three in company upon pain of the severest punishment.

And to the end the said non-commission'd Officers and private Soldiers may be sensible of the care we have taken of them upon their dismission, you are to cause these our directions to be read at the Head of each Company for a more ready Compliance with our Pleasure hereby signified, and see the same be put in Execution.

Given at our Court at St. James's this 31st day of January, 1763, in the third year of our Reign.

By his Majesty's command,

W. ELLIS.

To our Trusty and Welbeloved George Beauclerck, Esquire (commonly call'd Lord Geo. Beauclerck), Lieut.-General of our Forces, or to the person or persons appointed by him for the Service above mentioned.

The regiment thus reduced was the first of the Fencible Regiments raised in Sutherland. The others were the Sutherland Fencibles of 1779, the Sutherland Fencibles of 1793, and the better known Reay Fencibles of 1798, the "brave and honest Reays" of General Lake, whose story has been so well told by Mr. John Mackay of Hereford.

All these regiments did honour to the county of their origin, and it was mainly from the disbanded regiment of 1793 that the gallant 93rd Highlanders, the famous "Thin Red Line," now the 2nd Battalion Argyll and Sutherland Highlanders, was recruited.

Of the 80,000 men raised in the Highlands between the years 1759 and 1814 the county of Sutherland contributed her full share, and there is little doubt that much of this military patriotism was due to the example of that famous Scots Brigade, whose name is writ large in the military annals of Europe, "Mackay's Regiment."

London.   ERIC MACKAY.

TO CORRESPONDENTS.

All Communications, on literary and business matters, should be addressed to the Editor, Mr. JOHN MACKAY, 9 Blythswood Drive, Glasgow.

TERMS OF SUBSCRIPTION.—The CELTIC MONTHLY will be sent, post free, to any part of the United Kingdom, Canada, the United States, and all countries in the Postal Union—for one year, 4s.

THE CELTIC MONTHLY.

MARCH, 1899.

CONTENTS.

OUR NEXT ISSUE.

NEXT month we will give plate portraits, with biographical sketches, of Captain Murdoch Mactaggart, Bowmore, Islay: Messrs. Duncan Davidson of Tulloch, and John M'Kerchar, London.

"LOYAL LOCHABER."—We were pleased to hear Dr. Fraser-Mackintosh, at the Invernessshire Gathering, make such a kindly reference to this delightful work. The book, we are informed, is selling well, and we hope Messrs. Morison Brothers will be called upon soon to issue a second edition.

THE CALEDONIAN MEDICAL SOCIETY have offered a prize of Five Guineas for the best essay on "The Ethnology of the Scottish Gael," not to exceed 20,000 words, and must be written in English. The competition is open to all Highlanders, and papers should be sent to Dr. S. R. Macphail, Derby.

THE CLAN CAMPBELL SOCIETY held their eighth annual festival in the Queen's Rooms, Clifton St., Glasgow, on 27th January. Dr. Gilbert Campbell presided. There was an attendance numbering between five and six hundred, among whom were many prominent clansmen from all parts of the country.

THE CLAN CHATTAN have issued a tastefully got up little volume on the "Proceedings at the Dinner of the Clan in Edinburgh" recently, when Cluny was presented with a handsome shield-salver. The various speeches are given in full, as well as the paper on "Cluny of the '45" which was read at the meeting. We are pleased to notice that the Macphersons have given that venturesome scribbler, Mr. Murray Rose, a rather vigorous handling in the columns of a northern paper for his ill-natured reflections upon the chief of the clan in the '45 rising. No reputation seems safe from the reckless assaults of this amateur historian.

KINTYRE CLUB.—The annual general meeting of this Club was held in the Religious Institution Rooms, Glasgow—Mr. David MacDonald presiding over a large attendance of members. The Treasurer's accounts showed that the Club had expended during 1898 :—In charity, £84 18s. 6d.; in bursaries, £54 7s. 4d.; and in prizes and medals to Kintyre schools, £13 16s. 5d. The funds of the Club now amount to £4816 13s. Mr. Daniel MacMillan was elected president for 1899; and Dr. J. M. MacMillan and Mr. Robert Wyllie were appointed to the two vacancies on the board of directors. The treasurer, Mr. William Ferguson, C.A., and the secretary, Mr. R. Harvey Pirie, LL.D., were re-elected.

THE ROSS-SHIRE GATHERING, which was presided over by Captain Macleod of Cadboll, was a great success.—THE CLAN MACKINNON had also a very successful Re-union. The Rev. Hector Mackinnon presided, and in his spirited address gave excellent reasons to justify the existence of clan societies. Other speakers followed, and a very pleasant evening concluded with an assembly, which was well attended.—THE COUNTY OF SUTHERLAND ASSOCIATION met on the 8th ult., the lecturer being Mr. John Mackay of the *Celtic Monthly*, who spoke on the subject of "Clan Banners, their history and romance." He traced the use of flags from the Ossianic period to Culloden, and referred to the few now remaining of the old clan standards.

CLAN MACKAY AND ROB DONN.—There has been a somewhat excited controversy going on in most of the Highland papers as to whether the Reay Country bard was a Mackay or a Calder. The Rev. Adam Gunn, of Durness, has very cleverly exposed the Calder sham, which was actually evolved from register entries which did not exist. Mr. Hew Morrison has not taken up Mr. Gunn's challenge to produce the Murray *aliases*, and so the great Calder theory shares the fate of many another humbug.

THE MACKAY BANNER controversy has still to be settled. Rector Macbain of Inverness, who poses as a sort of "Gaelic Mogul," some time ago published several insulting references to the rendering which the Rev. Angus Mackay, M.A., gave of the inscription on the ancient banner, and submitted one of his own. Mr. Mackay, however, referred the matter to two of the leading specialists on old lettering in the British Museum, who have declared his version to be correct, and Mr. Macbain's to be a far-fetched theory. Their evidence as to age of the flag proves it to be without doubt the historic *Bratach Bhàn* of the Clan Mackay, and no more belonged to the Grays of Skibo than to the Mikado! After all his spiteful and sneering remarks the "universal arbiter" on all Highland matters has only succeeded in making his vaunted scholarship a subject of general amusement.

THE CLAN MACKAY, through the patriotic exertions of Mr. John Mackay of Hereford, have now ten Gaelic classes formed in the Reay country, attended by 300 pupils, to whom text books were supplied gratis. It has been decided to send a deputation in the autumn to examine these classes and award suitable prizes. A great Highland Gathering is to be held at Tongue, at which handsome prizes will be offered by the clan for pipe music, Highland dancing, and the various athletic events. A large sum will be required to meet the expenses. Subscriptions should be sent to Mr. John Mackay, Hon. Secy., 9 Blythswood Drive, Glasgow.

HOW HECTOR OF MAMORE BECAME A SILENT MAN.

IT is a hard thing for a man who is living in the towns of the south to know what quietness is. For there is no silence at all in the big cities. But in Lochaber a man may bide by himself in places where he will be bothered with nothing but his own company. And if strangers will keep saying that the mountain dwellers are too silent, it is because the folk that write about us come themselves from places where men hustle one another and are so full of little thoughts that they cannot keep from chattering in the ears of each other when they meet. It is the man who will be always speaking that is the weak

GLEN NEVIS HOUSE.

HEADQUARTERS OF THE HIGHLANDERS DURING THE SIEGE OF FORT WILLIAM, MARCH, 1746.

man. And so we have a proof word among ourselves when we wish to know if a man is to be trusted. We say "Can he keep his lips!" We measure a man among the hills not by what he says, but by what he keeps himself from saying.

And there was one man in Lochaber who was more silent than any other. It was Hector Cameron, the keeper who lived among the stags at the back of the Mamore Forest.

Those who have trodden the deep snows that never leave the summit of the Hill of Heaven even on the hottest summer day, and looked down on the great desolations of the Mamore, will know that it is one of the wastes of the world where silence and thunders and solitudes get leave to reign in undisputed possession. And yet, it is not so desolate either. For on its fringes there are some of the bonniest bits of moorland and seaboard that can be seen anywhere.

All along the north lies the Silent Glen of Heaven, and where it leaves off, the line of the Amhuinn Reidh continues to where it flows out of Loch Treig, beyond which lie the lone moors of Rannoch and Corrour. The blue waters of Loch Linnhe on the west from Corpach to Corran, and Loch Leven on the south with a line running on to the Amhuinn Reidh again—that is the circle of Mamore. And Mamore in the good Gaelic means the Great Waste.

This was Hector Cameron's sanctuary. It is

a pleasant place enough so long as you keep to the Glen of Heaven, or by the shores of Linnhe or Leven, where the corn grows and the wee ones laugh. But it was not often that Hector of the Few Words was seen there. His road lay more among the wildernesses of Stob Ban and Sguir Amhuinn and Binnein Mor, where the iolair makes its nest on the beetling crags and the big stags stand in the light of dawn and wake the echoes with a hollow roar.

It is told of a man from Lochiel who was once through the Mamore in the first month of the year but one, that when he came back to Fassifern he was saying to the schoolmaster, that the Mamore must have been the last place that God made when He was going away home tired on the Saturday night.

But Hector of Mamore was not always a silent man. The time was when he would dance a reel and send a laugh round with the wildest lad in Lochaber. And at the piobaireachd on the pipes there was none to beat him. But that was before it all happened.

They say that a woman is at the bottom of everything in the world. And whiles we are for believing it. But at least, it was a woman that made Hector Cameron a silent man and yet, small blame to her. In Lochaber some of us are Catholics and some of us are not. But in Lochaber love counts for more than a man's kirk, and both priests and parsons are chief enough. In sooth there are many houses where

MEALL AN T-SUIDHE, FROM NEVIS BRIDGE.

a man is a Protestant and his wife a Catholic, and the other way of it as well. But for all that, we are peaceable enough; only, when we fall out, there is no bottom to a man's rage.

Hector of Mamore was a sound Protestant, but, as fate would have it, he fell in love with Aileen MacDonell—a sweet little lass of Keppoch—who, like all her family, were good Catholics. In eleven cases out of the dozen there would have been no ado made at all. But Hector's case happened to be the twelfth. And the MacDonells opposed the match. Aileen, they said, must wed one of her own folks. And Hector was sent back one day to Mamore with a curse on his lips and love leaping like fire in his heart. But he had seen Aileen in the wood at Keppoch, and this is what she said—

"Hector, it is I that love you well enough to leave Keppoch for ever for the sake of you And if they will be keeping us apart one way, we can just go about our courting in another."

It was the very word that Hector was wanting her to say—the brave little lass !

"Aileen, my treasure, you will listen now to me. And if it is not brave enough that I am to stand between you and any danger whatever, then may the lightnings of Mamore strike me dumb." And he proceeded to lay before her a plan. For a long while they were at the talking, and then with a last kiss they parted. And they knew that the next time they met it would be by moonlight, and Aileen would be seeing Keppoch no more.

It is a long way for a man to come a courting, from the back of Mamore to Keppoch, whether it be by the track over the hills or round by the road and up the Glen of Heaven. And no man will cross fifteen miles of wild bogland and forest to see a lass for sport alone. And as Hector Cameron walked up the glen the day after he had seen Aileen his mind was full of heavy thoughts.

The glen road, as every Lochaber man knows, stops about ten miles up from the Roaring Mill. After that there is but a rough track along the river leading up to the head of the glen, where the mountains come down on every side to bar the way. But on the eastmost side, through a narrow and fiercesome crack in the hills, the river comes tumbling down in waterfalls and wild cascades, and it is only by creeping along the side of this gully, and high up above the river too, that any man can win out of the glenhead, and find a path that will lead him up the Amhuinn Reidh to Loch Treig.

This beetling path was the only way to Hector Cameron's shieling. A stranger would think that no man could live in that wilderness of solitudes. The French might invade England and a man at the back of Mamore would be none the wiser. In the hard months of winter the folk down at the Fort would walk up with Hector's supplies and leave them in a small cave where the road stops, and when a fine day came round Hector would come down the gully from his shieling and fetch the things home. Home to him meant silence, two brace of dogs—and Mamore. And it was for this that Aileen MacDonell was willing to leave the sweet vale of Keppoch. Indeed, there is no understanding the way of a man and a maid.

When Hector reached the gully on his way home, he began to creep along the face of the cliff on the rocky path that he knew so well. It was almost dark, and a wan, weird light was playing mysteriously away up above the jet black crags. Down below him the river roared in its abyss; and all around him was the gloom of the glenhead. Just when he reached the corner, Something white made him lift his eyes.

BEN NEVIS, FROM CORPACH.

Rare and Interesting Highland Books for Sale.

— ◇ —

Rare and Interesting Clan Histories for Sale.

Mr. John Mackay, Editor, 'Celtic Monthly,' 9 Blythswood Drive, Glasgow, will be glad to forward any of the undernoted books,, on receipt of the price stated (postage extra).

Clan Mackay.--History of the House and Clan of Mackay, by Robert Mackay, Thurso, with Genealogies of all the Chieftain Families, 4to, 30s. 1829.

Clan Mackay.--Life of Lieutenant-General Hugh Mackay of Scoury, Commander-in-Chief, 1689, Colonel of the Scottish Brigade in the service of the States General, by John Mackay, of Rockfield, with Appendix and Portrait, large paper copy, 4to, 10s 6d. 1836.

Macky (John), "The Jacobite Spy," Memoirs of the Secret Services of, during the Reigns of King William, etc.; 8vo, calf, 10s. 1733.

Maclean's Historical and Traditional Sketches of Highland Families and of the Highlands; 12mo. 6s. Dingwall, 1848.

Clan Maclean A History of the Clan Maclean, including a Genealogical Account of the Principal Families, etc., by J. P. Maclean, illustrated with Maps, Portraits, etc., limited edition, 25s. 1889.

Clan Maclean.--An Historical and Genealogical Account of the Clan Maclean from its first Settlement at Castle Duart in the Isle of Mull to the Present Period, by Senachie, 8vo, very scarce, 25s. 1838.

Macdonalds of Keppoch, a Family Memoir of the, by Angus Macdonald, M.D., with Notes by Charles Edward Stuart, Comte d'Albanie, 8vo, cloth, scarce, 25s. 1895. Printed for private circulation, only 150 copies printed.

The Last Macdonalds of Isla, chiefly selected from Original Bonds and Documents sometime belonging to Sir James Macdonald, now in the possession of Charles Fraser-Mackintosh, LL.D., profusely illustrated by fac-simile portraits, &c., very fine, 21s. 1895.

Clan Macdonald, by Rev. A. Macdonald, 570 pages, 40 illustrations, royal 8vo, cloth, gilt top. Volume I. ready, 22s. 3 vols., 55s post free; edition de luxe, 63s per vol.

Life of Flora Macdonald, and her Adventures with Prince Charlie, by the late Rev. Alex. Macgregor, M.A., with an Account of Flora Macdonald's Descendants, their Marriages, Professions, &c., &c., and a Life of the Author. By Alex. Mackenzie, F.S.A. (Scot.) Inverness, 1896. 8vo, cloth, gilt, 2s 6d.

Macdonalds of Glengarry, by Alex. Mackenzie, 5s 6d, 1881.

Macdonalds of Clan Ranald, by Alex. Mackenzie, 5s 6d. 1881.

Clan Chattan.--The Minor Septs of Clan Chattan, by Charles Fraser Mackintosh, LL.D., illustrated with eight coloured plates of clan tartans, and many facsimiles of ancient documents, relics, clan antiquities, &c., printed on finest calandered paper, and handsomely bound, gilt top. 21s. Treats of the following Septs:--Cattanach, Clark, Crerar, Davidson, Farquharson, Gillespie, Gillies, Gow, Maclean or Macbain, Macgillivray, Mackintosh, Macphail, Macpherson, Macqueen, Noble, Shaw.

Macraes.--History and Genealogy of the Clan Macrae, by the Rev. Alex Macrae, B.A., demy octavo, map of Macrae country, numerous illustrations, 21s.

Macgregor.--History of the Clan Gregor, from public records and private collections, by Amelia E. Murray Macgregor, 21s; fine paper copies, 42s.

Macgregors.--Life and Exploits of Rob Roy, and Historical Account of the Clan Macgregor; and Manners, Customs, and History of the Highlanders of Scotland, by Sir Walter Scott, Bart., published at 6s, for 4s, nicely bound, new. 1893.

Mathesons.--Sir James Matheson, of Lewis, Bart., and his descent from the Mathesons of Shiness, by Alexander Mackenzie. F.S.A. (Scot.), privately printed, 8vo, paper, 1s.

Campbells.--In the Press--Crown 4to, Gilt Top, Elegant Binding, 21s.--Argyll's Highlands, or Mac Cailein Mor and the Lords of Lorne, with Traditionary Tales and Legends of the County of Argyll and the Campbells and Macdonalds, by Cuthbert Bede author of "Glencreggan, or a Highland Home in Cantire;" profusely Illustrated, with Annotations by J. Ronald M. Macdonald, of Largie Castle.

Campbell (Lord Archibald).--Records of Argyll. Legends, Traditions, and Recollections of Argyllshire Highlands, collected chiefly from the Gaelic, with notes on the antiquity of the dress, clan colours, or tartans of the Highlanders, printed in a sumptuous style on hand-made paper, and illustrated with 19 exquisite etchings by Charles Laurie; handsome 4to volume, issued to subscribers at 52s 6d, for 30s. 1885.

The 'Red and White' Book of Menzies, a History of the Clan and its Chiefs, by D. P. Menzies, F.S.A., Scot. Numerous portraits, views, and coloured plates of the Tartans, and 41 illustrations in the text. 4to, cloth, Glasgow, 1894, 42s.

Mackenzies History of the Mackenzies. The volume contains several new Family Genealogies, 648 pages. Price 25s net; large paper, 42s.

Chisholms.--History of the Chisholms, with authentic Genealogies of all the Families of the name north and south, 232 pages, demy 8vo, top gilt. Only a very few copies now remain for sale. Demy 8vo, 15s; large paper, 21s

Munros.--History of the Munros of Fowlis, with Genealogies of the Principal Families of that name, to which are added those of Lexington and New England, by Alexander Mackenzie, gilt top, edges uncut, 25s; large paper, 42s.

Monroes of Fowlis.--Doddridge's Life of Colonel Gardner, with an Appendix relating to the Ancient Family of the, 2s 6d. 1817.

Frasers.--History of the Frasers of Lovat, with Genealogies of the principal Families of the name, to which are added those of Dunballoch and Phophacy, by Alexander Mackenzie, gilt top, edges uncut, 25s; larger paper, 42s.

Camerons. History of the Camerons, with Accounts and Genealogies of all the Families of the Name, by Alexander Mackenzie, 8vo, roxburgh binding, gilt top, edges uncut, 25s.

Browne's History of the Highlands, and of the Highland Clans; 1st edition, 4vols, 8vo, cloth, 21s. 1854.

The Clans of the Highlands of Scotland, illustrated by 72 full-length figures in authentic Tartans, with their Armorial Bearings, etc.; 2vols, crown 8vo, halfmorocco, 21s. 1862.

What is my Tartan? or the Clans of Scotland, with their septs and dependents, badges, pipe tunes, slogans, decorations of chiefs, crests, etc., by Frank Adam, F.S.A., Scot. 3s. 3d., post free.

Stewart (Charles).--The Gaelic Kingdom in Scotland: its Origin and Church, with Sketches of Notable Breadalbane and Gleulyon Saints; crown 8vo, cloth, 5s, rare. 1880.

Kintyre.--The White Wife, with other Stories, Supernatural, Romantic, and Legendary, collected and illustrated by Cuthbert Bede; First Edition, sq. fcap. 8vo., orig. cloth, 12s 6d; very rare. 1865.

Young's Anglers' and Sketchers' Guide to Sutherland 2s. 1880.

When he saw It, he slipped—and had he not clutched at a piece of rock in time, it is a dead man that Hector Cameron would have been.

The wraith of Aileen MacDonell stood before him, dancing slowly up and down in mid-air. He could see her pale face all drawn with fear. Her black hair was hanging down over her white shoulders, and the hands of her were stretched out as in deep despair. Round her shining neck was a rosary, and at the end of it hung a crucifix. And through the filmy wraith the man could see all the time the black points of the hill beyond.

Hector stood shaking and without a word. He was waiting. Waiting with a terror in his eyes to see which way the ghost would go. He was not much of a praying man, but it was now he was praying with all his might to God that It might come towards him. But still It only stood and danced gently in mid-air.

Then—It began to recede! Slowly getting further away from him, and dancing all the while with an awesome look of fear on the face of It until It vanished altogether. And Hector knew beyond all doubting that he had seen the ghost of his sweetheart dancing the dance of death.

* * *

A week later he was standing late one night in a wood near Keppoch holding a horse by the bridle. Presently a small, dark figure came creeping stealthily along the path. It was a woman in a dark cloak.

VIEW AT INVERLOCHY

"Aileen!"

"Hector!"

And in another moment they were both on the back of the horse as it galloped at full speed along the road to Inverlochy.

"We are safe now, Aileen, my treasure," whispered Hector.

"Aye, Hector, but why will you look so feared?"

"Feared, lass! I am just the happiest man in Lochaber, and there is no fear at all in me!"

And two lies lay burning on the man's soul after he had spoken.

After a bit he lengthened the stirrups without stopping, for they had a long way to go, and it is only a foolish man that will try to ride a long way with short stirrups. So gathering up the snaffle rein again in his hand he set the horse to an easier gallop.

At Inverlochy the moon was high, and they continued at a canter. At the entrance to the glen, where the road lay like a white ribbon in the moonlight, they dismounted and had ten minutes of a rest. Then remounting they began the long ride up the Glen of Heaven, and now the horse was put at a steady trot. But it was Aileen that did most of the talking, for the love in her heart had driven out all the fear.

The moon was beginning to wane when they reached the waterfall of the Three Sisters, and by the time they had got to the end of the road the dawnlight was moving above the hills like the quivering of the lids of the eye of day. At the first pale flushing of light a chill was sent through the night air like a cold shaft, and somewhere far away in the shadows a grouse cock crowed.

They dismounted and turned the horse loose to find its way home to the Fort. Then began the long rough walk up the stony track to the gully.

"Come, my little one," said Hector with a strange sound in his voice, "in another hour you will be stirring the peats on your own fireside, where no man in Lochaber will venture to vex you."

"Aye, it is glad I am, Hector, that our troubles are all ended, and it is to the other side of the world I would go out of love for you."

And the new day blushed again when it saw the two lovers embracing one another in that wild courting hall.

"Now, Aileen, you will watch me closely and you will follow every step I take."

"Yes, Hector, I will follow."

So the man went first and the brave little lass crept cautiously behind him.

Just when they had reached the corner Hector thought he felt in the air Something white. But though he felt it, he dared not look up. Whatever it was he would defy it and keep quiet for Eileen's sake. But there was a mighty shaking all the while in the limbs of him as he crept on.

There was a scream—a wild piercing scream at his back, that made the blood freeze in his veins!

"Ah! ah!! ah!!! Hector—do you see It? A-a-a-ah!"

And when he turned quickly to clutch at the

girl his hand closed on empty air. And the next moment he saw her falling down, down, down into the awful darkness below. O God! how he strained his ears to listen! Twice he heard a cruel thud and twice a pitiful cry coming up to him. And then—the murmur of the water filled the glen again with an audible silence. And the day broke!

* * * * *

That was what made Hector of Mamore a silent man. Every time he came down to the world he had to pass the corner of the precipice, and it is said that he never passed it in the dark without seeing a white light that danced up and down. It was his curse. And it made him a speechless man to the end of his days.

TORQUIL MACLEOD.

THE SOCIAL CONDITION OF THE HIGHLANDS SINCE 1800.

BY A. J BEATON, F.S.A. SCOT., F.G.S.E.

(*Continued from page 85*).

VIII.—EMIGRATION.

" From the lone shieling on the misty island,
Mountains divide us, and a waste of seas,
But still the blood is strong, the heart is Highland,
And we in dreams behold the Hebrides."

BETWEEN the years 1773-1775, 30,000 persons from various parts of the Highlands crossed the Atlantic, but it was not until about the beginning of the present century that the tide of emigration reached its full height, when the crofters were swept away to make room for the wealthy sheep farmers from the southern dales who invaded the Highlands, and offered an enormous increase for the summer "shielings" of the poor crofters. The late Dr. Carruthers, of Inverness, quotes an instance in which a sheep farmer from the south offered no less a rent than £350 for a cattle grazing belonging to the men of Kintail who only paid an annual rent of £15 for it. To impecunious lairds such temptations were beyond their power to resist.

"Then it was that the more active and enterprising of the people had emigrated; and the few that remained squatted down in lethargic contentment, so long as their miserable patches of half cultivated lands yielded them a few potatoes and sufficient corn for some meal, with an occasional shoal of herrings throwing themselves within the weirs of the lochs; and thus the people struggled on in that lethargic manner,

never endeavouring to elevate or improve themselves above the customs and manners of their forefathers. They married and multiplied; the crofts were sub-divided, and additional huts thrown up to accomodate an ever increasing population, which, notwithstanding the moderately steady drain of emigration and military employment, still went on growing till the townships failed to support a population now double that of its original settlers. No opportunity was given for spreading out from their confined area; and as they depended wholly on potatoes as their staple food, which now failed them, in 1846, when the destitution crisis began and became so unequalled for intensity, and which involved both chief and clan, landlord and tenant in irretrievable embarassment and ruin." And though the immediate distress was mitigated by the generosity of the British public, its effects are still more or less chronic; and ever and anon the sad case of human destitution and starvation occur, and will continue to do so, until permanent remedial measures are introduced that will for ever place it beyond the possibility of recurring.

The natural aversion Highlanders have to emigrate, further suggests that some improvement of their condition at home should be first attempted before the adoption of the extreme measure—emigration; for when the late Sir James Matheson of Lewis offered to cancel all arrears of rent, forgive all debts, purchase the stock, and provide a free passage to Canada, to any of his tenants willing to emigrate, his generous offer was only accepted by a few. As I have already observed, men who emigrate and have their whole soul concentrated on "The old country," cannot be expected to labour with that energy which is necessary to cope with the difficulties of a new country, and to make them successful in proportion to the troubles they have undergone.

Dr. Norman Macleod illustrates this in that graphic and pathetic style so peculiar to him. "To Highlanders," he says, "emigration has often been a very passion—their only refuge from starvation. Their love of country has been counteracted on the one hand by the lash of famine, and on the other by the attraction of a better land opening up its arms to receive them with the promise of abundance to reward their toil. They have chosen, then, to emigrate, but what agonising scenes have been witnessed on their leaving their native land? The women have cast themselves on the ground, kissing it with intense fervour. The men, though not manifesting their attachment by such violent demonstrations on this side of the Atlantic, have done so in a still more impressive form in the colonies—whether wisely or not is another question—by retaining their native language and cherishing feelings of the warmest affection for the country which they still call 'Home.'"

In his "Reminiscences of a Highland Parish," Dr. Macleod, in describing the departure of some emigrants, says:—"Among the emigrants from 'the parish' many years ago was the piper of an old family which was broken up by the death of the last laird. Poor 'Duncan Piper' had to expatriate himself from the house which had sheltered him and his ancestors. The evening before he sailed he visited the tomb of his old master, and, playing the family pibroch while he slowly and solemnly paced round the grave, his wild and wailing notes strangely disturbed the silence of the lonely spot where his chief lay interred. Having done so, he broke his pipes, and laying them on the green sod, departed to return no more."

THE "CAS CHROM," OR OLD HIGHLAND HAND PLOUGH.

IX.—INDUSTRIES.

AGRICULTURE.

The Highlands of Scotland, being a purely agricultural and pastoral country, and its prosperity closely linked with those industries, we should naturally expect that the development of agricultural and grazing pursuits would be the chief aim of its inhabitants, and that numerous experimental farms and agricultural colleges should be scattered all over the country, but it is not so. The Highland and Agricultural Society, established over one hundred years ago, undoubtedly has done much good, and to some extent has stimulated farmers to practise improved methods of husbandry; but the local associations, or farmers' societies, have done little more than create a wholesome rivalry among the few cattle breeders, and it is only in some localities here and there that experimental work has been carried on with anything like scientific precision.*

° In this respect the Welsh are far in advance of us, for this year (1898) a fully equipped experimental farm has been established in connection with the North Wales University College. Bangor, which has only been in existence 16 years.

(To be continued)

JOHN MACGREGOR, CRIEFF.

MANY notable members of the Clan Gregor have appeared in our "Gallery," but hitherto no representative of the name resident in the Macgregor country has been given. It therefore gives us pleasure this month in honouring that popular and respected Highlander, Mr. John Macgregor of Crieff. There is perhaps no one of the name so well known in Perthshire as the subject of this brief sketch Mr. Macgregor was born at Glenquaich, Perthshire, on 15th August, 1830, his father being from Lochearnside, and his mother a Crerar—a sept of Clan Chattan very numerous in the glen sixty years ago. In his boyhood he was fonder of the excitements of archery and shinty contests than of the dominie's instruction. After leaving school he occupied several situations, until in 1864 he came to Ochtertyre as head keeper to Sir Patrick Keith Murray, Bart., in whose service he remained till recently, when he retired. Being in charge of the grounds, which were open to the public and visited by thousands of pleasure seekers annually, he was widely known and popular. Mr Macgregor comes of a gifted race, being himself a poet of no mean repute, and cousin to that talented Highlander, Mr. Duncan Macgregor Crerar of New York, whose name is a household word among Gaels in Canada and America. We may fitly conclude this brief sketch by quoting a few lines sent by Mr. Crerar to his kinsman on his birthday :—

Ah, many years have gone since we
Two merry boys together,
Did gaily rove o'er fell and lea
And gambolled in the heather :
Free were our hearts from wordly care,
Free too they were from sorrow,
As we to-day our joys did share,
So shared we on the morrow.

Though wide since then between us two
Has rolled the roaring ocean,
Our friendship has but grown more true,
And deeper our devotion ;
Oft has my exiled heart been cheered,
By tokens of thy giving,
Reminders some of kin endeared,
Those gone before, those living.

A TOAST: "TO THE HIGHLANDS."

HERE'S a health to Highland bonnets,
Here's a health to Highland men,

Here's a health to the lads o' the kilts and
the plaids,
From the mountain and the glen !

To the lads o' the thews and sinews ;
To the lads o' the brawn and thigh ;
To the lads who were bred on the bannocks o' meal
In the land for which they'll die ;
To the men o' the croft and shieling ;
To the men o' the oar and sail ;
To the leal-warm heart and the leal-warm hand
O' the friendship-loving Gael.

Here's a health to Highland fellowship,
A health to Highland cheer ;
To the light o' heart and the lithe o' limb
In the home o' the mountain deer !

To the lads o' the pibroch music
That rouses the heart to fire,
With the tender tale and the plaintive wail
O' the songs that souls inspire ;
To the lads o' the Highland schottische,
The reel and the Highland fling ;
To the coronach moan and the bonnie strathspeys
That the pipes and violin sing.

Here's a health to Highland bonnets,
To the lads o' the dirk and targe—
Oh ! the foemen feel the might o' the steel
In the cataract o' their charge !

In every loch there's a spirit
As dark as its depth below ;
In every glen and lonely ben
There are legends of long ago ;
And they tell them still in the twilight,
In the peat fire and the mist,
When the pine-tree sobs to the wail o' the wind
And the children o' nature list.

Here's a health to Highland bonnets,
Here's a health to Highland bros.,
To the land o' peat and the land o' heath,
And land where whisky *grows*!

To the lads o' the floods and torrents
And rivers rushing free ;
To the lads o' the speech that's music,
And deep as the sough o' the sea ;
To the banished sons o' the mountains,
And over the earth they roam,
But they hear the streams and torrents, *in dreams
When their spirits wander home.*

Here's a health to Highland bonnets,
To the lads afar that roam ;
To the land they love and will ever love,
And the land that's aye their home !

To the children of clans and chieftains
Of a former pride gone by ;
To the stalwart man and the red-cheek'd maid
Of the dark romantic eye ;
To the men who have died for country,
And proved their right to the soil ;
To the hardy sons o' the hardy north,
The men who can fight and toil.

Here's a health to Highland bonnets,
Here's a health in Highland song,
To the men o' bone and the kindly heart,
To the true men and the strong !

BERNARD GEORGE HOARE.

JOHN MACGREGOR.

GILLEASBUIG MAC-NA-CEARDADH.

Is ann le cridhe trom, smuainnach a tha
sinn a' cur an cèill d'ar luchd-leughaidh
gun do chaochail an Gàidheal fiùghail
Gilleasbuig Mac-na-Ceàrdadh, clo-
bhuailtear a' mhìosachain so. Ged a bha
e gearan ré na bliadhna so chaidh, agus
gu sònraichte ré a' gheamhraidh le cuing-
analach cha robh beachd aig a chàirdean gu'n
robh an t-eug cho teann air. Chaochail e air
a cheud là de 'n mhìos so chaidh, aig aois
ochd agus dà fhichead bliadhna.

Rugadh 'athair agus a mhàthair ann an
"Heath ghlas an fheòir" agus ged a rugadh
am fear nach mairionn ann an Glaschu bu
Ghaidheal e gu 'chùl, agus b' Heach e na
chainnt 's na cho fhaireachdainn. Bha
'athair na chlo-bhuailtear ann an Glaschu,
far an do chuir e suas air a laimh fhèin
anns a' bhliadhna 1818. 'Nuair a
chaochail e anns a' bhliadhna 1870 cha robh
Gilleasbuig òg ach na ghiullan maoth, ach
chuir e dhruim fo 'n eallaich gu duineil
agus ann am beagan bhliadhnachan uidh
air n-uidh fhuair e suas am bruthach.
Chaidh e air imrich do bhùth bu mhotha,
far an do chuir e suas innleachdan clo-
bhualaidh ùr agus annasach, a thug an
comas dha an tromlach de na leabhraichean Gàidhlig a chaidh a bhuileachadh
oirnn ré ioma bliadhna air ais a chlò-
bhualadh gu snasmhor, comhlionta. Bha e
fhèin na dheagh sgoilear Gàidhlig agus bha
bhlàth 'sa bhuil sin air gach leabhar Gàidhlig
a thàinig troimh làmhan. Tha grinneas a
làimh ri fhaicinn anns an leabhar òran eireachdail sin ris an abrar an "t-Oranaiche," an t-aon
luach peighinn Gàidhlig a's fearr a chaidh riamh
a bhuileachadh air Clann nan Gaidheal. Am
measg nan leabhraichean Gàidhlig a chlo-bhuail
e tha "Laoidhean Spioradail" leis an Urramach
G K. Mac-Callum, "An t-Eileanach" le Iain
MacPhàidein, "Clàrsach an Doire" le Niall
MacLeòid, "An Celtic Garland," agus "Leabhar
na Céilidh" le "Fionn," "Baird Uist" leis an
Urramach G. Mac Dhomhnuill, "Eachdraidh
Beatha Chriosd" leis an Urramach Iain Mac-
Ruaraidh, " Leabhar Urnuigh na h-Eaglais
Shasunnaich ann an Gaidhlig " "Dàin agus
Orain a' Bhàird Ilich," "Laoidhean Gobhainn
na h-Earradh," cho math ri iomadh leabhar
luchmhor Beurla a tha buntainn ri eachdraidh
"Thìr nam Beann."

'Nuair a chaidh an Comunn Heach a
chuir air chois ann an Glaschu anns a
bhliadhna 1862, bha ainm seann Ghilleasbuig
agus Ghilleasbuig òig air an càradh air clàr a'
a' chomuinn agus bho sin cha robh anns a'
chomunn fear a bu dhìlse dha, no a rinn uiread

air a shon. Bha e 'na cheann-suidhe air a'
Chomunn Ileach agus na Iar-cheann-suidhe aig
Comunn Gàidhlig Ghlaschu. B' e h-aon de
luchd-dreuchd a' Mhòid Ghaidhlealaich, agus
Comunn Earraghaidheil. Bhuineadh e do
dh' Eaglais Chaluim Chille, agus bha e na riagh-
lar anns an eaglais sin ré iomadh bliadhna,
agus cha robh ceangailte rithe fear a b'
fheàrr ainm na 'b' àirde cliù. Bha e da-
rireadh air thùs 's air thoiseach anns gach
deagh oibre, agus cha do dhiùlt e cuideachadh
riamh le cùis no aobhar a bha e meas a bhiodh a
chum math a luchd-dùthcha.

Cha robh e na inghnadh mata 'nuair a
thàinig an là anns an robh e ri bhi air a chàradh
fo 'n fhòid gu'n do thionail na Gaidheil ás gach
cèarna de 'n bhaile gu meas a chur air a chliù, is
am bron airson a chall a nochdadh. Cha robh
Comunn Gaidhealach an Glaschu nach do chuir
h-aon no dha a dh' ionnsuidh a thòrraidh, oir bha
iad uile eòlach air mar Ghaidheal teò-chridheach
fialaidh. Chuir an Comunn Ileach agus an
Comunn Gàidhlig cho math ri càirdean eile
blàth-fhleasgan eireachdail air uachdar na ciste-
mhairbh. Air blàth-fhleasg nan Ileach bha na
facail so—"Gilleasbuig Mac-na-Ceàrdadh, ceann-
suidhe a' Chomuinn Ilich. Sàr mhac an deagh-
athar. Gàidheal blàth-chridheach, suaireeil 'aig

an robh cridhe fial 'an com na céile, bithidh a
chuimhne buan-mhairionn am measg Chlanna
nan Gaidheal."

Am measg an luchd dàimh 's nan dlùth-
chàirdean aig an tòrradh bha ceathrar mhac an
fhir nach mairionn—balachain mhaoth - agus a
bhràithrean-céile, an t Urramach Iain D. Mac-
Neill, Chaladair, an Lighiche Maclain à Heath,
agus Seumas Izat   Bha an t-Olladh Urramach
Iain Mac 'Illeathain, ministear Eaglais Chaluim
Chille aig ceann na seirbheis ann an tigh a'
bhròin, agus rinn an t-Urramach Iain D. Mac-
Neill ùrnuigh Ghàidhlig aig an uaigh fhosgailte.
Cha robh sùil thioram anns a chladh, no cridhe
mu 'n uaigh nach do thaisich 'nuair a ghuidh e
gu 'm bitheadh Dia tròcaireach dhaibh san a
bha fo bhròn, agus gu 'm bitheadh e, a reir a
gheallaidh, na chéile do 'n bhantraich agus
'na athair do na dilleachdain, a toirt dhaibh
" maise an àite luaithre, oladh aoibhneis an àite
bròin, agus éideadh mholaidh an ait' spiorad
airsneil."

Dh' fhàg am fear nach mairionn bantrach,
aon nighean, agus ceathrar mhac ga chaoidh,
agus tha sinn cinnteach nach 'eil neach a
leughas so nach guidh gu 'm bi Dia fhein maille
riu aig an àm so, agus cha 'n 'eil Gaidheal a b'
aithne ar caraid nach cuir clach na chàrn.
Faodaidh sinn a ràdh gu cinnteach -

" Dh' fhalbh cùl-taice na Gàidhlig
An là 'chaidh a chàradh fo 'n fhòid."

FIONN.

MINOR SEPTS OF CLAN CHATTAN.

BY CHARLES FRASER-MACKINTOSH, LL.D.

No. XVIII.—THE "KITH AND KIN" OF CLAN
CHATTAN.

MR. ALEXANDER MACOMIE, in
Glenshee, was, in 1693, one of the
patriotic protestors against the English
opponents of the Scots Darien Scheme; and
was father of Elizabeth MacOmie, whom
the Rev. Lachlan Shaw mentions as wife of
Captain Duncan Mackintosh, 3rd son of the
third Borlum. Being my great-great-grand
parents, I must be excused for noticing that
with the bride came from Glenshee to Inverness,
some of her name, who settled chiefly in the
heights of Borlum, in the Fealmi now called
Drumashie; and of them descended the Mac-
Omies in Balnagaig of Dunain, the late Mr.
Alexander Mackintosh, retired teacher, for many
years resident at Culcabock, and others now

named Mackintosh, but known amongst themselves and neighbours as MacOmies.

III.—Mackintoshes of Dalmunzie.   They
descend from Angus Oig, 3rd son of Angus, 6th
Mackintosh.   They removed to Perthshire, and
since 1502 have been proprietors of Dalmunzie.
Duncan Mackintosh, of Dalmunzie, is found as
proprietor, and signs the Bond of Service to
Mackintosh, as his chief, along with MacOmie
of Glenshee, as formerly mentioned.   **Three**
generations bring us to John, who, in 1665,
with three of his sons, appear supporting Mackintosh in the field in Badenoch and Lochaber.
Two years later he supports his chief under the
following circumstances :—

" In September, 1667, a party of Lochaber
men came down to Glenisla, about the time
Mackintosh had married Edzell's daughter, and
took away a spreath of goods from Edzell's
tenants.   Mackintosh took this, as it really was, a
great affront, and resolved to repair Edzell's loss,
or have full satisfaction from the actors.   After
a deal of time was lost, and with several crosses,
he sets out for Lochaber, accompanied by Invercauld, Aberarder, Corrybrough Mor, Inverey,
Nuid   younger, Balnespick, Dalmunzie, the
Tutor of Dunmaglass, and others -in all, 300
able men and marched from Garva, in Brae
Badenoch, to Brae Lochaber, where his tenants
of Glen Roy and Glen Spean, to the number of
six score, meet him in good order; and, in
December, kept his first Steward Court on the
lands of Keppoch, and having gotten all due
obedience in that place, thereafter caused restore
the pre-mentioned spreath, which Huntly's
tenants lately before had taken out of Glenisla."

It was on the above occasion that Mackintosh
appealed to the Earl of Mar, hereditary friend
of Mackintosh, who, in reply, addressed to him
the following letter, the spelling being partly
modernized :-

" MUCH HONOURED COSEN,

In obedience to your intreaty, Sir, I have
written to Invercauld, to take alongst with himself,
my whole vassals and feuars in Braemar, Strath
Dee and Glengairne to attend you, and accompany
him in what you have to do in Loughaber.   And
as this is the best and most effectual order I can
send them to make intimation hereof, as my will
by Invercauld, who is my Bayliffe in this country,
so shall I be ready, Sir, to witness my respects to
you in a greater manner when occasion offers, Sir,
your most affectionate cousin to serve you.

(Signed) J. MAR.

TILLYFOUR, 26th November, 1667."

Addressed—
" For my much Honoured Cosen, the Laird of
Mackintosh, these."

The Farquharsons, who accompanied Mackintosh in this expedition to Lochaber, included

Invercauld, Invercy, and Monaltrie from Aberdeenshire, and Mackintosh of Dalmunzie from Perthshire, and the prominent and valuable assistance given by the Farquharsons on that and other occasions is gratefully remembered to this day, and heartily acknowledged.

One of the family, Robert Mackintosh, advocate, was for some time Governor of the York Buildings Company ; and a later member, Lachlan Mackintosh, was for many years editor of the *Morning Post*. The present representative is Mr. Charles Hills Mackintosh, who, though a resident in England, is an enthusiastic clansman, and justly proud of representing a family which, even two hundred years ago, the Kinrara historian describes as having " flourished a long time in great account and estimation."

IV.—The Toshes, or Toshachs, Glennies, and MacGlashans, etc.—The Toshes, the oldest cadets of the house of Mackintosh, breaking off before 1220, being descended of Edward, son of Shaw, 2nd Mackintosh, settled in Perthshire, and for a considerable period held a good position in Monzievaird, Culcrief, Pittenzie, and Glentilt.

In 1599, Lachlan Mackintosh of Mackintosh is entrusted by them—then sore pressed by powerful absorbing neighbours, the Drummonds of Perth and the Murrays of Atholc—with the custody of their title deeds. This inventory, including some very ancient documents, came into my hands some years ago, at the cost of a few pence.

In 1450, Andrew Toshach grants the lands of Brewlands and others to the Monastery of Inchaffray. In 1502, Finlay Toshach is described as Thane of Glentilt, his lands extending to three davochs. In 1509, Andrew Toshach, upon his own resignation, gets a new grant of the free Barony of Monzievaird and free forestry of Glentorade. In 1596, Duncan Toshach of Pittenzie is mentioned, and as early as 1371 Eugenius, Thane of Glentilt. Connected with the Toshes, or Toshachs, were the old family called the sons of Adam, first Ayson, latterly Esson.

The Glennies. This family, once influential on either side of the Aberdeenshire Grampians, has in course of time disappeared from their original duchas. Many rose to a high position in England, in the church, army, and law. Amongst them may be named that learned scholar and good Highlander, Mr. J. Stuart Glennie, who cherishes the connection of his family with the Clan Chattan.

The MacGlashans, as well as the MacKerrachers, are considered to be of Clan Chattan.

[CONCLUDED.]

LETTER TO THE EDITOR.

THE CHIEFSHIP OF CLAN DAVIDSON.

NEW YORK.

DEAR MR. EDITOR—In the *Celtic* for this month I notice a letter from "Quebec" in which, speaking for himself and a large number of the Aberdeenshire and Badenoch Davidsons, he states that Tulloch's position as Chief of Clan Dhai is not beyond dispute. Does Mackintosh, the High Chief, exercise undisputed sway over Clan Chattan? Ask the Macphersons. Does Queen Victoria, the most beloved of Britain's sovereigns, reign so supreme even in her Island Home, that not a jar is felt? Mark the spasms of dissent which ascend from Old Erin and the occasional growl emitted by Merry England. No, dissenters (called "kickers" by the Americans) appeared almost at the opening of the Garden of Eden. They will flourish to the crack of doom. In many respects they are as essential to healthy progress as salt is to meat. Scotland owes much of her virility to this essence. If it were not for the "pin pricks" of the kickers our self-sufficiency as a people would lead to retrogression, and mark the beginning of that long and silent march to the tomb of dead races. I thank "Quebec" for coming kicking into the peaceful forum of the *Celtic*, for thereby we may be enabled to more firmly establish the right man in the right place.

"Quebec" wants proofs produced in support of Tulloch's claims. That he comes of the main branch of the clan all writers on the subject have freely admitted. Before the destructive fire which occurred in his castle some fifty years ago, documentary proofs were in evidence of an honourable family history extending backwards over several centuries. Happily, these can still be verified to a certain extent from the annals of another country. Some of Tulloch's ancestors performed distinguished services to the King of France, a land which, in days gone by, excelled in the art of burnishing Highland steel. But, although the Scots illustrated the quality of their blades, before they could be ennobled they had to prove their descent noble for at least six generations prior to July, 1620. This they did as will be shown by the " Livre d'Or " in the public archives of France.

It is the descendant of these men whom "Quebec" would have the Canadian Davidsons desert for the line of Seumas Laghach, the name by which the last Davidson of Invernahavon was commonly called. Well, there is no accounting for tastes. If such is their choice I will put them on the trail. The great-grandson of Seumas Laghach—John Macpherson) of Invernahavon—was living in 1758. But I shall venture to assert that the other Davidsons will have none of a line whose sire was ashamed of his name, thereby forfeiting whatever rights he had to the chiefship. Let that line rest in the oblivion into which Seumas crept. We want live men for chiefs, men who are proud of their name and who will abide by their clansmen through storm and sunshine. Such are the Davidsons of Tulloch. In those days in which England is trying to wrench the very name from off Alban's door, let us stand fast by Tulloch, one of a gallant band battling against Sassanach approach. Too many, alas, of these sheltering mountains, among which the Gael was bred and nurtured, have already passed into possession of the stranger.

12th January, 1893.   MAC PHAIL.

THE RIVER NAVER.

THE following verses were composed by the late George Mackay of Farr, Sutherland, upwards of fifty years ago. George left his native place when a young man and settled in Edinburgh, where he composed this poem. After some years' residence in this city he built a house in his native hamlet of Farr—the first slated house in the district—where he generally spent his annual holidays. It was in 1854 I first made his acquaintance, and our friendship continued until his death in 1863, when he died at Farr, aged 54. He was a very intelligent man, and "nature's gentleman." He was a genial and warm-hearted clansman, and many were the pleasant hours we passed together. His daughter, Mrs. Mackay, gained the second prize for Gaelic reading at the competition held at Farr by the Clan Mackay last autumn. The verses are of considerable merit, and I trust *Fionn*, or some other of your gifted contributors, may

A GLIMPSE OF STRATHNAVER AT SYRE.

favour your readers with a Gaelic translation

Edinburgh.   ALEXANDER MACKAY.

THE Dee, the Don, and bonnie Doon,
  Have all been sung with favour,
But ne'er a lyre has yet been tun'd,
  To sing my Highland Naver ;

But thou dear wild romantic stream,
  My rustic muse inspiring,
Shall yet be sung in numbers sweet,
  Till all shall gaze admiring.

Thy varied scenes for every mood
  Some new delight presenting,
Relieving care and cheating woe,
  And pleasure still augmenting.

When tyrants' laws—enforced by knaves
  Proud, cruel, self-conceited—
Have lash'd my soul to frantic rage,
  I've to thy banks retreated.

Thy headlong torrent rushing down
  To the exhaustless ocean,
Has with my feelings harmonised
  In fierce and wild commotion.

I've followed moodily thy course,
  Till through some valley wending ;]
I've felt my heart with thy mild flow
  To gentler feelings bending.

Again at peace with all mankind,
  My mind with joy elated,

I've gazed with rapture on the scene
  While on thy margin seated.

Beneath the speckled silvery tribe,
  Their sportive play pursuing,
Transporting me to youthful days
  Ere grief or care ensuing.

Around a thousand fragrant flowers
  Thy verdant bank adorning,
All glistening with the crystal dew
  They kiss the lord of morning.

Thy shady groves on every side
  With sweetest music ringing,
The little warblers to engage
  Each other's love are singing.

Thy ambient heath-clad hills and knowes,
  With crimson bells abounding—
The startled deer and nimble roe
  Across their summits bounding.

Far up thy course the mountain peaks,
  The distant skies embracing,
The eagles in their rugged clefts
  A sure retreat possessing.

Though now far off from thee I roam,
  My love shall never waver ;
Thy scenes are graven on my heart,
  My native Highland Naver !

CAPTAIN MURDOCH MACTAGGART.

MRS. MURDOCH MACTAGGART.

THE CELTIC MONTHLY:

A MAGAZINE FOR HIGHLANDERS.

Edited by JOHN MACKAY, Glasgow.

No. 7. Vol. VII.]　　　　　APRIL, 1899.　　　　　[Price Threepence.

CAPTAIN MURDOCH MACTAGGART.

THERE is not a better known man in Islay than Captain Murdoch Mactaggart, Solicitor and Bank Agent, Bowmore. Born on the 15th August, 1862, at Fern Cottage, near Bowmore—the birthplace also of Pattison, the poet—he has spent most of his life in his native island. He comes of a family devoted for generations to agriculture, several of his relations having been well-known gentlemen farmers in Islay, while some of the best worked farms in the island at present are in the hands of near relatives. His only brother is the respected minister of Glenelg Parish, Inverness-shire.

Mr. Mactaggart was educated at the Bowmore School, which in the course of its history has sent forth a large number of scholars who have made their mark in the different professions, conspicuous among them being the Rev. Professor Taylor of the Edinburgh University, and that enthusiastic Highlander, the Rev. Dr. Blair of Edinburgh.

On leaving school Mr. Mactaggart entered the office of the late Mr. Peter Chisholm, a gentleman who united in his own person almost all the public appointments in the island, and whose eminent business qualifications and ripe experience were in the highest degree helpful in the training of the young clerk. In 1884 he entered the Edinburgh office of the North British and Mercantile Insurance Company, but in the following year, on the death of Mr. Chisholm, he was offered most of the appointments which the latter had held, and, though it cost him a pang to turn aside from what promised to be a very successful career in the insurance line, he accepted the offer.

To enumerate his present offices is no easy task: he is a Solicitor, Agent for the Royal Bank of Scotland, Clerk of the Islay District Committee of the County Council, Clerk to the Parish Councils and School Boards of the two Parishes of Kilarrow and Kilchoman, Sheriff Clerk Depute, J.P. Clerk, etc. As may be inferred from the number of his offices, he is an excellent man of business, and possesses the entire confidence of the Boards under whom he serves. On the death of Mr. M'Lullich two years ago he was offered, but declined, the Procurator Fiscalship of Argyllshire. In politics Mr. Mactaggart is a Liberal Unionist, and at the General Election of 1895 acted as Agent in Islay for Mr. Nicol, M.P. He is an enthusiastic volunteer, and is Captain of the local company of Argyll and Bute Volunteers, whose efficiency has twice within the last three years gained them the Regimental Trophy. An elder in the Bowmore Parish Church, he has represented the Presbytery of Islay in the General Assembly.

Mr. Mactaggart is married to a daughter of the Rev. John M'Gilchrist, the respected minister of Kilarrow. She belongs to a family who have gained the highest academic honours, one of her brothers being the cultured minister of Fodderty, and a younger brother having within the last few years carried off about a score of medals in his medical classes at the Edinburgh University. Mrs. Mactaggart has herself taken the degree of LL.A. of St. Andrews.

LINES ADDRESSED TO MRS. BLACKIE.

WHEN thoughts of thee my spirit fill,
　　A finer essence they distil,
　　　Then all things seem so calm and clear
Because thou art so very dear.
Tell me, dear heart, for thou dost know,
Why is it that I love thee so?

Blindly we walk on by the mind,
By love alone soul-sight we find,
This missing, we have surely lost
The jewel rare of highest cost.
Tell me, dear love, for thou dost know
Why is it that I love thee so?

Oh, subtle power, though unseen,
More truly felt, yea, doubly keen,
More real thou than ought we see
Because thou art so dear to me.
Tell me, dear heart, for well you know,
It is because I love you so.

ROBINA FINDLATER.

Jess of Culreigrein.

—:o:—

A TRUE STORY OF THE HEBRIDES.

—:o:—

CHAPTER I.—THE PARTING.

IT was a straggling line of a dozen or more crofts, which lay, as the name signified, "At the back of the Sun." Across a narrow ford, the open sea thundered on the white-shelled shore of Mellost. Southward, some two miles distant, stood the capital, with its several streets and innumerable stores, its court-house, its five churches, and its great turreted castle, flanked by the rocky headland of Arnish, where an arm of the Minch, lulled from its turbulency to a lake of glass, formed the most beautiful natural harbour in the three kingdoms. Eastward, stretched a road, which terminated at the Point of Eye. Westward, twelve miles of boggy moorland separated where the wide Atlantic washed the sands of Barvas.

It was here, at Culreigrein, the lovers parted, while the kindly shades of dusk deepened to cover their last embraces, and the wintry wind blew shrilly and drowned the maiden's sighs. For this was their first severance since they had plighted their troth at this very ingle, when Ewan Morrison came back from the East Coast fishing, where all the fascinations of the fair maids of Wick had failed to banish from his memory the homely grace of Jess Maclean.

True, his sweetheart's charm was not that she was beautiful; for the figure of Jess was short and sturdy rather than *petite* and delicate, her shoulders already a trifle bent by the burden of many a stack of peats from the moors to the little homestead which she shared with her aged father, and of which she performed all the multifarious duties of crofter and housewife in one. What if her cheek betrayed somewhat the harass of over-work, combined with the rough vigour of health inured to storm and sunshine, and her large dark eyes that melancholy, which seems to come naturally to these far dwellers by the sea. What cared Ewan for peach-bloom complexion or sparkling eye when he had discovered the truest heart in all the island to beat in the bosom of Jess Maclean?

And who so comely in the eyes of Jess as the stalwart Ewan, so tall and straight and gallant to look upon in his sailor uniform of blue? For Ewan was one of the envied body of Royal Naval Reserve, the seamen's volunteer force so dear to the ambition of the Gaelic fishermen, and whose badge was a sure passport to their women's hearts.

But now those blissful four weeks of courtship were over, in which Jess had been wont to kiss good-bye to her lover each day as he went on his way so blithely to drill at the battery half a mile distant; or, when evening came, to pass a halcyon hour over Jess's peat fire on his walk homeward, watching her nimble fingers ply her knitting-needles, while he recounted stories of the mainland, or now and then joined Jess in crooning some plaintive Gaelic melody, while the old father, in his great chair on the other side of the hearth, dozed and nodded approval in turn. To-morrow there would be no such happy hour as this, for Ewan was to join the haddock fishing fleet which would sail out from the Broad Bay at early dawn.

It might be many days, even weeks, ere they would so enjoy each other's society again.

Ewan's home lay six miles farther in the country, and the strong young lover was not one to neglect duty for pleasure when the harvest of the sea lay waiting a rich recompense for hours of danger and toil. And now each undertaking of his willing hands meant a step nearer the fulfilment of wedded happiness; for though the little croft, of which Jess was sole mistress, stood ready to acknowledge him master, Ewan would have scorned to come to any maid without that competence, however small, which should give an added worth to his advent.

"And it is not long that you must be thinking, Jess, my woman," he adjured, as they clasped hands at Jess's door for the twentieth time, "for it iss you that will be saying when I will be coming back that it iss a ferry good thing whateffer that there will be the haddock fishing to put by the winter till I will be goin' on drill again."

And though Jess shook her head a trifle sadly, murmuring shyly in her dulcet Gaelic something equivalent to a protest, that Ewan could not be dearer to her if he brought her back his weight in gold, in her heart of hearts she was none the less happy because Ewan refused to eat the bread of idleness on her account. So it was a proud lass indeed who watched her lover out of sight that night— her lover so strong and clever, who had learnt to talk that difficult English language so beautifully since he had begun to wear the magic badge of R. N. R. upon his breast, and who, as an outcome of his industrious exertions, would put to sea on the morrow in a bran new smack of his own, in which he and Jess had already enjoyed a first secret sail, lest, as superstition decreed, spectators should covet her.

"Good-bye!" came the fisherman's strong young voice midway across the ford; and bravely went Jess's answer, despite its sadness:

"Slàn-leat" (farewell).

CHAPTER II To the Rescue

THERE had been little warning of the hurricane before it rose. A cold, still night, a pale moon flooding the wide wastes of newly fallen snow, the great sea asleep. By early noon a raging tempest, a dark rack scurrying across a darker sky, the broad Minch a seething whirlpool.

Jess stood at her little doorway as the short afternoon closed quickly in, and gazed upon the scene with fear and trembling in her eyes. She was no coward. She had struggled through storm and snow to bring home the cow which she throve so wondrously on the only pasture she had ever known—the sea-wave strewn shore. She had baked and brewed, and busied herself with the old man's comforts, and crooned a snatch of song through it all, too; musing on Ewan, and with never a thought of danger in her heart. For her the ocean had no terrors. Her cradle-songs had been the lullaby of billows. As a child she had sported with the breakers, or woven fairy tales out of the lapping of waves. In calm or storm it was her beloved world still, the world which was her life.

But now as she clung, beaten by the hurricane, to the rough boulder-work of the cot wall, her bosom heaved and two tears stood in her brave brown eyes. Out of a dozen or more fishing-boats driven before the gale in the Broad Bay this morning three of the number had not succeeded in making land, and, indirectly, it had come to the girl's knowledge that Ewan Morrison's was among the missing.

It was but four days since the lovers had bidden each other farewell. Jess was telling herself now, with the pitiful resignation so characteristic of the Hebridean, that it had been for ever. Her years had been made up of toil and privation, of inurement to the hazard of

"They who go down to the sea in ships, that do business in great waters." She had known so little of joy till Ewan came and wrapped it about her life, that her despair resembled more the awaking from a happy dream than the realisation that her heart must break should Ewan come no more.

Outside the wind howled; while ever and anon the distant thunder of the sea roused Jess from her slumbers on her lowly pallet where she had laid down to rest at last, dressed as she was, overcome by forebodings and fatigue.

It was close upon midnight when Jess awoke suddenly with the sound of loud knocking ringing in her ears. Her first sensation was of incredulity and alarm. For an instant she sat up trembling, waiting for its repetition; then reproving herself for her fear, she sprang to her feet, undid the latch, and threw open the cabin-door.

A sharp gust of wind blew out the newly-lighted candle she held in her hand, but by the pale gleam of the moon she saw the snow had not long ceased to fall, and lay a pure, untrodden track before her. No human foot had traversed this white carpet. That knocking must have been a dream, the outcome of her anxious fears for her lover's safety. Yet she closed and barred the door reluctantly; the awakening had been very real, the summons imperative. True, it might have been one of the peats composing the thatch which had become dislodged, which the wind lifting had rebounded along the roof. Jess, being a sensible lass, tried her best to convince herself of this matter-of-fact explanation of the mystery, and stretched her weary limbs anew in search of rest. She had undergone a long day of hard toil, and wakeful as her harrowed brain was, Nature asserted itself in her tired body, and in a few moments she was sleeping profoundly.

How long she slept she knew not. The same loud knocking as heretofore brought her struggling, but half awake, with latch and bolt.

"Who is there!" she panted, in her native Gaelic, while yet the door was barely open.

No one was there.

The shivering girl looked out upon the same untrodden stretch of snow. The moon gleamed above her, lighting up the dark ford, the white shore beyond. There was the sound of the wild sea beating there—there was the low sobbing of the wind—and Jess stood paralysed.

This time there was no doubt in her mind— those knocks were a reality. They had broken in upon a happy dream. She was at the ingle waiting for Ewan, as he came marching blithely towards her from the drill battery, with the sunlight glancing on his bonny suit of blue and his boyish face gleaming beneath his cloth bonnet.

He called to her in his fine English : " Iss it you, Jess ! "

Then the knock came. Jess shivered.

The Celtic heart is a strong heart ; it loves passionately, it suffers proudly ; but is essentially superstitious. Jess, while she feared neither cold nor tempest, trembled at the touch of Fate— for she felt it was Fate. That knocking was a warning. Ewan was in danger! Ewan was dying ! Ewan was calling upon someone even now to save him.

The wind whirled in at the open doorway, and filled the place with curling smoke from the ruddy peats. She shut the door and knelt down by the fire to replenish it, and, as she knelt, she prayed fervently, and with the flutter of hope at her breast, though the tears were streaming down her cheeks. She was praying that if Ewan was in peril that summons should come again as a sign, that she herself should be empowered to go to his aid.

And even while she prayed the knock came. Then Jess rose up without hesitation.

This time she never essayed to go to the door. She entertained no thought of appealing to others for help. Ewan was almost a stranger to all save herself at Culreigrein ; could she expect any to feel the intense solicitude for his welfare which filled her own soul? Had it been the signal gun of a ship in distress which had broken in upon her rest, she knew there would have been no lack of support in answer to her call from the brave fellows around her to whom fear or selfish consideration was unknown. But was it not impossible to arouse even one friend at the dead of night on the mere plea of presentiment ?

Mechanically she began to pin up her rough homespun skirt fish-wife fashion, leaving exposed the shorter coarse blue petticoat, which custom proved more serviceable for walking use. She knotted a little tartan shawl about her head and neck. She wrapped a large plaid around her body, and stuffed a small bottle of whisky within her bodice. Then, perhaps, more from habit than forethought, she lifted her empty creel from the corner and swung its band over her shoulders. She wore neither shoes nor stockings ; they were a luxury identified with the gown which lay in the oak chest, to be donned only on Sabbath and fast days. She threw a few more peats on the fire, cast a last glance round the cabin, softly opened the door, fastening it on the outer side by means of a piece of rope, and passed out into the night.

Instinctively her steps turned towards the ford. She felt led by a magnetic influence, whose power she was unable to resist. The tide was at the ebb. At times she trod on dry ground ; at others the water washed her ankles ; once it rose almost to her knees.

Still the girl went on. The track would have been familiar to her on the darkest night had there not been a moon to light it, and no fear, save for Ewan, was in her heart.

She went on, on along the great white beach of Melbost. Against the clear horizon the wide sea broke like a black cloud. Nearer, the foaming breakers reared and plunged, their thunder waking drear echoes along the shore. Now and then there would come the cry of the curlew, again the twitter of the mavis ; but otherwise, in this cold world Jess seemed to breathe and live alone.

She had walked, perhaps, half a mile, gazing always to seaward, till her eyes were growing dim and strained, when suddenly her heart stood still.

A few yards before her a dark *thing* lay huddled in the snow, motionless, and she ran forward with a wild cry and lifted up its face to the moonlight. It was Ewan Morrison!

CHAPTER III.—WAS IT TOO LATE?

JESS knelt and drew the passive form to her warm young breast. She cradled the head upon her arm. She kissed the white lips reverently, as one kisses the dead. For in that awful moment she believed him dead. She told herself agonisedly that she had answered his call too late. His clothes were soaked with brine, and little icicles had formed upon his damp, dark locks. His hands were blue and frost-bitten.

"'Luaidh mo chridhe! (my darling) that I should live to let you die like this!" was the plaint of Jess's piteous Gaelic which thrilled the great silence.

O ! merciful Heaven ! He *could* not be dead ! He should not die !

She put her hand upon his heart. Was there a flutter there, or was it but her own pulses throbbing with the fire of passion and despair? She took the flask from her bosom and tried to force a drop or two of the strong spirit through the set teeth. It was of no avail ; the liquor streamed back upon her own arm.

Suddenly, then, Jess released herself and rose up. She swung her creel to the ground, took off her great plaid, and, stooping, bound it tenderly about the prostrate man. To lift him into the creel in his stiff and crouching attitude was a more difficult feat ; but where even Jess's strong young arms might have failed, her stronger will accomplished. Then she knelt for a moment on one knee, placed the creel's rope round her neck, and struggled slowly to her feet with its load upon her back.

The return along the path whence she had come proved long and arduous. The wind beat in her face and baffled her steps. The snow began to fall, fluttering flakes at first, becoming

DUNCAN DAVIDSON

gradually larger and denser. To Jess the cold night air seemed to grow warm and stifling. Frequently she stopped short to utter an overpowered sigh, only to plod on anew through the deep snow with numbed feet and panting breath. The swish of the water about her ankles told her at last that she was re-crossing the ford. She waded forward, her sight blinded by the white drift of snow-flakes, but her feet following intuitively the unmistaken track.

It was accomplished! Her fingers were tearing at the bit of rope which bound the cabin door. She carried her heavy burden in, and stretched it upon her own pallet before the glowing peats. Then she fell beside it in an agony of suspense. Was it too late?

* * * *

No, happily it was not too late. When

'East and west without a breath
Mixt their dim lights like Life and Death
To broaden into boundless day,'

Ewan Morrison re-awoke to consciousness to bless the noble girl who had braved her life for his.

In later hours Jess shed many a pitying tear for her lover's comrades who had perished in that pitiless sea, and she could not but think with regret of the gallant craft which represented years of the young fisherman's economy and toil, and had swept to the bottom with it such hopes of near prosperity. Yet, after all, what was the loss of anything in comparison to her joy when the cruel ocean, which had taken so much, had cast upon its shore her truest treasure!

"It wass you that will be forgetting to be putting the crookit sixpence in the keel of the bonnie boat, and so the ill-luck will be offertaking you," an old mariner told the happy pair, with a wise and solemn shake of his hoary head. But Ewan answered:

"I will not be thinking it ill-luck at ahl, at ahl, since I, who might haf died in the snow, was carried home in her creel by the bravest lass in the Lews." MAVOR ALLAN.

SHINTY CHAMPIONSHIP.—The final contest for the Camanachd Association Cup was played on the North Inch of Perth on 18th March, the teams representing Kingussie and Ballachulish. After one of the most keenly contested matches on record, Ballachulish won by 2 hails to 1. In the evening Lord Provost Dewar entertained the teams and over 100 gentlemen connected with the various Shinty Clubs to Dinner in the Salutation Hotel, Mr. John Sime presiding. The toast of the Camanachd Association was proposed by Mr. John Mackay, Editor, *Celtic Monthly*, Mr. John Macpherson Grant of Ballindalloch replying. Mr. John A. Stewart, Solicitor, proposed the winning team, and Mr. Macdonald of Keppoch the losing team, the respective Captains making suitable reply. A specially hearty vote of thanks was given the referee, Mr. D. P. Macgillivray, late Secretary.

DUNCAN DAVIDSON OF TULLOCH.

IT may be appropriate in view of the interest created by the controversy as to the Chiefship of Clan Dhai or Davidson, to give some particulars regarding the present head of the ancient family of Tulloch, whom many believe to be the rightful Chief of the Clan.

The Davidsons of Tulloch stand high among the old landed families of the Highlands. About the year 1790 Alexander Davidson of Davidston in Cromarty married Miss Bayne of Tulloch, and purchased the estate from his father-in-law. The Baynes of Tulloch were for many generations of great position and influence in Ross-shire, being a sept of the Mackays, and claiming direct descent from a chief of that powerful clan. The castle is of ancient date, the keep having been built in 1166, and other parts of it in 1665. In 1845 a considerable portion of the castle was burned, many valuable relics and other property being destroyed, but it was restored eight years ago and is now, together with the shooting, under lease. Many interesting anecdotes are related regarding the grandfather of the present Tulloch, who was considered the handsomest man in Scotland. He was married no less than five times, and on his death the Queen sent his widow a letter of condolence.

Duncan Davidson, the present head of the family, was born at Tulloch Castle, near Dingwall, on 3rd October, 1865, and was educated at, among other institutions, The College,

MRS. DAVIDSON OF TULLOCH.

Inverness, and by private tutors. When 18 years of age, at his father's wish, he entered the Commercial Bank of Scotland, and served four years under the late Mr. MacBean Ross, whose father, the late Provost Ross, was for forty years factor for Tulloch estate. His father succeeded to the estate in 1881, and eight years later was succeeded by his son, the present Tulloch. He found the property, however, like many other Highland estates, so heavily burdened that he found he could not live at the castle in a manner becoming his position, and so put it on lease. With praiseworthy independence Mr. Davidson has devoted himself to business, in the hope of being able to live some day in the old home at Tulloch, and is a director of Messrs. Malcolm Kearton & Co., Ltd., West India Merchants. He lives in Hampshire, travelling

TULLOCH CASTLE, ROSS SHIRE.

to business in London four days each week, and spends his well-earned holiday in the autumn at Tulloch Cottage, the residence of his mother, which is within the castle grounds. Mr. Davidson is considered one of the best shots in Scotland, and has been frequently one of the judges for piping and dancing at the Northern Meeting.

On the 15th November, 1887, he married Gwendoline Mackenzie, eldest daughter of William Dalziel Mackenzie of Fawley Court, Bucks, and Farr, Inverness-shire, a young lady of remarkable beauty and accomplments, and the daughter of one of the most esteemed and popular of Highland lairds. Into the merits of the Chiefship question we have no desire to enter, but if the Clan consider that he is the rightful Chief, Tulloch is well fitted to do honour and credit to the position.

TURUS CLANN MHIC-AOIDH DO THIR AN SINNSEARA.*

By REV. ANGUS MACKAY, M.A.

SANN mu dheireadh an thoghair so 'chaidh ghluais carrann araidh de Chomunn a' chinnidh so do 'n Taobh-tuath. Bha 's a' chuideachd Ian Macaoidh a Hereford, Seumas

* Read at the last Meeting of the Gaelic Society of London.

Macaoidh a Lunnain, Ian Macaoidh a Glaschu, Alastair Macaoidh a Duineidin, Dr. Macaoidh Dingwall a Renton, Dr. Adhamh Macaoidh a Latharna, agus mi fhein. Thug sinn 'n ar coise Ruaraidh Macloid a Innernis, fleasgach de mhuintir Asainnt, a thug brath-gill air na bha aig a' Mhod 's an Oban an uiridh a' seinn orannan Gaidhlig. Bha sinn air ar tarruig Tuath le da iarrtas. Bu mhiann leinn duthaich ar n atbraichean fhaicinn, far 'na ghabb na suinn chombnuidh, a ghleidh le neart gairdein agus faobhar claidhimh, an cuid 's an coir air iomadh blar gort. Bha tlachd ro mhoir againn 'bhi faicinn gach beinn agus gleann ann an tir

Mhicaoidh, agus ar cas fhaotainn aon uair eile air an fhraoch a bhuineadhd huinn. Fhuair sinn sin, agus cha robh fear 's a' chuideachd nach robh ag radh gu-n do chuir sud bliadhna r'a laithean. Ach thuilleadh air so bha sinn ag iarraidh 'dhol do thir Mhicaoidh chum bhi brosnachadh gach oig fhir is tè gu bhi leughadh na Gaidhlig, agus gu bhi seinn bardachd cheol-mhoire ar n-athraichean. Bha, agus tha sinn de 'n bheachd nach fhaigh a' Ghaidhlig, a tha cho aosda agus cho eireachdail, bas, o fhuachd agus acras, aig lamhan na tha an diugh g'a bruidhinn 's an Taobh-tuath. Chuir sinn romh-ainn a bhi 'togail suas, cha-n i mhain "bratach bhan Mhicaoidh," ach brataich is sine, fo am faod gach Gaidheal tionail, na bratach air am bheil mar shuaicheantas "A' Ghaidhlig a bard-achd 's a ceol." Ged nach robh sinn ann ach ochdnar, gu bhi 'togail teisteis air taobh na Gaidhlig, bha duil againn 'n uair a ruigeadh sinn Duthaich Mhicaoidh gu-n tionaileadh na sloigh mu-n cuairt oirnne. Agus mar shaoil thachair. 'N uair 'rainig sinn *Portskerra* bha coig ceud duine agus bean, le piobairean is brataichean a' feitheamh oirnne, agus thug gach creig freagairt chridheil do 'n iollach chairdeil a fhuair sinn o na bha cruinn. Cha b' i failte nan Gall 'bha sud idir, ach failte cho Gaidhealach agus a fhuair cuideachd dhaoine riamh.

Mach thun a' bhlar a ghabh sinn agus thois-ich saothair an latha. Fhuair sinn dearbhachd ann an sin gu bheil a' Ghaidhlig beo, agus gu bheil da rireadh. Bha caileagan agus balaich, nach b' airde na chrios, g'a leughadh cho milis poncail 's gu-n chuir iad sodan air ar cridhe. Bha seanairean agus sean-mhathraichean cheart cho eudmhoire gu bhi 'toirt dearbhachd dhuinn air 'n comas ann a bhi 'leughadh na Gaidhlig. Cha bu leabhraichean furasda idir thug sinn daibh r'an leughadh ach orannan "Alastair Mhic-Mhaighstir Alastair" agus orannan "Dhonnachaidh Bhain." Gidheadh bha moran diubh comasach air an leughadh ro ghasda gu cinnteach. Na dheigh sin chuala sinn iad seinn, agus 's an aca fhein bha 'n guth. N' am faigh-eadh iad teagasg tha seinneadairean treuna 'n am measg, ach tha iad a dh' easbhuidh luchd-teagaisg ciuil.

An ath la chaidh sinn air ar n-aghairt gu Bun-Srath-Neamhair, aite comhnuidh nan Abrach, agus ma fhuair sinn failte 'am *Port-skerra* cha bu lugha idir an te fhuair sinn 'an so. Bha brataichean geala ban sgaoilte o gach cnoc is creig, mar a bha sinn tighinn dluth air an aite-comnuidh. Bha sean mhnathan agus daoine, nach b' urrainn coiseachd gu aite a' chruinneachaidh, 'tighinn a mach gu 'n dorsan, mar a bha sinn dol seachad, agus a' guidhe beannachd oirnne. Anns an aite so thainig corr air tri fichead pearsa air an aghairt gu bhi air an ceasnachadh ann an leughadh Gaidhlig, agus 's ann aca fhein bha ghnothuich ris. Cha-n fhaighear ni 's fhileannta air leughadh Gaidhlig an au cearn eile de 'n Ghaidhealtachd, ged is mor am facal e. Air son ceathar nairean de 'n uaireadair bha sinn air a' bhlar, agus cha-n aithnichear air aon diubh gu-n robh iad air sgiosachadh. Bha 'n cridhe da rireadh 's na bha dol air aghairt. 'N uair thainig am feasgar, 's ann sin bha 'n aoidheachd—an sluagh coir g' ar n-iarraidh gu 'n tighean chum gu-m bristeadh sinn aran. Ach 's an b' eudar falbh, le iomadh beannachd dol 'n ar coise.

Chuir sinn seachad an t-Sabaid ann an Ceann-taile Mhicaoidh fo sgeile beinn Laoghail agus Chnoc an Fhreacadain. 'S ann an so, air son iomadh ceud bliadhna, bha triath agus uailsean ar cinnidh a' gabhail taimh, ged a nis, mo thruaighe! tha talla na mor-chuisean falamh dhiubh. Ach taing do Dhia, ged dh' fhalbh ar triath cha d' fhalbh ar cinneadh. Tha iadsan 'an so fhathasd cho smiorail, cruaidh, blath-chridheach agus a b' abhaist. Tha meas aca air cliu an athraichean, air a' Ghaidhlig, cainnt am mathraichean, air bardachd agus ceol na duth-cha. Tha iomradh anns gach aite mu 'n cuairt air piobairean Taobh-Mhilnis, agus fhuair sinn dearbhachd an la sud air mar a' lainnhsicheas iad a' phiobh-mhoire. A Milnis, air taobh thall a' chaoil thainig piobairean gun aireamh, agus bheireadh an dara fear brath-gill air an fhear eile. Bheir mise mo bhoid gu-r iad thein a thug an fhuaim a craicionn caorach an la ud. Buaidh is piseach air na sgoid : 's iad a chuir an fhaoilte air a' chuideachd. Aig a' cheasnachadh Ghaidhlig bha iad 'an so cheart cho sgiobalt agus a bha iad ann am *Portskerra* no ann am Fairc. Leugh sean is og carrannan de na bard Ghaidh-ealach bha r' an leughadh, agus sin gu poncail. Aig a' choinneamh aidhche fhuair sinn aithne air cia nar a sheinneas iad 'an Ceann-t-saile. Tha luchd teagaisg aca 'an so, agus bha sin gu soilleir ri fhaicinn, oir bu ghasda thainig daibh orannan Gaidhlig a sheinn.

Mu 'n dh' fhag sinn Ceann-t-saile chaidh sinn a dh' fhaicinn Blar-Druim-nan-Coup, astar choig mile, troimh fhraoch is gharbh-chriochan, far an dh' thug Macaoidh buaidh ainneamh thairis air sluagh an Taobh-Chataich; anns a' bhliadhna 1427. Bha moran an crochadh air a' chatha so. N' an robh an la air dol leis an namhaid chaill-cadh Macaoidh 'fhearann; ach cha deach. Thuit ar ceann-cinnidh, Aonghas Du, air a mharbhadh le saighead, ach fa-dheoidh chuir am bagannach grinn sin, Ian Abrach a mhac, an ruaig orra agus ged a chaill e 'n gairdean ceàrr, le beum tuaighe, lean e 'n fhaogaid air ceann a dhaoine air son iomadh mile, 'sileadh fola mar a bha e. Sloinnear, gu-s an la 'n diugh, Abraich *Shra-Neamhair* o 'n latn so, agus ni iad iomradh air

Druim-nan-Coup mar ni Albanaich air *Bannock-burn*. Shiubhail sinn, am blar air fad, agus 'n uair rainig sinn na h-uaighean anns am bheil na gaisgich air an adhlaiceadh, thug sinn dhinn ar n-eideadh-cinn. Ach b' i cheisd a nis tilleadh dhachaidh troimh na mhonadh, is an aidhche air tighinn. Bha cuid againn air an robh coisbheart freagarrach gu leoir 'falbh shraidean Lunnain, ach gle mhi fhreagarrach airson garbhlach Dhruim-nan-Coup. Mu-n d' rainig sinn Ceann-t-saile bha cuid gun raic bhroige orra, agus cuid eile le 'n eudach lan cabair is mointich, ionnus gur ann a bha sinn coltach ri daoine sgith, leonta, 'tilleadh o la-blar. Gidheadh cha robh neach de 'n chuideachd an aithreachas gu n d' thug sinn 'n cuairt ud, agus cha do mhill e cail no slainte aon fhear.

Thug sinn a nis aghaidh air Diùrnais, ach "bha cù eadarainn is conart." Bha caolas mor Erriuboil againn ri dhol thairis ann am bata beag, agus cha b' i sin a chuis fhanaid air la garbh gaothach. Bha 'ghaoth 'n ar n-aghaidh, direach 'n ceann oirnne, am muir ag eiridh 'n a thonnan uaine, agus dol suas na still gu ruig mullach a' chroinn. Rinn sinn an seol cho beag 's ghabhadh deanamh, agus bha feum air. Cha robh sinn fada bho thir 'n uair bha dara leth na cuideachd 'n an luidhe le tinneas mara. Dh' fheuch am bard Macleoid air oran a sheinn, ach cha b' fhada gu 's an robh port eile aig. Bha an da leighe bha air bord, "mar bha Fionn 'n tighe a' Bhlar Bhuidhe, gu-n chomas eirigh no suidhe." Bha am ministear a bha air bord, le taoman 'n a dhorn a' cuir a mach an uisge a bha tighinn a steach 'n a bhalagannan. Mu dheireadh fhuair sinn gu tir air sgeir creige, ach 's ann an sin a bha 'n obair a' streap suas, agus a' cabhair cuid a bha gun chomas gluasaid.

Rainig sinn Diùrnais mu fheasgar, agus bu mhoir an fhàilte a chuir an sluagh coir oirnne. Dheasaich sluagh an aite suipeir air ar cinn, anns an tighe-osda, agus phaigh iad air son so le airgiod a thionail iad 'n am measg fein. Ged a tha iad a chomhnuidh dluth air a' Pharbh fhiadhaich, cha-n eil cridheachan ni 's blaithe na tha aig sluagh Dhiùrnais 'r am faighinn air feadh Dhuthaich Mhicaoidh. Chuir sinn cuid de 'n aidhche seachad ceasnachadh ann an Gaidhlig, na thainig air an aghairt de shean agus òg. 'S ann aca fhein tha mheur air leughadh Gaidhlig, agus is e bha duilich a dheanamh a mach co a b' fhearr diubh. Sheinn iad mar an ceudna gu loinneil orannan Rob Duinn, agus bha 'n guth blasda ceolmhoire. Anns a' mhaduinn thug sinn sgriob gu Baile-na-cill, far a bheil uaigh Rob Duinn baird Duthaich Mhicaoidh, agus chunnaic sinn aitean adhlaic dhaoine ainmeil eile. Dh' fhag sinn Diùrnais air Di-ciadain, chuir sinn an aidhche seachad anns an Ri-coinich, agus air Diar-daoin chaidh sinn troimh an *Direadh-mhoir* gu ruig Oversgaig. Air Di-haoin rainig

sinn Lairg, far an robh coinneamh ciuil againn m-fheasgar ann an talla mor bha lan de shluagh. Air Di-sathuirne thainig sinn gu Raoghairt, chum sinn ceasnachadh Gaidhlig ach cha robh iad comasach air a' Ghaidhlic a leughadh 'an so mar a bha iad anns an Duthaich mu thuath. Chuir sinn an t-Sàbaid seachad 'an Raoghairt agus air Di-luain sgaoil sinn o cheile, duilich gu-n d' thainig sinn gu crich ar turuis.

Air mo shon fein faodaidh mi 'radh, le m' uile chridhe, nach deachaidh mi riamh air cuairt o 'n dh' fhuair mi uiread de shòlas tiomail, agus nach do thachair mi riamh air cuideachd de dhaoine uailse 'bheireadh barrachd air a' chomunn ud, ann am modhalachd, ann an stuaimeachd no ann an cairdeas. Cha chuala mi droch fhocal, no focal feargach, o' aon de 'n ochdnar re fad nan naoi la 'bha sinn comhla. 'S e *Hereford* bha 'n a cheann oirnne, agus cha-n fhaighear ni b' fhearr. Tha e eudmhoir gun bhi amaideach, tha e tialaidh gun bhi sgiotach, agus tha e stuama gun bhurraidheachd. Bha 'fhocal 'n a lagh dhuinn, ionnus gu-n robh sinn ullamh gu radh ris, " 'S i do thoil se ar taitneas a' Chaptain Mhicaoidh," mar thuirt cuideachd de Reismeid Mhicaoidh ri 'n ceannard air blar *Oldenburgh*, is e air foighneachd dhiubh an leanadh iad e ann an oidhirp chunnartach. Choisinn *Hereford* gradh, is meas, is urram na bha sinn ann, agus mar a b' fhaide 'bha sinn comhla ris 's ann is mo bha sinn smuaineachadh dheth. B' i so ar cainnt air a' chul-thaobh, agus gabhaidh mise orm fein a nis an sgeul aithris fa chomhair. 'S i ar durachd da, durachd Rob Duinn do Sheoras :—

> Saoghal sona 'n deagh bheath dhuit
> 'S deadh oighreachan bhi t' ait
> Buiread eile dh' ionndrain orra
> 'S an àm an faigh iad bàs.

(*Gu bhiodh air a chriochnachadh*).

"WE ENGLISH."

NEW YORK.

SIR,—In the New Year's edition of the *New York World* it had letters from celebrities from each side of the Atlantic, including one from the Duke of Sutherland, in which he used the expression—"We English." Considering that he owes his chief title to Scotland and has also a position as a great Highland Chief to support, the above expression to the average Scotsman will appear intensely absurd. It is such examples which encourage the imitative American in "Englishing" every animate or inanimate thing which hails from the British Isles. For a steady supporter of the name "Britain" commend us to Andrew Carnegie. After Mackays the Mackay country can receive no better immigrants than he. Hoping the clan may so prosper that some day they may claim Strathnaver as their own,

I remain, faithfully yours,

B. D.

THE OUTLAWED MACGREGORS.

FEW clans have more interesting legends connected with them than the outlawed Clan Gregor. The stories of wanderings in the mountains and hair-breadth escapes never fail to rouse a feeling of sympathy towards the noble Clan Alpine.

Before the Campbells came to power, the mountains and glens round Loch Awe were the property of the Macgregors; but now not a vestige of the old dwelling can be seen in Glen Strae. Traditions of their bravery and deeds of valour are still current in the region where they once flourished; and in a wild corrie of Ben Cruachan is pointed out a rock, from behind which the last Macgregor that was hunted as a beast of prey, shot the blood-hound that was set upon his track.

Near Ben Lomond is a dark, wild loch, called Loch Chon or the dog's loch; so named because there were blood-hounds kept there specially for the purpose of chasing the Macgregors. These dogs were trained so that, it is said, they knew a Macgregor from anyone else. One day an individual of the proscribed clan had ventured down to the clachan of Aberfoyle, when he saw in the distance a hound approaching; he immediately took to the mountains, and fled in the direction of Loch Katrine. But the pursuer was steadily gaining on him, so he turned round and waited for his enemy, drew his sgian dubh, and stabbed the dog near a spring, situated at the road from Aberfoyle to the Trossachs, now called Rob Roy's Well.

The son of the last laird of Glen Strae had gone out hunting one day with young Lamond of Lamond; they had rested in a hut near Tyndrum and were dining, when a quarrel arose which ended in the death of young Macgregor. Lamond immediately fled, pursued by some of the murdered laird's followers, and at length succeeded in reaching the house of old Macgregor. Seeing Lamond approaching in such haste, the old man called out, "You are safe here whatever you may have done," and led him into the house. The pursuers arrived soon after, told the father what had taken place, and demanded young Lamond. "Let none dare touch him," said Macgregor, "I have promised him safety, and he shall be safe in my house." The old man afterwards escorted Lamond home, and in bidding farewell said, "I cannot protect you farther, keep away from my clan, and may God forgive you for what you have done." Not long afterwards the name Macgregor was proscribed, and old Glen Strae was a wanderer without a home. But Lamond now returned the kindness which had been shown to him, by sheltering Macgregor and his family.

ERIC STAIR KERR.

THE OUTLAWED MACGREGOR'S VOW OF VENGEANCE

TO CORRESPONDENTS.

All Communications, on literary and business matters, should be addressed to the Editor, Mr. JOHN MACKAY, 9 Blythswood Drive, Glasgow.

TERMS OF SUBSCRIPTION.— The CELTIC MONTHLY will be sent, post free, to any part of the United Kingdom, Canada, the United States, and all countries in the Postal Union—for one year, 4s.

THE CELTIC MONTHLY.

APRIL, 1899.

CONTENTS.

OUR NEXT ISSUE.

NEXT month we will give plate portraits, with biographical sketches, of Messrs. George W. Mac-Lean, Newcastle-on-Tyne; M. Macleod, Cheltenham; and M. Macbean, Ontario, Canada.

NEW CAITHNESS.—A subscriber in Queensland writes us as follows:—"We are all very Scotch here, and look forward to getting our *Celtic* every month. I am a grazier, and hail from Caithness. One part of this run is named Reay, and others Wick, Watten, Canisbay, and Thurso, all places in the neighbourhood of my old home in "Bonnie Caithness." This information will doubtless greatly interest our many Caithness readers at home and abroad.

STAND FAST, CRAIGELLACHIE!

IT has often been remarked of the late General Ulysses S. Grant that while of strictly American stock—his immediate forefathers having been settled in the States for a period of probably 150 years—he took exceeding pride in his Highland ancestry. The following incident, well known to Scottish circles here but perhaps new to *Celtic* readers, will show how forcibly this trait in his character was once brought out on a certain occasion. It has not been an infrequent custom of the Presidents to make a tour of doubtful States just before the eve of an election, in order that they might come into direct touch with the people. Worthy of all emulation is this time-honoured custom of the old Scottish Kings, so long as it is employed in the cause of common weal.

General Grant once made a tour such as that described, travelling on an observation train, his political friends delivering the addresses to the awaiting crowds from the car-platform. It is need-less to explain that the grim, silent soldier knew little of the art of speech-making. He came of that race of eagles whose swoop was more potent than their scream. Standing in the crowd at a certain station were two friends—an American and a Scots-man—the former remarking what a strangely taciturn man Grant was, unresponsive and seemingly void of all human emotion. "I disagree with you," replied the Scotsman; "I believe that I could recall something to his memory which would prove other-wise." His friend laughed derisively. "Now look here," continued the Scotsman, "I am prepared to bet that I shall do more than awake some outward show of feeling in the General—I shall arouse his enthusiasm." "Done" was the reply. The approaching train with the Presidential party standing on the car-platform stopped, whereupon the Scotsman, lifting his hat, called out lustily—"Stand Fast, Craigellachie." Had the summons come direct from far Cairngorm the effect could not have been greater on the General—a glow suddenly appeared on his face, gone was the warrior's grim-ness and, returning the salutation, he smilingly bowed his most gracious acknowledgments.

When the American had somewhat recovered from his astonishment he asked for an explanation of the magic which lay in the words uttered. "It is simple," was the answer, "what you heard is the war cry of Clan Grant."

The bet was paid.

New York.   MAC DHAI.

CLAN DAVIDSON.

CANADA, 1st February, 1899.

SIR—It will no doubt interest your readers, especially those of the Clan Davidson, and their friends, to know that there is in the Canadian military service a smart kilted regiment, the 48th Highlanders, raised about six years ago, uniformed in Highland costume complete in every respect, excepting in winter when they wear trews instead of kilts, and this regiment wears the Clan Dai tartan, with the MacDhai crest and motto as a regimental badge, all of which was adopted when the regiment was raised, as a compliment to their first commanding officer, Lieutenant-Colonel John Irvine Davidson.

Yours very truly,
GEO. A. SHAW (Tordarroch),
Lieutenant-Colonel.

KILCATTON CLAN.

LONDONDERRY, 11th March, 1899.

SIR—I have been reading in your *Monthly* about the above clan, but it will doubtless interest some of your readers to learn that we have a Kilcatton about six miles from this city. Did the Kilcatton clan come from Ireland, or were they of Norse origin? I shall be glad if your Quebec or New York corres-pondents can inform me if Davidson of Tulloch is of Celtic or Scandinavian origin; if the former why change the "Mac" to "Son" (Davidson)? Both are synonymous terms. I could understand people from the Orkneys or Shetland calling themselves Davidson, but in Ireland, where the name has been anglicised, we use Devett, Devette; or the Keltic form MacDevette, meaning MacDavid.

Yours truly,
JOHN MACDEVETTE, J.P.

THE MACDONALDS OF ACHTRIACHTAN.

By CHARLES FRASER-MACKINTOSH, LL.D.

EVERY Highlander has an interest in, and warm feeling towards the Macdonalds of Glencoe, of which house Achtriachtan is a cadet.

There seems unfortunately, perhaps necessarily on their part, at the present day among certain of the baser class of Scotsmen, pottering amongst old papers, unable to discriminate but ready to wound, an inclination to besmirch the good name of prominent Highlanders, if Jacobites. The infamous writings and doings of the Dutchman and his willing tools have by certain writers even in the 19th century undergone white washings, though the more this is attempted the deeper are the stains.

William intended the expropriation of the Glencoe men and carried it out to the last.

Even after the lapse of two hundred years justice has not fully overtaken the destroyers, from the usurper downwards to the meanest of his engaged assassins.

By what authority did the Dutchman take it upon him to give direct orders for the massacre. There was, at least nominally, legal authority in Scotland through which all orders for the carrying out of prosecutions for non-submission, fell to pass. The Privy Council of Scotland existed, through whom all such orders could alone be legally directed. What were they, if Secretary Johnstone willed it otherwise? What could, however, be expected from Scottish spirit after the Revolution, trampled into dust as were all Scottish rights. A few ambitious Scottish nobles, affecting sympathy, joined those conventiclers, who again lifted their heads, and steeped in fanaticism and blind-folly, prepared the way for the adoption of Patronage.

That odious step, the direct consequence of the Revolution of 1688, came about within twenty-five years, and by destroying the independence of the church, has proved such a curse to Scotland, that even to this day its prejudicial effects are seen everywhere patent and visible, unceasingly disturbing the land. No regular Parliament was constituted in Scotland during William's and Mary's reign.

The Mac-ic-Iains continued, despite all, to flourish, and did so until the time of Alexander Macdonald of Glencoe, who died early in this century, and who, engaging deeply in the nefarious trade of extensive sheep farming, with its eviction of people, all over the Highlands, impoverished his estate. Though the name was kept up the male line terminated without lawful issue in the person of Dr. Macdonald, son of the above named Alexander Macdonald.

The estate now belongs to a successful Canadian, who has shewn excellent signs of wholesome Highland feeling, and has it in his power to

From R. R. M'Ian's]   MACDONALD OF GLENCOE.   ["Clans of Scotland."

revive much of the glory of its historic past.

The old Highland feeling, which allowed to the stranger, without question, protection and hospitality, was infamously taken advantage of, and the actors cannot even shelter themselves from their ill act, under pretended sense of duty.

And though in them Glencoe's devoted men
Beheld the foes of all who bore their name,
Yet simple faith allowed the stranger's claim
To hospitable cheer and welcome kind."

In 1692, at the time of the massacre, Alexander Macdonald of Achtriachtan was amongst those murdered. In the accounts of the day, it is stated "that a party under Sergeant Barker fired upon a number of Glencoe men, killing the Laird of Achtriachtan and several others. This gentleman had a protection in his pocket from Colonel Hill."

I do not find anyone of the family proprietor before the above Alexander, who, described as "eldest lawful son of John Macdonald in Achtriachtan," enters into a feu contract with John Stuart, Fiar of Ardsheal, receiving in feu :—

"All and haill the three merk land of Achtriachtan, and all and haill the merk land of Kinlochbeg in Glenco, with houses, biggings, yards, milns, multures, and with the third part of the fir and oak wood of Kinlochbeg in Glenco, and with other woods, isles, rocks, fishings, pertaining and belonging to the said four merk lands, all lying within the parish of Kilmolowack, Lordship of Lorn, and Sheriffdom of Argyle. And also the salmon fishings upon said Alexander, his own side of the water of Leven, and salmon fishings of Achtriachtan." This contract of feu is dated 4th February, 1686.

The lands of Kinlochbeg had previously pertained to John Cameron of Kinlochmore in virtue of wadset thereof in his favour by Robert Stuart of Appin. Cameron having disponed to Achtriachtan, the latter's brother and successor, Angus, the second Achtriachtan, received a Precept of Clare Constat from Appin upon 8th January, 1704. He was probably the fortunate person of whom it is recorded as follows :—

"A brother of the Laird having been seized by Barker (before alluded to), requested him as a favour not to dispatch him in the house, but to kill him outside the door. The Sergeant consented, as he had received some kindness formerly, but when brought out he threw his plaid, which he had kept loose, over the shoulders of the soldiers appointed to shoot him and escaped."

The extent of the lands of Achtriachtan and Kinlochbeg may be inferred from its taking two days, 14th and 15th January, 1704, to take infeftment upon the above Precept.

There appears to have been some doubt as to the title to Kinlochbeg, as it was found necessary for Angus Cameron of Kinlochleven, son and heir of the above John Cameron, to grant formal renunciation and discharge of any right or pretension he, the said Angus Cameron, or his father, John, had over Kinlochbeg.

Angus Macdonald must have possessed the estate for over fifty years; and by repeated statements on the part of Miss Fraser Macdonald after mentioned, daughter of the fourth and last Achtriachtan, to her kinsman, Mr. Alexander Cameron, Accountant, Rose Villa, Balligeary, Inverness; Angus, a staunch, hereditary Jacobite, took up arms for Prince Charles, being then over seventy years of age, and was killed at Prestonpans in 1745.* By his wife, Flora Cameron of Callart, he had two daughters, and dying without male issue the succession passed to another Angus Macdonald, the third Achtriachtan, who, described as "nearest heir male to the deceased Angus Macdonald, his grand-uncle's son," received a Precept of Clare Constat from Dugald Stuart of Appin, the Superior, dated 26th July, 1751, upon which Angus Macdonald was infeft upon the 27th July. Angus Macdonald, third Achtriachtan, the heir male, married as his first wife his cousin, eldest daughter of the second laird. The second daughter, Margaret, married Angus Macintyre in Comasnabarrie of Callart, ancestress of Mr. Alexander Cameron above mentioned.

Prior to Achtriachtan's making up titles, he, upon 22nd January, 1751, negotiated with Dugald Stuart of Appin for an exchange of Appin's lands of Leckentuim with the lands of Kinlochbeg. The exchange was advantageous to Achtriachtan, for Leckentuim was a two merk land, while Kinlochbeg extended only to one merk. Achtriachtan was afterwards infeft in "the two merk lands of Leckentuim, with the whole pertinents thereof, lying in Glencoe, parish of Lismore and Appin, and shire of Argyle." 27th July, 1751. He also had a long lease of the farm of Achnacon.

In 1754 he had some business transactions with Alexander Stuart of Acharn. This name brings up a frightful instance of Campbell atrocity. The Lord Justice General Isla's monstrous behaviour at the trial of James Stuart of Acharn has not even in these white-washing days, been yet attempted. That it may not be attempted would be unsafe to say.

According to the Bighouse Papers, edited by Captain Douglas Wimberley of Inverness, the Earl of Breadalbane, writing to a confidant under date 21st November, 1752, shortly after Acharn's judicial murder, narrates with satis-

---

* Some trinkets found on the body were taken care of by the deceased's friends, and continued as treasured heir-looms in the family, and by none with greater pride and affection than by their ultimate possessor, Miss Fraser Macdonald.

faction an interview with the Lord Chancellor, in which the latter, though well aware that an innocent man had been executed, felt no pity for him, no, his whole mind, as well as that of his concurring auditor, was this:—

"That he wished heartily that the principal actors, and more of the contrivers of that horrid fact, could be found out and brought to justice, that more examples might be made besides James Stewart."

So much for the Lord Chancellor, now for the noble Earl's own views:—

"In answer to another letter which I writt to him after the other, in which I advised taking proper methods to pursue this affair further while it is warm, he says that I am certainly in the right in thinking that the utmost diligence and vigilance ought to be exerted in finding out the other persons concerned in this barbarous murder, not only in order to punish them for that crime, but to exterminate them out of the country, but that stronger orders can not be framed than those which have been sent from London to all the King's officers, civil and military, in Scotland, for both those purposes, and he thinks they ought to be reminded of them."

"I have transcribed his own words as far as can be done in an extract."

"He says he has given a hint (as I writt to him) that enquiry should be made in France relating to Allan Breck's being come back to his regiment, that we may be able to judge if he is still in this country."

Leckentum lay well into the estate of Dalness, and how the best part of the whole estate fell into the hands of poor Achtriachtan's law agent and confidential adviser, Coll Macdonald, W.S., of Dalness, is mentioned hereafter.

Achtriachtan proper had a fine sheiling attached called "Grianan." Achtriachtan married, secondly, Anne Campbell, daughter of John Campbell of Ballivcolan, and a post-nuptial contract betwixt them with consent of the lady's father bears date 10th December, 1753. She appears to have been first married to Stuart of Appin.

The connection of a Macdonald with a Campbell seldom boded good to the former, and in this case the small tocher brought was dissipated by the Campbell connections.

Achtriachtan had lawyers busy in Fort-William, Glasgow, and Edinburgh, getting more involved every year, but struggled on until his death on 28th December, 1798.

A friend in Edinburgh, under date 4th January, 1799, is found writing:

"Poor Achtriachtan died here this day eight days after a very short illness. The bursting of a blood vessel was the immediate cause of death."

Among the papers delivered up by his Edinburgh agent after his death, there was a bundle "No 5, consisting of papers relative to Ach-triachtan's processes with Cameron of Kinloch-leven, being in number forty-three."

(*To be concluded.*)

THE CAMERONS OF GLEN NEVIS.

DEAR SIR,—I am interested to learn from your correspondent, Mr. Donald Cameron, that one at least of the old Glen Nevis family is to the fore, and I trust that his letter in last month's issue will lead to some light being thrown upon the history and origin of *Siochd Shomhairle Ruaidh*. Mr. Cameron takes my expressions "extinct" and "vanished race" too literally. I did not intend to convey the idea that the race was altogether blotted out, but that, as far as Glen Nevis is concerned, no remnant of this historical family now dwells on the land from which their territorial designation was taken.

An authentic account of the origin of *Siochd Shomhairle Ruaidh* would be of the greatest interest to students of Highland history, as the whole matter is at present shrouded in mystery. From the Gaelic patronymic I certainly favour the Macdonald origin, as the name Somhairle (Norse, Somerled; English, Samuel) is almost unknown in early Cameron history, whilst quite common among the ancient Macdonalds. This taken in conjunction with the fact that John, Lord of the Isles, granted land in Glen Nevis to a Somerled in 1466 (from whom probably the designation *Somhairle Ruaidh* is derived) is almost conclusive, and if further proof is necessary it will be found in an extract from the Register of the Privy Council given in full on page 421 "Loyal Lochaber," in which the name of the Glen Nevis chieftain is mentioned as "Alester M'Alester M'Donald," and the tutor of the family as "Sorle M'Conill (MacDonald) Maklane." This is during the chiefship of *Domhnull Dubh Mac Dhomhnuill*, XV. of Lochiel, during the sixteenth century. Another extract from the same source, dated 1598, gives the chief's name as "Allaster M'Allaster Vc Coneill of Glennyves." The first mention of the name of Cameron in the glen, as far as I have been able to trace, is in 1612, when the Privy Council issued an order denouncing Cameron of Erracht for refusing to assist the Government in their action against the Clan Gregor; in this document we find mention made of "Allaster M'Allaster Vc Donald Camroun of Glenneves," by which it would appear that the name Cameron was then added to Macdonald and from thenceforward always used. The late Rev. Dr. MacIntyre, minister of Kilmonivaig, who had a most intimate knowledge of Lochaber, always asserted (on what grounds I am unaware) that the Glen Nevis Camerons were originally MacIntyres.

In conclusion I would add that your correspondent is quite correct in his statement that the last of the old family who lived in the glen was John, brother of Patrick, son of Ewen, son of Alexander, who was chief during the the '45 but was not "out," his brother Alan taking his place at Culloden, where he was killed. John sold the family estates to Sir Duncan Cameron of Fassifern and became a planter in the West Indies, where, I believe, he married, but of this I am not certain.

Yours faithfully,

W. DRUMMOND-NORIE.

Deeds that won the Empire. ✸

By JOHN MACKAY, C.E., J.P., Hereford.

Capture of Martinique, 1762.

(Continued from page 107).

THE futile attempt made by General Hopson to capture this island in 1759 has been described in a previous chapter. The result was to warn the French, and they were not slow to see the weak points in their fortifications. They at once set to strengthen them, and erect other entrenchments on every vantage point round the coast, and reinforce their garrisons.

In the last chapter it was shown what, in spite of all these obstacles, a handful of brave determined men gallantly led can effect, and how quickly Dominique was captured, with its Governor, staff and troops, but the expedition was too feeble in numbers to undertake further operations, the reinforcements expected from home not being sent.

The "Great Commoner," the matchless orator, the organiser of victories, was foiled in his views and martial projects. He clearly saw that Spain was about to side with France, and he wished to declare war upon her, seize her gold fleets from the West Indies, and attack her in all her vulnerable parts. The boldness of the scheme frightened the young King, never famed in the best of his days for mental sagacity. Pitt resigned, and in a short time Spain declared war. His successor found himself compelled to adopt Pitt's plans and declare war with Spain in 1761, and a fleet was sent to watch its coast. Amongst the ships of that power taken by the British cruisers was a rich galleon from the West Indies with an immense treasure on board, which gave the fortunate captors, crews of two frigates, no less a sum than £519,705 in prize money. The shares of the two captains being £65,000 each, lieutenants, £13,000, warrant officers, £1800, and seamen, £485 each.

Early in January, 1862, a British fleet of 18 ships of the line, besides frigates and other ships, commanded by Admiral Rodney, anchored in St. Anne's Bay, Martinique. The land forces, among whom were the "Black Watch" and Montgomery's Highlanders, consisted of about 14,000 men, and were commanded by General Monckton, the comrade of Wolfe on the Heights of Abraham. The greater part of the army were immediately landed near Cas de Navire, under Morne Tortueson and Morne Garnier. These forts commanded the town and citadel of Fort Royal, and were its chief defences. Great care had been taken to improve their natural strength, which from the deep ravines surrounding them was very great. General Monckton resolved to attack Fort Tortueson first. He ordered a body of 800 marines and other troops to advance on the right towards the town along the sea-side, for the purpose of attacking two redoubts near the beach, to support this movement, he at the same time directed flat bottomed boats, carrying a gun each, manned with sailors, to follow close along the shore.

A column of light infantry was to get round the left of the enemy, whilst, under cover of the fire of some batteries raised by the perseverance of sailors from the fleet, on opposite ridges, the attack in the centre was to be made by the Highlanders and grenadiers, supported by the main body of the army. The contest was arduous, but at last the enemy were driven from the Morne Tortueson, but a most formidable operation was still to be performed. This was to gain possession of the other eminence, from which, owing to its greater height, the enemy greatly annoyed the British troops. Preparations were made at once to carry this post, but before they had been completed the French descended from the hill and attacked the advanced posts of the British. The attempt was fatal to the French, who were instantly repulsed. No sooner were they seen to retire, than the Highlanders, drawing their claymores, rushed forward like furies upon the French, and being supported by the grenadiers under Colonel Grant and a party of Lord Rollo's brigade, the hills were mounted, the batteries seized, and numbers of the French, unable to escape from the rapidity of the attack, were taken. The French regulars escaped into Fort Royal, the militia fled and dispersed themselves over the country. This action proved decisive, for the town being commanded by the forts on the heights, now in possession of the British, surrendered on the 5th February. This point being gained the General was preparing to move on St. Pierre when further proceedings were rendered unnecessary by the arrival of deputies to arrange terms of submission for St. Pierre and the rest of the island, together with the islands of Grenada, St. Lucia, and St. Vincent. In this spirited enterprise the Highlanders lost 2 officers, 1 sergeant, and 12 rank and file killed, 10 officers, 3 sergeants, and 72 rank and file wounded.

With the capture of Martinique France lost all her West Indian possessions.

In the next chapter will be shown what humiliation was inflicted upon Spain, how Havana and Manilla—names recently, and even yet, themes for newspapers all over the world—had been captured, and France as well as Spain begged for peace, which they had wantonly broken.

(To be continued).

THE WITCH'S ISLE.

A KINTYRE LEGEND.

" INTO the lonely loch it glides
　　When darkness covers land and sea,
　Upon the sullen water rides
　　That wondrous isle of mystery.
And who shall dare the witch's ire
　Before the white cock hails the morn,
Shall win perchance, his heart's desire,
　Its price the soul of the Unborn."

Young Kenneth heard the cailleach* speak,
　" I love a maiden, high and proud,
I'll to the witch, her aid I'll seek,
　To win fair Margaret's love I've vowed.
Poor though I am she'll be my mate,
　Proud though she be I'll bend her will
To mine, and rule her future fate
　For weal or woe—for good or ill."

Where breakers foam round dark Kintyre,
　Where hidden rocks to death beguile,
To win his love—his heart's desire,
　Young Kenneth sought the Witch's Isle.
No moon upon his pathway shone,
　No mortal eye his purpose scanned,
By stealth, in silence, and alone
　Fearless he trod that eerie strand.

* Old Woman.

" Grant me, oh witch! the boon I crave,
　And whatsoe'er the price may be,
Or great, or small, that shalt thou have,
　I, by thy Master, swear to thee."
Loud laughed the hag from out the gloom,
　Hoarse croaked the raven overhead,
" Hold thou to that, or dree thy doom,
　My Master's price is high," she said.

" Seal thou our compact with his sign,
　Nor book, nor bell we need to bind,
Swear thou thy first-born shall be mine,
　My Master's kain is paid in kind."
Dim grew his eyes, he heard a name,
　While round him seethed a sea of fire,
But Margaret's face before him came,
　Dear Heaven! *he's won his heart's desire.*

Joy reigned within the chieftain's hall,
　Fair Margaret shone, a happy bride,
And grandest, goodliest of them all
　Young Kenneth moved his love beside.
" Sweet wife," he spake with accent fond,
　Then shuddered as a whispering breath
Fell on his ear, " Thou knowest the bond,
　In joy she'll taste the cup of death."

And death in joy she found, alas!
　As bending o'er his sleeping face
She heard such words as dared not pass
　His lips when waking-sense held place.
" Ah, woe is me! my love is given
　To one whose soul is lost—undone,
To whom is barred the gate of heaven,
　Who owns as lord the Evil One."

Slowly the months rolled on, her eyes
　Grew wild and dark with dread and pain,
As one to whom lost paradise
　May shine afar, but shine in vain.
" Why should such awful blight be laid
　On this poor life of mine forlorn?
The price to Hell's dread Master paid,
　The sinless soul of the Unborn."

And sadder grew young Kenneth's heart,
　And blacker still the shadow fell,
" Oh! grant me strength to do my part,
　And brave the awful powers of Hell.
No penance done, no cleansing fire
　Can purge me of my guilt, I trow,
I sought, and won, my heart's desire,
　And with it won eternal woe."

Once more to seek the witch's den
　He hied him forth at midnight hour,
When deeds are done beyond our ken,
　When evil spirits wield their power.
The beldame's laugh, the raven's croak
　Came hoarsely through the brooding gloom,
As by the witch's blasted oak
　He waited for the words of doom.

" Harken, oh witch! the prayer I make,
　Unasked I pay thy Master's dole;
But, for the price I promised, take
　In free exchange, my own dark soul.
Love bade me buy my heart's desire,
　Love prompts the deed to cast it down,
Love taught my soul by sorrow dire
　To lose for love my heavenly crown."

Loud yelled the witch, the thunder's roll
　Crashed overhead, the lightening gleamed,
"Knowest not," she shrieked, "by soul for soul,
　By life for life, the bond's redeemed.
Learn, hateful one ! vain are thy toils
　For souls by Love Eternal stirred,
Thy Master's power, my Master foils,
　Soon as thy first-born's cry is heard."

"Go ! get thee hence," the raven shrieked,
　Foul shapes his homeward flight pursue,
But vain the beldame's wrath was wreaked,
　For shrill and clear the white cock crew.
When in the east a glimmering spear
　Of light proclaimed the day begun,
Fell on his eager, straining ear
　The wailing of his first-born son.

Fair Margaret smiled, strange peace she felt,
　When to her chamber dim he came,
And contrite by her pillow knelt,
　And softly, fondly, called her name,
"Sweet wife of mine ! I sought thy troth
　To buy and keep, with wicked hire,
Now, by the bond that holds us both,
　I win indeed my heart's desire."

　　　　　　　　　　　JANET A. M'CULLOCH.

JOHN M'KERCHAR, LONDON.

MR. M'KERCHAR hardly requires an
introduction to a Highland audience,
for as Treasurer of the Gaelic Society
of London, and as a prominent leader in matters
of Highland interest in the Metropolis, his name
is familiar to his countrymen at home and abroad.
That he is physically a typical representative of
the Gaelic race, is evident from the portrait
which we have pleasure in giving this month.
He was born at Croftmartaig, Kenmore, Perthshire, in 1850, and was educated at the F. C.
School, Acharn. After acting for some time as
pupil teacher at Aberfeldy, he decided to adopt
a commercial career as being more congenial to
his tastes, and received an appointment with
Messrs. Peter Lawson & Son, Edinburgh, the
well-known Seed Merchants. From there, in
1873, he removed to Chester, where he was
offered an important position in the employment
of Messrs F. & A. Dickson & Sons. It was
during the eight years which Mr. M'Kerchar
spent here that he acquired a taste for Natural
History, the study of which he prosecuted with
great energy and success, and the fruits of which
he embodied in various valuable botanical papers
which he read before the Chester Society of
Natural Science and Literature.

Chester was, however, only a stopping place
on the highway to the great Metropolis, and
there, in 1881, our friend found himself, having
accepted a position of responsibility and trust in

the firm of Mr. B. S. Williams, the great Orchid
Specialist and Horticulturist of Upper Holloway.
In his professional capacity as a trained seeds-
man, Mr. M'Kerchar has travelled a great deal,
on the Continent as well as in the United Kingdom, and has earned the esteem of all with
whom he has come in contact, ever ready to
help those deserving of his generosity, and
ungrudging of his friendship and assistance.

He had not been long in London when he
joined the Gaelic Society, the oldest of the
London Scottish Societies, and now acts as
Honorary Treasurer. (And let us remark in
passing that every true Highlander in the
Metropolis should be a member of this most
useful institution, which does so much for the
preservation of our mother tongue.) He is also
President of the North London Scottish Association, and Vice-President of the Breadalbane
Society, and takes an active part in the further-
ance of all Scottish matters, being a member of
the committee, formed at the instance of the
Gaelic Society, to entertain Brigadier-General
H. A. Macdonald to a banquet and present him
with a Sword of Honour. He is a well-known
and welcome figure at the social gatherings of
Scotsmen and in connection with his profession,
his humorous and eloquent speeches being always
enjoyed by an appreciative audience. In 1897
when the Gaelic Society sent a deputation to
the Secretary for Scotland to advocate the
teaching of Gaelic in Highland schools, Mr.
M'Kerchar's address was one of marked ability,
creditable to himself, and most gratifying to the
members of the Society. Mr. M'Kerchar is still
in the prime of life and has, we hope, many
years of usefulness before him.

LETTER TO THE EDITOR.

THE M'HARDYS.

THEIR ORIGIN AND TRADITIONS.

HELENSBURGH, 7th March, 1899.

DEAR SIR—My attention has been drawn to a
paragraph in your *Celtic Monthly* of February last
to the effect that Mr. Macbain of Rainings School,
Inverness, has suggested that the name M'Hardy
may be derived from the Pictish "Gart Naigh,"
pronounced Gratney, changed to M'Cartney, and
ultimately before 1587 into M'Hardy. Mr. Macbain is further represented as saying that the late
Donald M'Hardy of Daldownie, who died in 1870,
claimed to be head of the M'Hardys and that he
owned no other chief than The Mackintosh.

A statement such as this is very misleading,
besides being unfair to the M'Hardy clan if allowed
to pass unchallenged, and as a humble member of
that sept, hailing from Braemar, I beg to state that
Mr. Macbain is in error.

Yours faithfully
John McKerchar

The M'Hardy clan is undoubtedly a branch sept of the ancient Clan M'Leod of Rasay (now extinct), and the old Braemar tradition is that while King Malcolm Canmore was subduing some of his rebellious chiefs in the north, he took captive to Braemar several clansmen of whom were M'Leods as a guarantee for future good behaviour. The "Legends of the Braes o' Mar" gives the following account of how the name was changed to M'Hardy, viz:— "Malcolm Canmore felt an enormous fancy to the taming of a huge monster called the 'Tad-Losgann' (the toad-frog); others say a wild-boar; and the people round about were taxed, each in turn, a cow or bullock, for its maintenance. It is said to have lived about the rocks of the River Cluny, on which the castle was built. If it could be possible to account for its being there, the name and description of the monster would indicate a crocodile very exactly. Some years previous to this time, a poor man, a M'Leod, had established his household gods in a cottage on the castle plain. He died, leaving his widow with an only son, who grew up a sturdy youth. This youth, imitating the fashions of his fathers, married, and in due time had a son. When the widow's turn to supply the tax in favour of the monster drew near, having but one cow and few merks to purchase another one, she cried out in sorrow and rage—'*Nach truagh nach eil a h-aon de shiol Thorcuill beo, a mharbhadh an Tad-Losgann*' ('What a pity there is not one of the Siol Torquil alive to kill the Tad-Losgann').

This hint at degeneracy from his father's valour fired the young man's blood, and on the morning for the surrender of his mother's cow, it was found the Tad-Losgann had bid adieu to the land of the living—not, by any means, of his own accord. The King frowned and fumed and stormed, and doomed the murderer of his monster to the death. A gibbet, high and strong, awaited him on Craig Choinnich. He was led out by the north gate. The King attended in state. A crowd of nobles surrounded him, and the poor country-folks hung timidly on the flanks. Just at that moment the procession was to start forward, a woman, with an infant in her arms, rushed shrieking through the crowd. She threw her arms round M'Leod.

'Spare him, spare him,' cried she, turning to the King, 'and take everything else we have.' When the soldiers offered to separate them, she clung to him more firmly. 'My love,' said the poor fellow, 'go in peace, and my blessing go with you.' 'No, no,' exclaimed she frantically, 'I will not leave you; I will die with you.' Malcolm was moved to compassion for the wife's sake, but he hated the fellow. 'It's a pity,' said our friend Allan Durward, 'to hang such a splendid archer.' 'A splendid archer, eh, Allan!' replied the King; 'I've an idea.' He had indeed a few, and no wonder, with such a head. The procession wended slowly down to the Dee. Arrived on the nearer bank, the young wife, with her child in her arms, was put across on horseback, and placed on Tom Ghainmheine. M'Leod must pierce with an arrow an apple placed on the head of his son in his wife's arms. The width of the Dee must separate him from his mark. He asked for a bow and three arrows, all of which he examined with the greatest care. Of the spare two, one he took between his teeth, and the other he stuck into his side belt. He aimed, but his body trembled like

the leaves of an aspen, and he drew back, crying out, 'This is hard!' Again he placed himself, but he trembled still. He turned round to the King, and repeated in a low voice, 'This is hard!' There was no relenting in the King's face. For the third time he fell into the attitude. A voice, hoarse, and lowly distinct like the roll of distant thunder uttered, 'This is hard!' Everyone of the spectators trembled and withheld their breath. His son stretched out his arms on the opposite bank, and the mother covered her eyes with her hand. His sinews stiffened like tightened cords, and stood out from the surrounding flesh like willow-wands: the arrow parted like a ray of sunshine the apple fell from the child's head in two equal parts; the mother seized her child with a cry of delight, pressed him to her bosom, and covered him with kisses. The murmur of applause rose into a shout of triumph. The King approached, and seeing the last traces of agony passing from the face of M'Leod—'Why,' demanded he, 'did you ask for three arrows, you so sure of hand and keen of sight?' 'Because if I had missed the apple, or hurt my wife or son, I was determined not to miss you.' The King turned pale; but imagining that a man like this would perhaps be as valuable to him as the Tad-Losgann—'Friend,' said he, softening his voice, 'I receive you into my bodyguard, in which you will be well provided for.' 'I can never love you enough,' answered the undaunted Celt, 'to fight in your defence, after the painful proof you have put my heart to.' The King turned away in amazement, crying out, 'Hardy thou art, and Hardy thou shalt be.' The descendants of this M'Leod were called Hardy's son, which in Gaelic is MacHardy."

The version here given has a resemblance to Tell's exploit, still this origin is so strongly corroborated by the fact that the Clan M'Hardy crest and motto are identical with the crest and motto on the ancient arms of the M'Leods of Rasay, and the M'Hardy Buies, as they were termed of old, have always adhered rigidly to this version; and they can trace their descent back in Braemar to a very remote period.

There are many instances to be seen in the old R. C. Registers of how Macleod *alias* M'Hardy Buies are entered. Notably—the Rev. Wm. M'Leod *alias* M'Hardy (a near relation of my grandfather), who was priest for many years at Tornahaish, Corgarff, about 1745, and was afterwards priest in Braemar, in which latter place he died in 1809, at a very old age; and he almost invariably signed his name Wm. M'Leod. Many of his relations (M'Hardys) are still living in Braemar and Corgarff districts.

There is, however, another account given of the origin of M'Hardy which is believed in by some, viz. That the name originated from a Frenchman named Hardie to whom King David II. granted certain lands in Corgarff about the middle of the 14th century. There were no doubt several families in Strathdon who were called M'Hardy, *alias* Dhu or black M'Hardys, but they were a different race from the M'Hardy Buies; some of them became connected with the Buies through marriage. These M'Hardys *alias* Dhu, I believe, claimed their descent from the French origin.

In 1715 the M'Hardys and all the Braemar men

rose to a man under the Earl of Mar's Standard, the Laird of Inverey being Colonel, and his brother, James of Balmoral, aide-de-camp to the Earl of Mar. In 1715 the Braemar, Strathdee, and Glengairn men, including the M'Hardys, rose with the Farquharsons, who were then the leading clan in the district, and those of Strathdon, Corgarff, Glenlivat, Tomintoul, etc., under Lord Lewis Gordon and the Laird of Glenbucket, and not under The Mackintosh as has been erroneously stated—see position of Highland clans at Culloden in "Historical Geography of Clans of Scotland," by F. B. Johnston, Esq., F.R.G.S., etc., and Colonel Robertson, F.S.A.S., Edinburgh—it being a well-known rule amongst the clans that where the powerful or leading clan of a district had to be raised all the smaller adjoining clans and tenants bound themselves to join in with the leading clan for their own safety and protection. After 1715 the Earl of Mar's estates were forfeited, and M'Hardys and other tenants who had formerly held lands off the Earls of Mar had in 1745 become tenants of Farquharson of Invercauld and others. In no case can it be shown that the M'Hardys owned Mackintosh as their chief, so that Mr. Macbain's statement that Donald M'Hardy of Daldownie owned no other chief than Mackintosh is not correct.

That M'Hardy, Daldownie, claimed to be chief or head of the M'Hardys is perfectly true. Daldownie and my father were brothers' sons, and consequently he was well known to myself and brothers, five of whom are still living. He was also uncle to Mr. Peter Coutts of Ballater, who resided with him from 1827 till his (Daldownie's) death in 1870, and being now 84 years of age and in full possession of all his faculties can testify, with my family, that M'Hardy, Daldownie, never owned Mackintosh as his chief; but that he adhered most rigidly to the M'Leod-M'Hardy tradition, both as to sept and clan tartan. The M'Hardy clan tartan was worn and preserved by the M'Hardy Buics and by them only.

There is no doubt but that this Donald M'Hardy's father, Donald, and his grandfather, Alister Mòr, alias "Ballochbuie," were recognised leaders, as several stirring tales are related of this "Ballochbuie" when acting in that capacity with the Braemar men on occasions when raids or creachs were made upon the people in that district. His success in restoring the creachs to their lawful owners was often told.

This Alister, "Ballochbuie," had three sons, viz: (1) Donald, of whom are descended the family of Daldownie and the family of John M'Hardy at Invercauld; (2) Alister of Auchallater, of whom are descended my own family and the family of the late Alister M'Hardy of Newe, Strathdon (who was leader of the Lonach men for upwards of 40 years), and others; (3) James of Inverey, of whom are descended the M'Hardys of Viewmount, Braemar, and that of Braemore and Plockton, Ross-shire, and others. Ballochbuie had a brother, George of Dalchork, who had two sons: (1) Donald of Gleneye, of whom are descended the M'Hardys of Tomintoul and Croftmicken, etc.; (2) Charles of Dalvorar, of whom are descended a M'Hardy family in Dundee.

Another important fact which shows the M'Hardys owned M'Leod as their chief is that

when the Press Gang Act, as it was called in the Highlands, became law (which compelled anyone to enter the army if called upon, even against their will), my grandfather and his brother Donald, "Daldownie," happened to be in Perth. Donald had gone out early in the morning for a stroll, and was met on the old bridge by twelve men of the press gang, who demanded him in the King's name to join them. On his refusal an attempt was made to compel him by force, which resulted in a serious melee. Daldownie having succeeded in making his escape made a hasty retreat over the hills to Mar, arriving at Gordon's of Abergeldie the same evening, a distance of 60 miles. The Dragoons, who were in hot pursuit, failed to capture him, and Daldownie was put to the horn as an outlaw. On this fact becoming known in Mar, the Braemar men rose in rebellion against this obnoxious Act, and were led by James of Inverey, who marched down to Crathie and took possession of and destroyed all the official papers found there relating to the Press Gang Act. On continuing their march towards Aboyne Castle, with the view of soliciting the Marquis of Huntly's influence with the Government to have this offensive Act cancelled, they were intercepted by the Dragoons who had been communicated with. They met on the Moor of Dinnet, and the result was that James of Inverey and John Bowman, leaders, etc, were taken prisoners and lodged in Aberdeen gaol. On my grandfather learning what had occurred, he forthwith went direct to the Chief of the Clan M'Leod (whom he owned as his chief), and laid the whole of the facts of the case before him. M'Leod, "Chief," assured him of his sympathy and support, and being at the time in favour with the Crown, used his influence with the Government, the consequence was that James of Inverey and Bowman, etc. were liberated from prison in due course. This experience of my grandfather and his brothers was often told us by my late father; and there are people living still to whom my grandfather told the same tale—repeatedly too—adding that he would never forget the hearty welcome he received from the M'Leod Chief at Dunvegan Castle on that occasion.

It would ill become us, M'Hardy Buics, if we failed in the least iota in adhering to the old traditions of the M'Hardy clan, which our forefathers held so long and true under many trying circumstances.

There are many other M'Hardys deserving of special notice, but I have only referred to the head of the Daldownie branch and his near relations, as he happens to be the person specially mentioned in the paragraph referred to. I trust Mr. Macbain will now feel satisfied that there are a sufficient number of Donald M'Hardy, Daldownie's, relatives still living who are quite willing and able to uphold and guard the old traditions of the Clan M'Hardy at all hazards.

CHAS. M'HARDY.

CLAN MENZIES SOCIETY.—Lieut. D. P. Menzies, Hon. Corresponding Secretary, has just received from Dr. W. F. Menzies, Chedleton, a donation of Ten Guineas towards the Clan Benevolent Fund inaugurated by the Chief, which now amounts to £100. The Society is making excellent progress.

THE SOCIAL CONDITION OF THE HIGHLANDS SINCE 1800.

By A. J. BEATON, F.S.A. Scot., F.G.S.E.

(Continued from page 116).

IX.—INDUSTRIES.

AGRICULTURE.

WHEN comparing the present condition of agriculture with what it represented at the commencement of the present century, notwithstanding the inferior nature of the soil and the ungenial climate, many Highland farmers, by their shrewdness and resolute determination, although labouring under so many difficulties, have distinguished themselves more than any other class of farmers perhaps anywhere, and the great progress which agriculture has made in the north-eastern parts of Scotland during the last hundred years testifies to the high position which these Highlanders now occupy as agriculturists. In the poorer localities, particularly among the crofting class, especially in the outer Hebrides, little advance has been made during the past one hundred years. At the commencement of this century, agricultural prices were exceedingly high. In 1812 wheat fetched 126s 6d per quarter, but gradually it fell until in 1822 it declined to 44s 7d per quarter, while in 1841 wheat sold at 26s per quarter. Notwithstanding these fluctuations, we find that the rentals of Inverness and Ross-shires stood as follows:—

Rentals, 1815. 1873. 1887.
County of Inverness £185,565 £417,951 £420,892
Ross and Cromarty 121,557 298,325 310,150

Showing an increase in the 72 years of £235,327 on the rental of Inverness-shire, and for the combined counties of Ross and Cromarty £188,893; from these figures—after making a liberal deduction for increase in Burghs and valuation of Railways— we must infer that farmers, seventy years ago, must have had a good time, or that to-day the tillers of the soil must be labouring for nought.

Agriculture during the present century has had a series of revivals and of corresponding depressions. The most notable depression began about the year 1879, when a series of bad seasons came in succession, till affairs became so desperate in 1879 that a Royal Commission of enquiry was appointed to enquire into the prevailing agricultural distress; and the Commissioners' report, which was issued in 1882, pointed out that two of the most prevalent causes of distress were bad seasons and foreign competition, aggravated by increased cost of production and heavy loss of live stock from disease.

On the strength of the Commissioners' report Mr. Gladstone's Government, in 1883, passed the Agricultural Holdings' Act, a measure tending in the right direction, but conferring on the tenant, but few of the privileges which he contends he is entitled to. Of the other legislative measures passed during this century I need hardly mention the repeal of the Corn Laws, the Abolition of Hypothec, the Ground Game Act, the Abolition of the Malt Tax,* and the Cattle Diseases Act of 1884, all measures having a tendency to ameliorate the condition of the tenant farmer.

About a quarter of a century ago agricultural prices stood at a remunerative figure, and the demand for farms far exceeded the supply, resulting in fabulous prices being given for land; and at the same period landlords were seized with a mania for creating large farms and consequently hundreds of the small tenants were evicted, and sometimes as many as a dozen holdings were rolled into one vast farm. Men of capital readily took up every farm in the market, many of them on long leases; but a series of bad seasons landed most of the large farmers in bankruptcy. Some managed with difficulty to carry out their agreement, but on the expiry of their lease they quitted as ruined men, while others failed to complete any more than half the terms of their contracts.

Big farms have therefore proved a failure,

---

* Some contend that the Abolition of the Malt Tax has been injurious to the farmer by removing what used to be a practical bounty on British barley. But if this was its effects, the intention of it was undoubtedly good, and the effect unforeseen by the promoters of the Act.

HIGHLAND CATTLE

and several causes can be assigned for this. The chief cause may, however, be attributed to cost of production together with low prices; because the big farmer when not near a town must employ a large permanent staff, whereas in the days when he was surrounded by small tenants and crofters he could secure labour just as he required it.

The landlords also made a fatal mistake when they converted the small and middle class farms into extensive holdings. No doubt they considered it more economical, as one set of offices would serve where perhaps five or six steadings would be required were the various farms to be re-let, the buildings of nearly all the smaller farms being in a most dilapidated condition at that period. How far their economical policy has benefitted them they themselves know; but now they are compelled to sub-divide those farms as well as to erect premises and offices; and thus it appears to have been simply a case of putting off the evil day for a short period, and during that period the evil was accumulating. Had the small farmers been left in their holdings they would in all probability have weathered through the storm of depression.

X.—CATTLE BREEDING.

With the exception of a few well-known herds high class breeding of cattle does not receive the amount of attention in the Highlands which the beef producing counties of Aberdeen, Banff, Forfar, etc. devote to this branch. Indeed, in these days what with foreign competition and low prices, it does not pay the trouble and risk involved in rearing fat stock.

The West Highland ox, with his shaggy coat and picturesque appearance, is the breed most profitable and best adapted to the Highland counties. In 1884 Argyllshire alone had 660,500 head of best Highland cattle.

Sheep farming is an equally if not more important industry than arable farming. In 1884 it was estimated that in the Highlands there were 6,983,293 sheep, of which 2,393,826 were lambs.

The once remunerative business of sheep farming induced landlords to convert whole tracts of territory, then under cultivation, into extensive sheep runs; and sheep farmers are therefore looked upon by the crofters of Scotland as the primary movers or originators of evictions.

Sheep farming, as well as the kindred branch of agriculture, has suffered in the general depression aggravated by the large importations of foreign mutton and wool. The estimated quantity of wool grown in Scotland in 1884 was about 34,500,000 lbs., and the estimated weight of wool imported from Australasia in the same year was 400,000,000 lbs.†

Again the fabulous prices offered for sporting estates led to the breaking up of sheep farms and the converting of them into deer forests, so that to-day there are about 2¼ millions of acres occupied as deer forests in the Highlands of Scotland.

Before leaving the question of sheep I must allude to the great "Wool Fair" held at Inverness in July of each year. There are hundreds of thousands of sheep sold annually at this market, and yet not a head is exhibited. "This market is peculiar," says a well known writer, "in so far as no stock whatever is shewn, the buyer depending entirely upon the integrity of the seller together with the character the stock is known to possess." "It is a great source of pride to the farmers in this part of Scotland to be able, as they are, to say that no question involving legal proceedings has ever yet arisen out of a misrepresentation of stock sold at this market, which has been in existence since the commencement almost of this present century."

Dairy farming is not carried on scientifically nor to any great extent beyond the requirements of local consumption, and only in a very few localities is cheese manufactured, beyond what is required for home use. There is wide scope for developing this industry, for in many of the English counties the farmers are solely dependent on the manufacture of cheese as the means of paying their rents.‡

On the rich alluvial lands skirting the shores of the Cromarty and Moray Firths, and indeed throughout the Highlands generally, where farms attain an area of any considerable extent, cultivation is carried out on the most improved principles; and large sums of money have been expended on draining, trenching, and squaring lands. The modern improvements in agricultural machinery have materially assisted the farmer in bringing the soil to the present high condition in which we find the arable lands in those districts referred to.

"No account of the agriculture of Scotland," says the late sub-editor of the "North British Agriculturist"—Mr. James Landells—"would be complete without some reference to the peculiar condition of the smaller tenants of the Highlands and Islands. The system of agriculture pursued by the crofters, or the smaller tenants, is of the most wretched description."

---

† Vide Ordnance Gazetteer.

‡ Co-Operative Dairies, with Central Creameries, have been established in Ireland and prove most remunerative investments. There is a wide field in the Highlands for the establishment of similar manufactures.

(To be continued).

MATHEW HENDERSON.

THE CELTIC MONTHLY:
A MAGAZINE FOR HIGHLANDERS.
Edited by JOHN MACKAY, Glasgow.

No. 8 Vol. VII.]   MAY, 1899.   [Price Threepence.

MATHEW HENDERSON,
PRESIDENT, GLASGOW COWAL SOCIETY.

IT has been estimated that about two-thirds of the population of Glasgow are of Celtic name, and a glance at the directory will be sufficient to convince one that a very large proportion of these are of West Highland origin. To the young and ambitious Gael in the remote clachans of Argyllshire and the Western Isles, Glasgow offers attractions compared to which even the great metropolis must be content to occupy an inferior place. The Northern Highlands sends the bulk of its young men to Edinburgh and London, while the Western Highlands pours the best of its strong and energetic manhood into St. Mungo's city, where its immense commercial connections offer plenty of scope for their energies and talents. Even Glendaruel, that secluded and beautiful little spot in Cowal, sends its annual contingent city-wards—probably inspired with the spirit of "The Lost Pibroch", the strains of which seem to fire the ambition and adventurous desire of the youth of every Highland village.

Among the many men of note which Cowal has presented to Glasgow, there is no one better known than the genial Highlander whose portrait we give this month. Mr. Mathew Henderson was born in "The Glen," the son of a farmer, and came of a sturdy stock. As a boy he acquired proficiency in those two qualifications which are expected to equip the Highland lad for the battle of life—a good education and a reputation as a crack shinty player! They indicate a healthy mental and physical condition. When twenty years of age, Mr. Henderson came to Glasgow to serve his apprenticeship as a joiner with the firm of John Nairn & Sons, on the completion of which he accepted a partnership with John Lamb & Co.; and since the retiral of Mr. Lamb forty years ago, Mr. Henderson has carried on the business in his own name. His career has been very successful, his firm to-day occupying one of the foremost positions in the trade in the West of Scotland. Many of the finest buildings in Glasgow bear evidence to his energy and skill; while some of the largest erections on the Clyde are examples of his enterprise.

The enthusiasm which characterises Mr. Henderson in his business pursuits he carries with him into all matters in which he may be interested. In recognition of the high position which he occupies in his trade, he was elected a Deacon of the Wrights' Incorporation; and a similar honour was conferred upon him by the ancient Society of Anderston Weavers. To Highlanders, however, he is popularly known as President of the Glasgow Cowal Society, a position which he has worthily held during the past two years. This society enjoys the reputation of being one of the most useful and successful of the Highland organizations of Glasgow; and it is interesting to mention that Mr. Henderson has made his term of office the most prosperous in the history of the society. At the Annual Business Meeting, held last month, he was elected Hon. President.

He occupied the chair at the recent large Annual Concert of the Cowal Shinty Club, his amusing reminiscences of how shinty was played in his younger days in Cowal being one of the most enjoyable features of the evening.

Some years ago he built a beautiful house at Drumchapel, where Highland friends always receive a hearty welcome from the Deacon and his hospitable wife.

AN APPRECIATION. That the *Celtic Monthly* is welcomed in distant lands is amply evidenced by the following extract from an American letter:

"The *Celtic* is good throughout, the illustrations 'second to none.' The short stories which appear from month to month are selected with excellent judgment. Whenever Torquil Macleod appears with one of his quaint but graphic stories, which are singularly appropriate to the columns of such a magazine, the land of the 'Almighty Dollar' is forgotten for the nonce, and we are again back in the land of beetling crags and dark mantling woods. The late Alexander Mackenzie never dreamed that the successor to his magazine would turn out to be such a beauty, in accomplishments as well as in appearance. You have good reason to be proud of the *Celtic*."

Deeds that won the Empire. ✸

By JOHN MACKAY, C.E., J.P., Hereford.

Capture of Havana, 1762.

(Continued from page 135).

THE expedition destined for this undertaking consisted of 19 ships of the line and 18 frigates carrying 2042 guns, under the command of Admiral Sir George Pocock, K.C.B., with 150 transports, having on board 10,000 land forces. These were joined by 3000 more from America, and the Highlanders from Martinique. The troops were commanded by General the Earl of Albemarle. The armament assembled off the north-west point of Hispaniola, and for the sake of expedition was skilfully conducted through the old channel of Bahama, arriving on the 6th of June in sight of the far-famed Havana. The object of their long and perilous voyage and of so many ardent hopes, was now before them.

The appearance of the city at the entrance of the port is one of the most picturesque and beautiful in Equinoctial America. The strong fortifications that crown the rocks on the eastern side, the noble internal basin, where more than a thousand vessels might anchor sheltered from every wind, the majesty of the groves of palms which there grow to a vast height, the city itself, with its white houses all of Gothic and Saracenic style, with quaint galleries and deep red roofs, the pillars and pinnacled towers and domes, half seen and half hidden amid the forest of masts and sails, seen under a clear and burning sun, all conspired to present a most imposing spectacle.

The north side of the entrance to the harbour is formed by a high ridge called the "Cabana," the face of which is almost perpendicular, and crowned by bastions that overlook the city and the sea. At the extreme point of the entrance stands the Moro. This range of fortifications, together with Fort Principe and the Castle of Altares to the west, some ridges of low elevation and rows of palm trees, encompass the plain on which, on the western side of the harbour, stands the city in the form of a semi-circle, with its suburbs in the rear.

The Moro Castle was then, and still is, an edifice of great strength, having two bastions towards the sea, and two more on the land side, with a deep wide trench cut out of the solid rock. The opposite point of the entrance was secured by another fort called the Puntal, which was girt by ditches, and in every way calculated for co-operating with the Moro in defence of the harbour, and it had also batteries that faced the country and enfiladed the city wall, but the latter and the fortifications of the city itself were not in good repair, the ditch was a dry one and the covered way was nearly in ruins.

It was therefore thought by some officers that the town should have been attacked by land, especially as it was impracticable to assail it by sea, the entrance to the harbour being subject to a cross fire from the Moro and Puntal, and defended by 14 Spanish ships of the line, three of which were afterwards sunk in the channel, across which a boom was thrown. Either from being ignorant of the real state of the defence or from viewing objects differently, Albemarle resolved to begin with the reduction of the great Moro, the fall of which he thought would ensure that of the city. On the other hand it was alleged that if the city had been attacked, its wall could not have been defended for twenty-four hours. If the Earl made mistakes, the Spaniards were guilty of greater. Though timely informed that Britain had declared war against Spain they were not roused from their apathy, and when the British armament was off the shores of Cuba they had taken no means of defence. All was confusion and alarm when the sails of the hostile fleet were first descried covering all the sea between the old channel and the Gulf of Florida. Instead of having their ships at sea and ready for action, they were retained in the harbour. A naval victory, even dearly bought, might have saved the city.

but now, the city and harbour once taken nothing could save the fleet.

When the troops were ready to land, the Admiral, with a large portion of the fleet, bore away to the west and made a feint of disembarking, while a detachment, protected by Commodore Keppel, approached the shore to the eastward and landed without opposition ; a small fort that might have opposed them had been previously destroyed by the British ships. It was on this side that the main body of the troops were meant to act. They were formed in two columns, one being immediately occupied in the attack on the Moro, the other in covering the siege and protecting the foragers who procured water, wood, and provisions. The former column was led by General Keppel, the covering force by General Elliot, while a detachment under Colonel Howe was encamped near the west end of the city to cut off its communication with the country, and to divide the attention of the Spaniards.

The hardships sustained by the troops during the siege operations were incredible. The earth everywhere was so thin that it was with the greatest difficulty they could make their approaches under cover, the want of water and the great heat were most distressing. Fatigue parties had to carry water from a great distance, so scanty and precarious was the quantity that the troops had frequently to be supplied from the casks of the shipping. Roads had to be cut through the dense woods that grew in all the rank luxuriance peculiar to a tropical climate, and the artillery had to be dragged by pathless ways from a rough and rocky shore.

In these painful efforts under a burning West Indian sun, many of the seamen and soldiers, worn with toil, drenched with perspiration, maddened with thirst, dropped down dead in the drag-ropes, in the trenches, at their posts, slain by sheer heat and fatigue ; yet every obstacle was at last overcome, as they always were, and ever will be, by the happy unanimity that existed between the two branches of the service, seamen and soldiers, and batteries were at length erected along a ridge on a level with the fort, and from these, on the 20th of June, bombs were first thrown. The ships in the harbour were driven back so that their guns could not molest the besiegers, and a sally made by the garrison was repulsed with great slaughter by the the trench guards.

On the 30th three British ships of the line moved up to the Moro to breach the wall, but the Spaniards defended the fort with great bravery, and the ships, after a cannonade of six hours, had to sheer out of range, after suffering severely in loss of men and damage to the ships.   (*To be continued*).

THE SOCIAL CONDITION OF THE HIGHLANDS SINCE 1800.

By A. J. BEATON, F.S.A. Scot., F.G.S.E.

(*Continued from page* 140).

THE chronic state of poverty associated with the crofting class is alluded to in an earlier chapter. The land agitation, which had been smouldering over the Highlands during the past fifteen years, at length broke out in the wild and distant township of Valtos in Skye, and from there it spread rapidly all over the Highlands and Islands.

It was not till 1882 that the agitation reached its climax, when the "Battle of the Braes," near Portree, began, where a force of seventy policemen arrested a number of crofters accused of having deforced a Sheriff Officer : they were, however, all acquitted, except two, who were fined. In the autumn of same year another campaign was commenced at Braes, and similar riots broke out in Glendale ; and the turbulent spirit was spreading all over Skye, until it was found necessary to despatch H. M. gunboat "Jackal" with a special Government Commission on board to remonstrate with the inhabitants. The agitation had by now raised such a feeling in the country, and so attracted even the attention of Parliament, that in 1883 the Government appointed a Royal Commission to enquire into the condition of the crofters and cottars of the Highlands and Islands of Scotland. The Commission, with Lord Napier as chairman, found "*that the crofter population suffered from undue contraction of the area of holdings*, insecurity of tenure, want of compensation for improvements, high rents, defective communications, and withdrawal of the soil in connection with the purposes of sport." "Defects in education and in the machinery of justice, and want of facilities for emigration, also contributed to depress the condition of the people, while the fishing population, who were identified with the farming class, were in want of *harbours, piers, boats, and tackle for deep-sea fishing, and access to the great markets of consumption*." The Highland Land League was now organised ; and at Martinmas, 1884, a "no-rent" manifesto was issued ; and many tenants absolutely refused to pay any rent until the land was fairly divided among them. Raids were made on deer forests, march fences were demolished, and lands were forcibly taken possession of, until the whole of Skye and the Long Island were in a complete state of chaotic anarchy. Attempts were made to serve summonses of removal, but the officers were mobbed and deforced. In November, 1884, it became necessary to send a military expedition to Skye with four gun boats and five hundred marines. This formidable force restored order, and the crofters accused of acts of deforcement submitted to be quietly apprehended.

In face of the recommendations contained in the report of the Royal Commission accentuated by those riots in the Hebrides, Parliament in 1886 passed the Crofters' Holdings (Scotland) Act, whereby three Commissioners were appointed to fix "fair rents" and deal with the question of arrears, and at the end of year 1887 the Commissioners had examined 1767 holdings, and for year ending 31st December, 1888, they examined and awarded decisions on 2185 holdings, being a total of 3952 cases dealt with from the opening of the enquiry, having 7621 applications to be still dealt with as at 31st December, 1888.

I append a table shewing number of holdings for which "fair rents" have been fixed, and amount of arrears cancelled.

Year ending	No. of Holdings.	Present Rent.	Fair Rent.	Arrears Cancelled.
31st Dec., 1887,	1767	£12,457 16 0	£8,617 6 0	£14,418 5 1
31st Dec., 1888,	2185	£11,882 1s 8	£8,280 1 11	£16,897 4 5
Totals,	3952	£24,340 s 8	£16,897 7 11	£28,315 9 7
			£16,897 7 11	
Permanent Reduction of Annual Rent,		£7,349 0 9		

This gives an average reduction of rent of 30·15 per cent on the total number of cases examined, and an average of 64·82 per cent of cancelled arrears. These judicial decisions prove that the crofters had just cause for complaint; and although I shall not attempt to justify the means which they adopted for the purpose of getting remedial legislature, still I will venture to say that our legislators are pursuing a false policy in allowing bad laws to goad the people to the verge of rebellion before they introduce measures of reform; for this gives an excitable race the idea that nothing for their benefit can be obtained without becoming turbulent and riotous.

I have already shown that in many parts of the Highlands agriculture made rapid strides during the present century; yet in the Hebrides, and, indeed, among nearly the whole crofter community, little if any progress has been made. In the first report issued by the Crofters' Commission we find the following paragraphs:—"The land, both in Skye and in all the other islands visited, is subjected to a process of continuous cropping which is disastrous. There is no particular shift or rotation adopted, the land being continuously cropped as long as it will grow anything. The consequent waste and

* The total permanent reductions in rent for the nine years 1886-87 to 1895-96 = £21,387 16s.—and the amount of arrears cancelled in same period = £123,469 2s. 10d.—*Vide* Parliamentary Return, 6th April, 1897.

deterioration of the land, especially the weaker kinds, is enormous. This observation, however, is not true to the same extent of Skye as of South and North Uist, the soil in Skye being generally of a stronger nature."

"It may be added that in Skye as in some other places we found great room for improvement in the matter of leading drains. It frequently happened that a crofter suffered from his neighbour failing to make and keep these in a state of efficiency. It also frequently occurred that a crofter waited for years on his landlord getting such drains scoured out in reliance on some real or supposed obligation to do so, instead of putting them in working order himself and thereby greatly improving his croft."

The Duke of Argyll, in a very learned article in the "Nineteenth Century" of January 1889 on "Isolation," after deploring the alarming increase of the population on the barren shores of the wild Hebrides, says:—"But there was another cause that effected the whole of Scotland, where the rising tide of innovation and improvement did not reach and did not submerge it. This cause was the profound and almost unfathomable ignorance and barbarism of the native agriculture, together with a traditional system of occupation, which, as it were enshrined and encased, every ancestral stupidity in an impenetrable panoply of inveterate customs." This language may sound harsh, or even unjust. And so it might be, if such language were not used in the strictest sense, and with a due application of the lesson to ourselves. We are all stupid in our various degrees, and each generation of men wonders at the blindness and stupidity of those who have gone before them. Man only opens his owlish eyes by gradual winks and blinks to the opportunities of nature and to his own powers in relation to them. Let us just think, for example, of the case of preserving grass in "silos," a resource only discovered, or, at least, recognised, within the last few years, yet a resource which supplied one essential want of agriculture in wet climates at no greater cost of ingenuity or of trouble than digging a hole in the ground, covering the fresh cut and wet material with sticks, and weighting it with stones.

THE CLAN MACKAY SOCIETY held the last meeting of the season in Edinburgh on 21st April, Major A. V. Mackay, president, in the chair. The controversy regarding the Mackay banner was discussed at considerable length, Rector MacBain's references to the relic in the *Northern Chronicle* as the "Skibo" flag, on the most frivolous grounds, being warmly resented. The Rector's readiness to accept every statement made by Mr. Murray Rose as correct has had its inevitable result; he has associated his name with arguments which have been proved untrue, and has accepted as genuine arms which are bogus.

FINLAY ALEXANDER MACRAE.

FINLAY A. MACRAE, LONDON.

 MR. FINLAY ALEX-ANDER MACRAE was born at the Free Manse, Kilmorie, Arran, on 18th November, 1858. His father, the Rev. Donald Mac-Rae, had been minister of the parish of Poolewe, Ross-shire, which he left at the Disruption, and was subsequently F.C. minister of Tarbert, Loch Fyne, and for twenty-three years of Kilmorie. His mother was a daughter of the Rev. Alexander Russell, of Gairloch, whose grandson is ex-Lord Provost Sir James Russell, of Edinburgh.

On his father's death, the family removed to Edinburgh, where Mr MacRae received his education. He served four years in a grain merchant's office in Leith, thereafter removing to London, where he has spent twenty years the last ten of which have been devoted to South African business, in which his firm is largely interested. On 24th January, 1893, at Crathie Manse, he was married to Myra, third daughter of the Rev. Colin F. Campbell, minister of Lamlash parish, Arran.

Mr. MacRae's name has been closely identified with athletics for many years past : indeed, it may be truly remarked that there are few sports in which he has not engaged and excelled. He has been successful on the running-path ; and as a player of Rugby football he was well known. In connection with cycling matters his name has always been prominent, having acted in 1887-88 as general secretary for the National Cyclists' Union. He has himself been a successful competitor in events from one mile to a twenty-four hours' contest ; and for seventeen years represented his club (the London Scottish B.C.) in the Union. He also acted for five years as secretary of the Records' Committee, in connection with which body he organised the system for checking road and path records.

This year Mr. MacRae has accepted a very important appointment, which is at present receiving his serious attention. We refer to the hon. secretaryship of the Scottish Gathering in London. He became a member of committee in 1890, and has taken a keen interest in promoting its success. This year, however, he has taken in hand the organisation of the great gathering for the 22nd of this month (Whit-Monday), and we trust that our readers in London will not fail to attend, and give Mr. MacRae their support. The object is a most deserving one. Nearly £1000 of the proceeds of the Gathering have been distributed between the aged pensioners of the Scottish Hospital, the boys and girls of the Caledonian Asylum, the West Highland Relief Fund, and other charitable institutions. Doubtless the MacRae and other tartans will be well represented at the gathering.

ISEABAL.

ISEABAL sat spinning in her lonely cottage, and as the wheel turned, thoughts of the news she had just heard came crowding through her brain; Moina dying and Nial killed in the war! But what did it matter? What was Nial to her, and was not Moina always a weak puny creature, not like the other women of the glen? Why had Nial married her? Was it not Iseabal that all the glen had named as Nial's wife, and was not she the only woman Nial had ever looked at since the days when they were children pulling the blackberries on the heathery braes and weaving wreaths of red rowans to crown Iseabal's dark curls? Then came the year she had spent in Skye with her mother's folk, and the news that came to her of Nial's wedding with Moina ; and now Moina, who had come between them with her childish face and clinging ways, was dying, and her baby only a week old.

Iseabal's wheel whirred on in the cheerful glow of the fire. Outside the wind blew keen and cold from the Firth of Lorn and trailed the white mists across the mighty shoulder of Ben Cruachan. Iseabal rose and looked out. It was going to be a wild night, and Moina would be alone, save for old Morag, who was still and frail. The snow had begun to fall in soft feathery flakes, and the wind was rising. As it moaned round the house it sounded to Iseabal like the plaintive sobbing of a little child. Would Moina's child cry and would anyone tend it, the little baby who would never know a father's or mother's love? Darkness was beginning to fall, but still Iseabal gazed at the snow as it drifted against the little window. There she stood dry-eyed and stern looking; but the heart within her breast was beating as if it would burst. At last she turned from the window and did a strange thing. She filled a bottle with new milk, and put it in a basket along with some bannocks ; then, wrapping herself in her plaid, she passed out into the drifting snow.

In the cottage by the loch side Moina lay weak and listless, with her baby on her arm, thinking bitter thoughts. Old Morag had fallen asleep by the fire, and heeded not the rising storm that blew the smoke of the fire down in clouds which lazily curled upwards again to the blackened rafters.

Moina started as a low knock came to the door. Who could it be on such a night?

Perhaps someone who had lost his way amongst the snow. Another gentle knock, and then the sneck was lifted, and a woman entered quietly as if she knew of the ailing one there. She threw off her plaid; and as she approached the bed Moina gasped faintly, "Iseabal, why have you come? Let me die in peace. I have been punished, Iseabal, I have. Leave me, leave me."

"Wheesht, wheesht and rest, I have come to help you in your trouble. You will let me help you, Moina? I have heard the news from the war about Nial;" and she turned away and shook the snow from her plaid and hung it to dry at the fire. Then coming to the side of the bed again she whispered, "Will you let me see your baby?"

Moina, who had been staring at Iseabal with wondering eyes, turned back the blanket and showed the little one sleeping peacefully in the warm folds. Iseabal bent down and stroked his little downy head and talked to him softly as if he understood.

"Iseabal," began Moina, "You are good to come."

"Wait till I have given you something nice to drink," interrupted Iseabal. "You must lie quiet and rest just now."

She stirred the fire into a blaze and put on more wood. As it crackled old Morag awoke with a start. "Iseabal," she cried, "is it you? You here? Well, well, glad indeed I am to see you. It is lonely watching here in the night, although" (she added in a whisper and glancing towards the bed) "it wont be for long now, poor lamb. I can see the shroud coming higher and higher."

"Morag, I have come to stay with Moina, to-night, so you can sleep, you must be weary."

"I am, a luaidh;" and muttering to herself about the strange ways of women, she lay down on a heap of hay in the corner, and was soon sleeping again, snoring deeply.

Moina lay with closed eyes, her long fair hair lying on the pillow limp and heavy. As Iseabal smoothed the blankets a great pity filled her heart for the girl who had come between her and her life's happiness. She was so young, so helpless, and so lonely.

The child wakened and was getting restless, and Iseabal lifted him from the hollow of his mother's arm, and sat down with him on a stool by the fire. As she drew the shawl closer round him, he opened his eyes and closed his warm little hand round her finger. The soft touch thrilled her woman's heart, and her eyes filled with tears as she clasped closer the baby of the woman she had hated. There she sat in the firelight bending over him and crooning softly old tunes with the sighing of the wind in them, the wind as it sweeps across the loch and bends

the rustling reeds, old songs of broken hearts and long farewells. Then she went on to a song Nial used to sing to her, with the refrain:

"Mo rùn geal dileas, dileas, dileas,
Mo rùn geal dileas nach till thu null,
Cha till mi fhin leat a ghaoil cha'n fhaoil mi
Ochoin a ghaoil seun tha mise tinn."

The tender words brought a crowd of memories with them. She was once more walking with Nial at her side, and the scent of the sun-warmed heather filled the air. Then there was the wedding of Mairi Nic Artair and the dancing afterwards. Och, the reels and the piping that made the rafters ring again and again. Was the like of it ever heard before in the glen? But everything was bright in those days.

A sigh from Moina awoke Iseabal from her dreaming. She rose and laid the sleeping child at the foot of the bed. "Iseabal," said Moina, holding out her hand, "I want to speak to you. You must let me speak while I am able. You don't know the wrong I have done you. You must listen," she said as Iseabal bade her keep quiet. Then she told the miserable story of how she too had loved Nial, and of how, when Iseabal was in Skye, she had told him that Iseabal had forgotten him, and was going to marry Donnacha Ruadh, the grand piper at Dunvegan. Then she told how she had gone to him with her sympathy, when his heart was sore, and pretended to comfort him. When the first wild burst of grief was passed he had been grateful to her. Bye-and-bye, when he offered her a home, she knew it was out of pity and gratitude; but she had hoped to win his love some day. "Then you came home, Iseabal, and I bribed that drunken bodach, Rory Dhu, to tell him you had got tired of the piper and his conceit; and that was the reason you hadn't stayed and married him. Then one night Nial met Rory, who had been drinking in the clachan and was very confidential, and he told him all, Iseabal. I will never forget Nial's face as he came home that night. He looked ten years older; and I knew something bad happened."

"Moina," he said hoarsely, "I have heard everything. Never speak to me of Iseabal again. You are not worthy to utter her name."

"It was all he said, Iseabal, but from that day there was a great gulf between us; and when the war began he was glad to go; and now he is dead. Oh, Iseabal, I suffered for my wickedness. If I could only live my life over again, I would try and make up for it. Oh, Iseabal," she sobbed, "can you forgive me before I die?" Iseabal, who had been listening as one in a dream, with a face white and haggard, clasped Moina's cold hand in her own, and whispered as the tears ran down her cheeks, "Moina, it is all past now. We will try and forget."

A movement in the corner made Iseabal turn round, and she saw that Morag had wakened and had heard all. Signing to her to be quiet, Iseabal laid the exhausted girl back on the pillow, soothing her with kind words of comfort, and when she had fallen asleep, Iseabal lay down beside Morag in the corner, and dreamed she was on a bed of down with guardian angels smiling on her.

In the morning Moina was weaker and as the darkness again fell, she sank rapidly. Iseabal and Morag were both by the bed watching the life that was quickly drawing to a close. Iseabal was holding her hand, and once Moina opened her eyes and seemed to know her, for she whispered "Iseabal." Then her breathing became fainter, till she fell into the sleep from which there is no awakening.

Next day the sun shone brightly over the snow through the window of the cottage by the loch side on a quiet figure lying on the bed covered with a white linen sheet. It was still shining when Iseabal went home carrying Moina's baby in the folds of her plaid.

* * * *

The last patches of snow had melted from Cruachan's peaks, and the air was sweet with the scents of spring. Pale green shoots were sprouting from the branches of the larches in the glen, and the rowan tree at Iseabal's door was sending forth bunches of fern-like leaves. Inside, in the cottage, all was bright and clean, and Iseabal was baking oatcakes on a glowing peat fire. Moina's baby was sleeping quietly in the box bed opposite the fireplace. Iseabal took the last cake from the fire, and scraping the meal from her hands, went to the open door to breathe the fragrant air. The sun had set, and the pines looked black against the lemon-tinted sky. Soon the early moon would be rising above Cladich, and making a silver pathway across the loch. How still everything was. A cry from the child brought Iseabal back, and taking the little bundle in her arms, she sat down beside the fire, smiling at him as he lay on her knee laughing and cooing, and stretching out his little feet in the warmth. A shadow crossed the window, then the figure of a man filled the doorway, and he gazed at Iseabal sitting there with the child on her knee. A minute or two passed; then he whispered "Iseabal."

She started, the colour slowly dying out of her cheek as she looked at the man standing there. Her lips parted as if to speak, but no sound came from them. The clock on the wall ticked on, but still she was silent.

"Iseabal," he said again.

"Nial, I thought you were dead." The words came with painful slowness.

"It was Nial MacArtair from Dalavich who was killed. Iseabal, as I came through the clachan I saw Morag, and she told me about you and what you did for Moina."

"Here is your baby, Nial," she said, holding out the child to him. He took the little thing in his arms, then crossed to the bed and laid him down. Coming back to Iseabal, who was still sitting by the fire, he knelt down, and laying his rough head on her breast said, "Iseabal, have you no welcome for me?" As she put her hand in his the unhappy past was forgotten, and a great peace filled their hearts.

ANNA NIC DHAIBHIDH.

THE CLANS: PAST AND PRESENT.

BY R. S. T. MacEWEN, of Lincoln's Inn,
Barrister-at-Law.

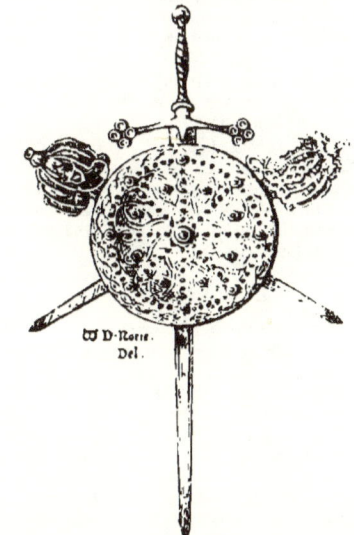

W D. Ross. Del.

FIRST APPEARANCE OF THE CLANS.

CLANS, as distinct and separate communities, distinguished from the ancient tribal divisions from which they descended, first make their appearance in history in the 13th century. Skene tells us that the first, of an earlier date, of which there is authentic information, is the Lowland Clan of Buchan in the time of David the First in the 12th century. The second instance is that of Clan MacDuff, in Fife, about the time of the first Earl of Fife. The Highland clans did not appear till the close of the 14th century. *Fordun's Chronicle of the Highlanders*, written shortly before 1385, makes no mention of clans beyond the Highland line, and Skene says they did not appear till after that date. In 1390, or within ten years after *Fordun's Chronicle*, a Highland raid was made into the Lowlands, and for the first time the raiders appear in the form of separate clans or septs. In that year the Wolf of Badenoch, with six principal and five adherent groups of men, made a raid into Angus. In consequence King Robert III. issued a brief directing the persons concerned to be put to the horn as outlaws. To those same groups or septs a number of clans have since been traced. The next important appearance is the combat of the two clans before the King and Court in the North Inch of Perth in 1396. This remarkable fight is a subject of controversy to the present day: for much has been written on the subject and the actors concerned in it. Later authorities trace the combatants to the raiders into Angus six years before, or to some of them, to Clan Qwhewl, since identified as the Shaws of Rothiemurchus, a sept of Clan Chattan, and to Clan Cameron, or a group from which a portion of that clan sprung, known at the time as Clan Clachiny or Clan Kay.*

From this period then, the beginning of 1400, the clan system can be followed with more or less of certainty, and occupies a large place in national history, for three and a half centuries, down to the breaking up of the clans in 1746, after Culloden.

CLAN PEDIGREES.

Much ingenuity and interest have been displayed at different times in tracing and building up the pedigrees of the clans and their founders. Skene tells us that 'in the early state of the tribal organization the pedigree of the sept or clan and of each member of the tribe had a very important meaning. Their rights were derived through the common ancestor and their relation to him and through him to each other, indicated their position in the succession, as well as their place in the allocation of the tribe land. In such a state of society the pedigree occupied the same position as the title-deed in the feudal system, and the Sennachies were as much the custodiers of the rights of families as the mere panegyrists of the clans.' The panegyrists at the same time were responsible for much of the legendary history attaching to the tribes, and the clans from which they sprung claimed their share in these past glories. The Irish Sennachies far surpassed their Scottish brethren in this kind of knowledge, were much resorted to, and after the feudal period, displayed the greatest ingenuity.

ACTS OF THE 16TH CENTURY AFFECTING THE CLANS.

With the feudal nobility and the feudal laws came three Acts of the Scottish Parliament, one in 1587, another in 1594, and a third in 1597, which had an important bearing upon the clans and clan property. The first two Acts brought the clans into direct contact with the Crown, and the third, which had the most pregnant effect, required—'That the inhabitants of the Ilis and Hiclandis shaw their holdings': in other words produce their titles, and that within a certain time, on penalty of forfeiture and loss of all pretended infeftments and other right and title they have, or may pretend to have, to any lands whatever they have holden, or pretend to hold, etc. This Act, says Skene, placed 'the greater portion of the clans in a most embarrassing and precarious position. Many who had charters had lost them in the troubles and conflicts, others had no rights except what was derived from forfeited lords. In other cases of disputed right to the clan demesne both parties had received at different times a quasi-title to them. In many cases the nominal superiority was feudally vested in an alien family, while the land was actually possessed by one of the clans, and in many cases there was no title but immemorial possession maintained by the sword. On the other hand those who possessed a nominal right to lands under feudal titles which they had been unable to enforce, or who saw a great prospect, through the threatened forfeitures, of acquiring possessions in the Highlands and Isles, would eagerly avail themselves of the opportunity afforded them by the statute. Compelled thus to defend their rights and compete with the claims of their opponents, and to maintain an equality of rank and prestige with them in the Herald's Office, the Highland chiefs, chieftains, and lairds had recourse to MS. histories, in some cases as imaginative as the legendary accounts of the old Sennachies, while in others spurious charters were set up. But the favourite form the genealogies took was that of making the male ancestor of the clan a Norwegian, Dane, or Norman, or a cadet of some distinguished family, who succeeded to the chiefship and to the territory of the clan by marriage with the daughter and heiress of the old Celtic line, thus combining the advantage of a descent which could (and no doubt in some cases did) compete with that of the great Norman families with a feudal succession to their lands. †

From these histories the later accounts of the clans have been compiled, and Skene thus sums

---

* Skene's *Celtic Scotland.*
† *Celtic Scotland.*

up the result: 'So far as they (the clan pedi-grees) profess to show the origin of the different clans, they are entirely artificial and untrust-worthy, but the older genealogies may be accepted as showing the descent of the clan from its eponymous or founder and within reasonable limits for some generations beyond him, while the later spurious pedigrees must be rejected altogether.'† Grant in his *Tartans of the Clans* comes to a similar conclusion. In other words the pedigrees dating from the chiefs and leaders of the clans in the 13th and 14th centuries downwards may be accepted, and in the case of a few, well established cases, for three or four generations further back. A distinguished modern writer says that 'only five out over five hundred of the oldest aristocratic families in England, at the present time, can trace their direct descent through the male line to the 15th century.'*

Mixed Character of Clan Descent.

The chiefs and people comprising the clans were not, even at this early date in clan history, the pure descendants of any one particular race. They were of mixed native origin, partly of Celtic (including the old Pictish element), Nor-wegian, Danish, Norman, and Flemish blood, with that of the old natives of the country; but the Celtic element and language prevailed. The great pre-historic tribes from which the clans sprung were the Gallgael in the West, Moravia in the Central and Eastern Highlands, and the North-Eastern tribes of Ross, Suther-land, and Caithness. After the Norman conquest of England in 1066 a number of Norman and Saxon adventurers, disappointed of favours from William, sought refuge in Scotland, and many of them were given territories and lands, and in time their successors took the chiefships of clans. In Mr. Adam's List of Highland Clans§ there are 64 clans, 44 with chiefs of Celtic and 20 of non-Celtic origin. The latter are Lowland (Norman or Saxon), Norse and Flemish.

Clan Divisions.

The clans are described as consisting of two divisions: the one of the kinsmen, or those of the blood of the sept, the other of the dependents or subordinate septs, who might be of different race.' Skene quotes the Gartmore MS. of 1747 as containing the best definition of the position of the chiefs and clansmen of the time: 'The property of these Highlands belongs to a great many different persons, who are more or less considerable in proportion to the extent of their estates and to the command of men that live upon them, or follow them, on account of this clanship. These lands are set by the landlord (the chief or chieftain) during pleasure, or a short tack, to people whom they call good men (duine wassel, or gentlemen), and who are of a superior station to the commonalty. These are generally the sons, brothers, cousins, or nearest relations of the landlord or chief. This by means of a small portion, and the liberality of their relations, they are able to stock, and which they, their children and grand-children, possess at an easy rent, till a nearer descendant be again preferred to it. As the propinquity removes, they become less considered, till at last they degenerate to be of the common people, unless some accidental acquisition of wealth supports them above their station. As this has been an ancient custom, most of the farmers and cottars (crofters) are of the name and clan of the proprietor.'.

Dependent Septs.

The dependent septs, families and 'broken men,' stood on a different footing. They were groups, families, and persons, either descended from the ancient occupiers of the land, or who had belonged to or descended from other clans, which had suffered in the conflicts of the times and were no longer powerful enough to maintain a separate independence. Their own chiefs had died out or been defeated, the clan lands had been lost, and in many cases they had become all but extinct. The remnants of these broken clans sought the protection of neighbouring chiefs and clans with whom they had been on friendly terms. Such a connection was a necessity of the times. Without it the weak were at the mercy of the first and strongest comer. Their position to the chief and clan whose protection they sought is exemplified by the Bonds of Manred or Manrent which they gave. The chief is declared to have been chosen of their own free will to be their protector in all great actions, they agree to do him homage and service, take up and fight for his cause and against his enemies when required; in return the chief agrees to give them lands, according to custom and usage, to protect them against their enemies and to treat them like his own clansmen. In course of time most of these adherents became merged in the principal clan, and took its name either in addition to their own or more commonly by dropping their own altogether.

(To be continued).

Mr. David Glen, 8 Greenside Place, Edinburgh, has just published No. 4 of his valuable collection of Ancient Piobaireachd, which contains fifteen of the most famous pipe tunes. We heartily recom-mend this work.

Social Evolution, by Benjamin Kidd.
§ *What is my Tartan?*
' *Celtic Scotland.*

TO CORRESPONDENTS.

All Communications, on literary and business matters, should be addressed to the Editor, Mr. JOHN MACKAY, 9 Blythswood Drive, Glasgow.

TERMS OF SUBSCRIPTION.— The CELTIC MONTHLY will be sent, post free, to any part of the United Kingdom, Canada, the United States, and all countries in the Postal Union—for one year, 4s.

THE CELTIC MONTHLY.

MAY, 1899.

CONTENTS.

OUR NEXT ISSUE.

NEXT MONTH we will give plate portraits, with biographical sketches, of Mr. George W. Maclean, Newcastle-on-Tyne; Mr. William T. Mackay, Middlesbrough; and Dr. J. Macrae, Huntly.

GLASGOW INVERNESS-SHIRE ASSOCIATION.—The Annual Gathering, which was held last month, was the most influential function of the season. Dr. C. Fraser-Mackintosh presided, and everyone was delighted to see him looking so well, and in such excellent spirits. He was supported by the leading officials of all the Highland Societies, who came to pay their respects to one of the greatest men of our race. Dr. Fraser-Mackintosh treated of a variety of interesting topics in his address, and took occasion to thoroughly expose as a fabrication the alleged secret order at Culloden not to give quarter to the royal troops. The Doctor proved conclusively that the order was a forgery. Mr. James Grant, the popular President of the Association, proposed the usual vote of thanks to the chairman, which was very heartily given. Messrs. Peter Grant, John Maclean, and other officials, deserve credit for the excellent arrangements of the gathering.

THE ST. ANDREWS HIGHLAND ASSOCIATION held its first Social Gathering in the Town Hall recently, which proved most successful. Provost Macgregor presided, and delivered a most interesting address; and was followed at a later hour by Mr. James Grant, Glasgow, and Mr. Donald Macmillan, both of whom gave rousing speeches. The Association has made an excellent start, the membership being already 150, and we have no doubt it has a very useful career before it. We hope all our readers in the district will join.

HIGHLAND TOMBSTONES IN BALLY-SHANNON CHURCHYARD.

DEAR SIR—Among the older tombstones becoming obliterated and liable to be dislodged at any time, in the Mullaghnashee graveyard, Ballyshannon, there are a few on which Highland names, etc., are inscribed. Perhaps the following are noteworthy, the first mentioned being headed with a coat of arms :—

"Here lyes Jean Bannerman, alias Forbes, who dyed September the seventh, 1681, aged 65."

"William Urquhart, Esq., late Captain in the Loyal Essex Regiment of Infantry, son to the late William Urquhart of Meldrum, Esq., Aberdeenshire, Scotland, died September 29, 1798, aged 42 years. This memorial was erected by his disconsolate widow.

How loved, how honoured once, avails thee not,
To whom related or by whom begot;
A heap of dust alone remains of thee,
'Tiss all thou art, and all the great shall be."

"This tomb was erected by the officers, non-commissioned officers and privates of the Light Company of the 91st Argyleshire Regiment, as a mark of their esteem and respect, in memory of Private David M'Intosh, who was drowned near Ballyshannon, 28 June, 1832, aged 38 years, after having served in the regiment at home and abroad during a period of 21 years."

"Here lies the body of William Bean, late private in the 79th, 1st company, who departed this life January 7th, 1804, aged 22 years. As a token of regard for their deceased comrade, this stone was erected by the non-commissioned officers and privates of the company."

As far as I can learn, no one has been known to claim any of the graves in question, nor can anything further be said concerning them than what they themselves record; and it is gratifying to know that the present minister of the parish of Kilbarron, the Rev. S. G. Cochrane, takes a great interest in their preservation. In my humble opinion, the inscriptions, with the verse of poetry, should be handed down, being of peculiar Highland interest, and I hope that, through *The Celtic Monthly*, this may now be duly accomplished. I shall be glad to give any assistance I can. In conclusion, let me say that the stone over Mr. Urquhart's grave is split right across the middle.—Yours truly,

Ballyshannon.   J. M. MACKINTOSH.

CLAN DAVIDSON.—Sir James D. Mackenzie of Scatwell, Bart., sends us some valuable information regarding the Davidsons of Tulloch. He says: "Harry Davidson, who bought the Bayne estates in 1763 for £10,000, was a son of Jean Bayne of Knockbayne, 2nd cousin of Kenneth Bayne, the last proprietor, who was a cousin of Sir David Bayne of Tulloch." He also remarks that the old property of Davidson, near Cromarty, was a small one, and an ancient possession of the Urquharts of Cromarty. The early castles in that part of Scotland were the original structures of Redcastle, Cromarty, and Dingwall; and to trace back Tulloch Castle to the time of William the Lion, is, he considers, incorrect.

THE MAN WITH THE CROOKIT NOSE.

CALLUM CAMERON was the simple man among us. He had the queersome bit in his soul that is not square with the reason. But like many another simple man, he at times would shew a wisdom that made the rest of us seem foolish. From a lad he was always getting in folks' way, and yet he was so taking that the very folks he bothered could not find it in their heart to be angered at him. He was a small man with a great head and very red hair, beneath which two black eyes looked out with a stare or a twinkle as the way of things might demand. His mouth, too, had a droll kind of pucker about it, and always he would be drawing the corners down tight-like before speaking.

But Callum's nose was the great thing about him. It was very long, very thin, and very pointed, with a strange crook about it that seemed to match the pucker at the corner of his mouth. When you looked at Callum, it was the nose of him that you always saw first. Some folks declared in Lochaber that it was the length of his nose that gave Callum the humoursome turn, and that it was the crook in his nose that gave him a silly soul. However that may be, the folks everywhere knew Callum Cameron as The Man with the Crookit Nose.

Indeed, I have heard it said that the very first Cameron that was, had a crookit nose, for the name is made up of these two words from the good Gaelic of Argyll—*cam*, bent, and *sron*, a nose. When the people of Lorn saw a Cameron for the first time they laughed and said to one another, "Oh, he is a fellow with a crook in the nose of him!" And the Campbells believe to this day that the Camerons have all a crook in their souls. At least so I have been told, but as I am neither a Cameron nor yet a Campbell, the tale has no great concern for me. It is only set down here because it was true of Callum Cameron—the Man of the Crookit Nose.

The first time that I saw Callum was at the pier one day, when he was saying good-bye to the preaching man who was standing for the church over at Corpach. Callum had been carrying the minister's bag, and when the minister was making a fine speech to Callum for carrying the bag, and not offering to give him anything else, it was then I saw the pucker at the corner of Callum's mouth.

"Blessings on you, meantime, my good friend, and I have enjoyed my stay in your beautiful neighbourhood more than I can tell."

"Aye, aye, Sir," said Callum, "we'll maybe see you back again, *and we'll maybe no!*" And the minister's face got as red as the lid of a grouse cock's eye as he stepped aboard.

Not so long after that Callum was walking up the glen one day when he stopped of a sudden and looked over the wall that is above the river. He was always stopping and looking at something. But this day he stood with his arms on the stone dyke for a more lengthy while than usual. It was the day after John Macdonald's sheep had been dipped, and Callum was standing there when John Macdonald himself came along with a drove of fine clean sheep.

"Callum," cried out Donald, "what is it that you are looking for to-day?"

"Aye, Donald, you may well be asking why I am wasting my time, but come here and look at this man. I have been watching him this hour and more, and he is up to the ankles in the water."

"Well, and if he is, Callum, were you never seeing a man standing up to the ankles in the water of a salmon river before?"

"Aye, Donald, many a time. *But this man is in head first!*"

And this was how the glen came to know that Hector Monro had drowned himself. Another man would have raced all the way to

RIVER NEVIS AT POLL DUBH.

the Fort, but the Man of the Crookit Nose stood for an hour looking over the wall and then spoke these gruesome words to Macdonald, who happened to pass first.

He was mightily feared of ghosts- this Callum. And there was one that he was more feared of than any other *bogan* in Lochaber. Callum called him The Man of Fire. But he meant the Devil.

The young lads at the Fort were very fond of Callum Cameron, but they are ever after some prank on the summer nights, and they set themselves to play a trick one night on the Man with the Crookit Nose. Every gloaming Callum went up to the hill to bring down Widow Macrae's black cow to the milking in the byre. He went up about the darkening and drew up the iron pin that held the long tether, and putting the rope over his arm he walked slowly down the hill leading the patient beast behind him.

The lads knew this, and two of them went and hid behind a rock on the brae face and watched Callum coming out from the byre. He came slowly up the hill and lifted the tether. Then he began to descend with his hands behind his back, and the cow quietly followed.

Then the lads went cannily down after the cow and slipped the halter from her head, and being particular to keep an even strain on the rope, Callum continued to go down the hill believing that the black cow was still following him.

Then when he had reached the door of the byre, the two lads gave a fearsome yell and pulled the rope with a quick tug as hard as they could draw, so that Callum fell back on his red head and lay sprawling in a puddle of muck and water, while the lads watched him from behind a wall, where they were holding their sides lest the big laughter would split them.

Callum rose slowly with a mighty pain in his head. There were maybe one or two cursings also on the lips of him. But when he turned round to look for the black cow, he saw her feeding quietly away up on the hill against the sky-line. His face became white and feared like. His eyes were big with terror. And as he stood there shaking, he was heard to say, "The Man of Fire! It is the Devil himself this time, and no mistake whatever. And it is I that will never be touching that black cow again!" And from that day Callum never led the black cow home to the milking.

But the Man with the Crookit Nose was to have a second encounter with the black cow before very long.

There was a small pond at the edge of Widow Macrae's field just where the wood begins to climb the hill. In this pond there was a mixture of all sorts of rubbish. An old tree had fallen into the water, and the constant soaking of the water had rotted the bark and filled the pond with the white phosphor fire that gleamed and glittered in the dark like a living thing when the water was troubled.

These were the days of the hot summer, when the cattle could not stand in the open fields for the fierceness of the sun. So Widow Macrae's black cow used to creep below the trees that were near the pond when the sun was too hot, and one afternoon she even walked into the pond and lay down on the edge and rolled herself like a horse in the cool water.

That night the clouds came up and there was a stillness like death hanging over everything. The folks said the rains were coming at last, and the very whaups were silent when the night came on hot and dark and with a heavy silence.

Callum was standing at the end of the byre watching the sky. The thunder began to mutter and roll far away among the hills. After the first peal the beasts that had been left out began to wander home. The black cow rose to her feet in the darkness. She saw something like fire on her legs. She looked round and flicked her long tail. It was flashing fire all over her back. Her whole body was ablaze. And the more she flicked her tail, the more fire was on her.

Then there was a second peal of thunder, and a bright sheet of lightning made the black cow see that she was standing in the middle of white fire. So with a frantic roar and a spring forward she began to tear through the darkness on the road for the byre—bellowing and snorting and flinging flame as she went.

Callum saw her in the dark. He heard the roar. White light seemed to flash from the head and tail and legs of the mad phosphor laden cow. Moreover she was charging straight for the place where Callum stood.

He let a yell out of him, and made for the hill crying as he ran, "The Man of Fire! The roaring fiery Devil is after me. The Devil himself is on fire! Help, help, help!"

Next morning, after the storm had passed, the black cow was found lying dead on the spot where Callum had stood, and her brains were splattered over the wall of the byre. This is how the Man with the Crookit Nose saw the Devil.

There are many other things about Callum Cameron which might be put down here, but it is not good that any man should be made too much of, even although he happens to have a Crookit Nose.

TORQUIL MACLEOD.

THE MACDONALDS OF ACHTRIACHTAN.*

BY CHARLES FRASER-MACKINTOSH, LL.D.

(Continued from page 133.)

NOTHING, however, had been sold, and had the eldest son lived, entire relief from pecuniary distress seemed certain. Achtriachtan had eight sons and three daughters, Isobel, Janet, and Betty. From a letter dated 14th August, 1817, it would appear the ladies had all married, but I have no information on this point. Of the sons, Alexander, the eldest, died unmarried in the East Indies in 1793. Adam, the second son, succeeded to the estates. Angus, the third, who had been specially called to the succession after the death of the eldest brother, died shortly before his father. James, the fourth son. I find a clerk in the Sheriff Clerk's Office in Inverness in 1781. The youth and his impecunious master, the Sheriff Clerk, for processes of debt became common in the Sheriff Court against the Keeper of the Records, naturally did not part on amiable terms. Allan, fifth son, John, sixth son, Evan, seventh son, and Robert, eighth son, all died without issue prior to 1815. Old Achtriachtan left a Trust Settlement in favour of Major John Campbell of Airds, Alexander Campbell, younger of Dunure, Captain Peter Campbell at Ardshiel, and others, including Coll Macdonald, W.S., named sine qua non, before and after alluded to.

Alexander, the eldest son, died as above mentioned in India, Captain in the East India Company's service. He left a considerable sum, but as a great portion was life-rented by his Indian housekeeper, "Julia," his heirs had much difficulty in forcing a division after Julia's

death by the surviving trustee, whose rank alone in the army, if otherwise destitute of honour, demanded a prompt settlement of his deceased friend's affairs. Had Captain Alexander lived to return to Scotland, Achtriachtan would in all probability have continued with the Macdonalds. But it was not to be, Captain Macdonald, disappointed in securing a passage by one of the latest vessels of the season, had to remain for a few months, and overtaken with fever, died. Upon the news reaching home, old Achtriachtan for good reasons, as may be judged from the sequel, called his third son, Angus, to the succession, but unfortunately Angus died very shortly before his father, who, even if he wished to do so, was then too ill to make a new destination.

I have no information regarding Allan, the fifth son. John and Hugh, the sixth and seventh sons, were in the service of the East India Company, and died there, their representatives in 1811 getting certain moneys from Chelsea Hospital and a share of the "Helder" money. Robert, the eighth and youngest son, ensign in the company's service, is specially referred to in the settlements of his eldest brother, Captain Alexander Macdonald.

The first notice I have of Adam, the second son and the fourth Achtriachtan, occurs in 1779, when he draws a bill for a small sum upon one Kenneth Stewart at Corran. At the time of his father's death Adam Macdonald was in the West Indies, and had been for some years in Jamaica, but judging from his after history he had realized nothing, in fact had to be assisted home by a brother Mac.

The only sensible thing I have to record of this last Achtriachtan was his marriage in 1801 to Miss Helen Cameron, eldest daughter of Ewen Cameron of Glennevis. To this worthy lady's credit it can be recorded, that during many trials and hardships she enjoyed the respect and friendship of all who knew her early and continuous troubles. One of Helen Cameron's sisters married the Laird of Glenmoriston, another, the Laird of Kilcoy. Adam Macdonald's sister married Cameron of Clunes, and was mother of the late Donald Cameron of Clunes, and Colonel Cameron, Clifton Villa, Inverness.

Achtriachtan I see thus described by one who knew him long and intimately, who, from his age and legal experience, was well qualified to judge:—

"Mr. Macdonald has shown from his youth the most flexible, facile, and unresisting disposition, a mind the most unsuspicious, weak and pliable, and a habit of life inconsistent with the ways of prudent men. In short he showed himself the easy victim of designing men, and especially of such as by connection and otherwise had title to the least

---

* Read at a meeting of the Gaelic Society of Inverness.

influence over his deliberations and actions. It is not wonderful that such a person as this should in his circumstances have soon felt the fatal effects of his facility. Accordingly he had been but a very few years at home when he became much embarrassed in his circumstances, and deeply involved in debt, arising from his cautionary obligations, into which he had been artfully inveigled, and from hopeless and ruinous law suits to which he had been most unproperly encouraged."

Had Achtriachtan settled down quietly he might have prospered, but, quite unfit to manage his patrimonial estate, he must needs not only give his name to needy and unscrupulous men, but actually enter upon unremunerative leases of sheep farms. Through his close connec-

tion with Alexander Macdonald of Glencoe, he doubtless imbibed the idea of making his fortune by sheep farming, and lost frightfully by becoming tenant or liable for sub-tenants of large farms in Strathconon belonging to General afterwards Sir Alexander Mackenzie of Fairburn. He had also a large farm from the Marquis of Tweedale, and took in as sub-tenants certain farmers named Rankin upon the advice of his law agent, which involved him deeply with the landlord. At the termination of the lease Achtriachtan's name, though he had ceased to have any interest, was used to defend some of the Rankins.

Mrs. Macdonald endeavoured in vain to extricate her husband, who still had faith in his agent

ACHTRIACHTAN LOCH, GLENCOE.

Achtriachtan had also a farm upon Ardsheal, where the family resided until Whitsunday, 1817, when it was by the exertions of the trustees sublet to Captain Cameron. Ten or twelve crofters had previously been ordered to be removed, "in case the incoming tenant should wish the farm clear." It further appeared a dozen servants and shepherds, about and on the farm, had been paid no wages for years past, and the annual loss in working of Ardsheal exceeded £200 and probably amounted to £300 per annum.

The estate of Dalness was large and important, but a shoe of Achtriachtan would come in very handy. The remainder of Achtriachtan might be depreciated by that operation, but that was

of no consequence to Dalness, whose plans had been long maturing.

Achtriachtan went to Edinburgh deeply embarrassed, and while there lost a heavy law suit, and sanguine and easy tempered as he was, became much dispirited. Anything to tide over present difficulties he was ready to grasp, and so without consulting or having time to see any friend he entered into an agreement for the sale of a large part of his estate. It specified the exact bounds, but as the acreage was unknown, while the whole estate was let as one holding, a pretence of fair dealing was made, viz., that the proportion of the whole rent should be allocated by accountants appointed by the purchaser, with whom alone they communicated, and twenty-seven years' purchase was fixed as the price. This allocation was hurried through and the title completed before the transaction became publicly known. The price worked out at £3,600, of which less than £100 came to Achtriachtan, all the rest going to purge an old debt of £2,000 incurred by Achtriachtan's father, and certain debts for which Mr. Coll Macdonald had become cautioner. This occurred in 1816, and the result was, that not only was the proportion of the whole rent of Achtriachtan applicable to the portion sold, unduly diminished, (working out at the twenty-seven years'purchase), but it proved an extraordinary bargain to the purchaser, and, at the same time, a serious loss to the seller, as afterwards shown when the remainder of the estate came to be disposed of.

This sale had one good result, in respect that it enabled Achtriachtan's trustees to dispense with the agent as such.

The dismissal was, however, resented, and the agent bought up some of the debts for a trifle, harassed the operations of the trust, prevented realizations and settlements, and heaped up expenses in form of reductions, multiple-poindings, etc.

Notwithstanding the sale to Dalness and that of Inshrigg to Mr. Downie of Appin, the trustees for a time had the hope of saving the last of the estate. It was found, however, that the expenses and obstructions to the working of the trust were insurmountable, and a sale by public roup in the month of June was ordered. The upset was fixed at £8,940, being with that given by Dalness the sum reckoned to be the value of the whole original estate. No purchaser appeared, and it then became clear that the sale to Dalness destroyed to a great extent the value of what remained. In the end the trustees had to accept £6,000, offered by Mr. Downie on 5th November, 1817, thus shewing that the private and secret sale to the agent involved a loss of nearly £3,000 in the ultimate realization. The persecution did not cease, for arrestments were laid on the price, and years of litigation ensued. In the end the ordinary creditors had to accept a composition, thanks alone to the reckless and wanton, but studied legal expenditure.

Achtriachtan and his family were reduced to depend upon the interest of Mrs. Macdonald's moderate fortune and upon her jointure, which was of course a preferable debt. I have seen a letter mentioning that Achtriachtan was buried in Eilean Mhunna with Highland honours, nine pipers accompanying the remains to their last resting place on Loch Leven's sacred isle.

After his death Mrs. Macdonald and her daughters lived much respected in Fort-William, were most hospitable and kindly in disposition, and were held in great esteem by all the people, not only for their unmerited misfortunes, but also for their own worth. The family consisted of three sons, Colin, John, and Hugh, and four daughters. The sons who survived left for the West Indies or Australasia, and the only reference I find among the papers to them is under date October, 1888:—

"On the 18th inst., at St. Faith's, Stoke Newington, by the Rev. Frederick Cox, Vicar of St. Philips, Dalston, Henry Edward, second son of the late John Bennet of Chester, to Isabel Jane, third daughter of the late Colin John Macdonald of Achtriachtan, Glencoe, Argyleshire.

The above Colin Macdonald, the eldest son, held a high position in the Post Office at Brisbane, New Zealand.

The eldest daughter, whom I recollect as a particularly handsome and stately specimen of the old Highland lady of the past, married Mr. Mackenzie, commonly called "Munlochy," brother of the late General Alexander Mackenzie and also of Mrs. Gibson, wife of the late Rev. Dr. Gibson of Avoch. Another of the Achtriachtan ladies married Mr. MacLellan, Officer of Excise, and some of their descendants have thriven in Australasia. The two youngest, Misses Isabella and Jane Fraser Macdonald, whom many will recollect, died unmarried, both accomplished women, and like their mother such charming exponents of the Gaelic that while even to hear them speak in that language was a pleasure, their old Gaelic songs were a still greater delight. At Inverness, where they lived for some years, their memory is still green.

That most competent, most delightful, most kindly delineator and exponent of the Highlands in the past and present, the Rev. Dr. Stewart of Nether Lochaber, mentions that old Achtriachtan was dead prior to the Doctor's settlement in Nether Lochaber, but he was well acquainted with the lady whom he describes as "a highly accomplished and charming old lady." Like her late husband she was interred in the sacred isle with all honour, for Dr. Stewart, who was present and officiated, states that it was the largest seen in Lochaber for sixty years, and conducted with all the music and profusion usual of old at Highland funerals of the "gentry."

The steady disappearance from the Highlands of old families of minor rank has been going on for a long time, whereby the country is so much the poorer. If their places were taken up by Highlanders there might not be so much to regret, but in few cases do new comers supply the loss of the old and careless, but kindly and sympathetic landlords, the ladies combining the courtliness of hereditary culture, with the warm and friendly intercourse so congenial to the Celtic race, knitting peer and peasant. All were "gentle" in its highest and truest sense.

[CONCLUDED.]

JOHN MACRAE, DUNS.

QUITE a number of the leading families of the Clan MacRae trace their descent from Fionnla dubh MacGillichriosd, who flourished in the 14th century, and his grandson, Farquhar, who was progenitor of the Torlishich branch. The subject of our sketch this month belongs to that famous family, his grand-uncle being Duncan MacRae of Torlishich, so renowned in the traditions of the clan for his great strength. Indeed, the MacRaes have always been specially noted for their remarkable stature and prowess. Mr. John MacRae was born at Strathanloan, Glenshiel, Kintail, in May, 1843, his father being Farquhar MacRae, who served three generations of the Lintons, the grazing tenants in that district, and died in Lochaber in 1882, aged eighty-five. Mr. MacRae joined the Constabulary in 1868; and eight years later was appointed Sanitary Inspector for nearly the whole county of Berwick, under a system carried out by the Commissioners of Supply—under the supervision of the then Chief Constable, Mr. List—to assist and enable the Parochial Boards, the then local authorities, to execute the Public Health Act in a more efficient manner than was generally the case at that early period of sanitation in many rural districts—a system which received the honourable mention of the late Sir John Skelton, of the Board of Supervision, in his valuable work on Public Health. After the County Council was established, Mr. MacRae was appointed County Sanitary Inspector, and Chief Sanitary Inspector for the three districts into which the county was divided for public health purposes. He had then to resign his police connection, and has since devoted his whole time to sanitary work. He enjoys a high reputation for the able way in which he has discharged his professional duties, the county standing high in sanitary matters.

We need hardly add that Mr. MacRae takes a deep interest in all Highland matters, and especially such as relate to his native county; and is in every way a worthy representative of the house of Torlishich.

THE HERO OF OMDURMAN. Brigadier-General Hector A. Macdonald is to receive a hearty Highland welcome from his countrymen. We are all very proud of Hector, for he has shown that the Highland race can still produce its heroes. The Highland Societies of London entertain him on 6th May; and on the 8th the Macdonald Society do honour to their clansman in Glasgow. Thereafter he visits his native county, where the proceedings will not lack in interest or excitement.

WELCOME, HERO, HOME!

Hero of Omdurman! welcome again
　To the land of your birth, the home of your
　　clan ;
Whose air, as a boy, you did drink with wild joy;
　Whose name you have honoured in deeds of the
　　man !

The rocks, her stern monitors, they have supplied
　Thy grandeur in daring, thy bold stubborn mood
Her tempests and torrents have mingled the tide
　That flows through thy bosom in proud stirring
　　blood.

Welcome ! we're proud of the lad we sent forth,
　Whose fortune is ours, whose deeds are his own ;
Welcome, brave Highlander, back to the North,
　Where your name is belov'd, your prowess is
　　known ! .

Oh, we'll sing of the lad that is gallant in war,
　The lad who in serving hath learned to command ;
The lad that we love, and the hero whose star
　Hath gilded with glory his brave native land.

The fame of Macdonald goes down the green glen
　The moor-fowl hath heard it ; the wild roaming
　　stag
Hath startled beneath it to bound up the ben ;
　The lone loch hath crooned it in dreams to the
　　crag.

Oh, how, when the hosts of the desert came down
　From the east and the south, on his flank and
　　his front,
He stood like a rock, and smote them and
　　changed
His thin line of heroes and gave them the brunt ;

How he changed his line twice, from the east to
　　the south,
　And twice in each spot did he swift overthrow,
With his swarth Soudanese and brave Fellaheen,
　The curse of the desert - the rallying foe.

And the Khalifa's might, that nodded like ears
　Of corn in the land, lay trampled and torn,
For the whirlwind encountered the rock where it
　　stood,
　And dashed its life out on its withering scorn.

Scotland, brave Scotland ! thy sons ne'er betray
　The land that they love ; where adversity breeds
The heath's purple bloom, they have learned to
　　obey,
　And the hour of thy triumph's the hour of their
　　deeds!

Hero of Omdurman ! welcome again
　To the land of your birth, the home of your
　　clan ;
Whose air, as a boy, you breathed with wild joy ;
　Whose name you have honoured in deeds of the
　　man !

Inverness.　　　　　　　BERNARD GEORGE HOARE.

JOHN MACRAE.

TURUS CLANN MHIC-AOIDH DO THIR AN SINNSEARA.*

By Rev. Angus Mackay, M.A.

(Continued from page 128.)

DH' FHEUCH mi, mar a b' fhearr a b' urrainn domh, cia mar shoirbhich leinne 'dol troimh Duthaich Mhicaoidh, agus cia mar a ghabh an sluagh cairdeil ruinn, ach cha-n eil 'au so ach leth mo sgeoil. Tha torradh mar tha 'an lorg ar turuis. Thug sinn dusgadh beag do Dhuthaich Mhicaoidh, agus thog sinn cridheachan nam muintir sin a bha feuchainn ris a' Ghaidhlic a theagasg do 'n àl og. Tha mi 'claistinn, agus gu dearbh tha mi toillichte, gu-m bheil, air a' gheamhradh so moran de 'n oigridh a tionail o oidhche gu oidhche, agus cuid a' tighinn astair fhada, thar chnuic is mhonaidhean, gu sgoiltean Gaidhlic cha chuir air bonn anns an tir mu thuath ud. Gidheadh cha bhi mi riaraichte ach an duisgear a' Ghaidhealtachd air far, o Mhuil-a'-Chinn-tire gu ruig sron a' Phuirbh 'an Cataobh. Cha-n-eil eileag bheo anns a' Ghaidhealtachd nach coir a seideadh, agus ma ni sinn sin cha chaill sinn ar saothair, oir tha Gaill is Gaidhil an diu 'cuir speis ann an nithe Gaidhealtach mar nach robh iad. Dh' fheuch luchd-riaghailidh na tire air ar smaladh 'n uair thug iad uainne ar feileadh an deigh Chuil-odair, ach chaidh car 's a' chuidhil o'n uair sin. Fhuair iad a mach gu-m bheil buaidh anns an fheile-bheag, agus gheibh e onair an diu air calbhsairean Lunain 'n uair a ghluais-eas gillean nam fuar-bheann gu farumach troimh na sraidibh. Chaidh Cluainidh, nach muirean, 'n uair a bha e'n a oifigeach anns an Reiseamead Du, gu damhsa ann am baile mor Sasunach, agus tha e air aithris nach robh bean uasal 's a chuideachd a sheasadh air urlar cnid ris, chionns gu-n robh e air eideadh 's an fheileadh. Cha thachaireadh sin an diu. 'S e bu docha gu-m biodh gog air na h-uile te gu greim fhaotainn air sgoid breacain.

Ma theid sinn ceithir fichead bliadhna air ais cha robh meas air Gaidhil, eadhon ann am bailtibh Dhuineidin agus Ghlasachu. Is gann gu-m faigheadh iad gu drench'd a b' airde na sgualaidh shraid, agus mar biodh an obair rapach cha-n fhaigheadh iad sin fein. Cha mho 'bha 'mheas orra aig an dachaidh. Bha meas air caoraich, ach cha robh air Gaidhil. Cha moran diubh fhuadach thar chuantan, gu nite a dheanamh do 'n chaora mhaol, agus rinneadh taire ro eagallach air cuid eile cha fhagail aig baile. Cha robh so gun dhroch bhuaidh 'bhi aig air an t-sluagh. Gun fhios daibh chaill iad am meas a bu choir a bhi aca orra fhein, mhuchadh an spiorad, agus mar sin fhuair an gradh a bu choir a bhi aca do chanain au mathair leon. Air daibh bhi faicinn an ciobair agus an chobhair gallda 'soirbheachadh, agus Domhnuil bochd a' dol an aghaidh a chuil, thainig iad gus a' cho-dhunadh gu-m b' fhearr a' Bheurla na 'Ghaidhlic Cha-n eil mise idir a' cur au aghaidh na Beurla, ach tha mi ag radh so: nach dh' fhuair a' Ghaidhlic ceartas, agus nach eil i a' faotainn a' cheartais a bhuineas di fhathast. 'N uair a bha mise 'dol do 'n sgoil—tha coig bliadhna fichead o 'n uair sin—cha-n fhaodadh neach againn focal Gaidhlic a labhairt 'an taobh stigh de bhallachan an tighe-sgoile, agus is iomadh buille choimheach a chunnaic mise eileagan is lulaich a' faotainn air son 'bhi bristeadh na aithne mhaslaich ud. Cha d' thug na parantan riamh an aonta do 'n dol air aghairt so, ach bha sud mar sud, agus cha-n iogantach leamsa idir ged nach eil a' Ghaidhlic anns a' Ghaidhealtas mar a bha i. Mur biodh gu-m bheil an sean-fhocal fior "theid duthchas an aghaidh nan creag" bha 'Ghaidhlic marbh air 'Ghaidhealtach gu so. Bhatar ag arach an ail oig anns a' bheachd gu-n robh a' Ghaidhlic taireil, agus 'n uair a thainig moran diubh gu aoise dhaoine agus mhnathan chuir iad cul rithe. Bha aig an oigridh ri 'dhol o'n dachaidh gu cosnadh, oir cha robh bheag ri dheanamh aig baile, agus air daibh tilleadh, 'an crann bliadhna no dha, 's e theireadh iad gu n robh iad air call na Gaidhlic. Is duilich leam a radh gu-n robh so fior gu h-araidh a thaobh nan caile-agan. Tha cuimhne agam air bana choimhears-nach araidh a thainig dachaid an deigh dhi 'bhi ochd miosachan deug air sheirbhis 'an Leodhas, agus air domh beannachadh dhi ann au cainnt a mathair 's e fhreagair i "O, I can't speak Gaelic now." Theirinn 's an dol seachad, tha beath no bas na Gaidhlic ann an lamhan nam boirionnach, oir 's ann aosa tha arach agus altrum na cloinne. Ma gheibh sinn na math-raichean gu tlachd a ghabhail anns a' Ghaidhlic tha na h-uile cuise ceart, agus cha bhi anns a' chath ach iomairt : mur faigh theid an la 'n ar n-aghaidh Tha sin cho cinnteach 's a tha 'ghrein 's na speuraibh.

Gidheadh thainig atharrachadh mor air cuis-ean seach mar bha tri fichead bliadhna, no idir deich bliadhna fichead air ais. Cuirear failte air na Gaidhil ann am bailtibh mor na Galldachd, bheirear daibh suidheachanan cho onorach 's tha r' an gabhail, agus gheibhear g' an lionadh mic is nigheanan an Taobh-tuath le mor chliu. 'S gann gu-m bheil baile mor mu dheas gun chomunn Gaidhealach, leis am bheil ar luchd-duthcha air an tarruinn ri 'cheil, agus air am foghlum gu meas chuir orra fein agus leantuinn gu dluth ri cliu an sinnsear. 'N uair a thig iad air ais gu-n dachaidh an diu, tha iad ni 's Gaidhealaich na 'n uair a dh' fhalbh iad. Sibhse 'tha 'measg nan Gall cumaibh taic ris na comunnan so, ch-n e

.uhain air sgath na buannachd 'gheibh sibh fein uapa, ach mar an ceudna air sgath na buaidh mholtaich tha aca air an duthaich o 'n tainig sibh. Cuinnichibh an tonn a thogas sibhse 'an Lunnain gu-m faod e gluasad eadhon gu ruig am Parbh 'an Cataobh. Air an aobhar sin guidheam buaidh is beannachd air gach comunn de 'n t-seorsa. Thainig mar an ceudna atharrachadh anabarrach air cor agus suidheachadh na tha chombnuidh mu thuath. Tha nis greim agus coir aca air an dachaidhean; tha guth aca ann an riaghladh na duthcha; tha foghlum 'fas ionnus gu-m bheil am paipear-naigheachd a' ruigh o thighe gu tighe, air a ghiulain tuath ann an carbadaibh an eich-iaruinn. Cha-n eil e ni 's mo fior "gur fad an cubh o Loch-Obha," oir tha Tuath agus Deas air an toirt dluth d' a cheile. Mar a tha 'n Gaidheal a' meudachadh ann an eolas, agus a' glacadh greim air a choirichean, tha e 'meudachadh ann an meas air fein; ach combhla ri sin tha e meudachadh ann an gradh do 'n Ghall, agus an Gall gu ghradhachadhsa air ais. Tha 'n gradh brathaireil so gu math, ach chionns nach eil math gun olc, tha cunnart ann gu-m faod air Gaidheal, o 'chairdeas do 'n Ghall, a Ghaidhlic iomlaid air son na Beurla

Tha cuid ann a their gu-m faigh a' Ghaidhlic bas, a dh' aindeoin oidhirp a bheirear gu 'cumail suas, agus 'n uair a thachras sin nach bi 'n call mor. Gheibh sinn uile bas, ach gidheadh tha e mar fhiachan oirnn, le lagh Dhia agus dhaoine, aire 'thoirt air ar beatha "chums gu-m bi ar laithean buan anns an fhearann." Am fear a chuireadh laimh na bheatha feih, chionns gu-n robh e cinnteach gu-m faigheadh e bas uair-eigin, chuntar e 'n a amadan agus 'n a aindiadhach. Eadar gu-m faigh a' Ghaidhlic bas no nach fhaigh, ma 's fhiach i, 's e ar dleasnas, mar Ghaidhil, a h-altrum cho fhada 's a tha i againn. Tha iomadh buaidh mhaith air a' Ghaidhlic, agus buannachd r' a chosnadh uaipe. Tha 'ciabhagan liath le b-aoise, troimh 'n a sheid gaoth na mile bliadhna gun bheud gun bhearradh. B' i caint na h-Albainn o shean—seadh caint nan righrean agus nan daoine 'rinn Alba 'n a h-Alba. Thug i thugainn air tus, aig lamhan Chaluim-Chille, 'n uair a bha sinn 'n ar sluagh borb aineolach, naigheachd mu 'n t-Slannighear, agus sgaoileadh leis a' Ghaidhlic solus agus eolas gu cearnan iomallach na h-Albainn. Tha i beartach le h-eachdraidh na Rioghachd, agus trom le sar obair nam bard Gaidhealach. Tha bardachd Oiscain, Alastair Mac Mhaighstir Alastair, Dhonnachaidh Bhain, Rob Dhuin, Iain Luim, agus aireamh mor eile, fo ghlais agus iuchair aig a' Ghaidhlic. Mu gheibh i bas tha sud uile air chall, agus co aig a tha 'dhanadas a' radh nach bu chall mor e? Tha tri nithe gu sonnruichte a bhuineas do dh' Alba—am feileadh breacain, a' phiob-mhoir, agus a' Ghaidhlic. Mu

nithear dearmad air a' h-aon diubh sud, cha bhi sin gu buannachd na Rioghachd air fad, oir tha gach aon diubh n a chobhair do 'n duthchas Albanach sin a rinn cho mor air son na tire mar-tha, agus air an cuir sinn a cheart uiread de fheum na dheigh so. Alba bhig rinn duthchas do chuid cloinne mor thu : na leigeadh Dia gu-n tig smal air an duthchas sin, no gu-m faigh e leon !

'S i cheist a nis ciod e bu choir a dheanamh gu bhi 'meudachadh graidh ar luchd-duthcha do 'n canain mhathaireil, agus gu bhi 'cumail taic rithe. Bu choir oidhirp a dheanamh air cothrom 'thoirt do 'n oigridh gu bhi foghluim na caint a leughadh. Tha 'n Crun Breatunnach a' toirt airgiod air son a bhi teagasg caint nam Frangach, caint nan Gearmailteach agus caint nan Eadailteach do ghinnealachd og ar duthcha. Tha gach misneach air a thoirt do 'n chlann gu bhi foghluim nan caintean sud, agus moran mhiltean pund Sasunach air an caitheadh orra gach bliadhna. Cha-n eil focal agamsa ri 'radh an aghaidh so, ach dh' fhaighnichinn ciod i a' mhisneach a tha 'n Crun a' toirt do theagasg Gaidhlic troimh na Ghaidhealtas? mo naire ! cha mhoir sin. Paidhear am maighstir-sgoile iomadh fillte ni 's fhearra airson teagasg Francais na airson teagasg Gaidhlic, agus tha e nadurrach gu leor gu-n teagaisg am maighstir-sgoile an rud a's fhearra 'phaidheas e. Cha-n eil an Crun a' deanamh dhleasanais ris a' Ghaidhlic. Tha cubh mhoir an trathsa airson saighdearan Gaidhealach, tha cuideachd 'dol an so agus an sud g' an sireadh, air chosd moran airgiod. N' am biodh dara-leth an airgiod so air a chaitheadh 'teagasg Gaidhlic do 'n al og, o leabhraichean freagarrach, cha bhiodh an saighdear Gaidhealach cho duilich 'fhaotainn. 'S gann gu-m bheil focal anns na leabhraichean sgoile mu eachdraidh, mu bhardachd, no mu chliu nan Gaidhil, agus a dh' easbhuidh teagaisg de 'n t-seorsa tha 'n Crun a' call seirbheis nan Gaidhil mar shaighdearan. Chuirinn mar fhiachan air na h-uile neach aig am bheil an comas a' chuis so 'dheanamh soilleir do 'n Chrun, agus a' sparradh air ar luchd-riaghailidh an tuileadh misnich a thoirt do theagasg Gaidhlic ann ar sgoiltean. Thoireadh iad luach a shaorach do 'n mhaighstir-sgoile agus gheibh a' Ghaidhlic a h-aite fein anns an sgoil. A thuilleadh air so deanamh gach cinneadh Gaidhealtach eile mar a' rinn Clann Mhicaoidh an uiridh. Cuireadh na Caimbeulaich, na Domhnulaich, na Camronaich, agus mar sin air aghaidh, cuideachdan troimh an duthchannan fein gu bhi misneachadh teagasg na Gaidhlic, agus duisgear na Gaidhil da rireadh. Bithidh an sluagh coir toillichte bhur faicinn, gabhaidh iad ar comhairle, agus gheibh sibh fein solas ro mhoir ag athurrachadh ur n-eolais air na glinn anns an do thuinnich ur n-athairichean.

A' CHRIOCH.

LETTERS TO THE EDITOR.

MACKAYS OF MUDAL.

Sir—Can you, or any of the readers of the *Celtic Monthly*, kindly inform me if William Mackay of Mudal, Strathnaver, had more than one daughter; and if so, whether married, and to whom. William Mackay was, I believe, maternal grandfather of Captain Donald Matheson, Shiness.

M. M'D.

THE GLENNIES.

Sir—In the concluding number of Dr. Fraser-Mackintosh's most interesting papers on the "The Minor Septs of Clan Chattan," published in your March issue, there was a brief note on the above-named family, the first sentence of which it may, perhaps, be worth while to correct. I do not find that we have ever been seated, as affirmed, on the Spey side of the Aberdeenshire Grampians; though on Deeside, and particularly on Donside, we have been settled for more than five hundred years. The earliest of the records published by Kennedy in his "Annals of Aberdeen" (vol. II., p. 471), is a Latin memorandum of a decision of the Burgh Court of Aberdeen in the case of "Willielmus Gleny *contra* Matthus Hulk", 20th October, 1399. Nor have we "in the course of time disappeared from our original duchas". There are, I believe, a number still of large tenant-farmers of the name—traditionally they were called the "Bonnie Glennies"—in Kildrummy, and the neighbouring parishes. They were "Out," one is glad to know, both in the '15 and the '45. After the latter date, many of them went south; and I have to thank Dr. Fraser-Mackintosh for his kind concluding remarks as to how they sped in the learned Professions, the Army, Navy, and Consular Service.

Of more general interest, however, may be a few remarks on the derivation of the name, and the dates to which it may be traced back.

The name was, I believe, originally "Ghlinne," the genitive of "Gleann" (*Fir Ghlinne*, "Men of the Glen"). This derivation was given by the late famous Clan historian, Alexander Mackenzie, familiarly known as "the Clach"; and it is in accordance with the opinion also of a still more authoritative Gaelic scholar—Mr. Alexander Carmichael, who has given me one or two instances of the name in its Gaelic form in comparatively recent times. This Gaelic derivation is confirmed by the appearance of the name in documents of the time of Robert the Bruce as "del Glen." In Ireland, however, we find it in its Gaelic form as the patronymic, seven or eight hundred years ago, of the famous gleeman, scholar and poet, to whom is attributed the monk-satirising *Aislinge meic Conglinne* ("Vision of MacConglinne") of the twelfth century, recently edited by Kuno Meyer (Nutt, 1892). In the beginning of the poem, we are told that "the place of its composition is great Cork of Munster, and its author is Anier Mac Conglinne of the Onaght of Glenowra"—*Loce don dudain so Corcach mor Mumun, ocus persu di Aner mac Congliude di Eoanacht Glennabracht*—"the son of the Hound of the Glen, of the Onaght (*recte* Eoghanacht) or descendants of Eoghan Mor, the son of

Oilill Olum, King of Munster in the third century," according to Hennessy. Still earlier does the name occur, in the eighth century *Historia Britonum* of Nennius, as the name of the river in Northumberland at the mouth of which was fought Arthur's first battle in the sixth century—"the river Gleni," now called the Glen, a tributary of the Till; but which originally must, I think, have been the *Abhainn*, or rather *Allt a' Ghlinne*—the river, or rather, burn of the Glen. And thus of the two names Glenn and Glennie, the latter does not appear to be a diminutive of the former, but the former an abbreviation of the latter.

J. S. STUART-GLENNIE.

Surrey, 9th April, 1893.

P.S.—I have read with great interest the letter in your current issue on the MacHardies, and can, from my personal knowledge, confirm most of the Braemar traditions which the writer recalls,

J. S. S.-G.

THE CAMERONS OF GLEN NEVIS.

DEAR SIR—Like Mr. Donald Cameron, whose letter appeared in the February number of the *Celtic Monthly*, I have read Mr. Drummond-Norie's charming work, "Loyal Lochaber", with great pleasure. From certain expressions in that portion of the book dealing with the Glen Nevis Camerons, I also understood him to speak of them as an extinct race. I am glad, however, to observe from Mr. Drummond-Norie's reply in your last issue, that he had no intention of conveying such an idea; but only that this branch of Clan Cameron has now quite disappeared from its ancient territory, which is doubtless the fact. I presume that your readers in general are interested in all details connected with old Highland families, and this is my excuse for mentioning other members of the Cameron Clan who are proud to trace their descent from the House of Glen Nevis.

My wife's father was so descended, being the son of John Cameron, an officer in the 79th Highlanders, who was head of the Dawnie family, an off-shoot of Glen Nevis. This John Cameron was the eldest son of Donald Charles Cameron, of Dawnie (a godson of Prince Charles Edward) by his marriage with a Cameron of Letter-Finlay. John Cameron's third brother, Donald Charles, went out to British Guiana at the beginning of the century along with his kinsman John Cameron, the last of Glen Nevis.

They both became sugar-planters in Berbice, British Guiana (Demerara), and whilst Donald Charles made a fortune which enabled him to purchase the estate of Barcaldine, Argyllshire, his relative, Glen Nevis, did not meet with similar success. He had not sold his property in Lochaber before going out to the West Indies, as the last sentence in Mr. Drummond-Norie's letter implies, but parted with it somewhere about 1850, to Sir Duncan Cameron, of Fassifern, owing apparently to financial straits, through want of success in the sugar enterprise. I believe that Glen Nevis ended his days in one of the Channel Islands, and if he left male off-spring I have never heard of them.

I am under the impression that there are descendants in the female line, but I know nothing certain on this point

An aunt of my wife now living in London, who

was born and spent her childhood in Berbice, remembers that Glen Nevis was generally esteemed in the Colony for his high and honourable character.

If it be the fact that there are no male descendants of this last Glen Nevis chieftain, there are yet other Camerons who can undoubtedly claim descent from earlier chieftains, as for example, the members of the Dawnie family, and I daresay there are representatives of other branches, as must be the case with your correspondent, Mr. Donald Cameron.

Donald Charles Cameron, of Barcaldine, my wife's great-uncle, left descendants; so did his next brother Ewen, of Tallisker, in Skye. The eldest brother, John Cameron (of the 79th), my wife's grandfather, married a Kennedy of Lianachan (mis-spelt Lismachan on p. 464 of "Loyal Lochaber"), and his eldest surviving son, another Donald Charles, became a successful colonist in Queensland, where he is now represented by his son, John Cameron, the present head of the Dawnie branch of Glen Nevis. The youngest son of John Cameron and Isabella Kennedy was my wife's father, Alexander Gordon Matheson Cameron, M.D., (born 1820, died 1884), who went out as a young man to Demerara with his family had been long connected as I have shewn. He married in Berbice (1855) Edith, third daughter of Richard Martin Daly, of Demerara, Attorney, by Sarah, his wife, only child of Thomas O'Brien, Captain R.N., son of John O'Brien, an officer in the Enniskillen Dragoons, and a cadet of the ancient House of Thomond.

By this marriage Dr. Cameron had, besides three daughters who are all married with issue, two surviving sons, the elder of whom, Alistair Cameron, occupies a leading position in Barbados, as managing attorney for the several sugar estates of an old West-Indian firm, and is married, with a family of one son and four daughters; whilst the younger, Evan Donald Cameron, holds a junior post on one of the estates of the Hon. W. A. Wolseley, in Demerara. I am, Yours truly,

T. CLARK SMITH, M.A. (Oxon.

THE JEW ADMIRES THE KILT.

A PARAGRAPH has more than once appeared in the *Celtic* calling attention to the fact how adroitly the Jews, when settling in an English-speaking country drop their "chosen" names and deck themselves with Highland names instead.

Of course, it is no news I give when I state that the Jews adore the tartan. Who doesn't! To-day the tartan waves in every capital in Europe: in every city in America. It is as much at home in the cloak-room of the Grand Opera-house as it is in the humble dwelling of the poor. No wonder, then, that the Jew—after all a most impressionable creature, with an eye as keen for the shapely turn of a ankle as for the colour of a diamond, should succumb to its seductiveness.

The oft-quoted saying, that admiration with the Jew is but the prelude to acquisition, led me to fear further conquests; hence I longed to ascertain his attitude towards the kilt. It has come; and with the knowledge appears a picture of the Jew in a new light. Chance furnished the opportunity, and a daughter of Eve the inspiration, for extracting an opinion on this interesting subject. It came

about in this way. Last autumn, I went down to see the Caledonian Games which were held in Ambrose Park, South Brooklyn. On the ferry-boat which conveyed the crowd of Caledonians thither, was another and gayer crowd bound for Manhattan Beach. Among the latter, I observed a handsome, well-dressed man whose Hebraic cast of feature was unmistakable. He was accompanied by one of these radiantly beautiful creatures—a summer girl. The twain were very happy together, and merry were the remarks passed on everything and everybody as we steamed down the bay. Suddenly she of the snowy raiment espied some stalwart Scots in the Highland dress. "Just look at them," she said, "I call that dress perfectly horrid; there is nothing more shocking to me than to see these men in their bare l-l-leg- (limbs, I mean) walking along Broadway." The Jew turned quietly around, looked at the offending Scots in a kindly, nay almost wistful, way, and remarked: "I beg to differ from you. Singular as it may seem, the appearance of that dress always raises strange thoughts within me, which would be hard for me perhaps to express, but I like the dress."

Such a tribute from a gentleman Jew shows that even to the stranger there is something in the Garb of Old Gaul which appeals to the imagination, some mysterious something hard to define, but which seems everlastingly entwined with feelings of a strongly martial nature. What would be the sensation of the same son of Israel on seeing a kilted regiment swing by? "The thin red line" would appeal to his mystic Oriental mind more as the forked lightning of the storm-cloud of war; while their tread would but awaken echoes of the rush of opposing hosts, the clash of steel, and the shout of battle.

It is said of the late President Grant when present at a review of British troops that he allowed regiment after regiment of the boys in breeks to pass by in stolid indifference, without a single comment, although their bearing was faultless; but the moment that the tartan swung into line, the eyes of the old general lit up as he exclaimed: "Ah! they have the sweep of empire in their stride!"

Free though some Jews of a certain class have been with Highland names, and much though they may admire the tartan, I now feel fully assured that they will let the kilt alone. Yes, I think it can be confidently asserted that when a Jew is seen prancing along the Glasgow Trongate in tartan array, the steady tramp of Macaulay's New Zealander can be heard in the distance as he goes marching on towards London Bridge.

New York.   MACDHAI.

THE CLAN MACLEAN have had a very successful year, the membership now being 460, and the funds £227, truly a very gratifying position. An "At Home" will be given in Glasgow in October, at which Sir Fitzroy and Lady Maclean will be present.

THE INVERNESS-SHIRE ASSOCIATION have also just completed the winter's work. The Association is second to none in this city, and has the promise of greater successes in the future. Mr. James Grant was re-elected president.

GEORGE W. MACLEAN.

THE CELTIC MONTHLY:
A MAGAZINE FOR HIGHLANDERS.
Edited by JOHN MACKAY, Glasgow.

No. 9. Vol. VII.]   JUNE, 1899.   [Price Threepence.

GEORGE WHITE MACLEAN.

NO better indication need be given of the great interest that is now taken in clan matters than the membership rolls of some of the clan societies. The clan sentiment appeals to the man of Highland name, no matter in what distant part of the world his lot may be cast. The Clan Maclean Society membership list is most interesting, as it shows how widely the Highland race has scattered; and how even among the sons and grandsons of these exiled Gaels the feeling of clanship is still warmly preserved.

In former issues, we have given sketches of Macleans in various parts of the kingdom; we have now pleasure in doing honour to a very worthy clansman, Mr. G. W. Maclean, of Newcastle-on-Tyne. He was born at Cowlairs, and educated at the Springburn and E.C. Normal Schools. His father was an engineer by profession, and died in 1888. After leaving school, Mr. Maclean went to live with relatives at Newcastle-on-Tyne, and was apprenticed to the wholesale and manufacturing stationery business carried on by his uncle, Mr. James Errington, on whose death he succeeded as managing partner of the extensive firm of R. Robinson & Co., which has now a large connection, and employs about 350 hands. Business matters have so fully occupied Mr. Maclean's attention that he has never found time to take an active part in public affairs, except on committees in connection with several philanthropic institutions of the city.

His wife is the eldest daughter of the late Mr. Sutton, of Houghton, and their family consists of two sons and a daughter. Naturally, their summer holidays are spent in the Highlands, first at a Clyde watering place, then on to Oban, and across the Sound to Mull the ancient home of Mr. Maclean's ancestors.

The subject of our sketch is a life member of the Clan Maclean Society, in the excellent work of which he takes the keenest interest. He cherishes the clan sentiment strongly, and nothing gives him greater delight than to spend a few days in Mull, among the places associated with the clan in the olden days.

OUR HERO'S WELCOME!

Dedicated, by permission, to Colonel H. A. Macdonald, C.B., D.S.O., A.D.C.; and sung by Miss Jessie N. Maclachlan at the Hotel Cecil, May 6th. Music by Colin MacAlpin.

From the crash of cannons' roar,
   And the flash of ringing steel;
Toilsome march and swift bivouac
   Broken by the trumpets' peal.
From the desert of Afric sands,
   Long renowned in battle story;
Omdurman's undaunted field,
   Where thy name is linked in glory.
     Ceud 's ceud mile fàilte.

Dear to soldier heart the laurels,
   When a glorious deed is done;
Dearer when from grim oppression's
   Broken chains the wreath is won.
Dearer still when hearts that love thee
   Honour in thy honours claim;
When the race of Conn, united,
   To the world their rights proclaim.
     Ceud 's ceud mile fàilte.

Maidens! softly touch the clàrsach,
   Sing your sweetest songs to-day;
Pipers! rouse the magic chanter,
   Loud Clan Colla's gathering play!
Clansmen! pledge with Highland honours,
   Highland cheers, our Hero's name!
Till the Highland hills re-echo
   Back again our Hector's fame.
     Ceud 's ceud mile fàilte.

       ALICE C. MACDONELL, of Keppoch.

THE CLANS: PAST AND PRESENT.

By R. S. T. MacEwen, of Lincoln's Inn,
Barrister-at-Law.

(Continued from page 149).

CLAN NAMES, LANGUAGE, AND CUSTOMS.

CLAN names, and the surnames of Gaelic origin, were entirely based upon the personal name. They were derived from the personal name of the founder or chief of the clan, and were in no respect territorial. In the Lowlands and in the north we find a few territorial names—such as Buchanan, Ross, Sutherland — with chiefs of Lowland, Norse, and Flemish origin. But although the Highland clans and chiefs in the eighteenth century, and long before that date, were of mixed race, the Celtic blood largely prevailed. They spoke the language and observed the rites and customs of their Celtic ancestors. The whole of the Highlands had been for so many centuries over-run and occupied by the Celtic races, that, long after their descendants had become a mixed people, the Celtic language and customs prevailed; and the language and literature survive to the present day.

EXTENSION OF CLANS AND SEPTS.

The Acts of 1587 and 1594 give the names of forty-two clans and "broken men." These represent the principal clans as known at the present time; but comparing these rolls with Mr. Adam's lists,* one is struck by the fact that several names which appear in the former no longer find a place amongst the present-day clans; while, on the other hand, a large number of clans, septs, and names appear in the modern lists which had no place in the earlier Acts. Instead of the forty-two clans and "broken men" of 1594, we now have seventy-eight -"each having its own tartan"—and some five hundred names of septs and dependents sprung from or connected with the larger clans. Some clans of an earlier date than the 16th century had become extinct by that time; others had been reduced and had become affiliated to larger clans, retaining only their original names. The great increase in the number of clans and clan septs in later times is thus accounted for; as time wore on, and just as clans developed from the tribes, so septs developed within the clans— the kinsmen of the chiefs who had acquired lands and founded families being the leaders. Under the feudal system, the land became hereditary in these families; and we find local chieftains and lairds all over the Highlands each with a following of his own -- in some cases

still continuing in the original confederacy and owning its chief; in others, setting up as separate organizations, with themselves as chiefs. Skene says: "The most influential of these was that of the oldest cadet in the family which had been longest separated from the main stem; and usually presented the appearance of a rival house little less powerful than that of the chief." He sums up the actual position by a quotation from a writer of the early part of last century, whose views he adopts: "The Highlanders are divided into tribes or clans, under chiefs or chieftains, as they are known in Scotland; and each clan again divided into branches from the main stock, who have chieftains over them. These are subdivided into smaller branches of fifty or sixty men, who deduce their original from their particular chieftains, and rely upon them as their more immediate protectors and defenders. The ordinary Highlanders esteem it the most sublime degree of virtue to love their chief and pay him a blind obedience, although it be in opposition to the government, the laws of the kingdom, or even to the law of God. Next to this love of their chief is that of the particular branch from whence they sprung; and in a third degree to those of the whole clan or name, whom they will assist, right or wrong, against those of any other tribe with which they are at variance. They likewise owe good-will to such clans as they esteem to be their particular well-wishers; and, lastly, they have an adherence one to another as Highlanders, in opposition to the people of the Low Country, whom they despise as inferior to them in courage, and believe they have a right to plunder them whenever it is in their power. This last arises from a tradition that the Lowlands, in old times, were the possessions of their ancestors."†

EMPLOYMENTS OF THE CLANS.

One would be apt to conclude, from a study of their history, that raiding their neighbours and fighting formed the chief business in life of the clans; and, no doubt, they did a good deal of this. Many of the clans had long and bitter feuds with each other. Raids and counter-raids, attacks and reprisals, were frequent and fierce, and often arose from the most trivial causes; as, for instance, the beheading of Alexander, chief of Clan Gunn, at Inverness by the Earl of Murray, for his audacity at Aberdeen, when, as a follower of the Earl of Caithness, he refused to yield "the top of the street" to the Earl. They were really, however, an agricultural people, and their wealth consisted in cattle and sheep. Their debts and fines were paid in kind. On the sea-board they added fishing to the cultiva-

---

* "What is my Tartan?"   † "Celtic Scotland."

tion of the soil. The Chiefs had their home farms, and received such rents as they could get from their clansmen. The Dhuine wassels had holdings next in extent to those of the chiefs. They paid little or no rent, and worked their lands by hired labour. The clansmen tilled their own ground. The women spun and made tartan clothes for their own and the men's wear. In later times, Chiefs and Dhuine wassels went further afield, and took service in home and foreign regiments, officered contingents sent abroad or raised to help continental sovereigns, and many became soldiers of fortune in foreign armies and in the continental wars. Others entered the church and the learned professions at home. They have filled the Highland manses from the Reformation next to the present time. In the towns of the country they became lawyers, doctors, and merchants, and held public appointments, legal and fiscal; until in course of time the Highland counties and towns became as quiet, orderly, and well-governed as any other part of the kingdom.

THE FIGHTING STRENGTH OF THE CLANS IN THE EIGHTEENTH CENTURY.

The number of fighting men in the clans mentioned in the Acts of 1587 and 1594 is not given; but, at a much later period, General Wade supplies a statement of the strength of the Highland forces which fought for King James in 1715:—in the islands and clans of the late Lord Seaforth (Mackenzie), 3,000; Macdonalds of Sleat, Glengarry, Moydart, and Keppoch, 2,820; Camerons, 800; Macleods, 1000; Gordons, 1000; Stewarts of Appin, 400; Robertsons, 800; Mackintoshes and Farquharsons, 800; MacEwens, 150; Chisholms, 150; Macphersons, 220; the Atholl men (more than half of whom were Robertsons and Stewarts), 2,000; and the Breadalbane men, 1000; in all 14,140.* This represents about twenty clan names on the Jacobite side at that time, and does not include several well-known and powerful clans—such as the Mackays, Gunns, Sutherlands, Murrays, Rosses, Munros—in the north, which numbered quite as many again. The total strength at this period was certainly not less than 30,000 fighting men, probably more.

THE CLANS IN THE '45.

In the engagements of 1745-46 we find Highlanders on both sides. At Prestonpans, on 21st September, 1745, the Prince had the Macdonalds of Clanranald, Glengarry, Keppoch, and Glencoe, Macgregors and other men of Perth, Stewarts of Appin, Camerons, Menzies, Atholl and Nairn men—in all, some 2,400. The Murrays fought for the Government. At Falkirk, on 17th

* Johnston's "Geography of the Clans."

January, 1746, the Prince was supported by the same Highlanders, with the addition of the Mackintoshes, Mackenzies, Farquharsons, Frasers, Macphersons, and some others; while the Munros were on the other side.

(*To be continued*).

"UNTO THE HILLS."
TALKS WITH HIGHLANDERS.

No. IV.—MOTHER EARTH. PART II.

DURING the bright summer weather of last year, when you were "doon the watter", I knew that you would not care to read about the green and purple dulness of country life, while exciting literature such as "The Scarlet Sin" and "Chuckles from a Cheery Corner" could be had for sixpence at the steamer bookstall; so I waited for spring-time and the rush of new Life before continuing my talks, and asking you once again to turn your hearts to Mother Earth and her homely nourishments of sight, sound, and contact. But now that the young men have long laid aside their braveries of Highland dress, with its harmless set of coast-cast weapons,* let us look together at another characteristic of the ancient Celtic ornament that we find in illuminated manuscripts, and covering porridge bowl and distaff, no less than shield and dirk and brooch, and the tombstones of those who have "gone before." Its freshness and variety we noticed before, but not yet its ENERGY. Through every page of the "Book of Kells", written in Ireland in the seventh century, the twisting ribbons run in and out among each other, with a quick turn here and a tight knot there, like honey-suckle trails among ivy branches—never losing their way, though it takes you half an hour to track out

* Folk in their twenties naturally go "brave"— in the second as well as the first meaning of the word, retained in the Scottish "braw"—and should shine, in every way, like Ian Aluinn. We want only the hand loom and natural dyes back again to give full colour to the "sett", and glint to the texture, of the tartan; and that the village blacksmith should become also a whitesmith, as he once was, able to put some heraldry of a young man's Spring fancies into the brooch at his shoulder or the sgian dubh at his knee—making the ornament as individual as the wearer (his sweetheart would have a still finer twist in her jewellery), a treasure for the present and afterwards an heirloom. Our fore-fathers were beginning to carve leaf and bird and beast patterns, instead of more complicated knots, when the Reformation came and turned all their curves into angles. Now we are starting again where they left off, for

"Jeanie MacRa' to the mountains is gaen,
Their Leagues and their Covenants a' she has taen;
She's got her heart and her mind at rest,
And as for her body, let the deil do his best!"

the course of one of them. The serpents coil and bite with the fiery grip of the wild man's heart and the fearless sweep of his hand—they are *his signature*, just as the regularly-crossed rug-straps and the "converted" nerveless beasts of the modern adapted work are the signature of a night-school student of design; not one whit more lifeful and vigorous than the hoops and loops in the tail of what is nowadays called a signature by the teachers of "good sound commercial handwriting."

Energy! life!—what a creature can do—strong and beautiful, or tender, or rigid, make us glad or sorry, kill or cure! These are its natural history; and the last point is the most important, whether we are considering honeysuckle or snakes, or the words of a man's mouth and the works of his hands. We don't want mechanical copies of old ornament back again, in a sham Celtic school organised by Saxons. What we do want is a new ornament, expressing happy sensations of our own, arising out of simple and healthy conditions of life and work to-day. The old ornament is a foundation and a starting point, because, like bodily gesture- of which it is an extension—its curves express accurately the natural directions of rhythmic energy in the race that produced it; but it must be filled with our wider sympathy and bent to our more pliable turn, before it becomes, in any true sense, *our* art or *our* possession; giving us hope once more of a living Celtic design, in which little children play with the biting serpents, and the intertwined ribbons spring into bud and blossom as "a root out of a dry ground."

Mechanical commercialism has driven out feeling from work and health from the body, and has set every man's wits against his neighbour's. Heart and hand united again in cheerful, affectionate work will yet change all that; and this work will become, in the near future, the first element in education.

But what is called education to-day? Your little girl goes to a Board school, and is examined in "physiology." She is foolishly asked to write down "what she knows about the functions of the cerebrum, the cerebellum, and the medulla oblongata." She remembers the badly printed woodcuts in her cheap text-book; and she has "heard tell" of the enlightened and liberal minister of information on the penny-in-the-slot principle, Mr. Mundella. So she sensibly writes down her general impressions, thus: "The cerebrum is white inside and grey outside, and the cerebellum is the other way; but the *Mundella* oblongata is between the two."[*] When she comes home from the examination, her own little cerebrum is far too full of muddled bunkum to allow her to attend to your sore leg. Now, would not the knowledge of how to use last season's hay to

the best purpose in feeding the stirk (I suppose, for the present, that you are unprogressive, and live in the country), and of how to boil up the flowers of the hay into a brown liquor which will instantly relieve your pain, be of more practical value to the household than anatomically decorative notions regarding the colour of the cerebrum or the cerebellum?—though I can't deny that the last is a very "fancy word!"

Under the present system of brain puzzling, children learn to talk confused jargon for a week or two concerning "brums and bellums," and then, happily, forget all about "physiology." They learn to pull a wild red rose "that's newly sprung in June" out of its little green cup, and "botanically" name the torn fragments a "calyx" and a "corolla"—getting as far from any real knowledge of the living creature as it is possible to go. Such visionless elementary cram may well be called, after the name of its most conscientious supporter, the Mundella-oblongata method. Compare with it the ancient Highland Ben Dorain manner[†] of Fair Duncan of the Songs. Duncan never heard any of these large bumbling "scientific" words, but he knew the character and humours and expression of every bird and beast and tiny plant upon his own hill; and he gives you complete record of it in two or three words, and often in one.

Suppose we try the first letters of a botanical A B C—founded, after his manner, upon observation and tradition only, for the use of children up to any age.

A, then, is for *Anemone (plùr na gaoithe)*, flower of the winds. You must look for it on a fine day; since before rain the light petals close firmly into a tiny pointed tent, where the fairies hide from the storm, pulling the fine spun rosy curtains in round their heads. Kneel down on the grass in the morning sunshine, and look closely at the pretty filmy pink and white star, hiding among its finely cut leaves in the hazel wood. Carefully pluck a few blossoms and a few leaves, saying to yourself as your fathers said: "I gather thee, fairy flower, as a remedy against disease." Take the anemones home, put some in a bowl of water, and dry the rest in the sun; then make a brown paper trumpet, fastening the loose corner with a pin, put flowers and leaves into the trumpet, stalks first, and tie them firmly in with a piece of twine round the narrow end, turn the point of the paper at the wide end neatly over at the opening to keep out the dust, and fasten on a little white label with the name of the flower in Gaelic and English, neatly written; for you will *do* the whole

---

[*] An actual answer to an idiotic question, as given by a clever country child.

[†] Duncan is no methodist.

JAMES MACRAE, M.D.

alphabet, I hope, in the same way soon—not only *say* it. Hang up the trumpet to the rafters; and, when you hear of whooping cough being in the place, boil a handful of your dry flowers and leaves for a quarter of an hour, and give the poor "whooper" a drink now and again, until the whoop has all gone, driven out by the power of the anemone. But the fairy flowers can do more for you. If you boil the flowers in vinegar instead of water, pour some into the palm of your hand, and snuff it up your nostrils at the beginning of a cold, it will cut it short there and then. Lang syne, the anemone was called the Pasque flower, or flower of the great Easter feast of the Resurrection, from the time of its blossoming. Pasque, or Càisg in Gaelic, comes, they say, from a Hebrew word meaning to "pass over"; and the fine and delicate flower of the winds may well remind us of the light aerial body in which, some day, helpful like an anemone, or helpless like a long word, we shall pass into the better life.

I should like to write a few more letters.[*] B for broom, C for chamomile, and a "big big D" for dock, which catches the "microbes" while the doctors are looking for them. Above all, H for heather—that sturdy red warrior of the hills. He only differs from his brother heathen by one letter. Both take their names from the wild places they inhabit; and neither of them has fallen under the civilising influence of the Young Men's Christian Association of New Jersey City, U.S.A., whose president, Rev. Mr. Hoagland, (he takes his name from a useful farmyard enclosure, though he "spells it with an a Saugny!") thinks dancing in the kilt "indecent", and would only allow a young Highlander to "have his fling" within the inexpressibly decorous restraint of Yankee bell-mouthed breeches. But the very thought of such virtuous enclosures as New Jersey City and their "associations" gives me, for the present, a "scunner" at literature; and sends me out to the heather, with a headache. No! with a slight congestion of the cerebrum, accompanied by a neuro-idiopathic determination to the cerebellum.

Tarnalt, Easter 1899.　J. A. CAMPBELL, of Barbreck.

*If anybody chances to want the others they will, I hope, find them before long in a little Herbary which the Peasant Arts Society of London is going to publish for me. I need not say that such an Alphabet for Highland schools should be in Gaelic.

THE CLAN MACMILLAN SOCIETY have just completed a very successful session. The membership roll has been largely increased, and the treasurer has a balance of £120 on hand. The Rev. Dr. Hugh Macmillan was re-elected chief; Mr. Donald Macmillan, Partick, president; Mr. Robert Macmillan, secretary; and Mr. Donald Macmillan, Main Street, treasurer.

DR. JAMES MACRAE, HUNTLY.

IN the country town of Huntly, Aberdeenshire, lives and labours Dr. James Macrae, the subject of this sketch. Of Highland descent from the Macraes of the Black Isle, Dr. Macrae is a typical specimen of his clan, which has always been conspicuous for the stature, strength and other physical endowments of its clansmen individually. Educated as a boy at the Grammar School, Aberdeen, James Macrae passed from that seminary to King's College, whence after taking the degree of Master of Arts, he proceeded to the study of medicine at Marischal College. In the Medical School as a student he highly distinguished himself in all his classes, being in the examinations always near the head of the lists, and not infrequently gaining a prize or a medal. Graduating Master of Surgery and Bachelor of Medicine in 1889, Dr. Macrae at once proceeded to London, whence, after gaining some experience in the hospitals there, he went on a sea voyage which extended over several months. He visited the Cape, Madagascar, and the Island of Mauritius.

On his return home Dr. Macrae was invited by Dr. Wallace of Turriff to act as his assistant, and this post he held for upwards of three years. In Turriff the doctor was one of the most popular men in the district. From the town of Turriff Dr. Macrae moved to his present abode, where he has been for the past five years; and where he has made for himself a name and reputation for skill as a medical practitioner equalled by few in the county. Possessed of a large and lucrative practice, the doctor devotes all his energies to his work; and in the wide district over which his practice extends there are few men who bulk so largely in the esteem and goodwill of the inhabitants as does Dr. James Macrae. The doctor is quite a young man yet, and there can be little doubt that, in the days to come, an even more prosperous future awaits him.

Dr. Macrae graduated Doctor of Medicine in 1898, and the photograph here presented was taken on that interesting occasion.

THE COMRADES:
A TALE OF THE 78th HIGHLANDERS.

THEY first met as recruits on the parade-ground of Fort-George. Ronald hailed from the banks of the Spean, Angus from the banks of the Findhorn. Their ancestors often met in deadly conflict in the days of old. Ronald's great-great-grandfather fell in a cattle-lifting expedition in the braes of Strathdearn;

Angus' great-great-grandfather fell at Mulroy, when the Macdonalds and Mackintoshes met for the last time as foes. Ronald was a typical specimen of his clan—tall and athletic, with square-cut face, fearless brown eyes, and dark hair. His every movement indicated dash and daring; but there was something in his face that told of a sympathetic, large heart. Angus was no less a good representative of his race—tall, lithe, fair, and sinewy, with firm mouth, and blue-grey eyes which at times sparkled with fun, but in which shone a steady light like that of the cleft granite of his native mountains. Deep down in both lay grand qualities that do not show themselves until the hour of adversity comes. Although they differed in creed, Ronald being a Roman Catholic, Angus a Protestant, they were early drawn together by county ties their regiment, the 78th, being chiefly composed of Ross-shire men—and that indescribable Jacobite sympathy that only those whose fathers fought and suffered for the exiled Stuarts can understand. Their Ross-shire comrades called them "Na h-Abaraich"—"The Lochaber men"; the black sheep of the regiment (what regiment is without a few?) jeeringly called them "Na h-Abaraich phròiseal"—"The proud Lochaber men." Proud they were—if that self-respect that does not allow its possessors to mingle with those of low tastes and low habits, is pride.

One night, when the regiment was at Edinburgh, and the two were making their way home to the Castle after a long walk in the country, they were stopped by half-a-dozen half-tipsy soldiers of their own regiment, who seemed determined on picking a quarrel with them—one, more insolent than the others, giving Ronald a slap in the face. In the twinkling of an eye, the aggressor lay stretched on the pavement. His comrades rushed upon the two, but the assaulted were instantly back to back; Angus hitting out quick and sure like the hill-cat of his clan, Ronald flooring whoever came within reach of his long arm. In two or three minutes the contest was over, luckily for all concerned before the policemen came upon the scene. From that day forth no one interfered with the Aberich.

When the two were off duty at the same time, they often ascended Arthur's Seat. The climb reminded them of stiffer ones on the slopes of Aonach Mhor and Monalia. They would at times sit down on the summit, look away over the Forth, and talk about scenes and faces far beyond the reach of their vision amongst the snow-capped hills of the North. The old stories and legends of their respective glens would be told, and the merits of bards and minstrels discussed. They were both lovers of song (what Highlander is not?) and both could compose

verse in praise of their sweethearts or native glens, when in the mood. On one of these occasions, Ronald seemed badly smitten with what Angus called the "Lochaber Longing." He sat for some time silent, but at length began singing the following lines :—

"Ri taobh abhuinn bhras-shruthach Spean mo ghaol,
Tha taighean beag boidheach, s e gealaicht' le aol,
'S anns an taighan sin maighdean og mhaiseach a tamh
A thug domh a cridhe 's a gheall domh a lamh."

Beside my loved Spean, the rapid, the clear,
Stands a little white house, wheredwells one to me dear;
The fairest, best maiden in all our broad land,
Who has given me her heart and has promised her hand.

Angus, with a mischievous twinkle in his eye, followed with :—

"Ri taobh abhuinn Eoin, nan tuil 's nan crag liath,
Tha maighdean na's boidhche na 'n Lochabar bha riamh.
A guth mar an smeorach, mar ghorm-speur a suil,
'S esan sheallas na h-aodann air each cuiridh cul."

On the banks of the Findhorn a maiden fair dwells,
That the maid of Lochaber in beauty excels,
With a voice like a mavis, blue eyes like the sky,
And he who beholds her all others pass by.

Ronald looked into the face of his fun-loving companion, with a flash of the old Lochaber fire in his eye, continued his song but changed the theme.

"Tha aite 'n Lochabar, do 'n ainm a Mhaolruaidh,
Far an liomhor na cinn a chaidh sgoltadh le tuagh,
'Us iomadh fear bosdail gu tosdach na shuain,
Os a chionn an dubh-mhointeach 's fraoch gasngach nain."

There's a place in Lochaber, Mulroy is its name,
Where cracking of skulls at one time was the game;
And the losers are sleeping beneath the brown heath,
Their boasting long hushed in the silence of death.

Angus, however, seemed to enjoy this thrust, for he had an arrow still in his quiver, and followed with :—

"Stad, stad, mo Raol ceolmhor, nach cuala thu riamh,
Mu 'Rathad na Meirleach' a Stratheirinn nam fiadh,
Far an iosal fir ghramail Lochabar nam beann,
Chaidh thogail nan creach anns na laithean a bh'ann."

Stop, stop, tuneful Ronald, remember the beaves,
And the track in Strathdearn named "Road of the Thieves",
Where your kinsmen are lying pierced with blue steel,
No more to go roving fat cattle to steal.

The two sprang to their feet, not to draw dirks, as their fathers would of old, but, with a laugh, to start running down the steep slope of Arthur's Seat. Ronald reached the Queen's Drive some yards ahead of his comrade, with the shout of "Lochabar gu bràth" (Lochaber for ever)—a shout his comrade would take up on another day, in a far distant land, where grimmer exercise awaited them.

Passing over several uneventful years in the career of our heroes, we come to that episode in the history of their regiment which Tennyson has put into immortal verse, and which encircles that kilted band with a halo of glory. At that time, the two well-behaved, handsome Highlanders were sergeants, Angus carrying the colours. Their ruddy faces had become sallow and deep-tanned with the Indian sun, their eyes sunken, their tartan tattered and dingy, but their heart were unchanged. In one of the many engagements in which they took part, Angus was shot in the leg. He limped on for a few paces, but another shot striking him on the arm, the colours dropped from his hand, and he fell. Ronald was at his side in an instant, whispered in his ear "I shall be back in a minute", picked up the colours and rushed on. Though sorely stricken, Angus raised himself on his elbow, shouted "Lochabar gu bràth", and fell back in a swoon. When the foe was repulsed, Ronald hastened back to his fallen comrade, and found the surgeon binding up his wounds. In the undoing of his coat, the small Gaelic Testament he carried in his breast had dropped out, and lay on the ground. Ronald noticed this, picked it up, and put it back in its wonted place, with the remark "We must not lose your book, Angus." These two leal comrades, although they differed in creed, had learned on many a long, weary march, and in many a hard-fought fight, that there is a brotherhood that oversteps all creed barriers, and even the dark river of Death, beyond which is a "City not made with hands, of many gates." The wounded were left behind under the protection of a small guard; but before Angus had recovered from the effects of his wounds, Ronald was carried back from the front, suffering from a severe attack of dysentery. The former rejoiced that, though still unfit for duty, he was strong enough to help his comrade. All that strong love, surpassing the love of women, suggested, he did. It seemed to him at times that Ronald would see Lochaber no more, and he would slip out of the tent to hide his grief from his stricken comrade. At times he would sit by his bed and read to him passages (perhaps not well chosen, but doing his best) from the Roman Catholic Breviary. At length Ronald's strong constitution began to shake off the malady that laid him so low, and Angus was relieved of his load of anxiety.

In a short time after this the mutiny was suppressed, the campaign ended, and the 78th returned home.

＊ ＊

On a bright spring day, when the woods of Dunain were ringing with song, Craig Phadruig standing out clear against a cloudless blue sky,

the tree buds bursting over the silent sleepers of Tomnahurich, and the river dancing and sparkling on its way to the sea, the loiterer on the Suspension Bridge of Inverness might have been roused from his contemplation of that scene of beauty and grandeur by the music of the bagpipes. Did it come from the east or west side of the river? From both though the tune was the same, a merry wedding one. A few minutes after, a small, gaily-dressed party might be seen coming down Bridge Street, headed by a piper; and a similar one marching up the western river bank, until they met in front of the Glen Albyn Hotel. One had come by boat on the previous evening from the braes of Lochaber, the other had come that morning by coach from the braes of Strathdearn. The bridegrooms were the heroes of our story, now pensioners after twenty-one long years of service, meeting on their wedding day, each proud of his bride brides whose faithfulness had stood a test by which only a few are tried. Not so fair and fresh, perhaps, were they as when their lovers sang of their charms on Arthur's Seat, but they possessed in a greater measure than at that time, charms more lasting. The two parties dined together (an arrangement Ronald and Angus had made on their way home from India). Health-drinking, Gaelic songs, and Highland reels, followed. Then they left for their respective homes, to prolong festivities amongst their friends; but the comrades never forgot each other.

A. G. M.

THE SOCIAL CONDITION OF THE HIGHLANDS SINCE 1800.

By A. J. BEATON, F.S.A. Scot., F.G.S.E.

(Continued from page 114).

"THERE is, however, something almost mysterious in the helpless ignorance of Scottish rural customs up to the middle of the last century. . . . In a country where there is a heavy rainfall, its inhabitants never thought of artificial drainage. In a country where the one great natural product was grass of exceptional richness and comparatively long endurance, they never thought of saving a morsel of it in the form of hay. In a country where even the poorest cereal could only grow by careful attention to early sowing, they never sowed till a season which postponed the harvest to a wet and stormy autumn. In a country where such crops required every nourishment which the soil could afford, to sustain them, they were allowed to be choked with weeds, so that the weed crop was heavier than the grain. . . They sow corn as if they were feeding hens, and plant potatoes as if they were dibbling beans. They think the more they put in the more they will take out. In short, we have here a survival of the wretched husbandry of the lowest period of the military ages staring at us in the fierce light of our own scientific and industrial times." Without a doubt, a great deal of the above is quite true; but then we know that however impartial His Grace may try to be, yet his judgment must be more or less biassed, as His Grace has anything but a favourable opinion of what he calls "the worst of all native customs" —"crofter" townships.

"The whole of the outer Hebrides, continues His Grace, "are mainly composed of the oldest, the hardest, the most obdurate rock existing in the world. It is the same rock which occupies a great area in Canada, on the north bank of the St. Lawrence. The soil which gathers on it is generally poor, and even what is comparatively good is often inaccessible. In its hollows, stagnant waters have slowly given growth to a vegetation of mosses, reeds, and stunted willows. Gradually these have formed great masses and sheets of peat. Only along the margin of the sea, where calcareous siliceous sands have mixed with local deposits of clay, are there any areas of soil which even skill and industry can make arable with success. The whole of the interior of the island is one vast sheet of black and

CASTLEBAY, BARRA, DURING THE FISHING SEASON

dreary bog. . . . To root them in that soil is to bury them in a bog—a bog physical, a bog mental, and a bog moral." So decides His Grace the Duke of Argyll; and yet Mr. Nimmo, one of the Commissioners appointed by the Government to enquire into the nature and extent of the bogs in Ireland, in his report, issued in 1813, says: "I am perfectly convinced, from all that I have seen, that any species of bog is, by tillage and manure, capable of being converted into a soil fit for the support of plants of every description; and, with due management, perhaps the most fertile that can be submitted to the operations of the farmer. Green crops—such as rape, cabbages, and turnips—may be raised with the greatest success on firm bog, with no other manure than the ashes of the same soil. Permanent pastures may be formed on bog, more productive than on any other soil. Timber may be raised especially firs, larch, spruce, and all the acquatics—on the deep bog, and the plantations are fenced at little expense; and with a due application of manure, every description of white crops may be raised upon bog."

The expense of draining and improving bog land as estimated by Mr. Griffith, one of the Commissioners' engineers, was about twenty-five shillings per acre, and he reckoned on receiving an annual rent of thirty shillings per acre, on a lease of twenty-one years.

Before the construction of the Grand Canal from Dublin to the River Shannon, a portion of the Bog of Allen called the "Wet Bog" was originally valued to the promoters of the Canal at one farthing per acre. It now lets for tillage and grazing at from thirty shillings to forty shillings per acre.

I may be pardoned for introducing this extraneous matter, as I wish to show the beneficial effect arterial drainage would have on the swampy lands of the Highlands. Stagnant waters produce one kind of unprofitable aquatic plants; vegetation is affected by the quantity as well as the quality of the moisture which it absorbs for its sustenance; and the cold damp exhalations from the swampy hollows have a most injurious effect on everything in their vicinity.

The draining of bog land in Ireland has proved remunerative, and were the Government to do for the Highlands and Islands of Scotland what they have on several occasions done for Ireland in the way of drainage grants, and a complete scheme of arterial drainage carried out in the Highlands, with a judicious planting of trees, we should have a more fertile soil, a healthier and finer climate, a more contented and industrious peasantry; and while the canals served as the means of carrying off the superabundant waters, they could at the same time be utilized as a waterway for the conveyance of the requirements of the districts they penetrated; or used as a motive power for mills, which might be erected along their banks.

The method of letting farms on long leases was, during prosperous years, considered one of the distinguishing privileges of Scots farms, but in recent years matters have entirely reversed. On the other hand, yearly tenancy has many objections. The uncertainty of tenure tempts the farmer to take all he can out of the soil, while he has the opportunity; or perhaps, when he has exhausted or impoverished the soil, he quits the holding. Of the two evils, therefore, it is difficult to decide which is to be preferred. The most satisfactory solution of the problem is the adoption of the principle embodied in the Crofters' Holdings Act—security of tenure and rent fixed by a Commission.

XI.—FISHERIES.

Another industry in the Highlands of equal importance with agriculture is the sea fisheries. The gross value of the sea fisheries of Scotland, according to the Fishery Board returns for year 1887, amounted to £1,915,602 10s. 0d., of which sum £1,128,480 8s. 0d. were accredited to the herring fishery. Now, as the herring fishery is chiefly confined to the Highland waters, it can

be readily seen what an enormous source of wealth this harvest of the sea yields to the country. The means of employment it also gives to the surplus population of the Highlands is very considerable, for no fewer than 49,221 men and boys were engaged in the sea fisheries in the year 1866. In addition to this number, 50,973 persons were employed in connection with the summer herring fishery. The estimated capital invested in boats, lines, nets, etc., is £1,712,349.

The herring fishery has gone on increasing at an enormous rate since the year 1809, when the total number of barrels cured was 90,185¼; in 1850, the number increased to 544,009¼; while in 1886 the number of barrels cured amounted to 1,103,424¼. Of this aggregate quantity, 865,911¼ barrels were exported to Germany and other places on the Continent; and a large proportion of the balance was sent to America and to Ireland.

If it were not for this industry, the Highlands —with its present low ebb in agricultural matters— would be in a most deplorable state of starvation and misery; but the All-wise Creator has compensated the poor Hebridean for his bleak and barren land by providing a rich and inexhaustible store in the precious treasures of the mighty deep.

Although the fisheries of Scotland have made extraordinary progress during the last fifty years, still there is much room for further development; and, to accomplish this, several things are necessary. State aid must be given for the construction of harbours and railways;* and existing railway companies should be compelled to carry fresh fish at a rate sufficient to pay them a fair percentage for haulage, without swallowing up the entire profits of the industry; and a suitable and central station ought to be selected on the west coast, where boats and steamers could land their cargoes so as to be dispatched by the most rapid and economical route to the great consuming centres of the Empire; and lastly, grants should be made to fishermen, on favourable terms, for the proper equipment of the fishing fleet.

The restrictions surrounding sums devoted by the Treasury under the Crofters' Holdings Act, have rendered it next to impossible to apply the money for what it was intended; and consequently, very few crofter fishermen have benefited therefrom.

(To be continued.)

*Since the above was written, the Government granted subsidies to the Highland Railway and West Highland Railway for extensions of their systems.

TO CORRESPONDENTS.

All Communications, on literary and business matters, should be addressed to the Editor, Mr. JOHN MACKAY, 9 Blythswood Drive, Glasgow.

TERMS OF SUBSCRIPTION.— The CELTIC MONTHLY will be sent, post free, to any part of the United Kingdom, Canada, the United States, and all countries in the Postal Union—for one year, 4s.

THE CELTIC MONTHLY.
JUNE, 1899

CONTENTS.

OUR NEXT ISSUE.

Next month we will give plate portraits, with biographical sketches, of Colonel Hugh B. Maclean, St. John, New Brunswick, and Messrs. Donald Fraser of Millburn, and Hector Mackay, Edinburgh.

DAVIDSON AND MACDEVETTE.

DEAR MR. EDITOR—In reply to Justice Mac-Devette's inquiry as to whether Davidson of Tulloch is of Celtic or Scandinavian origin, I would say that, as chief of Clan Davidson alone, he certainly comes from the former source. The Clan Chattan, of which the Davidsons are a sept, is always known as Celtic. Even if proved to be an off-shoot of the ancient Germanic tribe Catti, or Chatti, the Clan Chattan still remains Celtic. Tulloch's descent, traced by the female line, shows his mother to be a Mackenzie of Eileanach ; his grandmother a Mac-donald (daughter of the third Lord Macdonald); and so on to the Baynes, a sept of the warlike Mackays—they of the "strong hand." Thus it will be seen that Davidson of Tulloch is a chief of strictly Celtic race.

As to the name Davidson, while that of MacDavid is occasionally met with, and the MacDaids or Mac-Dades were numerous at one time in North Carolina, being early Highland settlers, the chief and majority of the clan have used the present form for a period longer than I can trace. And in adopting the affix "son" instead of the prefix "Mac" the Davidsons stand not alone. The Robertsons, Farquharsons, Fergusons, and Mathesons—all strong and independent clans in their day, and of which three claim to be Celtic—follow the same custom. The number of families with "son" to their names, springing from Celtic clans, in Scotland, is many, whatever may have been Mr. MacDevette's observations in Ireland.

Full information on the subject of Highland surnames can be had from Mr. Frank Adam's unique little work "What is my Tartan ?"—a work which can truly be characterized as the completest "Ready Reckoner" extant on everything relating to the clan system ; and is a task performed by the distinguished author which his fellow-Gaels fully appreciate.

New York, April 14th.   MacDhai.

THE SCOT ABROAD.

DEAR SIR—It is possible you may be able to find room in your magazine for the following :—

A SCOTTISH VOLUNTEER REGIMENT is being raised in Melbourne, Victoria, and a hundred men have already been enrolled. The Victorian Minister of Defence consented to the formation of the regiment, on the understanding that the country should not be called upon to provide the necessary uniforms, etc. The committee is now appealing for funds for clothing, general regimental and band expenses, etc. All monies contributed are deposited in the Government Savings Bank, vested in trustees—who are Sir John MacIntyre, M.L.A. (past president of the Caledonian Society), and W. H. MacLennan, Esq., of the Caledonian Society, Melbourne.

The sub-committee consists of Sir John Mac-Intyre, and members of the various Melbourne "Scottish Thistle" Societies and the Caledonian Society, and the Hon. Secretary is Yeats L. Cunningham, Esq., 195 Collins Street, Melbourne, who will acknowledge any subscriptions sent.

There are so many Scotsmen who are, or have been, resident in, or connected with, Australia, that if the subject be brought to their notice they may be inclined to contribute to this object ; and the day may not be far distant when the Australian volunteers may be called upon to take their part in the defence of the Empire. The offers of the New Zealand and Australian Governments to place what forces they have at the disposal of the Home Government, show that, if ever the need arises, they may be relied on to afford very practical aid to the Mother Country ; and Scotsmen connected with Australia, or Australians resident in Scotland, will be at least interested in the movement.—I am, Yours truly,

Lerags, Oban.   CAMPBELL MACKELLAR.

THE HERO OF OMDURMAN.—Colonel Hector Macdonald has doubtless found ere this that popularity has its drawbacks, and that defeating the Dervishes was a trifling matter compared to facing the series of receptions and dinners prepared for him by his enthusiastic countrymen! Well, Hector was worthy of it all, and has borne himself throughout the ordeal with a cheerfulness that denotes good nature. The London Scottish Societies first did honour to this gallant Macdonald ; then his clansmen in Glasgow presented him with a claymore, and an address designed by Miss J. M. Macdonell of Keppoch, before one of the largest and most enthusiastic gatherings of Highlanders ever held in this city; and later on entertained him to dinner. In Inverness and Ross-shire he received similar recognitions, and then the Aberdeen Highland Association took him in hand. Highlanders have shown that they know how to honour their heroes.

NEIL GOW.

WITH the exception of the greater lights, few men were better known in his day than Neil Gow, the famous Perthshire fiddler. This remarkable man and musical genius was born at Inver, near Dunkeld, on the 27th March, 1727; and rose—like one of the hills amongst which he spent his life—far above his compeers, and was acknowledged by his contemporaries and others as being the best player of Scotch Strathspey music that ever handled a bow. Of this there can hardly be a doubt, as there is abundant evidence, both direct and indirect, to substantiate it. His fame spread so rapidly that he was well known by reputation in every county in Scotland, and beyond the border as well. His parents first intended him to become a plaid weaver, but he showed at an early age such a predilection for music that the idea of his becoming a weaver was soon abandoned. He received no musical instruction until he was thirteen years of age, when he was placed under John Cameron, a follower of the house of Grandtully, who gave him his first lessons in violin playing, and from whom he probably acquired some knowledge of the elements of music. His progress was so rapid that he soon out-stripped his master and all the other players in his native county, which was well known to produce some of the best players in Scotland, and where his influence is felt even to the present day. The robust style of playing for which the violinists of that county have long been famous, was founded by Neil Gow, or, at any rate, greatly improved by him.

Out of his own county, he was perhaps as much admired in Fifeshire as anywhere. The writer of this notice was informed many years ago by an old gentleman in Fife, who knew several people who were intimately acquainted with Neil Gow, and had often heard him play, that there was something very uncommon about his playing—he seemed to produce an electrical effect upon his dancers; mentioning particularly that at the Fife Hunt balls a complete change came over the countenances of the people present the moment Neil struck up. The remarkable melodiousness of his playing, his forcible "up bow", and the animation of the assembly, added a charm to the music and a brilliance to the whole scene. When Neil Gow was at his best he generally, in the usual Highland fashion, shouted "Haigh" pronounced "Hy"—when changing from the Strathspey to the Reel, which of course added a stimulus to the heels of the performers. He was equally famous as a composer, having composed upwards of eighty-seven tunes—principally Strathspeys and reels many of which are almost unsurpassable. His first collection of music was published in 1784, and was dedicated to Her Grace the Duchess of Athole. Three others were issued during his life-time, in which he was assisted by his sons. He was twice married. His first wife was Margaret Wiseman, by whom he had a family of five sons and three daughters. The second wife, Margaret Urquhart, or Orchard, had no family. Four of the sons followed their father's profession, and became well known; especially Nathaniel, who was the most famous. Mr. John Glen of Edinburgh, in a critical essay on the Gows in the first volume of his fine "Glen Collection of Scottish Dance Music," gives a very full account of the Gows; and other interesting matter of a controversial nature which would be very difficult to refute.

On one occasion, Neil Gow was honoured by a visit of Robert Burns, the poet, who drew a sketch of him in his memorandum-book. Numberless are the anecdotes that have been related of him, and the smart things he said and did. He was a man full of quaint humour, honest and independent—which gained him the respect and confidence of many people of distinction. He was on familiar terms with the Duke of Athole, the Duchess of Gordon and other members of the aristocracy, and all the Perthshire county gentlemen. He was also quick of repartee, and given to practical joking of an innocent nature, which pleased and amused his patrons. Some of

NEIL GOW'S HOUSE.

the anecdotes connected with his name, Mr. Glen knocks over like a house of cards, as having no foundation in fact, but others were undoubtedly true. Mr. Alexander Troup of Ballater, who once lived for fifteen weeks in Neil Gow's house, informs me that the old walls are still standing, but that the house has got a new roof. The large stone opposite his house on which he often sat when practising, and the old oak tree—said to be over three hundred years old—under whose shadow he used to practise, and where he played many a Strathspey and reel for the village lassies, are still there—both within a short distance of the house.*

It was during the year of the great rebellion of 1745 that he first became known as a violinist, having competed in that year with nine others—amongst whom was his own tutor—and carried off the prize against all comers; being adjudged the winner by a blind and skilful musician named John M'Craw, who declared he could detect the stroke of Neil's bow among a hundred players. The above story and others are related in Drummond's "Perthshire in By-gone Days." The superiority he displayed at his first competition he maintained over all other players during his time, not only in Perthshire but throughout Scotland.

Living so near Dunkeld, his reputation attracted the Duke of Atholl, whose patronage—and that of his family, and the nobility and gentry of the neighbourhood—must have assisted materially in spreading his fame. He was presented with violins on various occasions from his patrons and admirers; but some of the stories

* See illustrations.

related in connection with them Mr. Glen, who is an undoubted authority, does not believe; but all are agreed that he exerted a considerable influence in rendering our national dance and music more popular.

His famous tune "Farewell to Whisky," was composed on the occasion of the distillation of whisky being prohibited in 1799, and it was published in 1801. Some of his other gems are "Neil Gow's Compliments to Mr. Marshall," "Neil Gow's Lamentation for James Moray of Abercairny," "Miss Erskine of Torry," "The Duchess of Atholl's Slipper," "The Brig of Ballater," "Mrs. Moray of Abercairny," "Mr. Robertson of Lude," "Miss Lucy Campbell," "Miss Stewart of Grandtully," "Lady Madelina Sinclair," "The Duke of Gordon's Favourite," "Miss Drummond of Perth," and many others.

His four sons—viz: William, John, Andrew, and Nathaniel—were also composers of music; especially Nathaniel, who composed upwards of one hundred and ninety-seven tunes, consisting of Strathspeys, reels, jigs, quicksteps, laments, waltzes, and slow airs. Many of his tunes are most beautiful, and fully equal to the father's—if not surpassing them. He was also in great repute, like his father, as a leader, and had a wide connection all over the country. Daniel, the youngest son, is supposed to have died in childhood. Andrew and John settled in London about 1780 as musicians, and became music-sellers, in 1788, at 60 King Street, Golden Square. A few years after, Andrew fell into bad health and died at Inver, whither he had come, on his father's advice, for change of air to his native place. His partner, John, continued to carry on the music business, besides being leader of the Scottish bands then fashionable, and is said to have amassed a considerable fortune.* Nathaniel is also said to have been worth upwards of £20,000 in his father's declining years.

Upon the whole, Scotland owes a great deal to the Gows for their splendid collections of music; for, with the exception of William Marshall's and Robert M'Intosh's, their compositions are the best of the old school we have got.

* See Mr. John Glen's Collection, volume II.

Their fame also increased the general taste for our national music; and as performers on the violin Neil Gow and his son Nathaniel had no equals, though there were many other good players throughout the country.

The following anecdotes regarding Neil Gow are said to be authentic.

On one occasion two gentlemen came from Glasgow to hear him play the violin; and when within half a mile of his house, they met a man on the road and asked him how far it might be to Neil Gow's house, as they had come all the way from Glasgow to hear him play. He replied: "I am Neil Gow; but I am sure I would not go so far to hear you!"

On another occasion, on his way to Edinburgh, every person he met addressed him as "Mr. Gow." At last he came across the Dunkeld carrier, who remarked: "Are you here, Neil?" "Whisht! whisht! man- I have been getting 'Mr. Gow' all day!"

Fishing one day with the Duke of Atholl on the river Tay, the latter killed two salmon, which Neil eyed with great satisfaction. At last he said: "Well, your Grace, if I had two fish, I would give you one of them." "O you want one, Neil," replied the Duke, and immediately handed him one of them.

On another occasion he bought a cow from a neighbouring gentleman for £5, which he was in no hurry to pay. The gentleman, seeing him one night at a grand ball, took a bet of £5 with another gentleman that he would make the great violinist blush; so the first opportunity he got he went up to Neil, and said: "Have you no word of paying for that cow you bought from me, Neil?" "Well," replied Neil, "I would have been the last man that would have spoken about it." His coolness served him well, and the gentleman lost his bet.

An endless number of similar stories are told of him all over the country, showing the estimation in which he was held by his countrymen. It is also said that "Athole Brose" was his favourite Strathspey; and that the last tune he played was "Pease Strae," a short time before his death. He was highly respected by rich and poor, and was considered a good neighbour and a thoroughly honest man. A biographical sketch of him by the Rev. Dr. Macnight, who knew him well, appeared in the "Scots Magazine" in 1809, couched in glowing terms as to his moral and religious principles. The same magazine records that though Neil Gow had raised himself to independent and affluent circumstances in his old age, he continued free of any appearance of vanity or ostentation. He retained to the last the same plain and unassuming simplicity in his carriage, his dress, and manners, which he had observed in his early and more obscure years.

THE OLD OAK TREE-NEIL GOW'S FAVOURITE SEAT WHEN PRACTISING.

His figure was vigorous and manly, and the expression of his countenance spirited and intelligent; and his whole appearance was a model of what national partiality conceives a Scottish Highlander to be. His portrait was painted by Sir Henry Raeburn for the County Hall at Perth, and separate ones for the Duke of Atholl, Lord Grey, the Hon. Mr. Maul Pansmure, and the Gow family. His likeness was also introduced into pictures by other artists, and an engraved portrait was published in 1815. There is also an excellent copy of the Raeburn portrait at Inverness, and another in the possession of the Earl of Moray. Our illustration is a photograph from one of the Raeburn portraits, and said to be a striking likeness. The original portrait by Sir Henry Raeburn is in the Scottish National Portrait Gallery, Edinburgh. It is nearly full length, and represents him seated playing the violin. It shows a full, honest, kindly face, dark brown hair touched with white, parted in the centre and rather long behind, greyish hazel eyes, dark eyebrows, shaven face, mouth dimpled at corners, double chin, dark bluish coat and vest with grey buttons, knee breeches and hose of red and green tartan yellowish brown back-ground canvas, 48½ by 38½. This portrait was formerly in the possession of Henry Raeburn, Esq., J.P., of St. Bernards who, in an autograph letter now in the hands of the Trustees of the Gallery, certifies that "This is the original portrait painted by the late Sir Henry Raeburn, my father; and that the other portraits of Neil Gow painted by him were copies thereof." Mr. Raeburn presented the picture to Robert Salmond, Esq., who lent it to the National Gallery of Scotland from 1871 to 1883. Engraved in mezzotint by William Say; in stipple by Scott; and as a vignette in line by Croll. Purchased, April, 1886.

Neil Gow died at Inver, near Dunkeld, his birth-place, on the 1st of March, 1807, full of years and honour, in his 80th year; and was buried in Little Dunkeld churchyard, where his

NEIL GOW'S GRAVE IN LITTLE DUNKELD CHURCHYARD.

sons, John and Nathaniel, erected a marble tablet to his memory.

We may conclude this notice of Scotland's greatest violinist, in his day, by quoting the following lines from the British Georgics, said to be by the late Rev. Mr. Graham.

" The blythe Strathspey springs up, reminding some
Of nights when Gow's old arm (nor old the tale)
Unceasing—save when cans went round—
Made heart and heel leap light as bounding roe.
Alas! no more shall we behold that look
So venerable, yet so blent with mirth
And festive joy sedate; that ancient garb
Unvaried—tartan hose and bonnet blue!

No more shall beauty's partial eye draw forth
The full intoxication of his strain
Mellifluous, strong, exuberantly rich!
No more amid the pauses of the dance,
Shall he repeat those measures that in days
Of other years could soothe a fallen prince,
And light his visage with a transient smile
Of melancholy joy—like autumn sun
Gilding a sere tree with a passing beam!
Or play to sportive children on the green,
Dancing at gloamin' hours; or willing cheer,
With strains unbought, the shepherd's bridal day."

K. N. MACDONALD, M.D.

DEEDS THAT WON THE EMPIRE.

By JOHN MACKAY, C.E., J.P., Hereford.

THE CAPTURE OF HAVANA, 1762.
(Continued from page 143).

FOR many days an unremitting cannonade was maintained on both sides with fierce emulation. In the midst of it all the principal battery of the besiegers, constructed chiefly of timber and fascines, caught fire. Dried by the intense heat, the material burned fiercely, and the battery was almost destroyed, the labour of 600 men for seventeen days was consumed in one hour, and had to be recommenced. This was a severe stroke of fortune, for it occurred at a time when the hardships of the besiegers were well nigh intolerable; increased by rigorous duty, the diseases incident to the climate reduced the army to half its strength. The provisions were bad, water more scanty than ever, and as the season advanced the prospects of success became fainter of Havana being reduced before the season of the West Indian hurricanes came on. Now another battery took fire, before the first had been replaced. The toil of the troops increased exactly in proportion as their strength was diminishing. Many fell into despair and died, overcome by fatigue, anguish, and disappointment.

But the riches of the Spanish Indies lay almost within the grasp of the survivors, and the shame of returning home baffled made them redouble their efforts. The batteries were renewed, their fire became more equal and soon proved superior to that from the Moro, its guns were silenced, its upper works dismantled and destroyed, and on the 20th July a lodgment was made by the troops in the covered way.

The darkest hour of night is before the dawn of day. Meantime some merchant ships escorted by Sir James Douglas arrived at Havanna, and supplied the besiegers with many conveniences for the siege, particularly bales of cotton, of the utmost service to the engineers in pushing their sap or approaches in the rocky trenches. Fresh vigour was now given to the siege operations, but an unforeseen difficulty suddenly presented itself, an immense ditch cut in the solid rock on which the Moro stands yawned before them, barring all advance. It was eighty feet deep and forty feet wide. To fill it up seemed an impossibility, and difficult as the toil of mining would be it was the only expedient, although exposed to the fire of cannon and musketry and showers of hand grenades. The engineers persevered and finally passed through the wall.

The close approach to the Moro so greatly alarmed the Spanish commander of the city of Havana (harbour) that he attempted to do something for its relief. He sent out a body of 1500 men and attacked the British lines at three points. The attack upon the trenches was gallantly resisted by the trench guards, and though taken by surprise they so resolutely defended themselves that the Spaniards gained no advantage and finally retired. The other posts thus attacked were soon reinforced by the covering column, from which four companies of the 1st Royal Scots were despatched, and again the Spaniards were driven down the hill at the point of the bayonet, with great slaughter, losing one third of their number in this well conceived but badly executed sally. Lord Rollo of Duncrub was one of the officers wounded in this gallant affair.

This was the last attempt made to raise the siege of the Moro, its garrison held sternly and sullenly out notwithstanding their being abandoned by the city and its walls being undermined by the enemy, but on the 30th July the mines were fired. A dreadful roar and a hideous sound were heard, and when the smoke and dust cleared away there was seen in the massive walls of the Moro a breach, "just practicable for a file of men in front."

With all their bayonets glittering in the sun, the Spaniards were seen crowding resolutely about the gap, ready to defend it with vigour. The Royal Scots with other two regiments, supported by the 56th, had been detailed for the assault, led by Lieutenant Charles Forbes of the Royal Scots. Mounting the breach untouched amid the storm of musketry that swept it, Lieutenant Forbes with signal gallantry formed the survivors of his party on the summit, and with the bayonet at the charge scoured the whole line of the rampart. "The charge was so impetuous and so vigorous," wrote the Earl of Albemarle, "that the enemy were instantly driven from the breach, and His Majesty's standard was instantly planted upon the bastion."

Thus was the Moro won, with a comparatively trifling loss—another instance of the virtue of impetuosity and audacity in attack in seige or battle. As Lieutenant Forbes and two other officers were congratulating each other on their sudden and splendid success, the two latter were shot down by a party of desperate Spaniards, who fired from an adjacent building. Forbes was so exasperated by the death of his friends and comrades, that he attacked the building with a file of his Scots, and put all within it to the sword.

No sooner did the Spaniards in the city and Fort Puntal see the British colours flying over the Moro, than they directed all their fire upon it. Meanwhile, the victors, encouraged by their success, were employed in remounting the guns of the Moro, and in erecting batteries upon an eminence commanding the city; and very soon sixty heavy pieces of cannon were ready to open upon it.

Albemarle, anxious to spare unnecessary carnage, sent a aide-de-camp on the 15th of August with a flag of truce, to summon the Governor to surrender, and to make him certain of the destruction that must fall upon the place if he resisted; but the Spaniard proudly replied: "I am under no uneasy apprehension, and shall hold out to the last extremity." But he was soon brought to his senses. The batteries opened fire, and were so well served by artillerymen and seamen, and the effect was so great, that, in less than six hours, all the guns in the Puntal Fort and the north bastion were completely silenced.

White flags of truce were now displayed on every quarter of the city, and a cessation of hostilities took place. As soon as the terms were adjusted, the magnificent city of Havana, with a district of 180 miles to the westward included in its government, the Puntal Castle, and all the shipping in the harbour, were surrendered to His Britannic Majesty.

The Spaniards struggled hard to save their war-ships, and have the harbour declared neutral; but after two days of vehement altercation they were compelled to submit. The garrison was allowed to march out with the honours of war, and to be conveyed to Spain. The money and valuable merchandise, with the naval and military stores, 361 iron and brass guns and mortars, three millions sterling of money, nine ships of the line fit for sea, were taken—three had been sunk, and two more on the stocks burnt, by the sailors.

So fell Havana; but our losses in its capture amounted to 1,800 officers and men killed and wounded in action, exclusive of those who died of fever, fatigue, and sunstroke. The hardy Highlanders of the Black Watch and Montgomery only lost eighty-five officers and men in killed, wounded, and diseases. The prize-money actually paid to the land and sea forces engaged in the conquest of Havana amounted to £761,000. Spain paid dearly for aiding the French in a quarrel with which it had nothing whatever to do. Manila shared the same fate as Havana—which will be the next theme.

(To be continued.)

DUNCAN MACKINNON.

THERE are few Highlanders better known to their countrymen in Glasgow than Mr. Duncan Mackinnon. His genial presence is always welcomed at the social gatherings, where his handsome figure, attired in the Highland dress, generally commands attention. He was born in the Island of Mull, on 12th May, 1838, his father being the late John Mackinnon, of Kilpatrick, Brolas, chief of the Gribun branch of the clan. Educated at the local parish school, he left home in 1856; and, after filling different situations, joined the Glasgow Police in 1862. He was appointed detective officer in 1876, and for twenty years acted as clerk of that department; was chairman of the Police Friendly Society; and acted for fifteen years as secretary of the Athletic and Rowing Club, in which capacity he officiated as judge at Highland gatherings in all parts of the kingdom.

It is, however, of Mr. Mackinnon as a Highlander that we desire here specially to speak. An ardent student of Celtic literature, he is well informed on Highland history and clan lore, and many were the keen controversies in which he has played a successful part. He was one of the founders of the Mull and Iona Association in 1866, of which he acted as secretary in 1878-81, vice-president in 1888, and president in 1895-97. The Clan Mackinnon Society, of which he was first president, also owes its origin and prosperity largely to the efforts of this worthy clansman.

Last year, to the regret of a large circle of friends, Mr. Mackinnon retired from the police service on pension, and took over a business at Crossmichael, Kirkcudbrightshire. The large number of valuable presents of which he was the recipient bore ample testimony to the high esteem in which he was held by all with whom he came in contact. Among others, he received presentations from the superior officers of police and friends; the Police Athletic and Rowing Club; Superintendent Mackintosh, president of the Clan Chattan Association; from the Clan Mackinnon Society, a gold hunting lever watch and a purse of sovereigns, and for Mrs. Mackinnon a gold ring; while the Hon. Mrs. Mackinnon, wife of the eldest son of the chief,

presented him with a beautiful silver-mounted paper-knife on the occasion of the social gathering of the clan last year.

Since settling at Crossmichael, he has taken an interest in local affairs, and is vice-president of the Literary, Reading, and Recreation Club connected with the parish.

Mr. Mackinnon is married to Mary Ann Macgilvray, daughter of Mr. Archibald Macgilvray, Glasgow, and grand-daughter of the late Neil Macdonald, Ardiona, Iona.

A NOBLE ACHIEVEMENT.
A HIGHLAND STORY.

By AGNES WALKER.

CHAPTER I.

IT was early afternoon, and the bright August sunshine was falling softly on the grey, weather-beaten walls of Auchnasheen Castle. It was an old building, with a battlemented front and square corner towers, standing on a high hill on the coast of Argyllshire, a few miles to the south of Loch Etive; and it had been, with its lands and all pertaining to them, in the possession of the Grahams since 1710, at which time they had been granted to Archibald, a scion of the house of Montrose, for services rendered at the Union, and who was afterwards raised to the peerage by the title of Baron Dunallan.

In her sitting-room—a fine old oak-panelled apartment, furnished with exquisite taste—Lady Dunallan sat alone. She was a tall, slender, graceful woman of twenty-five, with a sweet, refined face—a glance at which told there was Jewish blood in her viens; and she had the dark hair and the bright dark eyes of her race. She was sitting at the window, which was open to admit the pure, soft air. On her knee lay an open book, but she was not reading. She was leaning back in her chair, with her face towards the window, gazing outside.

And the view which met her gaze was one which few could have beheld without admiration —certainly none without interest. Away in the distance, the peaks of Mull and Morven rose up into the clear blue above; right in front, and stretching away on each side far as the eye could reach, was an expanse of sea with the islands of Lismore and Kerrera in the foreground—the one low-lying and fertile, the other a rugged mass rising abruptly out of the water; while, by slightly turning the head, could be seen the blue waters of Oban Bay, though, except for one or two buildings occupying lofty sites overlooking the water, nothing was visible of the

DUNCAN MACKINNON.

little town itself, which at this season would be gay and thronged with visitors.

There was no spot which Lady Dunallan loved so well as her home in the Highlands. Only the day before she had come back to it from the great English metropolis longing for its rest and its quiet, for a sight of the purple hills which rose around it, and for the sound of the waves on the white beach below; and so, just to sit where she now was, beside her open window, and yield herself to the influence of the beauty and the grandeur of the scene spread out before her, was happiness unspeakable. It was at such a moment that the burden of care and sorrow which pressed with such crushing weight upon her was lifted for a space; and that, unconsciously to herself, she gathered strength and endurance for a lot that was heavy and hard and bitter.

Presently she was roused by a knock at the door, and in answer to her "Come in", her maid entered the room.

"If you please, my lady, Mrs. Macdonald from Scarba has come to the Castle, and has asked if she might see your ladyship. Her son is one of the crofters there."

"Mrs. Macdonald from Scarba?" said her ladyship. "Oh yes! That will be old Mrs. Macdonald — Duncan Macdonald's mother. Very well then, Whitson, just bring her in here. That will be best, I think."

A few minutes later, a tall, thin, white-haired old woman, dressed in black, and carrying in her hand a small leather bag, was ushered into the room. Lady Dunallan rose and came towards her visitor, a smile of welcome on her face.

"I am very pleased to see you, Mrs. Macdonald," she said, in the gentle, kindly way so characteristic of her, as she put out her hand to the old woman, who was visibly trembling. "And won't you sit down?" she added, leading the way to where a couple of chairs stood, and seating herself on one of them. "I came back here only yesterday, so have had no time yet for going about and hearing any news. But you are all well at home, I trust; and everyone in and about Scarba likewise?"

"Yes, thank you, my lady. We are ahl well at home. And there iss not anyone ill at Scarba that I hef been hearing about. Not anyone at ahl." Her soft tones and Highland accent made her speech both attractive and pleasing. "And I hope your ladyship will pardon me for coming here and asking to see your ladyship. But, indeed, I did not know what else I could be doing. For it iss a terrible thing that has come upon us, whatever. And I hef come to ask a favour of your ladyship—a very great favour."

She paused, looking confused and troubled, and cast her eyes down.

"If there is anything I can do for you, Mrs. Macdonald, I shall be most happy," said Lady Dunallan, in a tone of kindly encouragement.

Opening her bag, the old Highland woman took from it a letter, which she held out towards Lady Dunallan with a shaking hand.

"If your ladyship will be so good as to read this," she said. "It was the factor sent it to my son, and we are sore troubled about it. And if your ladyship will be so good as to read it, mebbe your ladyship will be able to help us."

Lady Dunallan unfolded the letter and read:

"Auchnasheen Estates Office, Oban. "Duncan Macdonald, Scarba.

"Sir,—I am directed by Lord Dunallan to inform you that the notice to quit which was duly served on you must take effect, and your tenancy of the croft cease in November. His lordship also directs me to say that further appeal against this decision will be useless; and he requests that no letters referring to the matter be sent either to him or to me, as they will receive no notice. Yours truly, John Haggart, Factor.

There was silence for some moments. Then, turning towards her visitor, who was watching her with an anxious and eager look, Lady Dunallan said gravely:

"I do not know anything about Lord Dunallan's transactions with his tenants—these are matters I never hear discussed; but it appears from this letter that your son has received notice to quit his croft, and must leave it in November."

"Yes, my lady, that iss so," said the old woman piteously. "And what I am wanting to say iss this," she went on entreatingly, "if your ladyship will be so good as to ask Lord Dunallan not to be putting us out of the croft? For it iss not what we are deserving of. Oh, not at ahl. There iss not anyone in Scarba but would be telling your ladyship that. And if your ladyship would only think?—there has never been anyone but a Macdonald that has lived on the croft. My husband he has lived on it; and there was his father before him, and his grandfather too, before that. And now it iss my son But there iss no need for me to be telling your ladyship ahl that, for your ladyship knows it ahl already. And it would chist be breaking my heart, it would, to be going away from the croft. For I hef lived on it ahl my married life—that iss fifty-one years, my lady. That iss a long time to hef been living on the croft—ay, a long time."

She paused a moment looking before her with tear-dimmed eyes.

"And I was not thinking to be leaving the croft until I was tekken away to be laid beside my husband. It iss four years since my husband died. He was a good man—my Hamish! But it iss not wishing him back again I would be, ah, no!—and ahl this trouble to be coming upon us. It iss little he thought a Macdonald would live to see this day!"

The tears were now streaming down her wrinkled cheeks.

"Does your son know why he has been given notice to quit? Has there been any trouble in connection with the croft? Anything about the rent, or any quarrel of any kind?" Lady Dunallan asked, very gently, after a pause.

"My lady, it iss the truth I will be telling you," said the old woman, drying her eyes, and making an effort to overcome her agitation. "My son he iss not one to be holding his tongue when he sees there iss any wrong that iss being done. And he did hef a quarrel with the factor. But it was not about the croft they were having the quarrel—oh, no. Your ladyship will be remembering old Mrs. M'Callum that lived in the little thatched house close to the sea at Scarba? Well, it was about her that my son was having the quarrel. Your ladyship will not be knowing that her son Archie, that was in Glasgow, has been killed? It was a big building they were putting up in a street there, and he fell off the roof. It was a very sad thing, whatever. And he was a good son to his mother was Archie. It was not wanting for anything that he could give her she was. And he was ahl she had. But there iss not anyone in Scarba that would hef let the old woman starve, when her son was dead. And the factor was knowing that very well. But when he knew her son was dead, he would hef her away to the poorhouse at Oban, and she was not wanting to go to the poorhouse—ah, no!"

"Mrs. Macdonald, what is this you are telling me about old Mrs. M'Callum?" interposed Lady Dunallan, her eyes full of bewilderment and indignation, "her son dead, and she in the poorhouse at Oban?"

"Yes, my lady, that iss chist what I am saying," was the answer, "and, as I was telling your ladyship, the factor he would hef her away to Oban when he knew that her son was dead. And it was not to the poorhouse she was wanting to go—oh, no. And when they were tekking her out of her house to go away, she was crying sore, that she was. And my son he could not bear to see the old woman being tekken away. And he went up to the factor before ahl the people, and he told the factor that it was a black shame to be tekking the old woman away, and that it was to the poorhouse he should be tekken himself. And the factor he was very angry, and he told my son that he was an impertinent fellow, and to mind his own business. But my son he was not caring for that; and he chist told the factor what he thought of him, and spoke very plain.

And they had hot words, the two of them, and the factor said he would make my son rue it. He was angry because it was before ahl the people. He know that everyone was against him for tekking the old woman away, though it was only Duncan who spoke. And then it was chist the next week that my son got the notice to quit. We were knowing very well why he got it. But, for ahl that, my son he would go to Oban to see the factor. 'It iss the truth I am wanting, and it iss the truth I will hef,' he would be saying. But when he went to Oban he did not see the factor—the factor was away from home. And then my son wrote to the factor, and that was the answer he got—the letter I gev your ladyship. And so that was the quarrel they were having, my lady. They did not hef any other quarrel, and it was not about the croft they were having it—oh, not at ahl!"

The old woman paused, and there was silence again for some minutes, Lady Dunallan sitting with her fixed on the ground. Then, looking up, she said, with an air of quiet resolution, though her face was very pale and grave,

"Mrs. Macdonald, I shall keep this letter. Lord Dunallan returns to the Castle to-night, and to-morrow I will speak to him and see if your son cannot be allowed to keep his croft."

Tears rose to the old woman's eyes again, and a look of gratitude, very touching to see, came into her worn face. But before there was time for a word of thanks, Lady Dunallan was saying:

"And now I shall ring for Whitson, and she will take you to Mrs. Duncan and you will get a cup of tea before you go away. But how have you come from Scarba to-day? Did anyone drive you over?"

"Yes, my lady, it was in Dr. Buchanan's gig that I came," the old woman made answer, "the doctor he iss ahlways very good, and when he knew I was coming to the Castle to-day, he said that he would send his gig, and that his man would drive me over."

"That was very kind of Dr. Buchanan—very kind and thoughtful of him indeed," said Lady Dunallan, warmly.

Then Whitson was summoned, and after bidding her take Mrs. Macdonald to the housekeeper's room to get a cup of tea before she left, Lady Dunallan turned to the old woman, who had risen from her seat, and putting out her hand, said impressively:

"And now good-bye, Mrs. Macdonald. I am very glad you came to me to-day; and whatever I can do to prevent your son being turned out of his croft, rest assured, will be done."

In low and broken tones the old Highland woman strove to utter a few words of thanks.

Then she turned and followed the maid from the room.

When the door closed behind her visitor, Lady Dunallan stood still for some seconds, then she turned round, crossed over to the window, and, sitting down, leaned her arm on the sill and looked out. But it was not of the distant mountains, nor the stretch of blue, sun-lit sea she was thinking as she sat there. It was of the task she had undertaken—a task the delicacy and the difficulty of which she was but too well aware.

It was four years since her marriage with Lord Dunallan; and with what hopes she had then looked forward to the future, and how these hopes had ultimately been destroyed, only she herself knew. She had pledged her faith and given her hand to the young peer believing that she held the first place in his heart, as he held the first in hers. How could she think otherwise! There was no one to tell her that, since the days of her girlhood, her father (old Simon Levi, the wealthy London banker, and whose only child and heiress she was) had set his heart on realizing through her his great ambition—an alliance with some noble house. And would she have believed that even if she had been told? No. That her father should so far be found wanting in honour—should so far forget his duty to his motherless daughter—as to play the part of money-lender to a young impoverished nobleman, in order that, when repayment of the loans became impossible, he might urge, as the only alternative, a marriage with his daughter—was something which, had it been told her, she would have repudiated with scorn.

But it *was* the truth; and when, some months after the marriage took place, a few words accidentally overheard one night confirmed the terrible suspicion which had taken possession of her, it was then too late for anything but to endure and make the best of things. Not that she had anything to complain of in her husband's behaviour towards her. He had never given her a harsh word; and his manner to her, if cold, was never lacking in courtesy. But it was only too evident that she had not that place in his heart which she craved. She was his wife—but in name only. And as time went on too, and she saw how lightly his duties as a landlord were regarded by him, and that the management of the estate was wholly in the hands of the factor—a man arrogant, harsh, despotic—her heart grew more heavy and sorrowful still. Nevertheless, the knowledge of it all did not utterly crush her. What she wanted was her husband's love. And to win that, and to be the means of turning him from his gay and idle and purposeless life, and of rousing him to a sense of the duties of his high position, became her dominant desire.

And now, as she sat by the open window, with the factor's letter lying on her knee, the thought that it was possible her effort on behalf of the distressed family of Scarba might prove to be the first step towards the attainment of that which lay so near her heart, was every moment growing stronger and stronger. With all his faults, Lord Dunallan, she knew, was neither callous nor unjust; and that, if the real facts of the case were set before him (for there was no doubt in her mind as to the true cause of the eviction, however the factor might have justified it to Lord Dunallan), he would allow Macdonald to be turned out of his croft, she refused to believe. And if the affair should lead to further investigation into the factor's dealings with those over whom he was placed, what might the result not be? Her heart thrilled at the thought. Still, to go to her husband and say to him all that she must and would in connection with Macdonald's case, would be no easy matter. It was something which, she knew, would tax her courage to the utmost. Nevertheless, what she had promised to do that she would do; and as to the result, she could only hope and pray that it might be the desired one.

(*To be continued*).

LINES TO KINCHYLE.

The Old Home of the MacBeans.

Old home of the warlike and trusty Clan Bean,
In youth I oft played on thy carpets of green,
And, light-footed, wandered where deep lay the shades
Of pines that encircled thy flower-spangled glades.

The martial glory around thee that shone,
Though treasured in story, had long ago gone ;
And aliens flourished in latter-day style,
On acres that nourished the race of Kinchyle.

Yet around thee there lingered tradition and song,
That told of the dauntless, devoted, and strong ;
The dance and the revel of long-vanished day ;
Clan Chattan's stern muster, the foray and fray.

Thy song and thy story, related or sung
By lips of the hoary, delighted the young ;
Fit men were thy heroes the youthful to fire,
And, far from Strathdurris, their lives to inspire.

Thy matchless brave Gillies in vain did not fall
Defending the breach in Drumossie's grey wall :
A hundred years later a clansman of fame
Again with fresh glory encircled thy name. °

Sound, sound, be your slumbers, departed Clan Bean,
Not soft have your pillows in olden times been ;
Brave, leal, enterprising, your offspring the while ;
And green be thy pastures and woodlands, Kinchyle !

Hatfield.   Angus Mackintosh.

General MacBean, of Indian Mutiny fame, who by slaying, single-handed, eleven Sepoys at the storming of one of their strongholds, almost equalled the feat of his famous clansman of the '15.

AN OLD FAIRY LULLABY.

THE following sweet and simple *Taladh* or song of caressing is worthy of preservation on account of its inherent beauty, but to me it has a peculiar interest, because I got it from the late Sheriff Nicolson, that gifted son of Skye, who produced one of the most interesting books in the Gaelic language, I refer to his "Collection of Gaelic Proverbs." Writing from Kirkcudbright in October, 1879, Sheriff Nicolson says:—"I have much pleasure in giving you the words of that little *Taladh* you enquire for. It is one of the sweetest things I ever heard, and brings moisture to my eyes at this moment crooning it all to myself, partly perhaps because it reminds me of the kind, genial soul from whom I got it in 1865, the late Rev. John

MacDonald, in whose manse of Harris I stayed for several nights, spending the time every night till all hours in the morning talking of Gaelic things and singing Gaelic songs. He had a good voice, and I can remember the two of us chanting away at that *Taladh* together at two in the morning, he pacing up and down the floor and I stretched on a sofa. He was dead within a year of that—from the result of an accident. That is the only *Taladh* I know that I haven't seen in print."

The *Taladh* is supposed to have been sung by a good fairy, who, having entered a house, found a baby sleeping in a cradle, its mother having evidently deserted it. The translation is somewhat free, but will be of service to your musical readers whose Gaelic education has been neglected.   FIONN.

TALADH—A FAIRY LULLABY.

KEY A. *Tenderly, beating twice in the measure.*

Chunnaic mi seachad mu 'n taca so 'n dè,
Duine mór foghainteach, làidir treun,
    Le 'bhogha 's le 'shaighead,
    Le 'sgiath is le 'chlaidheamh,
'S mór m' eagal gu 'n tachair do mhàthair ris.
    Thàlaidhinn thu, etc.

Yesterday even' I heard them say.
A braw and brave gallant gaed by this way,
    Wi' bow and wi' arrow,
    Wi' sword keen and narrow,
I'm feared that your mammie's awa wi' him.
    Fondle thee, etc.

COLONEL HUGH H M LEAN.

THE CELTIC MONTHLY:

A MAGAZINE FOR HIGHLANDERS.

Edited by JOHN MACKAY, Glasgow.

No. 10 Vol. VII.] JULY, 1899. [Price Threepence.

COLONEL HUGH H. M'LEAN, NEW BRUNSWICK.

COLONEL HUGH H. M'LEAN, 62nd St. John Fusiliers, was born in 1855, and is a great-grandson of Lieut. Archibald M'Lean, Royal Navy, who settled in New York and was married there at Trinity Church in 1780, and after the war of the rebellion was granted a large block of land in Queen's County, in the Province of New Brunswick. His grandfather, John M'Lean, was for many years Judge of the Court of Common Pleas.

In 1878, war being imminent between Britain and Russia, Colonel M'Lean raised 100 men, and tendered his and their services to the Imperial Government, for which offer he received the thanks of the Imperial authorities. He was appointed adjutant of the battalion raised for service during the north-west rebellion, consisting of fourteen companies.

He was appointed this year in command of the Bisley team, which is composed of twenty of the best rifle shots in Canada, and is sent over by the Dominion Government. Colonel M'Lean will be at Bisley during the competition, and as he is Vice-President of the Clan M'Lean in North America, and a life member of the Clan Association in the Old Country, will be delighted to receive any members of the clan who may find time to call upon him.

Colonel M'Lean, who is a barrister-at-law, and Q.C., has large and important business connections. Among others, Counsel in New Brunswick for the Bank of Montreal, Canadian Pacific Railway Company, Dominion Express Company, Pullman's Palace Car Company, the Alexander Gibson Railway and Manufacturing Company, Guardian Assurance Company, New Brunswick Railway Company, Union Insurance Company of Bangor (Marine), Caledonian Insurance Company of Edinburgh, &c.

He is largely interested in railway enterprises, and is Vice-President of the Shore Line Railway, President of the Fredericton Branch Railway Company, Director of the New Brunswick Railway Company, the Canada Eastern Railway Company, Alexander Gibson Railway and Manufacturing Company, and Treasurer of that company. He is on the executive board and a director of the Saint John Railway Company, this company being a consolidation of the Electric Light, Street Railway, and Gas Companies; a director of the Saint John *Daily Telegraph* Publishing Company, Saint John Bridge and Railway Extension Company, and of the Grand Falls Water-Power and Pulp Company.

It is interesting to add that this clansman took a prominent part in arranging for the great reception which was given to the chief, Sir Fitzroy Donald Maclean, C.B., when he visited Chicago some years ago, at the invitation of the Macleans of Canada and the United States.

TOIMHSEACHAIN.

C.—Chi mi thugam, chi mi bhuam,
Da-mhile-dheug thar a' chnain,
Fear gun fhuil gun fheoil gun anam
'G-iomairt air an talamh chruaidh.
F.—Clachan meallain.

C.—Chi mi thugam thar an t-sàile
Fear mar àilleagain na grèine,
Fear a' choitlein uaine,
'S snàthainn dearg a' fuaghal a bhinn.
F.—Am bogha-frois.

C.—Chaidh Fionn do'n Bheinn,
Cha deachaidh Idir,
Dh' asaideadh bean Fhinn
'S cha d' asaideadh Idir.
F.—'S e Idir a b' ainm do ghaladh Fhinn.

THE SOCIAL CONDITION OF THE HIGHLANDS SINCE 1800.

By A. J. BEATON, F.S.A. Scot., F.G.S.E.

THE DEVELOPMENT OF THE FISHERIES.

(*Continued from page* 169).

(*Continued from page* 169).

I APPEND the most interesting statement made by Professor Ewart before a committee of the House of Lords, in evidence for the proposed railway for the West Highlands, in March, 1889.

Professor Cossar Ewart, of the Scottish Fishery Board, said "that great shoals of herring were to be found all along the West of Scotland; and both inside and outside the Long Island there were immense shoals. There were always large shoals running up the coasts of Coll and Tiree. Many of them pass along between Skye and the mainland into Lochs Hourn and Nevis, and others skirted the outside of Skye. There was a sort of concentration of herring shoals on the inner coast of Skye, especially upon the southern part. In 1882 there were cured from Lochs Hourn and Nevis no less than 80,000 crans of herring. The fishing in the following year did not prove quite so good; but there was no reason to suppose that the number of fish had decreased. Hitherto, except in certain cases, the fishermen of the West had received little encouragement. On the coast the number of fish taken has enormously increased during the last fifty years: some years as many as one

THE HERRING FLEET AT STORNOWAY—EVENING.

million crans were taken. In his opinion it was impossible to diminish by any means in our power the number of herrings on our coasts. Even when the herring did not enter Lochs Hourn and Nevis they were to be found in abundance in the vicinity; but the fishermen in the district were not equipped in such a way as enabled them to follow the fish, their boats being too small and their gear insufficient. On the East Coast the fishermen with their large boats scoured the whole of the north seas in search of the herring going out as far as fifty or sixty miles; and they followed up the shoals wherever they might go. The West Coast fishermen were an entirely different class. Fishing had never been prosecuted by them in any systematic manner. It is difficult to learn the trade of fishing; but the men of the West Coast were

taking advantage of the example shown them by the East Coast fishermen who had migrated there, and already there was a number of very expert fishermen belonging to Stornoway and other centres. Hitherto, except in certain cases, the fishermen of the West had received little encouragement. They had been standing, if he might say so, with one foot on the land and the other on the water, unable to make up their minds whether to engage in fishing or to work their crops. He had known men who, after having the necessary lines and hooks, had forsaken their resolutions to become fishermen and reverted to their crofts. The difficulty was that they had no prospect of disposing of the fish with any profit after they were caught. Little was known about the white fish banks on the West Coast. He knew, however, of a large bank lying to the north-west of Coll. The bank ran up to Canna and outwards, and had a depth of from 11 to 50 fathoms. In addition there were banks extending south-west towards Skerryvore and Dhuheartich Lighthouses. So famous, indeed, was this bank that East Coast fishermen found it paid them to go round to Coll, build themselves huts, and fish for cod and ling, which they dried and took home with them, or exported to the Continent. Undoubtedly these men would prefer to have a market to which they might send the fish in a fresh condition. The white fishing on the West Coast had not been developed in the least, because as long as herring paid well fishermen preferred to keep to that branch of the industry. After suitable boats and gear, what the fishermen on the West Coast required was ready and cheap access to the markets. The existing railways of course performed valuable work, but there was a large district between Strome Ferry and Oban totally unprovided for. Roshven he regarded as an extremely suitable place for a harbour connecting with a railway line. It was convenient for all the fishing grounds within the Hebrides, and it could readily be reached from outside. The development of the fishing industry on the West Coast was only a question of time. Already English fishing schooners visited the Hebrides, and Irish vessels came to Tiree. He had had some experience of Norway, and he found that it cost less to convey herring to London from Norway than from any part of Scotland.

"A scheme of co-operation should also be organised by the fishermen, whereby they could establish a central depôt with a responsible agent in every large town, by these means complete train loads of fresh fish might be despatched at cheaper rates than by sending in driblets, and the various agents could keep the senders fully apprised by telegrams of the demands of their respective markets."

XII.—MANUFACTORIES.

The Highlands are singularly destitute of manufactories, at least to any appreciable extent, for, with the exception of a few wool mills and several distilleries, there is no other branch of the manufacturing industry in the country. Shipbuilding was at one period—before ironclads were introduced—carried on in the Highlands; and we find it recorded by Matthew Paris that, as far back as 1249, a magnificent vessel (Navis Miranda) was specially built at Inverness for the Earl of St. Pol and Bloise, to carry him with Louis IX of France to the Holy Land. As far as Inverness is now concerned this industry is extinct. I have not seen a

vessel on the stocks for years. In so extensive a wool-growing country as the Highlands, with its unlimited source of water-power, one would naturally expect to find the country studded with woollen factories; but it is not so. Sir George Mackenzie, in his "Survey of Ross and Cromarty, 1810," complains bitterly of the total want of encouragement by the inhabitants of the country, and from the proprietors, in supporting a woollen manufactory started at Inverness by himself in conjunction with other gentlemen who thought the inhabitants of the Highlands would eagerly encourage home industry.

About the beginning of this century there were a good many woollen mills scattered over the Highlands: but improved machinery caused the old-fashioned hand-loom to go the way of the world, and they have fallen to decay; and neither sufficient energy nor capital has arisen to replace them.

As an example of the decline of the manufacturing industry, let us take the case of the Black Isle, where at this date not a factory of any description exists.* At Avoch, fifty years ago, there was a large woollen mill in operation; and the manufacturing of coarse linen from home-grown lint was carried on; and herring and salmon nets and fishing tackle were extensively made, and several carding mills were scattered over the peninsula. At Cromarty, less than eighty years ago, "there was a mill for carding wool and jennies for spinning it; also a wauk-mill, two flax mills and a flour mill," . . . "a large brewery, and houses for hemp manufactory. From the 5th January, 1807, to 5th January, 1808, there were imported 185 tons of hemp; and about 10,000 pieces of bagging were sent to London, which were valued at £25,000. During the same period were exported 1550 casks and tubs containing 112 tons of pickled pork and hams, and 60 tons of dried cod-fish. There is also a ropework in operation, and shipbuilding just begun."† To-day, I daresay, there is not another town of the size of Cromarty in Scotland more destitute of commerce, nor more deserted. One may well ask the question, whence this decay? It is simply isolation, and what is here true of Cromarty and the Black Isle is also true of many other isolated districts in the Highlands.

(To be continued.)

* Through the enterprising efforts of Mr. J. Douglas Fletcher of Roschaugh the Avoch Woollen Mills have been recently equipped with new machinery, and a considerable amount of business was being done.

† Sir George E. Mackenzie's "Survey of Ross and Cromarty, 1810."

THE HIGHLANDER ABROAD.

MAJOR-GEN. ALEX. MACDOUGALL.

WE frequently meet with the name of General MacDougall in the history of the American Revolution. While his career was not marked with any brilliant exploits, and his labours did not command public attention, yet his services were valuable, and his character reliable. Like many others, he has been unfortunate in not finding a biographer. In a letter to the President of Congress, under date of June 29, 1780, Washington speaks of him as a man "of approved bravery."

Thacher, a surgeon in the revolutionary army, makes the following note of him in his journal:—"General Alexander MacDougall is the son of a Scotchman, whose employment was that of a milkman in the city of New York, and the son was sometimes his assistant. The general at an early period was distinguished among those who adopted the Whig principles, and known to be a jealous advocate for freedom. Principle and sense of duty led him to the field of contest, and in August, 1776, he was by Congress appointed a brigadier general, and by his intelligence and active spirit he has acquired a reputable standing as a general officer. He displays much of the Scottish character, is affable and facetious, often indulging in pleasantry, and adverting to his national peculiarities and family origin; at the close of which he adds—'Now, gentlemen, you have got the history of Sawney MacDougall, the milkman's son.'"

General MacDougall was born in the island of Islay, Scotland, in 1731. His father, Ronald, emigrated to the province of New York in 1755, where he purchased a farm in the upper part of Manhattan Island, now covered by the city of New York. At first Alexander followed the sea, and in the war of 1756 was commander of the two privateers, "Barrington" and "Tiger." Subsequently he became a successful merchant in the city of New York, and was ardently attached to the cause of the colonists. When the Assembly faltered in its opposition to the usurpations of the Crown, he issued an address entitled, "A Son of Liberty to the Betrayed Inhabitants of the Colony," in consequence of which he was arrested and imprisoned for twenty-three weeks, and thus became the first martyr in the patriot cause. Immediately on obtaining his liberty he opened correspondence with the leading spirits in all parts of the country, and on July 6, 1774, presided at the meeting "in the fields" that was held preparatory to the election of delegates to the first continental congress. He was appointed colonel of the first New York regiment June 30, 1776, brigadier-general on the 9th of the following August, and major-general October 20, 1777. He was actively engaged at Chatterton's Hill, near White Plains, New York, and was in command at Peekskill in 1777, but was compelled to retreat before a superior British force. He performed distinguished service in the battles of White Marsh and Germantown. March 16, 1778, Washington appointed him to the chief command in the Highlands (back of New York). Owing to some general changes made by Congress, General MacDougall again took the command of his old division in the army under the immediate command of Washington. Without delay he forwarded to Washington the treaty made with France, which was acknowledged by the commander under date of May 1, 1778. We find him actively engaged at Hartford and in the Highlands, and on the exposure of the treason of Arnold he was directed to take command of West Point until the arrival of General Arthur St. Clair. In 1780 his military service was interrupted by his election as a member of the Continental Congress. By that body he was elected Minister of Marine, but, preferring active service, he resigned in order to take the field again. July 2, 1781, he was ordered by Washington to bring the militia to his support. At this time he was at West Point. The same month he was given command of the New York and New Jersey troops. In 1783 he was one of a committee of three to present the grievances of the army to Congress, and a year later was again a member of that body. After the close of the war he became a member of the New York Senate, of which body he was a member at the time of his death. He was the first President of the New York State Society of the Order of the Cincinnati.

General MacDougall died in New York city June 8, 1786. Washington, August 1, 1786, in communicating the news to Thomas Jefferson, speaks of him as "a brave soldier and a disinterested patriot."

Elizabeth, the only daughter of General MacDougall, married John Laurance, who presided as Judge Advocate-General at the trial of Major André. His son John died in the Canada Expedition at the head of Lake Champlain in 1775; and his cousin John, the son of John MacDougall, was blown up in the frigate "Randolph," in its engagement with the British frigate "Yarmouth" on March 7, 1778.

Ohio.   J. P. MACLEAN.

A GRAND CONCERT, under the auspices of the Highland societies of Glasgow will be held in November, to provide funds to encourage Gaelic teaching in the Highlands.

CAPTAIN JOHN CAMERON.

CAPTAIN JOHN CAMERON, FORT-WILLIAM.

CAPTAIN JOHN CAMERON, who has just been promoted to the command of E Company of the 1st Volunteer Battalion of the Cameron Highlanders, enjoys a popularity equalled by few in Lochaber. Born and reared near Aberfeldy, Perthshire, he entered the service of Mrs. Campbell Cameron of Fassifern and Callart when twenty years of age, and for the last thirty years he has acted as overseer and under factor for her estates, and holds the same position under Mrs. Cameron Lucy, who succeeded to the property. By all the tenants on the estates Captain Cameron is held in the highest respect and esteem. He has taken a very active part in public affairs, being a bailie of the Burgh of Fort-William, and was last November offered the provostship by his brother commissioners Being unable to spare the time for the discharge of such onerous duties he had to decline the honour.

In volunteer matters the captain is an enthusiast. He joined E Company in 1871, and after ten years' service was promoted colour-sergeant. In 1890 he received his commission as lieutenant, in recognition of his services. The advancement was well deserved, and afforded his superior officers the greatest gratification. His skill as a marksman is known far beyond Lochaber, the cups, medals, and other valuable trophies which he has won being too numerous to mention The rifle club of the regiment receives every encouragement from him. He took part in the Royal Review in 1880, and in the Jubilee Review held in Inverness seven years later. He was in command of the detachment of volunteers who ascended to the summit of Ben Nevis on Her Majesty's Diamond Jubilee, and who, standing knee-deep in fresh snow, fired a *feu-de-joie* from that, the highest point in Her Majesty's home dominions. It may be also mentioned that he wears the medal for long service. The Lochaber games, which have proved such a great success, owe much to Captain Cameron's exertions.

In the ranks of his own clan his services were recently recognised by his election to the office of Vice-President of the Clan Cameron Society. The clan could not have chosen a clansman more worthy of the honour.

MR. JOHN MACKAY, Hereford, who has been seriously ill for some time, has made a rapid recovery, and is now busily engaged making preparations for the Clan Mackay tour in Sutherland in September.

SOUGH O THE SOUTH.

ALASTAIR MEAR was the swanky fellow. You would see him go swinging along the road by the shores of Loch Linnhe, throwing a gallant word to the girls and passing the time of day with the old women as he went. He was the breezy man, too, the man with the cheersome soul who went through the world with a laugh that had no fear in it. Clean-limbed, shapely in the build, with the fine eyes that can turn a woman's heart to water—the lasses of Lochaber were all wild for the love of him. But, for all their coaxing looks, Alastair Mear went his own way, and had a word of daffing always ready for every comely woman betwixt Corpach and Corran.

Alastair's hut was on the shore, just outside the town. Every man, when he felt a longing to go out and see for himself what the world was like, would go down the lochside and past the white hut, wearing all the while a queer look. And at the bend of the road, where you get the last sight of the town, it was there that the world began for a man.

"Alastair, my son," the old *Cailleach* would say, as she looked out at the door, "there goes Callum Beg, with the fever in his soul, and Linnhe town will be seeing him no more. *Ochanorie*, but its the way with all the men when they hear the sough o' the south. They rise up and take the bend of the road to the south, where there is aye plenty of fighting and money, and their hearthstane kens them no more. You, my son, will some day take the road, too."

"Now, it is the foolish woman that you are! Have I not told you often that the shores of Linnhe are the place for me for ever and a day. I am never hearing this soughing sound that you speak of, and it is a silly fellow that would be breaking his word to his own mother."

"Aye, Alastair, my son, you have the tender heart, but many's the man that has laughed at the sough before, and went round the bend of the road all the same when it came to the bit. Alas, for my trouble! It is alone and blind I shall be when you hear the strange sound."

Then Alastair would stride away up the lochside with a protest in the heart of him that he would never leave Linnhe town for ever and a day. For no man likes to think that there is a thing that may come to him any day and take away his freedom altogether.

Two nights after, Alastair was at the change-house in Linnhe town drinking a cup with his mates. It was a fine summer evening, and the noise of the merry fellows escaped through the open windows of the inn and was wafted down to the shore of the loch on the light airs. It was all laughter and merriment indoors, and without, the night began to be full of stars and the scent of peat reek and sweet-smelling sea-wrack.

Hector Cameron had come across from Camus-na-gaul with his pipes, and was playing a pretty quickstep that was full of grace notes and turnings. The feet of the roysterers inside were moving unconsciously to the beat of the music, as Hector stood outside and played. In many a house nearby the lasses were kilting their coats and thinking of the fine steps they would dance when next they were asked to take the floor with Callum, or Paraig, or Ruari. And even the bairns that were abed heard a skirling in their dreams as they turned on their pillow. For Hector was a namely man for piping in Linnhe town.

But, with a sudden squeal, the music stopped, and the world seemed to be clean emptied of sound for a while. In the silence the little waves could be heard lapping the stones on the seashore and wooing the brown wrack with a cold clean kiss under the stars.

Then Hector of Camus-na-gaul entered the change-house with the pipes under his oxter and a strange man at his heels. Instinctively every man put down his beaker and looked at the foreign fellow.

"A good e'en to you, landlord, and a glass for every cheery lad here, and a health to the skilly piper."

A magerful man was this stranger, and no mistake.

He was tall and thin and spare-like, with a bronzed face and keen twinkling grey eyes. His jerkin had a foreign cut about it, and underneath his long cloak the scabbard of a sword stuck out and clanked noisily on the stone floor as he sat down on a bench. But his face had so much good cheer in it that every lad turned in expectation to see what he would do next.

"You are in a snug little world up here all by yourselves, my merry fellows, and better ale I never tasted even in the Low Countries."

"You are from the south, then?" said Alastair Mear.

"Aye, sir, where would a man of fortune come from if not from the south? I come from a land of Great Sights, and in my time I have seen everything that it is worth a man's while to see."

"Have you been to the wars?" asked one.

"Bless you, yes!" and he rattled the scabbard on the stone floor. "It is little, I tell you, that I have not seen, and, if it please you, I will tell you of a land where the women are the finest and the booty is the richest in all the world. Have I your ear, landlord?"

"Aye, we are all keen to hear you, good sir. Say on."

Then the foreign fellow took a long deep drink, and with a royal wave of the hand, began. He told them tales of blood and war that made the men forget their drinking. He spoke of lands where there were fine fields and slow-running rivers, and spice-laden barges sailing up to the very gates of the great cities. He described a way in which the men grew rich beyond the dreams of any man in Lochaber, and always he would rattle the scabbard on the floor and sweep in the whole room with his grey eyes until every man felt at the hearing of such tales that Linnhe town was a poor world indeed to live in when there might be gold, and fighting, and broad fields to be had in the south.

Again and again he called for ale and threw down a handful of gold pieces on the table, as if they were of no more value to him than the froth droppings of ale that fell on the flags. Hour after hour passed, and still the foreign fellow told his tales. And then when he was done he rose, and in breathless silence whispered a word that no man in Linnhe town had ever heard before! After that there was not a man but felt that the thing that may come to him any day to steal away his freedom had come to him at last.

Then the stars began to pale. A cold wind came up from the sea, blowing out of the mouth of day. The foreign fellow rose and went out. Hector, the piper, was the first to follow him. But no man spoke. Each rose in a while and went out into the street of Linnhe town, which seemed so small and poor and narrow now. And soon there was no one to be seen at all in the grey town by the northern sea.

But a *Cailleach* looking out of her white hut away down by the foreland saw a queer fellow go by in the dawning, with a smile on his face and a scabbard dangling under his long coat. Then came a man with his pipes tucked under his oxter. Then another, and another—each alone and silent. But when at last a fine swanky lad came striding along, the *Cailleach* rushed to the door and cried—

"Alastair! Alastair! son of my heart, come back!"

But he only turned whiter in hue and went on with a quicker step, looking neither to the right hand nor the left, until at last he disappeared round the bend of the road that brings dool to every woman and bairn in Linnhe town. And that was the last of Alastair Mear.

TORQUIL MACLEOD.

Legends of Perthshire.

FAITHFUL UNTO DEATH: A STORY OF THE '45.

PERTHSHIRE—extending from east to west for seventy miles, and from north to south for sixty-six miles, occupying that portion of central Scotland through which the southern chain of the Grampian range divides the fertile Lowlands from the rugged Highlands—for variety of scenery cannot be surpassed in Britain. It comprises within its limits the rich cultivated plains of Gowrie, Strathearn, and Strathallan ; the wild passes of Glenlyon, Killiecrankie, and the Trossachs ; the towering peaks of Ben Lawers. Schiehallion, and Ben-y-Gloe, and numerous others scarcely less lofty ; and the desolate moor of Rannoch. Within its area lie the beautiful fresh-water lakes, Loch Earn, Loch Tay, and Loch Rannoch, part of Loch Ericht, the Balquhidder Lochs, and several smaller sheets dear to the disciples of Isaac Walton.

The country is not less interesting in its history or the character of its people. It was in past times peculiarly the trysting place of the Saxon and the Gael ; where was laid the scene of the combat between Fitz-James and Roderick Dhu ; and where many another conflict took place between the representatives of the old patriarchal system, and the more modern feudal one. The inhabitants of the towns and villages lying at the southern base of the Grampians, notwithstanding the large admixture of Celtic blood in their veins, consider themselves ultra-Saxon ; and four decades ago or more looked with supreme contempt upon the poor Highland lads and lassies who used to come down in bands together, through the Sma' Glen, or Glenshee, to seek for a fee or a job at the harvest. Perth people knew that their town had been more than once taken by the ancestors of those same Highlanders—notably so in 1745, when it was held for a time in the name of "Bonnie Prince Charlie." Crieff annals recalled the burning of their town during the Jacobite rising of 1715 ; while the Gaels, on their part, cherished no kind memories of the "Kind Gallows" of Strathearn's capital. There was no great love lost between the two races ; but the *bodaich ghalltla* required workers to secure their harvests, while the Highlanders, on their part, were quite as anxious to carry off a few pound notes and a smattering knowledge of English, alias broadest Doric. Then the Celts

of Atholl, Breadalbane, and Rannoch, on account of their insular situation, were as free of any admixture of Saxon or Norse blood as any of their race in Britain. Modern means of communication—and many a shaft from Cupid's bow—have since played sad havoc upon the state of matters then existing ; and it is to be feared that the language and customs of the Gael fare but badly with the change.

It is, therefore, time that the traditional tales and songs of love and war, of patient suffering, noble daring. and faithful devotion, should now be told, ere they should be entirely lost, or a garbled version of two or three of them mixed together be allowed to go down the stream of time, to excite the wonder and incredulity of future generations.

The rising of 1745 was fruitful of cases of faithful devotion on the part of the Highland people to their Prince and the chiefs who led them. It will ever redound to their credit that a reward of £30,000 was not enough to induce the poorest person in the land to betray Prince Charles. The faithfulness of Flora MacDonald, Neil MacEachan, and the young man who suffered death on account of his resemblance to the Prince, will be told to the end of time ; and no unearthing of Pickles on the part of over-inquisitive scribes will ever rob the Gael of Scotland of their good name in that respect. Where instances of such faithfulness were so numerous, the following story will bear comparison with the most striking of them all.

James Menzies, of Culdares and Meggernie Castle, in Glenlyon, took part in the Earl of Mar's Rising in 1715, and was taken prisoner at Preston, in Lancashire, whence he was carried to London, where he was tried and condemned to death, but afterwards reprieved, principally on account of his youth. Grateful for this clemency, in his maturer years, when the standard of the Stuarts was unfurled in Glenfinnan in 1745, he remained at home ; but retaining an affection for the old cause, he sent a handsome charger as a present to Prince Charles, when advancing through England. The horse, which is often yet referred to in the traditions of Glenlyon as "*an t-each odhar*" or "the dun horse," was entrusted to the care of John Macnaughton, a son of one of Menzies' tenants. This young man had received a better education than most of his class at that time, having served for some time as a watchmaker in Edinburgh, and thus knew the south of Scotland well. Macnaughton was successful in delivering the horse over to the Prince, but was subsequently captured and handed over to the Hanoverian Government, under circumstances that need not here be related, and which reflect no credit upon those concerned in the capture. He was taken to

Carlisle, where he was tried and condemned to death.

"To extort a confession as to who sent the horse, threats of immediate execution in case of refusal, and offers of pardon on his giving information, were held out ineffectually to the faithful messenger. He knew, he said, 'what the consequences of a disclosure would be to his master, and his own life he considered as nothing in the comparison.' When brought out for execution, he was pressed to inform on his master. He asked if they were serious in supposing him such a villain! If he did what they desired, and forgo this trust, he could not return to his native country, for Glenlyon would be no home or country for him, as he would be despised, and hunted out of the Glen. Accordingly, he kept steady to his trust, and was executed."

The above quotation is taken from General Stewart of Garth's "Sketches." General Stewart, whose accuracy as a historian and patriotism as a man and a soldier are well known, was in a better position to ascertain the facts of this story than any subsequent writer. He knew personally a brother of Macnaughton, who was blacksmith on the Garth estate. Regarding him, General Stewart says "that he reminded him more of the old race of Highlanders than any man he had ever known, and that he walked about with an air and manner that might have become a Field Marshal."

After reading this story of faithfulness, all readers of the "Celtic Monthly" will doubtless cherish with enthusiasm the memory of "Mac-Neachdain an cich uidhir," another of the brave heroes of 1745.

Glenlyon.　　　ALEXANDER STEWART.

DEEDS THAT WON THE EMPIRE.

By JOHN MACKAY, C.E., J.P., Hereford.

THE CAPTURE OF MANILA, 1762.

(*Continued from page 174*).

HIS town was founded by the Spaniards in 1571. It was the capital of the Spanish possessions in Eastern Asia, and the chief town of the Philippine Islands, divided into two portions by the Passig river. On the south bank is the palace of the archbishop, numerous churches and monasteries, university, observatory, arsenal, and the garrison barracks. On the north bank are the modern suburbs, Binondo, &c., the palaces of the governor-general and the admiral of the station, the commercial and native quarters. The city is liable to visitations of earthquakes, hurricanes, and thunderstorms, of exceptional violence. In 1880 a violent earthquake caused very great damage,

whilst in 1892 a hurricane ruined half the city. The population is estimated at 300,000, for the most part native Tagals, some 25,000 Chinese—a large number descendants of these two races—and about 5000 Spaniards. One-half of its trade has been in British hands, one-fourth Spanish, and one-seventh American. The Spanish authorities have always been jealous of foreigners. The city has an export trade valued at £3,400,000, and an import trade of nearly the same amount.

The losses at the Havana, though immense and crushing to Spain, were not the only ones she was fated to suffer, through her alliance with France. A plan for invading her Philippine Isles, that immense and extensive archipelago in the eastern seas, north of Borneo, was submitted to the Ministry by Colonel Draper (afterwards Sir William Draper, K.C.B.), of the old 79th of the line, then in India, and disbanded after the peace of 1763, a regimental number replaced by the Cameron Highlanders in 1793. Colonel Draper received permission to put his plans into execution. No man was better qualified by military talent, and the most accurate local knowledge to give them effect, than this spirited officer.

The "Seahorse," twenty guns, commanded by Captain Grant, was first despatched to cruise off the Philippine Isles, and to intercept all ships bound for Manila. On the 21st July, 1762, the first division of the fleet sailed from Madras, and on the 1st August Admiral Cornish, who had lately succeeded to the command in the East Indies, and Colonel Draper followed with the remainder. The land forces consisted of 2300 Europeans and Sepoys. The Admiral had under his command fourteen ships, ten of which carried fifty guns and upwards. His flagship was the "Norfolk," seventy-four guns, of which the gallant Kempenfelt, who in 1782 perished with the "Royal George," was captain, the whole carrying 4330 men.

When the fleet anchored in Manila Bay on the 23rd September, the Spaniards were totally unprepared to receive them. A summons to surrender having been refused, preparations were commenced to land the troops, as it was resolved to attack the city itself in the first instance, and, after its capture, a fortified suburb and citadel, called Carvéte, which commanded the entrance to the inner harbour. Owing to the rough weather the landing of the troops occupied three days, but, notwithstanding the heavy surf, they were landed by the boats of the fleet under the direction of Captain Kempenfelt. The Spaniards had collected in force, with both infantry and cavalry, to oppose the landing, but, under a brisk cannonade from the frigates it was successfully achieved, and next day a reinforcement of 1000 seamen and marines was landed to co-operate with Colonel Draper.

On the 25th September a fort named the Polvérista, abandoned by the Spaniards, was seized as a place of arms, while Colonel Monson was detached with 200 men to reconnoitre the approaches to Manila, the spacious suburbs of which were now sheeted with fire, as the Spaniards had given them up to the flames, and the houses of the natives, built of nipa, covered with leaves, and raised on wooden pillars 10 feet from the ground, blazed away like tar barrels.

The Hermita Church and the priest's house, 900 yards from the city walls, were taken possession of by the 79th Regiment, as to maintain that post was of the utmost importance, for now the monsoon had broken out, the surf was more dangerous than ever, the whole country was deluged by rain, and at times there were the most dreadful thunder and lightning while the artillery and stores were being landed. The activity of the seamen, as usual, surmounted every obstacle, every difficulty.

The blinding sheets of rain that fell without ceasing compelled the troops to seek shelter anywhere. They frequently occupied scattered houses that were under the fire of the city bastions, much nearer them than the rules of war prescribed. The battalion of seamen was cantoned between the 79th and the marines.

Four hundred Spaniards with two field guns, under the command of Chevalier Fayette, issued forth and began to cannonade the invaders on the 26th, but they were roughly driven in by the pickets of the 79th, with the loss of one of their guns.

Colonel Draper now discovered that the fortifications of Manila, though regular, were not complete. In many important places the ditch had never been finished, the covered way was out of repair, the glacis was too low, some of the outworks were without cannon, and the now half-ruined suburbs afforded shelter to the besiegers.

The garrison consisted of 800 purely Spanish troops, but there were many half-castes, and to their assistance the country had poured in 10,000 Indians of a race who were remarkable for their ferocity, hardihood, and supreme contempt of danger or death.

The Governor, who was the Archbishop of the Philippine Isles, united in his own person, by a policy that was not without precedent in the colonies of Spain, the command of forces, together with the civil power and the ecclesiastical dignity, "however unqualified by his priestly character for the defence of a city attacked, he seemed not unfit for it by his intrepidity and resolution."

(*To be concluded.*)

LINES TO THE CLAN DAVIDSON.
ON THE CHIEFTAINSHIP.

SONS of warlike David, waken
From your sleep, where'er ye be—
Be it glen of pine and bracken,
Or far land beyond the sea.

Break from out the mists that settled
Long ago upon your clan,
Leal as when your fathers battled
In Clan Chattan's plaided van.

Chieftainless ye long have slumbered,
Now the time has come to wake,
And beneath some gallant leader
Of your own your place to take.

If the line of brave Black David,
Near or far ye cannot trace,
There are noble men amongst you
Worthy of the Chieftain's place.

In your choice be wise, united,
If a choice ye have to make,
And the motto of your fathers—
"Shoulder up to shoulder"—take.

They, from fields of olden story,
Disunited did not fly,
But enwrapped in martial glory
Like true men together die.

"Hail! Clan Chattan!"—chief and clansmen
Wait to greet your chosen man—
You and they, united kinsmen,
Have for ages long been one.

On that day the bonnie tartan,
Fringed and plaited, gay shall swing
To the martial strain of chanter,
And the gleesome note of string.

Highland toast, with Highland honours,
Gaelic cheers to rend the sky,
Sounding pipes, and waving banners,
Hail the Chieftain of Clan Dai.

Hatfield.   ANGUS MACKINTOSH.

MESSRS. BOTTOMLEY & LIDDLE, 154 St. Vincent Street, Glasgow, have patented and put upon the market for sale a most useful needle threader. The "Gem" is a very simple little article, and can be used by anyone. You put the head of the needle in a hole, pass the thread over it, and on withdrawing the needle it is found to be duly threaded. To the aged and those of defective sight it will prove a decided boon.

"AN DOTAIR BAN: A BIOGRAPHICAL FRAGMENT, BY HIS GRANDSON," is the title of a delightful little work published by Dr. M. D. Macleod. It was read at a meeting of the Caledonian Medical Society, of which Dr. Macleod is president, and gives an account of the life and work of the *Dotair Bàn*, whose name is a household word in every cottage in Uist, and whose memory is likely to be long cherished by the natives. Dr. Macleod has done a graceful act in collecting so much interesting information regarding his grandfather's labours in the Outer Hebrides, and putting it in a permanent form.

TO CORRESPONDENTS.

All Communications, on literary and business matters, should be addressed to the Editor, Mr. JOHN MACKAY, 1 Blythswood Drive, Glasgow.

TERMS OF SUBSCRIPTION.—The *CELTIC MONTHLY* will be sent, post free, to any part of the United Kingdom, Canada, the United States, and all countries in the Postal Union—for one year, 4s.

THE CELTIC MONTHLY.

JULY, 1890

CONTENTS.

OUR NEXT ISSUE.

Our next issue will take the form of a Grand Summer Number. Plate portraits, with biographical sketches, will be given of Dr. and Mrs. J. Campbell Maclean, Swindon; Colonel J. Bain Maclean, Montreal; and Major Mackenzie Kennedy, India.

"TRANSACTIONS OF THE GAELIC SOCIETY OF INVERNESS."—The 21st volume, just to hand, can favourably compare with any of its predecessors: if anything it is bulkier, and the papers fully maintain the high standard of excellence which is usually associated with the Gaelic Society's annual volumes. Dr. Fraser-Mackintosh contributes the opening paper on the "Cuthberts of Castlehill;" Provost Macpherson, Kingussie, continues his valuable "Gleanings from the Cluny Charter Chest;" Mr. J. L. Robertson, H.M.I.S., writes on "Early Sources of Scottish Gaelic;" Rev. J. Macrury and Mr. Neil Macleod are responsible for Gaelic articles, while dialect and philology are ably represented by Mr. Alex. Macbain, M.A., and Rev. C. M. Robertson; folklore by Rev. James Macdonald, Miss Goodrich Freer, Messrs. Alex. Macdonald, and Charles Ferguson; Gaelic ballads by Rev. John Kennedy; and papers on other interesting topics by competent contributors. It is probably not overstating facts when we say that the "Transactions" of this society form one of the most valuable literary collections connected with the Highlands, and as the small subscription entitles each member to a copy of these handsome volumes the wonder is that the roll of the society is not treble what it is.

"EARLY GAELIC SYNTAX, Popularly Treated for Beginners," by J. G. Mackay.—Mr. Mackay, in this most valuable work, has taken up the study of Gaelic from the English standpoint, and has treated his subject in an able and scholarly manner. His system has the recommendation of being simple and yet serves its purpose much better than those based on more complicated methods. It is effective, for it is the result of the author's own experience, which is at all times the most practical standpoint from which to judge of such matters. We heartily congratulate Mr. Mackay on the very useful work which he has published, and hope that it will have a good sale. It is published by Mr. David Nutt at 1s. 6d.

"THE PROPHECIES OF THE BRAHAN SEER," by Alex. Mackenzie, with an introductory chapter by Mr. Andrew Lang, has been issued by Mr. Æneas Mackay. The fact that so many editions have been published and found a ready sale is proof that Highlanders are fascinated with the life and prophecies of Coinneach Odhar Fiosaiche, and the fate which overtook the great house of Seaforth. The volume is nicely got up, and will no doubt find many purchasers. (Price 3s.) Mr. Mackay also sends us a very interesting work on "Scottish Life and Character, in Anecdote and Story," by William Harvey. The stories are very interesting, and cannot fail to attract Scotsmen.

LETTER TO THE EDITOR.

SOME HIGHLAND QUERIES.

SIR,—I shall feel much obliged to any of your readers who will kindly give me any information upon the following points:—(1) Order of battle of the Highland army at Culloden. According to Browne it was as follows:—Athole brigade on the right; then from left to right of first line, Camerons, Appin Stewarts, Frasers, Mackintoshes, Maclachlans, Macleans, John Roy Stewart's regiment, and Farquharsons, "united into one regiment;" Macleods, Chisholms and Macdonalds.

What was the composition of the Athole brigade, and which of the above-mentioned clans were formed into one regiment, as it is not clear from the text whether the Farquharsons only are meant, or all the clans from the Camerons to the Farquharsons?

Are there any more exact data available as to the strength of the various battalions and companies, and the designation and strength of the various septs in each unit, with especial reference to Clan Chattan?

(2) A few years ago there was an interesting discussion in one of the Scottish newspapers—I think the *Scotsman*—as to the exact route followed by Montrose in his march from the Great Glen to Inverlochy, 1645. What, if any, conclusion was arrived at on this point?

(3) What is the meaning of the piobaireachd known as "The Gathering of Clan Chattan" (*Cruinneachadh Chloinn Chatain*)? Who composed it, and when, and by what sept or septs was it used? From its resemblance to "Cluny's Salute," I have hitherto been inclined to attribute a Macpherson origin to it.

(4) What is the best and most authoritative work upon the tartans, with plates?

Thanking you in anticipation for the insertion of this letter.—I am, sir, yours faithfully,

Nova Scotia.   W. A. MACBEAN, *Capt.*

THE CLANS: PAST AND PRESENT.

By R. S. T. MacEwen, of Lincoln's Inn,
Barrister-at-Law.

(*Continued from page* 163).

THE CLANS AT CULLODEN.

AT Culloden, on the 16th April, 1746, that day so fatal to the Stuart cause and to the clans, the same clans were again engaged, reinforced by the MacLeans, MacLeods, and other western clansmen. The Highland host, according to one authority, numbered at the time 8000, but 3000 were not in the field, 1150 took no part in the fight, and only 3850 were actually engaged against the Duke of Cumberland's 9000 well disciplined and appointed troops. The Highlanders were worn out, famished, and dispirited by a fruitless night march, and had barely got to the ground when they were attacked by the fresh, active, and well-fed English troops. Each side lost about 600 in killed, so that the English, with all their advantages, suffered as severely as the clansmen fighting with everything against them. Yet they behaved with high courage and splendid endurance.* When the condition and number of the combatants is considered, the wonder is, as a writer on the subject has observed, "not that Prince Charles lost the battle, but that the Highland army was able to offer the resistance that it did." Indeed, but for certain unfortunate incidents at a critical moment of the fight, the Prince would have had the best of it. He won both at Prestonpans and Falkirk, and had misfortune not attended him he stood

*In the "Hardwicke Papers," a notice of which has appeared, a letter from the Hon. Joseph Yake, A.D.C. to the Duke of Cumberland, is given, in which it is stated that there were 2000 rebels killed and only 44 of the royal army. This is an English account, and wholly inconsistent with the reports of the period.

an equally good chance at Culloden. That such a result would have made any permanent difference may well be doubted. The Prince's exploit to win back his kingdom and heritage was a desperate adventure, hastily conducted and badly managed, and without external support from France or elsewhere, could not have succeeded permanently, and his party in England was neither numerous or influential at the time. It is not necessary to follow the wanderings and fortunes of the Prince and the remnant of his scattered followers, for they are matters of history. It is sufficient to say that Culloden spelt death to the Stuarts, and to the clans as fighting organisations in their own country. Yet the Stuart cause still lingers as a pleasant memory in the North, if not a potent force. On 16th April last, the 153rd anniversary of Cul-

MACKENZIE—AN INCIDENT OF THE '45.

loden, a number of representatives of Jacobite societies made a pilgrimage to the Memorial Cairn, on the historic battlefield, to the stirring strains of Jacobite music, and placed wreaths upon it, in demonstration of loyalty to the cause. The Scottish, English, and Irish branches of the Legitimist Jacobite League of Great Britain and Ireland, and the Order of St. Germain, were all separately represented by wreaths. The Chief of Clan Menzies also sent one on behalf of Clan Menzies Society, "In memory of 200 Menzies' who fell at the battle;" and Mr. Theodore Napier made a stirring speech. The Stuart sentiment and the glamour attaching to the name of "Bonny Prince Charlie" still live in the Highlands.

THE EXTERMINATING ACTS.

Several of the chiefs and chieftains concerned in the rebellion were forfeited and lost their estates, although some were afterwards restored; and two Acts were passed shortly after Culloden, with the object of exterminating the clans. The first was an Act of 1746, which has been described as the most "brutal" in conception and design which has probably ever found a place on the Statute Book. It provided for the disarmament of the Highlanders, proscribed the wearing of the Highland dress and everything connected with it, required the registration of all schools, a certificate and oath from all clergymen, schoolmasters, teachers of youth, private chaplains and tutors in families, while parents were prohibited from sending their children to any but registered schools and teachers; prayers were enjoined for His Majesty, his heirs and successors, and for the royal family whenever a prayer was said. Infringement of any of these provisions entailed heavy pains and penalties. The country was harried by English soldiers in search of arms. For having or bearing arms or warlike weapons the penalty was £15, and for concealing arms £100: on non-payment the convicted persons, if fit, were sentenced to serve as soldiers in America. The Government knew their fighting qualities—they had had enough of them—and considered this a good way of recruiting for America, where British soldiers were then badly wanted. They got rid of many by this means. If unfit for soldiers they were to suffer imprisonment for six months and find bail. In the case of women convicted they were, in addition to the fine, to suffer six months' imprisonment in the nearest Tolbooth. Second offences were punishable with seven years' transportation beyond the seas. But the most diabolical part of the proceedings was the oath of "good affection" (!) extracted from them, which was in these terms: "I, A. B., do swear, as I shall answer to God at the great day of judg-

ment, I have not, nor shall have, in my possession any gun, sword, pistol, or arm whatsoever, and never use tartan, plaid, or any part of the Highland garb; and if I do so may I be cursed in my undertakings, family, and property; may I never see my wife and children, father, mother, or relations; may I be killed in battle as a coward, and lie without Christian burial in a strange land, far from the grave of my forefathers and kindred; may all this come across me if I break my oath." Those who refused to take this awful oath were treated as rebels. No wonder that within a short time the Highlands were cleared of fighting men. For the first ten years the Act was vigorously enforced, and it was not till 1782 it was repealed. The second Act was passed in 1748, and abolished the heritable jurisdiction of the Highland chiefs. These two Acts gave the death-blow to the clan system.

THE HIGHLAND EXODUS.

At first the Highlanders, we are told, bore their wrongs patiently, but between 1763 and 1775 upwards of 20,000 emigrated across the Atlantic. Referring to later emigrations, Mr. Frank Adam says: "Another large exodus of Highland families took place between 1810 and the middle of the present century. The Act of 1748 had, by 1810, borne the fruit which the the Government had counted on. Many chiefs had ceased to be solicitous for the welfare of their clansmen. Many, too, preferred the luxury of the English Metropolis to the homely joys of Highland life, and needed money to indulge in the luxuries and pleasures of the south. To increase their revenues, many Highland landowners, during the period above alluded to, cleared out their tenantry from large tracts of country, in order to make room for extensive sheep farms. The result of these proceedings was a wholesale emigration from the Highlands. In some cases entire clans sought new homes in the colonies. In Canada especially, large tracts were colonised by Highlanders driven from home, not by war, nor, at this time, by Government, but by their own chiefs and by sheep."* And, it may be added, to make way for deer forests. Instead of soldiers for our army, the Highland hills and straths are now peopled by sheep and deer. In this magazine for March of this year, Mr. Beaton, in his article on "The Social Condition of the Highlands Since 1800," says that between 1773-75 30,000 persons from various parts of the Highlands crossed the Atlantic, but it was not until about the beginning of the present century that the tide of emigration reached its full height, when the

---

* What is my Tartan.

crofters were swept away to make room for the wealthy sheep farmers from the southern dales which invaded the Highlands;" and he gives an instance, quoted by Dr. Carruthers, of a grazing in Kintail which paid an annual rent of £15, for which a rent of £350 was offered.* In the same number of the magazine, in an article on "The First Sutherland Fencible Regiment, 1759," Mr. Eric Mackay says that between 1759 and 1814 80,000 men were raised in the Highlands for the army. In nine days, in 1759, the Earl of Sutherland alone raised and marched to Perth at the head of a regiment 1500 strong. He quotes from General Stewart's statement: "The martial appearance of these men when they marched into Perth in May, 1760, with the Earl at their head, was never forgotten by those who saw them, and who never failed to express admiration for their fine military air. . . . There was no light infantry company; upwards of 260 men being above 5 feet 11 inches in height, they were formed into two grenadier companies on each flank of the battalion." What Highland chief could raise such a regiment in the present day? Not that Highlanders are less loyal and brave than they were in the past, but the country no longer contains them in the same numbers.

(*To be continued*).

A NOBLE ACHIEVEMENT.
A HIGHLAND STORY.

BY AGNES WALKER.

CHAPTER II. (*Continued from page 179*).

THE morning had been grey and dull, and some rain had fallen, but now (it was about eleven in the forenoon) the clouds had rolled away to the south; from the castle windows the distant hills of Morven and Mull were visible again, and there was every promise that the day would be a lovely one.

In the library, a long and lofty room with windows looking north and west, Lord Dunallan, who had arrived at Achnasheen the night before, was seated. In front of him stood a writing-table, on which were some newspapers and magazines; while a couple of magnificent deer-hounds lay at his feet. He was a tall, distinguished-looking man of eight-and-twenty, with grey eyes, and blonde hair and moustache. His face, handsome and clear-cut, was somewhat marred, however, by an expression of indolence

---

* For the latest and most authentic information relating to the present condition of the crofters in the Highlands and Islands, see the "Report of Lord Napier's Crofters' Commission."

and hauteur. He had just returned from a visit to the stables, and having lit a cigar, had taken up a newspaper and was reading.

He had been sitting thus, smoking and reading, for fully fifteen minutes, when the door, which was slightly ajar, was pushed open, and Lady Dunallan entered.

"I hope I am not intruding, but I wish to speak to you about a matter of some importance, if it should not be inconvenient?" she said, when she had taken the chair which her husband had placed for her; and the two hounds, who had jumped up at her entrance and bounded towards her with every manifestation of delight, were restored to quietness.

"Oh, I'm quite at your service," said Lord Dunallan, leaning back in his chair and looking at her.

There was a slight pause.

"What I wish to speak about is a matter in connection with one of the crofters at Scarba—Duncan Macdonald." She spoke quietly; but the colour had deepened on her cheeks, and her hands were tightly clasped in her lap, as if to keep them from trembling. "It appears that he has been given notice to quit; and yesterday his mother came to me in great distress about it."

Lord Dunallan gazed at his wife, astonishment, which quickly changed, however, to disgust and annoyance, depicted on his face. A business matter to discuss was, of all things the most repugnant to him; besides, he had a rooted conviction that for a woman to meddle with these things was to muddle them. After a moment or two, he said:

"One of the crofters at Scarba has received notice to quit, and his mother came to you about it? What tomfoolery is this? If the man has been given notice to quit, then something must be wrong. Haggart's not the man to take such a step as that unless there is some reason for it. If the man has got notice to quit—he must go. There's nothing more to say about it."

There was silence for a few minutes.

"I have no wish to interfere between you and any of your tenants, and I have never yet sought to do so," said Lady Dunallan, in a voice which was not quite steady, though otherwise she betrayed no sign of agitation; "but in the case of Duncan Macdonald I feel that a great wrong is being done to a decent and hard-working family, and that I must speak. May I ask what the factor said to you about Macdonald—what the complaint was against him?"

"Oh, I know nothing about the matter—have never heard it mentioned," said Lord Dunallan, curtly. "I daresay Haggart will say something about it. But it's of little consequence—he understands these things better than I do."

"The factor has said nothing to you about the

matter, hasn't mentioned it?" said Lady Dunallan, slowly, her eyes, full of wonder and incredulity, fixed on his face. "That is strange—very strange indeed!" She unfolded the factor's letter, which she had brought with her into the room, and held it out towards him. "May I ask you to read this?" she added.

He put out his hand for the letter, wondering vaguely what all this was to lead to, and cast his eyes upon it. Watching him intently, and somewhat anxiously as well, while he read, Lady Dunallan saw his expression change and the colour mount to his brow. The next moment, with anger flashing from his eyes, he sprang to his feet and threw the letter down on the table in front of him.

"The confounded scoundrel!" he exclaimed. "What does he mean by penning a letter like that and sending it to anyone on the estate?" Then, after a pause, turning towards his wife and sitting down in his chair again, he added, "What can you tell me about this, Miriam? Who brought the letter? What did they say?"

Lady Dunallan's heart gave a great leap. Was the task which a minute ago she was feeling so hopeless about, and on the success of which she had built so many hopes, to be easy of accomplishment after all? In her quiet and simple way she proceeded to tell of Mrs. MacDonald's visit to her the day before, and of what had passed between them in conversation, dwelling a little on the old woman's agitation and distress; and she concluded by saying that it was her belief MacDonald was being turned out of his croft because of the factor's anger and malice against him for the part he had taken in connection with old Mrs. M'Callum.

When she had finished speaking, Lord Dunallan sat silent and thoughtful for some minutes. Then he picked up the factor's letter and glanced at it again.

"I knew nothing of this—nothing whatever," he said, with his eyes still on the letter. "And yet the factor states plainly here that he is acting under my instructions, and tells MacDonald that no notice will be taken of any letter he may send! But he shall answer to me for it all, and that before long."

"And I shall have something to say to him too," said Lady Dunallan. She spoke with a vehemence quite unusual with her. And it seemed, too, as if some change had been wrought in her. Her timid and anxious manner was gone. There was a new light in her face; her eyes were full of gladness. Altogether, she had the look of one who sees that some great and desirable end will be attained—that victory will be sure.

Lord Dunallan looked at her inquiringly.

"I mean about Mrs. M'Callum—the old woman who has been taken away to the poorhouse at Oban," she went on. "She is not the first on the estate who has been treated in a like manner. Just about a year ago, two old women—twin-sisters, named Janet and Mary MacLean—living at Fasdale, were taken away to Oban. They had been in domestic service, and when too old for work had come back to live at their native place. But, through the failure of some bank, all their savings were lost, and they were destitute. And when the factor knew of this, instead of waiting to see whether anything could be done for the poor creatures, he had them removed to Oban, and their furniture taken away to be sold. Fortunately, I came to hear of the matter, and so took steps at once to have the old women brought back to their home, and their furniture restored to them. And, at the time, I said to the factor that such a thing was not to happen again, that I could not bear the idea of anyone on the estate being sent away to a poorhouse, and that all cases of illness and poverty on the estate were to be reported to me, and what was needed I would supply. And yet, in spite of what I then said, this poor old woman, left desolate and destitute owing to the death of her son, has been taken out of her home and placed in a poorhouse. But I shall insist on reparation being made to her. And all matters of that sort must be taken completely out of the factor's hand."

"Decidedly, most decidedly," said Lord Dunallan, with promptitude. "I had no idea such things went on on the estate. Haggart's power must be curbed." Then, after a pause, he added, "And about MacDonald? I suppose intimation will have to be sent to him that he is not to be turned out of his croft? As his mother came to you, perhaps it would be better the intimation should reach them through you. Will you undertake to see that a message to that effect is sent?"

"I shall only be too delighted," said Lady Dunallan. "But——" She paused, and was silent for some moments, with her eyes cast down. Then, looking up, she said, in a somewhat diffident and hesitating way, "But if I may make a suggestion—do you not think, Kenneth, you could take the message to Scarba yourself? You could easily ride over. And you would hear the whole story from MacDonald's own lips, and would see things there for yourself, and thus be better able to come to a right decision about the matter."

Lord Dunallan deliberated for some minutes.

"Yes, you are right, Miriam," he said, with decision. "It's the best thing to do. I shall go to Scarba myself. Why, it will be quite a revival of old times. It's ages since I was in any of the tenants' houses; but when I was a lad I went about with my mother constantly. There wasn't a man, woman, or child on the estate she did'nt know. And there was nothing she wouldn't have done for any of them; while they, on their part, simply worshipped her. The *Baintighearna*—that was what they called her."

He had turned towards the portrait of a fair-haired, gentle-looking lady which hung above the fire-place, and was regarding it with eyes which had a curiously softened expression.

"I often wish I had known her," said Lady Dunallan, softly. She had turned, and was gazing at the portrait also. "I have heard so much about her from everyone here. She must have been all that was good."

Half an hour later Lord Dunallan, accompanied by a groom, was on his way to Scarba.

It was lovely out of doors. The promise which the later hours of the morning gave had been fulfilled, and the day was a typical August one—breezy, and bright, and warm. The road to Scarba ran close by the sea, which lay, a blue shimmering expanse, under the brilliant sky, but was not always visible to the two horsemen as they rode along—a high hill, purple with heather, sometimes rising between. But always they could hear the murmur of its waves along the shore; and now and then the shrill cry of a sea-bird as it flew from one rocky islet to another. Save for these, and the clatter of the horses' hoofs on the hard ground, other sounds there were none.

Scarba, which was the name given to a few scattered crofts and fishermen's huts facing a sheltered bay, was soon reached; and Lord Dunallan, dismounting and leaving his horse in charge of the groom, walked away in the direction of MacDonald's house, which an old woman standing at the door of one of the cottages had pointed out to him. It had a rather better appearance than its neighbours. It was somewhat larger; had a slated roof; while its thatched barn and byre were in a less dilapidated and tumble-down state than were most of the others.

On reaching it and being admitted, Lord Dunallan at once asked to see the crofter. He very soon made his appearance—a tall, broad-shouldered man of middle age; and he looked apprehensive and troubled, as if not very sure what this unexpected visit might portend. But any fears which filled his mind were quickly allayed by his lordship's frank and cheerful greeting, and by the announcement that he had come to see why such an old tenant as Duncan MacDonald had been served with a notice to quit. And presently Lord Dunallan was listening to an account of the factor and his doings on the estate, which raised his indignation against that individual to a white heat.

"Well, MacDonald, I am very glad to know all this," said Lord Dunallan, when there came a pause. "There are a good many things that will have to be seen into, and, as far as possible, remedied. And as for yourself, remember this—that so long as you wish to remain on the croft it is yours. I'll have no one turned off the estate to suit the whim or caprice of any man."

Then there was some conversation about other matters—the crops, the fishing, the moors; and by-and-by Lord Dunallan took his leave.

Needless to say that, after his lordship's departure, there was much rejoicing among the members of the little household. And of course the good news had to be communicated to anxious and inquiring neighbours; for his lordship's arrival at the little hamlet and visit to MacDonald's house had caused great excitement among the cottagers, and many eager and curious eyes had watched him as he rode away. And the unexpected turn which affairs had taken, and, above all, the fact that Haggart was "found out" at last, caused the keenest delight and satisfaction.

"I will tell you what it is I am thinking, Duncan," said old Murdo MacLean, the fisherman, as he sat, along with a few others, in the crofter's house that night discussing matters—and of course the conversation was in Gaelic. "I will tell what it is I am thinking, Duncan. I am thinking it was a very good thing the factor was giving you a notice to quit. For it has let his lordship know a good many things he was not knowing before. And it is not the factor that will be getting all the power now. Maybe the power will all be taken away from him. Mark my words, Duncan—the factor's day is over."

And the old fisherman's prediction would have been hailed as a veritable fact, had the little company known that immediately after Lord Dunallan's return to Auchnasheen a groom had been despatched to Oban, bearing a note to the factor requesting that gentleman's attendance at the castle on the following day.

(To be concluded.)

"THE GAELIC NAMES OF PLANTS," by John Cameron, Sunderland. A revised and enlarged edition of this valuable work is now in the press, and will be ready on 1st August. While the volume is written in English, the names will be given not only in Scottish Gaelic, but also in Irish, Welsh, and Manx, together with a most interesting collection of Highland plant-lore, from the Gaelic bards, proverbs, &c. The volume will be one of the most scholarly ever published on the Highlands, and will rank with "Nicolson's Gaelic Proverbs" as a classic. It is got up in attractive style, and as only a limited edition of 350 copies is being published, intending subscribers should send their names at once to John Mackay, 1 Blythswood Drive, Glasgow. Price to subscribers, 7s. 6d.

HECTOR GRAEME MACKAY.

MR. H. GRAEME MACKAY is a representative of the ancient family of Melness, one of the oldest and most influential branches of the Clan Mackay. The Melness chieftains were descended from the Hon. Colonel Æneas Mackay, second son of the first Lord Reay the famous Sir Donald Mackay, whose Strathnaver regiment achieved such renown under the great Gustavus Adolphus, of Sweden. The Mackays of Melness stood high in the clan, and produced many men who distinguished themselves in military and civil pursuits. The stately old mansion-house of the family is one of the most prominent features on the shores of the Kyle of Tongue, and appears to be still in as good a state of preservation as when built many generations ago. The house and lands, unfortunately, no longer belong to the Mackays, and the members of the ancient race of Melness are to be found scattered in all parts of the globe.

MELNESS HOUSE.

Mr. Hector Mackay, whose portait we give, was born in Liverpool, his father, Mr. Isaac Mackay, being a native of Leith. Mr. Isaac Mackay settled in Liverpool, where he established a successful business as a grain merchant. The subject of our sketch was the youngest of three sons, and was educated at Birkenhead Having developed marked literary tastes, he resolved upon adopting literature as a profession, and entered Liverpool University College, where he studied for a year. Thereafter he decided to proceed to Oxford, preparatory to taking up press work, but his stay there was of short duration, having contracted a severe illness owing to overstudy. A voyage to the Cape restored him to health, and last year he entered Edinburgh University, where he is now completing his studies in medicine.

Mr. Mackay is a life-member of the Clan Mackay Society, and takes a deep interest in the good work which that society performs. His relative, the late Mr. John Mackay (Ben Reay), claimed to be head of the Melness branch of the clan, and was perhaps the greatest authority on matters relating to the Mackays. He had been engaged for over twenty years in collecting material for a new history of the clan, and it is to be hoped that the results of his labours may yet be given to the public in a permanent form.

THE BATTLE OF THE WINDS.

WILL tell you the true tale—and true it is indeed—of the Battle of the Winds on Lochnagar.

On a day, Ruadri, son of Martach, was pursuing deer on Lochnagar. The light, active, nimble, swift-running, swift-following son of Martach, of shining limbs, was pursuing the chase on Lochnagar. To the lofty, white, purple, summit went he in pursuit of deer. There heard he the winds talking angrily one to another. Said the South Wind: "She is certainly mine; for, whenever I go near her, she smiles upon me. I give her the cool, refreshing, gentle rains of the heavens. The bright dews of the grass are my tributes, and the sound of my voice is as the sweet music of birds. She is mine! she is mine!"

Then cried the West Wind: "Not so, brother: you are mistaken. She loves me!" Then sang he:

"From the Golden West I come,
From my cave by the edge of the sea.
The blue of the sky is my gift.
She loves me! she loves me! she loves me!"

But the North and the East Winds laughed these two winds to scorn. Then fell they to disputing violently with each other.

Roared the North Wind: "She rejoices to see me race across the dusky plain of winter. In my strength is her delight. Trees root I up and rocks cast I down, for her pleasure. She claps her hands for joy when she sees me descending in my might from my lofty seat among the angry heavens. The waves of the ocean rise up and roar when they behold me; and I can make the swift rivers flow back to their sources in the high mountains. She loves me! she loves me!"

Then spoke coldly the East Wind: "I am her lover. Me only she fears; me only she loves. When I go near her, she holds her breath for fear and awe of me. I breathe upon the green fertile plain, and behold! it is turned to black. In my gift are the frost and the snow, and the cold, icy blasts of winter. In my gift, too, are the hot, scorching winds of summer; and, when I list, my breath is as the stagnant heat of sandy, desert places. I am her lover!" proudly said he.

And the South and the West Winds, because they were not of themselves strong enough to contend against either of the other two winds, and because each secretly hoped to gain some advantage over his rivals by such an artifice, took sides—the South Wind arraying himself on the side of the East Wind, and the West Wind arraying himself on that of the North. Then began the terrible Battle of the Winds on Lochnagar.

The noise of the shock of the contending winds was louder than the loudest thunder. For a year and a day they fought—like great, wild, savage beasts. Lightning streamed from their wounded flanks. The sun fled in fear of the conflict, and went and hid himself in the west. The moon and the stars forsook the skies. The top of the mountain smoked with the heat of the battle. The moisture flowed from them in torrents. It filled the lochs and rivers, which devastated the plains. As the hound shakes his quarry, so the winds shook the mount. Great rocks and stones went bounding down from top to bottom. Trees were snapt off at the stems, like brittle faggots in the hands of the husbandman. Oaks on the plain were bent and twisted by the mere breath of the conflict. It happened that an eagle which flew into an eddy was cast away, like the down of the hill.

Ruadri lay beneath a rock whilst this terrible battle was going on. But, by a miracle, he escaped. The half of his two strong arms was buried in the soil beneath the rock, and he himself with the stout grey rock of gigantic weight and strength to shelter him. Yet was he in danger of being dashed to pieces by spent breezes, once or twice.

At last, at the end of a year and a day, wearied of the useless conflict, and almost breathless, cried the North Wind: "Oh, brothers! it seems to me that we have waged war long enough. Let us now, therefore, conclude a peace."

Then said the East Wind: "I have but a sorry ally in this combat, so we will conclude a peace as soon as you please." And the South and the West Winds, because they saw that there was no advantage to be got out of the conflict, and because they feared the other two winds, gave a ready consent. So a peace was presently concluded between them. And by this peace it was agreed that the North and the East Winds should possess the beautiful maiden of the fair, smiling, sparkling countenance for the greatest part of the year, and the South and the West Winds for the rest. And because all were a little jealous of one another, it was further agreed that, sometimes, the winds should visit the maiden in consort. That is to say, sometimes the East and the North Winds should go together, and sometimes the South and the West. And, as a variation of this plan, it was also consented to by all, that, if at any time it seemed good to them, the winds should have liberty to visit the maiden in the order in which they had fought. Then was peace concluded between the winds and there was silence on Lochnagar.

This is the true tale of the Battle of the Winds, which Ruadri, the son of Martach, witnessed on Lochnagar. STUART ERSKINE.

CLAN EWEN.
MacEwens in Lochaber.
SLIOCHD EOGHAIN.

By R. S. T. MacEwen.

IN the article on Clan Ewen, Eoghan na-h-Oitrich (August, 1898*), mention was made of "Sliochd Eoghain" and of the frequency of the name MacEwen in connection with the Camerons. It is now proposed to trace this connection, and the origin of the name in Lochaber.

Keltie, in his History of the Highland Clans, says the original seat of the MacEwens was in Lochaber. This must have been anterior to the thirteenth century, for we find them at Otter, in Cowal, in 1222; when, with other western clans, they suffered severely in the conquest of Argyll by Alexander II. According to the MS. of 1540, the Siol Gillevray—from whom the MacEwens, MacNeills, and MacLachlans are derived—are descended from a certain Gillebride, King of the Isles, ancestor of the MacDonalds. Skene doubts the Gillebride genealogy, and favours the descent from Anradin, as given in the first article, "but, nevertheless, the traditionary affinity which is thus shown to have existed between these clans and the race of Somerled at so early a period, he thinks seems to countenance the notion that they had all originally sprung from the same stock."† The MacNeills were certainly vassals of the Lords of the Isles; and according to Keltie, the Camerons were connected with the House of Islay in the reign of Robert Bruce, and their modern possessions, Lochiel and Locharkaig, belonged to the Lords of the Isles. They are said to have deserted Alexander, Lord of the Isles, for James I. MacKenzie, in his History of the Camerons, also says that the MacLachlans of Strath-Lachlan are said to be descended from the Camerons and related to the the MacLachlans of Cornanan, "and this may have been the link which led Donald Dubh, the celebrated 'Taillear' Cameron warrior, to Cowal when he tired of a fighting life in Lochaber."‡

It is curious that tradition should have associated the *three* Siol Gillevray clans—which are western clans--with the Camerons in Lochaber—which is a Moravian clan—if there was no connection existing between them; and that Donald Duibh should have fled to and settled in Cowal, where the MacEwen and MacLachlan territories lay, if he was not sure of a kinsman's welcome. Again, the name Ewen is very common in the Cameron family. It first appears in 1219, when Sir Ewen de Cambron, third son

○ "Celtic Monthly," vol. VI., p. 207.
† Keltie, vol. II., p. 162.
‡ "History of the Camerons," MacKenzie.

of Arbroath. Up to the close of the fourteenth century, the history of the Camerons is meagre and imperfect, and the name does not appear again till we come to Ewen, eldest son of Allan, the ninth chief. This Ewen became tenth chief (1390-96), and was the chief in 1396 when the fight on the North Inch of Perth took place. From this time, for a long period, the name is common amongst the Camerons, both as a first or Christian name, and as a surname, with the prefix Mac. Since then, there have been four chiefs of the name, of whom one, Sir Ewen Cameron, seventeenth chief, is a historical personage, with a distinguished record. Of younger sons, and sons of cadets of the family, there are numerous Ewens. Ewen, the thirteenth chief, by his second wife, Marjory Mackintosh, had a son, also Ewen, the progenitor of the Erracht family, known as "Sliochd Eoghain." Ewen "Beag," fourteenth chief, met an early death. He had a natural son by a daughter of Mac-Dougall of Lorne, Domhnull MacEoghain-Bhig — Donald MacEwen Beg — better known as "Taillear Dubh," and Mac-Domh'uill Duibh (Black Donald), a celebrated warrior. So successful was he that he was suspected of a fairy origin, with a special charm upon him, and he has been the subject of much romantic history. He it was, who, getting tired of fighting, retired for a time to a monastery in Cowal, but subsequently returned to the world, married and settled in that district, and left issue.* The Rev. Malcolm Campbell Taylor, D.D., Professor of Church History, Edinburgh University, is said to be a descendant of his—the name Taylor being derived from "Taillear."

Keltie also has it that after the breaking-up of the other clan some followed MacDougall Campbell of Craignish into Lochaber. Could this have been the MacDougall of Lorne whose daughter was the mother of the "Taillear Dubh"? He was Donald MacEwen Beg.

In 1576-77 we find one "Allaster M'Ewin, of Camroun," applying to the Lords of Council for release from the Earl of Athole, who held him and others in confinement at Blair Athole; and in 1598 there was a raid by the Lochaber clans on the Dunbars of Moyness, which formed the subject of complaint to the Privy Council, and amongst those charged are a number of MacEwans.

But these are not the only traditionary and historical instances of connection between the Camerons and the western Celts. According to the best received Cameron tradition, the first Cameron was a western Celt from Dumbartonshire. An early tradition is that he was a younger son of the Royal Family of Denmark, who came over

○ Mrs. Mary Mackellar's Tradition.

the fourth chief, is mentioned in the Chartulary in 404 to assist Fergus II.; that he married the daughter and heiress of MacMartin of Letter-finlay, and thus acquired the property and chief-ship of the clan; and was called Cameron, in Gaelic, from his crooked nose." The author of the memoirs of Sir Ewen Cameron and modern clan authorities, however, favour the later tra-dition that the first Cameron was a Celt and not a Dane; and the chief has been handed down in history as of Celtic origin. The "broken nose" too, as we shall see, had no connection with a Prince of Denmark. The later tradition will be found set out at length in Mackenzie's History of the Camerons. Shortly stated, it is this:— The first Cameron was much renowned for feats in arms and prodigious strength, marvellous instances of which are given. He entered the lists with the most famous champions of his day. In one of these encounters he received a violent blow on the nose, which set it awry, and from this circumstance was called Camshron, or Cameron, "Knight of the wry nose". The name was, therefore, not Danish or a first or Christian name, but a Gaelic sobriquet arising out of the injury to his nose. The tradition proceeds: "Our hero was now arrived at the thirty-fifth year of his age, and had given many signal proofs of his valour, so that his name became terrible all over the country. But having little or no paternal estate, he began to think it highly necessary for him to join himself to some great and powerful family, the better to enable him to distinguish himself more eminently than it was possible for him to do as a single man, without friends or relations, or at least such as were of little or no account. He had spent his life in the shire of Dumbarton; but, as he had no family or inheritance to encumber him, he resolved to try his fortune in the world, and to go in search of a wife."

(*To be concluded.*)

ALMA.

WHO will face the fiery ordeal,
　Who will beard the Russian bear,
Who will scale the heights so dizzy,
　Who will do, and who will dare!
Britain's stately Guards are reeling,
　Backward fall the sons of Wales,
'Neath the fire so close and deadly;
　See! the Light Division fails.

Cambridge sees our heroes falling
　'Neath the steady leaden hail,

---

* As to the way clan pedigrees were constructed in ancient times, see Skene's "Celtic Scotland", and "Clans Past and Present" in "Celtic Monthly" for May, 1899, p. 148.

Is the Briton's vaunted courage
　Now no longer of avail?
Must our army now be beaten?
　Is there nothing now but flight?
Shall it be that Britain's driven
　From the fiery field of fight?

No! the hero heart of Campbell
　Still is beating true and fast,
He will never think of yielding,
　He will battle to the last.
He has fought and bled for Britain,
　Now his blood's at fever heat,
His brigade must face the foeman
　Ere he orders a retreat.

He will neither shrink nor falter,
　He will never ask for aid,
He will win or lose the battle
　With his own beloved brigade.
Thousands see and thousands tremble;
　Is he rash or is he mad?
Can he turn the tide of battle
　With his heroes, tartan-clad?

Scotland's best and Scotland's bravest
　Plaided clansmen in their pride,
They will die for dauntless Campbell,
　They will ne'er be swept aside,
Dancing plumes and waving tartans,
　Hero-hearts and Highland steel,
Campbell leads and they will follow,
　They will fight for Britain's weal.

See! the kilted force advances
　Steadily, as on parade;
Comrades tremble, foemen wonder
　Are the kilted lads afraid?
Dare they face the massive columns
　Waiting them in proud array?
Dare they? can they ever triumph
　In the hopeless, bloody fray?

Dare they! See! the plumes are waving,
　Waving proudly up the hill,
They have never feared a foeman.
　They can conquer, and they will.
Campbell's eyes are proudly flashing,
　Dauntless is his rugged brow,
Let the Czar's most vaunted legions
　Face him, ay! and turn him now.

Backward, backward, ever backward,
　See! the massive columns reel;
Upward, onward, ever onward
　Sweep the tartan and the steel;
Death has never been a laggard
　When the tartan takes the field,
Now the plumes are proudly waving
　And the Russian's doom is sealed.

Alma's won! The plaided heroes
　Well have stood the bloody test;
They are trusty still and fearless,
　Britain's bravest, ay! and best.
Alma's won! O'er foes unnumbered
　Scotsmen triumph once again:
History will sing their praises—
　Colin Campbell and his men.

Trancnt, East Lothian.　　　JAMES MILLAR.

GOID BEAN NA BAINNSE.

Le Eòghann Mac Colla.

(Arranged by Malcolm Macfarlane, Elderslie).

Gleus F. *Gu sunndach.*   Air fonn "Piobaireachd Dhòmhnuill dhùibh."

Seisd—

```
|s  :   m : m |l : — t  d' | s : —. m : m | m : r  : d  |
 "Hug   ag - us hó   ro   i!    'ill -  can 'si  'bhan - ais  i!

|s  : —. m : m |l : —. t  d' | s :     m : d | r  : — : d  |
 Hug   ag - us hó   ro   i!    ith - ibh  is  òl - aibh!

|s  : —. m : m |l : —. t : d' | s : —. m : m | m : r  : d  |
 Hug   ag - us hó   ro   i!    slàint - e  is  son - as di—

|r  :   r : m |f : —. s  l | s :     m : d | r  : — : d  ||
 Bean - bainnse lur - an - ach Bar -   an   na   Sròin - e!"
```

Rann—

```
.d'| d' : —. s : s | d' : —. l : l  | d' : —. s : s | m : r  |
Ach com - a   cia sùrd - ail bha'm Bar -  an  'sa   lùchairt,

:d | d : —. s : s | d' : —. l : l  | s : —. m : d | r  : — : d |
Cha b'ann  mar sud sùrd  na   h-òigh chiùin  bu chuis glòir   dhaibh.

   | d' —.  s : s | d' : —. l : l | d' : —. s : s | m : r : d |
De     so dhuisg smal - an  di, 'n dùil - eag 's ann dh'aindeoin di

   | r :   r : m | f : —. s  l  | s :     m : d | r  : — : d ||
   Thàr - ar 'ga ceang - al ri  Bar -  an   na  Sròin - e.
```

"Greas ort, a Dhòmhnullain, greas thar a' mhunadh ort !
Stigh air Gleann-fionnart gu h-ealamh gu 'd Mhòraig !
Greas ort, a dhuine, mur math leat a' chruinneag ud
Nochd a bhi laidhe le Baran na Sròine !

Gun éisdeachd ri tuilleadh, gu h-aigeantach, ullamh
Chaidh Dòmhnull do 'n mbunadh le buidhinn mhaith còmhl 'ris :
Sud mar an dealanach, null thar a' bhealaich iad !
Eiridh an donas do Bharan na Sròine.

Cluinnibh sud ! Cluinnibh sud ! Cluinnibh a' bhruidinn ud
Grad a' cur stad air gach cleasachd is òran !
"Theich a' bhean òg mar ri Dòmhnull nan Tulachan !
Clis as an déighidh, gach duine 'san t-seòmar !"

B' e 'n sealladh b' fhiach fhaicinn an iomairt bha aca
Feadh chàrn agus chnocan gu teth anns an tòir ud,

'S am Baran, gu treunail, 'nam meadhon ag éigheach so
"Buaile bho-laoigh dha bheir greim dhomh air Dòmhnull !"

'S mall, 's gu ro mhall e, a bhodaich, mar leanas tu ;
B' fhearr dhuit bhi tilleadh ; 's dean cailleach a phòsadh !
Mur math leat droch dhìol bhi ort féin is na bhuineas dnit,
Mholainn duit fuireach fad claidheamh o Dhòmhnull

Bha fathast na reulta 'san athar 'n àm tournadh
Do Dhòmhnull 's d'a cheud rùn air taobh eile Chòmhaill.
An ruig mi leas innseadh mu 'n bhanais ùir rìomhaich
Gle luath bu cheann-crìche do threubhantas Dhòmhnuill.

DR. J. CAMPBELL MACLEAN.

MRS. J. CAMPBELL MACLEAN.

THE CELTIC MONTHLY:

A MAGAZINE FOR HIGHLANDERS.

Edited by JOHN MACKAY, Glasgow.

No. 11 Vol. VII.] AUGUST. 1899 [Price Threepence.

DR. J. CAMPBELL MACLEAN.

DR. JOHN CAMPBELL MACLEAN is the son of the late Rev. Peter Maclean, one of the most prominent and powerful preachers of his day in the Free Church of Scotland, and whose fame as the possessor of a vigorous mind and a warm heart was well known. He had charges in Cape Breton, America, Tobermory, and at Stornoway, as well as being deputed by his Church to visit the Canadian Provinces.

Dr. Maclean's mother was one of the Campbells of Craignure and Knock, a branch of the House of Argyll, and one of the most distinguished of the old military families in the Highlands, three of her brothers having been in command of the 46th and 61st Regiments. Her liberal support of every scheme intended for the religious and material benefit of the country, or the amelioration of the condition of the poor, without respect of denomination, was proverbial in the Highlands.

The subject of our sketch was born in Tobermory, Island of Mull, in 1849. He received his early education at home under private tutors. After studying for some years in the Port-Glasgow Academy, he entered the arts classes in the Edinburgh University. Deciding on the medical profession, he went through the usual curriculum, gaining honours and prizes in surgery, botany, and chemistry, and finally qualifying as Bachelor of Medicine and Master in Surgery in 1868. In the following year he joined Dr. Gay, of Swindon, Wiltshire, as assistant. On the death of that gentleman

he started on his own account, and although several tempting offers to go to London were made him he preferred the more free but harder life in the provinces to the more conventional life in town. In 1871 he married Emily, daughter of Mr. T. C. Hine, architect, Nottingham, and their family consists of one daughter, who in 1892 married Mr. Ellis H. Pritchitt, architect. For relaxation from work, Dr. Campbell Maclean prefers active pastimes, and takes part in fox-hunting as frequently as his professional engagements will allow. He is an excellent shot, and finds ample opportunity for gratifying his love of field sports during the shooting season.

As an enthusiastic Freemason he has more than once passed through the chair in Craft Arch, Rose Croix, and Knights Templars; was elected some years ago by Lord Methuen as Senior Warden of the Province, and later by Lord Thynne to the highest obtainable position in Arch Masonry. We need hardly add that the doctor is an enthusiastic Highlander, animated with a love for everything that belongs to his native land. He is a member of the Clan Maclean Society, and is at present spending a holiday with his wife in the romantic land of his clan in Mull. We trust that he will enjoy many visits to *an-t-Eilean Muileach*, and continued prosperity and success in the profession to which he is so ardently attached.

THE WISH OF DONALD ROBERTSON.

Lay me with the rolling turf
　　Green above my head,
　Where the Garry's deeps are brown,
Girdled with the silver surf,
　　There I'll lay me down
　　With the Highland dead.

Let the ancient cross of Christ,
　　Gray on hills of heather,
　Guard me till our sleep be done,
Guide us till we keep our tryst,
　　Not as death slew, lone,
　　But kind kin together.

SARAH ROBERTSON MATHESON.

KINTYRE STORIES.

By Cuthbert Bede.

How MacEachran's Daughter saved a Bannock and lost a Laird.

YOU have all heard of the MacEachrans, and perhaps you are acquainted with Duncan MacEachran, the blacksmith in the Long Row. Honest man, he is the last of his family, though the clan was once a proud one, and held up their heads with the very best in Cantire. Shall I tell you how it was that they came south and settled at Kilellan? It must have been at least eight hundred years ago, and MacEachran was then the laird of Craigneish. It was there, at the spot they call Barbreck, that the king of the Scots killed Olaff, the king of the Danes, in single combat, and they buried Olaff under the mound called Dunan Aula, near to Dail-nan-Ceann, "the field of heads," where the Danes that had fallen in battle were buried. The Campbells of Jura have held Craigneish since then, though not of late, and this is how it came about.

MacEachran of Craigneish was unmarried, but he had a niece who lived with him as his adopted daughter. A Campbell came to court her, she accepted him, and they were married. But, as MacEachran did not care to part with her, he bargained that the young married folks

DALARUAN,   CAMPBELTON.

should live with him at Craigneish. They agreed to this, and for some little time all went on well. But MacEachran soon found that, although it was his own house, he was looked upon as one too many in it, so he made up his mind to leave Craigneish. They did not oppose his wish, and the only stipulation he made with them was that, whenever he came to Craigneish, he should sit at the head of the table, in token that he was the laird. Then he packed up his goods in a couple of creels, which he slung across his horse's back, securing them with girths of " woodies " (bark-bands), and he determined within himself that he would continue his journey until the woodies broke, and that he

would take up his abode at the place where they gave way. So he turned his back on Craigneish, and, keeping near to the coast and the Sound of Jura, went straight on, across where the Crinan Canal now is, and then down through Knapdale, and on to Tarbert, and still the woodies held firm. So on he came all through Cantire and reached Campbelton, and the woodies still held firm. So on he went towards the Mull, and began to think that he should find his resting-place in the sea, when, just as he had got to Kilellan, on the road to Southend, the woodies broke. Well, MacEachran made himself so comfortable at Kilellan that he never went back to Craigneish to take the head of the table, and his niece and her husband settled there and founded the clan of the Campbells of Craigneish. MacEachran himself got a wife to his taste, and he married and had a large family, and that was the rise of the MacEachrans of Kilellan. Well, time passed on, and brought its ups and downs to the Clan MacEachran, like it does to poorer folk, and I'm now going to tell you of some of the ups and downs it brought to a daughter of one of the MacEachrans. She was not only his only daughter, but she was his only child, and he looked to her to be making a fine marriage for herself. It happened on a day that she was baking oatmeal bannocks, and there came to the door a tall, strong-limbed man, who had a gold ring on his finger and a gold chain on his neck, but who wore neither bonnet nor shoes, and when he asked MacEachran's daughter to give him a bannock, the girl made answer to him with the proverb, "*Fàinne mu'n mheur is gun snaithne mu'a tòin.*" ("A bare back and a ring on the finger is a paradox throughout the world.") The stranger would not be put off with a proverb, but again asked the girl to give him a bannock, and when she would not do so, he took one from her by force, and went out. The girl called out to her father that there was a strange man who was taking away the bread, and MacEachran went after him and made him give up the bannock.

Some time after this MacEachran saw a company of soldiers at his door, with their commander, demanding food and lodging. MacEachran made them a feast, and provided beds for them, and gave up his own bed to the commander. In the morning, before they set out on their march, he gave them all a good breakfast. MacEachran's daughter had waited on them all and seen to their wants, and she found the commander so polite that she quite fell in love with him, and she told her father that he was just the man whom she should like to marry."

"We must first find out whether he is married already," said MacEachran.

After breakfast, when MacEachran's daughter had again waited on the commander, and shown him, as plainly as looks could speak, that she loved him, the commander said to MacEachran that he should like to have a word with him and his daughter in private. So she thought within herself that she knew very well what he was about to say, but in this she was mistaken, as you shall hear.

"Do you not know me?" said the commander. "Neither I nor my daughter have ever seen you until last night," replied MacEachran.

"You may think so, but you are mistaken," said the commander. "Do you remember a man without bonnet or shoes, who came to your house and asked for a bannock, and when your daughter would only give him a proverb the man seized the bannock, and she cried out, and you came and took the bannock away from the stranger. Perhaps your daughter will remember that, even if you don't."

"I remember it well," replied MacEachran. "Was that man a friend of yours?"

"The best friend that I have on earth, for it was I, myself, and I never thought to be so treated by you, for we had been friends up to that day."

"I had never seen you till that day," said MacEachran.

"But your factor had, for we have exchanged some land. You might have known my ring. Every one knows Macdonald."

When MacEachran knew that it was the great Macdonald, he was very sorry not to have recognised him, and he begged him to stay there on a visit, and promised that he and his daughter would do all they could to make him comfortable. She, too, urged him to stay, and looked at him with loving eyes.

"It is too late," said Macdonald. "These soldiers are my Irish friends, who have come with me from Ireland to fight for me, and I must go with them. Your daughter would not give me a bannock for my bare head, though she might have done it for this gold ring on my finger. It will never go on to her finger now. She saved her bannock, but she lost Macdonald."

With that he went away, and MacEachran's daughter had to look elsewhere for a husband.

THE COGE-MAKER'S TRIAL.

James *nan Gogain*, the coge-maker, or as he was commonly called, James Cogie, was a native of Campbelton, and by trade a cooper. He made a tolerable livelihood by making *gogain*, or cogee, which were small wooden dishes made up of staves, and without handles. Clay-ware was not much used in those days, the dishes adorning the dresser and table were usually a few pewter plates, surrounded by a great many coges. Indeed, every child had it own coge to suit its own size, to hold its porridge, milk, sowens, and every kind of soft-food; so that there was always a great demand for *gogain*, and the coge-maker's was a good trade. It was a proverb in Cantire, when one was angry with another, that he should take a stave out of his coge for that; meaning thereby that such an one would be lessened of his enjoyments.

James Cogie wrought at his trade with diligence, and would also occasionally go to the North Highlands with a herring-fishery vessel where he could act as cooper, and receive very good wages for making the herring-tubs. James Cogie was not very scrupulous in observing the eighth commandment; for whenever he saw a piece of wood that was suitable for his own purposes he would secure it. One day, being ashore in one of the fishing lochs, he saw a beautiful tree growing near to a gentleman's mansion. He used the freedom of cutting it into junks and concealed them, in order that he might take the fine wood home to Campbelton and convert it into coges.

The gentleman missed his tree, and made a search to find out the depredator to have him punished by the law. The law at that time was, that any person found guilty of cutting a tree without the liberty and consent of the proprietor, should lose his right hand by having it cut off at the wrist. The gentleman summoned one by one the crews of the fishing-vessels in the loch. James Cogie was conscious that he was

the cutter of the tree, and he had scruples of conscience about giving a false oath; but he was very ingenious, and pretended that he was perfectly ignorant of an oath. When his turn came, he appeared very awkward. The judge told him to swear.

"I never swore in my life," said James.

"Say you as I say, and do as I do," said the judge. "Hold up your hand."

"Hold up your hand," said James, quite seriously.

Said the judge—"Tut, man! say what I say!"

Said James Cogie—"Tut, man! say what I say!"

"Put out that stupid man!" shouted the judge, pointing at James.

THE HARBOUR, CAMPBELTON.

"Put out that stupid man!" shouted James, pointing at the judge.

In this way James Cogie was dismissed, for which he was very glad; and, when people asked him how he got on with the judge, James would answer—

"I sware at the judge, and the judge sware at me!"

James Cogie had a beautiful daughter who had many suitors, and he proposed to give her to the best of them who would put a hoop on a coge. So they assembled and did their best,

but broke the hoop on driving it on. One of the suitors was a greater favourite with the girl than all the others, and before his trial, she whispered to him—

"'N uair a sguireadh an caoval ri dol, Sguireadh m' athair fàin g'a char."

("When the hoop did cease to go, My father ceased to drive, I know.")

Taking the hint, the young man gained the daughter, and her words continue to this day to be repeated as a proverb by the coopers in Cantire.

MAJOR MACKENZIE KENNEDY.

MAJOR MACKENZIE KENNEDY,
Norfolk Regiment.

MASTER MACKENZIE KENNEDY.

CAN myself lay no claim to being Scotch, for my father was of French origin, his ancestors having come over from Normandy at the revocation of the Edict of Nantes, but for my husband's and the children's sake I take a great interest in clans and Highland customs, and in the staunchness, bravery, and independence that seem to appertain especially to all that is Scotch.

The Marquis of Ailsa is the head of their family, but their more immediate relations have been scattered abroad in all parts of the world. Many have been in the army, and some have died young. It was gratifying when I took our eldest boy and girl on their first visit to the north of Scotland, to see as we walked out of one of the large railway stations a more than life-sized statue of the well known and much beloved Dr. Kennedy, and to be able to tell them he was their great-great-grandfather.

There were also tablets inscribed to the memory of their grandfather and their great-grandfather, the one a clergyman and the other a major in the 1st Royals, in the Inverness Cathedral.

But the story they love most to hear is of their brave young great-uncle, brother to the above, who carried the colours at the battle of Waterloo, when only fifteen years of age. How, when wounded in the arm, he was sent back to have it dressed, and instead of remaining with the invalids, he had it hastily bandaged, and rushed back again into the thickest of the fight, bearing the precious colours bravely aloft in triumph with the uninjured arm. Soon afterwards he was mortally wounded, but even in death he held the token of victory that had been entrusted to his keeping so firmly that it could not easily be taken from his grasp. How, seeing this, a comrade lifted both his lifeless body and the colours, the sign of Britain's honour, from the ground and carried them silently off the field, and the enemy, touched by the spectacle of such extreme youth and so much bravery, ordered the "cease fire" to be sounded for them to pass! Some artist, I am told, made it the subject of a beautiful oil painting, although I have never seen more than a crumpled and discoloured print, a small copy very likely of the painting, but I hope we shall come across the original some day. We Kennedys shall never forget the young boy's heroism.

My grandfather was also at Waterloo, an ensign in the 40th Regiment, and maybe they knew each other and were friends. The life of one was made complete in a very few short years, the other lived to fight and be wounded in many other battles for his country, his king and his queen, and then to enjoy a peaceful old age.

He was indeed a credit and an ornament to his noble line of ancestry, and we must hope that the younger members of his clan, though living, happily, in more peaceful times, will each in their several ways try to follow his example, ever upholding a high standard of right, ever ready to fight against tyranny and oppression, be brave to endure pain and discomfort if it is for the good of others, true to duty and honour even unto death, and transmitting, we will trust, the feeling that "noblesse oblige" in its deepest sense to their children's children for many generations.

India. SARA MACKENZIE KENNEDY.

THE CLAN DONNACHAIDH SOCIETY.—The annual gathering was held at Dunkeld last month, and was well attended. Struan, chief of the clan, occupied the chair. Mrs Robertson Matheson reported that 86 new members had joined, and the balance at the credit of the society was £204.

THE SOCIAL CONDITION OF THE HIGHLANDS SINCE 1800.

By A. J. BEATON, F.S.A. Scot., F.G.S.E.

XIII. DISTILLERIES.

(*Continued from page 183*).

THE most extensive industry in the Highlands is the distillation of whisky, and so enormous has the demand been for Highland Whisky that in the year 1884 the quantity of spirits produced in Scotland amounted [to] 20,164,962 gallons, by far the greater quantity of which was manufactured in the Highlands. In the year 1825, when the duty was reduced from 6,2 to 2/4 per imperial gallon, the quantity distilled was only 4,324,322 gallons The Government duty per imperial gallon now is 10 4 per proof gallon. Smuggling or illicit distilling is carried on to a considerable extent in the remote districts of the Highlands at this very hour; and although the Revenue Officers make many captures, yet the practice can never be suppressed so long as there is so high a duty on whisky. By evading this high duty, the profit is so remunerative as to tempt many a poverty-stricken crofter to venture the risk of capture that he may be enabled to meet his obligations, and in many cases he depends on

THE CRINAN CANAL AT ARDRISHAIG.

the sale of his smuggled whisky for the money with which to pay his rent.

Smuggling is an evil which cannot be too much deprecated, for it not only demoralises the manufacturer but often leads to intemperance and immorality in communities that might otherwise be sober and industrious.

XIV.—KELP.

The manufacture of kelp at the beginning of this century was one of the most remunerative industries ever established in the Highlands; and maritime proprietors have suffered material loss from the abandonment of this manufacture. The product of the alkaline sea-weed was used in the manufacture of plate-glass and soap; but scientific research discovered a cheaper substitute which, together with the reduction of duty on Spanish barilla, completely outworked the profitable production of kelp in the Highlands. As a source of income it was enormous, especially when the price ranged from £15 to £20 per ton; it however gradually declined to £4 and £5 per ton, and now little if any kelp is made in Scotland. I recollect seeing some burnt in Orkney about thirteen years ago. Lord Teignmouth in his "Sketches of the Coasts and Islands of Scotland," states "that the number thrown out of employment by the failure of the kelp manufacture in a memorial prepared at Edinburgh, in the beginning of 1828, by the proprietors of the western maritime estates amounted to 50,000.

XV. DEVELOPMENT OF THE HIGHLANDS.

MEANS OF COMMUNICATION.

From the peculiar configuration of the Highlands, this region of Scotland was completely isolated from the rest of the kingdom, until the disturbed state of the country in 1715 forced the government to consider a scheme for the construction of military roads in the Highlands, so that the Royal forces might with ease be able to enter a hitherto impenetrable part of the kingdom. General Wade was therefore commissioned to construct about 250 miles of roads in the Highlands, and although we cannot rank the General as a first-class engineer, yet as the "Irish" couplet puts it :—

"Had you seen these roads before they were made
You would lift up both hands and bless General
Wade."

It was not, however, until the year 1803 that any material benefit was derived from the construction of roads; for General Wade's roads, well suited as they were for military purposes, were from the nature of their construction entirely inadequate and unsuited for the commerce of the country. It was left to Thomas Telford to intersect the Highlands with a network of roads which to this day stand unrivalled in Scotland.

In 1803 parliament passed an act granting £20,000 towards making roads and bridges in the Highlands, and for enabling the proprietors to charge their estates with a proportion of the expense of maintaining the different lines of communication.

Subsequent grants were made for the same purpose, and by 1820 no less than 875 miles of road were made, at a cost to parliament of £267,000, to the counties of £214,000, and to individual proprietors of estates of £60,000. The whole of these lines were then under one management, and the maintenance cost about £10,000 per annum. This amount was chiefly raised by tolls, which, however, was considered such a grievance that a Royal Commission was appointed in 1859 which recommended the total abolition of tolls in Scotland. In 1883, under a general act passed in 1878, tolls ceased to be collected on any road in Scotland, and these are now maintained by a general assessment, and managed by County Road Boards.

"The extent of roads, completed by means of the Highland Road and Bridge Act, and absolutely placed under our care by the Road Repair Act, is no less than 400 miles, and 60

miles more await only the formality of exonerating the contractors. Besides these, 270 miles are under contract and in various stages of progress, and at least 170 miles more will hereafter be placed under contract and finished, presenting a total of 900 miles, and proving how eagerly the inhabitants of the Highlands have availed themselves of the liberal assistance held out to them by the government for the improvement of their country. Independently of the above extent of roads, the bridges built and constructed under distinct contracts have cost the public £30,000 and the contributors upwards of £40,000." *

It may be imagined what an impetus would have been given to commerce in the Highlands after thus being intersected with so many roads. Before the commencement of the present century no public coach or other regular vehicle of conveyance existed in the Highlands. In 1800 an attempt was made to establish coaches between Inverness and Aberdeen, but from the wretched state of the roads at that time and the little intercourse that took place, it was found necessary to discontinue them, and it was not till 1806 and 1811 that coaches were regularly established on this route. In 1832 no less than seven different stage coaches passed to and from Inverness, making forty-four coaches arriving at, and the same number departing from it in the course of every week. Three of these included the mail run between Inverness and Aberdeen, and between Inverness and Perth over the Highland road; two between Inverness and Dingwall, Invergordon, Cromarty, and Tain; and the mail coach between Inverness, Wick, and Thurso, extending from London made in a direct line above eight hundred miles. There was also a coach from Inverness to Oban, which ran over a considerable part of the military road.

CANALS.

The next step towards opening up the Highlands was the construction of the Crinan and Caledonian Canals. The Caledonian Canal is the largest of its kind in the United Kingdom, and passes through some of the most picturesque and romantic scenery in the Highlands. The estimated cost of constructing the work was £474,531, whereas the actual expenditure amounted to about one and a quarter million pounds sterling. From the Canal Commissioners' report in 1831 it appears that the total expenditure from 20th October, 1803, to the 1st May, 1831, was £990,559 10s. 9½d. The total length of the canal from east to west sea is 59 miles, 16 chains, of which distance 37 miles 41 chains is

* Vide Report (7th) of the Commission on Highland Roads and Bridges, 1815.

formed of natural waterway, leaving 21 miles 55 chains required to be cut. Throughout the entire canal there are 29 locks, each being 40 feet wide and 172 feet long. At the Inverness entrance of the canal from the Beauly Firth there is a large basin or floating dock covering 32 acres.

The Caledonian Canal was opened in October, 1822, by Charles Grant, Esq., one of the Canal Commissioners, and for a long period member of parliament for Inverness-shire. The canal has done a great deal towards opening up and facilitating intercourse with the central Highlands, but still the anticipations of the promoters have not been fully realised. It was expected that all the coasting trade would pass along this waterway and thus save rounding the stormy Cape Wrath, but a very small proportion of this class of vessels patronises the route, although the Commissioners gave every inducement by lowering the dues to a minimum with little good effect. As it is the concern is a dead loss to the nation. Mr. David MacBrayne's excellent fleet of Highland steamers ply regularly through the canal between Inverness, the Western Isles, and Glasgow. It is a favourite tourist route, and for grandeur and picturesqueness in scenery without a rival in Scotland.

(To be concluded).

"MHARI": A SKETCH.

ABOUT eleven o'clock one fine August evening, two men were sitting on the deck of the S.S. Clansman as she rounded the dark Mull of Cantire. Sea, sky, and mountain lay around them veiled in the shades of night, like some mystic shadowland. Silently they glided in the dim darkness across the breast of the sleeping waters. The vessel's dark reflection pursued them like a phantom ship, while the Aurora's changing lights shot across the starlit sky. There was no sound save the thudding throb of the engines' mighty heart, and the unceasing low swish of the waters where the vessel broke through their calm. The passengers had gone below excepting these two men, who, in spite of the exquisite beauty of the scene, seemed guilty of dozing. Suddenly the younger of the two spoke in a half soliloquising fashion, "it seems strange to me, old man, for all this not to be mixed up with a girl, for in the old days when I left the Highlands there was always a girl in the case. A scene like this would keep me up all night dreaming of *her*, don't you know. By jove! life gets awfully practical when a fellow marries and settles down," he added regretfully. His friend not replying, he continued more briskly. "By-the-

bye, Campbell, I never told you how I met 'my wife.' It's ten years ago, this very month, and this is the identical spot on board the S.S. Clansman. How time flies! I had been up in Glen Eila for a month or two's shooting, and had there fallen in love (or imagined so) with a little Highland girl—an old crofter's daughter. Poor little Mhari! There's something awfully fascinating, don't you know, about these Highlanders. I remember I thought her accent perfectly charming; I should probably call it broad now," he added, laughing. "What a fool I was! Yet, after all," he continued vigorously, "there's something about that sort of love affair you don't get in a more reasonable one. But to return to the point. I left the Glen after a stolen interview with my little sweetheart, a hundred vows of undying love and speedy return on my lips, and joined this steamer at Oban. It was a night like this. I never left the deck. It seemed like some strange poem, and Mhari was the heroine. Mhari breathed in the air, Mhari shone in the moonlight, the very engine seemed to speak her name with every throb. At five o'clock in the morning I was pacing the deck (Mhari still) when an apparition issued from the deck cabin, formidably frowned on perceiving me, and then beat a hasty retreat. It was a girl with dark hair fastened across her forehead in some wonderful contrivances of steel. A yellow shawl imparted a ghastly hue to her complexion, and as she bestowed the favour of her frown on me, I involuntarily exclaimed, 'I pity the poor fellow who marries that girl.'

"As the passengers assembled on deck, I found among them an old friend of my father, who having made a pile in America had come back to spend it. We watched the early sun as it caught the summit of Ailsa Craig and transformed the dark rock into a blaze of living gold. Then we went down to breakfast together. There we were joined by his daughter, who, as I was introduced to her, held out her hand saying, with a ripple of silvery laughter, 'we are friends already, are we not? three hours old, at any rate.'

"You know my wife, Campbell, so a description of the transformation is superfluous. The memory of the apparition soon became obliterated from my memory, or rather perhaps, I never succeeded in identifying it with Miss Lowe, whom in less than a year I married. With the apparition faded another memory, Mhari, now, I hope, the wife of one of my old rivals."

Leslie's reminiscences ended, the two men went below, and next morning Campbell bade his friend good-bye, saying, "don't let Mhari keep you in Glen Eila."

About ten miles from the dainty town of

Oban lies Glen Eila. Lonely mountains rearing their lofty heads shut out the little Glen from the surrounding world. As far as eye can see stretch those lone hills with their heather clad brows. Sometimes as you stand and listen in vain for some sound of human life, the silence suddenly oppresses you until you long to scream and break the awful stillness; and as you gaze on the interminable hills you want to rush wildly on and on till you get to the world beyond them.

It would seem as if earth's sin and sorrow could not pierce the mighty barrier to curse with their load the lonely lives spent there. Yet there, where God's very presence seems embodied in the sublimity and grandeur of nature, there they sin and suffer, there they sorrow and die.

When Leslie returned to Glen Eila he entered the Glen by the mountain pass he knew so well. Unbidden the past came back again, and the flood gates of memory were opened. The remembrance of his early passion tinged every scene. Here and there a tree, a mountain burn, marked some once hallowed spot. An old man by the roadside greeted him with the characteristic phrase, "it's soft the day," and as he heard the quaint speech, he felt a boy in Glen Eila again. After exchanging a word or two with the old man, just to refresh his ear with the old accent he was about to go on his way, when by his side, he noticed a strange looking man of middle age. He had a long shaggy beard and unkempt hair. His clothes of rough tweed hung loosely about him. His figure, gaunt and lean, was strangely bent, and his dark sunken eyes he scarcely lifted from the ground. As Leslie paused, he slouched up to him with fists slightly clenched, and muttered something unintelligible in Gaelic. The old man pulled him away, and at his touch he seemed docile as a child. Then turning to Leslie he apologized, saying, "he will do you no harm, Sir, he will be for thinking that it wass the bad Sassunach that took his lass from him whateffer. There wass not any finer lad in all Argyllshire, and it iss a proud man I am thinking I would be this day, but he wass just daft about yon bit lassie." Seeing a look of interest on Leslie's face he continued "she wass a bonnie bairn, and it iss a good husband he would hef been to her whateffer, but one of yon fine English gentlemen comes to Glen Eila, and iss courting the lass with his fine speeches, and iss saying he will be coming back for to marry her. Then he went away, and it will not be ferry easy for a young lass to forget, but what is the use of fretting, and fretting. But it is not effery one will be able to put such things out of the mind. It wass a bad day the day that Mhari Og saw the Sassunach in Glen Eila, for it iss no news that

came from England, and the poor bairn iss yonder in the kirk-yard, and it iss Jamie who is daft-like since." It was enough, Leslie could stand it no longer; hastily pulling out a sovereign he would have thrust it into the old man's hand, but the latter drew back saying "no, no, I'm no wanting the money, I'll die on the road, but they'll no hef Jamie in the poorhouse; when I am gone the Almighty will do the rest."

Hurrying away Leslie did not stop until he reached the little churchyard on the hillside. No trim walks and gaily blooming flowers gave a living look to this wild spot. It was indeed a "city of the dead." Desolation and decay marked all around. Rank grass, among which were almost hidden the stone slabs, green with moss and dark with age, covered the dreary waste. No church cast its holy shadow over the sleeping dead and sanctified their resting place. Yet Leslie felt on holy ground as stumbling over hidden graves and broken tombstones in search of what he dreaded to see, he paused at last before a simple stone that stood out in snowy whiteness among the time-worn tombs around. Mechanically he read the short inscription—

MHARI,

Only Child of Duncan and Jane Macintyre, Born June 1st, 1879 : Died January 3rd, 1898. That was all, but Leslie read between the lines, read there the story of a broken heart, a shadowed home, the loss of a strong man's reason, through lightly held and long forgotten vows.

IMRICH NAN RADAN.

'Luchd nan earball fada direach,
Nam busan 's nan geur ghoileachan,
Tha mise 'toirt bàirlinn laghail dhuibh.
Sabhal an duine bhochd bhriouaich a sheachna'dh
A chaill a shlàinte, 's nach do ghlèidh i,
Mur an d'thuair e sguabag bho na càirdean air an dèire'.
Theirigibh thairis do Dhun-ghormaig ann Muile
Far a bheil Calum MacPhail 's na gleannaibh ;
An truilleadh mhosach bhriuideil bhodaich—
Siol ainm 'us a shloinneadh—
Thoiribh bhuaithe gach ni th'aige,
'S na fagaibh mias no meudar,
Liath no ladar, nach cream 's nach cagainn ;
Bhonaid 'tha nm cheann na beiste cuiribh an straic oirre,
Agus 'n uair ghabbas each nn thàmh 's mu'n cadal,
Thoiribh an aon sguirt-sgairt feadh an fhodair.

THE GAELIC MÒD will be held in Edinburgh on 5th October. A complete programme of the competitions and prizes will be found in our advertising pages. The proceedings promise to be of the most interesting and successful character, and we hope our readers will make a point of attending.

TO CORRESPONDENTS.

All Communications, on literary and business matters, should be addressed to the Editor, Mr. JOHN MACKAY, 1 Blythswood Drive, Glasgow.

TERMS OF SUBSCRIPTION.—The CELTIC MONTHLY will be sent, post free, to any part of the United Kingdom, Canada, the United States, and all countries in the Postal Union—for one year, 4s.

THE CELTIC MONTHLY.

AUGUST, 1899.

CONTENTS.

ANNUAL SUBSCRIPTIONS.

NOTICE TO SUBSCRIBERS.—Our next issue completes Volume 7 of the "CELTIC." *Subscribers who desire to renew for another year are requested to send their subscriptions (4s. post free) to the Editor, John Mackay, 1 Blythswood Drive, Glasgow, at their earliest convenience. If readers would kindly give this matter their immediate attention, it would obviate the trouble of sending notices each month to those in arrears, and considerably lessen our labours.*

OUR NEXT ISSUE.

The portraits in our next issue will be of particular interest, as the Highlanders whom we intend to honour are all resident in distant lands, and bear the names of historic clans—Colonel C. R. Macgregor, D.S.O., and Mrs. Macgregor, India ; Mr. Hugh Cameron, Montana, U.S.A.; and Mr. Wm. C. Munro, Hawkes Bay, New Zealand.

MRS. FARQUHARSON OF HAUGHTON.—At the International Congress of Women in London, Lady Marjorie Gordon read a paper on the work of women in biological science, by Mrs. Farquharson of Haughton, who was unavoidably absent through illness. In the course of her paper, Mrs. Farquharson urged the desirability and importance of duly qualified women having the advantages of full fellowship in scientific and other learned societies. The paper was very enthusiastically received.

THE MACDONALD SWORD OF HONOUR.—At a meeting held at the Scots Corporation Hall, of the Committee of the combined Highland Associations of London of the above fund, on the 21st inst, the honorary treasurer, Mr. Donald C. Fraser, submitted his financial statement duly audited by Messrs. James Fraser & Sons, chartered accountants, which showed the highly satisfactory result that after defraying all expenses, there remains a surplus of 60 guineas, which will be used in presenting Colonel Macdonald with some suitable souvenir of the occasion, to be selected by the gallant officer himself.

MR. R. W. FORSYTH, RENFIELD STREET, GLASGOW, whose reputation as a maker of the Highland costume and its accessories is world-wide, has just despatched to the United States, the entire uniforms of two Highland volunteer regiments which have been recently formed by our kinsmen in the New World. During the past year Mr. Forsyth has been entrusted with several important commissions of a similar character, the goods, we need hardly say, having given the greatest satisfaction. Those of our countrymen abroad who are interested in the establishment of kilted volunteer corps could not do better than place their orders in Mr. Forsyth's hands. We can guarantee satisfaction. His reputation as a Highland dress specialist is so well known to our readers at home, and so many have had experience of his tasteful workmanship, that we need hardly refer here to his business.

"THE BRAVE SONS OF SKYE," BY LIEUT.-COLONEL JOHN MacINNES.—This work will be welcomed not only by Skyemen, but by Highlanders all over the world. It is a valuable contribution to the literature of the Gael, and contains a mass of information which cannot be had elsewhere, and which represents the results of patient research extending over many years. The volume is got up in handsome style, the text being illustrated by a hundred portraits of sons of Eilean-a-cheo who have distinguished themselves in martial fields. Colonel MacInnes has rendered a service to his native island which Skyemen cannot fail to appreciate—but who will now write the records of the brave sons of Sutherland, Ross, Inverness, or Argyll? Skye has shown a worthy example.

LETTER TO THE EDITOR.

SOME HIGHLAND QUERIES.

THE CLANS AT CULLODEN.

SIR,—With reference to one of Capt. Macbean's queries in your last issue, the Atholl Brigade at Culloden consisted of four battalions. The fourth of these was never completed, and was composed not only of the Duke's own followers, but also of Menzies of Weems men, under Menzies of Shian, and of Struan men, under Robertson of Woodshiel. Lorn Nairne was colonel of the 1st Battalion, Lord George Murray of the second, William Jacobite Duke of Atholl of the third, and Thomas Blair of Glasclune of the fourth. No less than thirty-eight of the Duke's vassals brought their men to fill up the effective strength of the brigade, and the published "Jacobite Correspondence of the Atholl Family" makes it abundantly clear that nowhere was the work of recruiting and of whipping up deserters more actively pursued than in that district. The numerical strength of the Atholl Brigade can only be matter of conjecture.

With regard to another part of his query, the Camerons, Frasers, Mackintoshes, and the Stewarts of Appin certainly formed separate clan regiments. The Maclachlans and Macleans fought as a united regiment, as did John Roy Stewart's and the Farquharsons.   W. A. M.

THE CLANS: PAST AND PRESENT.

By R. S. T. MacEwen, of Lincoln's Inn,
Barrister-at-Law.

(*Continued from page* 193).
CHARACTER OF THE CLANS.

FOR three and a half centuries up to
Culloden the clans had been in constant
opposition to alien governments. They
were certainly a wild and turbulent race, but a
free, proud, and independent people. The
times, however, were wild and turbulent, and
there was not much to choose between them
and their lowland and southern neighbours.
In those days might was right; the sword was
the only arbiter. Civilization, as we know it,
was then in its infancy. It
is only necessary to refer to
the oath of "good affection"
(save the term!) required by the
Christian government of that
Christian monarch, George
II., and to the conduct of the
Duke of Cumberland and his
Christian soldiers at Culloden,
to guage its standard in war,
even so late as the middle of
last century. In the account
given by Johnston in the book
already referred to we read:
"Of the barbarities committed
after the battle this is not the
place to speak, but we cannot
help contrasting the behaviour
of the 'cousins' in the hour of
victory. Cumberland superin-
tending, with evident satisfaction, the murder in cold blood
of the unfortunate prisoners
and wounded that had fallen
into his hands (many of them
gentlemen of high standing
and undoubted courage), nay,
even 'insulting the slain'
On the other hand Prince
Charles remaining on the
fields he and his gallant
followers had won, to protect
the prisoners and wounded,
and to soothe, as much as
possible, the distress of the
vanquished. The Prince never
forgot that his enemies were
still his countrymen: the
Duke forgot that they were
human beings." *

* Geography of the Clans

Our partial historians have, however, not
refused their mede of praise. They allow
Highlanders some sterling virtues: strength,
valour, love of kindred and home, fidelity to
chiefs and clansmen, hospitality, splendid dis-
regard of hardships, and indomitable courage
and will in the most desperate circumstances.
Macaulay, himself one of the race, depicts the
Highlander of the seventeenth century in highly
rhetorical but impartial language. He describes
his local surroundings, passions, weaknesses,
and follies, but recognises his virtues and makes
due allowance for his environment and the
habits of the age. It is not an "attractive
picture," as he truly says, and "yet an
enlightened and dispassionate observer would
have found in the character and manners of
this rude people something which might well

THE CLAN MURRAY.

excite admiration and a good hope. Their courage was what great exploits, achieved in all quarters of the globe, have since proved it to be. . . . His predatory habits were most pernicious to the commonwealth. Yet those erred greatly who imagined that he bore any resemblance to villains who, in rich and well governed communities, live by stealing. When he drove before him the herds of lowland farmers up the pass which led to his native glen, he no more considered himself as a thief than the Raleighs and Drakes considered themselves as thieves when they divided the cargoes of Spanish galleons. He was a warrior seizing lawful prize of war, of war never once intermitted during the thirty-five generations which had passed away since the Teutonic invaders had driven the children of the soil to the mountains. . . . . It was not just to class him morally with the pickpockets who infested Drury Lane Theatre or the highwaymen who stopped coaches on Blackheath. . . . It must in fairness be acknowledged that the patrician virtues were not less widely diffused among the population of the Highlands than the patrician vices!" * This would seem to be the true verdict of history.

In 1716 the clans were considered a special danger to the Hanoverian King of England and his dynasty, and therefore the severest measures were adopted against them. The curtain has long since dropped on the last act of the old drama. During its long and troubled course of centuries the history of the clans has been the history of Scotland, and they are inseparably connected with all the great national events of by-gone days.

Present Position of the Clans.

The clans are not now as numerous as they were in their ancient ancestral homes; some have lost their territorial position altogether; but others still live on the land occupied by their forefathers. We have seen that clansmen emigrated in large numbers, first after Culloden, and again at a later period in consequence of the Highland clearances. The spirit of adventure, once aroused, has kept on ever since, and seems likely to continue, so that they are now scattered all over the globe, while the large towns throughout the kingdom have attracted many more. The great centres of trade and industry everywhere abound with them, for with the spread of education and the ready means of locomotion they have taken advantage of all places open to them.

Clansmen in the Army.

After Culloden the clans accepted the settled

---

government and the altered state of things. The chiefs and dhunivassals entered largely the commissioned ranks of the army, while their followers became private soldiers. They were formed into Highland regiments, and supplied the British army with some of its finest troops. They have fought with the spirit and determination of their race, and gathered laurels on every "stricken field" since then down to Omdurman. We have still our Argyll and Sutherland Highlanders (the "thin red line,") Black Watch, Camerons, Gordons, Seaforths, and Scots Guards. If there are not as many Highlanders in their ranks now as in the past, it is due to circumstances already noticed and to no want of loyalty on the part of the Highland people. They do their part in the service of the country as volunteers and militiamen. There is no longer a "Highland line" in the old sense; no more feuds, raids, and "fightings" between Highlanders and Lowlanders and between clan and clan. All claim an equal patriotism, and in this unity there is the greater strength. Have they not united and together defended and won the National Challenge Shield, and only this year brought it back to the capital for the ninth time.

Clansmen in Civil Life.

In the peaceable walks of life at home and abroad they are very numerous. In church and state, in the learned professions, public services, science, literature and art, mechanical appliances, commerce, trades, industries, and all the vast businesses and callings, they are, at the close of the nineteenth century, leading and busy men.

Clan Sentiment.

Nor, during the wonderful process of evolution which has been going on, has clan sentiment diminished. It is one of the curious things connected with the race that, notwithstanding the convulsions of the past and the age of universal brotherhood at which we have arrived, clan sentiment is still a potent and vivifying force Speaking at the dinner of the Edinburgh University Celtic Society lately, Emeritus-Professor Masson pointed out that "clan patriotism was an important force in modern society and was a thing to be conserved." That it is so, and is being not only conserved but advanced, one has only to look at the Celtic revival of recent years; at the interest displayed in Celtic literature, poetry, and music, in clan histories and lore, in the encouragement given to the Gaelic language, mòds, clan societies and associations generally, and to the revival of tartan

Dress and Tartan.

It is hardly necessary to insist upon the remote antiquity of the "garb of old Gaul" at

---

* Macaulay's History of England (ed. 1889), pp. 30-1).

the present day. History and the sculptured stones of Scotland establish the fact that the kilt or belted plaid was the ordinary dress of the Celtic Highlander from the earliest time of which we have any knowledge. The Dupplin Cross, which is assigned to the ninth century, represents figures in Highland garb armed with target and spear; and there are numerous other monuments, some of which Robertson considers to be of earlier date. Other parts of the dress and the arms have changed from time to time, and become more elaborate in the course of centuries, until they have attained their present fashion. Originally the kilt and plaid were one piece of cloth, two yards in breadth and four in length. It was wound round the waist, one end falling in plaits or folds to the knee, and was secured by a belt buckled tight round the body. The other end was carried up to the left shoulder, thus leaving the right arm free and at full liberty. In wet or cold weather the plaid could be thrown loose and cover the shoulders and body, and when the use of both arms was required, it was fastened across the breast by a large silver bodkin or circular brooch, often enriched with precious stones or imitations of them, having mottoes engraved, consisting of allegorical sentences or mottoes of armorial bearings, and they were used to fix the plaid on the left shoulder.* Mr. Adam quotes from a book by the Rev. W. Gilpin, prebendary of Salisbury in 1776, containing an extract from an account written in the time of Henry VII. (end of the fifteenth century), thus: "They (the Highlanders) are clothed in military cloak (or plaid) and inner tunic, with their legs bare to the knees. Their arms are bows and arrows, sword somewhat broad, and a dagger." In modern times the kilt and plaid have become separate articles of dress, and the kilt is often worn without the plaid, but the full dress includes the plaid, sporran, arms, and ornaments.

The word tartan is derived from the French: *tiretaine*, linsey-woolsey; the Gaelic name being *Breacan*. When the Anglicised word came into use does not appear, but France and Scotland have been connected from the earliest times, and the word was in vogue in the fifteenth century and probably earlier. The fabric itself is of much greater antiquity, and has been the material from which the Highland garb has been made from the remote past. There is ample evidence that in the fifteenth century it was manufactured in different "setts" or patterns and varying colours. Mr. Campbell, in the chapter on Celtic dress, in his "Tales of the West Highlands" (vol. iv., p. 366), furnishes further proof of its antiquity. He says there

* What is my Tartan?

are a number of old "setts" which are of unknown antiquity, although "every year produces a new crop." The old "setts" were made in particular glens and islands, and "came to be the distinctive uniform or dress of the families or clans who lived in the glens or islands, and who carried on the manufacture of tartan, spinning on distaffs, and weaving on hand-looms at home;" and he applies this test: "the oldest tartan 'setts' ought to be those which can be made from native dyes, and this test will weed out a considerable number which profess to be 'clan tartans.' Tartans, therefore, especially some 'setts,' ought to be old. If not as old as the seventh century, they are at least as old as 1603, according to the author of 'Certayn matters concerning Scotland.'" There are a number of old pictures at Taymouth Castle in which the Highland dress is represented, and Mr. Campbell says that between 1633-41, Jamesone, the Scottish painter, worked at Taymouth, and in 1635 executed a family tree "in which Sir Duncan of Lochow, the great ancestor of the family, is represented in a red plaid and kilt, with a shirt of mail, checked hose, and bare knees. It is at least certain that before Jamesone's time kilts were worn by the nobility and were supposed to have been worn by their remote ancestors." Mr. Adam in his work gives extracts from the accounts of the treasurer of James III. (1471), showing items paid for *tartane* for the king's wardrobe, and similar entries in the reign of James V.

The prevailing colours were blue, red, green, yellow, black, brown, and their compounds. They were prepared with great skill, and retained their brilliance for years in a way modern dyes do not. Logan mentions that a gentleman had assured him that he had seen a garment upwards of two hundred years old the colours in which were still admirable. He tells us "the pattern of the web was not left to the weaver's fancy. He received his instructions by means of a small stick, round which the exact number of threads in every bar was shown, a practice in use to the present day."

In early times every Highland man and woman was known by the tartan they wore, and it was easy to distinguish friend from foe. This custom led families and clans to have their own particular "setts," and to the adoption generally of clan tartans. The tartans of the principal clans are probably as old as their own separate organizations; but there are others of later date, and there is evidence of changes and "blendings" of old "sets" to suit modern tastes.

THE REVIVAL OF TARTAN.

The revival of tartan in a marked degree as an article of wear and the more frequent use of the picturesque Highland dress, afford further proof of clan sentiment. Besides the principal clan tartans many others have been revived or designed within recent years. The princes of the present royal family, unlike their immediate predecessors, have shown their appreciation by wearing the dress during their visits to Scotland. Her Majesty has her Balmoral Highlanders dressed in it. It is largely represented in the draperies at the castle. She rarely goes out or appears in public without being attended by one or more Highlanders in full Highland costume, and her pipers accompany her wherever she takes up her residence. How different from the spirit which prevailed a century and a half ago and conceived the act of 1746.

Mr. Adam regrets that while the *men's* dress has been so honourably perpetuated, the dress worn by the *women* has now become entirely a relic of the past. This is no doubt true so far as the old *Arisad* is concerned; but fortunately Highland ladies are not, even in our day, without a sentiment in favour of tartan. They may not wear the *Arisad* of primitive days, for various reasons. It would hardly suit nineteenth century ideas of a lady's costume; but tartans are used for various parts of a lady's dress, and a modern "tartan warehouse" will produce in homespun or silk any tartan garment that may be desired. Cloaks, jackets, and ribbons are fashionable, and coming greatly into use. It is good for the home industries in the Highlands and Islands, and on this account ought to be encouraged and supported. Those who may be in doubt as to the clan tartan they are entitled to wear cannot do better than consult Mr. Adam's work, to which reference has been made, on the point. They will there find the fullest information on the subject.

(*To be concluded*).

ORAN DHONNACHAIDH SIOSAL.

DUNCAN CHISHOLM'S SONG.

ABOUT sixty years ago, a poor cottar named Duncan Chisholm, who lived on The Chisholm's estate in Strathglass, was caught by one of the estate officials in the act of carrying away a stick from the woods. An altercation ensued between the two which ended in Duncan threatening to strike the official on the mouth. Proceedings were taken by the estate Law-Agent to eject the poor man from his cottage. In his distress he went for advice to the late Mr. Alexander Fraser, tacksman, Mauld—Fear Mhault—a gifted enthusiastic large-hearted Highlander, held in high esteem by the family of Chisholm of Chisholm. Fraser, to begin with, adopted a novel method of helping Duncan. On the spur of the moment he composed some verses, which he could do with ease; got Duncan to commit them to memory and adopt them as his own. The Chisholm of the day—Captain Duncan Chisholm of the Coldstream Guards—did not often visit Strathglass, but happened to do so at that time. Fraser immediately took advantage of this, and taking Duncan along with him—having drilled him for this occasion—made his way to the Castle. He laid the case before The Chisholm, adding that although the poor man was nervous and awkward in the presence of noblemen, he was a long way above his fellows in intellect and intelligence, a bit of a bard; and had put his distress, fears and hopes on that occasion into verse. Duncan was brought before the Chief, recited the verses Fraser composed, and went home with the assurance that he would not be turned out of his cot. I herewith give the song which is well worth preserving in the *Celtic Monthly*, where it now appears for the first time in print, and also a free translation which will give the English reader some idea of its contents. I often heard some of the verses in my boyhood's days in Strathglass, and lines of them are still fresh in my memory, but for the entire song I am indebted to Mr. James Fraser, Mauld, a worthy son of the worthy father who composed it.

A. M.

DHAOINE, chuala sibh 'n lonnsaidh
 Thug a' bhruid Ballingall.
Air mo chur as an dùthaich,
Ged b'e m' dhùthchas bhi ann,
Ach tha sgeul ann a chàirdean
Gum beil furtachd air bonn;
Ann an caisteal a shinns'radh
Tha mo ghaol am fear donn.

Ga m' chur à làirich mo bhothain
'S e air torran bochd lom,
Gun àirneis, gun earras,
Gun fhear ann gun fhonn;
'S mi gun dò-bheart gun dolaidh,
Gun choire gun chall,

YE have heard of the effort
 The lowlander made,
To deprive me of country,
Of shelter and bread;
And yet in the castle
I'm hopeful there's aid,
In the halls of his fathers
Still rules the brown-hair'd.

To turn me out homeless
From hearth and from cot,
That stands poorly furnished
Upon a bare spot,
Because, when provoked,
A slap on the mouth

Ach gu'n do thogair mi leog
Thoirt do bhlad an fhir Ghalld'.

'S e ri gleadhraich 'us mionnan
Air son bioran gun suim,
Ach ciod a b' urrainn mi dheanamh
'N uair bha maid' air mo dhruim?
Thubhairt e mòran droch oilean
Nach aithrisear leam,
Cuir thir air mo chinneadh,
Cantainn " Hielanman " rium.

Gu 'n deach' clèirich a' sgriobadh
Domh bàirlinn bha cruaidh,
'S thàinig carraid dha liubhairt
Ma' ri dithis dhe 'n t-sluagh,
Ainm siorraim 'us " nòtair "
Ann an òrdugh chuir suas,
Ach 's e deireadh mo sgeuil duibh
Thàinig m' èudal gu tuath.

'Se mo cheist am fear duineil,
Fear daimheil gun ghruaim,
Fear fearail, fear smiorail,
Fear is aithne do 'n t-sluagh ;
Fear an fhòghluim 's an oilean
'S am beil aithn' agus uaisle,
Ceann-cinnidh nan Glaiseach
An Siosalach suaire'.

Ceann-feadhna mo chinnidh,
'U s ceannas mo shluaigh,
Fear m' ainm 'us mo shloinnidh,
Gu 'n chuir sid orm uaill ;
Ma ni thusa rium fàbhar
Fhir mo ghràidh 's mi 'n càs cruaidh,
Cha dàn le Mac Thàmhais,
Ciod 's bochd mi, mo luaidh.

Mo cheist teaghlach na h-aoidhe
Cha be ghnàth dhuibh bhi crion,
'N uair bhiodh éiginn no càs oirnn
Do 'm b' àbhuist ar dion ;
Na bhur glinn 'us bhur giùbhsaich
Gheibhte craobh agus fiadh,
Gun eagal gun chùram,
Gun iomaguin 'gun fhiamh.

Ged tha Donnachadh bochd Siosal
Gun mhisneach gun treòir,
Tha Donnachadh Siosal 's a' chaisteal
Tha tapaidh gu leòir,
Na mhaith'nas mòr farsuinn
'N tir Ghlaisich nam bò,
'S cha chuir e fhear-cinnidh
Air imrich ri 'bheò.

Nach leat fhein Inbhir-chanich
'Srath, monadh, 'us glinn !
'S leat Afric àrd mbolach,
'S leat Comar 's Cnoc-fhinn ;
'S leat dà thaobh an t-srath bhoidich,
'S gur a sòlasaich leam,
'S cha 'n fhaod an Gall salach
Mo chuir dheth do ghrunnd.

I threatened to give
The rude churl from the South.

He was noisy, offensive,
Abusive to me,
Because I had taken
A worthless small tree ;
He spoke with contempt
Of my country and clan,
And called me, with bluster
And scorn, " Hielanman."

A summons, regarding
My taking the tree,
Was served by a legal
Stern bailiff on me,
Scribe, Sheriff, and Lawyer
Left nothing undone ;
But the best of my news is
My lord has come home.

My lord is the manly,
The kindly, the true,
The noble with virtues
Possessed but by few,
The learned, the accomplished
Refined gentleman,
The pride of his kinsmen,
The chief of my clan.

High chief of my people,
Exalted and dear,
Whose name and whose surname,
I'm proud that I bear,
If thou wilt befriend me
In this my sad plight,
Thy hard-hearted servants
My life cannot blight.

Not wont were thy fathers
For tree or for deer,
From glen or from clachan,
Their clansmen to clear,
Large-hearted, free-handed
They always have been,
And ready from hardship
The needy to screen.

Though poor Duncan Chisholm
Lacks courage and might,
Duncan Chisholm of Erchless
The wrong shall put right ;
His pardon extendeth
Where e'er dwells his men,
And he shall not send Duncan
Away from the glen.

Is not thine Invercannich
And far reaching glens,
Knockfin, Comar, Affric,
Green meadows and bens ;
Both sides of the valley,
Tracts bonnie and grand,
And shall a low Southron
Turn me off your land.

'Nuair bu Chaiptein 'san arm thu
Gum b' ainmeil thu, luaidh,
'S gum bu mhiosal thu, ghraidh,
Ann an Geard-nan-Sru'-fuar,
Bha thu duineil mar b' àbhuist,
'S bha thu tlath mar bu dual,
Nis bho 'n shealbhaich thu d' oighreachd
Gun robh'n " stoil " ud dhuit buan.

'Se sgeul ùr tha ri aithris
Chuir mi 'n àrdan 's am fonn,
Tha sinne 'n ar Gaidheil
'S tha e nàdurra dhuinn—
Mac an ionad an àrmuinn
A bha ghnàth os ar cinn,
An tir mhearail nan àrd-bheann
Far an d' àraicheadh sinn.

Bheireadh aigneadh 'us inntinn
Dhuinn striochdadh gu rèidh,
Agus seasamh gu dileas
Ri cinn ar cuid trèubh,
Mar rinn m'athair 's mo shinns'readh,
'S mo mhuintir gu lèir,
Mar dh' aithn' Maois anns a' Bhiobull
'Sa dh' fhag e sgriobta na dhèidh.

Ach a dh' aindeoin an t-saoghail
No aon ni tha ann,
Na caill daimh do dhùthchais,
Na d' dùthaich nam beann,
Ach cuimhnich a ghaolich
Sliochd nan laoich a bh' ann,
'S na bi call do chuid daoine
Air son slaodairean Ghall.

When thou captained the "Coldstreams,"
The brave and the smart,
Thou wert famed 'mongst thy comrades
For kindness of heart ;
And the virtues that always
Adorned thy race
Are thine, and well fits thee
To fill the chief's place.

The theme is a new one
That runs through my song,
But still to the race
Of the Gael we belong,
And joy to have o'er us
Unbroken thy line,
In the land of the torrent
High mountain and pine.

Whatever befalls us
'Tis ours to submit,
For this we're commanded
In Holy old writ ;
And to stand by our chiefs
Ever faithful and true,
This our fathers have done
And we also shall do.

But whate'er be the trend
Of the world in thy day,
The olden traditions
Put thou not away,
Forget not the offspring
Of heroes of worth,
Nor lose them for slouchy
Soft sons of the South.

M. MACRAE, GAIRLOCH.

MR. MURDOCH MACRAE traces his descent from one of the most prominent families of the clan. He is fifth in direct line from " Iain Breac," Chamberlain to, and foster brother of, Kenneth Mòr, third Earl of Seaforth. Iain Breac was the youngest son of the Rev. Farquhar Macrae, progenitor of the Inverinate branch, who claim the chiefship of the clan.

Mr. Macrae was born on 17th December, 1847, at Wester Keppoch, Carr, Kintail, of which his father, William Macrae, was joint tenant with his two brothers. His mother was also of the clan. He was brought up at Achnagart, and attended school at Shiel-bridge and Plockton, Lochalsh, where he gave promise of a successful career. He next proceeded to Edinburgh University, and took up the study of medicine, although his strongest desire was to follow the military profession. It is probable enough he would have given scope to his martial ambition had it not been that he met with a great misfortune which entirely altered his prospects. He caught a chill during the session of 1864, which brought on acute inflammation, followed by paralysis, completely prostrating him. He has never recovered the full use of his limbs, and can hardly move hand or foot. Mr. Macrae's noble struggle to support himself in spite of such overwhelming difficulties is a reflex of the indomitable and independent spirit of the man. To most people such an effort would seem hopeless, yet Mr. Macrae set himself cheerfully to the task, and, we are glad to say, has achieved a surprising measure of success. Settling at Gairloch, in his native county. he started fishing stations there, and in various parts of the Highlands, and while earning his own livelihood has done much to improve the condition of the fishermen, by procuring for them better boats and gear. He had his "ups and downs," as all business men have, but that he has earned not only his subsistence but the respect and confidence of all with whom he came in contact, reflect the greatest credit upon the integrity and high principle of this worthy clansman.

He has taken his share in public affairs, and has done good service on the school and parochial boards. While a Unionist in Irish politics, he is a thorough Liberal in all matters affecting the welfare of his countrymen. His report to

M. MACRAE.

the Royal Commission on the Highlands and Islands on the crofting and fishery questions was admitted to be the best of the hundreds of papers sent in.

We hope that Mr. Macrae will enjoy long life and prosperity. To those who lose heart and falter in the hard struggle of life Mr. Macrae's example should prove an inspiration and encouragement. No one need despair when he, with so many disadvantages, succeeded.

DEEDS THAT WON THE EMPIRE.

By JOHN MACKAY, C.E., J.P., Hereford.

THE CAPTURE OF MANILA, 1762.

(*Continued from page* 189).

IT was now evident that the Archbishop would defend himself to the last. The operations against the city were pushed forward with unremitting vigour, and after batteries for cannon and mortars were raised, the bombardment continued day and night.

"The front we were obliged to attack"-- wrote Colonel Draper—"was defended by the bastions of St. Diego and St. Andrew, with willous and retired flanks, a ravelin which covered the Royal Gate, a wet ditch, covered way and glacis. The bastions were in excellent order, and lined with a great number of fine brass cannon."

The Colonel's force was too small to completely invest a city of such magnitude as Manila, two sides of which were constantly open to those who poured in provisions, and to the hordes of armed militia, of whose services the Marquis de Villa Medina, commandant of the place, fully availed himself. The attacks of those hordes from time to time molested rather than obstructed the progress of the besiegers, and by frequent acts of savage cruelty provoked the most dreadful retaliation. Several British seamen when straggling along the coast were murdered by them. They even perpetrated the same cruelty upon an officer, Lieut. Tryar, whom Colonel Draper had sent to the city with a flag of truce, accompanied by the Archbishop's nephew, who had been taken prisoner. Tryar's body was mutilated "in a manner too shocking to mention, and in their rage and fury, they mortally wounded the other young gentleman who tried to save him."

On the 1st October there was a dreadful tempest of wind accompanied by a deluge of rain; the fleet was in great peril, and all communication with it was cut off. To raise the spirit of the people the Archbishop announced "that an Angel from Heaven had gone forth to destroy the British like the host of Sennacherib." This illusion was of brief continuance, for, notwithstanding the fury of the tempest, the soldiers and seamen completed a new battery for 24-pounders and one for 13-inch mortars, the roaring of the waves on the beach preventing the Spaniards from hearing the workmen who toiled at their task all night with unflagging energy.

About three hours before daylight on the 4th, more than 1000 Pampangoes, or native soldiers, attacked the cantonment of the seamen. They were encouraged by the conviction that the incessant rain would render firearms useless, and they stealthily approached, favoured by a quantity of thick bushes that bordered a rivulet by the bed of which they crept unseen during the dark. Our gallant seaman though taken completely by surprise, and unable from the darkness to learn who or where their assailants were, maintained their ground till daybreak, when a strong picket of Draper's own regiment attacked the enemy in flank and completely routed them with a loss of 300 killed. Although armed only with bows, arrows, and lances, they rushed up to the muzzle of our muskets and died like beasts of prey, gnawing with their teeth the bayonets that pierced them. In this affair Captain Porter of the Norfolk, man-of-war, and many seaman were killed.

At the same time when the Pampangoes made this sortie, another was made by them at a different point. The Sepoys who occupied a church gave way before them, and the building was instantly taken possession of by Spanish musketeers of the Royal regiments. The field-pieces were brought up to dislodge them. They were driven back with the loss of seventy men, but not before Captain Strachan of Draper's regiment, the old 79th, and forty more men were killed and wounded. After this the Pampangoes lost heart, and all of them except 1800 fled from the city and left it to its fate.

The fire from the garrison now became faint, while that of the besiegers became stronger than ever, and ere long a practicable breach was made. In such circumstances it might naturally have been expected that the governor would have offered to capitulate to save the lives and property of the inhabitants. No such proposal was made, and what was still more strange, the Commandant neither attempted to repair the works nor made any preparation to defend the breach. Colonel Draper, therefore, determined to bring matters to a speedy issue. At daybreak on the 6th the troops were under arms, and advanced towards the breach in the Bastion of St. Andrew, where a body of Spanish troops appeared, but on a few shells exploding amongst them they retired. Says Colonel Draper:—"We took immediate advantage of this, and by the signal of a general discharge of our artillery and mortars, rushed furiously to the assault under cover of a thick smoke that blew directly on the town. Sixty volunteers of different corps under Lieut. Russell of the 49th led the way, supported by the grenadiers of that regiment. The engineers, with the pioneers and other workmen to clear the way, enlarge the breach and make lodgments in case the enemy should have been too strongly intrenched in the gorge of the bastion, followed. Colonel Monson and Major More were at the head of two grand divisions of the 79th, the battalion of seamen advanced next, sustained by other two divisions of the 79th, the Company's troops closing the rear." In this order with bayonets fixed, they rushed onwards with incredible ardour, and swarmed the breach with loud cheers; the Spaniard fired a scattered volley upon them and retired. But little resistance was offered, except at the Royal Gate, where Major More was shot dead by an arrow, and in the Grand Square from the galleries and lofty houses of the Regiment Royal of Spain, from which a brisk fire came, and the arrows of the Pampangoes were shot, with deadly aim.

In the Guard House above the Royal Gate 100 Spaniards who refused all terms were put to the sword, and 300 more, endeavouring to escape over the rapid river, were drowned. The Archbishop and principal officers retired into the Town-house, where after a time they capitulated. The humanity and generosity of the British Commanders saved Manila from general pillage, but a ransom of four million dollars was demanded for this relaxation of the laws of war. The Spanish officers, to the number of 88, were all released upon their parole of honour, amongst whom were Spanish nobles of high rank. There were taken no less than 554 pieces of brass, iron cannon, and mortars, and a vast quantity of all kinds of munition of war.

The old 79th, Draper's regiment, to which he was much attached, was greatly commended by its gallant Colonel for its services in India and at Manila. He stated in his despatch that since it left England it had lost 23 officers and 800 men in various battles, and extended the glory of His Majesty's Arms to the verge of Asia.

But the regiment was reduced, when after the peace of 1763, all corps above the No. 70 were disbanded.

(Concluded).

THE CLAN GREGOR SOCIETY spent recently a delightful day in the Macgregor country. The young chief, Sir Malcolm Macgregor, Bart., and many distinguished clansmen from all parts of the kingdom, took part in the gathering.

A NOBLE ACHIEVEMENT.

BY AGNES WALKER.

CHAPTER III.—(Continued from page 195).

WHEN Mr. John Haggart, land agent, stepped into the conveyance which stood waiting for him next day at the door of his chambers in Argyle Square, Oban, and was driven off in the direction of Auchnasheen Castle, he felt no uneasiness as to the cause of the summons he had received, or anticipated any trouble for himself in connection with it whatsoever. The truth was, he had been so long accustomed to act in all matters connected with the estate precisely as he pleased, and without any fear of interference from his employer, or being called to account for anything he did, that the fact that he was about to suffer for his misdeeds—that justice had at last overtaken him and would crush him relentlessly, was something which lay very far indeed from his thoughts. But when, on arriving at the Castle, he was shown into the library, and found himself in the presence not only of Lord Dunallan but of Lady Dunallan as well, the surprise he felt gave place to a feeling of uneasiness which showed itself in a certain embarrassment of manner as he advanced into the room, and was in contrast with his usual air of self-complacency and self-importance. He was a short, stout man, of a rubicund countenance, with iron-grey hair, and deep-set blue eyes which had a cold steely glitter in them.

When greetings had been exchanged, Lord Dunallan at once plunged into matters by requesting to be informed why Duncan MacDonald had been served with a notice to quit.

The factor's face grew a shade paler, and for a few seconds he was too much taken aback to be able to think of any reply. Then he pulled himself together, determined to meet and overcome all difficulties. He knew he was in a fix; but it was not the first time in his life he had been in that position and out of which he had triumphantly brought himself; consequently, he did not contemplate failure now.

"My lord," he began, blandly, "I am very glad to have an opportunity of speaking with you upon this matter. I intended, as soon as I knew your lordship's arrival here, to seek an interview for the purpose of laying before your lordship the whole facts of the case. It's just this, my lord, there's not a more discontented, more dissatisfied, and more troublesome lot on the face of the earth than crofters; and if there's one of them more discontented, more dissatisfied, and more troublesome than any of the others — it's Duncan MacDonald. There's nothing that goes on in and around Scarba but he must have his hand into and his say about.

A quarrelsome, interfering man, for ever meddling with things he has no business with whatever. In fact, if there's mischief to be made anywhere, he's the man for it. However, his quarrelsomeness and his meddlesomeness might have been put up with had other things been right. But there's one thing that must be done—the property on the estate must be looked after. And it's just because I'm determined this shall be done, and that those who won't will have to make room for those who will, that Duncan MacDonald was served with a notice to quit. There's no other way, my lord, of keeping things right. And the fact is, MacDonald's letting everything on the croft go to wreck and ruin."

"What!" said Lord Dunallan, sharply. "MacDonald letting everything on the croft go to wreck and ruin? Why, I was at Scarba yesterday and saw the place for myself, and was much struck with the well-cared-for-look which everything about it had."

"Oh, that's easily explained, easily explained," said the factor, unabashed, after a minute's hesitation, lifting his hands and letting them fall again. "If MacDonald knew your lordship was to be at Scarba he'd have everything in readiness for the visit. Trust MacDonald for that. But, of course, if your lordship wishes it, the notice to quit can be withdrawn. The MacDonalds have been long on the place; and I know your lordship doesn't like to part with old tenants. And I may say, too, that though the notice was sent there was no intention that it should be enforced. All that was meant was just to give MacDonald a bit of a fright, and to see if he couldn't be induced to give a little more attention to his own affairs, and a little less to other people's."

"There was no intention that the notice should be enforced?" said Lord Dunallan, whose patience was fast giving way. "Perhaps you will tell me whether this reads as if the notice had not been intended to be enforced?"—putting into the factor's hand his own letter. "I should like an explanation of it!"

The factor stared at the letter which he held in his hand, his face pale to the lips. He had not calculated upon the production of this condemnatory bit of evidence; and for a minute or two he remained as if all power of movement and speech had left him. Then with the look of a man, despairing and desperate, he said, "My lord, I admit that I did wrong in writing this letter. But if your lordship will have patience with me for a little, I think I shall be able to explain everything satisfactorily. The fact is, in dealing with MacDonald's case, I felt that only strong measures would be of any use. And I must now tell you, my lord, what I had hoped would never require to be told, that

MacDonald is in the habit of speaking about your lordship in the most disrespectful terms. I have myself heard him——."

He got no further, for Lady Dunallan had risen to her feet.

"This is intolerable, simply intolerable!" she exclaimed. "I will not believe that Duncan MacDonald, or, indeed, that anyone on the estate ever said a disrespectful word of Lord Dunallan. The tenants and others on the estate do not know everything; but they know enough to be aware of the fact, that many things have been done in Lord Dunallan's name which, had he known of, he would neither have consented to, nor tolerated. And why are you so anxious to rid the estate of Duncan MacDonald? What is it he has done? Only shown himself to be brave enough and manly enough to stand up in defence of a helpless old woman who was being dragged out of her home and taken away to a poorhouse. And why was Mrs. M'Callum taken away to Oban? What was it I said to you a year ago? How have you dared to act in defiance of the orders then given? And had you no pity for a lonely old woman sorrowing for the loss of a son? But you will take immediate steps for the removal of Mrs. M'Callum from the Poorhouse. Lord Dunallan has given directions for her house at Scarba to be got in readiness for her; and by to-morrow we shall expect to be informed that she is again under its roof. After what has happened, it is of course impossible that you can continue to act as Lord Dunallan's factor. There is much that will have to be undone; but neither Lord Dunallan nor I will rest until what is wrong has, as far as possible, been put right. And if you are ever called upon to fill a similar position of trust and responsibility, let me urge you to prove yourself worthy of it. I know Lord Dunalla has some matters to talk over with you. So I will leave now, and will bid you good-bye."

She turned away—the cowed and miserable-looking man at the other end of the writing table not daring to lift his eyes to her, or to utter a word in extenuation of his misdeeds, or even to crave pardon for them.

* * * * * *

Since that day, a new order of things, bringing happiness and prosperity to all concerned, has been established and maintained on Lord Dunallan's estate. There is a new factor—a man very different from the old; but trustworthy and excellent as he is, it is in Lord Dunallan's own hands that the real management of his property lies. He has come to understand that if any good is to be looked for he must be at the head of affairs himself. And in the work to which he has so nobly set himself, he has found in his wife just the helper and the counsellor that he needed. Indeed, it is not too much to say that but for her he would never have accomplished what he has. And so greatly has he come to lean on her help and her guidance, that, in all matters connected with the estate, he will do nothing without consulting her; while the trust and the confidence thus inspired have given birth to that love and that reverence for his wife which makes Lady Dunallan account herself one of the happiest of women.

(CONCLUDED).

CLAN EWEN.
MacEwens in Lochaber.
SLIOCHD EOGHAIN.

By R. S. T. MacEwen.
(*Continued from page 199*).

He set out accordingly, and happened to light in that part of the country where Lochiel's estate now lies. Here he informed himself of the character and circumstances of the chief who resided there, and understood that he was a man of a large estate, and had a great number of friends and dependents, and withal had a fair and excellent young lady to his daughter. This was a foundation sufficient for our Wry-Nose Knight to build his hopes and future expectations upon." He accordingly made himself known to the chief, and as his fame as a warrior and man of great strength had preceded him, he was well received and hospitably entertained. This chief was MacMartin, Baron of Letterfinlay, and chief of a clan in Lochaber at that time. "In short, a bargain was soon struck for the daughter, who was as well pleased as the father with the offer of a husband so much to her liking; for strength of body, vigorous and sinewy limbs, and undaunted courage, were in those days the best qualifications to recommend a man to the affections of a lady." So, having married the daughter and led the clan in all their battles against neighbouring clans and enemies with conspicuous success, he eventually attained to the chiefship; and "this is the story which the Highland bards have recorded of this great progenitor of the Camerons."

Here we find not a Danish Prince of 404, arriving under kingly protection, and with an introduction from Fergus II., but a Celtic adventurer, many centuries later, from Dumbartonshire. Of his family history nothing is stated, but he was without estate or powerful relatives or friends. He was a soldier of fortune on the look-out to better his position, and in this he was successful. From the time he assumed the chief-ship, the Clan MacMartin and its dependent septs became known as Clan Camshron or Cameron.

This chief was not only skilful in war, but was a man of powerful physique and giant strength. Dumbartonshire in early times appears to have been the home of Celtic giants. We have this Cambro able to lift a 500lb. stone with the greatest ease. In the new Statistical Account of Scotland (Parish of Luss), we are told it was a place of refuge for the Highlanders from the earliest times. A powerful tribe of Celts lived at Dumfin, where there are traces of an ancient fortification. The chief, Fian M'Cuel, or Fingal, and his associates are represented as giants, of whom the most extravagant feats are related. An enormous stone or mass of rock is pointed out, which, it is said, Fingal, standing on the top of Benbui, took upon his little finger to throw to the top of Shantran Hill, a distance of several miles, but that not being rightly balanced, it fell into a small brook midway between the two! Then there is the tradition of the MacEwen giant who carried a stone coffin from the loch to the churchyard at Luss —having the coffin under one arm and the lid under the other. There is a curious similarity in these various feats of strength. Allowing for the necessary amount of fiction attaching to legends of the kind, we may fairly assume that these early western Celts were a powerful race, so distinguished for athletic performances as to render these worthy of transmission in Celtic folklore. It seems not improbable, too, having regard to the Cameron tradition, that Cambro was of this race of Celtic giants.

It is not stated when Cambro appeared in Lochaber, but it is manifest it could not have been so early as the time of Fergus II. (404), or for many centuries afterwards. It is more likely to have been in the twelfth or thirteenth century. Originally the septs of Clan Chattan and Clan Cameron followed the Maormor of Moray; and according to Gregory, separated about the middle of the fourteenth century. Mackenzie points out that Gregory, who agrees with the other authorities, states that the Camerons, as far back as he could trace, had their seat in Lochaber; and appeared to have been first connected with the Macdonalds of Islay in the reign of Robert the Bruce—that is to say, in the beginning of the fourteenth century.

(*To be concluded.*)

"Rob Donn's Songs and Music" is now published, the press reviews being of the most complimentary character. The Rev. Adam Gunn contributes a chapter which makes short work of the nonsense which one or two persons, who ought to have known better, published in regard to the bard being a Calder. Mr Gunn produces an array of evidence which proves beyond any doubt that the great Reay Country bard was a Mackay.

W. T. MACKAY.

MRS. W. T. MACKAY

THE CELTIC MONTHLY:

A MAGAZINE FOR HIGHLANDERS.

Edited by JOHN MACKAY, Glasgow.

No. 12 Vol. VII.]　　　SEPTEMBER, 1899.　　　[Price Threepence.

W. T. MACKAY, MIDDLESBROUGH.

THE ancestors of the distinguished family to which Mr. Mackay belongs, hailed originally from the neighbourhood of Tain, Ross-shire, and are believed to be cadets of the Melness branch of the clan. His grandfather, Andrew Mackay, LL.D., F.R.S., was a man of great scientific attainments, and in addition to a professorship of mathematics, held the responsible post of examiner for Trinity House, London, and also for the East India Company; and his father, George Gray Mackay, in conjunction with an elder brother, John Selby Mackay, took a principal part in founding the Grangemouth Coal Company. His brother, Major A. Y. Mackay, is the popular president of the Clan Mackay Society; while his cousin is Provost of Grangemouth.

Mr. Mackay was born 31st July, 1847; educated at Dollar Academy; and thereafter spent five years in the office of the Grangemouth Coal Company. In 1870, he went to Germany to study languages; but having heard on arrival at Hamburg that war was declared with France, he returned to Scotland with one of the last steamers which managed to escape the blockade of the Elbe. The two following years were, however, spent in Germany and France studying the languages. On 1st January, 1875, he settled in Middlesbrough as manager for the firm of George G. Mackay, the well-known ship-owner and merchant of Grangemouth. Eight years later he commenced business on his own account as steamship broker and commission agent; and also acts as agent for Messrs. James Rankine & Sons' well-known line of steamers to Rotterdam, and for steamers trading between Bilboa and Middlesbrough.

Although absent from Scotland for so many years, he has never ceased to take an interest in affairs affecting his native land. The Clan Mackay Society (of which he and his brothers and cousins are all life members), naturally claims his special interest, and he intends taking part with his brothers in the tour in the Reay country which the members of the clan have arranged to commence from Thurso on 5th September. Mr. Mackay has never seen the ancient home of the Mackays, and looks forward with keen interest to meeting his clansmen in the Mackay country, and to visiting the romantic places familiar by name to those acquainted with the history of the clan. He was present at the Clan Gathering held in Glasgow last winter, at which his brother presided.

In September, 1883, he married Lilian, second daughter of Mr. D. D. Wilson, Bon Accord Lodge, Middlesbrough, a native of Aberdeenshire (General Manager for the Stockton and Middlesbrough Water Board), and has three children surviving. We have much pleasure in giving Mrs. Mackay's portrait along with that of her husband.

AUTUMN IN THE HIGHLANDS.

AROUND the mountain's brow the mist wreaths twine,
Like ghosts of ancient storms they come and go,
Haunting the regions of eternal snow,
That weird, mysterious world whose border line
Man may not cross. On the wide slopes combine
Green brake and purple heather's vivid glow,
And stretching to the horizon's verge below
The crystal loch and dancing wavelets shine.
By hoary, lichened scaur, in dusky glen,
On shell-strewn shore on lonely, wind-swept isle—
On solitude of moor or lofty Ben,
The eager heart may cease from care awhile,
And con within its depths the calm content,
Of Nature's peace and grandeur eloquent.

JANET A. M'CULLOCH.

THE CLAN MACFARLANE.

THE early history of the Clan Macfarlane is so interlinked with the House of the ancient Earls of Lennox that the history of one family is practically the history of the other, until the extinction of the line with the eighth earl of the original House of Lennox.

The founder of the clan, one Gilchrist, was indeed the younger brother of Maldowen, the third Earl of Lennox, who granted him a charter making him overlord of the lands of Arrochar. If further proof of this near kinship between the families was required it is found in the Lennox charters, several of which Gilchrist endorsed as a witness. He is described therein as *frater comitis*—brother of the Earl. *Verbum sat sapienti.* Mr. Skene, the famous Highland historian, states that with the exception of the Clan Donnachaidh the Clan Pharlan is the only one the descent of which from the ancient earls of the district wherein their possessions were situated, may be established by the authenticity of a charter. Of all the native earls of Scotland those of this district alone have had a foreign origin assigned to them. It is supposed, runs the story, that Alwyn MacArchill, an Angle of Northumbria, was father of the first Earl of Lennox. The first known Earl of Lennox undoubtedly bore the name of Alwyn, as did the second earl, and it is equally certain that an Alwyn MacArchill repeatedly witnessed charters of David I. The Northumbrian's father was named Arkill, and he was connected with a certain Archillus, son of Aykfrith, a Saxon who had large estates in Northumbria and fled to Scotland in 1070 to evade the vengeance of William the Conqueror. Skene, however, scouts this suggestion, maintaining there is nothing to support the theory except the resemblance of names. He in his turn traces the origin of the family back to Lughaidh, King of Munster, of the line of Heber, through his son Corc, and gives the descent from father to son, through Maine Leamna, Machdovnaigh, Muredach, Alwyn, first Earl of Lennox, Alwyn, second earl, and Maldowen, third earl, whose brother Gilchrist, as we have seen, was the founder of the Clan Macfarlane. So much for what is almost pre-historic ancestry and dry reading at the best.

It was not until a great-grandson of Gilchrist's assumed the chiefship that the clan became known by the name it has since borne. This chief's name in Gaelic was Parlan or Bartholomew. The real founder of the clan is, however, considered to have been Malcolm, the son of Parlan, as it was he who received the charter, dated Bellach, May 1th, 1351, confirming him in the lands of Arrochar in return for service to the king.

The seventh chief of the Macfarlanes had not long succeeded to his inheritance when the ancient original line of the Earls of Lennox became extinct. This was in the year 1460, and the earldom and estates were claimed by three families, two of which were the chiefs of Macfarlan and the Stewarts of Darnley. The latter were successful and took possession in the year 1488, when the clans formerly allied to the earldom, of which that of Macfarlan was the principle, disassociated themselves from their former allegiance. The chief of Macfarlan's claim was that of heir male. Undoubtedly a just one from his point of view, and he took the field against the more successful heirs. The fighting that ensued proved disastrous to the clan. The chief and his family perished in defence of what they considered their just rights, many of the clansmen fell and the remainder were dispersed to find refuge in remote parts of the country. Happily for the descendants of Macfarlan to-day, their forefathers were saved from utter annihilation through the efforts of a kinsman, Andrew Macfarlan, who had a claim of gratitude upon the Stewarts, and furthermore had married a daughter of the House of Darnley, the new Earls of Lennox. He rehabilitated the clan and recovered most of their hereditary possessions. Andrew, though the saviour of his family, was not in the direct line of the chiefship and so jealous were the clansmen of preserving the direct line intact that they refused him the title and dignity of chief, he and his son, Sir John Macfarlan, merely bearing the subordinate title of captain of the clan.

The clan in gratitude for their salvation now returned to their allegiance to the House of Lennox, an unfortunate connection for them, as subsequent events proved. In the 16th century Duncan Macfarlan with 300 of his kith and kin joined Lennox and Glencairn's army of 1544, and, of course, was on the defeated side at the battle of Glasgow-Muir. Forfeiture of lands was again suffered, and only the intercession of powerful friends at court obtained their restoration under the privy seal. When Lennox returned from England, whither he had flown, Macfarlan could not join him personally, being strictly observed by the Government, but unshakenly loyal to his patron and preserver of former days, he sent his kinsman, Walter Macfarlan of Tarbet, with this time 400 men to swell the army of the invaders. It is stated by Holinshed that these Highlanders did very excellent service, acting as light troops and guides to the main body, which was composed of English troops loaned by Henry VIII. The warlike Duncan perished eventually at the battle of

Pinkie in 1547, on which fatal field many of his clansmen fell around him.

The battle of Langside was the next episode in the history of the clan, and this time they were on the side of victory. Indeed the clansmen of Macfarlan were instrumental in turning the tide of battle at the crucial moment. "Macfarlan," so the story runs, "came up with three hundred of his wild caterans in the hottest of the fight, and falling fiercely on the flank of the Queen's army, threw them into irretrievable disorder and thus mainly contributed to decide the fortune of the day." The clansmen took three of Queen Mary's standards in the fray,

which were preserved for many generations in the family. Macfarlan's reward for this notable achievement was not very tangible, and does not reflect creditably upon the munificence of the Regent Murray, being merely the bestowal of the crest below referred to, which sufficiently flattered the vanity of the chief. Doubtless the rank and file took part in the general loot which followed battle in those lawless days, and as fighting was as the breath of their nostrils to them, they would return to the wilds of Loch Sloy fully satisfied with their deeds. The Macfarlans were now as loyal supporters of the reigning House of Stewart as before they were

BANNACHRA CASTLE- ANCIENT SEAT OF THE COLQUHOUN CHIEFS.

uncompromising opponents, an attachment which however led to their ultimate dispersal.

But I anticipate. In the disturbed times following the decapitation of the unfortunate Charles I. of Great Britain, they remained Royalist to the core. Twice Macfarlan was besieged in his own house by the Roundheads, and his castle of Invernglas was burned down by Cromwell's troops. It still stands a melancholy ruin. Although always a small clan, due to their constant engagement in every minor war which was waged in the neighbourhood, they were most turbulent and predatory. By the Act of the Estates of 1587 they were

declared to be one of the clans for whom the chief was made responsible; by another act passed in 1594 they were denounced as being in the habit of committing theft, robbery, and oppression; and in July, 1624, many of the clan were tried and convicted of these crimes. Many were punished, some pardoned, while others were banished to the Highlands of Aberdeenshire and to Strathaven in Banffshire, where they assumed the names of MacCandy, Greisock, MacJames, Stewart, and MacInnes. One of their forays, in company with an equally turbulent section of the MacGregors, which occurred in July 1592, is fully described. They descended upon the low country of Dumbarton-shire, and committed vast ravages, especially upon the territory of the Colquhouns of Luss and Rossdhu. Sir Humphrey Colquhoun at the head of his vassals, and accompanied by several neighbouring gentlemen, attacked the invaders and after a bloody encounter which continued until nightfall, the Colquhouns were defeated, Sir Humphrey retiring to Bannachra Castle which is situated—the ruins still stand—at the foot of the hill of Benibuie, on the north side, in the parish of Luss. A party of the Highland allies pursued him and sat down before the castle. Now occurred an act of treachery which cannot be palliated, the only excuse to be offered being the war customs of the period. One of Sir Humphrey's retainers agreed to turn traitor at a price. While conducting the knight to his sleeping apartment up a winding stair he caused the glare of his torch to reflect in such a way as to make his victim's position evident to the murderers without, when he was passing a loop-hole of the castle. A winged arrow true to its mark entered and pierced the unhappy knight to the heart. Macfarlans of to-day can only lay the unction to their souls that the treacherous shaft came from a Macgregor's bow. The fatal loop-hole can still be seen, though the castle is rapidly falling to decay.

In direct succession there were no less than twenty-three lairds of Macfarlan and the family held their lands, extending from Arrochar round the head of Loch Lomond, for 600 years. The lineal descendant of the chieftains cannot now be traced, and various claimants have arisen for what is now, alas, but an empty title. In a volume, "The Scottish Highlands," it is stated the last scion emigrated to North America early in the 18th century, and from him M. W. W. Macfarlan, a New York barrister, claims to rule. The Irish Macfarlanes claim the title from Macfarlan of Hunstown House, in the county of Dublin, a branch of the family having settled in Ireland in the reign of James II. of Great Britain. But as the clan existed at Arrochar until the fatal rebellion of Prince Charlie in 1745 when they were finally broken up, these claims seem to have but slight foundation. The true descendant will never be known, but as there is nought now to inherit, the lands of Arrochar having passed to the Colquhouns, the matter is not of vast importance. Indeed, perhaps it is better as it is, for each scion of the family can imagine to his satisfaction that he is the lineal heir. While they held sway in Arrochar they were a terror to the more peace-fully disposed farmers of surrounding districts. The peninsula of Rosencath was one of their favourite foraging grounds, and the natives must have been serenely glad when they were rooted out.

The devotional loyalty of the Macfarlans to whichever cause they espoused, the loyalty, approaching worship, of the clansmen to their chief, and their great bravery in every fight in which they took part, must call forth the admiration and applause of every reader. Had the chief succeeded to the Earldom of Lennox, to which according to modern ideas he was justly entitled, the family might now be as powerful as that of MacCailein Mòr himself. They were, however, unfortunately for them-selves, invariably on the losing side in political struggles, except upon the solitary occasion when they threw the weight of their support on the side of Protestanism and James VI. in the scalesagainst Queen Mary and Roman Catholicism. The Macfarlane tartan is not of the order "fashionable" and therefore has not been duly distorted from its original design to meet the exigence of certain garments. The groundwork is red crossed with four stripes, two of green and two of navy blue. The green stripes enclose the blue ones, while an indication of white completes one of the most artistic of the many Highland designs.

The coat of arms, to describe it in other than the somewhat involved and pedantic heraldic language, consists of a shield bearing the St. Andrews Cross upon its surface, and supported on either side by a Highlander whose feet touch a scroll. On the scroll is inscribed the famous battle-cry of the clan "Loch Sloy." Above the shield is a helmet with the visor down, while over that again is the crest earned from the Regent Murray at the battle of Langside for prowess in the field—a demi-savage holding in his right hand a sheaf of arrows and pointing with his left to an imperial crown. The motto, "This I'll defend," is borne upon a scroll above the head of the savage. The clan badge is the cloudberry bush.

Since the days of its greatness the clan has given at least one eminent man to Scotland. I refer to Mr. Walter Macfarlane, who was, as Mr. Skene says, as celebrated among historians as an indefatiguable collector of the ancient records of his country as his progenitors were among the Highland chiefs for their prowess in the field.

Helensburgh.   JAMES MACFARLANE.

"THE LAD WITH THE BONNET OF BLUE."—This spirited song, by Miss Alice C. Macdonell, of Keppoch, which first appeared in our pages some time ago, has just been set to music by Mr. Colin M'Alpine, and is published with pianoforte accompaniment, by Messrs. Cary & Co., London. The song itself is a delightful little composition with word music of it own, but we are pleased to find that Mr. M'Alpine has entered into the spirit of the theme and has wedded the verses to music which has a fine martial ring about it, appropriate to the sentiment of the words. We have pleasure in recommending the song to our readers.

GEORGE MACKAY.

GEORGE MACKAY, New South Wales.

HE LATE GEORGE A. MACKAY of Collwood, near Orange, New South Wales, was born at Dervaig, Island of Mull, in 1819. When he was three years old his father, Lachlan Mackay, removed to Coll. Lachlan was the youngest of four sons of Hugh Mackay, originally of Caithness, who with three sons, William, Donald and George, enlisted in the 79th Cameron Highlanders. Lachlan, the youngest son, also joined the regiment as a piper, his youth preventing him from following the example of his brothers. The father, Hugh, being deemed too old for active service did garrison duty at Malta for some years. Of his sons, William and Donald served through the campaign in Egypt under Sir Ralph Abercrombie, assisted at the bombardment of Copenhagen, fought through the Peninsular war, took part in the memorable retreat of Corunna, under Sir John Moore, and were in the battles of Toulouse and Salamanca. Eventually they had also the glory of participation in the famous fights of Quatre Bras and Waterloo. Throughout these stirring experiences neither of the brothers received a serious wound. George, the third son, meanwhile acted as a recruiting sergeant for the regiment, and the father and Lachlan, the youngest son, remained connected with the garrison at Malta, and afterwards successively in Scotland, Ireland, England, and Canada. One event of note in which the father and sons with their regiment took part, was the funeral of Lord Nelson.

Some years after Waterloo the whole of the members of the family obtained their discharge from the 79th regiment. William settled in Coll; Donald in Ireland; and George in Canada. The father, Hugh, died in Mull, having lost his wife previously at Malta.

Lachlan, the youngest son, on his return to his native land, was apprenticed to a blacksmith-farmer, and on the death of his master succeeded to his business. He married Anne Stewart of Coll; and his family, four sons and three daughters, were all born on that island with the exception of the two eldest sons, John and George, the latter of whom is the subject of this sketch.

In 1837, in response to representations made by Dr. Boyter, an agent of the government, the whole family decided to emigrate to Australia. They joined the ship "Brilliant" at Tobermory and sailed for Sydney, Australia, on 27th September, 1837, reaching their destination one hundred and twelve days later.

George shortly afterwards accepted the position of overseer of Dockairne Farm, near Bathurst. In 1849, on the discovery of gold in California, he sailed for San Francisco, but on reaching that place abandoned his intention of gold-seeking and accepted an appointment in a warehouse instead. Eighteen months afterwards on the outbreak of cholera in San Francisco he returned to Australia, where he continued to reside till his death. He married Margaret Maclean, daughter of Roderick Maclean, formerly of Skye and settled in the neighbourhood of Orange, a flourishing town in New South Wales.

Mr. Mackay took a fair share of the duties of good citizenship during his long sojourn in Orange. He was among the first batch of local town councillors and filled the position of Mayor in 1861. He was an alderman also for a number of years and was returned member of parliament for Orange in 1867. On the expiration of the term of parliament for which he was elected he did not again seek the suffrages of the people. He was a J.P., and took an active interest in various public institutions, and was also an active member of the school board. Throughout his life he was a strong supporter of the local Presbyterian Church in which he filled the office of elder for forty years. His family consisted of eight sons and two daughters of whom seven survive him. One son, a bank manager, met a tragic end at Barrata, N.S.W., a few years since, being shot dead by armed robbers while defending his trust. The surviving members of the family are holding responsible places in the various colonies. One is a bank manager in New Zealand; another a mining accountant at Kalgoorlie, Western Australia; while others occupy the following positions—solicitor, practising in Orange; one, chief draftsman in the department of mines, New South Wales; and another is engaged in the pursuit of horticulture in the same colony.

MR. MACBAIN'S "FURTHER GAELIC WORDS AND ETYMOLOGIES."

MR. MACBAIN'S fresh contribution to his philological Dictionary has been elsewhere gently overhauled by Dargo Duncanson. In the case of some of the disputed derivations it is possible that the final word has not yet been spoken. A wider knowledge of the dialectic varieties of the same word might in some instances at least contribute to clear their origin. Mr. Macbain, for instance, follows Dr. Gillies in giving sionn, fox-glove, as the derivation of breac-sheunan, freckles. Dargo Duncanson, with greater probability suggests sonn, E. Ir., sén, (blessing, sign, luck). Neither, however, takes notice of the form prevalent in the North Highlands (Sutherland, Caithness, etc.). There it is either *breacabhreannaidh*, or *breacabhiannan*. Is it not possible that the rather fanciful *fox-glove* and *luck* derivations must give place to the more prosaic *breac-a-bhian* or spotted skin, which is more direct and descriptive. The H. S. D. spelling of the word (breac-mheanaidh) is misleading. This genesis of breac-shianan is in accordance with well-known phonetic laws ; *b* of bian (skin) aspirates into bh or f ; f when aspirated (fh) is silent ; we thus arrive at breac-eunan or breac-ianan in those dialects in which phonetic decay is at a more advanced stage. This origin has the advantage of explaining the northern and southern dialectic difference of the vowel-sound (eu, ia), coming as it does from an Indo-European base, *breino*. It is hard to see how *sion*, fox-glove, would yield an eu-sound.

(2) *Slaman*, curdled milk, is referred by both authorities to *slam*, a lock of hair or wool. Such a connection, though possible is a little far-fetched. The northern form of the word is *lampan*, which curiously enough, escaped the notice of Dr. Mackintosh-Mackay, in the H. S. Dicty. ; m of lampan is probably intrusive (cp. tombaca from tobacco). *Slamagan*, the sediment of sowens, in the North Highlands, is the same word. The base is *lath-lu* whence *laban* mire, and its variants *lapan* and *lopan* ; also *lathach*. It is just possible that slaman and lampan come from the same root, s of the former being prosthetic (cp. slorg for lorg in Arran). The root meaning of a *thick liquid* is more satisfactory in the case of *slaman* than its resemblance to a lock of hair or wool. If these words have a common origin the intruding m has displaced *p* in *slaman*, and of course the connection with *slam*, a lock of hair, is more apparent than real.

(3) There are several words in Mr. Macbain's list to which some further consideration might well be given. It is difficult to believe that the Sutherland *badhan*, churchyard (rather *baghan*), is from Irish bàbhùin, m. Ir. bódhún (bo, cow, and dùn, a heap). There is no good reason to reject bàgh, bay, as the explanation of bàghan, churchyard. Mr. Macbain derives *pracadair* tithe-collector, from Sc. procutor, Eng. proctor, procurator ; but what about *prac* itself, *the tithes?* It is more scientific to say that *prac*, tithes, yields *prucadair*, tithe-collector, than the reverse. The *prac* was a tenth of the yearly increase, and the Sc. word *fract*, for *fruct*, increase, fruit, is a more likely origin ; *am fract* would easily pass into *am prac* by what is termed provection.

Eirbleach, crippled person, is unknown in the North Highlands, but *eirdeach* is very common in that sense. It is from Sc. birplock, hirple, and is interesting as showing Gadelic dislike of *p* (cp. Carbh, the Lewis name for Parbh, Cape Wrath).

Càpraid, which is also common in the far North, is derived by Mr. Macbain from Lat. crapula. There is a Sc. word *capper*, to seize violently, whose claim to this dialectic word should be considered. *Sèileann*, and *samhag*, two names for the *tick* or sheep-louse, are not etymologised ; to these may be added *sur* (*a* short and *r* slender) which is the Northern term.

One is glad to see so large a contribution of good Gaelic words rescued from oblivion by Mr. Macbain. There are still many claimants waiting for admission, and still some sins of omission and commission to be repented of. In "reading the marches" between Irish and Scottish Gaelic Mr. Macbain has done good service in clearing from our Scottish vocabularies scores of Irish words which never obtained a footing on Scottish soil. Very likely he has gone too far in this direction, but the remedy is easy. The suggestions offered by Dargo Duncanson of taking note of all unusual words in one's native dialect, and committing them to writing, if carried out by a score or two in different parts of Scotland, would very soon enlarge the dimensions of our only philological dictionary. Set phrases and peculiar idioms and words should have a distinct corner in the *Celtic Monthly*, and there is reason to fear that a dread of exposing themselves to the truculent methods of criticism adopted by some of our Gaelic *savants* prevents many from giving to the public their *amateur* attempts at enlarging our Gaelic vocabulary. It is in a study of the dialects that any further progress is to be made in Celtic philology, and in this connection one is glad to observe the paper of the Rev. Charles M. Robertson in the recent Transactions of the Gaelic Society of Inverness, on the Gaelic Dialect of Arran to which with your leave I may refer in a future issue.

Durness ADAM GUNN,

THE HIGHLAND CONTINGENT AT THE ROYAL NATIONAL EISTEDDFOD, CARDIFF.

THIS great and interesting Welsh festival was opened on the 18th July last, and continued on the 19th, 20th, 21st, and 22nd, with unabated vigour and unflagging interest. Present at it were strong contingents from Celtic Brittany, Celtic Ireland, a representative from the Isle of Man, while Celtic Scotland, whose contingent "all plaided and plumed in their array," was the most picturesque of all, as diverse in the hue of their tartans as they were in stature and countenance. The wearers of the tartan lent to the Eisteddfod a variety of colour and form never before seen at this ancient institution of gallant little Wales, all fraternising together in the most friendly manner. There was seen the Highlander conversing with the Breton in the mellifluous language of France, at another moment explaining to his countrymen in English or good Gaelic, the admiration of the Breton at the picturesque costume of the "Montagnards Ecossais," others of his comrades giving the hand of fellowship to the Welsh and Irish, with congratulations in good English or good "broad Scots." There were also seen and heard Breton, Irish, and Highland pipers discoursing the melodies of their various nationalities. The grand harp of Wales was also well to the front at the Gorsedd.

All assembled at the Town Hall, the Arch-druid—preceded by a brass band, and mounted police, the banner of the Eisteddfod, and sword-bearer—went first in a carriage, followed by the presidents and dignitaries of the Eisteddfod, also in carriages, then the chief bards clad in pure white. To the Highland contingent with its pipers was assigned the honour of leading the second division of the procession. Thousands swarmed round in front of the Town Hall. The interest created by Scotia's sons marching through the streets of Cardiff towards the Gorsedd, in their kilts, plaids, sporrans, brooches, plumed and crested bonnets, headed by six pipers playing the "Cock of the North," was extraordinary, indeed indescribable. The two tall Highlanders (Messrs. John Mackay, Hereford, and D. A. S. Mackintosh, Glasgow, both stalwart and handsome men), who led the van were the victims of many a snap-shot. One Cardiff journalist named them "Wallace and Bruce"; another reckoned their stature to be seven feet!

The streets from the Town Hall to the Gorsedd were so densely crowded that the drones of the pipes with their tartan bannerets floated over the heads of the crowd nearest the pavement, packed so dense that none of them could stir, while the cheers were deafening, almost silencing the resounding notes of the pipes.

Arriving at the park where the Gorsedd was held, the mounted police cleared the way to enter, and to march up to the outer circle of Gorsedd boundary, a veritable Stonehenge of erect pillars. Coming up to these formidable pillars, the pipers diverged to the left, and led the contingent three times, sun-wise, round the circle, playing as they marched. The surrounding crowds cheering them enthusiastically. Arriving opposite the Arch-druid, in the third round, the pipers ceased playing, fronted, formed up, and the whole contingent gave the venerable Arch-druid a military salute. Stately and venerable the grand old man looked, as he stood to return the compliment, clad in robes of pure white with a circlet of oaken leaves as a coronet, a golden breast-plate hanging from his neck, looking like a veritable Moses. More vociferous cheers for the "gallant Scots" were then given.

The work of the Gorsedd, with all its ceremonies and ceremonials was now commenced, by the Arch-druid invoking in sonorous Welsh the blessing of Heaven upon the work of the Eisteddfod. He then ordered the Gorsedd sword to be unsheathed and held aloft. Then turning to the cardinal points of the zodiac, east, south, west, north, each time in loud sonorous tones, inquiring, "Is it peace?" the bards and crowds surrounding, responding, "It is peace!" Then the venerable man, standing on the centre of the Logan Stone, ordered the sword to be sheathed, and again invoked the Deity to give peace to all the world, and His blessing upon the work in hand.

The Hirlas Horn, a cornucopia, filled with flowers and fruit was presented to the Arch-druid by Lord Tredegar, as a gift to the Eisteddfod, and the most interesting ceremony of the Gorsedd began. Lord Tredegar was the first to be decorated as a chief bard. Then the Arch-druid, in sonorous terms, to which the Welsh language and the Gaelic lend themselves on solemn occasions, invited all those who had given in their names for induction into the order of bards to come forward to receive from his hands their bardic names, countersign, and badges of degree, as the case might be—the latter wore white, blue, and green ribbon, tied by the Arch-druid on the right arm of each. Among those who were thus favoured was a daughter of Erin, a lady of fine form and charming countenance. When she was called upon, a movement was discernible amongst the "kilted Scots" who stood near her, putting their heads together, and seemed

to be discussing something of importance in their own language. A decision appeared to be instantly arrived at, for they were observed to form in rank prepared for action; those around them wondered what they were about to do, every one was on the tiptoe of expectation. They were not long held in suspense, for no sooner did the Arch-druid tie the green ribbon on the lady's arm, than the Caledonians with one voice lustily cheered the lady, repeated and repeated it, exclaiming, "Slàinte 'a furan do 'n bhean uasal. Erin gu bràth!" On being asked what it all meant, the reply was, "Health and good luck to the fair lady; Ireland for ever!" The whole Highland contingent were decorated by the Arch-druid.

The Gorsedd thus begun was brought to an end by another oration from the Arch-druid, and all entered the pavilion where thousands were already seated. Presently the martial notes of the Scottish pipers were heard outside, and the Highlanders again gave an example of good training, entering the pavilion in single file, pipers in front, they marched round the platform, while their kilted comrades filed off to the left and took their seats at the end of the orchestra. The pipers, finishing their round, marched out again in single file as they came in, evoking thunderous applause from the enormous audience.

Next day the whole Highland contingent, desirous of seeing the country round Cardiff, went in two brakes to St. Fagans. The intermediate country was much admired for its woodland and finely cultivated fields, crops nearly ripe. St. Fagans, one of the seats of Lord Windsor, was soon reached. It was ascertained that his lordship was at home. A respectful message was sent to him for permission to see the castle grounds; a genial reply was returned granting permission. The whole contingent, including the pipers, marched to the castle, and formed up in front of it. The delegates were introduced to his lordship. The pipers were requested to play the "Cock of the North" and other Highland airs, which brought Lady Windsor and the family to the front of the house. The "Sword Dance" was asked for and performed, followed by the Reel of Tulloch, Highland Fling, and a Strathspey, to the great admiration of Lady Windsor, who suggested a drink for the pipers, the "weather being very hot and pipe playing hard work." Great was her ladyship's surprise when the pipers would have nothing stronger than lemonade, except the pipe-major. Her ladyship was greatly interested in the pipes. The pipe-major explained to her all its parts, taking some parts of it asunder and showing the use of each, and their mechanism. Lunch was offered, but it was already provided for at the hotel. All were then taken by his lordship and Lady Windsor over the principal rooms in the castle, and finally the head gardener was sent with them into the gardens and grounds. After a repast at the hotel the contingent returned to Cardiff, visiting Llandaff Cathedral on the way, much impressed with the country, but much more impressed with the amiability of Lord and Lady Windsor.

The third day of the Eisteddfod was a repetition of the first, and need not be described. Next morning the Highland contingent returned home, greatly delighted with all they saw and experienced.

"UNTO THE HILLS."

TALKS WITH HIGHLANDERS.

No. V. BROTHER FIRE (BLUE, RED, COVERED, AND RADIENT).

"PRAISE be to my Lord for Brother Fire, who is fair, jocund, and most robust and strong." So sang St. Francis of the Poor, St. Francis of the Beasts and Birds, brother of pity, and true lover of life—not of *dogdrines* and of *dogmas*, as German theological lecturers call them. So sang St. Francis in the pure joy of his heart, greeting all the great powers of the Universe as friends and relations, in chiming Italian verse, lilted out after the manner of bards on the spur of the moment; when, after obeying literally his Master's orders to lay down all petty cares, he walked with his young companions across the mountains in the early morning sunshine, happy as a child, having nothing in the world (except " his song to sing, O!") and yet possessing all things. Freedom from worry—lightheartedness, it was the first treasure of early unendowed Christianity—homely and gentle, "warming both hands at the fire of life," without being obliged to calculate the price of coal, a religion of the fireside instead of the fire-escape, such as the modern street ranter curses and swears about under his dark lantern to the gaunt females with the hymn books, the stray pickpocket bribed by "a Sabbath free breakfast," and the chorus of laughing shop girls.

In the first days of religions the lilies and the birds, the bread and wine, the hearth and the well, preach the sermons to the heart and senses of everybody. In the last days of religions the clever, heartless scoundrels — who have destroyed these messengers of peace and desolated the land— send out missionaries from their respectable mansions, built upon the ash-heaps with the price of human blood, to terrify all happy and innocent creatures with nightmares of burning and wrath, reflections upon their distorted imagination of the monstrous physical conditions which they themselves have created.

I know that, in the Highlands especially, the question of "*Personality, who the Deffil he is?*" has long been a burning one, and I am the last to throw cold water upon it; for not only do I believe in the devil (like the P.'s and the Free's, and the U.P.'s and the "split P.'s"), but also that his nature, as well as his name, is Legion. Among the hills, experience goes to show that his power is strictly limited, but he has a grand wide sphere of orthodox temptation open to him in Pollokshields.

Some friends of mine had once the privilege of hearing a Lochaber minister preach a very incisive sermon about the arch-enemy. He told his people how a good man once lived simply in a little white-washed room in a Highland cottage, with a rough loft over it, under warm heather thatch, furnished only with a dresser, two home-made chairs, a wee stool, and a box bed, till his heart waxed proud, for he had been to Glasco for his holidays, and seen all the fine things in Glasco, and he craved after them, and the Lord sent his curse upon him, and he grew rich, and he began to furnish his room with grand fal-lals like the fine rooms in Glasco, and he laid down a carpet—"Oh, yes, a carpat!" And he hung up picturs on the walls on a new wall-paper. And he got the whole house to himself, and he had it swept and gyarnished, "Ou ay! swept and gyarnished," and then what did he do? (och, the poor man!) he wanted company, and there iss no people now in the country whateffer, so he took in seven deffils wis him into his fine house, under his noble red tin roof, and "*a fine time they have of it!*" That minister had perceptions of many valuable things hidden from the wise and prudent.

Up to about a century ago the orthodox devil of theology was almost a stranger in the Moabitish hill country, he was only a sort of a "bòchdan" (och, the poor man!) like the other "bòchdans" of the high rocks and desert places where the cattle would not feed, there was no *houfing* for him in all the sunny pastures of the upper corries or the cultivated fields below the head dyke. No room in the white cottages nestling with open doors among sheltering crooks of the glen, nor corner stool next the fire at the *ceilidh*. Healthy, happy people had absolutely no upkeep for old Hornie, since even the worst grass was all eaten by the tethered sheep and the real goats, and there was no black coal smoke for him and no sulphur. But his night was at hand and his "bield" prepared for him, even in the Highlands, behind the broken down dividing dykes of endless desolate moor, without one patch of cultivated ground, and with scarcely a man to inhabit them; while in the Lowlands around Glasgow the devil's own time had fully come at last, and he gathered his children together in deep sulphurous pits upon earth, where black and blue flame and grey ashes surrounded them for ever. No wonder if hell, thus realised in town and country, gave lurid colour and a horrible sense of desolation to the imaginary hell of the future. Pleasantness had gone from the world, and the gates of the elements by which the angels enter man's heart and senses were fast shut against them. North of Druimalban the stranger's sheep browsing in the green pastures. South of Druimalban no green pasture in which even a sheep might lie down, nor any still waters by which it could be led. Instead of them, smoke and vapour, and an horrible tempest everywhere. What remained for the scattered ¦Highland shepherds, and the small farmers banished to the sea-shore, except to listen, like the begrimed children of the pit, to the thundering of wandering gutter-bred preachers, and since it was almost impossible to live happily on earth, to learn to "spiritualise" everything into a vapour of black smoke, after the fashion of our good old Free Church cook, who earnestly desired to hear her minister "spiritualeeze a grand text, such as Moab is my wash pot, and bring forth the hidden treasure, and no be speaking aboot worldly things at all." The spiritualeezed treasure of a Moabitish wash pot! is that not indeed the shadow of a shade!

*If a priest holds up his fingers in sunshine, and gives the benediction in a finished ultramontane style, the shadow of the devil's horns falls upon the wall, so at least the Parisians pretend. Might he not put down his hand (the poor man!) and let the sun himself give a more thorough benediction? I fancy so, and that is one reason why I am writing these strange letters for your grandchildren to read when progress again means movement towards sunshine and simplicity. While it still means competitive elbowing Deucewards, it would be surprising were you to discover a "method in the madness."

Once upon a time while the sun, and the angel standing in it, lord of health and consumer of consumption, ruled the day, the red peats on the cottage hearths were all turned with their glowing red side outwards to welcome the stranger. When the sun had gone well away, and it was time for sleep, the glowing red side of the peats was turned inwards. The fire was covered with these enshrining words, which may not impossibly be learned by heart again, and the holy domestic Sacrament of the *Smàladh* celebrated nightly in every Highland household:—

†"Tha mi 'smàladh an teine,
  Mar a smàlar Mac Moire;
Gu ma slàn dha 'n tigh 's dha 'n teine,
Gu ma slàn dha 'n chuideachd uile.
Co sied air an làr? Peadair agus Pàl.
Co air a bhitheas an fhaire an nochd?
Air Moire mhin-gheal 's air a Mac.
Beul Dé a thubhradh, aigeal geal a lannradh.
Aingeal an dorus gach tighe,
'G ar còmhnadh 's 'g ar gleidheadh,
Gu'n tig là geal am màireach."

I cover the fire
As it is covered by the Son of Mary,
Blest be the house, blest be the fire,
And blest be all the people.
Who are those on the floor? Peter and Paul.
Who keeps watch to-night?
Beautiful gentle Mary and her Son.

The mouth of God tells of a white angel gleaming,
An angel in the doorway of every house,
To shield and protect us
Till the white day comes back again to-morrow.

In nature's school we saw that the first lesson is the noticing, admiring and handling of flowers and herbs; the feeding of beasts and birds, and healing of sick folk. The second lesson may well be the gathering of kindling and the carrying of peats. Then, as nature's long displaced code is gradually restored to its place, the angels begin again to gleam in the doorways, till the desolate nineteenth century night wears past, and the white light comes back again in the morning.

J. A. CAMPBELL,
Turnalt, Corpus Domini, 1889.   of Barbreck.

*A good priest, whatever his creed, is respected by everybody who can feel his worth. Such a helper is the one who lately gave his life for his people in the small-pox outbreak in Barra. Yet I remember being asked "vera seriously" by a stranger in a railway carriage whether I thought this priest would be "saved," being a "Roman Catholic?" I replied that, if not, I hoped that all my friends would be thoroughly well damned. The stranger was an upright commercial and theological Saxon, always occupied in "saving" pence, but no more of a hypocrite nor of a human creature than his own rigid shop scales.

Note.— It was held niggardly to make a black fire by reversing the peats, and keeping down the hospitable blaze.

† Discovered in use among the people of South Uist by Mr Alexander Carmichael. The feeling about fire is primitive and permanent. The names of the guardians vary from Ormuzd in Persia to the tender Christian names of Mary and her Son in South Uist; and perhaps instead of "Peter and Paul," sometimes Colin, my father, and Anne, my sister, in quite Protestant places on the mainland.

CLAN MACKAY SOCIETY.—A large and influential deputation of members of this Society have arranged to visit the Reay Country in September, for the purpose of holding competitions for Gaelic reading, recitation, writing, and singing, in the various parishes. Five great gatherings will be held, and 250 prizes—contributed by Mr. Mackay, Hereford, and other members of the Clan—will be presented. The deputation meets at Thurso on Tuesday, 5th Sept., and competitions will be held at Melvich on Wednesday; Farr on Thursday; Tongue, Friday; Melness, Saturday; and Durness on Monday. Thereafter, the party will probably attend gatherings at Rogart, Lairg, and other places in the south of Sutherland. The competitions are not confined to Mackays, but open to all residents in the Clan country. The gatherings held last year created a sensation in *Duthaich 'ic Aoidh*; but the large number of clansmen who intend going, and the interest taken in the proceedings, will make this visit even more memorable.

TO CORRESPONDENTS.

All Communications, on literary and business matters, should be addressed to the Editor, Mr. JOHN MACKAY, 1 Blythswood Drive, Glasgow.

TERMS OF SUBSCRIPTION.—The CELTIC MONTHLY will be sent, post free, to any part of the United Kingdom, Canada, the United States, and all countries in the Postal Union—for one year, 4s.

THE CELTIC MONTHLY.

SEPTEMBER, 1899.

CONTENTS.

ANNUAL SUBSCRIPTIONS.

NOTICE TO SUBSCRIBERS. - *The Annual Subscriptions are now due. Subscribers who desire to renew for another year are requested to send their contributions (4/- post free), to the Editor, John Mackay, 1 Blythswood Drive, Glasgow, at their earliest convenience. If readers would kindly give this matter their immediate attention, it would obviate the trouble of sending notices each month to those in arrears, and considerably lessen our labours.*

THE NEW VOLUME.

This number completes our seventh volume. Only one former Highland magazine, we believe, has had the good fortune to exist for so long a period. We are glad to think that the *Celtic Monthly* has gathered round it such a large circle of friends, both at home and abroad; and we have no doubt that it has many years of usefulness still before it. Many of our readers in distant lands have desired us to double the size, and make it a sixpenny magazine; but after serious consideration we have decided to make no alteration—this year, at least. It commands a popularity enjoyed by no former Highland monthly; and we would be very reluctant to make the price such as to preclude its being subscribed for by the poorest clansman, as well as by the wealthiest chief. It is welcomed in the Highland cot as heartily as in the castle; but we all know that while many a poor crofter might not hesitate to spend threepence on his *Celtic*, sixpence might not come so readily within his limited means. We think our readers generally will approve of our decision.

For next volume we have arranged for a large number of contributions by distinguished Celtic writers. Dr. Fraser-Mackintosh has promised a series of original papers on a subject of particular interest; Rev. Adam Gunn, M.A., will give several able Gaelic

articles on Sutherland topics; "Torquil Macleod" will continue to delight our readers with his racy stories, of which he has a fresh budget on hand—the result of a recent tour among the romantic isles of the west; while Mr. Mackay, Hereford, Mr. Henry Whyte (Fionn), Mr. Angus Mackintosh, and other talented contributors, have promised to fill our columns with interesting contributions in prose and verse. The artistic department will also be kept up to the present high standard.

VOLUME VII. can now be had, tastefully bound, 6s. 6d., post free, from John Mackay, 1 Blythswood Drive, Glasgow.

OUR NEXT ISSUE.

We will give plate portraits, with biographical sketches, of Colonel C. R. Macgregor, D.S.O., and Mrs. Macgregor, India; Dr. N. J. McKie, Newton-Stewart; and Mr. Hugh Cameron, Montana, U.S.A.

CLAN MACKAY SOCIETY.—Members of the clan will be pleased, no doubt, to learn that Sergeant-Major James Mackay of the Seaforth Highlanders (a native of Watten, Caithness, and grandson of Sergeant Mackay of the 42nd, "Black Watch," a Waterloo hero, whose monument may be seen in Reay Churchyard), has just been granted a commission as second lieutenant in the Royal Dublin Fusiliers, in recognition of his gallant services during the recent engagements at Atbara and Omdurman. Lieut. Mackay will doubtless endeavour to emulate the career of his distinguished countryman, General Hector Macdonald, whose success must be an inspiration to all Highland soldiers.—We are sorry to learn that Provost William Mackay, of Thurso, has had to resign his public position owing to ill-health. The learned provost has been in indifferent health for a long time past, and it is a matter of sincere regret to many friends to know that he is not improving so rapidly as they would wish.

THE WELSH EISTEDDFOD.—The Highland representatives seem to have taken a prominent part in the proceedings of the Welsh National Gathering last month. The pipers created quite a sensation by their playing, and aroused a perfect storm by their dancing! It appears that they gave one or two Highland dances; such a performance shocked the overstrung sensibilities of one or two of the officials, who at the business meeting made some rather rude remarks regarding the incident. The Highland Reel and Sword Dance are evidently not intellectual enough for "Mabon, M.P.," and savours of indelicacy! It is all very amusing to Highlanders, who are credited with being more strict regarding the proprieties than their neighbours. The objections raised were ridiculous. If dancing is not in sympathy with the Welsh national idea that is all right, but to insinuate indelicacy is a matter too silly for serious discussion. That Welshmen generally were delighted with the dancing is evident from a strongly worded note we have received from a Welsh reader in Dolyddelen who was present, and who offers to send us for publication a signed protest by many who saw the dance, against the insulting remarks made by the gentlemen whose sense of modesty was so rudely shocked at the sight of the Highland dress! We must clothe the limbs of the Gael in the immaculate trousers on the next occasion when Scotland is represented at the Eisteddfod.

THE CLANS: PAST AND PRESENT.

By R. S. T. MacEwen, of Lincoln's Inn,
Barrister-at-Law.

(*Continued from page* 214).

Clan Status.

IN 1852 the Court of Session defined the legal position of a clan at the present time. After pointing out that the progress of civilization, the influences of settled government, regular authority and settled law had destroyed the essential qualities and character of Scottish clanship, it held that a court of law was precluded from recognising clans as existing institutions or societies with legal status, membership of which can be acknowledged for ascertaining heirs to succession. They have never been known as institutions or societies having legal status, rights or functions, and when all military character, feudal subordination, heritable jurisdiction and independent authority of chiefs are extracted from a clan nothing remains of its essential and peculiar features. Clans are no longer what they were. The purposes for which they once existed are now unlawful, and they do not legally exist. The law knows them not. But "for peaceful pageantry, social enjoyment and family traditions, mention may still be made of clans and chiefs of clans. The Highlands of Scotland, no longer oppressed by arbitrary rule and the power of the sword, or distracted by feudal contentions, are now inhabited by loyal, orderly and peaceful subjects of the crown; and clans are not now corporations which law sustains nor societies which law recognises or acknowledges." It is now therefore in the form of useful and social organizations that the clans make themselves felt, and as societies for fostering and promoting all that is good and worthy of perpetuation in the old clan system.

Clan Societies.

A strong movement has taken place in recent years, with the object of gathering together the scattered members of the clans into 'clan societies.' There are some sixteen or more such societies at the present time, representing most, if not all, of the leading clans, besides county and district associations. These have their head-quarters in the principal towns of Scotland with local branches in the country towns; and London and other English towns, and centres in the colonies where clansmen muster in any force, have their own societies. The object of these societies is the fostering of clan sentiment, the cultivation of social intercourse among the members, the rendering of assistance to deserving clansmen, the encouragement of education, the collection and preservation of clan records and traditions, the investigation of clan and family histories, the revival, study and promulgation of Celtic literature, and the encouragement of Highland arts and industries.

THE CLAN GUNN.

The societies are non-political and non-sectarian. They are open to all persons bearing the clan name or bearing clan sept names or related to the clan by descent. The subscriptions are regulated on the lowest terms so that the poorest clansmen may become members, while the rich are furnished with an excellent object for their munificence. They have their chiefs, presidents and councillors to manage their affairs, their bards and pipers as of old, and three classes of members, life, extraordinary, and ordinary members. Their rules are framed, added to or amended at general meetings by a majority of clansmen present at the time. Their property and funds are vested in trustees; and they have their secretaries, treasurers, and auditors, all in business form. Their accounts are considered and passed at annual meetings; and there are frequent social gatherings throughout the year, so that all clansmen who have the opportunity may keep in touch with each other. They furnish to their members an annual report of their doings and proceedings. For the encouragement of education the societies give bursaries, varying in amount, tenable for one or two years, to enable deserving students to pursue their studies at a university, high school or technical college, and they give prizes for Gaelic and other branches of study. They render assistance to poor and deserving persons and in the large towns are often helpful in obtaining employment for clansmen. The county associations work on much the same lines and with similiar objects. The principal difference between the two being that membership of a county association is not limited to a clan or sept name or to relationship in any way with a particular clan, but embraces all connected by birth or relationship with or who take an interest in the county. But in the bestowal of benefits neither 'society' or 'association' differ. They both confer these without reference to clan or name. The county associations are not confined to the Highlands; the Lowland as well as the Highland counties have their associations; but in the Highlands the clan societies and county associations may be found working side by side. These bodies confer real and lasting benefits on the poorer clansmen and country people, fulfil a useful purpose and are deserving of every support. We cannot have too many such societies and associations.

THEN AND NOW.

A century and a half has passed away since Culloden. If clansmen were formidable warriors in the past they are no less formidable competitors in the struggle for existence in the different walks of life in the present day. Notwithstanding the severe measures taken against them they

have survived and flourished. They furnish a splendid example of the truth of the 'survival of the fittest.' In the 'social evolution' to which all races of men, since the world began, have been subject, the outstanding fact everywhere, especially in modern times, has been the struggle between the privileged and non - privileged classes and the victory of the latter. In the competition of life the stage of 'equality of opportunity' has been reached. In this struggle the Celtic race in this country have not been left behind. The days of privilege and interest are over. Men have no longer to beg their way upwards and to crave the interest and favour of patrons and persons in authority. Under the old clan system the further a man descended in propinquity from his chief the less considerable he became, until in course of time he arrived at the position of the poorest of the commonality. It may have been a matter of generations but the direction was invariably downwards. Now a man's ascent or descent in the social scale is dependent entirely upon himself and the use he makes of his opportunities. On the eve of the twentieth century we are all members, with equal rights and privileges, of a great republic; everything is open to us, and Celtic Highlanders are as alive and active to the fact, and as strong upholders of the principle as the people of any other race. Macaulay's "good hope" for the Highlanders has been realized.

(CONCLUDED.)

THE SOCIAL CONDITION OF THE HIGHLANDS SINCE 1800.

BY A. J. BEATON, F.S.A. SCOT., F.G.S.E.

XIV.—RAILWAYS.

(Continued from page 208).

BUT the most important factor in developing the Highlands has been the construction of railways, and, although the first portion of the Highland system of railways was opened in 1854, still at this date we have only a little over 400 miles of railway in the Highlands. At the same time, we feel truly thankful for what the noblemen and capitalists in the country have done for us, yet there is a wide field for developing railways in the northern and central Highlands. A comparison with any part of Ireland will illustrate how Scotland is comparatively isolated in this direction. I am glad to notice that the attention of the present Government is engaged at this moment in considering the advisability of granting a subsidy towards constructing railways and tramways in the Highlands and Islands,* and I fail to see how the loyal Scottish Celt is not as fully entitled to Government aid as his more boisterous brother beyond the Irish Sea. Before the opening of railways in the north, an inside seat in the coach from Inverness to Perth cost 60s, and an outside seat 35s. By rail you can now get a return fare to London for £3 ; and you can also perform the return journey to the metropolis in less time than the coach took to run from Inverness to Perth.

There are no minerals except granite in the Highlands of sufficient value ever to yield great wealth to the country ; and this region must therefore look largely to its fisheries as the future source of prosperity ; and it is most im-

portant that everything which science and money can accomplish should be employed in developing this great industry. The fishing centre should have direct railway communication with the interior of the country, and cheap and rapid means of transit to the large English towns and thickly populated districts ; and the Government should construct safe and commodious harbours, as well as make liberal grants to fully equip the fishing fleet. I should also like to see a fishery school established at Inverness, or some central station in the Highlands, where young fishermen and boys could receive technical training and instruction in making fishing gear, as well as in constructing and repairing boats. And last, but not least, all the tillable lands in

PEAT-CUTTING IN THE HIGHLANDS.

the Highlands should be allotted to the surplus population of congested districts, and light or narrow gauge railways constructed through these newly settled glens. When these things are done we shall have an enriched nation and a peaceful, contented, and prosperous peasantry —their country's stay and their nation's pride.

*As the result of the Royal Commission Enquiry a Light Railways Act was passed in Parliament, but instead of benefiting the Highlands in any way it has proved abortive. The failure is partly due to the smallness of the grant allowed by Government and partly to the unfounded apprehensions of the promoters, of "breaking the gauge." I have advocated in season and out of

XV.—PEAT.

There is another source of industry which might yield a large income if properly and scientifically developed. I refer to the thousands of acres of peat-mosses scattered over the Highlands. The primitive method of making peat suitable for fuel by cutting the turf into

season the advisability of adopting a 3ft. gauge for branch railways in sparsely populated districts in the Highlands. The inconvenience of transfer is small compared with the advantages derived ; and the saving in construction and maintenance is just sufficient to make a narrow gauge line a paying undertaking, where the standard gauge would be a financial failure.

rectangular blocks and drying them in small stacks in the open air and that in a climate so uncertain is so crude that, in an age steeped in scientific discoveries, one marvels that this remnant of what one might call barbarism should possibly exist, for no matter how the cubes are left drying, a large proportion of water will be retained. Notwithstanding this, thousands of tons of peat are annually consumed as a fuel; and in many districts in the Highlands of Scotland and Ireland this is the only fuel used. Experiments made by Sir Archibald Geikie put the constituent elements of peat after being dried at 100 degrees C. carbon, 60·48; hydrogen, 6·10; oxygen, 32·55; nitrogen, 0·88 The large proportion of water which cannot be extracted from peat is the great obstacle to its use as a fuel, but under a pressure of 6000 atmospheres, peat may be converted into as hard, black, and brilliant a substance, and having the same aspect as physical coal.

If a syndicate were formed having an efficient stock of cutting, compressing, and drying machinery, a lucrative enterprise might be established in the Highlands, benefiting both the promoters and the inhabitants. A fuel thus manufactured would be equal in many respects to coal, and the cost not more than half what that mineral costs. In the large peat-moss of Lancashire, lying between Liverpool and Manchester, a considerable trade is carried on in manufacturing the most fibrous portion of the peat into material for litter.

I fear some sceptical reader will say that many Highland proprietors have tried the "improvement scheme" with but poor success; Sir James Matheson of Lewis expended in six years the sum of £67,980 more than the entire revenue derived from his estate in three years. The late Mr. James Fletcher of Rosehaugh informed me that for twelve years after purchasing his Black Isle properties he annually expended over £10,000 on improvements, this being more than his entire rental, with the result that there is not at the present time in all the Highlands an estate so well equipped with houses and farm offices and intersected with such excellent roads. The Duke of Argyll between 1846 and 1852 spent £1790 in addition to the revenue derived from his property in the island of Mull; and the Duke of Sutherland spent £254,000 on the reclamation works at Lairg; while nearly every proprietor throughout the islands has spent more or less in developing and improving his estates. But can it be said that those sums of money were expended to no purpose? Certainly not; for, for every penny judiciously spent, the property was proportionally enhanced in value. A brief glance at the rental roll twenty or thirty years ago compared with that of to-day will

demonstrate that those expenditures were good investments, which, other things being equal, have paid well, or will pay well, in the end. Recent legislation on the land question now places landlords in a position from which we cannot expect them to expend much capital on improvements; and it is therefore the more necessary for them to allot their unoccupied lands at a fair figure, and allow the crofter to bring them into cultivation. The country will thereby retain the people, and the capital which they would take with them if they emigrated; and in the place of as now

"The flocks of a stranger the long glens are roaming.
  Where a thousand fair homesteads smoked bonnie
      at gloaming;
  Our wee crofts run wild wi' the bracken and
      heather,
  And our gables stand ruinous and bare to the
      weather."

We would then have instead of the dreary and barren moorland and deserted and lonely glen, rich fields of waving golden grain, and happy homes of virtuous women and brave and pious men.

(CONCLUDED).

A LESSON OF THE SEASONS.

I come, says the SPRING, to remind you
    That I am the season to sow
The seed that in season wild find you
    Glad reapers, when harvest will grow;
For they who will delve in due season,
    And toil when the loiterers sleep,
May hope, with appropriate reason,
    In due proper season to reap.

Withhold not your hands from the furrow,
    While yet it is time for the plough,
For weeds in the fields will soon burrow,
    Unless you will furrow them now;
Then plant them with prudence beseeming,
    With flowers as well as with corn,
And see that the soil be not teeming
    With briar and bramble and thorn.

So CHILDHOOD, remember, is ever
    The soil and the season to learn,
The soil being so easy to sever,
    The season so void of concern;
Then sow the good seed in the morning.
    When life is still tender and pure,
That so you may find it adorning
    The sunset and shadows obscure.

I come, says the SUMMER, in sunshine,
    For I am the season of heat,
When May in its glory and June shine,
    To rear up the barley and wheat;
Whatever in Spring was well planted,
    Well watered and nurtured with care,
Will grow with full vigour, undaunted,
    Refreshed by the midsummer air.

Then cease not to labour in earnest,
  And stir up the soil with the hoe,
For this is the time of the sternest
  Attention that you can bestow ;
Remove the wild weeds that be choking
  The plants which their creepers go round,
The tares and the thistles provoking,
  That cover and cumber the ground.

So Youth is the season of passion,
  And growth of both body and soul,
And therefore the season to fashion
  Our lives out of passion's control ;
Make use, then, of time in the manner
  Best chosen to cultivate truth,
With virtue displayed on your banner,
  To guard 'gainst the sallies of Youth.

I come, says the Autumn, to follow
  The footsteps of Summer at length ;
In me there is nought that is hollow,
  For I am the season of strength ;
The Spring and the Summer completed
  The way to establish my reign,
And much as they passed and were treated,
  Shall now be for profit or pain.

Though strong, I am far from a stranger
  To diverse diseases that blight,
As well as the floods that endanger
  The fields that be waving and bright ;
Then, prithee, be up and be doing,
  To guard against these as you may,
The path of true duty pursuing,
  And scaring the wild birds away.

So Manhood, arrayed in its glory,
  Is strong in the store of its might,
Yet, knowing how chequered its story,
  Its years should be ordered aright ;
Then work in the bloom of your power,
  With confidence, seasoned with care,
Lest enemies scale the strong tower,
  And leave it a wreck of despair.

I come, says the Winter, in wildness,
  With bane in my venomous breath,
And know neither meekness nor mildness,
  For I am the season of--death!
I strip the fair fields of their blossom,
  As onward I pass on my way,
And pressed to my merciless bosom,
  They shrink into sapless decay.

Prepare, then, the fields for the Winter,
  As best to encounter the blast,
Though sure it will shrivel and splinter,
  And doubtlessly conquer at last ;
Then meet it with courage undaunted,
  Accepting the fate from on high,
That all that on earth is implanted,
  Is destined as surely to die.

E'en so is Old Age, limp and hoary,
  The end and the winter of life,
When Manhood is past with its glory,
  And pains become woeful and rife ;
Then patiently watching and waiting,
  Prepare for your destiny's doom,
Since there is no way of checkmating
  The fate that consigns to the tomb.

L'ENVOI.

But Spring over Winter shall flourish,
  Reviving again the fair field,
And Summer shall nurture and nourish,
  And Autumn her harvest shall yield ;
And so shall the soul on high pinion,
  Survive after man's fleeting breath ;
Then where is, O Grave, thy dominion,
  And where is thy triumph, O Death?

                                JOHN MACGREGOR.

LINES TO THE CLAN MACGILLIVRAY.

A GALLANT sept of the Clan Chattan, many of which, including their Chieftain, are now scattered in distant lands, but whose hearts are still in the green dales of their fathers about the head waters of the Nairn.

Ye mountain torrents deep and strong,
  Ye rills that streak the brae,
Your voices mingle with my song
  On brave Clan Gillivray.

Though Gaelic bards no longer sing
  Of shield and keen claymore,
Around the Dun* traditions cling
  " Of the brave days of yore."

The echoes of these vanished days
  Still linger 'mongst the hills,
In martial stories, airs, and lays,
  The Highland heart that thrills.

And fancy hears the murmuring Nairn
  Still whisper of the strong
Who heard in ages old and stern
  Clan Chattan's battle song.

No clansman cradled in the Dun,
  Or green Dalcrombie's dale,
The mustering place was known to shun,
  Nor chief nor chieftain fail.

But armed with claymore, dirk and shield,
  Were valiant, leal and sure,
From Harlaw's stubborn gory field
  To bleak Drumossie's moor.

Whene'er from Moy's raised banner sprung
  The grey cat of the cairn,
MacGillivray plaids responsive swung
  Adown the vale of Nairn.

Waft, waft ye winds my Highland lay,
  O'er ocean's heaving breast,
To palm-fringed sunny Eastern bay,
  To forests of the West.

*Dunmaglass, the old seat of the MacGillivray chieftains.

A clansman's tribute to his kin
In distant lands that stray,
To sons of sires who held the Dun,
The brave Clan Gillivray.

Hatfield, Herts.　　　　ANGUS MACKINTOSH.

W. C. MUNRO, NEW ZEALAND.

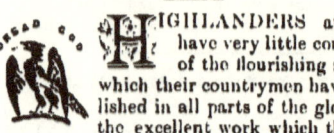

IGHLANDERS at home have very little conception of the flourishing societies which their countrymen have established in all parts of the globe, and the excellent work which they perform. Highland societies are to be found in the most remote regions, many of which possess a larger membership and are financially stronger than some of the leading societies in the mother country. Indeed, the Gael in Glasgow has only the most superficial idea of what his countrymen are doing abroad, and for that reason seem to think that Scottish societies in Canada, America, India, Africa, Australia, Siam and other distant lands, can only be of little account. We happen to know something of the splendid work which these organizations perform, for we have many readers of the *Celtic Monthly* in most of them, and we feel that it is a pity that so little should be known in Scotland of the practical outcome of that strong clannish sentiment which makes Highlanders band themselves together for mutual assistance, and to foster the national feeling, in almost every country where a few of them may cast their lot. It is our intention in the succeeding issues to give some particulars of these societies, with portraits and sketches of a few of the leading members.

There is no part of the world where the Scot has established himself more firmly than in Australia. Almost every leading town has its Caledonian Society, the Highland dress and the music of the pipes denoting the masterful presence of the Gael. There is a very powerful society in the district of Hawkes Bay, which includes in its membership some of the most enthusiastic Highlanders in New Zealand.

In this issue we have great pleasure in giving the portrait of a leading Gael in this province, Mr. W. C. Munro. He himself was born in 1855, at North Melbourne, Victoria, but his father sailed from the old country in 1853, on board the ship "Ida," 140 days being occupied in the passage. For some time he managed large sheep stations in the Wimmera and Murray districts, but in 1869 he removed to New Zealand, where he entered into pastoral pursuits, assisted by his son. Ten years later they removed to the volcanic district in the North Island, where they resided for a number of years. Here Mr. W. C. Munro witnessed the great eruption of Mount Tarawera on 10th June, 1886, a sight never to be forgotten. He was also one of a party who first penetrated to the destroyed site of the famous pink and white terraces, and saw the great openings in the earth which vomited forth huge rocks, hurling them hundreds of feet in the air. Shortly afterwards Mr. Munro removed to the East Coast, where he still resides. He takes an active interest in the meetings and Highland Gatherings promoted by the society, the great success of which is largely due to the enthusiasm with which the members enter into the work.

LEGENDS
of Perthshire.

II. HOW GLENLYON WAS NAMED.

BOUT the middle of the fifteenth century, Glenlyon, which had been for some time in the possession of the Stewart line of Lorne, fell into the hands of the Macivors, a sept of the Campbells, who usurped possession before it fell to that powerful clan through the marriage of Archibald Campbell to the heiress. At that time a feud between the Stewarts of Garth and the Macivors took place through the following cause:—The young heir of Garth had been nursed by a woman of the Clan Macdiarmid, residing at Craigianie, one of the ancient moathills where the family was represented until 1896. This woman had two sons, one of whom, foster-brother to the young laird, having been much injured in a dispute with Macivor, threatened to apply to the laird of Garth for redress. In those days a foster brother was regarded as a member of the family, and Macivor, well aware that the quarrel of the Macdiarmids would be taken up by his neighbour, ordered a pursuit. The young men being hard pressed, threw themselves into a deep pool of the river Lyon, where they hoped that their pursuers would not venture to follow them. The foster-brother was, however, desperately wounded with an arrow, and drowned in the pool, which is still known as Linne Dhòmhnuill, or Donald's pool. The other youth succeeded in reaching Garth. Determined to avenge his friend's death, Garth collected his followers and marched to Glenlyon. Macivor gathered his men, and met the invaders about the middle of the glen. The chieftains saluted each other, and held a conversation in order to settle affairs amicably. Stewart wore a plaid, the one side of which was dark coloured

W. C. MUNRO.

tartan and the other red. On going to the conference, he told his men that, if the result was to be peace, the darker side of the plaid was to remain outside as it was; if otherwise, he would give the signal for attack by turning out the red side.

They were still engaged in conference when Macivor whistled loudly, and a number of armed men started up from the adjoining rocks and bushes, where they had been concealed, while the main body were drawn up in front. "Who are these?" said Stewart, "and for what purpose are they there?"

"They are only a herd of my roes that are frisking about the rocks," replied Macivor.

"In that case," said the other, "it is time for me to call my hounds."

Then, turning his plaid, he rejoined his men, who were watching his motions, and instantly advanced. Both parties rushed to the combat; the Macivors soon giving way were pursued for eight miles further up the glen. Here they turned to make a last effort, but were again driven back with great loss. The survivors fled across the mountains to another part of the country, and were not again permitted to return. Macivor's land was, in the meantime, seized by the victors, and law confirmed what the sword had won. A charter under the Great Seal was passed by James III., dated 24th January, 1477, conveying the lands of Fothergall (now Fortingall), Apnadull, Temper, and others in Rannoch; Glenquaich, Wester Strathbrane, and Glenlionn, in the County of Perth, to John Stewart, of Garth and Fothergill, and Neil Stewart, his son and heir.

The names of the river and glen still continue memorials of this sanguinary fray. Duibh and Glen Duibhe (that is, Black Water and Glen), were their former names. When the Stewarts were returning from the last pursuit, they washed their swords in the river, which was discoloured a considerable way down on one side by the blood.

"This stream," exclaimed the chieftain, "shall no longer be called Duibhe, but Liobhann (Liobh is Gaelic for to wipe or polish). This change of name is commemorated by the Gaelic couplet—

"Bho latha liobhadh nan arm,
Bithidh Liobhann mar ainm air Duibhe."

"Since the day of the cleaning of arms,
Blackwater shall be called Leiven"

(now Anglicised into Lyon).

Before the combat commenced, Stewart's men pulled off a kind of sandals which they wore, bound round the ankles with thongs, and called in Gaelic cuaruin. Those they laid aside, close to a small rock, which to this day is called Leac-nan-cuaran, the stone or slab of the sandals.

The spot where they drew their swords is called Ruskich, to uncover or unsheath; the field where the rencounter commenced, Laggan-a-chatha, the field or hollow of the battle; and the spot where the last stand was made, Camus-nan-carn, the fork of the cairns, from the cairns or mounds of stones which cover the graves, and which, from their quantity, show the considerable number slain, which tradition says amounted to 140 on the side of Macivor."

This is the tradition current in the glen, as taken down by General Stewart, who found at this spot some old armour; and of "Sgiathanach," the Rev. Mr. Macgregor, then of Kilmuir, Skye, who wrote a Gaelic account of the feud for "Fear Tathaich nam Beann," published by Dr. Norman Macleod, senior, in 1849.

Another derivation of the name Glenlyon, given on such good authority as the Rev. John Maclean, of Grandtully, and Dr. A. C. Cameron, late of Fettercairn, now of Paisley, is that the word is derived from lithe, flood, on account of the rapidity with which the stream swells when heavy rain falls. They also quote the foregoing charter, and an earlier one given by King Robert Bruce, to William Olifaunt, who never took possession. His son David gave a grant of the lands of Glenlionn to John Macdougall, of Lorne. Glenlyon was known in Ossianic poetry as Crom ghleann nan clach, where the Feinne were said to have twelve castles, as commemorated in the lines:—

"Bha dà chaisteal dheug aig Fionn,
An Crom ghleann nan clach,"

that is, "Finn had twelve castles in the Crooked Glen of Stones."

Glen Duibhe and Crooked Glen were both inconvenient names to use in charters, so it is probable that the present name was first used in those documents, and that it was not until after this battle that it came to be used by the people.

Glenlyon. ALEX. STEWART.

CLAN EWEN.
MacEwens in Lochaber.
SLIOCHD EOGHAIN.

BY R. S. T. MACEWEN.

(Continued from page 220).

IN 1396, according to Mackenzie, there were four septs or branches of the clan, viz: Gillaufhaig or Gillonie (Camerons of Invermalie and Strone), the Clan Soirlie (Camerons of Glen Nevis), Mhic Mhartain or MacMartins of Letterfinlay (of which Cambro had been chief), and the Camerons of Lochiel. There were also dependent septs, the principal being Mhic Gilveil, or MacMillans. It is said to have been the head or captain of the first of these, Gillanfhaig (MacGillonies) or Maclanfhaigh—" Fhaigh " in its aspirated form being represented by " Hay " or " Kay " of the Chroniclers—who led the Camerons at the Inch of Perth.

Bancho (Shakspeare's Banquo), who was Thane of Lochaber in the time of King Duncan, and was slain by M'Beth because he was foretold that Bancho's posterity would be kings of Scotland -a prophecy which was fulfilled—had a sister Marion who married Angus, the first of the Cameron chiefs of whom there is any mention. From Bancho's grandson Walter, Great Steward of Scotland, which office became hereditary and turned into a surname, the Royal Stewart family and the Stewart Earls of Lennox were descended. Then, at a much later period, viz., in 1516, we find " Ewen Eoghain Mac-Ailein," the 13th Cameron chief, supporting the then Stewart Earl of Lennox in his rebellion, for which he was tried and executed. Here we have another instance of close connection between the Lachaber and Dumbartonshire chiefs and clans.

All these traditions and historic incidents, coupled with the fact that the first Cameron chief was of Celtic origin, point to a very early connection with the western clans—if, indeed, the progenitors of the first Camerons were not western Celts, who, in their early wanderings, settled in Lochaber, and for a time formed part of the Moravian host. Whether this circumstance, or the settlement of the MacEwens at one period in Lochaber accounts for the name Ewen amongst the Camerons it is of course impossible to say at the present day; but while the name has been common in the Cameron families and in Lochaber, it is very rare amongst the neighbouring clans of the district, who were previously connected with the Camerons under Moravian rule. It is not a common name amongst the Mackintoshes, or the minor septs of Clan Chattan, or the Moravian clans. It is of western origin, and common amongst the western clans, and the fact would seem to support Keltie's statement that the MacEwens had originally territory in Lochaber. In later times, the families of that name in Lochaber appear to have derived it, in some cases, from the Cameron Ewens, according to Celtic custom, for the " Sliochd Eoghain " were the children and descendants of the first Ewen, chief of Erracht. In others it doubtless had its origin in the later connection with the MacDougall Campbells of Lorne; and the "Sliochd Eoghain " was probably composed of the descendants of both. The MacEwen Camerons who took part in the Struan raid under Sir Ewen Cameron in 1666, were no doubt of this sept. The Skye Colony of

MacEwens may have been derived either from the Otter or Lochaber families, or both. In later years, they appear to have been numerous in Skye, for from General Wade's Statement of the Highland Clans in 1715 there were one hundred and fifty then in the island.

The MacEwens have been a scattered race since the early part of the thirteenth century, although the chief of Otter, "Eoghannah-Oitrich", managed to hold his own till the middle of the fifteenth century. They are not in the rolls attached to the Acts of 1587 or 1594—a proof that they were badly " broken" by that time. Tradition assigns their final ruin in Argyllshire to the Campbells in the time of Earl Colin's " redding up "; and it is on record that from and after that time a kinsman of his own was established at Otter—no doubt according to the fashion of the times.

The name is to be found not only in Argyllshire, Dumbartonshire, and the neighbouring counties, but as far north as Perth and Lochaber, and in the west in Skye.

HOW WE BRING THE WEE ONES HOME.

HE SEA! Ah, it is our own. We love it and we fear it, for it brings to us both life and death. It laughs cheersomely with a beautiful laughter among the shallows when the sunlight falls on the dancing waves, and the white-winged birds go skimming with delight above the shimmering plane of blue. The salt smell of it gets into our nostrils when as yet we are but bairns, and then it is that you will hear us laughing softly with a wonderful cooing sound before the words are formed on our lips. The blue grey glamour of the sea is reflected in the infant eyes that ever afterwards shine with the light and shadows of the waves. The sea steals its blueness from heaven, and the island dwellers steal the blueness of their eyes from the sea—because of their much gazing on the magic waters.

And when we be men and women, we are still drunken with a love of the sea wave. It tears our dearest ones away from our hearts for ever, and yet, above our terror of it, is our love. I have seen an islesman in an inland place stop of a sudden and sniff the winds of heaven with a bright light shining on the face of him. He had happened on a road that was but three miles from the sea. The smell of it was in his nostrils, and a mist of tears was creeping over his eyes. Go where we will, ours are the hearts that never can forget. The sea is our nurse that sang to us when we were bairns, and rocked us to rest with a gentle heaving. Aye, and there be some of us who would be glad enough at the last to lay down our toiling, and return to our nurse's arms when the night falls, and the sound of voices comes to us out of the darkness from a far off shore of dreams.

It is of the sea that I am wishful to tell you now. For in the Isle of Ridges we are lapped about for ever with a moaning and a sighing and a whispering of waves.

The sunlight was lying hot on the moors above Loch Seresort one Sabbath day. The air was as still as still could be. There was nothing heard but the soft calling of sea birds, like the sound of music in a sleep-world far away. Out across the waters to the north the Coolins lay on the horizon like big floating clouds, and straight away to the east from Kinloch to the point of Sleat stretched ten miles of shimmering sea, quivering in the sunlight like a flashing mirror. It was a sea of glass mingled with fire, such as the Holy Seer speaks of in the Book.

While I was lying on the warm rocks near the jetty, Ruari of the Dogs came along the shore with a pair of great oars over his shoulder. He was big and strong and silent, and a man namely at the *camanachd* and the *cabar* —but this day he had a look of dool on his face.

"What ails ye, Ruari, that on the day of peace you should be meddling with the boats at all?"

"Oh, it's yourself is it? I was not seeing you. I am for Armadale in the big boat, with Padraig Cam and Donald and Hamish. It is the doctor we are after."

"Who is ill, Ruari?"

"Big John's wife."

"And what ails Big John's wife?"

Ruari was silent for a moment, and then he answered slowly, as he walked away, without looking at me—

"Big John's wife will be worse before she is better."

"Aye, is it so?"

We understood one another in a twinkling—for it is a phrase with us.

"Then I will be going with you, Ruari," and we went down the jetty together, both of us hoping that it might not be too late when the doctor came. There was no more talk between us as we set about overhauling the tackle, and getting the four great oars out. We were both thinking about Big John's wife, for she was the gentlest woman in Kinloch.

Then Padraig Cam and Donald and Hamish came down the jetty and stepped into the "Star of Evening" for that was the name of Ruari's boat and soon we were in the middle of the loch, with the four great sweeps breaking the surface of the calm sea. It was twenty miles or thereabouts to Armadale, and before we reached

Kinloch again the new day would be breaking. And even then, who can ever tell when a boat will return to the harbour?

But a woman's life and a bairn's hung on the balance, so the rowers bent their backs with a will, and a man's heart was beating behind every stroke. We were all single men—unless Padraig Cam, who had married Aileen the Fair, and maybe that was the reason why Padraig Cam took the stroke oar and made the time.

All through the long summer afternoon we rowed over the sea of glass. Around us lay the fairest scene on earth—at least, to every isles-man's eye. Canna, Skye, and far off Uist to the west; and on our starboard the long rugged coast of the mainland about Arisaig, Morar and Moidart—steeped in the peacefulness of heaven, and shining through a veil of summer haze. There was no variation at all in the sounds that come to us out of this dream-world of beauty. The dull *thud-thud* of the oars in the thole pins, the measured splash of the blades in the sea, the constant *sweesh-h-h* of the water at the bow, with the broken conversation of the men now and again, while far up in the deep blue of the sky overhead the white birds went circling and crying, and diving and swooping, with a cease-less motion that was free and light and full of strength.

"Ruari," said Padraig, with a look away into the west, "did you bring the oilskins with you?"

"Aye, Padraig, and I'm thinking that before long we will need them."

"Aye, aye," answered all the men.

But to a landsman such a thought would have been out of place on such an evening as this.

We were creeping up the coast of Sleat, and the air was as still as the grave, and the heat was oppressive, and the sea was like a burnished mirror, and everywhere a kind of red mist was rising that gave the appearance to land and sea as if the sunset had thrown a red dust across the hot, airless world.

"It is a red evening," said Padraig, "and I will know always what that means. But we will get the doctor aboard, and be on our way back before it comes."

In another hour we were in at the green-shored bay of Armadale, waiting for the doctor to come down from his cottage. At last he appeared, and over his arm he carried a water-proof, and in his other hand a small black bag.

It took us two hours to get to the point again, and in the dusk we made out another boat being rowed quickly towards us.

"That is Big John's boat," said I.

The men stopped rowing and looked round.

"It is Big John himself!" cried Ruari, and in a short time we were within hail.

Then followed a flow of the good Gaelic,

which to my thinking is like the sound of sweet music in the ear. Big John's voice rose in the dusk with a fine note of triumph in it.

"Doctor Macdonald, there will be no need of you to come now, for the good wife is doing fine, and—and—doctor, *it is a boy!*"

"*Dhé*—but you are the rich man this day, John. Blessings on you, and it is I that know what you are thinking. *It might ha' been a lassie!*"

The doctor, good soul, was rowed ashore amid laughter and merriment, and left to trudge his ten miles home along the lonely road. When it happens to be men's work to go out of their way for nothing, it is little that they think about it.

But when we had fetched round the point, and were slowly rowing in the direction of the Isle of Ridges, the men in both boats stopped and began to put on their oilskins. The air was hotter than ever, and even more still. Not a seabird cried now. But out of the swelter of silence came at last a long, low muttering of thunder. The men in Big John's boat were setting their sail, and in a short while both boats were being rowed slowly into the gloom, with their close-reefed sails hitched up to the mast, and ready for the wind when it came.

We had not long to wait. After another peal of thunder, and a vivid flash of lightning that lit up the sea like the sun, a low moaning and hissing sound was heard coming up from the south through the mirk—growing louder and louder as it came—hissing like the red hot iron when it is plunged into water; so, mad with rage, the black squall came flying across the sea, tearing up the glassy deep as it flew, and lashing the waves into a yeasty pother of foam.

"Stand by, lads," cried Ruari, "put some way on her—quick, quick!"

The squall was on us at last, and with a rising shriek it struck the boat on the port side, and sent her heeling over to the gunwale before she gathered sufficient way to stand up to the wind. Then, like an arrow from a bow, through drenching rain, she shot forward into the jabble of sea and storm, the rag of her sail straining and creaking and bending the stout mast as a withy—plunging she went through the huge waves that buried us again and again in a smother of foam. Oh! but it was wild, mad, thrilling work! Now we were racing along the ridge of the seas, now we were down in the black hollows. *Thud—s-s-s-h!* *Thud—s-s-s-h!* plunged the boat, and all the while Ruari of the Dogs sat with his hand on the tiller, and said no word. A false move meant death to us all, but there was no fear at all, for these men looked death in the face every time they were caught in a squall, and the hand that held the tiller had a grip of iron, and the eye that watched the

waves was not less sure than the eye of the *iolair* when it looks in the face of the rising sun. *Thud—s-s-s-h!* *Thud—s-s-s-h!*

As we baled out the water, we knew that in the heart of us there was a wild thrill of relish as we lashed through the storm and cheated the Black Spirit of its prey.

"I can see the loom o' the land," shouted Duncan from the bow, and immediately he was drenched by a wave that leaped over him out of the night.

"Aye, aye, we are doing fine, lads," replied Ruari, and he in turn was answered by a cold shower bath that sent a shiver down the small of his back.

"We have the shelter of the hill now," said Padraig Cam, "and it is a dirty night that we have picked for our bit trip. I'm thinking that for all the wind and rain, Big John will be in before us, to see if the wee boy has the red hair on his head!"

"Look you, Ruari, that you fetch us in quick—" *thud—s-s-s-h!* and another drench of water— "before the other boat!" And Hamish was spluttering like a drowning puppy, with the salt water in his mouth.

"No, Hamish my man, I will not be able to out-steer any man who is sitting at the tiller with the love o' wife and child in his heart. I am a single man, and Big John has something ashore that is pulling him through the sea this night like a glare o' light. Is it not true, Padraig—you should be knowing it?"

"Aye, it is so," answered the One-eyed Man with a queer smile. He was thinking of Aileen the Fair.

And when the "Star of Evening" reached Kinloch at the dawning, her crew saw Big John standing on the shore waiting for them. He said with a laugh that the "Sea Maid" was a faster-built boat than the "Star of Evening," and that there was no credit at all in fetching the loch sooner than Ruari of the Dogs, who was the best sailor in Kinloch.

We did not contradict Big John. But as we wrung the water from our clothes, we knew that if Big John had been in the "Star of Evening" that night, or any other boat, he would have reached Kinloch first. It is strange. But it is true.

And this is how we bring the wee ones home.

                      TORQUIL MACLEOD.

GAELIC SOCIETY OF LONDON.—Many of our readers will regret to learn that Mr. W. A. Martin, who has so ably acted as Secretary to this society for a number of years, has just resigned office.

www.ingramcontent.com/pod-product-compliance
Lightning Source LLC
Chambersburg PA
CBHW020932030726
47496CB00005B/1148